Heroic Adventure Stories

From the Golden Age of Greece and Rome

Edited by
Mike Ashley

Robinson
LONDON

Robinson Publishing Ltd
7, Kensington Church Court
London W8 4SP

First published in the UK
by Robinson Publishing Ltd 1997

A copy of the British Library Cataloguing in Publication
Data for this title is available from the British Library

ISBN 1-85487-865-4

Printed and bound in the E.C.

CONTENTS

INTRODUCTION

The Golden Age

The time from the rise of the ancient Greek world to the fall of
the Roman Empire in the West spanned over a thousand years.
The two cultures, one so closely developed from the other, yet so
different in outlook, were to leave their imprint not just on Europe
but, eventually, on the whole world.

The period is rich in the strength and diversity of its historical
characters and, also, in its religious beliefs, ranging from the early
Greek myths and legends to the dawn of Christianity. All of this
has strongly influenced generations of authors and served as a base
for a tempting variety of fiction. The Greek and Roman myths have
furnished a wealth of novels and stories, some of which have sought
to rationalize the events, whilst others have taken the myths at their
face value. Perhaps the best known of these have been the novels by
Mary Renault, starting with *The King Must Die*, which looked at the
life of Theseus. Renault's books, especially those about Alexander
the Great, are probably the most popular of all books dealing with
the ancient world, although one should not forget *I, Claudius*
and *Claudius the God* by Robert Graves. In fact ever since Lord
Bulwer-Lytton wrote *The Last Days of Pompeii* in 1834 there has
been a fascination for novels set in ancient Rome. Other enduringly
popular works include *Ben-Hur* by Lew Wallace, *Quo Vadis?* by
Henry Sienkiewicz and *Spartacus* by Howard Fast, all well known
because of their translation into spectacle on the big screen. More
recently the novels by Colleen McCullough (starting with *First Man
in Rome*), Allan Massie (*Augustus* and *Tiberius*) and David Wishart
(*I, Virgil* and *Ovid*) have restimulated public interest.

This anthology contains thirty stories which explore that fascinating period of history. The stories are set in chronological order

and range from the time of the Trojan War to the establishment of
the Eastern Roman Empire at Constantinople. They include classic
stories by Naomi Mitchison, Lew Wallace and Robert Graves,
and more recent examples by Allan Massie, Vera Chapman and
Thomas Burnett Swann. Nine of the stories are published here
for the first time, and I am most grateful to L. Sprague de
Camp, Juliet Dymoke, Tom Holt, John Maddox Roberts, Darrell
Schweitzer, Rosalind Stewart, Keith Taylor, Peter Tremayne and
Derek Wilson for responding to my requests. I am particularly
pleased to include two lesser known items by Mary Renault. In
'The Fiction of History', which serves as an introductory discussion,
she explains her approach to historical fiction and the creation of
characters, whilst in 'The Horse from Thessaly' she recreates the
story of Alexander the Great's famous horse Bucephalus. I must
thank Richard Dalby for tracking down a copy of 'The Fiction of
History', Judith Higgins, for providing several ancient tomes and
less ancient suggestions, and Steven Saylor for a number of excellent
suggestions, including the story by Pierre Louÿs.

It is easy to think of the world of the Greeks and Romans as
something so ancient, so unfamiliar, that it is irrelevant to our
world; but they were men and women like you and I, and had
many of the same problems. In these stories, in some small way,
we can relive a thousand and more years of history and experience
the birth and death of civilizations.

Mike Ashley
May 1997

THE FICTION OF HISTORY

Mary Renault

Often I have found that the germ of a novel has emerged, in what has seemed an entirely accidental way, from some secondary theme, or bit of background material, made use of for purely functional reasons in some previous book. The selection of a theme, of course, is never an accident with any writer; its provenance, however, does sometimes seem to be thrown in one's way like a coin in the sand, which catches the light when one walks past at a certain angle.

A passage of dialogue and discussion among the characters of an earlier novel set in 1940, *The Charioteer*, gave the starting-point to my first historical novel, *The Last of the Wine*; and from this in turn grew *The King Must Die*.

The Last of the Wine is about civilized, highly educated Greeks of the fifth century, who lived much with the legends of their founding heroes, but had not, any more than had Shakespeare when he clothed Caesar in a doublet, knowledge enough to picture them in their real contemporary context. Between these Athenians and the Bronze Age, Homer with his mixture of authentic tradition, Dark Age accretions, and eighth-century [BC] personal genius, was the only link.

In classical Athens, Theseus was a household word. He was the first High King of all Attica, saviour of the land from tribal anarchy, establisher of Athenian pre-eminence, and founder, by tradition, of the rule of law; a just and strong ruler, upholding the Virgilian precept, *'parcere subjectis et debellare superbos'* [to spare the defeated and humble the proud], to whose sanctuary, for centuries after, maltreated slaves could fly for refuge. His shrines were dominant, his images were everywhere; but all, of course, in the visual idiom of the sculptors' own day; a young athlete with the proud unconcern at nakedness which marked out the 'civilized' Hellene from the white-skinned, over-clad, pudent 'barbarians' who had been stripped and mocked when they struggled ashore from their rammed ships at Salamis. Had these fifth-century sculptors been offered as their model a real Bronze Age warrior, in a helmet of hide stitched with boars' teeth, wearing embroidered *lederhosen* and massive jewels, no doubt they would have recoiled. Yet their idealized, nude victor still wielded in battle the weapon which had come down to them in his living tradition, the immemorially ancient Minoan-Helladic double axe, cult-object and royal mace of Crete.

Theseus had no place in *The Last of the Wine*, except as part of the stuff with which one had learned, in one's reading, that the characters' minds were furnished, as their rooms were furnished with supper-couches, red-figure rhytons, and household shrines. Sometimes they had occasion to remember him: 'There is a labyrinth,' says the Priest of Apollo to Alexias, 'in the heart of every man, and to each comes the time when he must reach its centre, and meet the Minotaur.' But while writing this, I still saw only the Theseus whom the priest and Alexias would know.

I cannot remember exactly when, or how, this face in the crowd came forward to take the stage. But about this time, the first Linear B decipherments were appearing, with their glimpses of feudal Mycenaean kingdoms; along with some dramatic discoveries of royal tombs. There began to be described a mainland culture different from the mannered elegance of the Minoan. Here with their skeleton hands still folded over their long gold-pommeled swords, lay the tall princes whose descendants took Troy; beside their domed tombs had stood the great stone walls of their fortress-palaces, the gates with their huge lintels, lifted no one knows how, and their lion-carved capstones. The written tablets shadowed a warlike society, well organized, aristocratic and art-loving, but primitive and barbaric by the standards of Crete's millennial sophistication.

At some stage of these thoughts, I began to picture the young Theseus, a product of this environment, making his appearance at Knossos as hostage, athlete or invader. But the moment of cross-fertilization, when I first knew what the book would be about and why, happened when after reading, if I remember rightly, Robert Graves's *The Greek Myths*, I was reflecting on the concept of the Royal Sacrifice. Clearly it had been sometimes enforced; just as clearly, it seemed to me, it must have been sometimes voluntary. When, and why?

Suddenly, everything fell into place. I could begin to guess at the way Theseus' mind was furnished, the kind of beliefs and aspirations and responsibilities which might have determined his actions; the tensions between victorious patriarchy and lately defeated, still powerful matriarchy, which could have underlain the love-conflict element in his legendary relations with women. The story became self-propelling in my mind and I started serious reading, in order to check errors before it ran away with me. But everything I read went along with the tale as I had conceived it, nothing against.

There was one more crucial turning-point, however, after the novel was actually in progress. I had written several chapters, presenting Theseus in the Greek heroic image; that is, the Homeric, with the build of the tall princes in the tholos tombs; adding, since he was a hero, a few extra inches for good measure. Somehow, I couldn't tell how or why, I found the story resisting me. Something was dragging, something stuck. I went on, with an increasing instinct that I was going to fetch up against some block or other which would refuse to be side-stepped and would make me a lot of work. I was, and it did. I had already accepted fully the view now held by most scholars that the tribute of youths and maids from Athens, prey of the Minotaur (which just means 'Bull of Minos'), the doomed company which Theseus joined as a volunteer, must in fact have been conscripts for the bull game, whose astonishing athletics are so dominant a theme of Minoan art. Two discrepant images had thus been wrestling in my subsconscious imagination. Among these light, slender, wiry young acrobats, who possessed the only possible physique for the bull dance, what on earth was this six-foot-three warrior doing?

Here it was. He had dragged on me because, though orthodox, he was unreal. Suddenly I saw Theseus as the kind of man his conditioning might produce, if his mind and aspirations had been those of a Helladic prince, but his body that of a bull-leaper; a body not of his own conquering race (and there was a mystery about his birth) but of the conquered Pelasgians. A constant element of the Theseus legend, I remembered, was that he had invented the science of wrestling. Why should a big man need to do that? It would much likelier be the resource of an intelligent lightweight.

I remembered Alexander; a man of just such slight limber build and lightning reflexes, with a face of striking beauty, of whom a contemporary would none the less record for later historians that his limbs were remarkable for strength rather than good looks, 'for he was not tall'. Height was, to the Greek, a *sine qua non* of physical prestige, even in women; a prestige perhaps historic and racial, as well as aesthetic, and having its origins in a day not far antecedent to Theseus' own. Legend was bound to confer this quality on a founder-hero; nothing else would be conceivable. But the real Theseus was a man who had made an asset of his liabilities, as so many real-life heroes do.

Obviously, there was now no alternative but to re-write from the beginning. But from this decision on, I started to enjoy myself. Nothing is more exciting, when one explores the past, than the sense of having, perhaps, found a new lead into truth. Someday, no doubt, new documents will be deciphered, which will restore the lost history of the Helladic age, and some or all of my guesses will be disproved. Never mind; it is better for us all, including me, that more truth be known.

I have never, for any reason, in any historical book of mine, falsified anything deliberately which I knew or believed to be true. Often of course I must have done through ignorance what would horrify me if I could revisit the past; at the best one is in the position of, say, an Indonesian resident who has never met an Englishman, trying to write a novel set in London from documentary evidence, pictures, and maps. But one can at least desire the truth; and it is inconceivable to me how anyone can decide deliberately to betray it; to alter some fact which was central to the life of a real human being, however long it is since he ceased to live, in order to make a smoother story, or to exploit him as propaganda for some cause. I have yet to be persuaded that the word 'committed', if analysis is pressed home, will ever be found to mean anything which does not boil down to, 'a state in which something else matters more than truth'.

There is nothing amusing about committal; the victims of that slaughter lie strewn around. But exhortations to be contemporary always strike me as irresistibly comic. When a lady blue-stocking announced in the presence of Carlyle that she accepted the universe, he remarked aside, 'By God, she'd better'. If one could, even for an instant, be anything but contemporary, one would have achieved omniscience. What a triumph of the historical imagination! Anyone now alive is contemporary whether he likes it or not, and any kind of creative work he does will show it. Kipling is wholly a man of his own world situation, while doing a first-class job of reconstruction on the life of a Roman-British centurion manning Hadrian's Wall; Spenser, painstakingly archaizing Prince Arthur in Fairyland, is quintessentially Elizabethan. Thackeray's characters listening to the cannon of Waterloo are all mid-Victorians; we are far nearer to Jane Austen's shore-leave naval officers who chat about their prizes in an English parlour.

We all bring to the past our own temperament, our own preoccupations, to limit the reach of our insight; our visual field at its widest will be small enough. It seems to me that it is in the struggle to stretch these bonds, to see the universals of human nature adapting to, or intractably resisting, the pressure of life's changing accidents, that the excitement of writing historical novels lies.

You cannot step twice into the same river, said Herakleitos. People in the past were not just like us; to pretend so is an evasion and a betrayal, turning our back on them so as to be easy among familiar things. This is why the matter of dialogue is so crucial. No word in our language comes to us sterile and aseptic, free of associations. If it was coined yesterday, it tastes of that, and a single sentence of modern-colloquial slang, a turn of phrase which evokes specifically our own society, can destroy for me, at any rate, the whole suspension of disbelief. Yet phony archaism merely suggests the nineteenth century instead, and actors in ill-fitting tights. If I wrote about the England of any earlier century, I should want to use, as far as it is still understandable, the actual speech of that day. That this can be done is proved by Rose Macaulay's magnificent *They Were Defeated* whose smell of authenticity quite goes to one's head. However, I was writing about people who spoke Greek. In such case all one can hope for is to be, as far as possible, transparent, not to intrude.

Greek is a highly polysyllabic language. Yet when writing dialogue for my Greeks I have found myself, by instinct, avoiding the polysyllables of the English language, and using, as far as they are still in the living language, the older and shorter words. This is not because the style parallels Greek style; it is entirely a matter of association and ambience. In Greek, polysyllables are old; in English, mostly Latinized and largely modern. They have acquired their own aura, which they will bring along with them. Their stare, like that of the basilisk, is killing. Take the following sentence, which I have just picked at random from a magazine: 'High priority is to be given to training in the skills of community organizing and conflict resolution.' It contains no concept which Plato did not know, or, indeed, did not in fact deal with. But it comes to us steeped in notions of the company report, the social survey, and so forth. When I see writing like this in a historical novel I know what the author is after. He wants us to identify with the situation of his characters as if it were our own. But it isn't, and identification thus achieved is a cheat. You cannot, as an advertising copywriter would say, enjoy a trip to fifth-century Athens, or Minoan Crete, in the comfort of your own home. You have, as far as your mind will take you, to leave home and go to them.

Does all this really matter? Yes, I think so; and not just aesthetically. Every era of man's development, from the palaeolithic upwards, is still in living existence somewhere on earth. Indeed, the metropolitan technocrats whom self-centred intellectuals glibly call Twentieth Century Man, are as few today in relation to all humanity, as the spores in a mould-spot on a grape where it has scarcely begun to spread. We live in blindness if we forget that history is not only vertical; it is also horizontal.

However, one does not go to the past as a public utility. So why? One can say, 'Because it is there.' But unlike Everest, not only is it there, but we are its products. We go, perhaps, to find ourselves; perhaps to free ourselves. It is certain we shall never know ourselves, till we have broken out from the brittle capsule of Megalopolis, and taken a long look back along the rocky road which brought us where we are.

March 1979

PARIS AND HELEN

Edward Lucas White

We begin our journey through history with one of the most famous events in both legend and reality: the siege of Troy. Not only did this give rise to one of the earliest classics of literature, The Iliad, attributed to Homer in the eighth century BC, but it also gave us one of the earliest strong female characters in Helen of Troy. In the legend, Paris was the son of King Priam of Troy. He was abandoned as a baby when his mother dreamed he would destroy the world, but he was rescued and raised as a shepherd before eventually discovering his own origins. Paris was asked to judge who was the fairest of the goddesses Hera, Aphrodite and Athena, and he chose Aphrodite when she promised him the most beautiful of women for his wife. When Paris sailed to the court of Menelaos, king of Sparta, he met the king's wife, Helen. He abducted her, and thus began the Trojan War. The date traditionally given to the fall of Troy is 1184 BC, but recent analysis of ancient historical records (especially those in Egypt) throws doubt over this dating and suggests that the events could have taken place as much as 250 years later, around the year 900 BC. This would place it only a generation or two before the time of Homer, who may have heard stories directly from the sons or grandsons of the heroes.

The extract that follows is taken from Helen *(1925), an episodic novel by the American, Edward Lucas White (1866–1934), who taught Greek and Latin at schools in New Jersey. He wrote two other novels, both of Roman life,* The Unwilling Vestal *(1918) and* Andividus Hedulio *(1921) as well as the scholarly* Why Rome Fell *(1927). White suffered from migraine throughout his life, which often gave him the most bizarre nightmares which he converted into horror stories, most of which were collected as* Lukundoo *and*

Other Stories *(1927). Continuing ill health led him to take his own life at the age of 67.*

In the following excerpt Paris is mourning the death of his brother Hector, the greatest of the Trojan heroes, who had been killed by Achilles. Paris feels he must avenge his brother's death.

'Hector's death,' said Paris, 'has shaken me more than I would have believed possible.'

'Despondency,' said Helen, 'I did not expect of you. I sympathize with your heart-ache, for I loved him dearly myself and I sorrow with you. But I had anticipated that you would, by this time, have recovered from your dejection and have resumed your habitual demeanour and way of life.'

'I have had,' said Paris, 'during the dreadful years of this interminable siege, many bereavements, each of which should have left me plunged in melancholy, but I could never see any good in being gloomy and have always been able to shake off my sadness. I have been accused of taking my losses too lightly, of being unfeeling and frivolous. For the first time I comprehended how my revilers felt, and I see that there was much reason in what they thought and said. They upbraided me and I could not discern why; now I am overwhelmed by self-reproaches bitterer and more crushing than their invectives. For the first time in my life I feel remorse. As I sit here or as I lie awake at night I review all the evil I have caused, the many times I might have helped Hector and yet failed to help him; all I have let others suffer for me without myself doing my duty from day to day. To begin with, I alone caused this devastating war.'

Here Helen interrupted him.

'You are altogether too severe on yourself,' she asserted. 'You heard and saw what I heard and saw the day after you brought me to Troy, when the people at their public assembly debated whether I was to remain here or be sent back. You heard all the speeches and you, like me, saw the people swept away by their admiration for me and heard them vote, vote overwhelmingly, to keep me and to fight for me. You yourself had urged them to ignore their love for you and to decide whatever was best for themselves. 'If their decision was dictated by enthusiasm rather than by discernment and sagacity it was not your fault, and you should not blame yourself.'

'I do blame myself, and with reason,' said Paris. 'If I had never brought you here they could never have been so carried away by your beauty and winsomeness as to vote to die for you. I should never have let my passion for you overmaster me as I did. I should never have lured you to yield to your feelings as I did.'

'How could you or I,' said Helen, 'withstand the power of the most potent of all goddesses? I am ashamed of how we came to belong to each other and often I blame myself. But neither you nor I are actually to blame, but the goddess who constrained us. You should not blame yourself.'

'I do blame myself,' said Paris, 'as does Father, and as do the rest of the family, even Mother in her secret heart, though she never hints it, let alone says it. And the people blame me, and rightly, though they have borne all the misery I have caused without reproaching me for it. What they have reproached me for and what I most reproach myself for is the indubitable fact that I have shirked much of what should have fallen to my share in the way of actual fighting.'

'You've done plenty of hard fighting,' said Helen, 'and some of it very brilliant fighting.'

'My two single combats with Menelaus, for instance,' Paris sneered bitterly.

'You did your very best in both,' Helen asserted. 'I, looking on, could see that in both combats you were almost his match. I prayed hard.'

'For which?' sneered Paris.

'For both, as I have often told you,' Helen stated. 'And my prayers were heard and were not in vain. I dreaded that he would kill you, for I love you so that nothing else in the world means anything to me except you and your welfare and our being together. But, while I passionately wanted you to escape alive and unhurt, I did not want Menelaus killed or even wounded. He did not deserve to have any harm befall him, does not and never has. I wish Menelaus were dead; for if he were you and I should be safe in our possession of each other and might have even a taste of real happiness, might even live out our lives happily together. But, while Menelaus is alive I do not, I cannot, wish for his death or for any harm to him. Vehemently and utterly as I love you I have an inextinguishable regard and affection for Menelaus. He was ardently in love with me and wistfully eager for me to love him. When he found that I merely tolerated him, though it hurt him acutely, it did not sour him or make him unkind to me, as would have been the result with most men. He was always not only punctiliously courteous but as unremitting in his attentions as any fervid suitor. In a very trying situation he behaved as well as possible. I admire and revere him.'

'You never did love Menelaus,' Paris amplified, 'but you respect him; you idolize me, yet you despise me.'

'I never said so!' Helen disclaimed warmly.

'No!' Paris gloomed, 'but I have seen contempt in your eyes more than once and you expressed it emphatically enough after each of my single combats with Menelaus, though, after you had cooled off, you have always made wifely excuses for me, both publicly and to me alone. Don't make any more just now, they only sharpen my self-reproach. I know you despise me, and you have a good right to feel contempt for me. I despise myself. I recollect Hector's chidings. He thought I ought to be as pertinacious at the war as he was. Hector was a wonder. He had heart in him as unweariable as the bronze edge of an adze; a shipwright hews with his adze all day and, at sunset, the adze is no nearer to being fatigued than it was at sunrise. Hector's courage was as staunch as the bronze of an adze. No more peaceable man than Hector ever lived, nor any man who less relished battle and even victory. But when, against his wish, and will, Mars hurled him into war, he fought the Greeks as a shipwright's adze hews oak, unfalteringly and unflinchingly. He was just as brave and gallant one day as another or at any hour of any day. He expected me to be like him, and reproached me because I was, as he said, erratic and unreliable. Because he was always ready to go out and fight, day after day, because he fought just as well one day as another, he expected me to be like him. In vain I told him that there was no use in my going out to fight on days when I knew that I was not merely not my best, but very far from my best. When I feel like fighting I am not only one of the best fighters Troy has, but one of the best she ever had. My arrow flies far and finds its mark precisely as I meant it should, and drives deep where it hits; my spear whirrs mightily and carries death on its point. My eye is so keen and my muscles so quick that no missile aimed at me has any chance of wounding me. But, when I do not feel like fighting there is no sense in my going out when I should be so sluggish at dodging that any tyro might kill me; when I should be certain to miss any foe whom I aimed at. When I am far from my best I should only mar our defence by taking my place among our fighters. Better for me to wait for the day when I feel my best; meantime I might just as well pitch quoits in the Palace courtyard or sit in the sun and twang my guitar. I used to say that to Hector, over and over, and I always thought him unreasonable and unkind when he reviled me; now I know how he felt, I comprehend how he felt, out in the field and in danger of death every instant, seeing gallant men perish daily defending Troy and me while I sat on the Palace terrace in the sun, holding your skein of yarn or playing you tunes on my guitar and singing to you. It not only looked unmanly but it was unmanly. If I had been a real man I should have been able and willing to fight in every battle, any day, as Hector was. I should have done my plain duty according to my capacities. I shirked it. I despise myself. I should have done my duty to Troy and the family and you, and I have not. I despise myself.'

'I do not see,' said Helen gently, 'how sitting here berating yourself helps you to do your duty to me or your parents or your brothers or Troy.'

'While I have been berating myself, as you call it,' Paris rejoined, 'I have been thinking out how far I can spur myself on and nerve myself up to help Deiphobus and Aeneas take Hector's place as leaders of our defence. On my best days as a spearman I have been excelled only by Hector, Deiphobus and Aeneas among ourselves and Sarpedon and Memnon among our allies; as an archer since Pandarus is dead, I have no rival among us, for no Trojan of my time has ever been able to equal me with the bow. Deiphobus is almost as good an archer as I, but not quite. I have been meditating on how many good men we have lost since the siege began on account of the way in which the two Ajaxes co-operate, big Ajax as a spearman, mortal in his aim, unassailable behind his great shield, and his compact cousin with him as an archer, watchful to right and left as is his tall partner to the front. We have never had such a pair on our side, but I am thinking that Deiphobus and I might make an even better team, for we are both superlative archers and capital spearmen.'

'On your best days,' Helen put in.

'I forecast,' said Paris, 'that I shall be my very best and keyed up to more than my best every day until I have avenged my brother Hector.'

Helen turned pale.

'Do you mean,' she cried, 'that you intend to go out day after day and seek an encounter with Achilles?'

'Not alone,' said Paris. 'That would be mere lunacy; as well might an osprey attack an eagle; but I mean Deiphobus and I together, one challenging as a spearman, well behind a shield, the other watching his chance with bow and arrows.'

Helen flushed.

'How brave of you!' she cried. 'How venturesome! Yet it is not a foolhardy plan. You two might have a chance so.'

Before dusk, however, she was panic-stricken with the conviction that any chance which Deiphobus and Paris or any other combination of Troy's best fighters would have against Achilles was too small to make her or anybody feel hopeful. She spoke to Paris of her feelings.

'It does not matter to me,' said he, 'if I go to certain and inevitable death; I go. I have been remiss too long. I am now thoroughly roused to do my duty as I see it. Since I have seen it, inaction means for me only the gnawing of remorse worse than countless deaths. I love you, and I love life, but every fibre of me is tense to avenge Hector. I shall defer to you in all else and cherish you as I may while I live. But do not seek to swerve me from my purpose or to tempt me to slip back into my self-indulgent, easy-going ways. I am resolute to dawdle no longer. Either I shall avenge Hector or I shall perish in the attempt.'

Helen, as always, almost as a child to her mother, turned to Aithre.

'I cannot help you in this, darling,' said Aithre. 'I ought not to try to help you and you should not ask if of me nor expect it. Paris is right. He should have done much better in this war, he might have done much better. If he had acted as he should his magnificent brother might be living now, might have lived to succeed his father as ruler of Troy. No wonder Paris mourns and rages. He is too much keyed up for any consideration save vengeance to affect him now. Let him alone. We can only watch and pray.'

Next morning Paris laid his idea before the assembly in his father's council-hall. Sultan Priam tugged his vast expanse of curly white beard and looked at his handsome son, a faint gleam of prideful approbation showing momentarily through the pathetic dejection of his grief. Deiphobus could never be enthusiastic, but he was as nearly hearty in his expressions of approval as was possible for his cold, reticent nature and his dry, weathered appearance. The old councillors approved the suggestion as offering some hope of revenge for their irreparable loss and for a successful defence of the city. Aeneas, after every possible speaker had said his say, stood up and spoke weightily:

'The plan,' he said, 'is good; even, I think, the best possible. But it can succeed only if the attack be delivered at just the right instant without anything to give warning of what is intended or to cause any suspicion that anything unusual is afoot. If you two go out together before the press of our young spearmen, one or both of you will perish, for the Greeks have a dozen champions any one of whom is superior to either of you as a spearman. If you wait among the press until you see Achilles approaching and then advance against him, both together or one before the other, he will slay one or both of you, for he is stronger, prompter, swifter and more deadly of aim than any man alive. Neither in succession nor simultaneously can you hope to overcome him if he sees you intending to attack him and prepares for your onset. But if he be flushed with victory and pursuing heedlessly you may kill him and come off unscathed. This is the only chance of your promising plan succeeding. If he be in his chariot one or both of you should be charioted; if he be afoot you may both be in your chariots or one afoot or both afoot. But he must be so intent on attacking or fighting or pursuing other men that you deliver your cast or shot before his attention shifts to you.

'This is my suggestion. We have been inactive several days in succession, solemnizing the funeral of our best warrior and best-loved prince. The Greeks, naturally, will rest until we again challenge them, for they know they can do nothing against our walls and gates, even if very thinly manned. I propose that to-morrow early I lead out the mass of our young spearmen and all our charioteers who are fit, and that we advance towards the camp of the Greeks, where their reed huts line the shore about the sterns of their beached galleys. To a certainty they will, as soon as they see us advancing, come up against us with most of their charioteers and chief champions and a cloud of spearmen afoot. I propose no long skirmish, but a prompt retirement, as dilatory and gradual as can be managed, so long as we do not lose too many of our gallant lads. I propose that not only the Scaean Gates be set and kept wide open, but also the Sigean Gate to the westward of them and the Dardanian Gate to the eastward, with a strong force of archers on the tops of the two towers flanking each gate, others along the wall above the long sloping ramp leading up to the Dardanian Gate and an adequate force of gate-guards at each gateway, including a body of practised and alert youths to shut and bar the gates neither too soon nor too late, and also big, burly fighters to hold off the press of foemen at the nick of time. Then our spearmen, doggedly retreating, will know that there is no danger of their being shut outside closed gates to be massacred by their pursuers, nor of being crushed in the press of their countrymen crowding to squeeze through a gateway, since laggards outside the Scaean Gateway may scamper westwards to the Sigean Gateway or trudge safely up the ramp to the Dardanian Gateway, for few Greeks will venture within arrow-shot of the men on the gateway towers or of the sentries behind the battlements of the wall above the sloping ramp.

'When our press of spearmen in its retreat is half already inside the city and Achilles is flushed with success, you two, ready by the Scaean Gate, neither too far from the city walls nor too near, may have an excellent chance at him as he recklessly urged his team or heedlessly follows afoot the press of his fleeing foes. Some such ruse as this might entrap him to his death.'

Ucalegon spoke after Aeneas, approving his plan.

Next day it was attempted, none of the fighters, except Aeneas, and Priam's own sons, knowing what was intended.

Priam himself, with Ucalegon and others of his councillors, looked from the highest of the wall-towers and on another tower-top was Hecuba, with Ilione, Andromache, Creusa, Helen, Aithre and others of the women of the Palace.

It is almost impossible for us moderns to conceive what war was like in those early days. The germs of strategy had already burgeoned. Men had learned to deliver their attack at one point, while attention was distracted by a feint at another point, as had Castor and Pollux at Aphidnae. Even a frontal attack masked behind a sham semblance of general onset, such as Aeneas proposed, was not an extreme rarity. But then only the veriest rudiments of co-operation, of subordination, of orders given and orders obeyed, had as yet developed. Discipline was unthought of, drill undreamt of. Men, men even with the best minds then on earth, went out to battle much as a crowd in one of our cities goes out to look at a fire, each man for himself. Organization there was none. Most men were afoot, armed each with a spear; the rich drove two-horsed chariots and had better arms than the commonality. The most the chieftains did towards commanding their warriors was to hold them in check until what seemed a suitable moment and then to give a signal for advance. At the signal, each thinking for himself, forward they went, at a cautious walk or at a helter-skelter scamper, according to their feeling at the moment; sometimes a press of crowded men afoot in front, sometimes with venturesome chariots in the lead, even far in the lead; sometimes with the best-armed champions far before the general rabble; but never formed by any system or according to the orders of any leaders.

The main gateway of Troy to seaward was not on the level of the plain, but on a steep hillside markedly above that level, and was reached by a long, sloping ramped roadway which left the plain about halfway between it and the next gateway westwards. This, being to the left of the Dardanian Gateway to anyone facing outwards from it, was called the Scaean Gate. It was, originally, the least important of the eight gateways in the outer city wall of Troy and was one of the two which were customarily kept closed in times of peace. For it had been built as a sally-port in times of war, because no sally from the Dardanian Gateway could surprise any foemen, since any warriors issuing from the Dardanian Gateway must run all the way down the ramped sloping roadway before they came to grips with any besiegers and must thus be in full sight of the enemy for a time long enough to enable their antagonists to make ready for their onset. As the Scaean Gate gave the promptest access to the plain between Troy and the Greek camp, most of the fighting during the long siege had been in front of it, since most of the Trojan sallies had been made from it and most of their retreats through it.

The morning was fair, with a deep blue sky flecked with a few small clouds of a dazzling whiteness. There was a light breeze, mitigating the heat of the brilliant sun-rays. As they meant the Greeks to be forewarned of their sally, the Trojans set wide all three gateways at once and the elders and ladies on the watch-towers presently saw spread from all three over the plain many war-chariots, their half-broken teams tugging at the yokes across their necks, the two-wheeled chariots jerked forward by the pole connecting axle and yoke, jolting, lurching and bouncing, the waving crests of the champions and charioteers flickering in the sunshine, their shields glittering. Behind the chariots came a rush of swift-running, agile young spearmen, behind them the main body of Troy's warriors, running too, but more evenly and steadily than the lads ahead of them.

Interspersed among the spearmen were archers, wiry callants, each entirely naked except for a leather cap, like half a melon, tight on his skull, and a scanty loin-cloth; and unencumbered by any equipment save a quiver of arrows hanging on his back, a short sword belted to his hip, and his bow in his hand.

The spearmen wore each a helmet of polished bronze with at its top a conical spike longer than a man's hand, supporting a curved, folded piece of bronze like a cock's comb, fashioned to hold a great plume of horse-hair. Every warrior afoot or charioted was protected by a leather corselet provided with a breast-plate and a back-plate of thin bronze not much thicker than a man's thumb-nail, and from the belt of which depended nearly to his knees a kilt of overlapping hand-broad straps of leather, the outer layer plated with thin scales of bronze. Each wore a pair of shin-guards, called greaves, made of tin as pure as the metallurgy of those days could smelt it, and therefore at once flexible and certain to cling fast to the legs. These greaves were not so much to protect the shanks from brambles and thorns as to keep the lower rim of the heavy shield from bruising raw the upper shin just below the knee.

One and all, from the youngest archer to Aeneas himself, the warriors were barefoot. Sandals were all very well for men on a journey or armies on the march, but to battle the men of those days went as barefoot as Zulus or Matabele of Africa in modern times.

Each corseleted warrior carried a great circular shield, its diameter such that it covered him from above the left shoulder to below the left knee, made of bullhide stretched over a rim of artfully bent wood, tough and reliable, and covered with a plate of bronze even thinner than that over the leather of his corselet. In his right hand each carried two spears, one to throw and one to use as a pike. The sword at each man's hip was not much longer than his forearm. All swords, spear-points and arrow-heads were of bronze, approximately such as that of which we make our least valuable coins; steel was as yet unknown, and iron known only as a rare, soft and costly metal, used chiefly for decorative inlays because of its greyish colour, contrasting with the hues of gold, silver, copper and bronze.

The watchers on the tower-tops had before them a wide and magnificent view across the plain to the Greeks' low huts and the high stern-ornaments of their ships, showing between the great mound by Rhœteum and the greater mound by Sigeum like the teeth of a titanic comb against the deep blue waters of the straits; beyond them the hills of the farther shore, then heavily forested, light-green oak, beech and chestnut woods below and black masses of pines above; the dark blue sky over all; the rolling country far off to the right; the open sea away and away to the left, beyond Tenedos.

This prospect they entirely ignored, intent on the outrushing thousands of their spearmen and the scores of chariots of their chieftains. The chariots they could make out individually, but from them, as from the masses of men afoot, the dominant impression was of innumerable waving helmet-plumes, some black, some blue, some green, some yellow, some white, but most, more than all the rest together, crimson or scarlet or vermilion, all tossing in the breeze, while from between them flashed the countless blinding sparkles of the sunrays on burnished helmets, corselets, shields, baldricks, kilt-straps, and greaves.

The Trojan host poured on down the plain like the waters of mountain torrents spouting from three gorges in the foothills and spreading over a level meadow. From the beach the Greeks rushed up to meet them like the foam of a great breaker lashing up a broad strand. There was no impact of the two hosts, no collision, no onslaught of either on the other, no engagement, no affray. Well out of the utmost reach of any arrow from the other host each host slowed its pace to a trot, then to a walk, till each was barely continuing its forward motion.

Then the watchers, even at that distance, could clearly descry a dozen chariots on each side make a curving dash noticeably in advance of their associates. In those days every man rich enough for his family to afford it and sufficiently endowed with strength, skill and valour to make the expense worth while, drove to battle in a war-chariot drawn by two swift and mettlesome horses, driven by a capable and expert charioteer. But those chieftains did not fight from their chariots; the chariot was a means of swiftly conveying pre-eminent warriors, unwearied and fresh, to the battle-line and of placing them just where they judged it was most advantageous for them. The practice was for the charioteer to direct his team, at full gallop, so as to swing outward towards the foe and return in a sort of loop, at the outer end of which the horses were slowed down, the warrior leaped to earth, ran a few paces, hurled his lance at the mass of the enemy's foot soldiers, if near enough to them, or at his chosen antagonist, if opposed by some charioted champion from among his foes; darted after his receding chariot, bounded into it and was whisked away out of range of his foemen. This exploit was regularly essayed with the turn to the right, so as to bring the shield-arm of the venturesome champion towards the foe at the critical interval between hurling his lance and regaining his chariot.

Great as was the distance the watchers on the towers could see this manœuvre performed by nearly a score of chariots on each side. But, after the exchange of aimed spears, while the Trojan chariots whirled about and carried their owners towards the mass of their countrymen, the chariots of the Greek champions, after picking up their masters, swerved again towards the city. This was the instant at which the archers on both sides would put forth all their strength, skill and audacity. But their gallantry was not visible so far away, nor was any effect from it discernible. On swept the Greek host, iike a tidal wave, and before them the Trojans receded like dead leaves driven by a great wind; fleeing, scurrying, scuttling, jumbled, jostling.

As the two hosts came on, pursued and pursuers, the watchers could see the most intrepid of their champions attempt to impede the Greek pursuit by having their chariots driven in circles, curving back towards the oncomers, and threateningly swooping towards them. These feints did slow down the pursuers opposite them and so retarded the general advance.

But that advance continued: from the tower-tops the watchers could see the fugitives dividing into three swarms, some making direct for the Scaean Gateway and others diverging to right and left, aiming for the Sigean Gateway or the ramped roadway leading to the Dardanian Gate. As the Greeks drew nearer, since, after years of warfare, all notabilities on either side were well known to all beholders, the watchers could recognize Ulysses, Diomede and Sthenelus guiding their teams in the hope of reaching the foot of the ramp before the fugitives or before the last of them; Idomeneus, Meriones and Teucer similarly straining after the swarm making for the Sigean Gate; while Achilles, the two Ajaxes, Menelaus and Agamemnon held on after those approaching the Scaean Gateway.

Already the Scaean Gate was choked with jostling, crowding, panic-stricken fugitives; the ramp filled with puffing men, already feeling safe and trudging unhurriedly under the arrow-points of the wall-guards; the flat, dusty, hard-trodden space outside the walls between the Scaean and Sigean gates was covered with spearmen streaming towards the Sigean Gate and safety; behind them the Greek chariots ever nearer, their charioteers lashing their teams, the champions brandishing their shields and spears and yelling, yelling so loud that they could be heard above the all-embracing insistent scream of the chariot-wheels.

Yelling loudest of all was Achilles, nearest of all, the scarlet plume of his helmet waving in the wind, the sun-rays gleaming on his burnished helmet, corselet, shield, kilt-straps and greaves; his face blazing with excitement and the anticipation of triumph, his yellow hair streaming behind him, his mouth half open, his right hand brandishing his great spear.

Up to that time human ingenuity had created no more formidable embodiment of military power than such a tall, strong, agile, swift, unerring, valiant warrior, charioted, armoured and armed. Achilles, as the paragon champion of his time, was more terrific than any portent then on earth.

When he was almost on his victims, out dashed, from where they waited under the walls to left and right of the Scaean Gateway, in the intervals between the three swarms of panic-stricken fugitives, Deiphobus and Paris, each in his chariot, behind swift mares guided by a dexterous charioteer. As they came he saw them, Deiphobus on his right, Paris on his left, approaching him from nearly in front.

All three charioteers made their loop and swerve at the same instant; at the same instant the three champions sprang to earth, Deiphobus a trifle nearer Achilles than was Paris. With unerring judgement Achilles faced the nearer adversary and Deiphobus and he, each with the short run of three or four steps always taken to add impetus to the flying weapon, simultaneously hurled their spears at each other. Just when Achilles had his right arm at its highest, just when he threw, his left arm concomitantly drooped as he balanced himself and the upper rim of his great shield sagging enough for Paris, spear and shield cast aside, feet firm on the ground, legs wide apart, curving his great bow into an arch as he drew the arrow till its barbs touched the fingers of his left hand, to send his light shaft true to a finger-breadth above the gleaming shield-rim and clean through Achilles' heart, till its feathers were left projecting hardly a hand's-breadth from the burnished bronze of his breast-plate.

So near was Achilles to the city wall that all beholders could see the whole manœuvre, the spear of Deiphobus flying past Achilles' throat over his right shoulder, the spear of Achilles grazing the corselet of Deiphobus under his right arm, Paris deftly tossing his strung bow to his charioteer and retrieving his own shield and spear from the ground; and Achilles, even as his lance grazed his antagonist like many another man shot through the heart, putting forth in his death-agony strength even vastly beyond the utmost he had ever exerted by intention and turning completely over in the air twice in succession in convulsions inexpressibly terrific before he sprawled horridly on the earth, twitching and heaving yet.

The watchers beheld Deiphobus possess himself of the great spear which Achilles had hurled at him, beheld Paris rashly dart towards the fallen hero, and, miraculously, before Ajax and Agamemnon, swiftly as their lashed teams came on, were near enough to prevent him, make off safe with his gold-crested, crimson-plumed helmet, the point of his lance, as he ran, neatly severing the chin-strap and picking up the prize. Both, after their trophies had been passed to their charioteers, turned, and, with Aeneas and a dozen more of Troy's mightiest champions, made a rush at big Ajax, Menelaus and Agamemnon and their comrades, standing over the body. Up flocked more Greek chieftains, more Trojan veterans. One side straining to make prizes of the dead man's armour, even to carry off his corpse bodily, the other to protect it, to rescue it and its accoutrements, they shot, lunged, thrust and hacked at each other, their clash becoming an affray and, as more and more men of each side joined in or pressed forward from behind, spreading to a general engagement, a furious mêlée. This lasted until the sun was declining, by which time scores of men on each side had fallen under the rain of arrows, the frequent spear-casts, the incessant pike-play and sword-play; not one of the most prominent champions on either side remained unwounded, and the fighters unhurt were utterly exhausted.

Then, toward sunset, the Greeks, by a spasmodic effort, drew off their champion's corpse and retired with it, the combatants thereupon separating.

All Troy was frantic to welcome Paris. He had always been their darling, but he had hitherto done little over which they might exult. Now, all at once, he had, in full sight of hundreds, carried to success a ruse as perilous as possible, had made a shot both difficult and effective, and scarcely to be surpassed by any bowman, had avenged his revered brother, and had rid them of their most baneful enemy; also he had been among the foremost fighters in the frenzied and protracted struggle for the body of Achilles, intrepidly active in the midst of that appalling mêlée, inflicting many wounds and safe out of it, though twice wounded.

The populace was delirious with rejoicing, the warriors jubilant, the chieftains exultant; all Troy, for the first time in years, positively hopeful. After an ovation in the city square their hero at length entered his home to relish Helen's congratulations and solicitude. Though merely flesh-wounds, the slash through his right shoulder and the tear along his right hip showed how dauntlessly he had faced the pikes of his foemen, how near he had been to death in the affray. Helen, for the first time was proud of Paris and showed it. She uniformly loved him, but rather shamefacedly and half against her will; now she admired him and glowed with her admiration. He revelled in the sensation of having made her esteem him.

Paris was entirely healed of both his wounds, in fact, not an unhealed scar was left on any Trojan champion, before the Greeks had completed their ceremonial observances honouring the funeral of Achilles. In the interval Paris had ample time to discuss with his brothers and father, with the Sultan's councillors, with Aeneas, with other chieftains, with Helen, his plans for another exploit.

'It would be silly as well as futile,' he said, 'to attempt to repeat our successful ruse. We must vary our methods. But there is no reason why we may not succeed in killing some notable Greek champion at our very next sortie. Deiphobus might be the archer and I the spearman. But I intend to try again a joint and simultaneous assault at any and every opportunity; it matters not which of us relies on his lance and which on his bow.'

'And which chieftain will you aim at this time?' Helen queried.

Paris looked her full in the eyes and then looked away.

'Obviously,' he said, 'there is only one man by killing whom I can end this war at one stroke.'

'I don't want Menelaus killed!' Helen protested.

'I know,' said Paris, 'and I aim to humour you in all things, in so far as I may. But, in this case, I must think first not of your wishes, but of what I may do to possess you entirely as my own, undisputedly as my wife, and of how I may deliver Troy from its long agony of siege and bereavements. If I kill Menelaus the league which menaces us ceases to have any reason for its existence; the oath which binds together its leaders lapses; the coalition will at once dissolve; Troy will be saved and you will be mine and I yours till old age brings death to one of us. I must scheme to compass the killing of Menelaus. But I must not miss a chance, if any offer, of mitigating the siege by killing any other champion. Deiphobus and I shall go out, certainly tomorrow, assuredly day after day, until both of us are killed or until we have seen Menelaus a corpse.'

Helen, her eyes downcast, found no words to utter in reply or comment.

At her first opportunity she spoke to Aithre.

'Fate,' said Aithre, 'is beyond the control of the gods themselves: how much further beyond any power of yours or mine to sway. What must be, must be.'

Helen, at once poignantly happy and painfully apprehensive, could not but exult at the adoration of Paris by all Troy.

Priam himself said to her:

'If your husband continues to do as well as he has lately I shall feel not merely justified in issuing but obliged to issue an edict naming Paris as my successor on the throne. Of course, until our stunning bereavement, we all assumed that Hector would survive me and succeed me. Now that he is gone Deiphobus is manifestly our pre-eminent warrior and also one of Troy's most eminent councillors. He is in all ways fit to succeed me except that he is not only the reverse of lovable, but is positively disliked by most of my people of every class: princes, nobles, commoners, yeomen and rabble. My Trojans would never accept Deiphobus, now my eldest surviving son, as their liege. If Paris had not so brilliantly distinguished himself I should probably have felt constrained to appoint cousin Aeneas as my successor, certainly as regent after me. But, with Paris in this blaze of renown and popularity, everything points to him as my natural successor. If all goes well you will be Queen of Troy.'

Helen, from the gallery of the council-hall, from her balcony, from the flat roof of the Palace, had abundant opportunity to rejoice over the position in the community to which Paris had attained at a bound. The old councillors listened to him with respect and even deferred to his opinions; the warriors honoured him; the populace idolized him. And Paris was not intoxicated by adulation nor puffed up with his prestige; he kept his head and was modest in his demeanour.

Very handsome he looked as he moved about among his adorers, far more solicitous about their equipment than his own, giving advice about fastening a new shoulder-strap to a corselet, absorbed in considering the balance of a spear-shaft, bending over the hub of a chariot-wheel. Wherever he was, all eyes turned towards him; wherever he went he was cheered to the echo.

Paris had always been unsurpassably handsome. But from his acceptance as a son of Priam and Hecuba and a legitimate prince of Troy, his beauty had been marred by an expression of easy-going, self-indulgent vanity, of indolent, languid sensuality. His face, handsome as it was, had been devoid of intelligence, almost vacuous. Now, transfigured by his popularity, responsibility and opportunities, his countenance was irradiated by ambition, self-reliance, and high resolve. He moved in a sort of prismatic halo, coloured by the lustre of his feat, the hopes he had aroused in his fellow-countrymen, and the dazzling possibilities of his future.

Especially was he magnificent as he moved towards the Scaean Gate for his daily sortie: his bay mares caracoling, the pompons on their crimson harness dancing, his chariot bright with polished wood and burnished metal, his greaves lustrous, his kilt-straps brilliant, his corselet and shield resplendent, his yellow hair waving, his cheeks aglow, his blue eyes asparkle, his helmet gleaming, its crest scintillating beneath his flickering scarlet plume.

It was thus, on his way to battle, that Helen saw him for the last time, caught her last glimpse of him alive.

NO PLACE LIKE HOME

Tom Holt

After the Trojan War the heroes made their weary way home. Not all arrived home successfully or happily. In the following story, Tom Holt (b. 1961) looks at the eventual arrival home of one of the best known of all heroes.

Holt is most closely associated today with his comic fantasy novels such as Expecting Someone Taller *(1987) and* Faust Among Equals *(1994), but he is a great devotee of the classical age and early in his career produced two novels set in ancient Greece,* Goatsong *(1989) and* The Walled Orchard *(1990).*

I have an idea that who we are depends very much on where we are.

I thought about this as I climbed up from the valley to the high steading where I hoped to find a man called Eumaeus.

The place wasn't hard to find – a big stone building on the hillside, with a good view over the valley, a large, well-designed courtyard and a stout thorn stockade. Inside he'd built twelve styes, each one large enough to hold fifty sows, with a pen outside for the boars. Eumaeus had been busy these last twenty years, and he had plenty to show for it. He could look at what he'd done and feel proud.

I found him in the shade under the wall, cutting sandals out of an oxhide. He was – well, obviously he was older now, but he carried the years well. Clean living, good food and plenty of work. He was in better shape than I was.

His dogs noticed me first and came rushing out in a frenzy of

barking, claws skittering on the paved courtyard. I kept perfectly
still while they growled at me, their ears back. That was as it should
have been because I was a stranger and not a particularly salubrious
one, at that. I approved of Eumaeus' dogs.

'What do you want?' he said, standing up and looking me
over.

'A drink and an hour in the shade,' I replied.

He looked at me carefully and saw a man of about fifty-five,
scruffy and worn with travel but wearing a good pair of boots
and a broad-brimmed leather hat; not a king or a prince or a great
lord, perhaps, but not a tramp either. He did the sensible thing and
withheld his judgement. 'I can manage that,' he replied, shooing the
dogs away with the rough tenderness of a man with his children.
I approved of that, too. 'Come on in, I'll get you some water.'

It was a fine house for a working man and a credit to its builder.
I mentioned this. He thanked me.

'No point in living in a dirty hut when there's all the timber
and stone I could want, and plenty of time as well,' he continued,
handing me the cup. I thanked him and took a long drink. 'And
I'm left pretty much to myself up here, which suits me.'

'Still,' I replied, 'it's not as if it's your own. I don't know that
I'd be in such a hurry to improve another man's property if I was
in your position.'

He shrugged. 'It may not belong to me,' he replied, 'but I live in
it. And I do a good job, though I say so myself, so I don't suppose
they'll be in any hurry to replace me. To be honest, I often don't
see anything of them from one year's end to the next. That's an
advantage of being up here in the hills.'

I nodded. 'What are they like?' I asked.

He poured himself a cup of water before he answered. 'Not my
place to say,' he replied.

'Like I told you, I don't have much to do with them; just once
or twice a month, when they send up for a hog for the table – '

'Once or twice a month,' I repeated, trying not to sound shocked
(and under my breath I muttered *the bastards!*) 'That's a lot of pork
for one household to get through, surely.'

He laughed. 'Oh, they do themselves pretty well these days. And
who's to say they shouldn't, at that? Pork's there to be eaten, after
all. And I've built up the stock over the years, so we can afford it.
They're not peasants, you know. An important family like that,
they should keep a good table.'

'Even so,' I replied, while in my heart I was thinking, *two hogs
a month, that's twenty-four a year, dear gods, twenty-four hogs a*

year, what do they do with all that food? 'Keeping a good table's one thing, but overdoing it's another. How many of them are there in the main house these days?'

He grinned at me. 'Well, you know what it's like,' he replied. 'It was different in the old man's day, but with the prince still just a kid and his mother supposed to be running things, it's only to be expected that there'll be a few of the big men hanging around, and not just for the free dinners.'

'What do you mean?' I asked.

'Use your head,' he replied, leaning back and cupping his hands behind his head. 'Not for me to say anything, of course, but sooner or later she's going to have to marry again. Why she's kept them all hanging around this long is anybody's guess. She can't still think the old man's going to come back, after all.'

'Quite,' I said. 'I heard he died in a shipwreck.'

He nodded. 'I heard that too,' he said. 'Also that he'd been killed in the war, he'd survived the war but got killed on the way home, that he didn't get killed but he's living with some beautiful goddess on an enchanted island in the middle of the great sea, that he sailed so far away to the West that he fell off the edge of the world. Everyone seems to agree he's dead, though. And that he's a big hero and we should all be very proud.'

'Why?' I asked.

'Not sure, really. Exactly what the advantage is in having a king who goes off fighting wars in foreign parts and getting himself presumably killed is something I've never quite managed to puzzle out. Which is probably why I'm up here, herding pigs – '

'And he's out there somewhere under the sea getting eaten by the crabs,' I said.

'Or living in pampered luxury with this fantastically beautiful nymphomaniac goddess,' he replied with a grin. 'None of my business, anyhow.'

I held out my cup. He filled it with wine this time; thick, dark stuff, nearly black. I'd forgotten how rough it was. 'I've heard a lot about him on my travels, of course,' I said. 'What they call a legend in his own lifetime.'

'That's how tales get about,' he replied with a shrug. 'They do say that the whole war was all about some prince running off with another man's wife.'

'I heard that too,' I replied.

He yawned and stood up. 'You're staying for something to eat,' he said. 'Company's all right for a change. No, you stay there. You look like you've come a fair way.'

'You can say that again,' I replied, as he pulled down a side of bacon from the rafters and cut a thick wedge. 'I'll be honest with you, I wish I was back home by my own fireside. No disrespect, but I'm sure you know what I mean.'

He laughed. 'Where are you from, then?' he asked, as he sliced the bacon.

'Crete,' I lied. 'Originally. Since then, any number of places . . .'

He pulled down a jar of barley-meal and sprinkled some over the bacon, then cut a chunk out of a big round cheese. 'Trader?' he asked. I nodded.

'Used to be, at least,' I added. 'Difficult to do any business when your ship's at the bottom of the sea and all your goods with it.'

'You're a long way from Crete here,' he said. 'This is Ithaca.'

'I know that,' I replied. 'But I've got friends here, or at least I used to have. If any of them are still alive and haven't completely forgotten me, I expect they'll see me all right. What about you? Were you born here on the island?'

He shook his head, then went on fixing the meal. 'Oh no,' he said. 'But you don't want to hear about me. Very dull subject.'

'I'll be the judge of that,' I replied.

He shrugged. 'Please yourself,' he replied. 'And you can believe it or not as you like. No, the truth is that I was born a free man, as good as any on this island, or better. Syria's where I'm from, and I'll bet you've never even heard of it.'

'Been there,' I replied untruthfully. 'You're a long way from home then.'

'Left there when I was a kid. Well, not so much left as got taken. But I don't like talking about it.'

I didn't blame him. His was, after all, a very sad story and sadder still for the fact that nobody but me would ever believe it. I knew it was true because I'd been there, twenty-odd years ago, when a Phoenician ship called here with goods to sell and among them a little ten-year-old boy in ragged purple clothes who cried all the time and swore blind in bad trade Phoenician that he was a king's son in his own country and he'd been kidnapped by these cruel pirates. I hadn't doubted it then and I don't now. Like I said, who you are depends on where you are, and when I'd bought little Eumaeus from the Phoenicians I sent him up here to the steading to learn swineherding. I was pleased to see that my faith in him hadn't been misplaced. And things hadn't worked out so badly for him after all. Here he was, a man comfortably placed with a pleasant enough life, able to spare food and wine to give me when

I was destitute. He could look back on the last twenty years and feel he'd made something of his life.

'So,' I said, changing the subject, 'tell me a bit more about what's going on at the main house. It helps to know these things when you're travelling round.'

He put the dish of food on the table between us and let me help myself first. 'There's quite a few of them taken up residence,' he said, 'all the local big men and a few from other islands, too. Some of them,' he added with slight distaste, 'not much older than her son. Still, that kind of thing doesn't matter so much in good families where there's property at stake.'

'And has she given any clues about which one she's going to marry?' I asked.

He spread his hands. 'I don't think it works like that,' Eumaeus replied. 'More a case of they can't decide among themselves who's to have her. It's all complicated negotiations and settlements and protocol and stuff, which thankfully is way over my head. Can't be much fun having to live like that,' he added, 'being argued over like you were some disputed boundary.'

'Mighty compassionate words coming from a slave,' I said, with a grin.

'The hell with you,' he replied. 'The way I see it, she's as much a slave as I am. Think about it, will you? When she was twelve-years-old she was bundled on board a ship and whisked off across the sea to a place she's never heard of and told she was going to marry a man she'd never seen whether she likes it or not, run his house, have his kids. Fair enough, so she's the Queen of Ithaca and she wears a linen gown and sits indoors all day spinning fine cloth with maids to wash her and put her to bed, but her body's not her own, even less than mine is. And now, when she's got a son full-grown and ought to know who she is, she's being sold on again like confiscated property after a man's been banished from the kingdom. I feel sorry for her and I don't care who knows it.'

'It's one way of looking at things,' I replied diplomatically. 'I'd heard they were going to decide the matter quite soon.'

Eumaeus nodded. 'They say that,' he replied. 'They say that she's promised to marry anyone who can string the old man's bow and shoot an arrow through the socket-holes of seven axes. If you went around believing everything you hear, gods only know what'd become of you.'

I wanted to smile at that because I remembered that bow. It was one I'd made myself, a fine piece of work if I do say so myself. I'd come across a pair of ibex horns, long as my arm and not too badly twisted, so I sawed them into strips and boiled them in a cauldron until they were soft enough to straighten; then I made some glue out of scraps of hide and dried blood and glued the strips to a thin core of cedar-wood, backed the limbs with dried, combed sinew in a base of thick glue, clamped it all up tight in a form to get the shape I wanted and left it for a month to set. When I took it out and flexed it on the tiller to train the limbs to bend without snapping, it came compass beautifully, a perfect crescent shape, right first time – I couldn't believe it. The only problem was that I'd made it so strong that I couldn't even bend the damn thing enough to string it. A complete waste of time and good materials, like so many things in my splendid and illustrious life; a magnificent result, but absolutely no use to me.

That set me thinking. No doubt about it, Eumaeus could have bent that bow – twenty years of hard work in the fresh air and filling in his spare time with building this place had given that little boy I'd left behind me shoulders like an ox and arms as thick as a young man's leg. But he was up here on the steading, not down in the valley where the quality lived, even if he was a rightful king in his own country. Or would have been, if things had been different. A king away from his kingdom doesn't stay a king for very long. I knew that, all right.

'This wine's gone off,' he said, with a sour grin. 'The hell with it, I'll open another jar.'

And what about me, I thought. I wasn't the same man I'd been twenty-odd years ago. Back then I'd been a king's son in my own country, and my exercise was all riding to hounds and throwing the discus and the javelin, fencing practice and the gentle arts of war. Twenty years on and my arms weren't quite so graceful and rounded. I'd been pulling oars and digging trenches, heaving rocks and cutting timber, and that comely bloom of puppy-fat we admire so much in a delicately nurtured youth had long since turned into hard muscle. No better than a peasant to look at these days; but then, none of us gets any younger. And of course, everything depends so much on where you happen to be at the time.

'What about the old man's son?' I asked. 'Strikes me he can't be much of a man if he lets an army of strangers take over his house and practically rape his mother. I don't suppose his father'd be very impressed with what he's turned out like.'

Eumaeus frowned at me. 'That's easy enough to say,' he replied. 'You try taking on twenty or so grown men on your own some time, see how you get on.' He swallowed some wine and made a face, which didn't say much for the quality of the new jar. 'Of course, they do say that if he'd been his father it'd all have been different, because of course King Ulysses was a hero and a big man, and he'd have had those twenty lords out of there just like *that*.' He snapped his fingers, close under my nose. I winced. 'And maybe that's true,' he added, 'and maybe it isn't. We'll never know now, will we? Fact of the matter is, we can't all be heroes. Gods help us if we were; there'd be nothing but fighting and killing, which is all that sort is good for, and hasn't there been enough of that already? Five hundred men he took with him from this island to the war and not one of them's ever come back. Maybe young Telemachus has got more sense, that's all. Isn't that what his name means, the man who stays away from the fighting?'

That was a notion that amused me – I'd never thought of it like that, but yes, the words could bear that meaning, as well as 'He who fights from afar,' such as an archer who bends a mighty bow.

'So what is he like?' I asked quietly.

Eumaeus shook his head. 'Don't ask me,' he said. 'If I've seen him ten times that's all, and that was mostly when he was a kid, and they're all pretty well the same until they're fourteen or so. From what I gather, he's nothing special. Not specially bad, not specially good. Not specially anything much. Probably have made a good king for that very reason. Then again, it doesn't take much to be a good king. All you've got to do is sit on your arse all day and not get in the way of people working.'

I nodded. 'You may well be right,' I said. 'I wouldn't know. Like I said, I've spent most of my life travelling around, never been in one place long enough. You know,' I added, standing up, 'you may think this sounds a bit strange, but I reckon you've got a better life than most here, being in one place and knowing more or less what it is you're supposed to be doing. Now you look at me, and what have I got to show for anything? Pretty well what I stand up in, and that's about it.'

Eumaeus shook his head. 'Things'd have been a lot different if I'd stayed in Syria,' he replied. 'I'd have had a better life there, that's for sure. I don't know; there comes a time when you look at your life and all you see is the edges, the places you've never been, the things you've never done. At least you've seen more than one rocky hillside and one valley. I'd stop moaning if I were you and count your blessings.'

There didn't seem much more to say after that, so I left him to get on with his work and carried on down the hill towards the town and the main house. The closer I got to the town, of course, the more I remembered, though it had been a long time, and of course things had changed. The sad thing was that nearly all the changes had been for the better – and what did that say about me?

They'll gladly tell you what I did next and how it all came out in the end, those singers of songs and guardians of the tales of ancient valour. Everybody knows the story, about the stringing of the great bow and the shot through the seven axeheads, the great fight in the hall, one man alone against twenty or so, and the utter defeat of the wicked suitors, the recognition and the reconciliation and even the happy-ever-after that the narrative tradition demands. To be honest with you, I don't remember it all that clearly. Perhaps I wasn't paying attention, my mind being elsewhere.

Like I told Eumaeus, the swineherd in Ithaca who had been a prince in Syria, when I was a destitute wanderer in Ithaca after my return from wherever in hell I've been these last twenty odd years, I've spent my life travelling around, never been in one place long enough. And if I'm right, if who you are does depend on where you are, then maybe that explains a lot about me and who I've become. As I walked down the hill towards the town that evening, almost at the end of the story, closing in on that happy ending like a wolf tracking a weak lamb, I tried to remember who I was. But all I could call to mind was who I had been – Ulysses, the son of Laertes, at one time king of Ithaca, a great captain in the armada of the Greeks against Troy, who after the ten years' war wandered another ten years in the furthest and wildest of places, finding all manner of wonders while seeking only the way home. I remembered that time when, in the great hall of King Alcinous of the Phaeacians, after my shipwreck, when I was washed up naked and half-dead and brought to the king's hall unrecognized and out of pity, I sat and listened to a minstrel who sang an old song, one he'd learned from his father, about the glorious deeds of Ulysses, the sacker of cities, who in the tenth year finally broke open the gates of Troy. . . .

I remember, that night I came home, standing in front of the gates of the stockade that surround the main house, wondering what manner of lofty folk must live in such a fine place. There was a dungheap just inside the gate, and on top of it was the fresh sweepings from the hall floor, rushes and scraps and bits of bone and a dead dog. Welcome home, I thought, and I couldn't help calling to mind the dogs who'd come bounding up to me at the steading, barking and wagging their tails and snarling, and caring who had just come into their territory. Down here, nobody seemed to give a damn. I suppose a great deal depends on who you are and where.

THE THREAD

Vera Chapman

If there is one Greek legend we seem to know from our earliest schooldays it is that of Theseus and the Minotaur. Like Paris, Theseus was another disowned youth, who was eventually reconciled to his father Aegeus, king of Athens. Theseus joined the seven youths and seven maidens who were annually sacrificed to the Cretan Minotaur. Ariadne, the daughter of the Cretan king, Minos, fell in love with Theseus, and gave him a sword to kill the Minotaur, as well as a ball of thread to allow him to find his way back out of the labyrinth.

That's usually what most people remember, though Theseus had many more adventures. He was one of the Argonauts with Jason in search of the Golden Fleece, and he seemed to enjoy abducting women, including the young Helen of Troy. It is something of that later life, and the continuing influence of Ariadne, that Vera Chapman considers in this story.

Vera Chapman (1898–1996) is best known for her trilogy of Arthurian novels The Three Damosels *(1978), though she has written other books, including* Blaedud the Birdman *(1978) and* The Wife of Bath *(1978).* The King's Damosel *(1976), from the Arthurian trilogy, has been adapted as an animated feature film by Warner Brothers. Vera Chapman was, for many years, the wife of a country vicar, but she later became a practising Druid, and was the founder of the British Tolkien Society.*

Naturally, Theseus had let go of the thread when he fought the Minotaur. A man couldn't fight for his life against that horror and

still hold a thread in one hand. Ariadne ought to have thought
of that.

And now here he was, in the glimmering twilight of that
subterranean maze, with the Minotaur dead at his feet, and its
decapitated head in his hand – lost in the dark.

He cursed, and flung the head away, and, pulling himself up
to the low stony roof, crawled out through one of the ragged
interstices through which a little light filtered in – and came to
the surface.

It was not an encouraging prospect. Far away to the northward
he could make out the palace – very dimly – the red and blue pillars,
the yellow architraves, gleamed; mere spots of colour, otherwise all
the rest was too far off to see. A long day's march if one could
go straight there, but – all the country between, he could see,
consisted of the broken ground under which lay the half-buried
maze he had traversed. The Old Palace, far older and vaster than
that where King Minos now lived, and totally unexplored except
by that repulsive creature, the Minotaur. As he pursued his quarry,
Theseus had taken note, in the practical way a hunter would, of the
nature of the place – dark tunnels, dark empty rooms, sometimes
faintly lit by light-wells, but these were mostly choked with the
heavy vegetation above them. Places here and there where the
track came to the surface, in a courtyard or a terrace, but all
buried in bushes and creepers and thorns, dense and venomous.
Stairways, and long, long tunnels underground, where sometimes
the roof had cracked and let daylight in – other places that seemed
to be deep below, under solid masonry. Down there, the beast-man
had led him along tracks which it knew, unerringly; the thread had
unrolled behind him, and of course this would lead him back the
way he had come – but the thread had run out – it wasn't long
enough – and had left him with no more than an awkward end,
and then he had dropped it, as anyone would . . .

No going back underground, then – and overground? miles of
treacherous underfoot jungle, sharp edges and ridges, pitfalls, screes,
precipices, wells, traps – as easy to try walking over a reef of jagged
rocks at low tide. No man could do it, and – the sun was past its
noon. A broken neck at the bottom of one of those concealed shafts,
that was the least horrible fate that awaited him.

He shuddered, and cursed again. Out there in the red-pillared
palace, they would wait for him, his loyal seven men and seven
women, who had conquered in the Bull Dance, and all those others,
slaves and captives and enemies of cruel old Minos; all those who
had only waited for Theseus the Prince to give them a lead. They

would be waiting and ready now, at the moment of sunset, to fire the palace, while the ships he had summoned in secret lay in waiting outside the harbour. But he would not be there. He'd be dying of thirst and hunger, out there in the rough country, and the hyenas would pick his bones.

And Ariadne would wait. Ariadne! Strange girl. Not really attractive to him – and yet, a pretty girl was a pretty girl – with her tiny waist, and exuberant breasts worn shamelessly bare. . . . She had come to him in prison, and coolly conspired with him to overthrow her father, and her father's kingdom, and her brother . . . Her brother! He shuddered again – that horrible half-human creature, *that* was her brother. Half-brother, then – of course that ridiculous story about Queen Pasiphae and the bull was just an obscene jest handed about among the people. The father of Minotaurus was the sea-rover who called himself the Bull. But, on the other hand – the people of Crete had a Bull-God. Such things had happened . . .

Ariadne – yes, a very strange girl. She had seemed so eager, amo-rous he would have thought, and yet – not quite that. Her eyes were far away, and she would not let him touch her. But she had begged him to take her away – to take her to Athens – and had promised him a rich reward if he would do so. Yes, and kill the Minotaur – her brother! – and for that purpose she had given him the thread, and planned everything. And now, because he had relied on that damned thread, he was to die here . . . Far off, the sight of the sea mocked him.

Oh well, just one more look and feel around. He descended, stiff with weariness, into the darkness the way he had come – and at first could see nothing, and stumbled over the corpse of the Minotaur. His fingers encountered the head. He lifted it by the hair. 'Oh yes, I'll have to take you with me, ugly mug, whether I like it or not,' he muttered. Something brushed his wrist, hanging from the creature's hair. It was the thread.

Through the darkness, the ships ploughed their way north and westward towards Greece. Behind them, Knossos was burning. The other ships surrounded and convoyed that on which Theseus and Ariadne sailed. They would hasten to Athens with news of Crete broken, Crete with its heart plucked out, Crete ripe for conquest by the kings of Aegina and Sparta and Mycenae.

At the stern of Theseus' ship a rich pavilion had been erected, closed all round with wooden lattices and embroidered curtains, and inside this, on a bed of down and silk, lay Ariadne, worn out with the fatigues and terrors of the escape from Knossos. She

had laid aside the belt that braced in her tiny waist, and her snake
bracelets and hieratic jewels; and her dark red hair lay spread on
the pillow. Theseus came quietly through the curtains. She gave a
cry, and covered herself with a mantle.

'Now, my love,' he said.

'No – no, Theseus. Never touch me. Leave me alone.'

'But my dear – I have rescued you as I said I would. You are my
bride – wasn't that your wish?'

'No. No. You don't understand. I never asked you that. I never
promised you that.'

'You promised me a rich reward.'

'You have a rich reward. Your ships are full of the spoils of the
palace. That's reward enough. I never promised –'

'Why, I understood –'

'You misunderstood. No, don't lay a finger on me. Don't come
any nearer. Theseus, I am consecrated. I am the bride of a god.'

'What is this? What god? Not the Bull-God?'

'Oh no, the Gods forbid. But Theseus, understand this. Many
years back, the holy Bacchus came to Crete – he is Dionysus and
Zagreus and Iacchos – he came with his band, bringing his message
of joy, and he absolved my sin.'

'Your sin? What sin?'

'A grievous sin. For it was I who loosed the Minotaur on the island.
He had been kept fast in prison, but I – in pity and foolishness – set
him free. And so he ravaged all Crete – and it was because of me.
None knew it, or I think the people would have stoned me to death.
But Bacchus cleansed me from my sin, and plighted me to him as his
bride. But that very night the Minotaur broke from hiding and slew
Bacchus. He slew my God, and rent him in pieces. – But I know
that Bacchus does not die. If I can go to his sanctuary at Eleusis,
by Athens, I shall see him again and be truly wedded to him. That
is why I prayed you to take me to Athens, and that is why you must
not touch me. Did you think that I was in love with you?'

He gave an inarticulate cry and turned from her.

'The Furies take you, woman! *Woman!* Who can understand a
woman? How could you serve me so? I don't know why I don't
throw you overboard –'

He looked back at her. That red hair, those protuberant eyes –
he recalled the Minotaur's head in his hand, and himself saying,
'I've got to take you with me . . . whether I like it or not.'

He went to the forward end of the ship – hardly master of his
emotions – and gave certain instructions to his servants.

*   *   *

When Ariadne woke, it was from a deep oblivious sleep. Her last recollection had been of one of Theseus' slaves handing her a cup of wine, spiced and very sweet. Now as she woke she was dull-witted and bewildered. She had no idea where she was. Silk curtains were all around her, and she lay on a silken bed, but she did not feel as if she were on the ship. The sun shone through the silk curtains – she was in a tent, and the sun was high. With her head still reeling, she rose, parted the curtains, and looked out.

She was at the door of a richly decorated pavilion – but she was alone. Quite alone. All round her was open grassland, overlooking the sea – certainly on an island, and for a long way around her, no trees, walls, houses – and no people. She could not take it in at first. Nobody? But how could there be nobody? She looked all round the tent, inside and out. It was firmly pitched, as to shelter her; there was a heap of vessels, jars of wine, bundles of various kinds of food, gold and silver vessels too, scattered in careless profusion, as if to leave her ironical gifts in her loneliness. Loneliness! All at once the full force of it struck her, and she sank to the ground with a sob.

Left behind. That was what he had done – left her behind, on this island. Gone, gone. And not a soul, not a living soul near her.

At first she sat, and tried to collect her thoughts, to control her rising panic. She would not shriek and run about – she would not. Come now, there was food and drink and shelter to last a day or two. Ships would come by – perhaps he would come back for her? But she knew only too well that he would not. Oh no, he would not come back for her.

The sun was high and fierce – she was intensely thirsty, and her head ached. She drank from one of the wine jars – it made her head throb and reel, and ache still more. She began to sob, quietly at first, then more and more wildly – then she walked, aimlessly, barefoot and lightly clothed as she was, along the line of the cliffs. Upwards, as the line of the cliff went. Was that music she could hear? Oh, if it were music – if only it were music! She quickened her pace, up the shoulder of the down. There she came to a place where her way was barred by a deep cleft, where the sea came in below. The other side of the cleft was another grassy slope, a fathom's length across the chasm. And along this grassy ridge she saw them coming – Bacchus and all his beautiful people. It was as if they grew out of the quivering heat-haze. There were the lovely long-haired Maenads, and the little Fauns, and the tall young men, the Kouri, and the jolly old men on donkeys – and there at their head was the Heavenly Lover, Bacchus himself – the face she had

loved long ago, once dead, now alive forever. He stood and called
to her across the gulf.

'Come across. Come to me, my love – it is only a step. Come!'

With a wild cry she stepped across the abyss – and was caught
up into great joy and felicity.

There were so many years behind Theseus now – twenty – thirty
years since Crete and the Minotaur. Years of conquest and kingship,
battles, love and death and heartbreak. Hippolyta had come and
gone out of his life, and poor Phaedra, and Hippolytus – ah, that
had hurt. He had forgotten that Phaedra was Ariadne's sister – it
was all so long ago.

Pirithous was his comfort now – Pirithous, whom all Greece
acknowledged to be the handsomest man in all the land, even now
when he was no longer young. They made a fine pair together.
Pirithous! Worth more to him than all the women. Pirithous kept
him young, led him into bold adventures and absurd pranks like
schoolboys. It was increasingly hard now to rouse his heart to feel
anything worth while – he had known everything. But Pirithous
found him new interests, new sensations – new vices, too. Theseus
was ruler of Athens – called without any resentment the Tyrant –
and could be held blameless for many things that no doubt ought
to have been blamed.

Yes, Theseus was bored, without denial he was bored. So he sat on
the porch of his great white marble house in Athens, and drank with
Pirithous, who alone could find means to relieve his boredom.

Below them they watched the long procession forming up, to set
out on the way to Eleusis for the Mysteries.

'I hate all that,' Theseus said. 'Priests and mysteries and
women.'

'Especially women,' said Pirithous.

'Yes. It's all dark, and devious, and secret – it gives me the horrors.
Why is it secret? If there's anything good in it, they should let all the
world know. If not, there must be something bad. Unspeakably bad.
– As Tyrant of Athens, I've tried to put it down, but the priests are
too strong for me.'

An uneasy silence fell. Below them a street singer passed. Not
everyone was occupied with the preparations for the Mysteries. This
man preferred the popular hero-songs about Theseus and Pirithous.
They heard him sing:

> Theseus and Pirithous, the lovers
> They are so brave they would go down to Hell

And drag up thence Persephone,
The Queen of the Dead herself . . .

The two men turned to each other and laughed.

'Why, that's what we ought to do,' said Pirithous.

'What do you mean – fetch up Persephone from Hell? We can't do that.' An unaccountable shiver ran over him.

'We can and we will – don't you see? Eleusis – the Priestess of the Mysteries. They say the initiates are taken down into Hell, through that cave they speak of – and there they come into the presence of Persephone, the Queen of the Dead. What else can she be but the chief priestess, whom no one ever sees? Theseus, you say you want to put down all this priestcraft and superstition. That's the way we'll do it.'

'But how? No one can go there but the initiates.'

'Then we'll become initiates.'

'What? No, we couldn't –'

'We could. We'll go through all their solemn mummery, and then we'll break the whole thing wide open, and bring this Persephone of theirs up to light – poor thing, you'd think she'd be glad to come! And perhaps, who knows,' he added with a sour laugh, 'we might induce her to make the spring stay all the year round.'

It caused a sensation when it was known that Theseus and Pirithous were candidates for the Mysteries. To their admirers, whatever they did was right. Many who admired them less took this as evidence that virtue and piety had won a victory over them. All rejoiced, and the number of applicants for the Mysteries doubled, and the gifts flowed into the treasury of Eleusis.

But certainly the two friends had to submit ·at least to the appearance of virtue. The preparation was long and serious. Fasting and watching, prayer and meditation, instruction and abstinence – they had to keep reminding each other of their eventual objective.

First came the Lesser Mysteries, in spring, when the holy image of Iacchos, or Dionysus, or Bacchus, was brought from Athens to Eleusis in procession. This was a cheerful seed-time festival, and Theseus and Pirithous went through the first degree of the Mysteries without much trouble. Afterwards in private, Pirithous laughed and made mockery of it. But Theseus' laughter began to be a little hollow. More than once he thought of leaving the whole thing – no, not to go through with it in earnest, but to withdraw from it altogether, driven by the sense of the uncanny, the holy terror, that began to haunt him. But once embarked on the Mysteries you could not draw back – he

had become a 'mystos,' one whose eyes and lips were sealed, and
he must go and become an 'epoptos,' one whose eyes were opened,
though never his lips. And Pirithous urged him on, and laughed at
his misgivings.

Autumn came, and the time of the Greater Mysteries. Now it
began – the long torchlight procession under the full moon, all the
people of Athens, men, women, and children, in holiday mood,
streaming out along the Sacred Way, with food and drink, garlands
and musical instruments, in feast-day clothes, bearing smoking
torches, making a cheerful babble along the brilliant ribbon of
light under the translucent dark blue sky. In the midst, in their
white robes, quiet in all the excitement, went the Mystoi. At the
Bridge there was the customary halt, where buffoons and clowns
broke upon the sacred procession with wild fooling and the most
obscene of jokes, for this was in memory of the Goddess's servant,
who had jested to her to make her smile, that she should not die
of sorrow.

'Laugh now,' said the hierophant priest who had charge of the
candidates, 'laugh your fill, for you will not laugh for many
days after.'

Pirithous nudged Theseus. 'Oh yes,' he whispered, 'we'll laugh
all right afterwards. That we will!'

But Theseus did not return the nudge.

Revelling and dancing and shouting, the crowd escorted the Mystoi
into the precincts of Eleusis at midnight. The torches marked the
sky with flame and smoke. The ritual words were said, and the
candidates for the Greater Mysteries – twelve in all, eight men
and four women – were led through the great swing doors that
creaked in their grooves on the marble floors. Dim lights showed
from inside, but the people outside tried in vain to get a glimpse of
what lay within. The same great doors closed behind the Mystoi,
inexorably. Outside, the folk would revel and feast till daybreak,
thankful to the Mystoi, who would ensure for them the fertility of
the Mother and the happy return of the Daughter next year. But
inside, the Mystoi must spend a holy night of quiet preparation.

Daybreak brought the echoing, hollow cry over the bay: 'To the
sea, all Mystoi!' and, hardly roused from sleep, they came, almost
naked, the men in one line, the women, far off, in another, and
with the early sun dazzling them, plunged into the cold sea. Each
one, grotesquely, carried a small squealing pig, for this was the
accustomed sacrifice. Theseus and Pirithous struggled awkwardly
with their pigs, and Pirithous swore, and hit his pig so violently

with the edge of his great hand that it was dead before he laid it in the sacrificial trench. Now they were all clothed in new white garments, as purified, and the rite proceeded.

In the afternoon they were allowed a rest in the little cells set up for them. As a rule the initiates were kept in strict seclusion, but because Theseus and Pirithous were who they were, the hierophants allowed them to spend an hour together.

As the door closed upon them, Theseus exclaimed, 'Pirithous, I'm not going on with this.'

'What? Oh, nonsense. I know it's tedious, but look, it's nearly over. It's just tonight, after midnight – first there's that interminable long procession, the "Search for Persephone" – then the initiates go down into the Cavern, two by two, and come before the Goddess – as they call her. That's our time. That's when we bring her out to all the people and show them she's no Goddess at all. Finish the whole sorry affair, once and for all. Everything you hate – priests, women, mysteries. And what a feast we'll have afterwards! Why, the people will call us Gods ourselves.'

'No.' Theseus stood up and confronted his friend, hands on hips, stubbornly.

'What do you mean – no?'

'I don't like it, and I won't go on with it. It's not right, it's not . . . well, I'm sure it's not lucky. Bad things will come of it. I feel it in my blood – it shouldn't be done. I'm going through with the Mysteries, but I'll do it properly, and I'll have no part in it – what you said we'd do.'

'Theseus!' Pirithous sprang from where he sat, and confronted his friend, red-faced. 'Do you mean to say – it can't be that you've let all this rubbish influence you? The oaths and all that? Words, Theseus, nothing but words. Easy enough to say. Why, you're not – afraid are you?'

Theseus gave a growl of rage and sprang with his hands at Pirithous' throat. Pirithous looked him straight in the eyes, and calmly put his own hands over his friend's hands that were about to throttle him.

'Oh, none of that, none of that. Don't be a fool.' The clutching hands relaxed. 'Don't you see – there's no going back now? I shall do what we planned, and if you don't, can you imagine what will happen?'

A loud knock on the cell door interrupted them. Their personal hierophant, robed in white and with his head covered, stood at the door.

'Pirithous, it's time you went to your own cell. Come with me.'

They had quickly turned their hostile grip into the semblance of an emotional leave-taking.

'Farewell, then, till we meet again,' said Pirithous. And a terrible foreboding of grief came over Theseus.

As dusk fell, out over the precincts of Eleusis floated a single lonely voice.

'Oi-moi. Oi-moi. Oi-moi.'

And a deep chorus of men's voices took it up, not loud, but penetrating. 'Oi-moi, oi-moi, oi-moi.' It was the chant of the forsaken Mother seeking the Daughter, Winter seeking Spring, Age seeking her own lost youth. As the moon rose, the procession wound its way along the dark pathways; the torches, always the torches, blinking in a windless night.

And now they reached the low archway of the cavern, the way down to the place where Hades was King – he whose name was so dreaded that it was never spoken – he was called The Rich One, Pluto. Here the procession halted while the ominous sacrifice of a black goat was made. In the dimness and crowd, all that most of the worshippers could see was the dark horned shape, rearing up and then falling – they could hear the hiss and splash of the blood as it ran into the low trench. Then, stepping over the trench where the sacrifice still lay, the first two initiates were led in, and the doors closed against the rest.

At first Theseus and Pirithous found themselves in total darkness – then, as unseen hands led them forward, they turned a corner, and there was a dim green light from a brazier.

It was a small, low room, and in it were just six people – their two selves, the hierophant who was leading them, and at the far end, up three stone steps, two tall guards, in the long straight dress that proclaimed them as eunuchs, stood each armed with a stone mace – and between them the High Priestess, the Goddess, with a black veil over her face.

'Now!' said Pirithous, and in one movement the two rushed forward. They had no weapons, but relied on hands and fists and the power of surprise. Pirithous, one pace in front of Theseus, seized the Priestess by the waist and the knees, and lifted her from the ground. She screamed on a piercing high note, and in the same instant the two eunuchs brought their maces down on Pirithous's head. As he fell like a poleaxed beast, the Priestess disappeared behind a curtain.

Theseus fell on his knees beside his friend.

'Pirithous, Pirithous – oh, the best friend a man ever had. Dead,

dead – smashed like an eggshell by a horrible eunuch!' His sobs broke the silence.

Then he looked up. The Priestess had come back. Without a word she resumed her throne and lifted her veil. She stood very still and looked down on the scene. Her snake bracelets were not bracelets but living snakes, and they hissed. He looked up and saw her face.

Worn and ravaged with years, the eyes blank, remote, crazy – still he knew her. It was Ariadne.

WHERE IS THE BIRD OF FIRE?

Thomas Burnett Swann

Here we move from the Greek world to the Roman, in fact to the founding of Rome itself. The Romans didn't seem to be any better at looking after their children than the Greeks. Romulus and his twin brother Remus were the children of Rhea Sylvia and Mars. Their uncle Amulius tried to drown them at birth, along with their mother, but the twins were saved and fostered by a she-wolf until they were found and reared by the herdsman Faustulus. When they were fully grown, Romulus and Remus expelled Amulius and restored their grandfather to the throne. They were then granted permission to build a new city on the Tiber. The following story explores the relationship between Romulus and Remus as well as the passing of the world of legend.

Thomas Burnett Swann (1928–76) wrote over a dozen stories and novels set in the ancient Greek and Roman world, but is best remembered for his Minotaur sequence, Cry Silver Bells *(1977),* The Forest of Forever *(1971) and* Day of the Minotaur *(1966). The following story was later rewritten with other material to form the novel* Lady of the Bees *(1976), but I retain a special fondness for this original version.*

I

I am very old by the counting of my people, the Fauns – ten full years. Hardly a boyhood, men would say, but we are the race with cloven hooves and pointed, furry ears, descendants of the great god

Faunus who roamed with Saturn in the Golden Age. Like the goats, our cousins, we count ten years a lifetime.

And in my years, I have seen the beginning of Rome, a city on the Palatine which Romulus says will straddle the orange Tiber and spread west to the Tyrrhenian Sea, south through the new Greek settlement at Cumae to the tip of Italy, and north through Etruria to the land of the Gauls. Romulus, the Wolf, says these things, and I believe him, because with one exception he has never failed. Now, however, I do not wish to speak of Romulus, but of his twin brother, Remus, who was also part of the beginning. Remus, the bird of fire. With a reed pen, I will write his story on papyrus and trust it to the coffers of time which, cool in the earth, endure and preserve.

My people have wandered the hills and forests of Central Italy since the reign of Saturn: the blue-rocked Apennines where the Tiber springs, and the forests of beech and oak where Dryads comb green hair in the sun-dappled branches. When invaders arrived from Africa and from the tall Alps to the north, Saturn withdrew to a land where the Fauns could not follow him. Forsaken, they remained in Italy, together with the Dryads in their leafy houses.

A Faun's life has always been brief and simple. We wear no clothes to encumber our movements except, in the winter months which have no name, a covering of wolf skin. Our only weapon is a simple sling with a hempen cord. We have no females of our own and must propagate by enticing maidens from the walled towns. I was born to an Alba Longan who had come to draw water from the Numicus River, outside her city.

Because the city was bowed under King Amulius, a tyrant who some years before had stolen the throne from his kindly brother Numitor and imprisoned him in the palace, she was willing to stay, for a little, with my father in the woods. But when she gave birth to me and saw my cloven hooves and pointed ears, she cried, 'I would rather nurse a goat!' and hurried back to her town and its tyrannical king. I was left to be reared by a band of Fauns, who had built a small encampment in the woods, with branches raised on stakes to shelter them from the rains of Jupiter, and a low palisade to guard against marauding wolves or unfriendly shepherds.

It was night and we had built a fire, not only to cook our supper but to comfort ourselves in the loneliness of the black woods. Evil forces had come with the flight of Saturn, Lemures or ghosts and blood-sucking Striges. My father, holding nine black beans in his mouth, made the circuit of our camp and spat them out one by one, mumbling each time, 'With this I ransom me and mine.' The Lemures, it was said by the shepherds who had taught him the custom, followed and ate the beans and were appeased.

This done, he bathed his hands in a clay vessel of water, clanged together two copper cooking pots left by my mother, and said, 'Good Folks, get you gone.' At six months old – five years or so in human terms – I was much impressed with my father's ritual. He had never shown me the least affection, but neither had anyone else, and a Faun's place, I judged, was to be brave and clever, not affectionate.

My father looked very gallant confronting the ghosts and very wise since, even while facing them bravely, he spoke with discretion. The other Fauns, eight of them, gnarled, brown, hairy creatures as old, one would think, as the oaks of the forest, squatted on their hooves and watched with admiration and also impatience, since they had not yet enjoyed their supper of roasted hares and myrtle berries.

But scarcely had my father uttered 'Good Folks' than a tree trunk crashed through the thin palisade and figures ran through the opening and thrashed among us with wooden staves. Lemures, I thought at first, but their staves and goatskin loin cloths marked them as shepherds. I heard the names 'Romulus' and 'Wolf' applied to the same man and guessed him to be their leader, the brawniest and the youngest.

The first thing they did was to stamp out our fire. I scrambled to shelter in a thicket of witch grass and watched with round-eyed terror and with ears quivering above my head. By the light of smouldering embers, I saw my father struck to the ground by Romulus himself. I roused myself and scurried to his side, but Romulus's brawny arms scooped me into the air. He raised me above his head, opened his mouth, and gave the high thin wail of a hunting she-wolf. Then with the camp in shambles and the Fauns either fallen or staggering, he leaped through the broken fence with me in his arms, and his shepherds followed him, hugging roasted hares.

I gave my captor a sharp kick with my hoof, but he squeezed me so hard that I gasped for breath, and I thought it best to lie still.

Through the woods we raced; through oak trees older than Saturn, and feathery cypresses like Etruscan maidens dancing to soundless flutes. At last the earth became marshy and Romulus's sandals squished in the sodden grass. I had heard my father speak of this malarial country near the Tiber, and I held my breath to avoid the poisonous vapours. Finally I grew faint and gulped in breaths, expecting the air to burn as it entered my lungs. Throughout the journey, Romulus never seemed short of breath, never stumbled, never rested.

We began to climb and soon reached the summit of what I guessed to be that hill of shepherds, the Palatine. On a broad plateau, hearth fires flickered through the doorways of circular huts. The jogging motion of my captor made the fires seem to dance and sway, and I blinked my eyes to make sure that they were real and not some feverish dream implanted by the swamp. From their pens of stone, pigs grunted and cattle lowed in resentment at being awakened.

One of the huts, the largest, seemed to belong to Romulus. We entered through a low door – though Romulus stooped, he brushed my ears against the lintel – and I found myself in a windowless, goat-smelling room with an earthen floor baked hard by the central fire. Romulus thrust me against a wall where a goat was nibbling a pile of straw. A hole in the roof allowed some smoke to escape, but some remained, and I waited for my eyes to stop watering before I could get a clear look at my captor.

I saw that the powerful arms which had held me belonged to one little more than a boy (at the time, of course, he looked overpoweringly adult, but still the youngest in the hut). Yet he was tall, broad, with muscular legs and with muscles tight across the bare abdomen above his loin cloth. A thin adolescent down darkened his chin, but the furrow between his eyebrows suggested ambitions beyond his years. His crow-black hair, unevenly cropped about an inch from his scalp, rioted in curls.

He stood in the firelight and laughed, and I dimly understood even then why men twice his age could follow and call him Wolf. His handsome face held a wolf's cruelty, together with its preternatural strength. Had I been older, I might have seen also a wolf's fierce tenderness toward those it loves; for this boy, though he loved rarely, could love with great tenacity. As it was, I thought him cruel and powerful, nothing more, and I cowered in terror.

An aged shepherd, his long white hair bound in a fillet behind his head, rose from the fire when Romulus entered with his five men. The five immediately began to laugh and boast about their victory over my people. But when Romulus spoke, the others were silent.

'The Fauns were driving out spirits, Faustulus,' he explained to the old man. 'Their leader said, "Good Folks, get you gone," and in we come! See, I have captured a baby.'

'In a year he will be full grown,' said Faustulus, whose face, though wrinkled like a brick shattered in a kiln, held an ageless dignity. He was no mere shepherd, I later found, but a man of learning from Carthage. Shipwrecked near the mouth of the Tiber, he had wandered inland to take shelter with herdsmen and married a girl named Larentia. When his rustic bride hesitated to return with him to Carthage, he remained with her people and learned their trade.

'What will you do with him then? Your nocturnal games are childish, Romulus. They bring you no closer to the throne of Alba Longa.'

Romulus frowned. 'Everything I do, Faustulus, brings me closer to the throne. Tonight we wrestle with Fauns. Tomorrow, soldiers. My men need practice.'

His ominous tone and the thought of what he had done to my father made me tremble. I burrowed into the hay where the goat seemed unlikely to eat (a foul-smelling beast, cousin though he was!) and peered out between wisps of straw.

Romulus saw my terror. To Faustulus he said, 'You ask me what I will do with our captive. Eat him, before he grows up! Goat flesh cooked on a spit.' When Faustulus seemed ill-disposed to the joke (or serious intention, I was not sure which), Romulus addressed a young shepherd with the stupid, flattened eyes of a ram. 'Faustulus, it seems, is not hungry. What about you, Celer?'

Winking at Romulus, Celer felt my arms and muttered, 'Too thin, too thin. Fatten him first, eh?' His speech was thick and slow, as if he were speaking with a mouthful of wine.

Romulus seemed to debate. 'No,' he said finally. 'He may be thin, but I am hungry. And I want to make a belt of his ears.' With that he hoisted me from the ground and lowered me toward the fire by the stump of my tail! I lay very still until I felt the flames singe my ears. Then I began to bleat, and Romulus and the ram-eyed Celer threw back their heads in merriment.

A voice spoke from the doorway, low but forceful. 'Put him down, Romulus.'

Romulus turned and, recognizing the speaker, tossed me back into the straw. With one tremendous bound he reached the door and embraced his brother.

'Remus,' he cried, 'I thought they had kept you in Veii!'

Remus returned his brother's embrace with enthusiasm, though his slight frame was almost engulfed by Romulus' massive hug. Like the others, he wore a loin cloth, but of wool, not goatskin, and dyed to the green of the woodpecker which haunts the forests of Latium. Over his shoulder hung a bow, and at his side, a quiver of arrows, their bronze nocks enwreathed with feathers to match his loin cloth. When I saw his hair, bound with a fillet but spilling in silken fire behind his head, I caught my breath. Picus, the woodpecker god,

I thought. Who except gods and Gauls, in this part of Italy, had yellow hair (and Etruscan ladies, with the help of their famous cosmetics)?

He released himself from Romulus' hug and walked over to my nest of straw. I squirmed away from him. A god he might be, but after all I had been kidnapped and almost cooked by his brother. I need not have feared him, however. He lifted me in his arms as my mother might if she had not disliked my ears. He cradled me against his smooth bronze chest – fragrant with clover as if he had slept in a meadow – and stroked the fur of my ears, smoothing it toward the tips.

'Little Faun,' he said. 'Don't be afraid. Tomorrow I will take you back to your people.'

'Take him back!' protested Romulus. 'I caught him myself.'

'Fauns are not animals,' said Remus. 'At least, not entirely. They have lived in this forest for centuries, and we have no right to capture their children.' He pointed to Romulus' bloody stave. 'Or fight their fathers.'

'They enjoy a fight as much as we do,' shrugged Romulus. 'We knocked them about a bit, nothing more. If I don't train my shepherds, how can they capture a city?' He grinned broadly, his sharp white teeth glittering in the firelight. 'If we don't take the city, what will we do for women?' Celer and the others – except Faustulus – whooped their approval. I was later to learn that these young shepherds, driven from Alba Longa and other towns of Latium for minor crimes, were womanless, and that Romulus had promised a house in the city and a wife for every man. Romulus winked at Celer. 'My brother knows much of animals, but nothing of women. We will find him a girl when we take Alba Longa – a saucy wench with breasts like ripe pomegranates.'

'Brother,' said Remus, a slow smile curving his lips. 'What do *you* know of pomegranates? You must have been gardening beyond the Palatine!'

'I know!' cried Celer. 'I know about them! The girls I remember –'

'And the girls I imagine,' sighed Remus.

'Remember, imagine,' said Romulus. 'One is as bad as the other. But once we take the city –! Now, brother, tell us about your journey to Veii.'

Romulus and the others seated themselves around the fire, while Remus remained standing. Clearly there had been an urgent purpose behind his visit to Veii, the Etruscan city twelve miles to the north. Even at my age, I sensed that purpose and, crouching at his feet, awaited his words more eagerly than those of my father when he told me stories of Dryads and river goddesses. What I failed to understand at the time was later clarified for me by Remus.

The brothers, it seemed, claimed to be sons of the war god Mars and a Vestal princess, Rhea, daughter of that same King Numitor whom Amulius had deposed and imprisoned in the palace. As Remus spoke, I learned how these royal twins in exile longed, above everything, to seize the throne of Alba Longa and restore their grandfather or rule in his place. Remus had gone to Veii to ask the *lucomo* or king to back their cause. It was a brazen thing for a young Latin shepherd, even a deposed prince, to seek audience with an Etruscan king and ask him to make war against a Latin city. But Romulus and Remus, after all, were very young.

I passed into the city (said Remus) with farmers taking shelter for the night. The palace astonished me. Its walls were of purple stucco, and terra cotta sphinxes flanked the entrance. I told the guards that I wished to see their king; that I could speak only with him. Would they tell him that Remus, exiled prince of Alba Longa, sought an audience.

'Yellow Hair,' one of them said. 'Our king is a jolly man. I will take him word. Your boldness will make him laugh.'

After a long time, the guard returned and said that the king would see me now – in his banquet hall. In the great hall, the ceiling was painted with winged monsters and strange enormous cats. The king was lying on a couch with a young woman at his side. She was almost unrobed. He motioned me to a couch next to him and laid his arm, heavy with amber and gold, on my shoulder.

'Remus,' he said, 'I have heard your story from shepherds who once served Amulius but now serve me. They told me how your mother, the Vestal Rhea, bore you to the god Mars and was buried alive for breaking her vow of chastity. How her uncle, King Amulius, ordered the shepherd Faustulus to drown you in the Tiber, but the shepherd set you adrift in a hollow log. How the log came ashore and a she-wolf suckled you in her cave and a woodpecker brought you berries, until Faustulus found and reared you as his own children.

'The story, it seems, is widely known in the country, though Amulius himself believes you long dead – for tyrants are rarely told the truth. I greet you as the prince you are. But we of Veii want peace with Alba Longa, our closest neighbour. Lead your shepherds against Amulius, if you must, and pray to Mars that the townspeople rise to help you. When you have captured the city, come to me again and we shall sign treaties of amity. Until then, let us be friends but not allies.'

I looked closely into his face, the short pointed beard, black as a vulture, the arched eyebrows, the almond eyes, and saw that he would not change his mind. I took my leave and followed the basalt road through the great arched gate and returned to you.

Romulus sprang to his feet, narrowly avoiding my ears. 'No help from Veii then. And we are not yet strong enough alone. Thirty shepherds at most, even if we scour the countryside.' He fingered the stubble on his chin, as if craving the ample beard – and the years – of a man. 'We shall have to wait at least a year before we attack,' he continued, with the heavy weariness of one who was not used to waiting – who, at seventeen, was something of a leader already and covetous of wider leadership. 'Gather more shepherds around us. Send scouts to the city and feel out the mood of the crowd.' Neither Romulus nor Remus had visited Alba Longa: their royal blood made it difficult to pass as herdsmen. 'Father Mars, let it not be long!'

He strode to the corner of the hut where a wreathed bronze spear, green with age, lay apart like a holy relic. Mars, as everyone knows, manifests himself in spears and shields. 'One day soon, Great Father, let me say to you: "Mars, awaken!"'

'But even if we take the city,' asked Remus, 'will our grandfather let us rule? The throne is rightfully his.'

'He is very old,' said Romulus. 'When he steps aside – and he will, very soon – we will build a temple to Mars and train an army even the Etruscans will fear.'

'And offer asylum to slaves, and even to birds and animals.'

'Oh, Remus,' chided his brother. 'This is a *city* we will rule, not a menagerie! For once, forget your animals.'

'But the city can learn from the forest! Remember when I cured your fever with berries last year? A bear showed them to me, growing beside the Tiber.'

Romulus shook his head. 'Remus,' he smiled, 'we shall have our problems ruling together. I sometimes wish that I had no brother or that I did not love him above all men. But let us capture the city – then we shall plan our government. Now it is late. Almost Cockcrow time.'

With a warm goodnight to Romulus and Faustulus, Remus gathered me in his arms and left the hut. Of course I could walk quite by myself, but rather than lose my ride I said nothing. Stumbling a bit with his burden, he descended the bank of the Palatine toward the Tiber, which looped like an adder in the starlight and swelled in places as if digesting a meal. Near the foot of the hill we entered the mouth of a cave where a small fire burned on a raised clay hearth. Remus stirred the fire.

'I hate the dark,' he said. 'It is sad with spirits. People who died like my mother, without proper rites.'

Sleepily I looked around me and saw that the earthen floor had been covered with rushes and clover, that a pallet of clean white wool lay in the corner, and that earthen pots lined the opposite wall. There was no one in the cave, but a large dog lay asleep beyond the fire. As we entered, the animal awoke and opened its eyes. A dog indeed! An immense wolf, its yellow-grey fur matted with age, rose on its haunches and faced us. Whether it snarled or grinned, I could not be sure. When Remus bent to deposit me on the pallet, I refused at first to let go of his neck.

'Lie still, little Faun,' he laughed. 'This is Luperca, my foster mother. It was she who found Romulus and me on the bank of the Tiber and brought us to this very cave. She is very old now. Sometimes she walks in the woods, but at night she shares my cave and my supper.' He knelt beside her and stroked her black-rimmed ears. In looking back, I can see the nobility of the scene, this boy with slender hands and hair as yellow as sunflowers, the aged wolf that had suckled him in this very cave. But at six months old, I saw only a flea-bitten animal which monopolized my friend's attention.

'My name is Sylvan,' I said haughtily. They were the first words I had spoken since my capture.

'I did not know you could talk,' he laughed, rising from my rival and coming to lie beside me.

'Nobody asked me,' I said, less haughty now that he had answered my summons. As the firelight dwindled, he talked of Alba Longa and how, when he ruled the city with Romulus, Fauns would be as welcome as men.

'You have surely seen the city,' he said, and before I could tell him yes, that my father had carried me once to see the walls and pointed, 'That is where your mother ran off to,' he continued. 'It is a very small city, really just a town. But its houses are white and clean, and its temple to Vesta is as pure as the goddess's flame. It is now an unhappy city. Amulius is a harsh ruler. He killed my mother, Sylvan. He laughed when she told him that Mars was my father. "You have broken your vow," he said, and buried her alive in the earth. Faustulus saw her before she died. Just a girl, really. Bewildered but proud. She looked at Amulius with her large black eyes and said: "Mars is my husband and he will look after my sons."

'Everyone believed her except Amulius. You see why I hate him. And I have other reasons. He taxes the vintners a third of their wine and the shepherds a fourth of their sheep. What do they get in return? The protection of his soldiers – when they are not stealing wine and sheep! But Sylvan, forgive me. I am keeping you awake with problems beyond your months. Sleep little Faun. Tomorrow I will take you home.'

But I already knew that I did not wish to return to my people.

II

Twelve months had passed. Growing two inches a month, I had reached a Faun's full height of five feet. Sometimes I looked in the stream that flowed near our cave and admired my reflection, for Fauns are vain as long as they resemble young saplings, and until they begin to grow gnarled – alas, too quickly – like the oaks of Saturn. My skin was the bronze of Etruscan shields. I wore my ears proudly, waving their silken fur above my head. I combed my tail with a hazel branch and kept it free from thistles and burrs. Remus was eighteen now but soon I would overtake him. Together with Luperca, I still shared his cave and we often hunted together, I with a sling, he with a bow and arrow. But at his insistence we hunted only the lower animals, and then from necessity – the hare and the wild pig. Bears and deer and even wolves had nothing to fear from us. Sometimes on these hunts I saw my father and called to him in passing. The first time he stopped to speak with me. I saw the scar which Romulus' staff had left between his ears. He looked much older than I remembered and a little stooped.

'Is it well with you?' he asked, ignoring Remus.

'Yes, Father,' I answered, half expecting him to embrace me. For I had grown used to Remus' affection.

But family ties among Fauns are usually shallow; we live such a little time. 'Good,' he said. 'I thought they might have killed you.' He galloped into the forest.

On the Palatine Hill, new huts had risen near that of Romulus and Faustulus. Sabine shepherds had moved there from a neighbouring hill, the Quirinal (named for their spear god, Quirinus), and also thieves and murderers from the forest, whom Romulus welcomed too readily into his group. When Remus objected, Romulus argued that thieves, much more than shepherds, could help to capture a town. They could move with stealth and strike with sudden fury.

As shepherds, of course, the brothers must care for a large herd of cattle and sheep, leading them from pasture to pasture both on and below the Palatine, guarding them from wolves and bears, and making sacrifice to the deities called the Pales. The herds they tended belonged to an Alba Longan named Tullius, who often sent an overseer from the city to count or examine his animals; hence, our source of news about Amulius and his increasing tyrannies.

One day the overseer complained that the king had doubled taxes, the next, that his soldiers had insulted a Vestal or executed a boy for petty theft. The soldiers numbered a thousand – all the able bodied men in town were subject to duty at one time or another – and by no means the whole number approved of Amulius or victimized civilians. But a hard core, rewarded with land, cattle, or armour (there was no coinage yet in Latium), served Amulius willingly.

Inflamed by word from the city, Romulus left his herds in the care of sheep dogs and drilled his men; he taught them how to climb rocky cliffs like city walls or move with the swiftness of wolves. On the hill called Aventine, Remus taught them to whittle bows from hickory limbs and feather their arrows for deadly accuracy.

One day, when Remus was resting from both the herds and the training of archers, we had an adventure which seemed at the time unrelated to war and conquest, though it later proved vastly important. I found Remus standing under the fig tree near the mouth of his cave. He called it the Fig-Tree of Rumina, the goddess who protected suckling infants, because he felt that she had watched over him and Romulus while they fed from the she-wolf.

Finding him preoccupied, I crept up silently, seized his waist, and rolled him to the grass. My disadvantage in such matches was my tail, which he liked to take hold of and jerk until I begged for mercy. This morning, however, I had caught him by surprise, and soon I was sitting on his chest, triumphant. Already I had grown to outweigh him, with my hooves and my slim but sinewy body.

'Enough,' he gasped. 'Let me up!' I rose and we fell against each other, laughing and catching our breath.

'The next time you turn your back,' he swore, 'I will pull out your tail by the roots!' Suddenly he became serious. 'Sylvan, my bees are dying.'

He had found the bees in a poorly concealed log, stunned them with smoke, and removed them to a hollow in the fig tree, safe from hungry bears and shepherds. For a while they had seemed to thrive and Remus had been delighted, taking their honey only when they had enough to spare. But now –

'Look,' he said, drawing me to the tree which lifted its broad rough leaves to a remarkable forty feet. 'The bees are very ill.'

I stood beside him, my hand on his shoulder, and peered up into the tree. The bees were carrying off their dead in great numbers. Two of them, overwhelmed by the weight of a third, fell to the ground at my feet.

'They look beyond our help,' I said. 'But there are other hives, Remus. There will be no lack of honey.'

'But I am fond of *these*,' he protested, turning to face me. 'They are my friends, Sylvan. Not once have they stung me, even when I took their honey.' He looked so troubled, so young and vulnerable, that I was speechless. In the year I had known him he had hardly changed. His face was still beardless, his hair like woven sunlight. Who could explain this blond, green-eyed boy, so different from Romulus, had been born to a dark Latin mother? Only Mars knew the answer. Yet Rhea, the gentle Vestal, and not the war-like Mars, seemed more truly his parent.

'Wait,' I said. 'Fauns love honey and sometimes keep bees. My father will know what to do.'

We went to find him in the forest south of the Aventine. Though a Faun without clothes and with only a slingshot to encumber me, I could barely keep pace with Remus, who raced through the woods as if he wore wings. As a matter of fact, he had sewn his loin cloth with those same woodpecker feathers he used to wreathe his arrows.

'Remus, take pity,' I gasped. 'I expect you to rise through the treetops!'

Remus laughed. 'They say a woodpecker fed me when I was small.'

'And gave you his wings.'

In the deepest part of the forest, the trees were tall as hills and older than Saturn. What they had seen had left them weary – bent, twisted, and sagging – but still powerful. Oaks were the oldest, but ilex trees, too, and grey-barked beeches mixed sunlight and shadows in a venerable mist of limbs. Blue-eyed owls hooted among the leaves and magpies, birds of good omen, chattered in hidden recesses. A woodpecker burned his small green flame against the greater fire of the forest, and Remus pointed to him excitedly. 'It was one like that who fed me berries.'

Remus might have wandered for days without finding my father, but Fauns have an instinct in the woods and I led him straight to our camp.

Outside the palisade, I bleated like a goat to signify kinship with those behind the barrier. A section was lifted aside and a Faun, knotty and mottled like the underside of a rock, filled the entrance. His ears quivered with suspicion.

'It is Sylvan,' I said. 'Will you tell Nemus, my father, I wish to see him?'

The Faun vanished without a word. Another took his place. To human eyes – to Remus, as he later confessed – there was nothing to distinguish this Faun from the first. But I knew my father by the scar on his head and by the length of his ears – they were very long, even for a Faun.

'Sylvan,' he said without emotion. 'You want me?'

'Yes, Father. This is Remus, my friend.'

'I have seen you together.'

'We need your help. Remus' bees are dying. We hoped you could help us save them. The hive is well placed. But a sickness has taken them. They are carrying off their dead.'

Nemus thought a moment. 'Ah,' he said. 'You must find a Dryad.'

'A Dryad, Father?'

'Yes. They speak to the bees. They know all cures.'

'But Dryads are rare. I have never seen one.'

'I have,' said Nemus proudly. 'Her hair was the colour of oak leaves, and her skin, like milk –' He broke off, as if embarrassed by his own enthusiasm. 'But I will tell you where to look. Two miles to the south of this camp, there is a circle of oaks. Some say Saturn planted them. At any rate, one is inhabited by a Dryad. Which one I cannot say. I saw her dipping water from a spring and followed her to a ruined altar among the oaks. There she escaped me. You must hide in the bushes and watch the bees for an hour or more. In the tree where the most of them light will be your Dryad. Taking her nectar, you know. But tell me, Sylvan, why are these bees so important? Let them die. There are others.'

Remus answered for me. 'They are friends. We like to hear them work outside our cave. Now they are almost quiet.'

'Friends, you call them? You are one of the Old Ones, aren't you, boy? Your hair is ripe barley, but your heart might have lived with Saturn. In the old time, there was love in the forest. So the records of my people say. A scrawl on a stone, a picture, an image of clay – always they tell of love. Fauns, men and animals living in harmony.' He turned to his son.

'Look after him, Sylvan. Help him to find his Dryad. Help him always. He is one who is marked to be hurt.'

I reached out and touched my father on the shoulder, as I often touched Remus. He seemed surprised, whether pleased or offended

I could not say. When he turned his back, we went to find our Dryad.

There was the ring of oaks, just as he had said. Not the most ancient trees, if planted by Saturn, but old nonetheless. In their midst rose a pile of crumbling stones which had once formed an altar. Fingertips of sun touched the stones and live plants overrunning them, white narcissi with red-rimmed coronas, spiny-leafed acanthuses, and jonquils yellow as if the sunlight had flowered into the petals. We did not explore the altar however, and risk discovery by the Dryad, but crouched in some bushes beyond the oaks and watched for bees.

Soon a faint buzzing tingled my ears. I cocked them toward the sound and nudged Remus. A swarm of bees was approaching the ring of oaks. We watched them circle and vanish in the oak tree nearest the altar, a large tree with a trunk perhaps twenty feet wide at the base, and a welter of greenery high in the air. Yes, it could easily house a Dryad. I started to rise, but Remus grasped my tail.

'No,' he whispered. 'Your father said to watch where the *most* bees go.'

We waited, I fretfully, since a minute to a man seems like ten to a Faun. Soon I grew sleepy and, using Remus's back for a pillow, slept until he shook me.

'Three swarms have entered that tree and left again,' he said. 'No other tree has attracted so many. That must be the one.'

We rose and walked to the tree in question. 'We forgot to ask your father how to get inside,' Remus said, staring at the great trunk. Apparently the bees had entered through a hole invisible to us and far above our heads. The trunk was much too rough and broad to climb, and there were no branches within reach of our hands. We circled the base, prodding among the roots for an entrance, but succeeded only in dislodging a turquoise lizard that ran over Remus' sandal and flickered toward the altar.

Thoughtful, Remus stared after him. 'Your father lost sight of the Dryad near the altar.' We followed the lizard to the crumbling stones and began to kick among the rubble, careful, however, not to crush the jonquils or narcissi. A field mouse, poised for escape, stared at us from the tallest stone. A honey bee surged from a shaken jonquil.

'Sylvan,' Remus cried at last. 'I think we have found it! Eagerly he brushed aside bushes and, head first, squirmed into an opening just large enough for one body at a time. I followed him without enthusiasm. Such holes concealed poisonous adders as well as harmless lizards and mice.

The walls were smooth; neither roots nor rocks tore at our bodies. But the journey seemed long and the blackness grew oppressive. I imagined an adder with every bend of the tunnel.

Suddenly Remus stood up and pulled me beside him. We had entered the trunk of a tree, the Dryad's tree, I hoped. Far above our heads, a light shone roundly through an opening. Climbing toward the light, wooden rungs had been carved in the side of the trunk.

'We have found it,' he cried, joyfully pulling my tail. 'We have found her house!'

'I hope she is more accessible than her house,' I muttered.

We started to climb and at once I felt dizzy, since the tree was very tall. I consoled myself that our Dryad would perhaps be beautiful. I had heard that they remained young until they died with their trees. Remus and I saw no women on the Palatine, and imagination was a poor substitute. I had seen him scratching pictures on the walls of our cave, Rumina and other goddesses. He invariably drew them young, beautiful, radiant, the image of Woman in his own young heart. Did such a woman await us now?

Through the circular opening, we drew ourselves into a room which roughly followed the shape of the trunk. Small round windows cut in the walls admitted sunshine. A couch stood across the room, with feet like a lion's and a silken coverlet prancing with warriors. The air smelled of living wood, and white narcissus petals carpeted the floor. Somewhat hesitantly we advanced into the room. At once I collided with a table and almost upset a lamp like a twisted dragon. Remus, meanwhile, had settled in a backless chair.

'It is citrus wood from Carthage,' he said. 'I saw one like it in Veii. But where is the Dryad?'

'The ladder continues,' I noted, hastily ridding myself of the dragon lamp. 'There must be a second room over our head.'

Remus walked to the ladder. 'I will call her. She must not think we are robbers.'

But he did not have to call, for we heard footsteps descending the ladder. I lifted the sling from my neck in case the Dryad should be armed. Aeneas, after all, had found a race of fierce Amazons in Italy. Dryads who lived alone, Amazons or not, must know how to fight for their trees.

The Dryad paused at the foot of the ladder and faced us. She was diminutive even to a five-foot Faun – no taller than four herself. Her hair fell long and loosely over her shoulders, green hair, a dark leaf-green that in the shadows looked black, but where the sunlight struck it smouldered like jade that travellers bring from the East. Her mouth was pink and small; her skin, the pure fresh white of goat's milk. A brown linen robe, bordered with tiny acorns, rippled to sandalled feet.

She waited for us to speak and explain ourselves. When we said nothing – what could we say? our invasion was evident – she spoke herself, slowly as if out of practice, but with great precision.

'You have violated my house. I was sleeping above when your clumsy sandals woke me. May Janus, the door-god, curse you with evil spirits!'

'I am sorry we woke you,' said Remus. 'As for violating your house, we were not sure it *was* a house until we found this room. Then we forgot ourselves in its beauty.' He paused. 'We have come to ask a favour.'

'A favour?' she cried. 'I can guess the favour you mean.' She fixed her glare on me. 'You are the worst, you Fauns. Did it never occur to you to cover your loins, as your friend does?'

'If you notice my nakedness,' I said proudly, 'perhaps it is because you admire it. Dryads need men, and Fauns need women. Why should they not be friends?'

'I have banqueted kings,' she spat. 'Shall I frolic with strangers who blunder in from the woods – a Faun and a shepherd?'

'We only want to ask you about our bees,' Remus blinked, a small hurt child scolded for a deed he has not committed. He stepped toward her and she did not move. 'Our bees are dying and we want you to heal them.' They stared at each other. Then, incredibly, unpredictably even to me, he took her in his arms. Like the scolded child who does the very thing of which he has been accused, he kissed her small pink lips. Quick as an adder her hand rose – for the first time I saw the dagger – and raked down his side,

With a cry he withdrew, staring not at his bloodstreaked side but at her, and not with anger but shame at his own affront. I seized the knife before she could use it again and caught her, struggling in my arms. Furious because she had hurt my friend, I pressed her wrists cruelly until she lay still. I felt her breasts against my flesh, and then, before I could want her too much myself, said:

'Remus, she is yours. Kiss her again!'

'Let her go,' he said.

'But Remus, she attacked you. She deserves what she feared.'

'Sylvan, let her go,' he said, a small boy, baffled, defeated, but not to be disobeyed. I released her. She stared at the streak down his side.

'Please,' he said to her. 'My bees are dying. Tell me what to do for them.'

She drew him into the clear light of a window and dabbed the blood with a corner of her robe. 'Burn galbanum under the hive and carry them clusters of raisins in leaves of thyme. They will heal and grow strong again.' Then she took a long, unhurried look at him, and I might have been in another oak, for all they noticed me. 'You are very young. At first you were hidden in the shadows. When you kissed me, I was sure you were like the rest.'

'I am,' he said. 'I came to ask you about my bees, but I forgot them. I wanted your body. You made me think of grass and flowers in the hot sun. I am like the rest.'

'But you told your friend to release me. Why weren't you angry when I hurt you?'

'I was. With myself.'

She held his face between her hands. 'You are fragrant from the forest. You have lain in clover, I think. Like Aeneas, the Trojan. I loved him, you know. He came to me just as you have. All Latium rang with his triumphs – Turnus defeated, Camilla's Amazons put to rout! He sat on my couch and said, "Mellonia, I am tired. Since the sack of Troy I have wandered and fought. I have lost my wife and my father and forsaken a queen of Carthage. And I am tired."

'I took his head between my hands and kissed him, my prince, my warrior. In the years that followed, I watched him grow old. He married the princess Lavinia to found a royal line here in Latium. But he died in my arms, an old man with hair like a white waterfall. And I cursed this tree which kept me young. I wanted to die with Aeneas. The years passed and I did not give myself, even in loneliness. I have waited for another Aeneas.'

She turned away from him and stared through a window at a swarm of bees approaching the tree. 'They are bringing me honey. My little friends. Your friends too.' She faced him again.

'Why are you young? Aeneas was grey when he came to me, older than I in wars and loves, though younger in years. Now I am ancient. But you are young. You cannot have waited for anything very long. Your eyes are naked, a child's. You have not learned to hide your thoughts. You want me and fear me. I could stab you with words more sharply than with this dagger. Why do you come here young and virginal? I will make you old. My face is a girl's, but my eyes are tired with waiting.'

Like round-built merchant ships laden with precious oils, the bees invaded the room and unloaded their nectar in a cup of agate. She held out her hand and some of them lit in her palm. 'To me, Remus, you are like the bees. Their life is six weeks.'

'Then help me to be like Aeneas!'

She reached up to him and loosened the fillet which bound his hair. 'It spills like sunflowers. I am cold, so cold. Give me your sunflowers, Remus. Prince of Alba Longa!'

'You know me?'

'Not at first. Only when I had hurt you. I knew you by your yellow hair and your gentleness. The forest speaks of you, Remus. With love.'

Their voices blended with the whirr of bees, and the scent of nectar throbbed in my nostrils like a sweet intoxicant. I had lingered too long. I backed down the ladder and returned to the pile of stones.

Much later, when Remus stepped from the tunnel, he said, 'Sylvan, you are crying!'

'I am *not* crying,' I protested. 'Fauns don't cry. We take things as they come and make light of everything. A bramble bush scratched my eyes and made them water.'

He looked doubtful but did not press me. In fact, he said little even after we left the circle of oaks and plunged into the forest.

'The Dryad,' I asked. 'Was she hospitable?' I pressed him with the hope that he would speak of her lightly, as a woman possessed and forgotten. I wanted him to reassure me that I was not replaced in his heart by a bad tempered Dryad older than Aeneas!

'Yes.'

'Remus,' I chided. 'Your spirits seem mildewed. Have you nothing to tell me about Mellonia?'

It was almost as if the aged Faustulus were speaking. 'What is there to say about love? It isn't happiness, altogether; it is sadness too. It is simply possession.'

'I should think you would feel like wrestling,' I said. 'Or drawing one of your goddesses. Or swimming the Tiber. You don't look possessed to me, you look vacant.'

'I am thinking of many things,' he said. 'Yesterday, I wanted to punish the man who had killed my mother, and I wanted to be king for the sake of Fauns and wolves and runaway slaves. Now I want to be king for her sake also.'

We were nearing the Palatine. At the mouth of our cave, he stopped and faced me and placed his hands on my shoulders.

'Sylvan, why were you crying back there?'

'I told you,' I snapped.

'Did you think she had driven you out of my heart, little Faun?'

He had not called me 'little Faun' since that night a year – ten years – ago, when Romulus stole me from my camp. 'Yes,' I said, losing control of my tears. 'And not to a girl but a witch! Or squirrel, I should say, the way she lives in a tree. Remus, she will bite you yet.' Being half goat, I always saw people as animals.

He did not laugh at me and try to make light of my tears, but touched his fingers, lightly as butterflies, to my ear. 'In the circle of oaks,' he said, 'there were jonquils and narcissi growing together. There was room for both. Do you understand what I am saying, Sylvan?'

Just then the ram-eyed Celer hurried toward us down the hill. If anything, his eyes had grown flatter and more stupid with the passing year.

'Remus,' he called in his thick slurred way. 'News from the city! Romulus wants you in his hut.'

III

In the early dusk, the hill lay shadowed and strange, and the hut of Romulus seemed misted to stone. Solemn and dignified, sheep roamed the paths and, pausing, were hardly separable from the low rocks which Vulcan, it was said, had thrust from his caverns in a fiery temper. Shepherds and those who had recently joined them, Romulus' latest recruits, loitered in small groups talking about the day's work or tomorrow's drill. The newcomers held apart from the original shepherds. Their garb was the same simple loin cloth, but their faces, though mostly young, were scared and sullen. One, I knew, was a murderer who had fled from Lavinium after killing his wife; another, a parricide from the new Greek colony at Cumae. It was men like these whom Remus wished to bar from the Palatine, and Romulus welcomed because they knew how to fight.

When the wife-killer saw me, he bleated like a goat. Remus wheeled in anger but I shoved him toward Romulus's hut. He must not fight on my account.

'You sound like a frog,' I called good-naturedly. 'Do it like this.' And I bleated so convincingly that she-goats answered from every direction.

A figure loomed toward us, a tall ship scudding in a sea of mist. It was Romulus. To me he nodded, to Remus he smiled.

'Brother,' he said. 'Gaius is here from the city. He has brought us news.' We walked into his hut, where a small, bearded man who reminded me of a water bug, so freely did he skip about the room, was telling a story he seemed to have told several times and would no doubt tell again. His eyes sparkled when he saw Remus and me, a new audience.

'Remus,' he said. 'And Sylvan, is it not? Listen to what I have seen! I met Numitor in the market yesterday with two attendants. Lately Amulius has allowed him considerable freedom. To appease the people, I expect, and keep them from growling about taxes. Anyway, a half-grown sheep dog was barking at one of Amulius' soldiers. A friendly dog, wanting to play. But the soldier did not. He raised his spear and drove it through the animal's heart. Numitor cried out in anger and raised his staff to strike the man. The soldier, far from cowed, drew his sword, but a barber and a vintner intervened while Numitor's attendants hurried him back to the palace.

'As the old man disappeared, I heard him shout, "If my grandsons had lived, there would be no soldiers!" Everyone who had watched the scene – myself included – was stirred by Numitor's courage. And everyone wished that there were truly grandsons to drive the soldiers from the street.'

With a vigorous skip, he ended his story and smote Remus' shoulder for emphasis. Remus' emotion was evident. His eyes, wide and troubled, mirrored the flames from the hearth: mournful lights in a green, sad forest. As far as I knew, no one had told the overseer the boy's real identity. But Gaius watched him with unusual interest. Perhaps he had overheard the shepherds.

Sparing Gaius the temptation to repeat his story, Romulus led him to the door. 'It is bad news you bring us, Gaius. Thank Jove we are kingless here! Do you wonder we stay in the country?'

Gaius smiled ironically. Doubtless he guessed that most of Romulus' men and Romulus himself avoided the city for reasons that had nothing to do with a fondness for the countryside.

'When I think of Amulius,' he sighed, 'I am tempted to stay here with you. They call him The Toad, you know, though he calls himself The Bear. But Tullius, my master, depends on me. His herds have multiplied, Romulus. I shall take him good news.' With a backward wave, he bobbed down the Palatine.

In Romulus' hut, Faustulus, Celer, the twins, and I gathered by the fire to evaluate Gaius's news. On such occasions, Remus always included me, though the first time both Romulus and Celer had objected to the presence of a Faun.

'We have waited with patience,' Romulus said with unsuppressed excitement. 'Now the mood of the city seems right. They will flock to our side the minute they know us! But they have to be told who we are, and our grandfather is the one to tell them. First we must identify ourselves to him. I will go to Alba Longa tomorrow and get an audience.'

'But he lives in Amulius' palace,' cried the aged Faustulus bent like a hickory bow but taut, like the rest of us, with the spirit of revolt. 'How can you get an audience?'

'He is right,' said Remus. 'You can't simply walk to the palace as I did in Veii and ask to see Numitor. Amulius' guards are much too suspicious. Your height and bearing set you apart at once. I should be the one to go.'

'You, Remus? What about your hair? Blond men in Latium are as rare as virgins in Etruria. They will take you for a spy from the Gauls! Even if they don't, how will you gain an audience with Numitor?'

'I have thought what I would do for some time. First I will dye my hair dark brown. You know the umber that's dug from the banks of the Tiber? I will rub some in my hair and disguise the colour. Then I will steal one of Numitor's cows. His shepherds will catch me and take me to Numitor. In the theft of cows, the owner and not the king has the right to pass judgement. Amulius will have no hand in this unless Numitor turns me over to him. I don't believe he will.'

'No,' said Romulus, 'it is much too dangerous. I won't let you take the risk.'

Usually I wanted to kick him with both my hooves. Now I wanted to embrace him.

'Remus is right,' said that idiot, Celer, mouthing his usual monosyllables. 'Old men love him. He's soft and polite. Let him go, Romulus. I have a stake in this too.'

Yes, I thought, cattle, women, and a house in town. That's all you want. What do you know about government? Remus, my friend, even if you win the city, you will not have won your justice.

'It is settled then,' said Remus with a finality that ended argument.

'And I will help you,' I said.

'No, I will do it alone. Fauns are not popular in Latium. The shepherds might kill you right off.'

Romulus looked troubled. He stroked his beginning beard and furrowed his brow. This fierce, ambitious young man, who feared neither wolves nor warriors, was unashamedly afraid for his brother. At last, like a father sending his son to fight the Gauls, he placed his hands on Remus' shoulders and said,

'Go then, Brother. But while you are gone, I will gather the shepherds. We will be ready to attack the city when you return with word from Numitor. If you don't return within three days, we will attack anyway. The gate is strong, but the walls aren't high to shepherds who live on hills.'

'Or to shepherds led by princes,' said Faustulus proudly, drawing the twins to his side. 'For eighteen years I have called you my sons.

In fact, since I found you in the cave at the breast of Luperca. After you had fed, she let me take you – she, your second mother, knew that the time had come for a third. And I carried you back to this very hut and to Larentia, my wife. When Larentia died a year later, I brought you up myself. Now, like the wolf, I must step aside and return you to your grandfather. You will not shame him.'

In our cave the next morning, Remus veiled his head in a cloak and addressed a prayer to the god Bonus Eventus, whose image he had scratched on the wall. No one knew the god's true appearance, but Remus had made him young and round-cheeked, with a spray of barley in his hand. Holding out his arms and quite oblivious to Luperca and me, Remus prayed:

'Bonus Eventus, god who brings luck to the farmer with his barley and his olive trees, bring me luck too; send me safely to my grandfather!'

After the prayer, he set a cup of milk before the image, for everyone knows that the gods, whether human as Remus and the Etruscans supposed, or bodiless powers in the wind, the rock, the tree, demand offerings of food. (Luperca eyed the milk, and I hoped that the god drank quickly!) Then he attended to his bees, burning galbanum under the hive and carrying them raisins in thyme.

'Look after them, will you?' he asked. 'And Luperca too. You may have to feed her from your hands. She is very feeble.' (Not too feeble to drink that milk, I thought.) 'And Sylvan. Will you tell Mellonia where I have gone? I had meant to visit her today.'

I stamped my hoof in protest. 'The squirrel lady?'

'Goddess,' he corrected.

'Goddess? She will live no longer than her tree!'

'But her tree has lived hundreds of years, and will live hundreds more. Till Saturn returns. Then he will find her another.'

'Is that what she told you? What about lightning? And floods? And woodcutters?'

'Your ears are quivering,' he grinned. 'They always do when you are angry.' And he began to stroke them with his irresistible fingers. 'You will see Mellonia? Promise me, Sylvan.'

'Don't do that,' I cried. 'You know how it tickles.'

'But you like to be tickled.'

'That's my point. You can make me promise anything.'

'Would you rather I yanked your tail?'

'All right, all right. I will see Mellonia. Now go and steal your cow.'

*   *   *

Of course I had meant all along to help him. My problem was how to remain hidden until he had begun his theft, then run out and implicate myself and share his capture. I followed his tracks at a safe distance. In the marshes, I was careful not to let my hooves squish noisily, and among the Sabine burial mounds, some fresh, some covered with grass, I steeled myself not to take fright at the presence of spirits and break into a gallop. I was careful to keep a tree or a hill between us. He moved rapidly, as always, but his tracks and my keen sense of hearing kept me on his trail.

Numitor's shepherds lay asleep in the shade, three gnarled men as ancient as their master, who, it was said, hired only the old to work for him because the young reminded him of his lost daughter and grandsons. At the feet of the shepherds lay an aged sheep dog who also seemed to be sleeping. I hid behind an ilex tree and waited for developments.

Remus advanced into the herd and singled out a thin, black cow with a shrunken udder. The dog stared at him sleepily as the three shepherds continued to drowse.

'Ho there, cow, off with you!' Remus cried, scuffing through the bushes with a great racket. Like a child chasing geese, he seemed to enjoy himself.

The dog made no move until he saw the shepherds open their eyes. Then he hobbled forward and warily circled the intruder. The men rubbed their eyes and began to shout, 'Thief, thief!' Remus pretended to be bewildered by their cries and ran in circles around the cow. I sprang from my ilex tree and joined him.

'I told you not to come,' he whispered, as angry as I had ever seen him.

'Two of them,' croaked a shepherd. 'And one a Faun. They might have made off with the herd!'

They cautiously approached the spot where we circled the cow, who, unperturbed by our sallies, continued her breakfast of grass, while the dog, preening himself on his vigilance, barked from a bed of lupin.

'Brave dog, brave Balbus,' the shepherds muttered, stroking the animal on its flea-bitten head. One of them fetched some leathern thongs from a lean-to beside the pasture.

'Now,' said the least infirm of the three, who seemed their leader. 'Tie their hands.'

Without resistance, we offered our hands. While a shepherd bound them, the leader waved his staff threateningly and the dog rushed in and out barking, then withdrew to catch his breath.

'They are just boys,' said our binder, craning his neck and squinting for a clear look. 'Need we take them to Numitor in town? It's such a long walk, Julius. A good thrashing may be all they need.'

Remus hurried to speak. 'My father thrashed me once. That is why I ran away. It made me rebellious. No, I am afraid you must take us to Numitor, unless you want every cow stolen and sold to the Etruscans across the river.' He looked very fierce and tilted his head as if to look down in scorn on these men who dared call him just a boy. 'And my friend here, the Faun. Would you believe it! Young as he is, he has already carried off six maidens.' He added wickedly, 'I have carried off seven. But then, I am older.'

'Boys they may be,' sighed the leader, 'but dangerous ones. Numitor will have to judge. Can the two of you get them to town while Balbus and I watch the herds?'

The old men looked at each other and then toward town, as if weighing the effect of twenty-four miles on their weathered ankles. One of them prodded Remus with his staff, the other me. We lurched forward obligingly. 'We will try,' they sighed.

'Give them a whack if they talk,' advised the leader, and off we went to find Numitor.

Alba Longa, the city of Romulus' and Remus' dream, which I myself had seen only from the woods at the foot of its plateau, was in truth a modest walled town of five thousand people. Its rock walls, though tall, were starting to crumble, and its streets grew grass between their cobblestones. Nevertheless the houses glittered whitely with plaster and looked to us both like little palaces.

'And their roofs,' Remus whispered. 'They are covered with *baked clay shingles*.' We were used, of course, to the thatched roofs of shepherd huts. 'No danger of fire, no rain soaking through.'

'Ho there, thieves, get on with you,' our captors shouted, and prodded us with their staves. Everywhere the people stared at our advance, to the obvious pleasure of the shepherds, who cried the more loudly, 'Ho there!' A vestal with a black Etruscan vase almost spilled her water. A vintner dropped his pig-skin of wine and a thin red stream trickled among the cobblestones. There were barbers in stalls by the road, and sellers of vegetables holding great melons in their hands; children, sheep dogs, and asses; and, brash and numerous, the soldiers of Amulius. In most Latin cities, I knew, there was no standing army, no soldiers except in wartime. But Amulius' men, brandishing spears tipped with bronze, marched through the city as if to say, 'We march

on the king's business, and it is not for civilians to inquire its
nature.'

'Ho there,' shouted our captors once too often, and a soldier
swatted them both on the head with the shaft of his spear. 'Be
quiet, old men. You are near the palace.' Chastened, the shepherds
fell silent and ceased to prod us.

To the left lay the temple of Vesta, raised by Etruscan architects
on a stone platform, with four square pillars across the front. Its
pediment twinkled with orange terra cotta but not with the images
beloved by the Etruscans, for the Latin goddess Vesta lived in the
flame of her hearth and had no physical semblance. Opposite the
temple crouched the palace of Amulius, a low white rectangle
distinguished only by size from the houses we had passed. It
was whispered that one day Amulius hoped to build a true
Etruscan palace, multicoloured instead of white, with frescoes
and colonnades, from the cattle he took in taxes; he would trade
them to the Etruscans for architects and stone.

As a start, at least, he had flanked his gate with bronze Etruscan
lions, slender and lithe-legged, their tails looped over to touch their
backs, their eyes almond-shaped like those of the men who had made
them. In front of the lions stood a pair of human guards, only less
lordly than the animals.

'Have you business in the king's palace?' one of them demanded.
His jerkin was leather, his crested helmet, bronze.

Our captors had not recovered their composure since the scene
with the soldier. They stammered awkwardly and Remus had to
speak for them.

'They caught us stealing Numitor's cattle. They want to receive
his judgement.'

At mention of Numitor, the guards softened. One of them leaned
into the gate and called, and a withered attendant appeared from
the interior. Guard and attendant whispered together; attendant
disappeared and shortly returned. He led us down a hallway
supported by wooden timbers and into a garden behind the palace,
enclosed on three sides by a brick wall. Roses rioted in vermilion
chaos and crocuses spilled like golden goblets. It was the first flower
garden I had ever seen. I wanted to roll in the blossoms, thorns and
all, and kick my hooves in the air. Then I saw the king of the garden
and forgot to dream. He sat in a backless chair and stared into a
milky pool. His white curving hair was hardly distinguishable from
his robes, which billowed around his feet and hid his sandals.

He seemed unaware of us. The attendant drew his attention.
'Prince, your shepherds have brought two thieves to receive justice.'

He raised his head and looked at us without expression. His face was as yellow and cracked as papyrus, laid in a tomb by pharaohs older than Saturn; god-men ruling the Nile before the Etruscans had passed through Egypt and brought her lore to Italy. A face like papyrus whose writing had been erased by time; inscrutable.

'Bring them forward,' he said. We knelt and Remus took his hand.

'My king,' he said, nothing more, but with infinite sincerity.

Numitor withdrew his hand and motioned the boy to rise. 'I am not your king,' he said stiffly. 'I never was. You are much too young – the age of my grandsons, had they lived. And they were born after I had lost my throne. Tell me, boy, why did you steal my cattle?'

'Because I wanted to see you.'

'To see me? I don't understand.'

'As a thief, I knew they would bring me to receive your judgement.'

'You were right. Before I deliver judgement, what favour do you ask? I warn you, I have few to give.'

'Your blessing. Your love.'

'An old man loves his children. I have none. His grandchildren. I have none. My heart has rid itself of love. A nest without swallows. But what is your name? Something about you stirs me to remember –'

'A shepherd named me Remus, and my brother, Romulus. We are twins.'

The names, of course, were meaningless to him, but he caught at Remus' last word. 'Twins, you say?'

'Soon after we were born, our mother was buried in a pit and we were taken to be drowned in the Tiber. But Faustulus saved us and made us his sons.'

Numitor groaned and surged to his feet, like the geysers of Vulcan, white with borax, which roar from the earth and shudder in the air.

'What are you saying?' he thundered. 'You lie as well as steal. I saw my grandsons when Amulius took them from my daughter. One had dark hair, darker than yours. One had gold, gold like this flower.' He crushed a crocus under his sandal. 'A gift from the god, his father. Which are you?'

'The gold-haired.' Remus fell to his knees and ducked his head in the pool, which began to run rivulets of brown. He rose and shook out his hair. Though streaked with umber, it glittered yellowly like gold among veins of iron.

I watched the papyrus mask. The worn and time-veined surface

trembled and softened, the forgotten language of love spoke in
misting eyes. He ran his hand through Remus' hair and felt the
molten umber between his fingers.

'Time,' he said. 'Give me time. I am not used to tears. They burn
like wine.' An old man sightless with tears, he took the boy in his
arms. 'Rhea,' he whispered, 'your son has come back to me.'

'You are a senile old fool,' a voice croaked from the door. 'This
boy has played a trick on you. He should be taught a lesson.'

I recognized Amulius though I had never seen him. I knew him
from the veined toad eyes which never blinked, the hunched and
dwarfish shape. Amulius the Toad.

'Guards!' he called.

'Go to Romulus,' Remus whispered. 'I will hold them off.'

Behind me a prince and a tyrant grappled in roses and thorns.
With a single thrust of my hooves, I clutched the top of the wall
and drew myself up the bricks. 'Bonus Eventus,' I prayed, 'help me
to bring him help!'

IV

I landed in a narrow street behind the palace and my hooves clattered
on the cobblestones. An old woman, carrying melons from market,
paused in surprise, then trudged down the street with a shrug that
seemed to say: 'Let Amulius protect his own palace. If Fauns can
rob it, good for them.' There was no one else in sight, but an ass,
tethered to a stake, watched me vacantly. His master, it seemed, had
business in the shop of a dyer, which reeked with decaying trumpet
shells, much prized for their purple dye.

Remus had given me seconds. As soon as the guards overpowered
him, they would follow me or send their friends. I must reach the
gate quickly; I must run. But a running Faun, in a city of soldiers,
would look suspicious. They would take me for a thief. Nibbling
grass between the stones, the tethered ass browsed in the sun. I
loosed his rope and kicked him with the full force of my hoof. He
galloped down the street.

'Whoa, whoa,' I shouted, galloping after him as if to recover my
own escaping property. Round a bend he sped and into the central
street and straight toward the towers of the gate. When he slowed, I
slowed. When he quickened, I quickened and yelled 'Whoa!' A hand
reached out to stop him; I caught my breath; but he burst free and
charged for the gate. The guards laughed and spurred him on with

a slap to his flank and a cry of 'Giddyap!' Upsetting a potter's cart, laden with orange clay lamps, I hurried after him.

'May thieves crack your skull,' cried the potter. I waved without looking back and raced down the hill toward the forest. To the left of me, Lake Albanus glittered in the afternoon sun, and skiffs of hollowed alder poised like dragonflies on its molten turquoise. Ahead of me dusky cypresses signalled the path to the Palatine.

I found Romulus with Celer and the herd at the foot of the Palatine. When I told him what had happened, he turned very pale and drove his staff into the ground.

'I *knew* I should have gone.'

'Never mind,' I consoled. 'Who can say no to Remus?'

'If they harm him, I will burn the city! Celer, watch the cattle.' He hurried me up the hill, making plans as he went. 'We will attack tonight. In the dark, we may be able to climb the walls before we are seen.'

'But the people won't know us. Remus had no chance to tell Numitor about our plan.'

'No matter. We can't delay. Once in the city, we will shout his name – 'Long live Numitor!' – and hope to rally support.'

Romulus was right, we could not delay. But what could we do against walls and soldiers? If we battered down the gate with a tree, soldiers would surely be waiting. If we climbed the walls, they might see us and still be waiting. Since Alba Longa stands on a ridge, it is difficult to reach the walls without detection, even at night. I said nothing; Romulus knew the dangers. But I could not risk Remus' life with such a puny effort.

I descended the Palatine and headed for the cave. I wanted to, think. On the way I passed Celer with the herd. He leaned against a rock, staff in hand and a straw between his teeth. Complacent oaf, I thought. Calm as a sheep when Remus' life is in danger.

'So they shut the Woodpecker in a cage,' he grinned. 'Big games tonight, eh?' Before I could hoof him, he changed the subject. 'Sylvan, I hear you found a Dryad. Where's her tree?'

'She is Remus' Dryad,' I said indignantly.

'And yours,' he smirked. 'And mine, if you show me her tree.'

'North of the Quirinal,' I lied. 'An ilex tree with a lightning mark on the trunk.' I lowered my ears to muffle his answer and hurried to the cave. Inside, I threw myself on a pallet of clover, but the fragrance reminded me of Remus and clouded my thoughts. I paced the floor. Luperca crept from the rear of the cave and pressed against my leg. I knelt and took her head in my hands.

'Luperca,' I said. 'Remus has gone to the city. They have taken him captive. What shall I do?' She looked at me with such intelligence that I felt she understood my words; she began to whine and I wished that I understood hers.

Then I heard a swarming of bees outside the cave. I walked out and looked at the hive in the fig tree. Mellonia's remedy had worked. The bees were recovering their health. Mellonia! She was the one to help Remus. She had cured his bees. Might she not have secrets to release him from prison? After all, she had loved Aeneas, the incomparable warrior. I galloped for the circle of oaks. Behind me, a conch shell boomed from the Palatine, and I knew that Romulus was summoning his men.

I stood at the foot of her oak and called: 'Mellonia, I have come from Remus.' No answer.

Again I called. A voice, muffled by branches, answered. 'I am coming down. Wait for me by the altar.'

In a surprisingly short time, she emerged from the tunnel. She was not the Mellonia I remembered, hard and queenly, but a pale tree child blinking in the alien sun. She raised a hand to shelter her eyes.

'He is hurt?'

'No. But Amulius has taken him prisoner.' I told her about his capture.

'What does Romulus mean to do?'

I explained his plan – as much as I knew.

'Romulus' shepherds,' she sighed. 'I have seen them drilling in the woods. They are brave but they have no armour. They have no spears. Only their staves and bows. What good are bows against walls, or in fighting hand to hand through the streets? They will cost Remus his life.'

'Mellonia,' I cried desperately. 'You can save him. I know you can.'

She touched my cheek with the tips of her fingers, like little blades of grass. 'You are a good friend to him, Sylvan. You and I and the forest, we are his friends. Perhaps we can save him. Go back to Romulus now. Say that when Arcturus shines directly over the temple of Vesta, I will come to him in the woods below the city gate. Let him do nothing till I come, but have his men in readiness.'

I pressed her hand; it was warm and small like a swallow. 'Mellonia, I have not been kind to you.'

'Nor I to you. But Remus has made us friends. You are his brother, Sylvan. Far more than Romulus, the Wolf. Trust me.'

I turned to go and she called after me. 'Sylvan, wait. In truth I am afraid for him. The forest is restless. The cranes have been flying all day, as they do before a storm. But there has been no storm. And all last night, owls cried in my tree. I have looked for vultures, birds of good omen. Especially for woodpeckers. There are none to be seen.'

'Good omens?' I cried. 'You are Remus' good omen!'

Tall above Alba Longa, the temple of Vesta burned in the moonlight, and orange Arcturus, the star of spring, climbed above the stone pediment. Fifty shepherds crouched in the forest below the gate: Romulus with his ancient spear consecrated to Mars; several with bows and arrows, the use of which Remus had taught them; but most armed only with knives, staves, or slingshots. The bodies of all were bare except for loin cloths – no greaves on their legs nor metal corselts to hide their chests and backs from the plunge of an arrow or the bite of a sword.

Their battering ram was an elm tree cut in the forest; their ladders looked as frail as saplings untested by storms. How many shepherds, I wondered, would survive the night? I was glad that the bent Faustulus, at Romulus' insistence, had remained on the Palatine. A momentary pity possessed me. Who could blame them, rough though they were, for wanting houses in town and women to tend their hearths?

'We can wait no longer,' said Romulus. It fretted him following orders from a Dryad he had never seen. Nothing but concern for Remus, I think, and knowledge of his own inadequacy, could have made him listen at all.

'But Arcturus has just now risen above the temple,' I protested. 'Before, it was still climbing. I know she will come!'

'What can she do if she does? We are fools to try the gate, which seems to be her intention. We should scale the wall on the far side.'

Then I heard the bees. 'Hush,' I said. 'She is coming.'

My ears quivered. The droning grew louder; curiously the men peered into the forest. I felt like a traveller approaching a waterfall. At first he hears just a murmur, faint and distant. Then the trees fall away and the murmur roars in his ears.

Now they surrounded us, bees beyond counting. Kindled by the moonlight, they curved like a Milky Way above our heads and wove a shield from the darkness. Mellonia led them. She seemed to be made out of leaves and mist and moonlight. She walked in a cloud of bees, and I had to look closely to see that her feet touched the ground. The men gaped at her; Romulus too, and that stupid Celer most of all.

'Is that your Dryad?' he whispered. 'She looks like a goddess!'

I gaped too, but less at her beauty than at the dark stains on her face – were they blood? – and at her torn, dishevelled robe.

'It is nothing,' she whispered, passing me. 'Part of my plan.' She singled out Romulus. It was not hard for her to recognize him, the brawniest of all of the young men and the only one with a spear.

'Romulus,' she said. 'Brother of Remus, I salute you. When the gate is open, I will raise my arm. Enter with your men.'

Before he could question her somewhat cryptic directions, she was gone, climbing the hill toward the gate. The bees swirled high above her; their droning died, their fires flickered out in the darkness.

'What does she mean to do?' Romulus gasped. 'Sylvan, she is mad.'

'Or a witch,' cried Celer, staring after her.

The men shuddered and whispered among themselves. Something moved in the forest. Shapes inseparable from the trees, not to be seen, scarcely to be heard. Something breathed.

'Striges,' went the whisper. 'Vampires.'

'Lemures. She sent to make us follow her!'

Now she was midway to the gate. 'Guards,' she called out, her voice broken as if with pain, yet strong enough to be heard in the towers that flanked the gate. 'Help me. I am hurt.' She fell to her knees. 'Help me.'

Silence. Then a voice, hesitant, testing. 'Who are you?'

'I have come from Veii. Wolves attacked my escort in the forest.'

Creaking, the gate swung inward on its massive stone pivot. A lamp flickered in one of the towers, vanished, reappeared on the ground. Its bearer paused in the gateway. Mellonia rose, staggered, fell again. 'Help me.' The guard walked toward her, sword in hand.

She raised her arm.

'They will shut the gate in our face,' groaned Romulus. 'We can never climb the hill in time!' But his hesitation was brief. Whatever his faults, he was not a coward. With a low cry to his men, he raced up the hill toward the gate. I ran beside him. The hill swelled above us, endless and black. I felt like a swimmer in the trough of a mountainous wave. Would we never make its crest?

Kneeling beside Mellonia, the guard raised his head and saw us. 'Shut the gate!' he shouted. He scurried to safety; the gate swung inward, monstrous, implacable.

Then a shadow crossed the moon. I looked up; my ears stood on end. Mellonia's bees! In a deadly amber stream, they poured from the sky. A shout, a thrashing in the tower. The gate groaned slowly to silence, half open.

I dug my hooves in the turf, kicked aside stones, drove myself furiously forward. Romulus tripped and I heaved him back in the path. Through the half open gate, I saw the movement of men, the flash of a spear, the swirling of bees and bronze. Then we were in the city. The bees withdrew and left us to fight our battle.

A soldier charged me, levelling his spear and grinning like the demons of death in Etruscan tombs. I raised my sling and caught him in the teeth. He stopped, a round black hole where his teeth had been, and stared at me. Blood gushed out of the hole. Like a broken bow, he fell at my feet.

'We have them outnumbered,' Romulus shouted. 'They are falling back!' Spears wavered, shields swung aside. The street near the gate lay empty except for ourselves.

'Numitor!' 'Numitor is king!' Romulus began the cry, and the rest of us took it up. 'Numitor is king!' Dazed with too easy a victory, we surged toward the heart of town, the temple, the palace, and Remus.

But the street was barred. A row of spears glittered across our path, like the oars of a galley raised from the sea in sparkling unison. A wall of spears to bar our advance, and behind them another, another, and finally a row of archers, grim as Etruscan bronzes. The soldiers we had routed were few. Now we must meet an army. Already our limbs were streaked with blood. We had spent our wind in the climb and the fight at the gate. We had lost some men – six I counted with a hasty glance in the street. We were tired, outnumbered, and armourless. How could we shake those fixed, immovable spears?

'Where are the bees?' I cried. 'Mellonia, where are your bees?'

Then I saw the wolves, thudding through the gate and into the street. Muffled as raindrops, their feet padded on the stones. My nostrils quivered with the scent of fur, grassy and wet from the forest. I felt hot breath and smelled decaying flesh. We crouched against the walls to let them pass. The wolves ignored us. Straight toward the soldiers they went, the levelled spears and the tightening bows. Mellonia and Luperca followed them.

Mellonia spoke so softly that I could not make out her words, or should I say incantation. It is said that the Etruscan princes, when they hunt, bewitch the animals with the piping of flutes and lure them into their nets. Mellonia's voice, it seemed, had such a power over wolves. Sometimes, it is true, an animal balked or threatened to turn from the pack. But Luperca, surprisingly agile, snapped at his heels and hurried him back into line. The venerable wolf who had suckled my friend in a cave and the aged, ageless Dryad: both were queens.

The line trembled, the spears wavered, like oars engulfed by a wave. The long taut bows swayed in the archers' arms. And the wolves attacked. High above the wavering spears, a body spun in the air. Spears shot up to ward off its deadly fall. The line was broken. The archers never fired. Men and animals rolled in the street; armour clattered on stones and weighed men down; animals sprang on their chests and tore at their naked faces. Spears were useless, arrows worse. A few had time to draw daggers. Most used their hands.

Some of the men broke free and began to run. Wolves loped after them. Wounded, in pain, the soldiers reeled against doorways and beat their fists for admittance. The doors remained shut.

The city had wakened. On the rooftops, torches flared, people crouched behind them and stared at the rout of the tyrants who, a few hours ago, had tyrannized Alba Longa. Now a weird procession formed: Mellonia and Luperca with the wolf pack, a cloud of returning bees above their heads: Romulus with his shepherds, raising their staves in token of victory.

But an army's march is slow, and Remus was still in the palace. Ignoring the wolves, I pushed to Mellonia's side.

'Come ahead with me,' I urged.

She nodded. 'Luperca can watch the wolves.'

In a cloud of bees, we raced through the market of silent stalls, where tomorrow the vintner would hawk his wine and the farmer his gourds and grapes. A terrified soldier reeled from our path. A sheep dog snapped at our heels but, hearing the wolves, ducked in an alleyway.

The palace was almost dark. The temple of Vesta, across the road, lent a fitful light from its eternal hearth. The Etruscan lions growled in brazen impotence. They had no soldiers to guard them. The gate was unbarred. We entered the central corridor and, following a light, turned aside into a large hall.

'Amulius' audience room,' Mellonia said. She pointed to a curule chair of gold and ivory raised on a stone platform. A tall candelabrum, hung with lamps, cast mournful flickerings on the tapestry behind the throne. Seeing that the room was empty, I turned to continue our search. Mellonia stopped me.

'We will lose minutes. Let my bees find him.' She raised her arms and inscribed in the air a series of circles and lines, like the loopings of bees when they tell the location of flowers. The bees understood and swarmed from the room.

We looked at each other. Where was the powerful sorceress who had opened the gate of a city to admit the forest? Like a swallow after a storm, beaten and bruised, she sank to the floor. I motioned her to sit in the chair.

'No,' she said. 'Amulius sat there.' She stared at the plum-coloured hangings behind the chair. 'Even his dye is false. Not Tyrian purple, the colour of kings, but the dye of trumpet shells.'

I sat beside her and rested her in my arms. 'It will be all right,' I said. 'Soon we will have him back again.'

'Now perhaps. But later? He will always be hurt, always be threatened.'

'We will look after him.'

'We are vulnerable too. Even now I am weary for my tall bark walls. I cannot leave them for long.'

Abruptly the bees returned, circling in the doorway to catch our attention. In the dark corridor, we lost sight of them, but their droning guided us through several turnings and down a stairway redolent of rocks and moisture. We stepped into a cellar lit by a single torch, smoky and pungent with resin. The room opened through a barred door into a small cell. The door swung wide on its pivot and Amulius' body, clutching a dagger, hunched like a bloated toad across the sill. Remus stood in the cell beyond the body.

'He came to get me,' he said, dazed.

'And you had to kill him?'

'No. They did.' He pointed to the bees which had lit on the pallet in his cell. I knelt beside the body and saw the red welts, a hundred or more, and the closed swollen eyes.

'He unbolted the door and said that my friends were coming; he was going to make me his hostage. I stepped backward. He drew his dagger, and they hit him from the back like a hundred hundred slingshots. He scraped at his eyes, groaned, and fell to the floor. Then you came.'

'The bees love you,' Mellonia said proudly. 'Some may have come from your own hive. They sensed your danger.'

He buried his face in the fall of her hair and she held him with exquisite tenderness. For the first time, I loved him loving her. Two children they seemed, warm in each other's arms and forgetful that love, however strong, is also brief, because it is bound by the frailties of the flesh. I wanted to enfold them in the magic circle of my own love and blunt, like a ring of shields, all menacing arrows. But I was a Faun, briefer than men.

At last she drew apart from him. 'How pale you have grown, shut up in the palace. In a single day, you wilt like a lotus.'

'Come,' I said. 'We must find Romulus. He is much concerned.' We climbed the stairs.

The palace thundered with men. Their shadows bristling on tapestried walls, they stalked through the rooms with torches and gasped at treasures which, to the eyes of a shepherd (and mine as well), rivalled the riches of Carthage. A fan made of peacock feathers. Pearls as big as acorns. A mirror whose handle was the neck of a graceful swan! Guards and servants were nowhere in evidence. They must have fled with our arrival, and the palace lay temptingly accessible. The shepherds seemed to forget that they had come to liberate and not to loot.

We found Romulus in Amulius' audience room, and I must say for him that he was not himself looting, but, torch in hand, trying to organize a search for Remus. He was having trouble; his men were more concerned with found treasures than with lost brothers. When he saw us, he whooped like a Gaul on the warpath. Throwing his torch to me, he lifted his twin from the floor and hugged him with brotherly ardour. Often he seemed the crudest of warriors, a brash young wolf who, in spite of his tender years, had somehow missed youthfulness. But with Remus he was youthful as well as young, and only with Remus could I like him.

'We have taken the city,' he cried, while I steadied his torch and shielded my eyes from its sputtering resin. 'Brother, Alba Longa is ours!'

'And Numitor's,' Remus reminded us. 'Has anyone seen the king?'

In a room at the back of the palace, we found him on a couch, his white beard overflowing a crimson coverlet. He had slept through the fall of the city, and he thought himself still asleep when Remus explained what had happened and said, 'This is your grandson, Romulus.'

At last the sleep had cleared from his eyes. He held out his arms to Romulus, though clearly he was ill at ease with this great muscular grandson, smelling of wolves and blood, who came to him from the forest.

Romulus and Remus supported the king between them and, with Mellonia and me, headed for the gate. Along the way, in corridors and sleeping chambers, Romulus gathered his men, and a sizeable procession emerged from the palace. Beyond the Etruscan lions, twenty or more shepherds lounged or sat in the street, placed there by Romulus and awaiting his signal to enter the palace. They stared at Numitor with mild curiosity.

On the roofs of the houses, the townspeople waited too. But Mellonia's wolves still prowled the streets, and the timorous Alba Longans, though visibly moved at the presence of Numitor, were not yet ready to risk descent.

Romulus stepped forward with Numitor and raised the aged king's arm into the air. 'People of Alba Longa, your king is restored to you!'

With a slight motion, Numitor released himself from Romulus' support and stood alone. He straightened his bowed shoulders and lifted his weathered face. Forgetting their timidity, the people cheered as if they themselves had restored him to his throne. The shepherds were silent; it was not Numitor they wanted but Romulus. Had they fought to restore an old man to a throne he had lost before they were born? I watched Romulus' face and saw his impatience for Numitor to address the people and abdicate in favour of his grandsons. The Wolf had done the honourable thing; he had proclaimed his grandfather king. The next move was Numitor's.

Meanwhile, Mellonia had left us. I saw her in the street with Luperca, gathering her wolves and bees as a shepherd gathers sheep. Remus saw her too, but she shook her head: he was not to follow.

'She is tired,' I whispered. 'She wants her tree.'

'People of Alba Longa,' Numitor was saying in a clear, resonant voice. 'Amulius is dead. My grandsons have come back to me. A staff in my old age, they will help me to live out my years – to rule wisely if only for a little while. As king of Alba Longa, I hereby declare an amnesty to all who supported Amulius. I will end my reign with peace, even as I began it. The years between are forgotten.' He paused, I should say posed; and lifted his arms with the studied flourish of a mime. A king, it seemed, even in exile, never forgot the gestures of royalty.

The applause was vehement.

'Long live Numitor!'

'King of Alba Longa!'

The people clambered from the rooftops and thrust their way through Romulus' men to the feet of the restored king. Remus tightened his hand on my shoulder. Romulus paled. A mutter, lost in the general cheering, ran among the shepherds. We had rescued Remus; for me, that was enough. But the shepherds wanted more, and rightly, while Romulus and Remus had dreamed of a throne since childhood.

At last the old man's strength was failing. 'Help me to bed, will you, my grandsons? Tell your men the largess of the palace is theirs. The wines, the fruits, the venisons. Tomorrow I will rule – with your help. Now I will sleep.'

When Numitor slept and Romulus' men roamed the palace, a sausage in one hand, a cluster of grapes in the other, Romulus, Remus, and I talked in the garden. The jonquils, beaten gold goblets by day, had paled with the moon into silver and seemed to be spilling moonlight into the pool.

For once, Celer was absent from our council. Romulus assured us that he had not been wounded, but no one had seen him since Numitor addressed his people.

'Chasing some wench,' I muttered.

Our conversation turned to Numitor.

'Did you see his excitement?' Remus asked. 'He will reign for years!'

'Then we will build our own city,' Romulus announced. 'Even if we reign with Numitor, we can't have our way in Alba Longa. What changes can we make while an old man holds the throne? His people will not accept changes as long as he lives. They have had a tyrant; now they want a venerable figurehead. Let them have what they want. We will build *our* city on the Palatine. Already we have a circle of huts. Next, add a wall, then a temple to Mars, then a place of government –'

'And a shrine to our mother,' said Remus, kindling to the plan. 'A temple to Rumina and a park for the birds and animals. I think, though, Romulus, that the Palatine is not the best hill. True, there are huts already. But some of the owners are thieves and cut-throats, as you well know. Let them keep their huts, but in our new city there will not be room for such men. Why not build on the Aventine? It is almost as high, and closer to the forest, to Mellonia and her friends, who won us our victory.'

'Ask Father Mars who won our victory,' Romulus snapped. 'Mellonia helped, it is true. But my shepherds, Remus, took the city. The men you call thieves and cut-throats.'

'Men like Celer make good warriors,' Remus granted. 'But not good citizens. I mean no disrespect to the man. But Romulus, can you see him worshipping in a temple or sitting in a senate house? Give him a woman and herds, but leave him on the Palatine. Build our city on the Aventine!'

'Ask for a sign from heaven,' I interrupted. The gods, I thought, should favour Remus, who worshipped all of them and not the war god only. 'Consult a sheep's liver, as the Etruscan augurs do, or watch for birds of good omen.'

'Very well,' said Romulus reluctantly. 'We shall ask for a sign. Early one morning – the best time for omens – we shall climb our respective hills and watch the sky for vultures, the luckiest of birds. Whoever sees the most shall choose his hill for our city. Now, my brother, let us sleep before we quarrel.'

The palace abounded in couches; I chose one with feet like an eagle's and fell asleep, dreaming of vultures.

V

With less reluctance than the brothers anticipated, Numitor received their declaration that they wished to build a city on the Tiber. Doubtless realizing that such a city would stand as a safeguard between Alba Longa and the Etruscans – now friendly, but expanding – Numitor had promised to send workmen and materials, and he had already purchased the herds of Tullius and given them to the twins who had long been their shepherds.

But first a site must be chosen. At sunrise three days after the capture of Alba Longa, Remus and I stood atop the Aventine, watching for vultures. The day had been chosen because it was sacred to the Pales, deities of shepherds who had given their name to the Palatine. Before sunrise, Remus had fumigated his herds with sulphur to drive out evil spirits and scattered the stalls with arbute boughs, beloved by the goats, and wreaths of myrtle and laurel. Later the shepherds on the Palatine would leap through bonfires and, facing the east, pray to the Pales. A lucky day, one would think, for omens. But for whom?

'I wonder why the gods favour vultures,' I said, wrinkling my nose as I pictured the birds at a feast. 'Such an ugly creature.'

Remus laughed. 'Ugly, yes. But helpful. They rid the forest of carcasses. And they never kill.'

'Which way will they come?'

'They may not come at all. They are very rare in this country. Mellonia says to watch the river, where the animals go to drink and die.'

He had visited her daily since the fall of Alba Longa. Her name had grown pleasant even to my long ears. Instead of his usual loin cloth, he was wearing a tunic, almost sleeveless and falling just below the thighs, which the Dryad had woven from rushes and leaves. Soon it would wilt, but Mellonia had promised him a leaf-coloured garment of wool to take its place. 'Now you are part of my tree,' she had said. 'Green leaves, green tunic. You carry the forest with you.'

'But how will Romulus know if we *really* see the number we say?'

'He will take our word,' said Remus, surprised.

'And you will take his?'

'Of course.'

'It means a lot to him to build on the Palatine.'

'I know. But he would never lie to us.'

'Remus. Have you ever thought of building your own city – without Romulus. It won't be easy to rule with him. If you win your hill, it will be even harder. And men like Celer, how will you keep them out? Or make them behave if they enter?'

'I will build with Romulus or not at all. He is my brother. Do you realize, Sylvan, I shared the same womb with him? We have never been apart.'

'You love him deeply, don't you?'

'He is one of three. You, Romulus, Mellonia. I love Mellonia as someone beyond me, a goddess or a queen. Green leaves in the uppermost branches of a tree. I love her with awe and a little sadness. I love you, Sylvan, as someone close and warm. A fire on a cold night. Barley loaves baking on the hearth. You never judge me. With you I am most myself. And Romulus? The stone pillars of a temple. The bronze of a shield. Hard things, yes. But strong and needed.'

'You are very different from Romulus. He is not always a shield. He is' – I chose my words carefully, not wishing to offend him – 'rash in some ways.'

'I know,' he said sadly. 'And I try to temper his rashness. In return, he gives me courage.'

'Courage, Remus? You have strength enough of your own. I never saw you hesitate when you knew what was right.'

'You can't see my heart. It leaps like a grasshopper sometimes! Romulus, though, is fearless.'

Then you are the braver, I thought. You conquer fear, while Romulus' courage is thoughtless, instinctive. But I said nothing; he would only make light of himself.

And then we saw them: High above the orange turbulence of the Tiber, six vultures glided to the north. Clumsy birds, ugly – I had not changed my mind – but oh, how welcome.

'Remus, you have won!' I cried. 'Even if Romulus sees them, we saw them first. They are flying *toward* and not away from him.'

We raced down the hill and scrambled up the Palatine, a few hundred yards to the north.

'Slow down, Woodpecker,' I shouted. 'Your tunic has given you wings.'

He laughed and tore me a leaf from his waist. 'Catch my feathers and fly!'

In a flurry of leaves and dust, we burst through the circle of huts and found Romulus, waiting with a small band of men, on the highest part of the hill.

'Six of them,' Remus cried. 'Romulus, we saw six at once!'

Romulus looked surprised, but he spoke blandly. 'So did we. Just before you came.' His face at last showed the start of a beard, a small black V below his chin. The ambitious boy, impatient but waiting, had hardened into a man who, no less ambitious, had ceased to wait.

'It must have been the same six. They were flying this way.'

'No matter. They still count.'

'Then we are tied.'

'No,' put in Celer. 'We have seen *twelve*.' He twisted his mouth to the caricature of a smile, but his flat eyes were cold.

'Twelve? There have never been so many near these hills!'

Romulus started to speak, but Celer continued. 'Today there were. The six that just passed, and before them, six more. Even larger – as big as eagles. They circled twice to be sure we saw them. Sent by the gods, eh, Romulus?'

'Is it true?' Remus asked his brother.

Romulus glowered. 'Of course it is true. Celer has told you. And the city is mine to build where I choose.'

Remus paled and spoke with an effort. 'Build it then.' It must have been clear to him that Celer had lied and that Romulus, though hesitant at first, had repeated the lie. 'Sylvan,' Remus said to me, 'I am going to the cave.'

We started down the hill. Behind us Romulus was giving orders. 'Find me a bull and a heifer. We will plough the boundaries of our new city. But first we will celebrate the feast of the Pales. Celer, break out the wine. And the rest of you, build us some bonfires.'

The men whooped approval and scuffled about their work. After the feast, Romulus would yoke the animals to a bronze-tipped plough and drive them around the base of the hill where he meant to build his walls, leaving a space for the gate. The area enclosed by the plough would be fortunate ground. Whoever crossed the furrow instead of entering by the designated gate would shatter the luck of the builders and allow the invasion of hostile spirits.

Remus was silent until we reached the cave. He threw himself on his pallet and Luperca, as if she sensed his trouble, crept beside him.

'You can build your own city,' I suggested.

'No, I will help Romulus. But first I must understand him.'

'I know how you feel. Your hill was the best.'

He looked up at me. 'The hill is not important. Romulus lied. That is important. He is building his city on a lie and the men know.'

'No one objected. They like the Palatine.'

'That is the harm. They knew and said nothing.'

I left him alone all morning and waited under the fig tree. Once I looked in the cave. His eyes were open, but he did not appear to see me, nor to hear the merriment on top of the hill.

'Rumina,' I said, more in conversation than in prayer. 'You are the goddess of the suckling herds. But your tree stands right at our door. Neglect the lambs for a while and help my friend.'

In the afternoon, I climbed the fig tree and captured some honey in a round clay bowl. The bees, sensing perhaps for whom it was meant (or instructed by Rumina herself), made no objection. In the cave I knelt beside Remus.

'Eat it,' I said crossly. 'You have brooded enough.'

He smiled, sat up, and took the bowl from my hands. He tilted it to his lips as if it were milk, for he relished the honey from his own bees, and drained the bowl.

'Now,' he said, 'I will help Romulus with his walls. But first I want to see Mellonia.'

'I will wait for you here.'

'No, come with me.'

'You must have things to say in private. Who wants a Faun's big ears at such a time?'

'She has grown to love you. Besides –' His smile faded. 'I want you with me. It is something I feel – a loneliness, a fear – I am not sure what. I want you with me.'

In the woods beyond the Aventine, we encountered Celer and three of his friends, leaning on each other for support and thrashing through the undergrowth with such a racket that turquoise lizards flew in all directions. When they saw us they stopped, and Celer looked momentarily sobered. He forced a grin.

'Big Ears and Woodpecker,' he said. 'You missed our feast. The gods will be hurt.'

'They are hurt already,' said Remus, without slowing. 'But not by Sylvan and me.' The revellers made for the Palatine with surprising directness.

Suddenly I remembered that Celer had asked me the location of Mellonia's tree. I had not told him, but the night of the wolves he had vanished from Alba Longa. Had he followed her home, I wondered, and then today, emboldened with wine and friends, returned to invade her tree?

'Remus,' I said. 'Do you think he has found her tree?'

We began to run.

The branches of Mellonia's oak tree sprawled like a city which has grown without planning, its temples and archways mingled in artless beauty. From a distance, there was nothing to hint an invasion.

We approached the trunk.

'That lowermost branch,' said Remus tensely. 'I think it is starting to wilt.'

'Too little sun,' I said, but without conviction.

He began to call. 'Mellonia!' 'Mellonia!'

I searched the ground for traces of a fire or other means of assault, but the trunk was untouched. Around the altar, however, there were definite signs of Celer and his friends – jonquils in crushed profusion, rocks overturned, and, yes, they had entered the tunnel; it reeked of their wine.

Mellonia's room lay hushed and broken. We found her beside the couch, a white small body blackened with bruises and cradled, incongruously, in a bed of narcissus petals. Remus lifted her on to the couch and smoothed her tangled green hair, in which petals had caught as if to take root in its venture. She opened her eyes.

'Little bird,' she said. 'Who will look after you?' That was all.

He covered her body with petals and kissed her on the mouth which could no longer feel bruises. 'I had never meant to outlive you,' he said.

I turned my head but I heard his tears. Or was it the column of bees that swayed through the open window, the forest grieving for its queen, and for the king who had loved her? The shepherds say that bees speak only what is in our hearts – our grief, our joy, not theirs. That their murmur is always the same, and it is we who darken or lighten it to our mood. Perhaps, then, I heard my own tears.

We left her in the tree with the bees. 'She would not want to be moved,' Remus said. 'The oak is dying. They will go to earth together.'

We stared at the tree and already, it seemed, the wilt was stealing upward to the green and sunny towers.

'Did you hear what she said?' he asked.

I pressed his hand. 'Yes. Yes, little bird.'

* * *

When we reached the Palatine, Romulus had driven his team around the foot of the hill. For one short space, the gate, he had left the earth unbroken. Stripped completely in the hot April sun, he leaned on the plough, his massive thighs diamonded with sweat. Drops rolled down his beard. He looked very tired – and very royal.

With mattocks and shovels, the shepherds were setting to work inside the circle. Romulus had captured the *numen* or magic of the gods. Now they must build strong walls and enclose the magic securely. They sang as they dug, Celer and his friends the loudest:

> Romulus, son of the spear god Mars,
> Nursed by the long grey wolf . . .

Celer looked up from his work and saw us. He dropped his shovel.

Pausing outside the circle, Remus cried: 'Romulus, your walls are useless, the luck is gone. A murderer stands inside!' He jumped the furrow. The shepherds stared at him in horror. I myself, midway to the gate, gasped at his daring. He sprang at Celer. Celer recovered his shovel but Remus parried, wrestled it from his hands, and felled him with a blow to his shoulder.

Romulus snatched a shovel from the shepherd nearest him. 'Idiot!' he shouted to Remus. 'It is you who have broken our luck. Fight me, not Celer.'

'Keep away from me,' Remus warned. But he made no move to defend himself from Romulus; he was waiting for Celer, dazed but conscious, to regain his feet.

Romulus struck him with the back of his shovel. I saw Remus' eyes. Surprise, that was all. Not fear, not anger. Then he fell. In the forest, once, I heard a she-wolf cry when a shepherd killed her cubs. All pain, all yearning. A cry from the vital organs of her body, as if their red swift pulsing could wrench her cubs from death. So Romulus cried and knelt beside his brother. In Remus' hair, the stains were of earth, not blood; the umber soil mingling with the sunflowers. But the stalk was broken.

I took Remus' shovel. 'Stand up,' I said to Romulus. 'I am going to kill you.'

He looked up at me through tears. 'Sylvan, I wish you would.'

I think it was Remus who held my hand. Born of one womb, he had said. Romulus, his brother, his pillar and shield of bronze. Instead of killing him, I knelt at his side.

Troubled and respectful, the shepherds surrounded us, and Faustulus laid his hand on Romulus' neck.

'My son, you meant him no harm. Let me prepare his body for burial.'

Romulus shook his head. 'I must make my peace with him first.'

'And you, Sylvan?'

'I will stay with Remus.'

The men climbed the hill. The sunlight thinned and shadows came to watch with us. Somewhere a cow lowed with quiet urgency. It is late, I thought. She is waiting for Remus to milk her.

'He must have a place for the night,' I said. 'He never liked the dark.'

Romulus stirred. I think he had forgotten me. 'The cave?'

'No. He would be alone there. We will take him to Mellonia's tree. Celer killed her, you know – he and his friends.'

He looked at me with stunned comprehension. 'Then that was why Remus attacked him. They will die for this, Sylvan.'

I kindled a torch in the cave with pieces of flint and returned to Romulus. Luperca followed me. Romulus stroked her head.

'Old mother,' he said, 'you loved him too.' He lifted his brother and held him lightly, with Remus' hair against his cheek. 'His hair smells of clover.'

'I know.'

We walked slowly – Luperca was very weak – and came at last to the tree. Trembling but quiet, she waited outside the cave.

We placed him on the couch beside Mellonia. I pressed my cheek to the shoulder where, as a child, I had clung to be warmed and loved. I crossed his arms as if I were folding wings.

'Little bird,' I said. 'You reproached Mellonia because you had to outlive her. But I am the one you punished. All of your life was loving – except for this. Where is your city, my friend?'

'In me,' Romulus answered.

I turned on him angrily. 'In you?' Then I was sorry. Tears ran out of his eyes. He made no effort to hide them. I thought that he was going to fall and held out my hand. He grasped it and steadied himself.

'You think I want walls and armies,' he said, 'and nothing more? At first I did. This morning I did, when I lied about the birds. But then I had Remus; it seemed I would always have him. Whatever I did, he would love me. He was all I needed of gentleness. Now he is gone – unless I capture him in my city. A great city, Sylvan. Men will call her Rome after me, and her legions will conquer the world – Carthage and Sardis, Karnak, Sidon, and Babylon. But her highways will carry laws as well as armies, learning as well as conquest. Sylvan, don't you see? Remus will live in us and the city we build. Come back with me, Little Faun!'

Where is the bird of fire? In the tall green flame of the cypress, I see his shadow, flickering with the swallows. In the city that crowds the Palatine, where Fauns walk with men and wolves are fed in the temples, I hear the rush of his wings. But that is his shadow and sound. The bird himself is gone. Always his wings beat just beyond my hands, and the wind possesses his cry. Where is the bird of fire? Look up, he burns in the sky, with Saturn and the Golden Age. I will go to find him.

Author's Acknowledgments

I wish to express a particular debt to Alan Lake Chidsey's *Romulus: Builder of Rome* and Carlo Maria Franzero's *The Life and Times of Tarquin the Etruscan*. T.B.S.

THE STORY OF GYGES

Herodotus

*The ancient Greeks were fascinated with their legends and delighted
in stories of their heroes and the early days of their civilization. Most
Greeks accepted these stories as true and few questioned them, until
the time of Herodotus in the fifth century* BC. *He travelled widely
throughout the Greek world, keeping details of the stories that
he heard and piecing these together in his* History. *He remained
open-minded and, though he reported all that he heard, he sometimes
questioned the stories and did not necessarily regard them as fact. As
a consequence, Herodotus is known as the 'Father of History' – he
was the first to systematically collect together facts and fiction and
endeavour to distinguish between the two.*

*The following story which he preserved, and which has had a
new lease of life because of the reference to it in the film* The
English Patient, *tells about the foundation of the new dynasty of
kings in Lydia, a major kingdom in what is now western Turkey.
The most famous king of Lydia was Crœsus, who was so rich that
his name has become synonymous with wealth. Herodotus's story
takes place in the year 685* BC, *over a century before the life of
Crœsus.*

The sovereignty of Lydia, which had belonged to the Heraclides,
passed into the family of Crœsus, who were called the Mermnadæ,
in the manner which I will now relate. There was a certain king
of Sardis, Candaules by name, whom the Greeks called Myrsilus.
He was a descendant of Alcæus, son of Hercules. The first king

of this dynasty was Agron, son of Ninus, grandson of Belus, and great-grandson of Alcæus; Candaules, son of Myrsus, was the last. The kings who reigned before Agron sprang from Lydus, son of Atys, from whom the people of the land, called previously Meonians, received the name of Lydians. The Heraclides, descended from Hercules and the slave-girl of Jardanus, having been entrusted by these princes with the management of affairs, obtained the kingdom by an oracle. Their rule endured for two and twenty generations of men, a space of five hundred and five years; during the whole of which period, from Agron to Candaules, the crown descended in the direct line from father to son.

Now it happened that this Candaules was in love with his own wife; and not only so, but thought her the fairest woman in the whole world. This fancy had strange consequences. There was in his body-guard a man whom he specially favoured, Gyges, the son of Dascylus. All affairs of greatest moment were entrusted by Candaules to this person, and to him he was wont to extol the surpassing beauty of his wife. So matters went on for a while. At length, one day, Candaules, who was fated to end ill, thus addressed his follower, 'I see thou dost not credit what I tell thee of my lady's loveliness; but come now, since men's ears are less credulous than their eyes, contrive some means whereby thou mayst behold her naked.' At this the other loudly exclaimed, saying, 'What most unwise speech is this, master, which thou hast uttered? Wouldst thou have me behold my mistress when she is naked? Bethink thee that a woman, with her clothes, puts off her bashfulness. Our fathers, in time past, distinguished right and wrong plainly enough, and it is our wisdom to submit to be taught by them. There is an old saying, "Let each look on his own." I hold thy wife for the fairest of all womankind. Only, I beseech thee, ask me not to do wickedly.'

Gyges thus endeavoured to decline the king's proposal, trembling lest some dreadful evil should befall him through it. But the king replied to him, 'Courage, friend; suspect me not of the design to prove thee by this discourse; nor dread thy mistress, lest mischief befall thee at her hands. Be sure I will so manage that she shall not even know that thou hast looked upon her. I will place thee behind the open door of the chamber in which we sleep. When I enter to go to rest she will follow me. There stands a chair close to the entrance, on which she will lay her clothes one by one as she takes them off. Thou wilt be able thus at thy leisure to peruse her person. Then, when she is moving from the chair toward the bed, and her back is turned on thee, be it thy care that she see thee not as thou passest through the doorway.'

Gyges, unable to escape, could but declare his readiness. Then Candaules, when bedtime came, led Gyges into his sleeping-chamber, and a moment after the queen followed. She entered, and laid her garments on the chair, and Gyges gazed on her. After a while she moved toward the bed, and her back being then turned, he glided stealthily from the apartment. As he was passing out, however, she saw him, and instantly divining what had happened, she neither screamed as her shame impelled her, nor even appeared to have noticed aught, purposing to take vengeance upon the husband who had so affronted her. For among the Lydians, and indeed among the barbarians generally, it is reckoned a deep disgrace, even to a man, to be seen naked.

No sound or sign of intelligence escaped her at the time. But in the morning, as soon as day broke, she hastened to choose from among her retinue, such as she knew to be most faithful to her, and preparing them for what was to ensue, summoned Gyges into her presence. Now it had often happened before that the queen had desired to confer with him, and he was accustomed to come to her at her call. He therefore obeyed the summons, not suspecting that she knew aught of what had occurred. Then she addressed these words to him, 'Take thy choice, Gyges, of two courses which are open to thee. Slay Candaules, and thereby become my lord, and obtain the Lydian throne, or die this moment in this room. So wilt thou not again, obeying all behests of thy master, behold what is not lawful for thee. It must needs be, that either he perish by whose counsel this thing was done, or thou, who sawest me naked, and so didst break our usages.' At these words Gyges stood awhile in mute astonishment; recovering after a time, he earnestly besought the queen that she would not compel him to so hard a choice. But finding he implored in vain, and that necessity was indeed laid on him to kill or to be killed, he made choice of life for himself, and replied by this inquiry, 'If it must be so, and thou compellest me against my will to put my lord to death, come, let me hear how thou wilt have me set on him.' 'Let him be attacked,' she answered, 'on that spot where I was by him shown naked to you, and let the assault be made when he is asleep.'

All was then prepared for the attack, and when night fell, Gyges, seeing that he had no retreat or escape, but must absolutely either slay Candaules, or himself be slain, followed his mistress into the sleeping-room. She placed a dagger in his hand, and hid him carefully behind the self-same door. Then Gyges, when the king was fallen asleep, entered privily into the chamber and struck him dead. Thus did the wife and kingdom of Candaules pass into the possession of

Gyges, of whom Archilochus the Parian, who lived about the same time, made mention in a poem written in Iambic trimeter verse.

Gyges was afterwards confirmed in the possession of the throne by an answer of the Delphic oracle. Enraged at the murder of their king, the people flew to arms, but after a while the partisans of Gyges came to terms with them, and it was agreed that if the Delphic oracle declared him king of the Lydians, he should reign; if otherwise, he should yield the throne to the Heraclides. As the oracle was given in his favour he became king. The Pythoness, however, added that, in the fifth generation from Gyges, vengeance should come for the Heraclides; a prophecy of which neither the Lydians nor their princes took any account till it was fulfilled. Such was the way in which the Mermnadæ deposed the Heraclides, and themselves obtained the sovereignty.

THE SLAVE OF MARATHON

Arthur D. Howden Smith

With this story we move into recognizable history and to one of
the most famous and decisive battles in the world, the battle of
Marathon. The battle was fought in the year 490 BC. At that
time Darius, the king of Persia, was expanding his empire, and
had already conquered Thrace and Macedonia. The intervention
of the Athenians caused Darius to turn the might of his army
against the Greek mainland. At Marathon, 10,000 Greeks, under
the command of Miltiades, defeated over 100,000 Persians. One
of the most famous episodes linked to the battle is the story of
Pheidippides. He was the courier who was first sent from Athens
to Sparta to request help against the Persians. He ran the distance
of 150 miles in two days, returned to Marathon (without help) over
the next two days and then, after the battle, ran from Marathon to
Athens to bring news of the victory. He collapsed and died on arrival.
It is the twenty-six odd miles from Marathon to Athens that is the
basis of the modern marathon event. Few athletes these days will
have already run 300 miles just before competing in the event.

Arthur D. Howden-Smith (1887–1945) was an American journalist and biographer and, in his day, one of the most popular
contributors to the American magazine Adventure. Today he is
remembered only by a small cult following for his book Grey
Maiden (1929), which traced the story of a sword (the Grey
Maiden of the title) down through the centuries. It is the episode
from that novel set at Marathon which follows.

Gray Maide men hail Mee
Deathe doth Notte fail Mee.

I

White tentacles of sea-mist fluttered out from the dense bank that
overlay the plain, and spiraled upward through the darkness along
the mountain slopes. A charred glow in the east, beyond the
invisible rim of the Aegean, was the first indication of the dawn.
Closer at hand, in copse and grove and thicket, fires were crimson
blobs against the green background of the foliage, and the men
who crowded each circle of warmth were specters, dwarfed and
distorted by the tossing shadows and the twining ribbons of mist.
It was very cold, a damp cold that pierced to the bone.

Glaucus squatted as close to his fire as he could come in the press
of slaves – and since he was a big fellow, that meant close enough
for comfort – and gnawed diligently at the handful of raw onions
and hunch of black bread which were the slaves' ration. The slow
grinding of their jaws sounded through the crackle of the flames
and the sullen murmur of comment.

'By Hercules, this onion is rotten –'

'Be content, Zike, the bread is also sour –'

'Yes, yes, any food is good enough for slaves to fight on –'

'Do you see the hoplites eating the dust from Antigonus' bins!'

Glaucus scowled at the last speaker.

'Go to the War-Ruler and demand us a sheep,' he sneered.

'No, no, it is you Callimachus consults,' retorted the other.

Gruff laughter applauded thrust and counterthrust. It was interrupted by a hail from the lower hillside.

'Ho, Glaucus! The slave of Aeschylus! Say to Glaucus that Giton
summons him.'

Glaucus stumbled to his feet, cramming the last crumb of bread
and sliver of onion into his mouth and trampling his fellows right
and left. He was a man of gigantic build, with a sour, resentful
expression, and the slaves made way for him, unprotesting.

'May the Furies tear his liver,' he growled. 'It seems I am to
have two masters, Giton as well as Aeschylus. A poet is no easy
task-setter, but a freeman who can not afford slaves of his own is
worse.'

The hail came again.

'Glaucus! Ho, Glaucus!'

'When the slave eats the master calls,' quoted a wit.

Glaucus replied with a curse, and crashed down the slope, forcing his way between the cedars and pines that rose above the lower shrubbery. He halted presently at sight of the glimmer of steel; and rounding a tree-trunk, came upon his master in converse with several higher officers.

'Giton is below,' said Aeschylus. 'Go to him, and say that I follow.'

Glaucus continued at a more moderate gait.

'This looks like battle,' he ruminated. 'And what have I done that I should be sent first to be slain?'

Steel glimmered ahead of him a second time – a broad belt of cuirasses – and he halted on the flank of a detachment of armored hoplites, leaning patiently on their spears.

'Ho, Giton!' he called softly.

'Is it you, Glaucus? Where is Aeschylus?'

'He follows,' answered the slave sulkily, as the thin figure of the freeman approached through the mist. 'What madness is he up to now?'

'No madness,' returned Giton, slinging his shield to his back. 'We are to prepare for the battle. As you know, the Plataens joined us yesterday –'

'A thousand men!' protested Glaucus.

'A thousand Hellenes,' agreed Giton. 'And if the sacrifices are propitious this morning –'

'We shall all go to our deaths,' exclaimed Glaucus. 'Eleven thousand hoplites, and it may be thirteen thousand of us slingers and javelin-men – and against us more Persians than there are folk in Athens!'

'If all felt as you do, it might be so,' rejoined the freeman. 'But the Persians can never stand against the hoplites.'

'The hoplites!' echoed Glaucus. 'It is all very well for them, with armor to protect them, but what of men like me, who must go naked?'

'I have no armor,' said Giton.

'You have a shield and a helmet – and a sword. That is something. I have my sling and a knife. The first Persian who –'

The voice of Aeschylus drawled quietly almost at the slave's elbow.

'Now, who would have thought you a coward, Glaucus, with that great body of yours?'

'I am not a coward,' snapped the slave. 'But I say it is nothing for men to go into battle armed as you are, while we slaves –'

'Can outrun us in retreat,' derided his master. 'But I did not come to listen to your woes. We are going down into the plain, a few of us, to determine if the Persians have cavalry in their camp and to make sure that the marshes on our right can not be crossed. Giton, you will see that Glaucus does not – ah – lose us in the mist.'

'Lose you!' rumbled Glaucus as he fell in with the freeman's little detachment of light-armed slaves. 'It would serve you right if I was killed, and you had to buy a Libyan to replace me. I have a good mind to complain of you to the Archons. You never had a slave who could work as hard as I, and instead of appreciating me, you must throw my life away!'

He turned to Giton.

'You are as crazy as any citizen of them all,' he went on. 'You were doing well at your carpentering until you had to march here. I don't see how you expect to profit from it.'

'I would have preferred to stay at my carpentering, but when the Persians came what was a man to do?' countered Giton.

'Let the citizens fight,' retorted Glaucus. 'It is they who get the advantage out of wars.'

'Are you sure? If the Persians conquered Athens my carpentering must suffer.'

Glaucus snorted contemptuously.

'Yes, for you are a freeman. I suppose they might make a slave of you. But it would be no disadvantage to us, who already are slaves, to change masters.'

'Are you sure?' the freeman challenged again. 'Did you ever know one who had been a Persian slave?'

Glaucus became thoughtful.

'Yes, that is so,' he acknowledged. 'That fellow, Zike, was bought from a Tyrian, and he said he would rather be a slave in Athens than a freeman in Tyre. But he is always trying to say smart things!'

'A Persian slave who grumbled as you do would be slain,' said Giton. 'And as for beatings, you would live on them.'

'Humph,' grunted Glaucus. 'Perhaps, but I still don't see what advantage you or I obtain by being killed to keep the Persians out of Athens.'

Giton was silent for a while. The eastern sky was one vast sea of fire from the mountain tops, but the column down in the plain of Marathon moved in a shadow-world of mist. The clanking of the hoplites' armor, the shuffling of feet, a few low-voiced orders were as distinct as thunder-claps in the quiet dimness.

'What is one man's life?' asked the freeman suddenly. 'What are many men's lives – compared with the State?'

The slave regarded him, puzzled.

'Why, a man's life is – is – his life. It's the only one he can have.'

'But how many men must die to make a city great?' persisted Giton. 'Think, Glaucus! There is Aeschylus, ahead of us. He writes poems that sweep all the people in the theater out of themselves. He is a greater man than I. But he ventures his life without thinking – that the city may be preserved.'

'Yes, and he has a fine cuirass to preserve himself, and a helm and greaves,' grumbled Glaucus, returning to his original complaint.

'He is a citizen; many men have lived and died to make him.'

'True, and there were those who came before me did not sleep in the slaves' quarters, but a slave I am.'

'That is the fate the gods send us,' answered the freeman. 'What the gods offer man must accept. Yet it must be pleasing to them to see men live and die, thinking of others than themselves.'

'If you do not think of yourself, who will?' demanded Glaucus.

'True,' admitted Giton. 'And if the City be not greater than any man, it is less than any man.'

'What care I if it be less than man or greater?' parried the slave. 'It means nothing to me.'

'But does it?' argued Giton. 'Without it you might not be sure of food and clothing and a kind master and laws to make a slave's life easy.'

'You may call my life easy,' growled Glaucus, 'but you are not a slave. What you say is all very well. It reminds me of what I have heard the philosophers disputing on the porch of the Acropolis. But as for the City, it sends me out here in a wool tunic, with a bag of stones, a sling and a knife, and if the Persians –'

A long-drawn, wailing cry came from the mist ahead of them, and the ranks of the hoplites clanked to a halt. Presently an order was whispered down the column:

'Giton's slaves are wanted up forward. Aeschylus bids them hasten.'

The freeman and his score or two of slingers and javelin-men trotted along the brazen line to where Aeschylus crouched behind a myrtle-bush, staring into the mist.

'Ho, is it you, Giton?' he murmured. 'Have you that big slave of mine? Then heed me. The Persians have an outlying force in front of their camp. That cry came from one of their sentries. It is my wish that your fellows should steal forward on the right, and take one of those sentries as soon as you have tested the morass under the foothills. Let Glaucus conduct your prisoner, but be sure to await

taking him until you have tested the morass. Lose no time, for if
the mist clears we dare not tarry in the plain, unsupported.'

Giton's spare, bony figure straightened.

'It shall be done,' he promised.

Aeschylus rose, and gripped his hand.

'I would go with you, if I might; but you must be free to run,
unhampered by armored men. It is for the City, Giton!'

The freeman's answer rang like a muted trumpet-blast.

'For the City!'

Glaucus smothered an exclamation of contempt. Citizen and
freeman were equally foolish. Why, they spoke of the City as if
stone walls were sacred as the very gods!

II

The wailing cries of the Persian sentries sounded faintly behind them
as the little band of slaves crept after Giton through the mist that was
beginning to turn ruddy overhead, where the sun's rays smote level
across the distant sea-floor. The course they followed trended to the
right, and soon brought them to the edge of the morass which ran
inland from the shore to the base of the mountains, a mucky slough,
impassable for men even as unencumbered as themselves. Satisfied of
this, Giton ordered the detachment to swing back into the middle of
the plain to undertake the accomplishment of its second task.

'Keep together, and be ready to run up if I call,' he said. 'I am
going ahead with Glaucus to capture a Persian, and perhaps have a
look at their camp. Remember, the rest of you, be quiet, and leave
the attack to me.'

The slaves mumbled assent, and lurched along in their leader's
tracks much like a herd of sheep. Glaucus was the only one to
comment on the situation. The big slave had recovered from his
early morning disgust, and was inclined now to savor the excitement
of the venture; but he could not resist a thrust at Giton on the score
of their previous argument.

'I see that you give the rest a chance to save their throats,' he
grumbled, 'yet I am to go into the Persian camp with you. A cheerful
enterprise!'

'You will do nothing that I do not do,' returned Giton.

'Ah! Much good that will do me when I am impaled. You may
talk all you please, but I –'

'The time is past for talking,' said the freeman curtly. 'You will
be silent. Do you want to warn the Persians we are coming?'

Glaucus accepted this rebuke with a frown.

'Oh, very well,' he answered, 'we'll see who is first when the trouble comes.'

And he made a considerable fuss over fitting a stone to the lip of his sling. But Giton continued without noticing the slave, sword drawn and ears and eyes alert.

The plain hereabouts was broken by the forked bed of a shallow brook, which tumbled down from the valley where the principal strength of the Greeks was concentrated, and Giton led his company into the meager shelter of the right fork, motioning to them to stoop low and make the most of the depression. The increasing power of the sun was burning the mist away, and occasional puffs of wind from the mountains tore lanes in the huge central bank which blanketed the country from the mountains' foot to the shore. One such lane opened up at this moment on the line Giton was following, and he and Glaucus had to fling themselves flat to escape detection, although the slaves behind them were still concealed by a tricky swirl of vapor. But the two took no thought to their companions, for they were occupied with the opportunity the wind had afforded them to spy on the enemy.

Where they crouched on the verge of the brook, they were raised slightly above the country nearer the shore, and the main Persian camp was plainly visible – a narrow huddle of booths and tents, swarming with men and backed by hundreds of galleys and transports, some beached and more at anchor. Six miles it stretched from horn to horn of the curving bay. Nearer, indeed, a scant bowshot from them, was the outlying camp, which Datis, the Persian commander, had formed to guard against a surprise attack at night. It was the sentries of this camp who had been hailing one another in the mist to give assurance that each was still alive and at his post. One of these men stood by the brook, leaning on his spear, so close that the watching Greeks could distinguish the pattern of his conical hat and long, quilted coat.

Glaucus wiggled in his excitement, and started to rise to his knees.

'I can take *him* for you, Giton! I'll knock him on the head with this stone. See!'

He lifted his sling.

'No, you would slay him,' objected the freeman. 'It is a live prisoner Aeschylus must have. The *strategoi* would question him.'

'I won't kill him,' urged Glaucus. 'That hat of his is padded like his coat. I'll strike him on it, and –'

He broke off amazed at an extraordinary spectacle which was

disclosed to them by another eddy in the mist. The outlying Persian camp was farther toward the foot of the mountain than they were; it projected past them, ahead of them and to their left, parallel to the course of the brook. The open area in the mist had widened abruptly, and revealed the progress of a strange rite or ceremony on the Persians' front. A considerable body of the long-skirted infantry were arrayed in line, and midway of them, facing the Greek position, stood a giant officer in brazen mail, upholding stiffly a lean, straight sword of gray steel. He was not brandishing the blade or gesturing with it, rather he appeared to be addressing it, and whatever he said, the soldiers at his back shouted some response.

'He prays to the sword,' murmured Glaucus.

'I never heard the Persians worshiped a sword,' answered Giton.

'But he does. Gods, but it is a good blade! Look to the sheen of it.'

'I am more interested in that sentry you said you could stun for me,' said the freeman. 'Show me your skill, and – Wait! Wait! What will you do?'

For the slave had risen to the straddled position of the slinger, and already was whirling his leathern weapon around his head.

'I am going to slay that Persian. He is a great man, Giton. Better to bring him down than a poor –'

'Hold,' remonstrated the freeman, jumping up in his dismay. 'No, no, we can never take that man. He is a *strategos*, at least. What use would he be to us, dead? At the other –'

It was too late. The stone whirred away into the air, and the huge officer dropped with a crash of mail as it rapped his helm. Giton wrung his hands.

'You fool!' he cried. 'Now, we shall be discovered. Quick! At the sentry. No, wait – he sees us – oh, go on, go on! Loose, fool, loose!'

The Persian officer was on his feet again, shaking his head like an angry bull, gray sword flashing as he peered this way and that to discover his antagonist. The sentry, too, was staring up the brook, and shouted a shrill warning at sight of the two Greeks. But Glaucus, to do him justice, was not behindhand in remedying his error. He had a second stone in his sling, and was whirling it to launch at the sentry even as he grumbled at Giton's unreasonableness.

'You are never satisfied. I was of a mind to have that sword. It has the look of a stout blade. Not that a sword means anything to you, who have one. Well, there goes your sentry. Shall I take him?'

'Who else?' snapped Giton. 'Be swift, and I will cover you.'

For the collapse of the sentry had drawn the attention of the

Persians in the outlying camp to the Greeks who lurked in the bed of the brook. Shouts and yells directed the officer of the gray sword to that quarter, and he led his men forward at a run; but fortunately a wind-puff from a different direction drove the mist swirling ahead of him, and friends and enemies were swallowed up again. A confused shouting echoed dully over the plain.

III

Glaucus found his victim without difficulty, ascertained that the man's heart was beating and slung him lightly over one broad shoulder, then trotted back up the brook until a hail from Giton summoned him to the left side of the watercourse.

'We shall be lucky to get off,' said the freeman unhappily. 'The Persians have been as far as this, but something distracted them. I think they have been fighting the rest of our party; I heard men calling to one another in Greek.'

'Oh, we shall get off,' replied Glaucus. 'If the Persians catch us you can carry this fellow I have on my shoulder, and I will teach them a lesson. Bah, you are fortunate to have me, Giton. I do not know what you would do elsewise.'

'You do not!' observed Giton. 'Suffer me to remind you that you require your wind to carry that sentry to Aeschylus. I will make good your retreat.'

The slave chuckled good-naturedly.

'That is to be seen,' he said. 'Up to this point it is I who have pushed the fighting. Ho, Giton, two Persians have I struck down!'

'It would have been better had you struck down the one I bade you to,' rasped Giton. 'In that case, we should have –'

One of the vagrant breezes that blew out of the mountain heights tore at the dissolving mists and rent them in twain. In a breath Giton and the slave were robbed of all protection; the plain lay bare around them, dotted with groups of friends and enemies. The other slaves were scattered in twos and threes, running for the protection of the small clump of hoplites Aeschylus led, who were formed up under the mountain wall. A horde of Persians were in pursuit, the foremost just across the brook from Giton and Glaucus, and in advance of all the giant officer with the gray sword, who howled exultantly as he veered to the left to cut them off.

'Can you run faster?' panted Giton.

'Easily,' boasted Glaucus. 'But instead, do you take this fellow as I suggested, and I will have another try at Gray Sword over there.'

The slave halted in his stride, fumbling for his sling with one hand while he balanced his captive with the other.

'Hurry,' he urged petulantly, 'I can't do everything.'

But Giton faced him with eyes blazing.

'Slave,' the freeman's voice was so cold that Glaucus involuntarily shivered, 'what I bid you to do that shall you do. Put up your sling, and run.'

'But I can kill him this time.'

'Run or I slay you as you stand!'

There was no uncertainty in Giton's gray eyes, and Glaucus ran; but the slave still had breath to spare for grumbling.

'Talking of killing me, eh? You couldn't get some one else to slay me, so you might as well do it yourself. This is fine treatment for an honest slave! Yes, yes, we shall see what the Archons have to say of it.'

'If you lose your prisoner, do not try to reach Aeschylus,' answered Giton grimly. 'You would die as surely at his hand as at the hand of a Persian.'

The freeman glanced back over his shoulder with a worried frown, for the Persians were gaining upon them; the officer of the gray sword was only a few spear-lengths behind, his immense black bush of beard bristling savagely, his face convulsed with fury. He shouted hoarsely as Giton looked around, and redoubled his efforts.

Giton measured the distance which was yet to be traversed to reach the protection of Aeschylus' spears, and shook his head.

'It is too much,' he said.

'Eh?' grunted the slave.

'I must stop and hold back that Persian who is so close on our heels,' explained Giton. 'You can never reach Aeschylus before he overtakes us.'

'Why does not Aeschylus come out to aid us?' snapped Glaucus.

'His men are too few. Go on, Glaucus. Run like Pheidippides.'

Glaucus looked back in his turn, and exclaimed in dismay.

'You can never stand up to that fellow! He is as big as I am – and mailed, besides.'

A faint smile showed in Giton's face.

'That is probably true, but this is one of those times when the City is greater than a man's life.'

He slackened pace, but the slave reached out a knotted arm and dragged him on.

'What? What's this?' growled Glaucus. 'You are no fool, Giton. The Persian will slay you. Hurry on with me. If he catches up we'll turn on him together.'

THE SLAVE OF MARATHON

'And lose the prisoner.' Giton twitched free of the other's grasp. 'On what that fellow has to say may depend whether the *strategoi* will decide for battle.'

The slave slackened his pace to match the freeman's.

'You'll be killed,' he babbled. 'That sword – Here, you take the prisoner, and let me –'

The steely ring gritted again in Giton's quiet tones.

'I am not strong enough to carry him. It is your part to run and live today, mine to die. We both fight for the City. The gods speed you safe, Glaucus. Run!'

Glaucus bent his head dumbly and ran. A moment later he heard the clatter of meeting blades, and Giton's voice, vibrant now with a triumph beyond victory:

'For the City! Back, Persian, back!'

The slave peered over his shoulder again. Giton was dripping blood, and his shield was split in two, but he hewed recklessly at the Persian, careless of his own body if he might only force his enemy to yield ground. Glaucus choked a sob. A sudden gift of vision oppressed him, and he saw, so clearly that it hurt him, the carpenter's tiny shop as it had looked when he visited it with errands from the household of Aeschylus. The clean smell of the cedar planks, fresh-hewn and stacked against the wall, mingled in his nostrils with the odor of the grease on the tools and the dusty perfume of the sawdust on the floor that was soft to his bare feet. Somewhere behind the shop he knew there was a wife, and he had heard a child's plaint.

A roar from the Persian sped him on. He fled through the gap the waiting hoplites opened to him, and cast his burden at the feet of Aeschylus.

'It was not right,' he stammered hoarsely. 'The Persian had a sword – they prayed to it – Giton was not big enough – I could have saved him.'

His master's shrewd, satirical face, lofty with a loftiness Glaucus had never understood, was grooved with bitter lines.

'A man has but the one death to die,' answered Aeschylus. 'Is it not well that he should be glad of an ending such as must rouse the applause of the gods? One who dies like Giton is never forgotten.'

'All for one prisoner,' protested Glaucus.

'Who knows what may come of this prisoner?' returned his master. 'Perhaps Hellas may be saved. Perhaps a slave's soul may be awakened. And I say again, Glaucus, a man who dies bravely never dies in vain.'

The slave lifted a clenched fist.

'Then the gods grant I may find that Persian, and slay him as Giton would not let me.'

Aeschylus eyed him curiously.

'When it is your task to slay him I hope the gods will show you their favor. Meanwhile pick up this captive, and complete the task that was set you. Close ranks, hoplites. Quickmarch!'

IV

Yesterday Glaucus would have glared sulkily at the haughty bearing of the group of chiefs who crowded about his master. He would have envied covertly their graven armor and splendid weapons. Now he gave them no thought. His mind was occupied with the shattered heap out on the plain that had been Giton, and the Persian who had hacked the freeman to pieces with his terrible gray sword. He hungered for the order to battle. In battle he might have the fortune to meet the Persian giant. He would show Aeschylus what a slave could do, unarmed, unarmored. By Hercules, he was as good an Athenian as any of them! If the City had more like him there would be no question of victory.

Then he heard Giton's name, and directed his attention to the report Aeschylus was rendering.

'– was slain, but he held back the Persians until this slave of mine escaped with the prisoner they had taken, as Miltiades directed. The slave declares the morass is impassable –'

'Did you, yourself, try it, slave?' interrupted Miltiades, who had been chosen to command that day.

'Yes,' answered Glaucus gruffly. 'Seeing that I was the heaviest of those with him, Giton sent me in until I was mired over the knees.'

'Good tidings!' exclaimed Miltiades. 'But what of their horsemen?'

'The prisoner said that the horses all had been sent to Eubœa for pasturage,' replied Aeschylus.

'What of that, slave?' interposed Callimachus, the Polemarch or War-Ruler, who represented the Archons in the counsel of the *strategoi*. 'Did you approach sufficiently close to see into the camp?'

'There are no horses in the camp,' said Glaucus.

'But how can you be sure?' demanded one of the *strategoi* who were of the party opposed to giving battle, a man named Lysimachus. 'They might be concealed.'

'When a score of men come out from a tent that is only large enough to house a score of men there are no horses concealed in it,' returned the slave contemptuously.

The *strategos* flushed.

'Your slave is free-spoken, Aeschylus,' he complained.

'He answered a question that was put to him, and with sense,' spoke up Miltiades. 'Thus it appears that we have not to fear the attack of the Persian horse if we bring on a battle. Also, that the plain is constricted in width by the morasses on either side – for I have already determined that the swamp on the left can not be crossed. The sacrificial omens are propitious, and therefore I urge upon you all, as I have urged before, that we seize this last opportunity to strike for freedom.'

'But if we wait until the full of the moon the Spartans will come to our aid,' objected the *strategos* who had complained of Glaucus.

'And it is equally likely that the Persians may be reinforced,' retorted Miltiades. 'They may bring back their cavalry from Eubœa. They may call in other forces. There are those in Athens who may be persuaded to make use of factional differences, and surrender the city by treachery.'

No man answered him, but after an interval the War-Ruler spoke:

'We have a serious decision to make. Let us vote upon it. Those of the *strategoi* who favor the advice of Miltiades stand with him; those who oppose him stand back.'

There were ten of the *strategoi*, one for each of the tribes into which the Athenians were divided, and they separated five and five.

'Yours is the casting vote, Callimachus,' said Miltiades.

The War-Ruler assented gravely.

'It is a great responsibility you lay upon my shoulders, Athenians. If harm comes of what I say my name shall be accursed.'

'And if you vote wisely, oh, Callimachus,' cried Miltiades, 'you will win for yourself an immortality of fame. For it rests with you either to enslave Athens or to assure her freedom. Never, since they were a people, have the Athenians been in such danger as they are at this moment. If they bow the knee to the Persians they will have set over them for masters the outcasts they have expelled from their midst. But if we fight, and are victorious, as I believe we can be, Athens has it in her to become the first city of Greece.'

'Not so! No, no!' cried several of the chiefs opposing him.

And Lysimachus called to Miltiades direct:

'How can you advise us to fight when we number at the most 11,000 hoplites? As for the light-armed troops, you are not so

foolish as to reckon them, seeing that almost all are slaves like
this fellow here.'

He pointed to Glaucus, who stood with arms folded over his
powerful chest a pace behind Aeschylus.

'I struck down two Persians out there,' growled the slave.

The *strategoi* regarded him in amazement, and Lysimachus reached
for his sword, then shrugged his shoulders, and said coldly to
Aeschylus:

'After all, he is your slave. Slay him yourself.'

'Why should I?' inquired Aeschylus. 'He spoke the truth.'

Even Miltiades looked aghast, and the War-Ruler protested:

'The fate of Hellas hangs upon what we do today. Shall we linger
to discuss the boast of a slave?'

Aeschylus pursed his lips in a whimsical grimace.

'Nevertheless, Callimachus, the gods have many ways of making
manifest their will. It is possible they speak through the mouth of
a slave.'

'You are pleased to talk as a poet rather than a warrior,' answered
the War-Ruler coldly. 'It is true that the Persians have no heavy
infantry to match the hoplites, as Miltiades contends, but of light
troops they have many more than we, chosen archers, freemen, while
we – But it is a purposeless discussion. They can sweep our slingers
and javelin-men from the field.'

'But how, if we contrived that in doing so they should cause their
own defeat?' proposed Miltiades. 'You smile, Callimachus. But I say
it can be done. Mass our strength on the wings, leaving the center
weak – five thousand hoplites on the right, five thousand on the
left, in the center a thousand hoplites backed by all the light-armed
troops.'

'We should be split apart,' derided Lysimachus.

'Yes, the center would break at the first shock,' agreed the
War-Ruler.

But Miltiades pointed down into the plain, which was spread out
at their feet.

'The mountains bend inward to the center,' he said. 'See! Below
us here the distance to be covered is twice that to right and left.
So the wings would meet the enemy first. They would be fighting
before the center engaged; the Persians would be fleeing from the
wings by the time the center came up. Is that plain?'

Strategoi of both factions nodded eagerly. The face of Aeschylus
was lit with high resolve. Only Glaucus stared moodily at the long
sweep of the Persian camp.

'The Persians will break the center, as Callimachus has said,' continued Miltiades. 'They will pursue it, and the wings can close in upon them in the midst of the plain and destroy them.'

'If they do not turn right and left upon the wings after defeating the center,' suggested Callimachus.

'That will be for the center to check,' answered Miltiades. 'The center may be defeated and broken, but it must die to a man sooner than leave the Persians free to turn upon the wings. And surely, the gods have veiled their faces from us if we can not find enough Athenians, free-born and slaves, who will dare all for the City!'

'Here is one slave,' growled Glaucus.

'And the slave's master,' added Aeschylus.

Several of the *strategoi* who supported Miltiades called that they would fight in the center, but the War-Ruler raised his hand for attention.

'Who is this slave who is so glib of tongue amongst his betters?' he asked fiercely.

'One of two men who have struck for the City today,' replied Aeschylus. 'If we ask his kind to die for us, and find them willing, we can do worse than permit them a free tongue – which is the least dangerous of all liberties, I think.'

'It is a good sign,' cried Miltiades. 'If a slave is fearless, can we be less so?'

Callimachus plucked at his beard, uncertain, pondering.

'Tell me, slave,' he asked suddenly, 'why are you anxious for battle?'

Glaucus answered hesitantly, like a boy conning a lesson:

'I – seek – vengeance – and – a sword.'

'But why, slave? Why are you willing to risk death?'

'Giton showed me,' said Glaucus simply. 'A man must be willing to fight for what he has. He owes it – to the City.'

'To the City!' repeated Aeschylus. 'Did I not say the gods might speak through a slave?'

'I am content,' said Callimachus. 'My vote is for battle. Miltiades, bid the trumpets sound.'

V

A confused clamor rippled from end to end of the Persian camp as the Greeks burst from the shelter of the trees; and solid columns of well drilled Medes filed out to meet the attack, attended by throngs of other troops, bowmen and javelin-men, representatives of half the nations of hither Asia and Egypt and Ethiopia – careless of order, but confident of the downfall of Hellas.

Across the plain the hoplites moved in compact masses of thousands, bristling with spears, except in the center where a bare handful were strung in loose formation to cover the unarmored freemen and slaves. Because of the longer distance the center had to cover, as Miltiades had predicted, the two wings were in action with the enemy before the center had established contact; but what Miltiades had not foreseen was that the remorseless pressure exerted by the wings tended to force the Persians in upon themselves, so that when the center finally came to the shock, it was opposed by an impenetrable array that increased from moment to moment.

Two columns, one of Medes and one of Dacians, lightly armored in comparison with the hoplites, to be sure, but disciplined and used to victory, converged upon the tenuous line which was captained by the *strategoi*, Themistocles and Aristides – Themistocles, who was to be the founder of the Athenian navy and the victor of Salamis, Aristides, who was to lead the hoplites twelve years later in the final overthrow of Persia on the glorious field of Plataea. The air was black with buzzing arrows almost before the Greek slingers realized that death was in their midst, and discharged their answering hail of stones over the heads of the hoplites.

Glaucus, behind his master, saw the slingers on each side of him pierced by the hard-driven arrows of Phrygian bowmen, saw hoplites collapsing in the ranks with shafts feathered in neck and armpit, groin and thigh. He whirled his sling as fast as he could unpouch stones, seldom attempting to aim – content to discharge his missiles into the dense ranks of their assailants.

But he had time only for half a dozen shots. Then the Persians and Dacians had lapped the flanks of the dwindling line of hoplites and repeated on a small scale the treatment their comrades to right and left were receiving from the Greek wings. The hoplites slew until their arms ached, Glaucus and his brethren fought with knife and javelin or such weapons as they might snatch from the fallen; but five Persians leaped to take the place of each man killed or crippled. And always as Glaucus fought, he kept a vigilant watch for the tall warrior of the gray sword.

The battle was still undecided when Giton's slayer appeared. By dint of heroic efforts, Themistocles and Aristides and their motley bands had destroyed the two columns of Persians and Dacians; to right and left the wings were forging ahead, bearing down the desperate enemy by the steady thrust of their spears. In the center the Grecks had given ground – it was part of the price they paid in stemming the first onslaught upon them.

And now Glaucus, panting beside his master in an interval of the combat, saw three fresh columns of the long-coated Persian infantry of the Immortals – tall men, with braided beards and high, peaked helmets and oblong wicker shields – tramping through the ruck to renew the assault. At their head strode the warrior of the gray sword, his brazen helm and mail agleam in the afternoon sunlight, his lean blade flashing above the chased brass of his shield.

As he came on he tossed the sword high in air and caught it again, brandishing it as if in invocation, and the men who followed him responded with a deep-throated roar.

'See,' whispered Glaucus. 'They pray to it.'

Aeschylus sighed and stepped into his position in the diminished rank of the hoplites.

'Perhaps,' answered the poet. 'Any man is to be excused for praying to any gods this day. Stand to it, Glaucus. Remember Giton.'

But the slave never heard him. Already Glaucus had his stone in the sling and was whirling it around his head.

'Ah!' he gasped with his effort, and released it; but it dinted into the brazen warrior's breastplate. The Persian scarcely felt it.

Grinding his teeth, Glaucus cast again, and struck his enemy's helm a glancing blow, no such outright rap as had knocked him sprawling that morning. The Persian shook his head like a bull that has been bitten by a fly, and strode on. He was singing now, his voice resounding above the clamor of the fray. Glaucus sought a third stone, placed it carefully in the lip of the sling and marked the range.

'Ah!' He let it go, and could have knifed himself as it shattered on the polished surface of the brass shield.

'The gods have deserted you, it seems,' commented Aeschylus, dressing the heavy spear that was the hoplite's chief weapon. 'Keep my back, for there are only enough of us for the one rank.'

'Yes, the gods will have none of my sling,' said Glaucus furiously, and he threw it from him. 'Sling, I am done with you! Henceforth I fight with what weapons I can come by.'

'Try for the gray sword,' advised Aeschylus.

'I will,' snarled the slave.

The three columns of the Immortals crashed into the slender line of hoplites, pushed it back and ground it up in a broken mass of light-armed troops, slaves and freemen – Persians and

Greeks, inextricably mingled. The center had caved in. Slingers and javelin-men broke and fled. The hoplites were running together in groups of a score or a dozen and standing back to back, prepared to die if necessary, determined to hold what was left of their position. Glaucus, a dead Persian's sword in his hand and a riven hoplite's shield on his arm, ran forward in the press to meet the giant of the gray sword, who was battering down all opposition that was offered him. The lean, straight blade sheared helm and breastplate – made nothing of tempered bronze and steel. Whenever it struck it maimed or slew, and its owner talked to it, sang to it, besought it at times, and the troops who followed him thundered the response Glaucus had noted before.

Afterward a slave who understood Persian translated invocation and response for Glaucus:

> Drink deep, O, Gray Handmaid of Death!
> Be a steep wall to protect thy wielder,
> Lead thy servants to the slaughter,
> Feed us who feed thee!
>
> We will not flinch from thee,
> We will come after thee,
> Handmaid of Death!

The gray sword had just lopped a man's arm as Glaucus came within reach of its owner, and the slave struck quickly, thinking to take the Persian by surprise. But with one of his bull roars, the brazen warrior spun upon his heel, and caught the blow on his ruddied blade. The slave's sword shivered into atoms, and Glaucus saved himself from the return blow by plunging head foremost over the ground. His hand clutched at the first weapon available, a hoplite's spear, and scrambling to his feet again, he ran back at the Persian, the spear leveled breast-high. But the gray sword's master laughed at this menace, caught the spear-point on his shield, and as it glanced, hewed off the head and two handbreadths of the shaft.

'No weapon touches me,' gibed the Persian in mongrel Greek. 'That is the virtue of this sword – and the name of it is Death.'

He struck again, and as he struck Glaucus hurled the hoplite's shield at his face. The Persian checked his sword-arm in air and raised his own shield to ward the clumsy missile – and Glaucus leaped like an angry snake, flinging his body low and hard, so that he dived beneath the Persian's shield, wrapped his arms around the brazen greaves and tossed his enemy, clanging, to the ground.

The gray sword faltered in its descent, and the edge was turned on its master's shield, which had slipped down over the Greek's loins. A startled bellow from the stricken giant became a snarling mumble of protest, a babble, a whine, a groan. To and fro they tussled in the dust, unheeded beneath the stamping feet of the combatants; and the Greek, half-naked, was always atop of the Persian, weighted by his mail.

Twice the brazen giant tore his sword-arm free, and slashed wildly at his nimble foe. Each time Glaucus twisted to avoid the cut. And after the last effort the slave succeeded in pinning his enemy's arms with sinewy knees, stabbed his thumbs into the hairy throat, and with a sharp wrench broke the Persian's neck.

Glaucus snatched the gray sword from the stiffening fingers, and tottered erect.

'So, Giton,' he murmured, 'rest at peace. Ha, I always craved a sword. By Hercules, what a blade!'

The metal was interlaced with thousands of little whorls and curling lines, and a sinister light flared in the dull heart of it. A tingle ran up the slave's arm from the wire-wrapped hilt, and that tingle became a fire, a flame, a gust of extraordinary energy and emotion.

He circled the blade around his head, exhaustion forgotten, his whole being exalted by the deadly purr of the keen edge, and he shouted hoarse phrases that were novel to his slave's tongue:

'Forward, Athenians! For the City! For the honor of your temples! For your fathers' graves! Hellas conquers! For the City! Forward!'

The weary hoplites took up the cry, the Immortals wavered, dismayed by the death of their leader, superstitions aroused by the glint of the gray sword in their faces. The freemen and slaves, who had thought only of flight, commenced to retrace their steps and drifted down to resume the attack. Themistocles succeeded in reforming a fragmentary line, which slowly advanced again. On the wings Callimachus and Miltiades wheeled their victorious hoplites against the flanks of the inchoate multitude of the Persian center. In the snap of a finger the Persian army dissolved into a herd of fugitives, each man intent on gaining a place in the galleys which were already pushing off from the beach.

VI

The *strategoi* were gathered before the tent of Datis, the Persian commander, when Aeschylus fetched Glaucus from the scene of the last struggle on the shore.

'This is he who made good the center when the rest of us had failed,' said the poet.

Callimachus offered Glaucus a hand nearly as blood-stained as his own.

'You have deserved well of the City, slave –'

Glaucus cast the hand of the War-Ruler from his, and Aeschylus explained quickly:

'No more a slave, Callimachus. I have freed him. Shall an Athenian hold for slave a man who has saved Athens?'

A murmur of approval answered the poet, and he dropped a friendly palm on the ragged shoulder of the man beside him.

'What said I when the sun was overhead, Athenians? That the gods might speak for us through a slave! And but for a slave I think we should be dead or disgraced who gather here, and Athens would be a city in mourning by the morrow.'

'No, no,' denied Glaucus in his rude slave's voice that had acquired a ghostly timbre of warrior's pride. 'Give the credit where it is due. Giton made me – Giton and this sword.'

Miltiades bowed his noble head in the twilight.

'What man shall estimate the sum of his deeds?' he exclaimed solemnly. 'We chiefs planned and wrought as best we could. But we must have failed, except that a poor freeman inspired a slave with the greatness of loyalty!'

'Any man may be a slave,' said Aeschylus, 'and any slave may be a king.'

'But not every king has a sword like mine,' boasted Glaucus.

Miltiades, the far-traveled, Prince of the Chersonese, bent over the whorled surface of the long blade, and pointed a finger to a series of tiny symbols etched in the gray steel.

'Yet has it been a king's sword, Glaucus,' he said, 'for there is the Egyptian "seft" for sword and some Pharaoh's emblem.'

The worn features of Glaucus were suffused with a dim light – like the light of the rising sun burning through a sea-mist heavy with the night dews.

'Henceforth it shall be an Athenian's sword,' he exclaimed.

And in truth, the Archons honored him with citizenship, and in after years a statue of him in his brown woolen tunic; sword in hand, was reared on the very spot where he turned at bay. But that statue long since became slaked lime in the wall of a Greek peasant's hut, and Glaucus was forgotten more completely than Aeschylus – only the sword of the one and the plays of the other lived after them.

THE KIDNAPPING

Margery Lawrence

The middle of the fifth century BC *saw Athens at the height of its power under the rule of the greatest of all its politicians, Pericles. During his command, when he ruled as king in all but name, Athens became an imperial power. Though its strength kept the Persian menace at bay, war broke out with Sparta which lasted, on and off, for much of Pericles' period of power. Nevertheless, it was during the Periclean age that Athens grew in wealth and culture and when many of the greatest items of Athenian art were created.*

Margery Lawrence (1889–1969) is an almost forgotten writer now though in her day she was popular both for her supernatural stories and her many historical novels, including Daughter of the Nile, *set in ancient Egypt, and* The Gate of Yesterday *from which the following extract is taken.*

Hunched-backed Timon, Arteus' slave, cocked a bright amused eye up at his master as he rode along on his new bay roan, carolling the latest song current among the gay young men of Athens. He had not long returned from a prolonged visit abroad. At Pericles' expressed desire he had been granted special leave from the army to make an extended tour of Attica's foreign settlements, garrisons and outposts, and bring back a detailed report of them, and he had made the most of his time. His tour had been both fruitful and adventurous, and Arteus, bronzed and handsomer than ever, was feeling very well pleased with himself. Spoilt and indulged from his

earliest years, but for the fortunate fact that he was an essentially
charming and kindly person, he would have been insufferable.

Pericles would be pleased to see him, the young man reflected as
he rode, and also glad to hear how well things were going with his
settlements and colonies, both great and small. Since his accession
to power, the statesman had thrown all his immense energy, his
charm and his unique gift of oratory into making the country,
and above all the capital he loved, the greatest in the world. She
was to be the very heart of civilization, and acknowledged as such,
and in pursuance of this ambition he had forced through many
much-needed changes and reforms in the system of government in
Athens, despite strenuous opposition from the more conservative
element, the nobles. For long political matters in Athens had been
balanced on a hairspring between two bitterly opposing parties,
Pericles' party, the Democrats, and the nobles; and though at the
moment things were quiescent, there was no saying how long the
uneasy truce might last. Did it break suddenly, it might well be
necessary for some of the leading figures in the defeated party to
seek refuge abroad as quickly as possible, and actually this was
one of the main reasons why Arteus had been sent abroad, to find
such a refuge for Leocrates and his family if it should be needed.
Leocrates was a shrewd man and well aware that, vastly popular as
were Pericles and his democrats at the moment, there were powerful
forces at work against him and it was almost inevitable that sooner or
later the time would come when his enemies succeeded in dragging
Pericles down and his friends and supporters with him; amongst
whom Leocrates, his cousin, figured very prominently.

So it was as well, thought Arteus as he rode along, that he had
succeeded so well in his mission and in his search for a suitable
property had headed for the oldest of Athens' colonies, in Magna
Græcia, where he had purchased a handsome estate in the large
city of Lydis, on the Gulf of Tarentum. If one were forced to leave
Athens, Lydis, with its luxury, culture and brilliance, was no bad
second, though Arteus devoutly hoped that no such eventuality as
having to leave Athens would ever arise. There was no denying that
he had enjoyed himself thoroughly during his nine or ten months
travelling abroad and had received much kindness and hospitality
from the Lydians. Not a few efforts had been made to secure him
as a son-in-law by parents anxious to match their pretty daughters
with so eligible a young man, but Arteus, who was well accustomed
to being pursued, had evaded capture by letting it be known that he
was betrothed to Agathea, the favourite niece of the great Pericles,
which left him free to pursue his own interests in women, secure

from any chance of being pinned down into marriage – and he had not neglected these interests, though they led him mostly into the company of women not noted for virtue.

He raised his voice in song again.

'On the banks of Ilissus I swore to be true,
  And now I'm returning, Quisana, to you,
So what do they matter, the girls I have known,
  Since now I've come back and I'm claiming my own?
My beauty, my loved one, the girl I adore,
  On the banks of Ilissus I'll kiss you once more!'

'Once mo-o-ore!' carolled Arteus, increasing his voice to a bellow on the last note – and broke off suddenly as a shout hailed him from a rider coming towards him round the bend of the road just ahead. A tall youth in a yellow tunic, riding a sorrel mare bare-backed, as all Greeks rode, with his brown hair blowing in the wind, rapidly approached.

'Arteus!' In his excitement and delight, Orontes all but pulled his beast up on its haunches and sat, beaming at his friend.

'Arteus – home at last!'

'Orontes, by all the gods – the very lad I wanted to see!'

The two friends clasped each other on the shoulder and sat grinning with delight, each surveying the other, appraising and approving. It was Arteus who spoke first.

'Oron, you've grown up! Where is the lanky, diffident lad I taught to handle a discus as it should be handled? Gone! – and in his place I see a young man that all the girls will be after! And now, where were you going, and what's the news? I've been away for so long that I feel I've grown colonial moss all over.'

'I was going home,' said Orontes. 'And you?'

'I was on my way to "the Three Graces" to meet Glaucus and some of the other fellows,' said Arteus. 'I arrived back at my parental home only yesterday and my father staged a most impressive welcome. I slept late today in consequence and then received a message from my revered Uncle Pericles, who has bidden me sup with him and the fair Aspasia tomorrow night. So as tomorrow night I shall have to behave myself properly, I thought that tonight I'd have a real celebration with some of my old friends.'

Orontes slanted a sidelong glance at him.

'It's early yet,' he said, and Arteus amusedly noted a hint of pleading in his tone. 'Did you tell Glaucus you'd meet him at any special time?'

'Why no,' said Arteus, 'he doesn't know I'm actually back yet, to be honest. I was just going to "The Three Graces" to foregather with whoever might happen to be there and I know Glaucus is generally there about this time, drinking toasts to the fair Lalage.'

'Then it wouldn't matter if you got there rather late, would it?' said Orontes eagerly. 'You could come back with me and have a drink and a talk before going to the Agora? Oh do! It is a good year since I've seen you and there is so much to talk about.'

For a moment Arteus hesitated. He had fully intended to get in touch with his ardent young admirer as soon as possible, having a genuine liking for him, but the picture of the merry group of friends gathered in the Agora lured him strongly. In his last letter Glaucus had mentioned a new and especially attractive girl who had recently joined the ranks of the hetairæ in Athens. He opened his mouth on a graceful excuse and then suddenly changed his mind. After all, he need not stay more than half an hour, and it would please the boy enormously. Also, now he came to think of it, he had heard from his sister, Elissa, in a letter, a very odd story about Orontes' sister, Xana, the child he once met, with a lovely skin and oddly attractive eyes. It might be worth lingering awhile to get at the truth of the story. He nodded and turned his horse round.

'That's a good idea,' he said. 'I shall be delighted. Let's send our men on ahead by a short cut, eh? They can tell your folk to get the wine cooled and ready before we come.'

Nothing loth, Demos and Timon went off, and together the two friends paced leisurely along the road, pleasantly shaded now by the giant pines in a strip of woodland through which the highway was winding. Arteus threw back his handsome head and luxuriously sniffed the scented air, strong with the aromatic perfume of the pines.

'I often grumble at my father for building a house out at Cephissia,' he remarked, 'but by Hera, there are times, Oron, when I think your father and mine had the right of it! When I think of the stinks of Athens . . .'

'Stop thinking about Athens and talk to me,' said Orontes. 'Why didn't you write to me, I should like to know? I wrote to you more than once and entrusted the letters to the captain of one of my ships with strict orders to see that they reached you.'

'He did,' said Arteus, 'and I ought to have answered them, I know, but I am hopeless at writing letters! That doesn't mean I was not interested in your news, and especially in what my sister has told me about Xana – amazing child! Though whether I approve of a well-born girl doing what she is said to be doing is another thing – frankly, I don't and I'm surprised that you do.'

'I don't!' said Orontes hastily. 'But you don't know Xana. If she wants to do a thing she *will*, somehow – and the worst of it is, she manages to persuade you she's right!'

Arteus's stubborn jaw set firm for a moment, then he laughed.

'I'll warrant she wouldn't persuade *me*, if I didn't think a thing was right, that it was,' he averred. 'But tell me more about this. I want to get the right slant on it as it's bound to be all over Athens in all sorts of exaggerated ways.'

Orontes looked rueful.

'I know,' he said. 'All that gossip, and three-quarters of it's not true. That's what worries me, and Edris, too. We'd hoped to be able to keep it to ourselves . . .'

'If you did you were optimistic, both of you,' said Arteus with a touch of scorn. 'Keep secret that a well-born girl has taken to healing as a career? That would be too much to hope for!'

'She only treats women and children, of course,' said Orontes defensively. 'She really *has* an uncanny gift, you know, and the slaves she cured talked, of course, and people from outside began to come for treatment more and more, and I simply *couldn't* stop it, much as I'd have liked to! All I could do was to insist that patients came to her, not she to them, so at least she treats them in her own home, with her own slaves to help and either my aunt or her mother always with her . . .' But Arteus shook his head.

'Even under the best conditions, it all seems to me *most* unsuitable,' he said gravely. 'If Xana were a mature woman, it would be rather different. But a young girl . . . however it's no business of mine to criticize, Oron, and I beg your pardon if I seem to have done so. I'm an old-fashioned sort of male, you know, and like women to conform to the good old ways, keep to their houses, learn to cook and spin, please their husbands and look after their children. That's the sort of wife for me.'

Orontes cocked a faintly malicious eye at him.

'Do you think that the fair Agathea will fill the bill?' he enquired. Arteus frowned faintly. The subject of his betrothed was something of a sore point with him.

'Our families certainly came to some arrangement about our marrying one day,' he said cautiously, 'but I'm not in any hurry, I like my freedom far too well! Also I'm bound to admit that Agathea, though a nice girl, is frankly as dull as ditch-water and there are times when I shudder to contemplate a lifetime spent with her!'

Orontes laughed out loud. It was well known in Athens that Agathea was not really the niece of Pericles, though she passed as such, but his illegitimate daughter by a girl of good family who, on discovering that she was pregnant, had hastily been married to a relative of his, Claudius Tellius; who, in return for that service, had received a handsome capital sum plus a coveted post in the government. On the birth of his daughter, Pericles had stood sponsor to her when she was named, and settled a handsome sum of money on her, which brought her plenty of suitors when she grew to an age suitable for matrimony. But though passably good-looking and an amiable girl, Agathea was so superflatively stupid, alas, as to be nicknamed 'The Great Goose', and it was only the fact that she was the apple of Pericles' eye that caused her list of suitors to be such an impressive one. It was plain that the thought of marriage with her depressed Arteus, and his next remark was a deliberate change of subject. What had Orontes been doing – had he been returning from a day at the Academia?

'No,' said Orontes. 'I've spent the day with Nestor down at the Piraeus and I'm really beginning to get a grasp of the business now, I think. But, Zeus, it was an uphill grind at first and I found it infernally dull!' He hesitated and went on, 'In fact, if it hadn't been for two things, I'd have backed out of it and stuck to sport!'

'What were the two things?' Arteus asked curiously.

Orontes flushed a little but answered honestly.

'Well, first of all, you. You'd advised me to tackle it and I didn't want either to disappoint you or let you think I was a quitter. And then . . .' he hesitated again and flushed a little more deeply, 'Nestor's daughter, Symian. You may have heard of her.'

Arteus shook his head, and Orontes went on, 'No, of course you wouldn't. Neither she nor her father would come your way. They're just our manager and his daughter.'

Noting his flush, Arteus wondered resignedly if he was doomed to have to listen to a lovelorn youth's recital of his first affair, but he said nothing and Orontes continued.

'Nestor's taught this daughter of his to be so infernally knowledgeable about the business that she knows far more about it than I do . . . and you know, that galls me like hell, Arteus! I hate a girl to know better than I do!'

'So would I,' agreed Arteus and the boy rushed on.

'Do you know, sometimes the buyers ask for her even when Nestor's there, to give her opinion on the quality of this and that, and she's a year younger than I am! And more than once, when Nestor has had to go to check a big cargo, he's handed me over to Symian, if you please, to go on with whatever we happened to be studying at the moment . . . imagine how I felt about that!'

'I can imagine how I'd feel about it, if the girl was anything to

look at,' chuckled Arteus, 'and what I'd do too! Did you make the
most of your opportunities, Oron?'

Orontes shook his head. It was strange, but the light comment
somehow gave him a little shock of distaste.

'Gods, no!' he said. 'She's not that sort of girl at all. She's a friend
of my sister's. Oh, Symian's a nice girl, though she wouldn't be my
particular choice at any time.'

'I gather, then, she's a plain-looking wench?' said Arteus, and
again the careless comment brought to Orontes an odd little sense
of shock.

'Oh, she isn't!' he said quickly. 'She's good-looking, in a sort of
foreign way. Her mother was a Syrian – she's called after her.'

'I wondered where she got that outlandish name,' commented
Arteus lazily. 'Dark-haired, I suppose?'

Orontes nodded.

'Yes, curly, and very dark eyes, and skin that is sort of golden,
rather like an apricot . . .'

'And tall, I imagine, and slender?' interjected Arteus, and laughed
outright as Orontes nodded again. 'Well, well it's obvious she's far
from plain, so I can't understand your coyness, Oron! If I'd been
in *your* shoes . . .'

'You'd have done precisely as I did – which is nothing at all!'
snapped Orontes. He felt oddly ruffled. 'Didn't I tell you she's not
that sort of girl? And do you think Nestor's such a fool as to leave
her alone with me? Not that he wouldn't trust me, but he knows
what would be said! No, old Thais, who was her nurse, looks after
them, and she's there to play propriety when Nestor isn't.'

'Well, well! Now I understand.' Arteus' tone was soothing. 'All
right lad, don't get annoyed with me when I tease you – you'll have
to get used to that . . .'

He was interrupted by a shout and, as they rounded a bend in
the road and came in sight of Orontes' home, they saw Demos, the
slave, running down the rough pathway that led from the road to
the gate. He was waving his arms and shouting.

'What on earth – ' exclaimed Orontes, kicking his horse fiercely
in the ribs and riding quickly up the slope. Arteus urged his
horse also up the sloping path, and came up in time to hear his
friend speak.

'But how in the world – I don't believe it . . .' he paused, for
from the house came the sound of a woman shrieking in hysteria.
'Oh, ye gods!' and Orontes was off his horse and away, running
into the house as the shrieks continued.

His curiosity now thoroughly aroused, Arteus dismounted also, tossed the reins to Demos, and following his friend into the house, sat down on one of the seats in the peristyle and prepared to wait. He wondered what could have happened in the stately home of Orontes to occasion such an uproar?

The woman who was creating the disturbance would be, he thought, the stepmother. Edris. It was not likely that a young thing like Xana would indulge in hysterics. He saw from the expression on Orontes' face when after a few moments he emerged from the women's quarters, that whatever the reason for the outburst it could not be disregarded. Half-way across the peristyle the boy burst out with his news.

'Arteus . . . Xana has been kidnapped!'

Arteus' jaw dropped and for a moment he looked completely blank.

'*Kidnapped?*' he said incredulously. 'Are you sure?'

'Of course I'm sure, you fool!' snapped Orontes angrily. 'Come and speak to the slave who's come back without her, curse him! If he wasn't so badly hurt already, I'd have flogged him until he couldn't move for leaving her. Come into the women's quarters with me. He's hurt and they're looking after him there . . .'

The two friends hurried across to the women's courtyard, to find a group of women headed by little Aunt Nœra gathered about the prostrate body of a dark-skinned slave who had obviously been severely injured in some sort of a fight. One arm hung awkwardly, plainly broken, his thighs and ribs were horribly bruised and his head badly cut, his hair caked and matted with blood and dirt. Aunt Nœra was kneeling and bathing his wounds while the maids stood holding bandages, a splint and the herbal lotions in which the little woman so heartily believed; but on the entrance of the two young men the treatment of the wounded man was instantly suspended, and Aunt Nœra rose to her feet as Arteus courteously saluted her.

'Forgive my abrupt entrance, lady, and my presence here, but Orontes insisted on my coming with him. Is there anything that I can do?'

'Yes, there is,' Aunt Nœra replied briskly, 'you can try to find out from Spiro here just what happened. He arrived only a few moments ago, all but crawling, in such a state of collapse that we could get nothing out of him but the bare word that my niece had been kidnapped and taken to Athens to be held for ransom – trapped by a false message calling for her help for someone in the city. And like the foolish, trusting child she is, she believed it and went!'

'Give him a glass of strong wine,' said Arteus. 'He's been badly injured, lady, and it must have been all he could do to get back here in this condition to try to get help.'

Aunt Nœra looked a little contrite.

'I am sorry,' she confessed, 'but I find it difficult to think of anything or anybody except my niece. Here, Spiro my poor fellow, drink this and try to tell us clearly all you know.'

As Spiro thirstily drank the wine offered him, Orontes spoke, and his voice was ominous.

'As head of this house and the guardian of my sister, I should like to be told precisely what has happened and how it was possible that Xana should be lured from her home?'

The little woman rose to her feet and faced her nephew squarely.

'I fear, Orontes, that I am largely responsible,' she said quietly. 'As you know, since her mother has no sympathy with the healing work, she will not come to the healings and, as a rule, I am always there with Chloe and Tasia here to help. But it was the end of the afternoon and only two patients remained and I thought I could be spared to go to Edris, who had a headache. The woman who acted as decoy to lure Xana away had not come, but I knew her – a woman called Phebe, seemingly respectable enough. She had been several times before, bringing a pretty child with her called Enoe who, she said, was ill though I personally could never see anything wrong with her . . .'

'Go on!' Orontes' voice was taut with hardheld impatience. 'This Phebe came after you left – who can tell me what happened then, if you were not there?'

The slave Tasia stepped shyly forward in answer to Aunt Nœra's beckoning hand.

'Lord, the woman came in, weeping and wringing her hands, saying her little daughter was too ill to come and would our lady go to her? She knew, she said, it was presumptuous to ask, but so hopeful was she that our lady's kind heart would let her come that she had ventured to bring a hired litter that was waiting in the road below . . .'

Orontes gave a furious curse under his breath.

'A plot – and the men with the litter in it!' he ejaculated. 'If she had to go, why in fortune's name did she not order her own litter and slaves, and travel in a style that befitted her?'

'I think, my lord,' said Tasia shrewdly, 'that our little mistress knew that to do that would be to start a bustle of preparation in the house that would come to the lady Edris' ears, and that she would be forbidden to go, for she would not let Chloe or myself go and ask the Lady Edris for leave. She said that her mother was ill and the lady Nœra was looking after her, and she would not have her disturbed. She would, she said, go straight to Phebe's house and come straight back, and there would be no need for her mother or aunt to know she had ever left the house .... Oh, we knew it was not right, lord, but who were we to argue with our Kyria or go against her will?'

Orontes nodded gloomily and motioned the girl to go on.

'So Chloe fetched our lady's scarf and the two men, Sesos and Spiro, and even more then we slaves felt there was something not right about this, for the woman Phebe frowned when she saw them and said something about an escort not being necessary ... and I could see that she was not pleased when Chloe mounted into the litter beside our lady, but she dare not say anything. We girls did not feel happy about our little lady's going away like that, but she had forbidden us to tell the older ladies, and indeed they suspected nothing. They thought our young lady was in the garden with Chloe until it began to grow late, and then suddenly Spiro returned in the state you see, and he is the only person who can tell you what happened after the litter left our gates.'

The wounded man, feeble but obviously much recovered, was now able to tell his story. It appeared that the litter, its leather curtains closely drawn, was carried along at such a pace by its four sturdy bearers that Sesos and his fellow-slave had trouble in keeping up with them. Sesos, the older of the two and a man of good standing in the Andronicus household, had not been at all happy at his young mistress setting forth in a hired litter with neither her mother nor her aunt to accompany her, but he had not dared to disobey Xana's orders. When the litter reached Athens, left the main street and plunged into the mass of evil-smelling alleys that was the Plaka, his uneasiness increased. The litter hurried on ahead and at a certain point the two slaves saw the woman Phebe poke her head out of the litter and beckon to a group of rough-looking men lounging together at a corner. These men rushed forward, tripped Spiro up and set about fighting his companion with the obvious intention of delaying them until the litter was out of sight.

Hopelessly outnumbered, both slaves were knocked out and left senseless in the roadway while their attackers took to their heels. Spiro, the younger man, revived first, and finding Sesos still unconscious, did the best he could for him, rolling his cloak into a pad for his head and bathing his wounds with water from the nearby gutter. He then managed to limp his way back to the Diometian Gate and back to the Andronicus homestead, where from shock and loss of blood, he collapsed.

At the conclusion of this tale, his hearers looked at each other in stunned silence. It was broken at last by Orontes, livid with rage and fear.

'The Plaka – my sister kept prisoner in some stinking hole in the most infamous district in Athens . . .'

Arteus, rising to his feet, strode up and down as he pondered, his brows drawn together in a heavy frown.

'It's plain that this is a carefully prepared plot,' he said at last. 'The wealth of the house of Andronicus is well known, and some rogues in the Plaka saw a chance and took it. They used the woman Phebe as a spy and decoy, posing as a patient and to insinuate herself into Xana's good graces . . . And the next stage is, of course, the appearance of a messenger demanding a ransom! Meantime, how the girl and her maid are faring only the gods know!'

'What are we to do – what?' Orontes' tone was frantic. 'Even the street-wards avoid the Plaka unless they are obliged to go there, and then they never go alone! The very thought of Xana in the hands of some frightful gang of criminals makes me mad! I'd pay anything, the whole of my fortune, to set her free, Arteus! And to think we have to sit here and wait . . .'

'We don't have to do anything of the sort,' Arteus said crisply. 'Where is Timon? – the devil's never here when he's needed!'

But Timon was already at his elbow. 'Lord, I am here. What shall I do to try and save the lady?'

'You can get on my horse this minute,' said Arteus, 'and ride like lightning home to Cephissia and bring back with you my dog Cerberus! Tie him to a long rope and let him run beside the horse when you ride back. Now hurry!'

The little hunchback ran like a hare out of the courtyard, and in the tense hush that followed Orontes looked at Arteus questioningly.

'Your dog – how can a dog be of any help here?'

'Don't count on anything, Oron, not yet.' Arteus' voice was gentle.

'But when I was in Lydis I bought a dog of the Molossian breed, bred for hunting and tracking. They can smell out the track of a person if they can first pick it up from something they have worn; and if you let my Cerberus get the scent of Xana from a scarf of hers . . .'

'But,' said Aunt Nœra, 'she was carried in a litter. How then can this dog of yours follow her scent if she did not lay one?'

Arteus looked stricken for a moment and there was a dreadful silence – when Tasia spoke timidly.

'May I speak, lord? When the men with the litter came to the gate we watched our lady and Chloe get into it, and saw one of the bearers had a bandage on one foot and it was torn and hanging loose. He tore it off and threw it aside when they left. If that would give the scent for the dog, perhaps it is still there. Shall I go and see?'

Arteus nodded and the girl ran out of the peristyle to return within a matter of seconds with a dirty strip of linen bandaging in her hand. Arteus pounced on it with a cry of relief.

'Thank the gods – and thank you, little maid, and your sharp eyes! Now Orontes, we have not long to wait! Pray the gods that Cerberus does justice to my faith in him.'

In a low-roofed stinking hovel in the back-streets of the Plaka, the worst slum district in Athens, Xana and her slave, Chloe, lay bound and gagged.

It seemed to Xana, lying in a corner on a pile of sacks and straw, crawling, she felt with disgust, with all manner of vermin, that she had been lying there for hours and hours, and yet it could not be more than two hours at most since she had climbed into that fatal litter. But what untold ages it seemed! She coughed and choked on her gag, a strip of dirty rag tied across her mouth. She should, perhaps be thankful, she reflected sardonically, that she had not had a piece of similar rag stuffed into her mouth as had happened to Chloe to stop her frantic screaming.

She turned her head with difficulty and stared anxiously into the far corner of the room where a motionless heap lying prone on the filth-encrusted floor showed where Chloe, worn out with her struggles, had fallen exhausted at last.

Though the shock of finding out the gross deception that had been practised upon her – and by one of her own patients! – had shaken Xana badly, oddly enough after that first shock she had felt no fear, only a wild surge of anger.

The truth of her situation had not dawned upon either Xana or her maid until their arrival in the Plaka, and it had been Chloe who had first realized it. The noise of the fight that had been staged to hinder Sesos and his companion slave from accompanying the litter any further had roused her attention, and she had poked her head out between the close-drawn leather curtains to see, to her horror and amazement, both their attendants being set upon by a group of strange roughs, but even as she cried out the hand of the woman

Phebe, who was riding with them in the litter, fell upon her knee with a crushing grip.

'Be silent, you!' hissed the woman. 'Yes, your men are being prevented from following you – for good reasons!'

Her thin lips twisted into a bitter sneer as she looked at Xana, at her gold ornaments, at the fine quality of her apparel and the even finer quality of the wide scarf or stole that Chloe had brought to protect her young charge from the coolness of the night on their return journey. Sheer blank astonishment kept Xana silent as the woman went on.

'Now, if you're wise, my young maid, no harm will come to you, nor to this silly girl either, though I didn't bargain, when we planned this thing, to have her on my hands as well. I'd forgotten that you fine ladies never move without a slave at your heels . . .' But by this time Xana had found her voice, which was quite steady . . . indeed, in an odd way Xana was more puzzled than alarmed. This was the very first time she had been brought face to face with class hatred, and though it shocked and startled her, she was too much interested to be frightened.

'What do you want with me?' she asked.

Accustomed to wealth as she was, the possibility of being herself an object by which money could be obtained had never dawned on her, and Phebe's hard retort startled her.

'If you don't understand why you've been brought here, you soon will!' was all the answer she was vouchsafed, and then the litter lurched, stopped abruptly as it was dumped down, and Phebe slipped to the ground and opened the curtains.

Before them loomed a low-roofed hovel, more like a stable than anything else, dark and evil-smelling, its floor littered with decaying vegetables and a thousand other oddments. Now for the first time Xana knew fear, and Chloe, terrified, began to scream, which was the worst thing she could have done, for from behind the litter three ruffians appeared, who seized her, bundled her bodily into the hovel and plainly muffled her in some way as after a few moments the sound of struggling and stifled cries ceased abruptly and the three men appeared, dusting their hands and grinning. One, a battered-faced villain of some fifty years, approached the litter where Xana still sat, frozen with horror, and spoke coarsely.

'Come quietly now! Or we shall tie up that pretty mouth as we've tied your slave's!'

'What are you going to do to me?' Xana's mouth felt dry – young as she was she knew something of the fate that might befall a girl alone in the hands of evil men and shuddered away from the thought.

'What do you want? Money, I suppose, before you let me go –
but I warn you, you are doing something for which you will be
terribly punished!'

The woman Phebe laughed brutally.

'Who is going to punish us when no one knows who has spirited
you away?' she demanded. 'All they know at your house is that I
came and besought you to come and heal my daughter, but they
do not know where I live, and after today Phebe will have vanished
into thin air. Oh no! We have guarded ourselves well, little lady.
Your slaves who would have followed us we held back, and now
nobody knows where you are. As to what we want . . .'

She stretched out a hand and snatched from Xana's neck the
cameo necklace that she wore and then took the twin gold clasps
that ornamented the shoulders of her pink chiton and the girdle that
matched her necklace. With a strange detachment, Xana reflected
that it was a pity she had put on her favourite ornaments on that
particular day, for as a rule she wore no jewellery on her healing
days; however; it was too late for regrets. She watched Phebe as she
tucked the jewellery into the folds of her shabby robe and spoke.

'These will do nicely for my little Enoe when she is old enough
to wear them, but they are only a first instalment. We are planning
to make much more money out of you, my little madam, than just
the price of these trumpery things!'

'You mean to hold me to ransom?' queried Xana. The palms of
her hands were wet with the sweat of fear, but her voice was steady
and controlled. The men laughed and muttered among themselves,
and their leader answered.

'That we do, and your rich family will have to pay out handsomely
before they get you back again! Even if . . .' he flung a meaning glance
over his shoulder to the two men behind him, 'even if they don't get
you back the virgin you came to us, which all depends! I may be
minded to lie with a fine lady just to see if she's made the same
way as our girls! Ha ha!'

'If you dare to touch me,' said Xana, 'I shall find strength
enough to tear out your eyes with my nails!' Her voice rang out
fearlessly, her grey eyes were fixed on his, and for a brief moment
the man's eyes wavered before hers and he spoke irritably, spitting
into the gutter.

'It's the money you're worth we're after, not your pretty body!
You'll stay here until we can get a message through to that mother
and brother of yours naming the price we want for your return –
money in cash to be left somewhere where we can pick it up. When
we have it, we shall clear out of here and they can have you back

and welcome. And now, mistress, I'll thank you to get out and into that room quick!'

The man laid a filthy hand on her shoulder and Xana suddenly lost her temper, struck the offensive hand furiously aside and sprang out of the litter with some wild idea of fighting her way through the group and taking to flight. But she was instantly seized and carried, fighting madly, into the den where Chloe already lay bound and muffled in a corner. She fought them, screaming all the time for help at the top of her voice, but the end was inevitable, and within a few minutes her wrists were tied behind her, her ankles tied together and a strip of foul linen stifled her cries. Phebe sneered from the background where she had been watching the scene.

'You're a little fool to have behaved like your slave! We'd not have tied you up if you had kept quiet. Maybe I'd even have given you a stool out of "The Cross-Eyed Dog" to sit on instead of those sacks.'

Xana lay glaring at her captors, but despite the tumult of her emotions she noted the comment and realised that it was probably the owners of 'the Dog' tavern who had planned her abduction. The man with the battered face confirmed her suspicions.

'Come on, lads, we'll go and drink to our success – and not a word to anybody, mind! If anybody comes making enquiries in the Plaka about this girl, who so innocent as the proprietor of "The Cross-Eyed Dog," who can prove he was conducting his business of selling drinks all the time. Lock these wenches in, Phebe, until we decide where to put 'em, until the ransom's paid.'

The heavy door was slammed to and locked and the two captives were left alone together.

Cautiously Xana tried the strength of her bonds, but the men had made certain their prisoner was not going to escape. At least the strip of rag around her mouth was within reach of her strong teeth, and despite the disgust she felt at the foul taste of it, she bit and worried at it until strand by strand the strip fell away from her face. Sickened, she cleared her mouth and spat vigorously, then spoke softly.

'Chloe, I've got rid of my gag. Can you hear me?' She listened eagerly and felt her heart bound with relief when a faint whimper indicated that her maid was at least conscious and, she hoped, no more than badly shaken.

'Chloe, I can't loosen the cords on my hands and ankles, but I'm going to try and roll across the floor to you. Then if I can, I'll bite through the bonds holding your hands, and then you can untie me. If your hands are tied behind you, turn over

on your face so that I can get at them. Get ready – I'm
coming . . .'

Hampered as she was by bound wrists and ankles, it was no easy
matter to get herself across the floor to the corner where Chloe,
to judge from the muffled sounds she was making, was doing her
best to obey her mistress's instructions. Moreover, the earthen floor
was littered with nails, broken potsherds, sharp bits of straw and
the like, so that as she inched herself towards Chloe, not only was
her robe torn, but her skin wounded and cut in many places; but
Xana, daughter of Paulus Andronicus, was made of sterner stuff
than most girls and set her teeth and struggled on until at last, to
her unspeakable relief, she reached the corner and found Chloe
lying obediently on her face in the muck, with her bound hands
uppermost. At once Xana set to work to try and gnaw through the
bonds, thanking her stars that these were of coarse rope and not of
leather! Her jaws ached furiously by the time she had succeeded
in freeing Chloe's hands. The slave's first action was to roll herself
upright and snatch the bandage from her mouth, then to fall upon
Xana's neck and prepare for an hysterical outburst of weeping, but
Xana was in no mood to tolerate any such display.

'Don't waste time crying, Chloe!' she said brusquely. 'And speak
low – we don't want those people to come in and ask how we come
to be ungagged! Untie me now and free your ankles, and then help
me to try to wipe some of this filthy stuff off my dress – I feel as
though I shall never be clean again!'

Chloe's attempt to tidy her mistress's hair and clothes was
singularly unsuccessful. Choosing a corner that seemed a shade
less foul than the rest of the place, they talked in low tones of
the terrifying adventure in which they were involved. Thanks to
her mistress's calmness, Chloe had regained her self-control but she
did not share Xana's serene certainty of rescue.

'How *can* we be saved?' she persisted. 'I saw Sesos and Spiro
fighting with those dreadful men, and when we turned the corner
they must have lost sight of us, and even if they had been able to
come running after us they would never have known which corner
to take!' Her lips quivered. 'Oh Kyria, what if they murder us? We
could easily be killed in this awful place and nobody would ever
know!'

'Don't be silly,' said Xana firmly. 'We are worth too much to
them alive.' She suppressed the uneasy thought that this did not apply
to a mere slave, and if Chloe proved too much of a complication
the ruthless group might have no hesitation in getting rid of her.
Hoping that this had not occurred to Chloe, she went on. 'We're

in an awful situation, I know, and it's all my fault for disobeying orders, but I was so eager to go I wouldn't face up to it, and now look at us! I'm sorry, Chloe, I shouldn't have done it.'

Overwrought by the tense situation into a demonstrativeness that normally she would never have dared to show, Chloe threw her arms about the girl and hugged her tenderly.

'Oh my little lady, it was your sweetness and kindness that made you go, and if this had to happen to you, I am proud to be with you! At least to be together is better than to be alone . . . . But how long are we likely to have to wait before rescue comes? Phebe said they would be sending a demand for a ransom "soon", and I know that your mother will pay anything to get you back. But only the gods know if we must spend the waiting time here or if they mean to take us somewhere else!'

Xana looked round the foul little den with real horror.

'If we have to be here long I really think we shall be ill! No decent places to sleep, or wash, or anything . . . I suppose they'll give us food but it will be as disgusting as the rest! Oh, if only Sesos and Spiro have been able to run back quickly and tell them at home what has happened, so that they can try to find us without waiting for this ransom business!'

She turned to Chloe, watching her with wide, fearful eyes.

'Let's pray to Hera, Chloe, to send rescue to us soon! After all, though I disobeyed orders by leaving home, I came because I wanted to help somebody I thought was in trouble, not for a selfish reason, and that *must* make a difference. Kneel down, Chloe, and pray with me.'

Together the two girls knelt on the rough floor and their voices spoke together softly, Xana's fervent, warm with the love and faith that were hers towards her goddess. Chloe's woeful and shaky with fear.

'Oh great Hera, save us, we pray you . . .' Chloe raised her head, listening, and spoke below her breath, laying her hand upon her mistress's arm.

'Listen, there is talking outside,' she whispered. 'What if rescue has already found us? What if Hera has sent us help before we even asked for it?'

Indeed, there was the sound of voices outside talking and arguing, and as Xana listened it seemed to her that some of them did not sound like the rough harsh voices of the Plaka! Leaping to her feet, she seized a heap of sacks and heedless of the loathsome vermin shaken out of it, dragged it over towards the little high-placed window.

'Give me more sacks – wood – anything you can find, Chloe,'

she ordered, in a whisper. 'I *must* see out. I dare not call until I'm sure, or they might come in and beat us . . .'

Panting with excitement, the two quickly built up a pile of sacks, boxes and odd bits of lumber beneath the window; but it was still too low and Xana stamped with furious vexation. Then seizing Chloe, who was fortunately a solidly-built young woman, she made her bend over, placing a hand on each knee after the manner of a man giving a 'back' to a companion playing leapfrog.

'Keep steady! I'll be as light as I can, but I *must* see out,' she ordered. Climbing carefully on to Chloe's back, she peered out of the tiny window and caught her breath with utter thankfulness. Outside in the yard stood Orontes and Arteus, parleying with the man in the leather tunic! Behind them stood a group of armed slaves and at Arteus' side stood a magnificent dog. It was rescue!

'Oron, Oron!' she screamed. 'We're here, Chloe and I! Locked in! Break down the door, quickly . . .' Her voice broke as Chloe, forgetting in her excitement to keep her hands braced together on her knees, suddenly collapsed and both girls went down together, laughing and weeping hysterically in their utter relief.

They could hear that an appalling din had broken out immediately following Xana's scream. Arteus and Orontes and their slaves had made a dash for the locked door, but the proprietor of 'the Cross-Eyed Dog' and his friends were putting up a fight; but after a few moments it seemed they were being outnumbered, and mingled with the sound of blows and running feet came the welcome thunder of blows falling upon the locked door till at last it fell inwards, and in the opening stood Arteus, an avenging young god, holding his sword in one hand, his great dog's collar in the other. With one arm about the shrinking figure of her maid, Xana faced him. The light behind him turned his curling hair to an aureole of gold, his blue eyes were ablaze with the fierce joy of combat, and the blade of his sword shone red, for the owner of 'the Cross-Eyed Dog' lay gasping his evil breath away in the yard outside, a sword thrust through his ribs.

As he stepped into the hovel, Xana released her hold on Chloe and tried to smile, and wondered dimly why, now it was all over, she was beginning to feel so giddy and queer.

'I – we – prayed to Hera,' she whispered, 'and she answered . . .' but she could say no more. Arteus caught her as she fainted, and turning towards Orontes, who had just appeared, stepped out into the yard. Chloe, pattering behind him with the blood-smeared sword that he had let fall, eyed him with admiration and trepidation, for surely it was Hera herself who had guided this god-like young man to the rescue of her lady?

'Orontes!' Arteus' tone was curt. 'I leave you to give those villains who still live, into the charge of the street-wards, to be dealt with later by the justices. I will carry your sister to the Ceramicus, where we can find a litter for her. Wait! Give me my chlamys to cover her. It is not suitable that she should be seen in this state . . . .'

In silence and a trifle awed by his friend's manner, Orontes obeyed, and watched the three depart, followed by Cerberus whose gift for following a scent had been so triumphantly vindicated, while Demos and his fellows rounded up the gang of ruffians and began to rope them together and, with the woman Phebe, marched them to the lock-up to await their trial.

He did not know that Arteus, carrying his limp burden, was watching the young face lying against his shoulder with eyes from which, as in the fairy stories, 'the scales had fallen' so that he recognized at last the girl of all girls he wanted to marry.

THE WEARER OF PURPLE

Pierre Louÿs

Despite the title, this story is not about the purple of the Roman emperors, but is a story of love and art at the height of the days of Greek classical sculpture. It is narrated by Bryaxis, one of the foremost of the Greek artists who worked on one of the seven wonders of the world, the Mausoleum at Halikarnassos. Bryaxis' story is set in the year 347 BC. Pierre Louÿs (1870–1925) was a leading French symbolist who produced a number of works using classical settings. The best known is his series of erotic prose poems The Songs of Bilitis *(1894).*

I

In the green gardens of Ephesus, the white city, we were employed, two youthful apprentices, in the service of the aged Bryaxis.

He had just seated himself in a stone chair, as pale in colour as his own face, and was silent, scratching the ground with the end of his worn staff.

Out of respect for his great age and for his great reputation, still more venerable than his years, we remained standing before him, leaning against two black cypresses and not venturing to open our mouths so long as he said nothing.

We gazed at him without moving, in a sort of awe of which he seemed to be aware. We were glad that he had survived all those we would have wished to know; we loved him to show himself to us, who were simple children born too late to hear the heroic voices of the past; and foreseeing the future, when he would be gone, we silently sought to recognize the invisible connection between his person and the glory of his achievement. That forehead had conceived, that very thumb had moulded in the clay of the preliminary model, a frieze and twelve statues for the tomb of Mausolus, the five colossal figures erected before the city of Rhodes, the Bull of Pasiphaë, a work over which the eyes of women dream, the tremendous Apollo of bronze and the Seleucus Triumphant of the new capital.

The more I contemplated their author, the more it seemed to me that the Gods must have fashioned with their own hands this sculptor of light, before descending to his presence that he might reveal them to mankind.

Suddenly we heard the sound of racing feet, a whistle, a laughing exclamation, and young Ophelion sprang into our midst.

'Bryaxis!' cried he. 'Listen to this! The whole town knows it already. If I am the first to tell you, I'll present our Lady Artemis with a broad bean! But first, greeting! I had forgotten.'

He gave us a rapid wink, which might pass for a greeting, unless it meant: Get ready for a surprise: and began at once:

'I suppose you knew, aged one, that Clesides was painting a portrait of the Queen?'

'I had heard so.'

'But have you heard the end of the story?'

'There is a story, then?'

'I should say so! Then you don't know? Clesides arrived eight days ago from Athens for that precise purpose. He was conducted to the palace, but the Queen was not ready: she condescended to be late. At last she appeared, accorded the painter a bare greeting, and began to pose, if pose it could be called. It seems she fidgeted the whole time, on the pretext that too much love-making had given her the cramp. Clesides continued to draw as well as he could in the midst of all this twitching, and was in a very bad temper, as you may imagine. His first sketch was not even made, when suddenly the Queen wheels round and announces that she wants to pose from the back!'

'Any reason?'

'Because her back, so she said, was as perfect as the rest, and ought to show in the picture. Clesides protested in vain that he was a painter, not a sculptor, that panels are not looked at from behind, and that it is impossible to draw a woman so as to be seen from every side in one picture. She replied that it was her will to be painted so, that the laws of Art did not apply to her, that she had seen the portrait of her sister as Persephone, and of her mother as

Demeter, and that she, Stratonice herself, would pose by herself for all three Graces.'

'Not a bad idea,' said Bryaxis.

Our friend became heated.

'Suppose Clesides had refused then? He could have done so, I presume. One does not give orders to an artist. That little thing gives them to us in a manner we are not going to put up with. Her father would never have behaved like that. Why, when he was besieging Rhodes and Protogenes was working there on his Iasylus –'

'I know,' said Bryaxis. 'Go on.'

'In short then, Clesides was very angry, although he did not show it. He finished his study of the back; the Queen rose. She asked him to return the next day; he accepted the invitation and left her. Good.'

Ophelion folded his arms.

'The next day, whom do you think he found? A serving-woman on a stool! "Stratonice," says she, "is tired this morning. She will not pose any more, master, and I am to be her substitute until the portrait is finished. Thus has she decided!"'

We burst out laughing, and Bryaxis himself joined in our mirth.

Ophelion continued gaily:

'The slave was not bad looking. Clesides was scrupulous enough to give her a stiff dose of cramp in order that she might bear a closer resemblance to her mistress. Then he explained dryly that he did not require her any longer, and returned to his lodging with his drawings.'

'He was right that time!' I exclaimed. 'The Queen was really making a fool of him.'

'On the way back, as he passed along the quay, he noticed a certain sailor who, so he had been told, was a secret visitor to the Queen, although no one could prove it. It was Glaucon; you know the man I mean. Clesides summoned him to his lodging, paid him, and got him to pose. Four days later he had finished two rude little pictures, which showed the Queen in the arms of this fellow, first from the front and then from the back –'

'Just as she had wished,' I interrupted.

'Pretty well. Last night, nobody knows just when, he fixed the two paintings on the wall of the palace of Seleucus: no doubt he managed to get away by sea after the publication of his revenge, for there is no trace of him anywhere.'

We all cried out:

'The Queen will die of rage!'

'The Queen? She knows already, and if she is furious in reality, she conceals it wonderfully well. All through the morning an enormous crowd passed in procession before that scandalous advertisement. Stratonice was told of it, and also wanted to look. Attended by eighty members of the Court, she halted before each painting, stepping forwards and backwards in order to criticize the picture by turns in its detail and in its entirety. I was there, and as I followed her movements with terror, wondering which of us she was going to put to death when her wrath should explode: "I don't know which is the best," says she, "but both are excellent."'

Bryaxis, in the midst of our delight at this, merely raised his eyebrows, wrinkling his aged countenance into the lines of surprise and approbation: 'She is evidently as witty as she is impudent,' said he. 'The story is really a curious one. But why are you so proud of it, my children? It seems to me that the artist's role is inferior to that of the model, in the anecdote I have just heard.'

'If the Queen had dared,' said Ophelion, 'she would have had Clesides pursued beyond the seas and killed like a dog. But in that case the whole of Greece would have considered her as a savage, and she likes to believe herself an Athenian because she happens to have been born in a Parthenon which has been turned into a brothel. Stratonice holds Asia in her hand like a bluebottle, and she has given ground before a man whose sole weapon is a lump of wax. Henceforth the Artist is the King of Kings, the only inviolable being under the sun. That is why we are proud!'

The old man made a slight grimace of disdain.

'You are young,' he answered. 'In my time, the same formula was current, and perhaps with more reason. When Alexander timidly endeavoured to explain "why" he liked such and such a painting, my friend Apelles silenced him by saying that he was making himself ridiculous in front of the boys who were grinding the colours. And Alexander apologized. Well! I never thought stories of this kind were worth the telling. Whatever may be the respect or the arrogance shown by the King to contemporary painters, the pictures are no better and no worse for it: all that is therefore of no consequence. On the other hand, it may be a good and even a great thing if an artist dares and can place himself, not above any king whose army happens to pass by his house, but above the laws of men and above the laws of Heaven, upon the day that his muses order him to trample under foot all that is not actually themselves.'

Bryaxis had drawn himself up.

We murmured: 'Who did so?'

'No one, perhaps,' said the old man with a dreaming look in his eyes. 'No one, except possibly Parrhasius. And then, was he right? I thought so, once. Today, I do not know what to think.'

Ophelion cast a glance of astonishment in my direction. But I could tell him nothing.

'We do not understand you,' I said to Bryaxis.

He decided to give us a hint.

'The Prometheus,' he muttered in a low voice.

'Well?'

'Don't you know? Don't you know how Parrhasius came to paint the Prometheus of the Acropolis?'

'We have never heard how it was.'

'You have never heard of that terrible drama? Of the tragedy of death and of shrieks whence that painting emerged in blood like a newly born infant?'

'Speak. Tell us the whole drama. We know nothing of it.'

For a moment Bryaxis rested his gaze upon our young faces, as if he hesitated to inflict upon our hearts such a recollection.

Then he decided:

'Well, yes! I will tell you.'

II

What I am about to relate, my children, took place in the very last year of the hundred and seventh Olympiad, the very year that Plato died; quite fifty years ago now.

I was at that time in Halicarnassus, and had just finished my portion of the work on the tomb of Mausolus the Long-haired: a thankless portion, if ever there was one. Scopas, who was in charge of us, had chosen to decorate himself the eastern front of the monument, which meant that at the hour of the morning sacrifices, our Master's marbles had the full benefit of the sun and actually one saw nothing else but them. He had allotted the side facing south, which was a little less interesting and twice as long, to his companion Timotheus. Leochares had undertaken the western face; and I had got what nobody wanted, the north side, which required a vast amount of work, and was in perpetual shadow. For five years, then, I carved Victories and Amazons that lived, while they were in the sun, like real women, but each time that I had to place one forever in the gloomy region of the Mausoleum, it seemed that I was witnessing her death, and I wept, my little ones.

At last my task came to an end. I busied myself with my return to Attica. That year, as now, the Aegean was unsafe. War everywhere.

Hate between city and city. Athens, by the way, had been defeated. On the day I wished to set out, I could not find any shipowner who cared to go to the Piraeus. The Carians, like good traders, were going over to the conqueror, and since the capture of Olynthus had led to the fall of Chalcis into the hands of the Macedonian, all the merchants of Halicarnassus were setting sail to Eubœa, where they intended to sell robes from Cos and courtesans from Cnidus.

I, too, set out for Chalcis, telling myself that the Euripus was not broad, and that I could soon reach Athens from Aulis by Tanagra and the Acharnian road.

The sea voyage was unpleasant. I had rather a bad time in my corner, though I took up little enough room. My name, no doubt, had then a different sound from that which it has today, and the Mausoleum was too new to demand an estimation of its worth. The other passengers were content to know that I was an Athenian citizen, and that was quite enough for them to ridicule me, since Athens was out of luck.

One morning when the sun had already risen above the crests of the eastern heights, we landed at Chalcis in the midst of an immense crowd. I plunged into it with delight.

In reply to my inquiries, I learned that outside the gates a slave-market quite out of the ordinary was being held. Philip, after the fall of Olynthus, had razed the town to the ground, and enslaved the entire population of about eighty thousand. The sale had been going on two days, and it was calculated that it would last three months.

The city was crammed, too, with foreigners, purchasers, and sightseers. My informant, who was a wine merchant, had no objection to these swarms of people; but he told me that his neighbour, who sold, as a rule, only the most expensive slaves, had been ruined in one night, so quickly had prices fallen. I can still hear the innkeeper saying, with much gesticulation: 'Then, a Thracian lad of twenty! Every one knows how much they are worth, by the Gods! When you bought twelve of them to work a field, you paid a full twelve bags of gold stamped with the owl!* Well, now go and look at the prices. The quotation has fallen to fifty drachmae! You can judge by that of the rest! It is unheard of! There are three thousand virgins in the market: they are being sold off at twenty-five drachmae apiece: don't think I am guessing, the price is twenty-two, twenty-five, or twenty-eight drachmae if their skins are particularly white. Ah, Philip is a great king!'

* The bird sacred to Athene.

I was disgusted with the fellow, and leaving him, I followed the crowd beyond the open gates into the vast sloping meadow in which the Olynthians were penned.

With great trouble, I was shouldering my way through the swaying groups of people, and wondering in which direction to continue so difficult a progress, when I saw passing before me a fanciful and majestic procession, before which the crowd drew apart.

Six Sarmatian slaves advanced two by two, each carrying a load of gold, and with swords stuck in his belt. Behind them a little negro held horizontally, like a libation-cup, a long crook of rose-coloured cedar with a gold riband: the sacred staff of the Master. Finally, gigantic, weighty, crowned with flowers, his beard saturated with perfumes, his shoulders upheld by two pretty girls, wrapped in a mantle of purple of enormous extent, and crushing the grasses with his great feet, Parrhasius himself appeared, like another Indian Bacchus, and his glance fell upon me.

'If you are not Bryaxis,' said he, frowning at me, 'how comes it that you permit yourself to appropriate his countenance?'

'And you, if you are not the son of Semele, who has given you those vast curls, that dionysiac stature, and that purple robe woven by the Graves of Naxos?'

He smiled. Without even disengaging his arm from the charming support which increased the appearance of its bulk, he held out to me, across one of the courtesans, his mighty hand, like a golden platter, loaded with rings, and clasped my own upon a bare breast.

'Chariclo,' said he to the girl on his right, 'lend an arm to my friend, and let it embrace him pleasantly. On with our walk; it will soon be too hot for your complexion.'

Arm in arm, then, we all moved on. Parrhasius imparted to our pace a vast and regular rhythm, pompous as a hexameter, in which the short steps of the women might be said to correspond to the beat of the dactyl.

In three words he asked after my work and my life. At each of my answers he said quickly, 'Excellent!' in order to cut short my explanations. Then he began to speak of himself.

'You must understand that I have taken you under my protection,' said he, 'for not one Athenian citizen except myself is safe in the hands of the Macedonian, and if the slightest quarrel had brought you before a court of law, I wouldn't have given two oboli this morning for your freedom. Henceforth you may rest assured.'

'I am not,' I answered, 'of a timid nature; but I can scarcely doubt that even here if you gave your name –'

'I have done so,' he declared. 'I announced myself. When Philip

heard that I was doing him the honor of visiting his new city, which
he is peopling only with rascals, he sent to meet me, at ten stadia
from the bridge of the Euripus, an officer of his household, who
presented me with the royal bounty, including six colossi of the
North and the two handsome girls you see – strength to clear my
way, grace to adorn my person.'

'Are the ladies from Macedonia?' I inquired.

They burst out laughing.

'If you call Rhodes Macedonia!'

With a generous gesture Parrhasius concluded the subject:

'They will attend you this evening. I have others, left behind with
my baggage; but you may be alone, my friend; accept from my hand
these roses. The skin of their young bodies should be extraordinarily
effective against a carpet of dark purple.'

We were now close to the great slave-market. He stopped and
looked at me.

'By the way, you don't ask what I am looking for here!'

'I did not presume.'

'Can you guess?'

'I certainly cannot; I do not think you require a slave, since Philip
presents you with his. Nor a woman, since these –'

'I have come from Athens to Chalcis to find a model, my young
friend. Ah, I thought that would surprise you.'

'A model? Why, are there none left between the Academy and
the Piraeus?'

'About four hundred and forty thousand for me,' said Parrhasius,
with pride; 'in other words, the whole population of Attica. Nevertheless, I am looking for a model in the Olynthian slave-market.
You will understand why, when I tell you –'

He drew himself up.

'I am painting,' said he, 'a Prometheus.'

As he uttered the great name, his mouth opened wide, and all
the horror of his subject appeared for a moment in the knitting of
his brows.

'As you know, there are studies of Prometheus in every portico.
Timagoras has sold one. Apollodorus has attempted another. Zeuxis
thought he could – but why recall so many miserable daubs? No one
has ever painted a Prometheus.'

'I can well believe it,' I replied.

'We have been shown naked peasants bound to wooden rocks,
with their faces twisted into some sort of indescribable grimace
which makes one think of the toothache; but Prometheus the
Fire-Smith, Prometheus the Creator of Man and his struggle with

the Eagle-God between the Caucasus and the Thunderbolt – ah,
no! Bryaxis, that has never been done. That mighty Prometheus I
see as clearly as I do your face, and I am determined to nail his
image upon the wall of the Parthenon.'

So saying, he withdrew himself from the support of the two
women, took his gold staff from its diminutive bearer, and traced
great lines in the air.

'I worked for two months; I had found magnificent rocks on
Crates' estate on the promontory of Astypalaia. All my studies
were finished. The background of my landscape, ready. The line
of the figure, in place. Suddenly I was held up. I could not find a
head. Of course, if it had been a matter of a Hermes, of an Apollo,
or of a Pan, any citizen of Athens would have been proud to pose
for me; but to take as model a man whose genius is like light upon
his face, and to bind such a man by the feet and by the wrists upon
the framework of a stage property, you can see well enough how
impossible that is. One can only subject the limbs of a slave to
dislocation of that kind, and they have all got heads like animals!
They might be called Enceladus or Typhon, but not Prometheus.
Why? Because we lack slaves who come from the free Hellene class.
Well, Philip is providing us with them; I have come for them to the
place where he sells them.'

I shuddered.

'An Olynthian?' I said. 'A conquered ally? Where are you going
to paint this picture?'

'At Athens!'

'On the soil of Athens your slave will be free.'

'He will be what I wish.'

'But then, if you treat him as a prisoner, are you not afraid of
the laws?'

'The laws?' said Parrhasius, with a smile. 'The laws are in my
hand like the folds of this mantle that I cast over my shoulder.'

And with a magnificent movement he swathed himself in the
sunlit purple of his robe.

III

The Olynthian slave-market stretched before us. As far as the eye
could reach, and forming in one direction six wide parallel rows,
platforms of boards had been raised upon low trestles which
were about on a level with the middle point of the thighs of
the passers-by.

The population of a whole town was collected there, in face of a second multitude: one merchandise, the other purchasers. Eighty thousand men, women, and children, their hands bound behind their backs, their feet tied loosely with cords, awaited, most of them standing, the unknown Master who was to conduct them to some mysterious quarter of the Hellenic world. One soldier was in charge of forty, and took the part of salesman. Behind the tables, servants, picked up in the suburbs, passed round the bread and water necessary for the sustenance of the enslaved host, and a loud and continuous uproar, like the ceaseless voice of a carnival, arose.

Parrhasius entered the principal fairway, where on either hand were exhibited, naked as a people wrought of marble, the young men and women who had been considered worth a high price. To my astonishment, I could see nothing mournful in their looks, which seemed more inquisitive than lugubrious. There is a limit to human suffering, and in youth it is soon reached. Since the ruin of their homes, these splendid creatures had completely exhausted the quota of days and nights which it was possible for them to devote to apprehension or to despair. No trace of such emotions was now visible in their appearance. The young men, no doubt, had regained confidence in the prospect of future escape. Perhaps the girls were thinking of the lovers to whom they were to be subjected, and were innocent enough to desire them, whoever they might be. In a word, whether it were ignorance or bravado, they seemed to put a good face on the matter.

The crowd surged about them, more anxious to examine than to buy. Few made their decisions quickly in the distraction of so extraordinary a market. The slaves were freely handled. The muscles of a leg, the delicacy of a skin, the firmness of a budding breast, or the breadth of a manly fist were carefully tested. Then the group would pass on to the next platform, hoping to find something still better.

Parrhasius halted for a moment before a young girl of remarkable height, whose tall white figure was an exact harmony.

'That is a beautiful girl,' said he.

Instantly the salesman sprang forward.

'She is the most beautiful in the market, lord. See how upright she is, and how white. Sixteen yesterday –'

'Eighteen,' corrected the girl herself.

'You lie, by Zeus! She is but sixteen, lord. Look at her black hair, gathered up with a comb. When she loosens it, it falls to her knees. Look at her hands, at her long fingers which have not even touched a distaff. She is the daughter of a Senator –'

'Do not speak of my father,' said the girl gravely.

'Whether I said so or not, you could tell she was,' declared the salesman. 'She is as beautiful as a Nereid, as supple as a sword, as gentle as a hind in a wood, and lastly, what is worth all the rest, virgin as on the day she was born.'

And with a rough and cynical hand, he proved to us the truth of his words.

Parrhasius struck the dry ground with the end of his heavy staff.

'Virgin or no,' said he, 'that did not trouble me. It was enough for me that she was beautiful. Free her of these degrading shackles, and let her put on her robe at once. I purchase her. What is her name?'

'Artemidora,' said she.

'Well, Artemidora, know that you are henceforth in the train of Parrhasius.'

She opened a pair of wide eyes, and murmured with naïve hesitation:

'You are – perhaps – the Parrhasius who –'

'I am he,' replied her master.

And dismissing her to the custody of his servants, he continued his progress.

Then he deigned to explain his purchase.

'Stretched on the Caucasus, that girl would make a delightful picture, but it was not with the idea of finishing by her aid the Prometheus of which I have told you, that I bought her. She will serve me as model for certain small pictures dealing with sexual subjects, with which I relieve the tension of my mind in my hours of leisure, and which are far, as you know, from being the least admirable of my works.'

For a long time we continued our walk among the trestles. The multitude had increased. The sun was becoming less and less endurable in this vast shadowless plain filled with a sea of people.

Artemidora had put on first her white tunic and then her virgins' belt drawn high beneath the breasts, and her hair was hidden in the end of a bluish veil which swathed her whole body. She often turned back to look at us, and I noticed then that with her raiment she had suddenly assumed what was practically a new personality. Her face seemed altogether different. She watched us with anxiety, as if she was wondering which of all these men was to insult her modesty, and already forgetting the nudity in which we had seen her, she continually twitched the folds of her veil with that delightful backward thrust of the left elbow which attempts to dissimulate the curve of the hips.

We were already half-way down the principal fairway when Parrhasius stopped.

'No,' said he, 'what I want is not here. A youthful frame and a fine head do not go together. Besides, Prometheus is not a boy. Let us turn off to the right and leave it to chance: it is more probable that I shall find my man among the slaves to be sold at a lower figure.'

Scarcely had we gone three paces into the second lane to the right when he stretched out his hands and cried: 'Behold him!'

I turned with curiosity.

The man to whom he thus drew my attention was about fifty. Well proportioned and of great height, he had a fine forehead, strongly marked and prominent brows, a nose at once powerful and of geometrically exact design, wide nostrils, and deeply hollowed ears. His hair was grey, his beard still brown and crisply curling, as striking as the rest of his features. The powerful sinews of his neck formed a sort of pedestal which lent, in some curious way, an additional authority to the intelligence of his eyes.

Parrhasius addressed him:

'What is your name?'

'No man.'

'I didn't ask you for a literary allusion, my good fellow, but for the name you received from your father. You will tell me that, I suppose?'

'For a month my name has been No man. If I am of an ancient stock, it is not my pleasure to reveal it.'

'Why not ?'

'Nor does it please me to give the reason, son of a dog.'

Parrhasius, beside himself, became more purple than his mantle. The salesman, very much alarmed, extended his arms in a gesture of supplication.

'Do not listen to him, lord. He speaks like a madman, and it is pure malice on his part, for he has more brains than I have. He is a physician. For knowledge and skill he had no equal in Olynthus. I am simply telling you what every one repeats, for he was celebrated even in Macedonia. I have heard that during the last thirty years he has cured more Olynthians than we managed to kill the day we took the town. He will be a valuable slave when you have chained him and made him feel the whip; he still plays the insolent, but he will change his tone like the rest. Then, if you know how to manage him, you will not make the acquaintance of death till your hundredth winter. Give me thirty drachmae and Nicostratus will be your property for life.'

'Nicostratus?' repeated Parrhasius, turning to me. 'I do, in fact, know the name. My indifference is complete in regard to his medical knowledge. All my drugs are in my cellar, and one cures me very well of the indigestions given by another. When, as sometimes happens, I have a cold, I do not make use of any other plaster than a fair warm-breasted girl to recline upon my bosom, and I am quite confident of living for a hundred years without the aid of this apothecary.'

Turning to the salesman, he ordered: 'Take off his clothes.'

Nicostratus, powerless but disdainful, made no resistance.

Parrhasius continued to issue orders:

'Face front, arms down. Good – sideways – back – now right side; front again; 'tis a bargain.'

He clapped me lightly on the shoulder and said in a low tone: 'Superb, my boy!'

And I did not answer, for I experienced an uneasy feeling which was almost one of envy.

Fifty years have passed – the space of a human life. I have seen thousands of models, never one comparable to this Nicostratus of Olynthus.

He was the statue of Man in all his greatness, at the age when strength becomes power. Parrhasius called him Prometheus, but any name of those that are eternal would have been no less fitting for his new slave. With that man in my studio for a year, I could have made enough preliminary studies to fill my whole career with statues of Zeus, of Pluto, of Poseidon, or of the fifteen grey-bearded Gods who are called the Lords of the World. He evoked all Olympus. When he stretched forth his arm, it held the Trident, and when he raised it, there was the Thunderbolt. The lines of his pectorals, where they joined the shoulders, were so majestic that all his gestures seemed divine.

Ah, I thought, Parrhasius offers me women, as if I were going to pass my evenings between the pillars of the Ceramicus, and it is clear that he does not understand that I would renounce love itself in return for his Nicostratus. Will the Gods ever inspire him to send me the man, were it but for a day?

Such were the pangs of jealousy that I secretly suffered; but I half consoled myself with the reflection that, if not in marble, at least in paint, a medium almost as pure, the deathless splendour that dwelt in him would be preserved.

Nicostratus was, in fact, lost for marble; I never had him as a model. The unfortunate man only posed once, and you shall hear how.

IV

I returned alone, on horseback, through Attica. During my five years' absence, my creditors had sold what little property I had, and I put up at one of the inns in the city, in very simple fashion, for the long weeks which would have to elapse before I could find a new home.

Parrhasius had followed me at a few days' interval. When he heard of my modest habitation, he desired that I should accept no other hospitality than his own, and sent word that he expected me. The next day I called upon him, unaccompanied, to decline his offer.

He lived half-way between the Ceramicus and the Academy, in a palace constructed of marble and bronze, near the small house occupied by Plato. His gardens stretched right down to the blue borders of the Cycloborus, and in the opposite direction, rising towards the road, they surrounded the white building with trees, which served merely for ornament.

Owing to a weakness, surprising in a man of his standing, Parrhasius was ostentatious in the display of wealth. His fortune was enormous, and he saw to it that no one had any doubt about the matter. In addition to this, he extracted its due proportion of delight from every pleasure, and desired to experience continually the freshness of marble, the fine texture of silk, the still more delicate material of virgin flesh, the colour of purple, so appropriate an adornment of the human countenance, and the incorruptible and sunlike quality of gold. For these reasons his house resembled the palace of Artaxerxes.

He welcomed me at the threshold of the great interior court which he used as a studio.

Erect, and draped as usual in his robe of red silk, a fillet like that of some Olympian God upon his forehead, he opened his great arms to receive me. I passed with him into the illustrious apartment, the womb of masterpieces, experiencing a deep emotion at finding myself there once more.

'My Prometheus?' he replied to my question. 'No, I do not feel that it is ripe for execution yet. That fellow Nicostratus requires a certain amount of study, and I foresee that my first conception of the subject will break down as soon as I introduce his figure into it. In a few days we shall see.'

I asked him if he was taking a holiday, but the question showed
how little I knew him. Painting was his very life. Returning from
his journey at midnight, he had begun a picture the following
morning.

'Come,' said he to me suddenly. 'I am glad you have the chance
to see it: that little sketch of mine is a marvel. I have never done
anything finer.'

It was another trait of his character to estimate his own works
at their actual supreme worth, and to understand the admiration
devoted to his great name by the entire population of Greece.

The panel which he had begun rested in a slanting position on
an easel of sycamore wood, whose twin supporting pieces, at the
point where they should have met, curved backwards in the form
of golden swans' necks.

I bent forward respectfully, and perceived a rather peculiar subject,
which, however, did not surprise me in the studio of Parrhasius.

His picture represented a vivid woodland landscape where a
sleeping nymph, arrows in hand, reclined upon her side. A satyr,
stooping before her, was in the act of raising her tunic to the girdle
with an expression of bestial and greedy delight. Behind her, a second
satyr, kneeling, was making a direct assault upon the virgin, without
producing any impression upon her youthful slumbers, which must
have been very profound. Such was the picture.

As I raised my eyes, I perceived a few yards away, lying upon
a bench, the abashed Artemidora between the two Sarmatian
barbarians who had been posing with her for the outline of this
sketch of life in the raw. Parrhasius explained:

'Yes, I am fond of these pictures dealing with intense feeling,
and I do not represent man's desire except at the moment of its
paroxysm, and of its fulfilment. Socrates, who had begun by being
a bad sculptor before becoming a good philosopher, wished to see
me paint the emotion of sexual love in looks and thoughts.* It was
an absurd criticism. Painting is design and colour; it only speaks the
language in gesture, and the most expressive gesture is that from
which its triumph proceeds. I have painted Achilles at the moment
when he is in act to slay. His anger, unexpressed in movement, I
leave to the poet. Still, enough of that, we understand each other.'

---

* There is a slight anachronism here. The year in which these events
took place is stated in the first paragraph of Chapter II to be
that of Plato's death, namely, 347 BC. Socrates was executed in
399 BC, and thus could not have known Parrhasius as an adult.
[Translator's note]

He seated himself before his easel and commanded: 'Recommence the pose.'

At this Artemidora raised her black eyes in our direction, and in a voice which rendered me uneasy, murmured: 'Before him?'

But Parrhasius was not listening. He was singing already. With his thin brush, whose handle was of ivory and hollowed like a reed, he added the last touches to the sketch in order to accentuate still more the purity of its impeccable design. Then two of his young apprentices brought him his instruments.

'As you see,' said he to me, with a smile, 'I no longer paint in distemper. Here are the irons and the wax in accordance with the new procedure. I shall beat these young people of the Sicyonic school on their own ground!'

And actually one would have said, to watch him, that he had always employed the method of Polygnotus which had recently returned to favour. His little wax-boxes were arranged in a small coffer already stained with use. He dipped carefully therein the thin rod, previously heated in the brazier, brought forth a tiny drop of coloured wax, placed it in position, and mixed it with the rest with a sureness of touch that drew from me from time to time a smile of enthusiasm.

As he painted, he told me how the wax was mixed with the colours, and which colours were the right ones, to the exclusion of all the rest. His white came from the island of Melos, that of Samos being too thick. He liked Indian cinnabar, which was more solid and also more costly than that of Ephesus. Flame-coloured sandarac and armenium, with its faint blue tint, were suitable for the habiliments of women. He realized the value of the ivory black recently discovered by the young Apelles, but preferred for his own part the black, easier to mix, which was manufactured, when one could get it, from the burned human bones taken from ancient sepulchres.

The day passed in this way without my noting the flight of the hours, except when Parrhasius gave the order: 'Rest!' and Artemidora, whose blushes deepened as the time wore on, hid her face in her hands.

Towards the end of the day he rose, calling to the apprentices: 'Heat the sheet!'

And turning to me, he said: 'It is done.'

The red-hot sheet, emitting sparks, was brought to him. He seized it by the eyebolt with long-handled pincers and moved it to and fro very slowly above the panel, which lay in a horizontal position. The wax rose to the surface and imprinted on the dry wood the multicoloured life of the picture.

And that is how, between the dawn and the dusk of a single day, the 'Nymph Surprised' of Parrhasius, which is now at Syracuse, was completed.

Parrhasius eyed his work with careless satisfaction, and shaking his beautiful and expressive hand, cried out as though to an audience of a hundred persons: 'Yes! It is an exercise before the battle!'

Inattentively I asked: 'What battle?'

He seemed astonished that I had not understood. With long strides he crossed the room and flung open a door. Nicostratus, in chains, looked up at us. At the sight, Parrhasius drew himself to his full height, and plunging his fingers into his beard, murmured as though to himself alone: 'My battle, as of a god, against this human soul.'

V

I was busy for a whole month at Athens with personal affairs, which prevented me from returning to visit Parrhasius.

The city was in deep mourning since the fall of Olynthus. The slave-market of Chalcis, the sale of an allied people, the scandal and insult offered at the very gates of Attica, was the subject of every conversation, the thought that filled every silence.

We could do nothing against Philip. Crates did not want war, and Demosthenes himself no longer demanded it, but Aeschines, on the way home from the Peloponnese, had met by the roadside flocks of Olynthians being driven like beasts, and it had been enough for him to relate that passage of a host of slaves for the indignation of the populace to be aroused, at his words, against the guilty cities.

One day, worse befell: it was discovered that, in the town itself, one of the citizens was treating an unfortunate Olynthian woman as if she had been a captive. The man was arrested, tried, and condemned to death immediately.

I was alarmed at this, and saw that a similar fate threatened Parrhasius. I left all my affairs to look after themselves, and went down to his palace in order to warn him if there were still time.

Doors were closed and curtains drawn when I arrived before the walls of his house. The slave did not want me to enter, and I had to insist, to show my anxiety, to declare that my business was a matter of life or death to his master. I got in at last, and running down the great empty gallery, lifted the hanging of the doorway.

I shall never forget the slow, grave look that Parrhasius turned upon me when he perceived my entrance. He was painting in an erect position, gigantic before a panel of black wood which was almost the same height as himself. The sky, which was ominous of storm, gave a superhuman aspect to his unusual stature. The serenity of his countenance was such that its characteristics were lost: the very wrinkles had disappeared, as may be observed in the corpses of very old men recumbent in the peace of death.

He did not speak to me nor look at me again. Holding the warm rod between his fingers, he carried the drops of wax between the box and the upright panel with a hand as sure and as steady as if he had created the world with blots of colour.

Then, as I followed his eyes, fixed by turns upon his work and upon a certain spot in the vast room, I perceived the naked and struggling form of Nicostratus, his four limbs spread out upon the hummock of an actual rock, all his muscles standing out in the effort to free himself from the four ropes which bound him.

For a long time I stood there motionless, holding my breath, forgetting what I had come to do and say. My whole attention was absorbed by the marvel of what I saw. My other senses abandoned me, and I had fewer thoughts than one has in a dream.

Suddenly Parrhasius uttered two words, at least I imagined I heard them. The words were: 'Cry out!'

His voice was as calm as his gesture and his face. 'Cry out!' repeated Parrhasius.

Nicostratus burst into a violent fit of forced laughter which shook the room. He exclaimed that he would not! That he was master of his features! That they could not be bound with ropes, like his limbs, to the rock! That he would prevent this picture being painted! Then he foamed at the mouth with rage, uttering a volley of abuse.

Not a line in the countenance of Parrhasius moved. He set down the rod he was holding, took up deliberately another, white-hot from the brazier beside him, and measuring the exact spot where the vulture of his picture was gnawing the liver of Prometheus, he said to a Sarmatian slave:

'Take this. To the right. Under the bottom rib. Touch lightly, without penetrating the skin.'

Nicostratus watched the fellow advance upon him. He managed to smile, but was very pale. The flesh shrivelled, and he did not utter a word. But, in a moment or two, his eyes darkened. A terrible sweat broke out upon his forehead. He began first to shriek, then to moan in a trembling voice, like a little child sobbing.

Parrhasius, impassive, observed the reaction of his features.

How long did it last? I do not remember. I think, until evening. Nor do I know when I had the strength to drag myself from the room, for I was faint from head to foot. At the very moment I passed through the doorway there was a sudden silence, then a voice at the end of the apartment:

'The fool!' cried Parrhasius. 'He died a second too soon!'

When next day it became known in Athens how Parrhasius had achieved the 'Prometheus Bound' which he destined for the Parthenon, a cry of horror arose from the whole city. Crowds swarmed out upon the road that ran beside the Cycloborus, and began to assault the house of the painter, whose doors were closed.

'An Olynthian! A Freeman! Taken by the Macedonian!'

'Prison for his murderer!'

I mingled with the hostile crowd, not in order to save my friend, for I too considered, at that time, that he deserved every punishment that could be devised, and the shrieks of Nicostratus still resounded in my ears. Yet I followed the mob, thrust hither and thither in the tumult, and arrived with it beneath the walls of the besieged mansion.

For a long time the shouts continued. The house seemed dead. Not a slave on the threshold. Not a voice behind the curtains which hung, drawn and motionless, between the columns.

At last two curtains on the first floor were parted, and Parrhasius himself appeared, his arms folded upon his royal robe and his forehead still bound with the sacred fillet.

A storm of shouts arose.

'Assassin! Barbarian! Ally of Philip!' yelled the mob. 'Where is the Olynthian? We will bury him like a victorious general. And for you, poison, poison!'

Parrhasius allowed their anger to escape and to subside. Then seizing, at his feet, by both sides of the panel, the 'Prometheus' which he had just painted, he raised it slowly and as though participating in a religious rite, at first above the balustrade, then above his own head, so that he was concealed by it, and the Work appeared in place of the Man.

An abrupt shock thrilled through the mob, and they came nearer. They beheld a prodigy; the picture of human suffering and of humanity's eternal defeat by pain and death seemed to throb into life above their heads. Before their countless eyes the height of tragic grandeur was unfolded there for the first time. The crowd shuddered. A few men wept. A silence as of a temple spread to the farthest of the multitude, and as the cries of menace attempted to break forth again, a thunderous acclamation extinguished them in a roar that is the voice of Fame.

THE GODS PLAY
FOR HIGH STAKES

Langston Day

This story works as a fine companion piece to 'The Wearer of Purple', as both explore the ancient Greeks' love for, and pursuit of, the artistic ideal. In the previous story it was sculpture – in this one it is music.

I have tried to find out more about the author, Langston Day, but without success and I would be delighted to hear from anyone who has any information. The following story comes from his 1951 collection Magic Casements, *which was highly regarded in its day.*

Glaucon, the father of Lysiteles, lived in a big house near the Itonian Gate which was rather like an ancient college building. A blank wall screened it from the dusty street, but the living-rooms opened on to a sunny courtyard with a family altar in the centre of it. If you went to call on Glaucon you knocked on a lion's-head knocker to arouse the porter, a surly Thessalonian slave, who was usually asleep and snoring like an owl. Waking reluctantly, he would scowl at you through his spy-hole, ready to loose a dog at you if he did not like your looks; but if he recognized you as an acceptable visitor he would unlock the door slowly and with a good deal of noise so as to allow the ladies of the household plenty of time to withdraw to their own quarters.

Naturally it would have been improper for any of the ladies to be discovered by a male visitor. So closely were they guarded that even Euphryne, the mother of Lysiteles, was not allowed to leave the house without Glaucon's permission. A thin, graceful lady with slightly protuberant blue eyes, she spent a great deal of her time fussing over her children, especially Lysiteles who was her favourite. When he was six, Glaucon, who detested fussing unless he was the object of it, sent the boy to live in the men's quarters. This made Lysiteles feel grown up and important, but it scarcely outweighed his chagrin at being separated from Melissa.

Melissa was a first cousin of about his own age whose father had died soon after she was born. Glaucon had added her to his family, which already included a number of poor relations, after marrying off her lovely young mother to a merchant who disliked other people's children. Euphryne thought this cruel of him and dared to tell him so.

'Name of Herakles!' he exclaimed testily, 'am I not the executor of her husband's will, and do men grow on olive trees who are willing to marry a dowerless widow? As for Melissa, she was lucky not to be potted.'

Euphryne sighed, for by 'potted' Glaucon meant 'left out of doors to die.'

'He must be heartless if he won't let his wife keep her own child,' she said. 'And besides, you tell me he is fat. How should I feel, Glaucon, if you were fat and disliked children?'

Her husband's frown disappeared, but he said in what he hoped was a stern tone, 'If I were a conscientious man I should not let you keep *your* children because you pamper them. See that you don't spoil Melissa.'

Euphryne promised that she would not, but by the time Melissa was three, Glaucon was spoiling her so outrageously that she had to speak to him about it.

As for Lysiteles, he was inseparable from her. They played with tops and go-carts and bowled hoops round the courtyard, swung each other on a swing under the veranda and played with the toy animals which Pollixena cut from pomegranate seeds.

Pollixena, the Phrygian slave who was nurse to both of them, could never make up her mind which of them was her favourite. Like most slaves she carried on a brisk retail business in fear and fantasy, and when they were in bed she told them frightening stories about fire-breathing Titans who cooked and gobbled up ship-wrecked sailors, and one-eyed monsters who lived beyond the Pillars of Herakles, with heads which grew from their chests. Glaucon, who was a Hoplite, also told them stories – rather long-winded accounts of his military adventures in the field. One story which he was for ever telling them was of how he had fought a battle against the Spartans and lost it because the enemy were cads enough to form up sixteen deep on the wing instead of eight deep according to the rules of civilized warfare.

But best of all, the children liked Euphryne's stories. Melissa's favourite was the story of Pandora, but Lysiteles liked the one about Orpheus who rescued his wife from Pluto's kingdom but lost her by looking back at the last moment. Melissa, always practical said it was silly of him to look back and he deserved to lose her. They almost quarrelled about it.

When Lysiteles was sent to live in the men's quarters he was so surly and fractious at being separated from Melissa that he was sent to school in the charge of a pedagogue, who acted as male nurse, chaperon and tutor. The older he grew the harder he found it to have any contact with Melissa, and but for Pollixena who acted as go-between he would never have seen her at all.

Melissa, whose mother came from one of the outer islands where convention was not so strict, chafed at being a prisoner in the house; for except when certain festivals came round in which the girls were allowed to take part, she saw nothing at all of the outside world. When with Pollixena's connivance Lysiteles came to see her, she would ask him to describe Athens minutely so that she could actually feel herself walking its streets.

Then he would tell her of the market-place where they sold you anything from a myrtle wreath to a Copaic eel, and where you could see the young dandies bargaining for scents, or a knight-at-arms, sent to market by his wife, making home with a dish of fried eggs in his helmet; the swarthy, trousered Scythian bowmen in their peaked caps who were the city's police; the painted colonnade full of philosophers who argued and expounded like noisy rooks; the gymnasium in which you practised wrestling naked with the other boys under a hawk-eyed trainer who stood ready to lash you with his forked stick; the bustling harbour of the Piraeus where you could talk to men who had sailed to Tyre and fought with pirates, or perhaps see a great trireme breasting grandly into port, to the faint sound below decks of the boatswain's call, 'R-r-rhy-pa-pài-a-pài!' which kept time for the chained oarsmen.

Melissa's eyes would sparkle with excitement. 'I wish I were a Spartan! In Sparta the girls are nearly as free as the boys, aren't they?'

'In Sparta you run away with the girl you want to marry and cut off her hair,' said Lysiteles with a glance at her red-gold curls.

Melissa frowned. 'Euphryne says my mother has hair like mine, and Glaucon married her to a fat, oily merchant from Megara. I expect he'll do the same to me.'

'No he won't. *I* am going to marry you – you know that.'

'Perhaps I shan't want you to. Then I suppose you'll get round Glaucon and he'll threaten me with a fat merchant as the alternative? You be careful, my boy, you don't know what a woman can do to you if you marry her against her will.'

By the time Lysiteles was seventeen he had done with school. In twelve months' time he must begin his two-year term of military service with the *Epheboi*, as the Cadets were called, but meanwhile he was free to enjoy himself.

At school he had made friends with a boy named Cleon who was so handsome that the sculptors took him for a model when he was stripped in the gymnasium. They hunted hares on Mount Hymettos, swam together in the warm, dark blue sea, and speared fish off the rocks. Sometimes they climbed the hills near Salamis and lay down among the cyclamen and the anemones, watching the sun glinting through the pine branches. But best of all they loved staying with Cleo's great uncle, Aristogeiton, who had a farm in the north.

Aristogeiton was old-fashioned and dogmatic, for ever talking of the Golden Age and vowing that Athens was going to the dogs. He wore linen instead of wool, bound up his long hair in a knob with a gold grasshopper pin, and swore with solemn Homeric oaths. He was strict as a priest about observing feasts and sacrifices, but he spoiled the two boys, letting them run wild on his farm. So in the summer they were happy as savages, hunting, snaring birds, riding on the farm wagons, lending a hand with the grape-picking and sometimes joining in the harvest celebrations.

One lovely evening in July Lysiteles said, 'I wish we could stay like this for ever.'

Cleon laughed in his mocking way and said that he had no imagination. When they were Cadets they would have blood horses to ride and fighting cocks to wager on; they would paint the town red with the other young dandies and go to banquets where you drank Chian wine and flirted with saucy flute girls; and perhaps they would have the luck to be in a scrap with the old Spartans.

'That's not what I want to do,' said Lysiteles.

'Zeus, what *do* you want, you old cockerel?'

Lysiteles did not reply.

Cleon made a comical grimace. 'Ehey, you're in love?' Then seeing his friend blush, he asked, 'Who is the lucky wench?'

Lysiteles had never spoken to him about Melissa, but now, suddenly, he felt the need of a confidant. So out it all came – how he and Melissa had been sweethearts almost since their babyhood, how she was as beautiful as Aphrodite, with hair the colour of the sun-shot clouds which gild the sky at sundown.

Cleon raised one eyebrow higher than the other, a trick he had for expressing comical dismay. In the distance they could hear Aristogeiton's slaves shouting 'Pente-hex!' 'Pentethettara!', as they gambled away their week's wages at a game called *Mora*. A young serving maid came with mincing steps and downcast eyes to tell the two handsome young men that supper was ready, and presently they were eating barley cakes, dried figs and curds in the vine-covered porch.

Next morning they went out hunting together, hoping for a hare or two. They carried javelins which both of them threw with skill. But though they tramped all day long until they were many leagues from the farm, not a bird or a beast did they see.

Suddenly as the shadows were beginning to lengthen, up jumped a couple of hares, and to their surprise one of them was jet-black while the other was snow-white. Away flew their javelins and each of them seemed to find its mark; but when Lysiteles ran forward, the white hare which he expected to find dead made off as if wounded. Snatching up his javelin he pursued the creature which gradually gained strength and loped along just out of range.

What a dance it led him! Over hill and plain he ran with the easy swing of limbs made supple by hard training in the gymnasium, but still the hare eluded him, until the sun went out like a snuffled lamp and the quarry vanished in the twilight.

Lysiteles lay down to recover his breath. The light faded quickly, as it does in southern latitudes, and when presently he stood up he realized that he was lost. There was nothing for it but to wait until Apollo drove his fiery chariot into the Eastern sky, but meanwhile he would be as well to find some sheltered nook where he could pass the night. He made his way down into a broad, flat-bottomed valley and soon he came to a temple standing beside a vineyard.

A tall, dignified man whom he took for a priest came forward to greet him and invited him in. There, in the inner court of the temple, a meal awaited him. It was almost as if he had been expected.

As soon as he began eating, the priest withdrew as silently as a cat but when the meal was finished he returned and spoke to him in a reverberant voice which reminded him of the hum of bees. He told him that his name was Menecles and that he was priest in this temple which was dedicated to Dionysos, the god of wine.

Lysiteles was a little surprised to hear this, for the cool walls of Pentelic marble breathed such an air of peace that it was hard to imagine any drunken orgies or wild dances in the moonlight such as he had heard Glaucon describe. Menecles, who seemed to know his thoughts, explained that in this temple Dionysos was worshipped according to the teachings of Orpheus.

Orpheus, he said, had been torn in pieces by the Thracian women just as Dionysos had been destroyed by the Titans. This fate had befallen him after he had lost his wife, Eurydice, in Pluto's kingdom. For many a month he had mourned her loss by the banks of the Strymon river, and in his grief he had avoided womankind, until malicious stories were told of him, and the fierce women of Thrace, resenting the aspersion on their sex, set upon him in a frenzy and tore him limb from limb. But before his death he had written many poems which for those who could understand them explained the mysteries of Heaven and Earth, and now throughout Hellas there were secret communities of Orphics whose religion was very different from that of Dionysos as it was known in public.

It was late when Lysiteles went to bed, and so still it was that he could hear a lizard rustling across the marble floor of the temple court. A white owl which crossed the full moon screeched as loudly as a tinsmith's file.

For a long time he lay awake thinking of what Menecles had said. At last he fell asleep and dreamed a marvellous dream.

He dreamed that Orpheus came to him and sang a song of such piercing sweetness that it melted his very bones. In every cell of his body it echoed, so that it seemed his heart would burst for the joy of it.

And then suddenly he was awake and knew that it was no dream; for Orpheus stood before him in a luminous cloud and the music which came to his ears was a thousand times more real than any that he had heard before. Unlike earthly music which fades and shivers, this music was solid and enduring, yet pure as a mountain spring and more potent by far than the enchantments of Circe.

How long the Singer sang to him he could not tell, for even Time stopped to listen; but at last the magical notes died away in the stillness and the very stones of the temple sighed with grief at their passing.

Then Orpheus spoke, and his voice was like the soft winds which sing through the pine trees. 'Go, Lysiteles,' he said, 'and learn to sing likewise.'

In the morning, Lysiteles awoke in a glow of happiness which puzzled him until, with a feeling well-nigh of awe, he remembered the song of Orpheus. Many years seemed to have passed since the previous day, but the future glowed before him as brightly as the painted palaces of Olympus. He sprang up and hastened to find Menecles.

The old priest listened calmly to his story but did not seem unduly surprised.

'Can it be true that I could learn to sing like Orpheus?' Lysiteles asked him.

'Hellas stands in dire need of such a singer.'

'But who could teach me?'

'It would be necessary to find a singing school, but a school of no ordinary kind.'

'Where may I hope to find it?'

'Men have travelled beyond the Pillars of Herakles seeking such a school, and they have failed to find it.'

These words Lysiteles found rather chilling, nor would the old man give him any advice or encouragement, but left him to eat his morning meal alone. However, when Lysiteles said good-bye and thanked him for his hospitality, Menecles said in his soft voice, 'The Gods work by contraries; if there were no darkness our eyes would lose their keenness.'

In daylight it was easy enough to find the way back, and before noon Lysiteles arrived at the farm where he was welcomed gaily by Cleon and with great relief by Aristogeiton.

'We were just coming to look for you,' said Cleon. 'We expected to find you with a broken leg at least, but you look as happy as a dancing master who has been invited to a banquet.'

Lysiteles hardly heeded the jest but at once told him of what had happened in the temple of Dionysos.

Cleon made a grimace. 'Well, well, what a dream the boy has had!'

'Oh no, Cleon, it wasn't a dream, it was more real than anything that has ever happened to me. I know what I want to do now – I want to sing like Orpheus.'

'Everyone to his taste. Myself I don't care much for music unless the wench who sings is bedworthy.'

Aristogeiton, who had been listening with compressed lips, laid a kindly hand on his shoulder. 'Don't let your head be filled with women's fancies, Lysiteles. There's far too much softness in the young generation. How can we expect to stand up to these Spartans if you young fellows grow effeminate? If I had my way, you would all be called up as soon as you left school. Be content to be a man, my boy, and leave Orpheus and his singing to the priests and poets.'

Lysiteles listened politely, but the old man's words fell on him as drily as autumn leaves; for still the song of Orpheus echoed in his ears with ineffable sweetness and potency.

A few days later he was back in Athens. A slight breath of coldness had blown between Cleon and himself and he longed to confide in Melissa. But arriving home he found his father in the house with a touch of the ague, Pollixena was in one of her surly moods, and it was impossible to arrange a meeting. At last for want of a more understanding hearer he confided in his mother.

Euphryne was alarmed and horrified. These Orphics, she said, were dreadful people with no dignity or self-restraint. They ate raw flesh, indulged in drunken orgies at which the most unspeakable things took place, and she had even heard that some of them were sorcerers who could change themselves into snakes and lizards. This priest was no better than the rest of them, you might be sure, and the vision of Orpheus was certainly the result of an evil spell.

Lysiteles did not argue with her but went to his father and told him of all that had happened.

Glaucon was hardly less dismayed than his wife. 'Learn to sing like Orpheus?' he exclaimed. 'Name of a dog, I never thought to hear a son of mine speak like this! Have you never heard of the doom which awaits the man who flies too high and incurs the envy of the Gods? Moderation in all things, my boy. You can play the *kithara* tolerably well. Be content with that and try to forget this silly dream which was certainly caused by over-fatigue at the end of a long day's hunting.'

Again Lysiteles felt the touch of cold fingers. Something had come between himself and Cleon; Aristogeiton was quite uncomprehending; and now a chilly mist was enveloping his own father and mother because their ears were closed to the music of Orpheus. Suppose Melissa did not understand?

Melissa, when at last he was able to tell her, turned very pale. 'What will you do?' she asked.

'I must find a singing school.'

'In Athens?'

He shook his head.

'Where will you go?'

'How can I tell? I must search.'

Silence fell between them. He looked at her uneasily. 'I *must* go. You do understand, don't you?'

'Yes, I understand,' she replied sadly.

'I won't be away for long. And as soon as I come back we'll get married.'

'If Glaucon doesn't marry me to someone else while you're away.'

'He would never do that. He knows I want to marry you.'

'Will you tell him you are going away?'

'I daren't. He would never understand. He has been giving me an allowance and I've spent hardly any of it. I shall just slip away quietly.'

'When will you go?' she asked in a small voice.

'As soon as I can get a passage on a ship.'

Melissa tried hard to control her lower lip which was trembling; but the thought of his leaving her, perhaps to be put to death by Scythian torturers or eaten alive by dog-faced cannibals with six arms and four legs made her begin to cry.

Lysiteles took her in his arms and stroked her lovely red-gold hair, promising to be back in two years, one year, three months perhaps, and she smiled bravely trying hard to believe him.

The minutes flashed by like shoals of little silver fish. He asked her to give him something which would remind him of her. She snipped off one of her curls, then kissed him and sent him away because it was better to get the parting over as quickly as possible.

Five days later he slipped out of the house at daybreak and boarded a merchant vessel bound for Miletus. Many a month went by and many a long journey he made afoot until at last he came to the ancient city of Memphis, in Egypt, and here he heard of a singing school about which the natives spoke with awe.

It was not hard to find. The school was an ornate temple on the outskirts of the city, and the teacher, a priest named Zedkhonsu, a lean man with hard eyes who claimed to know the secrets of Osiris, Lord of the Underworld. At first he was reluctant to accept Lysiteles as a pupil, but when he heard that he came from a good Athenian family and was able to pay the fees he haughtily consented.

The other pupils were young Egyptians of breeding, with a smattering of Persians and Greeks. The Egyptians wore elaborately curled black wigs, and around their necks brilliant collars of glazed beads. Some had enormous ear-rings of *faïence*; both sexes made up their eyebrows with *kohl* and painted their faces. They had all the aloof contempt of Brahmans and they treated him scornfully because he had no slave to attend him.

Lysiteles found that he was expected to undergo elaborate initiation ceremonies about which he was forbidden to speak under threat of the most terrible doom. Some of these were performed in the caverns beneath the temple foundations in an unknown tongue which Zedkhonsu said was the secret language of the ancient Egyptian priesthood.

The singing classes were held in the great court of the temple and the songs were mostly hymns of Osiris. One of them began:

> 'Praise to thee, Osiris! Thou lord of eternity, king of the gods!
>
> Thou with many names and lordly of being! With mysterious ceremonies in the temples.
>
> He it is that hath the noble ka in Busiris and the abundant sustenance in Letoplis; to whom men shout for joy in the name of Busiris, and that hath many victuals in Helipolis.
>
> Lord of the Great Hall in Hermopolis, and very terrible in Shashotep; lord of eternity in Abydos, that hath his seat in To-zoser.
>
> The firmament and its stars hearken unto him, and the great portals open to him; to whom men shout for joy in the southern sky. The imperishable stars are under his authority, and the never-wearying ones are his place of abode . . .'

All the pupils bellowed in chorus, but the harshness of their voices was drowned in a blare of trumpets and the rattling of siswa.

Lysiteles persevered, but the raucous sounds jarred on his ears and soon he was forced to admit that Zedkhonsu would never teach him to sing like Orpheus. So he left Memphis and once again set out in search of a true teacher, and after many months he heard tell of a Hebrew Prophet named Zaccur who taught singing in the land of Israel. It was a long time before he found him in an open camp in the mountains of Moab.

Zaccur was a grim-looking fellow with long matted hair and a bristling beard, but there was a terrible air of strength about him which gave Lysiteles hope.

'What do you want?' he asked sharply.

'To learn to sing with the voice of a god.'

'Thou heathen idolater! There is but one God – Jahweh, the God of Wrath.'

Lysiteles bowed his head submissively.

'Are you prepared to pay the price?'

Lysiteles began to explain that he had very little money left, but the Prophet interrupted him roughly.

'I do not teach singing for filthy lucre! If you wish to sing like the Angels of the Lord you must abjure money and all that money can buy.'

Lysiteles made no objection to this, and after some further conversation Zaccur sourly agreed to accept him as a pupil.

Then there began for him a life of such hardship as would have shocked a Spartan. All day long and far into the night. Zaccur's pupils were forced to hew great stones from a distant quarry and drag them up into the mountains to build a peculiar square tower without windows, but for what purpose none of them knew. They were given so little food that they scarcely had strength for the task, and they slept naked to the bitter night winds. Twice a month they were compelled to fast and forgo sleep. From time to time Zaccur would retire to a distant mountain-top where he was said to be in communication with Jahweh. On returning he would announce that God was angry with them for their transgressions and demanded some terrible expiation, which varied between floggings with ox-hide whips and searing the flesh with red-hot irons. Speaking was strictly forbidden, and as to singing they received no instructions at all.

One day Lysiteles lost patience and asked when the singing lessons would begin. Zaccur's only reply was a fierce reproof for breaking the rule of silence.

'But if I do not use my voice, how can it be trained?'

'Thou Son of Belial! Until thou canst sing in a manner pleasing to the Lord of Hosts it is a deadly sin to use it.'

At this Lysiteles became exasperated and said he wished to leave the school. Zaccur glared at him like a mountain cat and broke into a torrent of abuse. As he left the mountain he stood with all his pupils and cursed Lysiteles with uplifted hand.

For the third time, Lysiteles set out in search of a school, and after many months he came to the ancient city of Loyang in the Middle Kingdom where he found an illustrious Academy of Singing which was under the patronage of the Emperor. It was housed in a huge building and equipped with such an imposing variety of musical instruments that once again his hopes rose high. The grave Doctors of Music who staffed the Academy received him courteously and when they found that he was likely to be a serious student they admitted him to their classes. But they made him understand that nowhere else in the world did men teach the true Art of Music and that many years of intense study were needed before he could hope to master even the elements of it.

When his studies began he discovered that the sacred rules of Music in their entirety had been fixed for ever in the remote past, and that Music from time immemorial had been under State supervision to guard it against the slightest alteration contrary to ordinance.

Everything about it was orderly and logical. Each of the five notes in the muscial scale meant something matter-of-fact and no other notes were permitted. There were precisely eight sounds in Nature, namely, the sounds of Skin, Stone, Metal, Baked Earth, Silk, Wood, Bamboo and Gourd, and to produce these sounds eight classes of musical instruments had been invented. The sound of Skin, for example, was produced by a giant drum mounted on a pedestal, the sound of Bamboo by a hollowed-out pumpkin with twenty-four bamboo reeds set upright in a half-circle, and the sound of Stone by the *King*, which consisted of sixteen different-sized stones suspended in rows and struck with a mallet. Most of the musical instruments, which were played by blind musicians, were extremely ornate. Some of them were shaped like birds' eggs, writing tablets, or tigers; they were painted in bright colours and adorned with intricate carviings, tassels and ribbons.

Lysiteles had to learn all about the theory of these strange instruments and the ancient legends of their invention. His teachers led him through long mazes of philosophic doctrine which explained how Music was a code of Morality and Statecraft. Only occasionally was there time for a singing class, which usually took the form of chanting some ancient hymn in honour of ancestors. The singers accompanied by a small drum and a table-psaltery with twenty-five strings, chanted slowly and monotonously while the Doctor of Singing constantly interrupted them to explain some small point of musical theory. Lysiteles found it tedious in the extreme.

As the months went by a weariness and a boredom came upon him which slowly extinguished his last spark of optimism. He knew that these Doctors would never teach him to sing like Orpheus. They understood everything about Music except the soul of it, which defied their rules and conventions. So much for his hopes! His money was spent; sadly he decided to return home. His only consolation was the thought of seeing Melissa again.

And so he left Loyang, and many weeks later he reached the coast where with his last handful of obols he bribed the master of a corn ship sailing from Phocaea to take him aboard. After a calm voyage he was back in the Piraeus.

How excitedly he saw again the familiar bustle of the harbour – the garlic-chewing sailors lounging about the quay, the anxious merchants superintending the unloading of their wares, the idle, loafing crowd of onlookers who looked as if they had never done a day's work and never would, the thieves and swindlers awaiting their opportunity, the patient, sweating slaves staggering under immense bales of merchandize! He stood and watched it all in a happy glow of remembrance. But presently his ragged cloak was pulled from behind, and looking round he saw an old school friend who almost in the first breath asked him how he managed to escape service with the *Epheboi*.

He remembered then that if he went home he would at once be conscripted. It was unthinkable, for still the voice of the divine singer echoed in his memory, tugging at his heart-strings as a child pulls at his mother's skirts. He must have time to think. So quickly changing his mind he set out for Aristogeiton's farm. There he would be sure of a welcome, and for a few days at least he would be safe from the officers of the city.

Once again he took the road north, and because his purse was empty, hunger gnawed at him like a wolf. An empty stomach and a heavy heart are bad travelling companions, and several times he was on the point of turning back for Athens and the well-remembered house by the Itonian Gate. On the evening of the third day he was weak from hunger and in a gloomy mood about Aristogeiton who would have no sympathy with his desire to escape military service; but just as he was looking for a sheltered spot in which to pass the night, a hare jumped up at his feet – a snow-white hare!

This time he threw no javelin, nor had he the strength to run; but the hare loped slowly along and it led him straight to the temple of Dionysos.

There, standing at the entrance, was Menecles. He smiled a welcome, as if they had parted only the day before, and without a word led him inside where a meal was already prepared, which he left him to eat alone. When he returned, Lysiteles told him of all that had happened, but even as he was speaking he had the feeling that it was no news to the old priest.

'So now you will give up the search and return home?'

'No,' said Lysiteles, 'I want to sing like Orpheus.'

'But it is necessary to find a singing school, my son.'

'I will work until I have earned some more obols, and then I will set out again.'

The bright blue eyes of the priest rested on him for a moment. 'If you are willing to learn from me, I will teach you.'

Lysiteles was astounded. 'Can *you* teach me to sing? By the Gods, why did you not tell me this before?'

'Not until you have known false teachers can you value a true one. Sleep now for there are many hard tasks before you, each one harder than the Labours of Herakles.'

Without another word the old man left him, and in a very short
time Lysiteles was asleep.

Next morning the lessons began. 'Before it is possible to train
your voice,' Menecles explained, 'you must train your ears. It is
necessary for you to hear one thousand times more keenly than
the wild creatures, and to do this you must learn to close your ears
at will to all the common sounds which deaden your hearing. But
this is extremely hard.'

The months went by and Lysiteles was an apt pupil. After one
year he could hear a worm crawling through the grass. After two
years an ant's footsteps were audible to him as it ran along the
sunbaked earth. At the end of three years his ears were so keen
that they could catch the faint swish of the tiniest water-beetles as
they swam at the bottom of a pool, and even the subtle harmonies
of growing things.

Menecles was satisfied with his progress and began to teach him
to sing.

'When ordinary men sing,' he said, 'their voices are marred by
disharmonies which their ears cannot discern because they are too
gross. But you have ears which are keen, and they will teach you
to sing with purity. Yet to sing one perfect note is a task ten times
harder than the one you have accomplished, and you must work
ten times as fast. For tasks such as these make demands on the
gods, who unlike mortals cannot waste their time. Three years only
are allowed for this labour.'

Once again Lysiteles set to work. He worked with ten times his
former zeal and energy, obediently following the instructions of
his teacher, and when three years had passed he could sing a note
of such sweetness and perfection that the Orphic community who
worshipped at the temple listened to him entranced and the birds
flew close to hear him.

'That is well done,' said Menecles, 'but now comes the hardest
task of all. Your voice is a fitting instrument, and through you the
gods may one day sing the Songs of the Immortals as in days gone
by they sang through the lips of Orpheus. But this they cannot do
save by the power of Dionysos.'

Lysiteles was puzzled, and for once Menecles, usually so reticent,
explained what he meant. Long ago Zeus, King of Heaven, sent
his infant son, Dionysos, to rule over the gods. But in those
days there were giants upon Earth named Titans who lured the
child away, tore him to pieces and devoured him. Then Zeus
in a great rage destroyed those giants with a thunderbolt, and
from the smoking remnant of their brood sprang the human race,

which because the Titans swallowed the infant god is half evil, half divine.

So if Lysiteles wished to sing the Songs of the Immortals he must subdue the Titan blood in himself and enable Phanes, the Shining One, to shine through him as light shines through an untroubled pool. But this was a task one hundred times harder than the previous one, and he must work one hundred times as hard. Nor could he succeed alone. The Orphic community must help him to mature just as the roots, the stem and the leaves of a grape-vine help the grapes to ripen.

For the third time Lysiteles set to work and very quickly he knew that the priest had not exaggerated. The task was so difficult that many times he was in despair. Usually he seemed to work alone, but at such moments, Menecles was always at hand to warn him that if he failed, his failure would be shared by the whole community, for of what use is a vine if its grapes do not ripen? Then for shame he would continue the struggle, though his heart was sinking. Little by little the Titan blood in his veins became less opaque, until at last the Shining One shone through him like pure sunlight. When he sang now the singer was not Lysiteles but the gods themselves; hearing him the clouds stood still in the Heavens and the wind died away in a breathless hush.

Then Menecles told him that that the time had come for him to return to the outside world and use his voice to kindle the spark of Dionysos which slumbers ever in the hearts of men, though their deeds are the deeds of the Titans. For there were nights of darkness when the gods withdrew themselves from mankind, and days of hope renewed when the gods returned and spoke through the lips of mortals.

'Even the gods,' he said, 'are not omnipotent, for in their dealings with men they must use weak human instruments. They play for high stakes, and there is sorrow in Olympus when the game is lost, and calamity for the human tool which has failed.

'There is one thing more,' he concluded. 'A new life begins for you and all ties with your former life must be severed. If anything binds you to your former life, destroy it, for nothing must turn you from your purpose.'

Lysiteles bowed his head and obediently threw away a coin with a hole in it which Pollixena had given him for luck on his tenth birthday, and a gold ring wrought in the shape of two intertwined serpents, a present from his mother. But when it came to the lock of Melissa's hair which he wore always next his heart he could not bring himself to part with it immediately, and so from day to day he put off the evil moment until the resolution to throw it away faded from his mind.

He was very sad at leaving, for the Orphic community had become dearer to him than brothers; but who that possessed the voice of a god could be sad for long? Setting out for Athens one bright morning in Spring, he came to a wood where a great many birds were nesting, and sitting down on a tree stump he sang them a Song of Air.

The piercing sweetness of his song echoed through the trees and presently the whole wood was hushed to silence. Forgetting their nests, the birds came close to him. One by one they flew down and gathered about him in a charmed circle, and so long as he sang to them they were still and silent as spirits summoned by an enchanter. When his song was ended, fear returned to them and they flew away, but he sang a song and once more they came to him. Gradually they lost their timidity and perched confidingly on his head, his shoulders and his outstretched arms.

Then he sang a Song of Earth, and the hares, the moles, the foxes and the badgers drew near to him, forgetting their mutual enmities and mistrusts. He sang a Song of Water, and the myriads of creatures which swim in pools and rivers rose to the surface to hear him. Lastly, he sang a Song of Fire, and the great dragons and salamanders which dwell in the subterranean fires stirred their shining coils so that the Earth shook and all Nature trembled in ecstasy.

So he travelled in unhurried ease and as he sang, the bitter mistrust which divides mankind from the warm embrace of organic life gradually lost its sharpness and all Nature stirred, as a young bride stirs at her lover's touch.

When early one morning he came to Athens, he saw that something was afoot. Groups of men stood talking excitedly at the street corners, and he heard a water-carrier say that the signal was hoisted on the Pnyx, the flat space cut in the slope of the hill just beyond the market-place. Lysiteles followed the broad stream of people who were moving out from the city chattering and gesticulating like the true democrats they were. Two thousand years ago, Time, the modern dictator, was an easy-going patriarchal monarch. The crowd sauntered along and grouped itself in a crescent round the projecting slab of limestone, called the Bema, which served as an orator's platform. Lysiteles looked about him curiously. Here and there he saw a familiar face, but twelve years had passed since he first left Athens and no one recognized him.

Now fifty councillors in white robes, representing the Council of Five Hundred, came slowly over the crest of the hill and took their places above. A herald, speaking with a curiously mannered accent, shouted to the crowd to move forward, and along came another procession led by a priest whose acolyte bore the corpse of a little black pig. This procession made a circuit of the crowd, sprinkling blood as it passed along and so drawing a hallowed ring round the Athenian Parliament. A party of young rakes who looked as if they had been up all night jeered at this ancient ceremony and made noises like a litter of young pigs squealing.

An aged member of the Council whose beard wagged as he spoke announced in quavering accents that sacrifices had been made with successful results, at which the young men cheered ironically; and after certain dry formalities to which the audience paid not the least attention, the herald called out 'Who wishes to speak?'

There was a sudden hush as a tall man muffled up in a heavy red cloak and with a wide-awake hat over his long, unkempt hair, pushed his way through the crowd and mounted the platform. He was the spokesman of some Spartan envoys and in his rough dialect, which sent the young men into fits of laughter, he read a speech from his king pleading for peace with Athens.

It was difficult to hear what he said, for some applauded loudly, while others jeered and hooted. Tempers flared up and noisy quarrels broke out among the audience who were about equally divided. Then the Spartan envoy, looking bewildered, stood down and up jumped a little man on to the Bema, one of those mob orators now so common in Athens, who pandered to the war profiteers. He shouted, waved his arms and slapped his thighs in a most vulgar way. Soon he had the crowd in a ferment, and when he stood down there were angry cries against Sparta. The peace-mongers were shouted down.

But during the last speech Lysiteles had been edging his way forward, and now he climbed the steps cut in the rock and stood facing the people who stared at him with idle curiosity.

He began to sing. He sang a song of the Golden Age, a song which told how the gods came down from Olympus and dwelled on Earth, and all men lived in happiness; but how in the course of time the Titan blood rose in mankind so that the gods could no longer remain with them, and how on their departure the land came to be filled with bitterness, sorrow and strife.

As the last enchanted notes died away every man sat transfixed. Slowly the multitude stirred like men awakening from a dream. They looked about them and felt the warmth of human affection; they stared at the Spartan envoys and were unable to understand how they could have wished for war. One of the councillors rose and spoke a few stumbling words proposing a friendly reply to the embassy, and a great shout of approval went up from the crowd, which laughed, wept and cheered all at the same time.

As soon as his song was ended, Lysiteles stepped down from the Bema and passed quickly through the throng, which made way for him as if he had been a god. But as he walked between the gaping ranks he felt his cloak pulled from behind, and turning round he saw his own father.

Tears stood in Glaucon's eyes and for some moments he could not speak. But an Athenian could no more be silent for two minutes than a magpie, and suddenly the words gushed from him in a torrent.

Name of a Name! Where had Lysiteles been all these years? And where had he learned to sing like this? He himself had never been much of a one for music – soldiering was more in his line – but by Apollo, he had never heard singing like *this* before! Zeus strike him, it made him feel quite peculiar, as if the solid earth were giving way under his feet. It had shaken him. He had been all for sending those Spartan boors about their business, but now, by Pluto, he was not so sure about it. Archidamos wanted a friendly settlement. Name of a dog, perhaps he was right. And what a fine looking fellow Lysiteles had become! Euphryne would hardly recognize him. How she had worried about him all these years. Little else she had had to think about lately, for their children were fledged. His sisters were both married, yes, and to good husbands too. Trust his old father to manage things well.

'And Melissa?' Lysiteles asked with a sinking heart.

'Ah, Melissa. She's married to that young fellow who was such a friend of yours. What's his name? Cleon, son of Kallias. He asked me for her just after you disappeared. His father's dead now and he has a fine house in Tripod Street. She's a lucky girl is Melissa.'

Among a people so quick-witted and impressionable as the Athenians the singing of Lysiteles was naturally the talk of the town, and when on the next day he was seen in the streets a crowd quickly gathered about him and shouted for him to sing to them again.

He sang a Song of Phanes, the Shining One, whose warmth and radiance is in every heart, though the dark clouds of human passion obscure his light; and for a second time the magical notes sank into their very bones and the light of Phanes dispelled their sorrows like an Arctic sunrise. While he sang they were filled with unutterable happiness and so long as the faintest echo of his songs rang in their ears not one of them could feel the envy, malice and fear which poison the lives of men.

The singing of Lysiteles became a daily event and the force of it was so great that to this day men speak of the light which shone from Hellas in the time of her glory. News of his singing spread quickly to the islands and to the farthest boundaries of the mainland. It was reported in Cnossos and Syracuse and even noised abroad in Italy and round the shores of the Black Sea. Many a traveller braved the perils of shipwreck and of brigands in the hills to make his pilgrimage to Athens, and none who heard the Songs of the Immortals could ever quite forget the magic of them until the day of his death.

So Lysiteles sang and was happy in the knowledge that his last and greatest task had begun; but deep down in the innermost core of his mind was a dark feeling which he could never wholly uproot. In all these years the memory of Melissa had not faded, and although he had known she was powerless in Glaucon's hands yet he had clung to the hope that she would be free to marry him when he returned. Glaucon's news had shattered this illusion with a terrible bitterness. Not only was Melissa married, she was married to Cleon, the friend of his youth, who, knowing that they loved one another, had hardly waited for him to be gone before seizing her! At one stroke he had lost the two beings whom he loved best of all.

One day he happened to meet Pollixena, who had followed Melissa into Cleon's household. The old woman stopped dead and stared at him in comical confusion, torn between her love for him as a child and her awe of him as the divine singer. Lysiteles laughingly embraced her, whereupon she burst into tears, and then, quickly recovering, talked torrentially in her rough Phrygian brogue.

Cleon, she told him, was a gay young cavalry captain and a leader of the notorious band of rakes named the Triballi. Eh, but he was a one to paint the town red! If you mentioned his name the night-watchmen would tremble, and the *hetairai* told tales of him which you could not possibly repeat. All the same he was very fond of Melissa, although to be sure she had borne him no children, and Melissa was fond of him, as well she might be considering the behaviour of some disappointed husbands who should be nameless. Had she forgotten Lysiteles? Who could say. After her marriage she, Pollixena, had been forbidden ever to mention his name again. And quite right too, perhaps, when a young man disappears in the night like a fox without so much as saying good-bye and after arousing expectations, as you might say, and is never seen or heard of again for twelve years, though a poor woman might be crying her eyes out for a word from him . . .

Lysiteles felt his heart beating fast, and suddenly he asked Pollixena to arrange a meeting between them as she had so often done in the past. Melissa was a married woman now; surely it was possible for her to meet him, perhaps in one of the temples?

Pollixena protested violently, just as she had always done. Lysiteles continued to coax her, until at last she threw down the handful of obols which he had slipped into her hand, declaring that even slaves did not sell their honour for money; then briskly picking them up again she said she would think it over and meet him again at the same time and place on the following day. But next morning when Lysiteles came to the rendezvous, Pollixena told him that Melissa had turned very pale on receiving the message and had bidden her tell him that he must think of her as one who was dead.

Lysiteles was so sick at heart that he almost wished that Melissa really was in Pluto's kingdom, for then her tie with Cleon would be broken, and like Orpheus he might find his way to the Underworld and bring her back. But however bitter his sorrow, he had his fourth great task to perform. Day after day he sang to the Athenians, and while he sang his heart was lifted high above human sorrows; but in the long nights the lock of Melissa's hair which lay always against him seemed to scorch his skin, and because of this unbroken tie with his boyhood the light of Phanes would grow dim and his heart groped in the twilight.

Men were coming now to hear him sing from the very edges of the world, and there was a feeling of enormous possibilities, as when the February sun stirs the sleeping seeds. The poets and the dramatists walked in an Indian summer of inspiration, the philosophers saw eternal meaning in the very stones, and even the flowers and the trees responded to the songs of Lysiteles with a new and delicate flowering. Yet, such is the paradox of human nature, the giver of so much gladness was obsessed with a torturing sorrow. Every thought led him to Melissa, and at last he sent for Polixena and with great difficulty persuaded her to deliver a note to his beloved in which he implored her to send him a message, even if it were but a few words of farewell.

They arranged to meet again as before, but when he came to the meeting-place on the following morning, instead of Pollixena he found Cleon, very tall and elegant in a gold-bordered *chlamys*. Once and once only had Cleon heard Lysiteles sing, and the effects of his singing were profoundly disturbing to a young man of his stamp who scoffed at the poets and the philosophers and who jeered at singing as 'Egyptian', which was a byword for anything archaic. This fellow, he felt, was thoroughly dangerous with that extraordinary voice of his which sapped the military morale, so whenever Lysiteles sang, the Triballi plugged their ears and jeered at the singer, nicknaming him the 'Chorus Boy' and spreading rumours that he was in the pay of the Spartans.

Luck was with Cleon for on the previous day he had intercepted the letter to Melissa. Raising one eyebrow in the old mocking way, he greeted Lysiteles with elaborate courtesy pretending that he was overwhelmed by the invitation which had evidently been addressed to Melissa by mistake.

Lysiteles tried hard to control his rage and escaped from him as soon as he could, but from that hour the hostility towards him grew more quickly. A political faction was formed to work against him, and among the young men of spirit it became the fashion to say that Lysiteles was a Nine Days' Wonder for military shirkers and stone-deaf philosophers. At last the feeling against him rose so high that even Glaucon began to look at him uneasily. And so he made preparations to leave Athens and sing to the men of other cities. He arranged to sail to Corinth, but on the night before he sailed, as he lay tossing sleepless in the midsummer heat, an idea came to him with the suddenness of inspiration: he would go to Cleon's house and sing Melissa a Song of Farewell.

It was still and pitch dark, with a feeling of thunder in the air, as he groped his way to the house in Tripod Street. Arriving there, he walked slowly up and down under the blind wall which screened the house from view. The thought of Melissa so very near, yet for ever held apart from him by a relentless fate was bitter as gall. Did she love him still? Who could say. Yet at least it was in his power to let her know that his love for her burned as brightly as in the days gone by. Lifting up that magical voice of his he sang a Song of Farewell, a song which would have softened the heart of a Scythian savage, and the very stars in Heaven wept for the sweetness of it.

The last lovely notes died away on the stillness and there fell a silence deep as death. Had she heard him? Lysiteles listened – listened with ears sensitive to sounds so faint that magnified a thousand times they would yet have been inaudible to the ears of a fox. And from somewhere behind the frowning wall he heard Melissa sobbing and uttering his name in a broken whisper.

Then the light of Phanes flickered and expired, and the dark blood that was dormant in him coursed like a river which breaks its banks; and lifting up his voice again he sang a terrible Song of the Titans, calling down curses on Cleon and violently entreating Melissa to leave him. No words can describe one whit the volcanic force of it. The brutal urgency of a thousand war trumpets and all the passion and ferocity of the African jungle was in his song.

Everywhere within earshot men stirred in their sleep and awoke, feeling the hot blood throbbing in their veins.

Melissa lay still, her heart pounding like a mill-wheel, and suddenly she sprang up and ran down into the courtyard, but the outer gate was locked and the door-keeper had left with the keys of it. The song drew her like the traces of a war chariot and she wrenched at the gate crying aloud like a soul in Tartaros. The slaves of the household awoke, and running down to her some of them tried to lead her away. But she fought with the strength of an Indian tiger and their united force could not overpower her.

As a stone thrown into a pool raises ripples which spread in ever widening circles, the confused uproar spread quickly over the city. Dogs barked and howled, men shouted, and presently doors opened and people ran out into the streets. Rumours of a sudden calamity flew from house to house and soldiers stood to arms believing that an enemy was upon them. Fear gripped Lysiteles, and he went quickly home. But the echo of those cruel notes tore wolfishly at Melissa, and she raved and fought with such maniacal strength that it was a long time before she could be subdued, and on Cleon's orders, she was lashed to her bed with cords.

Of this Lysiteles knew nothing, for at daybreak he boarded a ship and sailed for Corinth, where huge crowds were gathered on the quay to welcome him. They hung garlands about him and led him in a triumphal procession to the Craneion; and on the steps of the Temple of Aphrodite he stood and faced the immense audience which had come to hear him sing.

He raised his hand for silence and a hush fell on the multitude. He looked at the sea of faces but felt no warmth of human affection, for the sobs of Melissa were still in his ears and the light of Phanes was dead. A storm was blowing up from the south and lightning cracked menacing fingers across the sulky sky.

And then he began to sing, and for a few moments he heard a voice which was so little like his own that it seemed to come from another's throat. It was cracked and toneless as a broken lute, and it trailed off into a dismal silence. The crowd gaped at him as crowds will. Suddenly from the black clouds which were massing overhead there came a blinding flash and a thunderbolt struck the temple. With loud cries of terror his audience fled.

Then Lysiteles felt a darkness within him like the darkness of the Underworld and all Nature wept with a sorrow more bitter than the sorrows of mankind. The rising wind groaned and the trees bowed their heads in mourning like a young bridegroom bereaved.

In utter dejection he returned to Athens, where he met Pollixena, who cried aloud on him like a sybil and told him that Melissa had never ceased to struggle and cry his name until death had mercifully put an end to her suffering. Cleon was now raising a great outcry against him and the fickle mob were calling for his blood.

The news of Melissa's death fell on Lysiteles like a bolt from Zeus, and in despair blacker than the Pit of Acheron he left Athens hurriedly and set out in search of the Temple of Dionysos. But this time no white hare sprang up at his feet to guide him and it was many a long day before he found it. Nor was this the end of his sorrow for he found the temple deserted. There he stayed none the less, hoping for death yet unwilling to take his life in case he might find means of expiation. In a little while the vine-dressers, taking him for a new priest, began to bring him offerings of food which saved him from starvation. And so once again he took up his abode at the temple – a temple silent and dark from which the life-spark had been withdrawn.

What heartfelt prayers he offered up to Dionysos that Phanes might return to him so that he could sing again! For many years his prayers remained unanswered, but one day as he walked sadly by the valley stream he became aware of the lock of Melissa's hair which still hung about his neck, and with a great wrench he tore it off and threw it into the water. At once to his great joy a faint spark glowed within him and he found that he could whistle a few bars of the Immortal Songs.

On making this discovery he went into the woods and whistled some notes of surpassing sweetness; and presently the birds gathered round him, just as they had done before, perching on his head, his shoulders and his outstretched arms. For several days he remained there, unconscious of hunger in his unbounded happiness; and as the days went by there came to him an idea – the idea of teaching the birds to sing.

Even to tell of how he did this would be a Labour of Herakles for it was a task which called for unending patience, and long before it was done he had lost count of the years.

Only a few of the birds were teachable. Those with gay plumage were too vain to learn, and the large ones were too slow in their wits. Others were too idle, and dilatory, and none of the sea birds came his way. The magpie and the jay listened to him in mere idle curiosity, the green woodpecker laughed at him, and the cuckoo having mastered two notes was so pleased with himself that he flew away convinced that he was the king of songsters. So he gave lessons to only a few of the birds, and to each one of them he taught a fragment of the Songs of the Immortals.

To the thrush he taught a ballad of fresh spring buds, and to the blackbird a lay of warm summer showers. The whitethroat learned a carol of may blossom, and the willow wren a song of dancing sunbeams.

But his aptest pupil was the little brown nightingale which never tired of learning and would practise all the night through. To the nightingale he taught a tiny fragment of the Song of Farewell, and to this day from some copse or thicket you may catch a faint, diminished echo of the notes that bewitched poor Melissa and made her sob and whisper in the stillness of the night.

THE HORSE
FROM THESSALY

Mary Renault

Alexander succeeded to the throne of Macedonia in 336 BC. He was to become the first great Commander of Empires, ruling a world which stretched from the Mediterranean to the Indian Ocean. Almost as famous as Alexander was his horse Bucephalas, which Alexander had tamed in his youth and which accompanied the king on his conquests. The horse died in northern India in 326 BC, and Alexander founded a city, Boukephale, in its memory. Mary Renault (real name Mary Challans, 1905–83), recreated the world of Alexander in her trilogy Fire from Heaven *(1970),* The Persian Boy *(1972) and* Funeral Games *(1981). In the following pages she concentrates on the story of Alexander's horse.*

In the year 343 BC, or thereabouts, a Thessalian horse-coper called Philonicus rode north over the passes, on a business trip, to Pella in Macedon.

Thessaly with its well-watered uplands had been the horse-pasture of Greece time out of mind. Its autocratic tribal chiefs rode before they walked, and disdained to put foot to ground, except indoors. Every kind of horse had its breeders there: fast ponies for racing chariots; race-horses; high-steppers for processions; war-horses broke to noise, up to the weight of an armoured man, and trained to leave him a free hand for sword or spear. One of these last, Philonicus had with him.

Greek bloodstock owners practised random breeding, within carefully hand-picked herds. Such strains were distinguished by a brand-mark, often of wide renown. A horse-dealer who could make good in Thessaly was in business anywhere. This was true of Philonicus, since the buyer he had in mind for his charger was King Philip II.

History says no more of Philonicus. About the horse we know rather more.

'In stature he was tall,' Arrian records, 'and in spirit courageous. His mark was an oxhead branded on him, and hence his name Bucephalas. Others, however, say he had a white mark on his head – the rest of him being black – which was just like an oxhead.' Very likely he had both.

How tall his stature really was, it is hard to say, since Greek breeds were small by today's reckoning; give or take a little, perhaps fifteen hands. Philip's portrait-head shows a stocky, solid build; he would have needed a good weight-carrier, though in the event this virtue was never tested. Certainly the horse must have been highly trained in the disciplines of his calling, for he was expensive, though nearly twelve years old.

This is the more remarkable, in that the Greeks disliked buying horses once they had lost their milk teeth; the veteran Xenophon, in his treatise *On Equitation*, strongly advises against it. One would question the age, but for the consistency of the records, and the fact that Arrian's source Ptolemy, later to found the dynasty which ended with Cleopatra, was a close connection of the Macedonian royal family – some say a bastard son of Philip's adolescence – and knew the horse's future owner from birth till death.

Accepting the age, however, one can hardly credit the asking price. Plutarch puts it at thirteen talents; which, allowing for purchasing power then and now, has been reckoned to equal about £25,000.

Life-expectation of Philip's war-horses was notoriously short. Still under forty, he was already seamed with war-scars. One eye had been blinded by an arrow, one leg lamed by a spear; he had had a badly broken collar-bone; we hear of one horse at least, probably two, having been killed under him. Evidently, he would value a steady, dependable mount; but this seems a pretty steep price to pay for it.

There may, however, be an explanation for the legend. Earlier in his reign, a racehorse of his had brought him the immense prestige of a win at the Olympic Games. Greek only by remote descent and regarded by southern Greeks as semi-barbarous, the kings of Macedon had barely scraped their way into the Olympic entry-list, which was open to Greeks alone. In spite of frequent snubs, Philip was almost touchingly philhellene; the victory had so elated him that he had had the horse put on his coinage. Then as now, a racehorse of this quality could well have changed hands at Plutarch's figure. This single remembered fact about it may have attached itself, over the generations, to a successor of more lasting fame.

News of the Olympic win had reached the King on a red-letter day. Before its sunset, two more couriers had come in. One announced that his general, Parmenio, had routed the troublesome Illyrians. The third message was from his Palace. His young Queen, Olympias, a beautiful Epirote princess whom he had courted on impulse after a chance meeting at a shrine, had been delivered of a healthy boy.

Some thirteen years had passed since these events. Philip had won no more Olympic races, but several more wars, and half a dozen more wives. Polygamy was a Macedonian royal prerogative. The wives were of minor rank; but Olympias, a proud and violent woman, found them an unforgivable affront, and a threat to the succession for her adored and only son. She had become the King's inveterate enemy. For years the boy had been torn between them, fought over and trampled in their wars like some disputed battle-standard. He had survived, on his own terms. If he carried deeper scars than his father's, they were out of sight. When Philonicus arrived, he was there to see the horses; quick-moving, restless, with grey eyes and red-gold hair; small for his age, though hardy; precocious and temperamental, with looks that favoured his mother.

In due course, the dealer produced his show-piece, the black horse with the white blaze. Philip eyed his points approvingly, and asked to see him work.

What paces he had been meant to show the King, we shall never know. From Xenophon's treatise we can conjecture some of them. Nearly a millennium had still to pass before some ingenious Celt invented stirrups; meantime, even to mount, a man needed much co-operation from his horse. Xenophon recommends that, if tractable enough, it should be taught to kneel, but that a horseman should be able, at need, to mount in the normal way: that is, if armed with a spear, he should take it in his left hand, along with the lead-rope, which would not be dispensed with till he was up; his right hand should grasp the reins, and the mane above the withers; he should then use the spear to vault. If unarmed, with the left hand free, he should use it to grip the mane between the ears. And he must try to take off with a good spring so as to keep his right leg straight; thus he would not 'offer an unseemly sight from behind' (Greek riding-tunics were short). The good soldier, prepared for all emergencies, would practise mounting on the off side as well as the near. As a last resort, when wounded or very elderly, he could train a groom to give him a leg-up in what Xenophon slightingly describes as 'the Persian way'.

Saddles were as far ahead as stirrups. Men rode either bareback or on a soft saddlecloth, using seat-bones and thighs to direct the horse, the feet hanging free except when using the spur. When the rider is up, says Xenophon, the horse should stand quiet while he gets the edge of his tunic out from under him, and transfers his spear to his right hand; to balance it, the horse should be trained to lead with the near leg. It should be worked across rough country, and over the natural jumps there; when jumping, or on steep slopes, the rider should grasp the mane, to ease the bit. (Good reasons for this injunction, besides the fear of falling off, will soon appear.)

The cavalryman whose horse has been trained thus to jump and scramble, should then accustom it to warfare, first by taking it through crowds, then by mock-duelling with a friend, casting blunted javelins, closing and wrestling, each man trying to unseat the other. But an officer, Xenophon points out, must aim at possessing a 'brilliant horse' which will do him credit at parades, though not all will have the needed qualities: 'you must have one naturally endowed with greatheartedness of spirit and strength of body'. Only such a horse was likely to be offered to King Philip. 'A curvetting horse is a thing so admirable that it captures the eye of all beholders, both young and old.' The black horse called Oxhead had probably had schooling, then, in airs above the ground.

The King, his party, and the dealer waited expectantly to see him justify his price by executing some, or most, of these manœuvres. Philip, with a game leg, would certainly be interested in the kneeling trick. He was to be disappointed. 'They went down into the plain', says Plutarch, 'to try the horse; but he was found to be so very vicious and ungovernable, that he reared up against all who tried to mount him, and would not so much as endure the voice of any of Philip's attendants.'

This was a highly priced animal, brought some distance for an important sale. Either he was, after all, an unbroken colt, and all the histories are wrong by ten years, which is unlikely; or something had lately happened to him. What it was, again we shall never know. Perhaps a wolf or leopard had frightened him on the way. It seems, however, that the enemy he loathed was man.

'The one best precept and custom', says Xenophon with emphasis, 'in treating the horse is: Never lose your temper. For anger is without foresight, and often does things which later will cause regret.'

Xenophon, however, for his day, was an exceptionally humane and patient horseman. 'If you ever wish to treat a good war-horse so as to make him more splendid and showy to ride, you must avoid pulling at his mouth with the bit, and spurring and whipping him, by which behaviour most people think they make their horses brilliant. For these people get results the very reverse of what they aim at.'

Some teach the curvetting action, he says, 'either by striking the horse with a rod under the hocks, or by having someone run alongside with a stick and hit him on the quarters. But I consider, as I keep saying, that the best training is to give the horse some relaxation whenever he does as the rider wishes.' What sort of grace, he asks, would one expect from a human dancer, if he were taught by whipping and spurring? With the spirited horse, he goes on to warn, one must especially be careful, for 'spirit is to a horse what anger is to a man'.

Someone, perhaps Philonicus himself, perhaps one of his men, may have neglected Xenophon, or thought his methods soft. Someone, in drunkenness or aggression (the sort of person who now overtakes on a blind rise) may have roused rebellion in the black horse, and with the sale so near had been in a hurry to enforce submission. He had got, if so, the reverse result.

For a spirited horse, Xenophon advises, a smooth bit is better than a rough. He speaks advisedly. Not for nothing, among the easel-painters of the time, was blood and foam on a horse's mouth a regular artistic convention. The 'rough' bits have to be seen to be believed in. Spiked rollers; barbed cheek-pieces squeezing the lips; projections of iron or bronze pulling up into the roof of the mouth; chain-bits with toggles in them; a collection of these things is an equine chamber of horrors. In the absence of the control which stirrups and saddle-tree give today, almost nothing human cruelty could devise had been left unused to curb a recalcitrant horse. This one, if he had been giving trouble before the sale, would certainly have a rough bit on, and probably a severe one.

The struggle to mount him continued vain. The royal party looked on; the King in growing impatience, the boy in growing distress. 'Spirit is to a horse what anger is to a man.' To the end of his short life, the intolerable tensions of his childhood, suppressed under a powerful self-control, would find release at long intervals in bursts of concentrated rage. Anger is without foresight, and does things which later will cause regret.

Meantime, Philip had had enough. He 'ordered the horse to be led away, thinking him entirely wild and unbroken'. It was at this point that the boy became difficult.

The King at first ignored his protests, which were impertinent; a boy of thirteen should not call out before his elders that a great horse is being lost for want of skill to handle him. However, 'he kept saying things like this, and seemed very much upset'. At length, in some exasperation, his father asked if he was finding fault with older people, in the belief that he could do better. 'I could with this horse,' he said.

Philip decided to take him up on it. It seems a risky challenge; but out of several successive Kings of Macedon, only one had died in bed; danger was a family way of life. The boy accepted with alacrity; if he won, the horse was to be his own. But, his father reminded him, this was a wager. What was *his* stake going to be? He answered, 'I'll pay the whole price of the horse.'

(This seems to dispose beyond doubt of the thirteen talents. He had been strictly brought up by a draconian tutor, who forbade not merely luxuries but even comforts. Any allowance he was getting at thirteen is most unlikely to have been of such an order.)

In any case, he had now ensured that he would own the horse, whether or not he mastered it. He was not one as a rule to cherish reminders of failure. It must have been love at first sight.

He may already have known his Xenophon, as he certainly did later, at any rate the *Persian Expedition*, and the *Life of Cyrus*, which seems to have been his bible next after Homer. But, whether or not he had read *On Equitation*, just now he probably did not need it.

He had noticed the horse shying at its own shadow, and turned it at once to face the sun. Then he eased the bit. Taking some reassurance from his touch, it let him stroke it. He allowed it to move forward a little; then, shedding his cloak, which apparently in his eagerness he had forgotten to do before, he gripped at the mane, and vaulted. Softly he took in the reins; the horse obeyed them. He kicked with his bare heel and gave the word to go. They dashed off at a gallop, but 'made the turn in the proper way'.

Thus Alexander the Great acquired Bucephalas.

One is struck by the detail, like that of an eye-witness, in Plutarch's account. Ptolemy may have supplied it; but my guess is that it came, in a manner of speaking, from the horse's mouth. Plutarch says later of Alexander that he would sit long over the wine, because he liked to talk; and that although in the general way no one had more charming conversation or delightful manners, when loosened by wine he would fall to bragging like a common trooper. Tiresome as it must have been for his entourage, it gives a moving glimpse into his boyhood's insecurities. He can be pictured in the royal tent, pitched somewhere in central Asia; the company of generals, satraps, visiting envoys and chroniclers sits at tables laden with gold vessels looted from Persepolis. Someone, who means shortly to ask a favour, brings up the subject of war-chargers. Alexander's eye lights up. 'You know my horse, Bucephalas? Of course you do. Now I'll tell you something. He'd have been hound-meat at the knacker's, but for me.' The guest, who has heard it from at least three other sources, expresses astonished curiosity. Tactless Cleitus gives an audible groan; wise Ptolemy hacks his shin under the table. The familiar tale proceeds.

At any rate, Bucephalas belonged already to Alexander when in his fourteenth year he went up to the hillside schoolhouse at Mieza, to finish his education with Aristotle. He rode him in his youthful wars under his father's standard: when, Regent of Macedon at sixteen in his father's absence, he crushed a border rising in wild country near today's Bulgarian frontier; when he reduced the rebel cities of the Chersonese and the tough mountain-bred Illyrians. Bucephalas, a still vigorous stallion of seventeen, carried the eighteen-year-old cavalry general in the great charge that broke the ranks of the Sacred Band at Chaeroneia. And when, at the last and most dangerous of Philip's weddings, Alexander threw a cup at the groomsman's head, just missed being spitted on his father's sword, and spent some months in bleak exile, Bucephalas cannot have been left behind.

In the critical time after Philip's murder by a cast-off favourite, when all the lands he had conquered rose at once in hopeful revolt, Bucephalas must have gone with Alexander through his lightning northern campaigns, and southward when he came down like a thunderbolt to wipe out Thebes. Indeed, it can be seen that the horse's greatest days were over, before the man's had begun.

For Bucephalas had reached the respectable age of twenty-one when, aged twenty-two, Alexander crossed to Asia. At the battle of Gaugamela, only three years later, we read already that 'as long as he was riding about to make his dispositions, addressing or briefing his men, or inspecting them, he spared Bucephalas, who was now getting old, and used another horse; but when he was going into action, he sent for him, and mounted him just before starting the attack.'

To be conspicuous in the field, for friend or foe, was part of the 'Alexander touch'. He wore white wings in a helmet polished like silver; his gorget and his belt were jewelled. Not all the adornments were for himself. 'Bucephalas when undressed would permit his groom to mount him; but when all caparisoned in his royal trappings and collars, he would let nobody near him but Alexander. If anyone else tried to come up, he would charge at them neighing loudly, rear, and trample them if they did not get away quickly.' For Alexander, he 'would even lower his body to help the mounting'. (Xenophon would have approved his pupil.) And if he could no longer endure the burden of a whole day's battle – it was another horse that was killed at Issus – we can guess that it was always he who appeared at the victory parade; curvetting, no doubt, to the delight of all beholders.

Gaugamela was the last of Alexander's great pitched battles till he reached India. After Gaugamela, Bucephalas kept him company, not as the fire-breathing warrior of romance, but as an indispensable old friend, nursed carefully over high passes and hot plains, as Alexander nursed along, sometimes with his own hands, elderly Lysimachus who had been the kindly pedagogue of his childhood. One probable reason why he had no tolerance for people who let him down, is that he himself was almost fanatically loyal.

In those gruelling marches, he must have changed horses several times a day (horseshoes were a Roman innovation). Bucephalas was being led by grooms through the densely wooded country of the Mardians, when raiding tribesmen swooped down, and carried him off.

'Because of this animal's superior qualities,' says Diodorus, 'the King was enraged, and ordered every tree in the country to be felled, while he gave out to the people through interpreters that if the horse was not brought back, they would see the land laid waste to its furthest end, and everyone in it massacred.' These measures were efficacious; before the hostages had done much tree-felling, Bucephalas was returned. 'He treated them all kindly', Plutarch contributes, 'and gave a ransom for his horse to those who had captured him' – no doubt in the reaction of relief. The fate of an old horse fallen among thieves must have been grimly predictable.

This was, as far as we know, Bucephalas' last adventure. Presently came the long pull up the Khyber. He was still alive at the time of the great battle at the Hydaspes against Porus and his elephants; but it is unlikely that the pensioned veteran took part, or that he sired on the local mares that host of foals, from which Afghan chieftains down to this day trace the lineage of their favourite steeds, as they claim to do their own from Alexander.

'In the plains where the battle was fought, and from which he set out to cross the Hydaspes, Alexander founded cities. The first he called Nicaea, from his victory over the Indians; the other, Bucephala, in memory of his horse Bucephalas, who died there, not wounded by anyone, but from exhaustion and age. For he was about thirty years old, and was the victim of fatigue.'

So too, after long labours, fevers neglected or ignored, and many wounds, was his master. He had only three more years to go.

'It is said too that when he lost a dog, named Peritas, which he had reared himself and loved, he founded a city and gave it the dog's name.' He might have done the same for the last of his three comrades, his friend Hephaestion, for whom he ordered the manes of all the horses to be shorn in mourning. But a month after Hephaestion's Homeric funeral rites in Babylon, Alexander was dead.

The site of Bucephala still eludes the archaeologists. But at Rawalpindi there is an ancient Buddhist *stupa*, in the shape of a low broad dome. For some reason lost in the mists of folk-tradition, the local peasants honour it as Bucephalas' tomb.

THE BANQUET OF DEATH

Peter Tremayne

After the death of Alexander the Great his empire crumbled in the hands of his successors. Other kingdoms came and went, all now bowing to the growing might of Rome. The strongest of these after Carthage was Pontus, in Asia Minor, whose king, Mithridates (or Mithradites), systematically enlarged his kingdom until he was ready to do battle with Rome. It is that preparation, and the banquet that precipitated the war in 88 BC, that is the subject of the next story.

Peter Tremayne, under his real name of Peter Berresford Ellis (b. 1943), is a highly regarded Celtic scholar, whose book, Celt and Greek, includes a more detailed study of the following events. Under his Tremayne alias he has written many novels of supernatural horror and fantasy and the books and stories featuring the investigations of the Irish advocate, Sister Fidelma.

'Will he come? Do you think he will come?'

Metis, the daughter of Mithridates, king of Pontus, turned from the sunlit balcony into the shade of her chamber where her maidservant was preparing a cooling drink. The sun was still warm although it was close to the tips of the western mountains, its light reddening across the white of the building. Metis was scarcely more than fifteen, the age when most girls in Pontus expected to be married. She was lithe and dark; of Hellenic beauty and yet – yet her features seemed to contain an intermix of some more exotic ancestry. It was true, of course, that Mithridates claimed direct descent from the former mighty kings of Persia.

Metis' dark eyes were flashing with excitement as she regarded her maid. The girl who was pouring the drink for her could not have presented a more marked physical contrast.

The girl was tall, red of hair and fair skinned with deepset green eyes. She was the same age as Metis but it was clear that each belonged to peoples who were as tangibly alien to one another as Hellene was to Ethiopian.

'Are you sure he will come?' demanded the daughter of Mithridates again, her excitement tinged with anxiety.

'I am sure,' the red-haired girl replied calmly.

Metis smiled as she reached elatedly for the drink. She sipped slowly at it before glancing towards the balcony where the lowering sun's rays were causing shadows to spread across its mosaic floor.

'But isn't it time they started to arrive, Aphrodite,' she went on restively. 'Surely it is time?'

The girl called Aphrodite did not reply immediately. She was, in spite of her name, a Galatian, a descendant of the *Keltoi*; tribes who had flooded through Greece and settled in Asia Minor over two centuries before. She glanced surreptitiously at her mistress from under lowered lids and sighed deeply.

'He will come, mistress,' she finally said, 'for didn't your father, the king, invite all the chieftains of Galatia to attend his banquet?'

Metis pouted.

'This is true, but Deiotaros is not a chieftain.'

'His father, Dumnorix, is king of the Tolistoboii, and Deiotaros is his heir elect. He will be there at the banquet. That is for certain.'

Metis smiled again as if this further assurance made her happy. Then abruptly she frowned as if a sudden thought had annoyed her.

'You will say nothing of this, will you, Aphrodite? If I catch you betraying me, I will have you flogged.'

The tall Galatian girl kept her eyes lowered in case her young mistress should see the anger and resentment burning in them. In her own land, the land of the Trocmi, she had been the daughter of a minor chieftain who had ruled at Ancyra by the sacred River Halys. Then the raid had ripped her from her family and she had been carried off to Pontus and into slavery. It was not the way of the Galatians to keep slaves and she had found it hard. She had only been ten years old when she discovered that she had been deprived of any right to be considered as a human being. Even her own name had been taken from her and she had been told that, henceforth, she would be called Aphrodite which was but a clumsy Hellenic synonym for her own name. At that point she had been ready to seize a knife and dedicate her life to Danu, the life-giver and life-taker – mother of all the gods and goddesses. Isolated, alone, she had no other path of hope left than to concentrate her belief in Danu. Her captors could not take away her unshakeable belief that one day Danu would show her the way to freedom.

That had been five years ago.

The High Steward of the household of King Mithridates, the sixth of his name to sit on the throne of Pontus, claimant to the glory of the empire of Alexander of Macedon, had bought her in the slave market to be a companion and maid for the daughter of the king. Metis was Mithridates' youngest daughter, and the daughter of his third wife who had died in childbirth. Life with Metis became tolerable – not good but tolerable.

Even so, there was never a moment when Aphrodite did not yearn for her homeland at Ancyra; yearn for her family, her elder brother whom she barely remembered and, above all, for her freedom.

And while she coveted freedom, her mistress, Metis, craved marriage. Not just marriage to anybody but marriage to a handsome warrior. In Pontus, marriage was always arranged by a woman's father or nearest male relation and she had no say in it. Now, as Metis reached the age of fifteen, she could expect a marriage arranged by her father. Metis' mind constantly turning over the procession of aged and ugly men who fawned at her father's court and dreaded the time when Mithridates would announce a decision.

That evening, as Metis and her maidservant, Aphrodite, stood watching the lowering sun casting its shadows across the balcony, they were, in reality, both awaiting the fulfilment of their respective dreams.

The young Galatian chieftain, Deiotaros, whom Metis was so anxious about, had already visited Mithridates' capital twice before as the envoy of his father, King Dumnorix of the Tolistoboii. Mithridates had invited the sixty chieftains who ruled the tribes of Galatia to a sumptuous banquet at his palace, declaring the gesture as an act of friendship to unite good relations between the empire of Pontus and its Galatian neighbours.

Deiotaros had acted as ambassador to conclude the arrangements for the visit of the distinguished chieftains. It had been during his two visits that Metis and Aphrodite had encountered Deiotaros in the palace gardens.

The meeting had been entirely an accident for in Metis' world the position of women was severely limited. Women were kept in seclusion in the home, having separate quarters in the palace. They could, at times, venture out but with their bodies and faces veiled. Usually, however, they remained in the palace, moving through a series of specially constructed passages along which no man might go. Women could therefore travel from one part of the palace to another without having to show themselves, and the entrances into common rooms, where men might be found, were hidden by tapestries or other drapes.

It had been the fault of a dilatory guard who had allowed the accidental meeting to happen. The guard had not ensured that the small palace garden was unoccupied before he allowed the Galatian chieftain to enter it. Deiotaros had expressed a wish to take the evening air before retiring. In truth, Deiotaros was a man who preferred the outdoors to the stuffy atmosphere of houses and palaces. The same guard had compounded his slackness by retiring himself and not accompanying his charge during the sojourn in the garden.

The moonlight had bathed the garden with its exotic flowers and herb-scented walkways.

Deiotaros stretched beneath the pale, cold rays of the moon, his face turned towards it. To his people the moon was the source of wisdom, the steed of Epona, the horse-goddess – for horses, in the time beyond memory, had enabled his people to rise from the ground and become the warrior nation, riding to the four ends of the earth.

It was a slight sound, perhaps a sigh, that had made Deiotaros wheel round, his hand dropping to his short sword.

It was then that Metis had come forward from her hiding place. She stood there, gazing at the warrior without any attempt to cover her face. She was an audacious girl for, as her mother had died at birth, she had been left much to her own devices and there had been no one to teach her circumspection. She saw the handsome young Galatian and was much attracted. And Deiotaros, son of Dumnorix, was similarly fascinated by the dark beauty and the alluring personality of the daughter of the king of Pontus.

Neither, in that first meeting, had taken any notice of Aphrodite, the resentful slave girl, standing in the shadows, waiting on the command of her mistress.

Aphrodite, too, had been more than aroused by the good-looking warrior. It had been years since she had seen one of her own people. Now here was a bold warrior and a pleasing young man at that. He was tall, dark haired but with bright, grey eyes and generous features. His muscular frame was every inch the figure of a hero. He wore his twisted gold torc around his neck showing that he was no pampered son of a chieftain, but had won his warrior's rights in trial and combat.

Aphrodite had watched him with covetous eyes, had examined the pale beam of the moon on his features, which gave him an ethereal quality. He looked like a god, a god of battles. When she heard that his name was Deiotaros, meaning 'the divine bull', she knew with a burning certainty that he was the hero sent by Danu, the mother goddess, to rescue her from her drudgery.

So Aphrodite had stood resentfully in the background while Metis flirted with Deiotaros. She had kept silent as they talked brightly of small matters, watching their animated faces with barely concealed envy. The shadows of the night had hidden her jealous features and Deiotaros had barely noticed her presence.

It was during the second visit that Deiotaros paid to the palace of Mithridates that she had a chance to talk with him. He had come with the final arrangements for the attendance at the banquet and Metis had sent her secretly to his quarters to bring him to an appointed spot so that they might talk again without anyone being the wiser.

'I am in love with him, Aphrodite,' Metis had confided. 'He is different to all the others in this palace. Soon my father will marry me off to some old man. I cannot bear it. Think me a fool, but my heart goes out to this Galatian. I must see if he feels the same, so that I might ask him to seek permission from my father to marry me.'

Aphrodite had sniffed less in disapproval than in rivalry.

'I do not think your father will be pleased with such an idea. He does not regard my people as worthy.'

Metis frowned momentarily.

'*Your* people?' She sounded surprised and then realized what Aphrodite meant. 'Oh yes. You were of Galatia once. Well, I am sure my father, correctly approached, will approve. Isn't he always talking about obtaining the loyalty of the Galatians to his empire. What better way of doing this than forming an alliance with the son of King Dumnorix?'

Aphrodite smiled thinly.

'I do not think that he had marriage in mind.'

'You are too impertinent, Aphrodite. Try my patience and you will be flogged. Now, be about the task I have set you.'

The Galatian girl glowered resentfully again yet she had obeyed Metis and gone that night to the guest room where Deiotaros was staying, using, of course, the secret passage through which women could travel unnoticed.

'My mistress, Metis, has asked me to bring you to her presence,' she announced as she stepped into the young Galatian's room, surprising him.

As she spoke his language fluently, Deiotaros looked at her closely for the first time.

'You are a Galatian,' he observed.

'I am of the Trocmi from Ancyra,' she answered proudly.

'What are you doing in this place?'

'I am a slave, what else?'

He caught the bitterness in her voice.

'So, you are not happy here?'

She smiled cynically.

'Are slaves meant to be happy? If I had an opportunity I would fly on the winds back to Ancyra. However, I am but an earthbound mortal and need help to escape my prison.'

Deiotaros regarded her in sympathy.

'How long have you been here?'

'Five years now. I do not even know if my family still live.' She was examining him speculatively. 'You are a compassionate man, son of Dumnorix. Help me to escape.'

He looked disconcerted for a moment.

'It might be done,' he conceded. 'We of Galatia do not believe in making slaves and to see one of our own suffering is a cause of distress. But we also believe in honour. Therefore any attempt to help you escape must come after the banquet when we have fulfilled our obligation as guests. We might be able to smuggle you out with the retinue of the chieftains after the feast.'

Aphrodite found her heart filled with happiness.

'Then you will help me escape? You will take oath that you will help me?'

'Unless the sky fall or the seas rise up and swamp the land, I shall not forget,' declared Deiotaros solemnly. 'And I am sure your mistress will be pleased that you will find your freedom.'

Alarm crossed her features.

'No. You must not mention this to Metis. She is a Pontian.'

'You do not like her?' Deiotaros asked in surprise.

'How can a prisoner like his gaoler however paternal. Freedom now, the desire for freedom, is something that is not understood by those who imprison others.'

'Do not worry, then. This shall be something only between the two of us.'

Nothing more was said and Aphrodite led Deiotaros to the assignation with her mistress, Metis.

Whatever Deiotaros had then promised Metis pleased the daughter of Mithridates greatly. So it was settled. Freedom for the slave; marriage for the mistress. And so, with their different dreams, Metis

and Aphrodite waited impatiently for the arrival of Deiotaros and
the Galatians for the great banquet.

So now they stood on one of the balconies of the palace, as the
sun finally sank below the western mountains, and witnessed the
arrival of the cavalcade of Galatian chieftains; lines of chariots
and horsemen, with their individual banners and emblems, which
proceeded sedately to the gates of the palace to be welcomed by the
High Steward of Pontus.

'I cannot see Deiotaros there,' exclaimed Metis anxiously, leaning
forward against the balustrade.

Aphrodite also peered forward.

'Nor I,' she conceded in disappointment. 'Yet he must be there.'

Metis turned impatiently to the red-haired girl.

'Listen carefully, Aphrodite. Go down into the reception hall. Do
not on any account let yourself be seen. Find out if Deiotaros is
among the chieftains and, if so, bring him to me before the feasting
starts. Tell him it is urgent so that I may instruct him what to say
to my father. The banquet will be the perfect time and place to
approach my father on the subject of my marriage. Go! Quickly
now, Aphrodite!'

Aphrodite made her way quietly through the hidden corridors
towards the reception halls of the palace. Her heart was already
beating a little faster as she anticipated her meeting with the
young chieftain of the Tolistoboii. But the anticipation of seeing
the handsome young man again was soured by a sense of bitterness
towards her mistress. That Deiotaros could care anything for Metis
of Pontus provoked a sense of angry injustice against her mistress.

Danu, the mother goddess, had sent Deiotaros to set her free.

She was passing one of the anterooms to the reception chamber,
where the Galatian chieftains would be received, when voices
interrupted her thoughts. Harsh male voices. She heard the guttural
tones of Zeumachos, commander of Mithridates' elite bodyguard.
She did not know what it was that made her halt. There was a
small air-hole in the corridor at this point which linked it with the
anteroom in which Zeumachos stood. Aphrodite glanced around,
found a small wooden stool and drew it under the square hole. She
did not know why she felt compelled to eavesdrop. Was it the tone
of Zeumachos' voice or was it some word, subconsciously ingested,
that acted as a mental warning bell? She drew herself up and glanced
through.

Two men stood in the room. She recognized the tall, muscled
form of Zeumachos, with his scarred face and haughty, dark
expression. He glanced around him as if to assure himself that

no one was within hearing before turning to the shorter man who stood facing him.

'Are you sure that it will work, majesty?' he demanded, though in respectful tones.

Aphrodite's eyes widened as she realized that the shorter man was none other than Metis' own father, Mithridates. He was an elderly man but his outward look of grey-haired fragility was deceptive. He had already reigned in Pontus for forty years and his grey hairs hid a will of iron. To achieve the throne he had incarcerated his own mother, murdered his brother and married his sister, Laodice.

Now Mithridates' empire extended all around the Black Sea. He was being called *Eupator*, 'The Great'. One by one, all the kingdoms of Asia Minor were falling to his armies, even Bythnia, which had boasted the support of Rome. But Rome was too occupied with its own internal problems at that moment to support Nicomedes of Bythnia. Token Roman armies, sent to protect the possessions of Rome in Greece, had been broken by his legions. Mithridates considered himself to be Alexander of Macedon and Darius of Persia reincarnate.

Yet to the south of Pontus, the state of Galatia had not yet felt the steel of his armies. Galatia lay on the central plain of Asia Minor and had been created over two centuries before by the eastern move of some of the great tribes of *Keltoi* who had devasted Greece in their surge towards new lands. The Trocmi had settled along the River Halys and built their great hillfort capital at Ancyra. The Tectosages had settled further east around Tarvium while the largest of the tribes, the Tolistoboii had settled along the Sangarios, where once the Phrygian kingdom had existed. The Tolistoboii had taken over the deserted city of Pessinus – deserted since Alexander had devastated it – and there they built the capital of Galatia, Drunemeton, the sanctuary of the oak. It was here that Gordius, father of Midas, had once tied a fabulous knot and decreed that whoever unravelled it would rule the world. Alexander had merely severed it with his sword. But that was a long, long time before. Now the tribes of Galatia sent their chieftains to sit in council at Drunemeton.

'I am sure, Zeumachos,' Mithridates was replying. 'I have spent much time on studying these Galatians. They are stupid but proud and have grandiose ideas of honour. They believe it is a sacrilege to their gods to enter a feasting hall with their weapons. So they bereft themselves of all defences save a small dagger with which to eat.'

'Then they are stupid, indeed,' agreed the commander of the bodyguard.

'Nevertheless, they are a fierce, warrior people,' Mithridates continued. 'Under the leadership of their chieftains, they once devastated these kingdoms. Never forget their reputation as warriors. Often they have served as mercenaries in the armies of the Hellenic kingdoms. They seem to have no fear. But without firm leadership they squabble among themselves. They become useless, without direction.'

'I am told that they believe they are immortal,' rejoined Zeumachos. 'Again, that is a stupid belief.'

'It is not quite so,' reproved the king. 'They believe that when they die, they are reborn again in another world and when they die in that world, they are reborn again in this one. That fact alone makes them a terrible enemy. They do not fear death and without a fear of death there is no task a man might not undertake. This is why we must act and cut off their head before we come to blows with the body.'

Aphrodite, peering through the air-vent, saw the commander of the bodyguard frown.

'Majesty, I am not sure how this will work.'

The king sighed deeply.

'We have invited all the chieftains of their nation to a banquet. Is that correct?'

Zeumachos nodded agreement.

'One of the peculiarities of these Galatians is that they do not have a single king. They are ruled by an assembly of sixty chieftains. From those sixty chieftains, they appoint three of their number, a triumvirate, each one representing one of the three great tribes which comprise their nation. Each of these takes the grand title of king, but has few rights of kingship that we would recognize. They hold office only so long as they please the people.'

'Yes, this much I know.'

'Well, if we destroy, at a single blow, all sixty chieftains and their triumvirate, who will lead the Galatians? As soon as we have destroyed them all, our armies will be able to march into their country, seize the land and there will be no one to organize further resistance against us.'

'The plan is good, majesty. I now understand it fully. But how can we be sure that it will work?'

'It will work because, as I have said, I have studied these people. The chieftains all responded to my invitation to come to my capital and be my guests at a banquet to celebrate our friendship,' Mithridates laughed, sharply. It was not a pleasant sound. 'Their pride thinks that I do them honour. They think that I have invited them as equals and friends. They think that I respect them, their warrior code, and would not act against them. They are arrogant fools, these Galatians.'

Zeumachos chuckled appreciatively.

'Well, it is true that they are all arriving. They have left their bodyguard, as requested, outside the palace, where our troops can quickly encircle them after the deed is done. But will these chieftains give up their weapons before entering the banqueting hall?'

'It is their custom. I am sure of it.'

'Then after the wine is circulated, my guards will act. I have appointed two to each chieftain, standing behind their seats at table. On a prearranged signal, they will step forward and cut their throats.'

'Excellent, Zeumachos. I will now go to meet with these arrogant fools. Make sure that nothing is said or done to arouse suspicion before the appointed moment. At dawn tomorrow our armies shall begin the march into Galatia.'

Aphrodite waited until Mithridates and Zeumachos had left the anteroom before she stepped down from her precarious perch into the corridor. She glanced up and down, assuring herself that no one had seen her act of snooping.

She felt strange; she was not exactly sure what she felt. She was not horrified by the revelation of the act of treachery which Mithridates contemplated. She was not even concerned with the planned fate of the chieftains of Galatia. She did not know them. What she found herself contemplating was the fate of one man – the handsome Deiotaros, the 'divine bull' who had been sent by Danu to lead her to freedom.

In him she had fixed her hopes for release from bondage; she had become infatuated by him or, rather, by her image of him as the saviour whom Danu had appointed for her and her alone. And now as she thought it through, she realized that it must be Danu who had revealed this trachery – and for a purpose! That purpose being to save Deiotaros, so that they might escape together from this evil palace of Pontus.

Determination flooded through her as she rationalized what she had heard.

Aphrodite kept to the narrow passages where no men were allowed. And because the women had been warned to avoid the feasting halls during the entertaining of the Galatian chieftains, no one was moving along them. Aphrodite travelled alone and unhindered.

She came to an entrance behind a tapestry which she knew gave access to the reception room adjacent to the feasting hall. Cautiously she peered around the corner of the tapestry and looked out into the room. There were trestle tables extending along the middle of the room which were piled high with body armour, helmets, swords, shields and a few spears.

There was no one in this room except for one young man who was unbuckling his sword belt. He was a red-haired Galatian who looked scarcely older than her, but she realized that he must be at least seventeen, for seventeen was the 'age of choice' when a boy became a man among her people.

Aphrodite slipped out from the cover of the tapestry.

'Son of Galatia!' she called softly,

The young man wheeled around in surprise. Aphrodite was, of course, dressed in the manner of the women of Pontus, her body cloaked in a long flowing garment and with a headdress and veil.

'Who are you?' he demanded, surprised at being addressed in his own tongue.

'It is of no consequence who I am. Do you know Deiotaros, son of Dumnorix?'

The young man nodded, frowning.

'Will you seek him out and tell him to come to me immediately? It is urgent.'

The young man examined her shrouded figure dubiously for a moment and then his face split into an understanding grin.

'I shall not stand in the path of love,' he commented. 'He has just gone inside the banqueting hall. I will fetch him for you.'

He turned and disappeared.

Aphrodite waited impatiently, having moved back behind the tapestry in case any of Mithridates' guards entered the room. She could hear the sounds of laughter and merry conversation from the next room.

It was barely a moment or two before the handsome figure of Deiotaros came hurrying into the room and halted, peering about in surprise when he saw it was empty.

'Deiotaros!'

He turned with a frown and his gaze lightened as Aphrodite stepped from behind the shelter of the tapestry.

'Metis? Is it you?'

His first assumption cut like a knife in her heart.

'It is not Metis,' she said, withdrawing her veil.

'Ah, Aphrodite, isn't it?'

She pouted slightly at what she saw was the disappointment in his face.

'Did you forget your oath to me?'

'Not I,' he replied with a quick smile of reassurance and she basked for a moment in that smile. 'But I said we would work a plan out after the banquet.'

'It might be too late . . .'

'What do you mean?' he demanded quickly and she regretted her formula of words.

'I only meant that my mistress, Metis, says that she must see you before you go into the banquet. Please leave your companions and follow me.'

'This is not good etiquette to leave the reception of the king.'

'He is not my king; not mine!' muttered Aphrodite. 'Come, my mistress must see you. You will not be missed for a few moments among sixty of your people.'

'In that case . . .' Deiotaros shrugged. 'But only for a moment or two.'

Aphrodite saw that he had left his weapons in the hall where all his companions had divested themselves of armour, swords and shields, just as Mithridates had predicted.

She motioned for Deiotaros to precede her and as he did so, she snatched up one of the abandoned short swords that the Galatians were so fond of using, hiding it beneath her long cloak.

She conducted him swiftly along the secret passage to the chambers of the daughter of Mithridates and then stood aside, controlling her simmering anger as Metis came running forward, hands outstretched, to take the hands of Deiotaros.

'Prepare a drink for my lord, Aphrodite, be quick about it!' Metis snapped at her as she led Deiotaros to a seat.

'I cannot be long, Metis,' the Galatian chieftain said. 'My father and my companions have already entered the great hall.'

'I shall not keep you long, lord,' Metis smiled reassuringly. 'But it is of the banquet that I must speak. Be seated here, next to me.'

Aphrodite moved to the tray of drinks on a side table and began to pour the drinks, furtively placing the Galatian sword to the side of the table, out of sight.

'What of the banquet?' demanded Deiotaros.

It was at that moment a strange cacophony came to their ears.

Deiotaros looked startled and rose to his feet.

'What is that?'

The sound grew in volume; cries, screams and pitiable howls rose from somewhere below in the palace of Mithridates.

Aphrodite felt emotionally cold as she recognized what was happening. Her head was clear. She turned to Deiotaros.

'The sounds come from the banqueting hall, Deiotaros,' she said softly in the language of the Galatians.

Metis turned to her with a frown.

'Speak Greek, girl! What is it you say?'

Deiotaros' face was suddenly drained of blood.

'Show me the way back, quickly!' he demanded.

Aphrodite shook her head.

'No need to rush back into danger. Keep your eye on her,' she gestured to Metis. 'I will find out what is happening.' She turned, picked up the Galatian sword and threw it to Deiotaros. He caught it deftly. 'I had a feeling that this might be useful. I think that you have been betrayed.'

Metis was looking confused.

'What is she saying?' she demanded.

'Stay still, Metis,' advised Deiotaros, 'until we learn the meaning of this disturbance.'

Aphrodite ducked into the hidden passage and moved back in the direction of the banqueting hall. She knew what she would find before she reached one of the hidden walkways which, through carefully hung tapestries, provided windows into the hall.

The hall was red with bloodstained bodies and the only people standing were the exhausted bodyguards of Zeumachos, their swords still running with the gore of their victims.

Satisfied, Aphrodite turned and hurried back to Metis' chamber. Now she had to put the plan she had formulated into action.

She looked expressionlessly at Deiotaros' anxious face.

'You have, indeed, been betrayed, Deiotaros. All your friends are dead, murdered by Mithridates' guards.'

'Dead?' gasped Deiotaros.

'Slaughtered like sheep,' affirmed Aphrodite. 'They were unable to defend themselves because they left their weapons outside the banqueting hall.'

'What is she saying?' cried Metis, trying to make sense of what was happening.

Deiotaros raised a hand to his head, shaking it as if he had received a physical blow.

'We must escape, Deiotaros,' pressed Aphrodite. 'You are in danger.'

'Yes, yes,' muttered Deiotaros. 'That is what I must do but my father, Dumnorix, and my brother . . .?'

'They are all dead,' the girl assured him. 'I know a way through the side gate of the palace. It will not be guarded now. There will be horses there. You must take me with you.'

'Of course, I gave my oath.'

Metis was still standing confused by this conversation which she could not understand.

Deiotaros regarded her in cold anger.

'Did you know of this treachery?' he asked, almost in a whisper.

'What treachery?'

'That your father invited us here to slaughter us like sheep?'

Metis' face was white.

'Of course, she did,' intervened Aphrodite in annoyance. 'No need to ask. She is Mithridates' daughter. Her blood betrays her.'

Metis' thoughts were scattered, trying to cling to some sanity. Her plans for the future had suddenly evaporated like the snow on the hilltops in spring.

'It must have been why she sent me to bring you out of the banqueting hall so that you would not be slaughtered,' offered Aphrodite, trying her best to convince Deiotaros who stood hesitating.

'My father and my brother are down there,' Deiotaros' voice cracked with emotion. Then his face lightened. 'If what you say is true, Aphrodite, then Metis attempted to save me.'

'Deiotaros, I love you!' cried Metis. 'I do not understand what is happening.'

'She is the daughter of Mithridates,' Aphrodite pressed again, 'of course she knew of the plan.'

'But she kept me alive by sending for me before the slaughter,' Deiotaros insisted.

'She has kept me alive these five years,' returned the slave girl, bitterly. 'She probably thought to save you from the slaughter and make you her slave. A selfish interest, no more than that. Come, Deiotaros, we should be gone from here . . .'

'No,' cried Metis, clutching at the Galatian chieftain's arm. 'This is not right. This is not . . .'

Her voice ended in a curious gurgle. She staggered back, her white dress suddenly stained crimson.

Aphrodite let the knife she was clutching drop from her hand. She turned a tragic mask of a face to Deiotaros.

'I had to do it. She was about to betray us.'

Deiotaros stood frozen as if unable to take in the tragic events of the last few moments.

'She said she loved me,' he said slowly.

Aphrodite shook her head.

'She would have used you only as a plaything. These people are not human, Deiotaros. You can see that for yourself, especially now after what has happened. I know these people. I have been a slave here for five years.'

'I would have married her,' Deiotaros went on, still staring down at Metis' body.

'I am sorry for the feelings that you thought you felt for her. She had little feeling for you. But now,' Aphrodite threw out a hand, gesturing to the door, 'we must leave before we are discovered.'

Deiotaros had been standing like a statue, his mind on fire as he tried desperately to adjust to his collapsing world.

'Deiotaros!' cried Aphrodite in her impatience, almost stamping her foot in despair.

The Galatian shook his head. It was as if he had made up his mind. His lips were thin and his face wore the impassive expression of a warrior about to join battle. He became a man of decision and action.

'You are right. We must get to our bodyguard outside the palace before Mithridates' men attack them,' he said. 'He probably plans to attack at dawn, at the time our warriors would expect the chieftains to return to the encampment. We must warn them and start back to Galatia to rouse our people.'

Aphrodite nodded, quickly smiling. *Our* people! How wonderful it now sounded. She was joined to him. Danu had shown her the way.

'Then follow me closely, Deiotaros,' she instructed.

She turned through the passage, moving in the opposite direction from the banqueting hall. She moved at a swift pace. An unearthly stillness had settled over the palace now. A voiced called out now and again. But a silence seemed to have shrouded the scene of infamy. Still, Danu be praised, no curious women were venturing through the passage and nothing impeded their progress until they came out into a small, dark courtyard.

The courtyard stood before a small gateway at one side of the palace. Aphrodite knew that it was here that Mithridates often entertained those he wished no others in the palace to see. The gateway gave on to the hills beyond and only two guards usually acted as sentinels. She paused and touched Deiotaros lightly on his shoulder.

'The stable is in that corner of the courtyard. There are horses there.'

Deiotaros acknowledged this silently and they moved stealthily through the shadows to the dark arches of the stable area. There was no one about except for the guards by the gate. Across the moon-dappled courtyard, they could see the gates standing open and the two guards lounging by them. They could hear their voices raised in some ribald conversation, coarse chuckles punctuating their remarks.

Reaching the stable, it was the work of a few moments for a trained warrior to saddle two of the better looking stallions that stood ready tethered.

Deiotaros glanced at the girl.

'How well can you ride?'

'Well enough,' she replied, for one of her tasks had been to accompany Metis on her morning rides.

Deiotaros helped Aphrodite up on one of the stallions and then swung himself up on the second.

He leant forward and whispered.

'You go first, for they will be taken by surprise. I shall follow. Head due south, that is where our bodyguard is encamped.'

At Deiotaros' command, Aphrodite kicked her beast into action. Her horse leapt forward across the paved courtyard, its hooves pounding, on towards the open gates. For a split second the guards were frozen in surprise and in that moment she was through the gates. Deiotaros, his sword swinging, followed closely. A guard jumped towards him with a yell of anger, making an attempt to seize the bridle of his horse but fell back screaming, a gaping sword wound across his face. There were cries and a hastily discharged arrow hissed through the air quite close, but then they were clear and heading into the embracing darkness of the night.

'Keep straight on!' cried Deiotaros.

Aphrodite glanced at him and raised a hand to show she had heard.

Deiotaros glanced over his shoulder but could see no signs of pursuit.

At that moment he found that he had ceased to feel any emotion other than rage as he thought of the treachery of Mithridates and of the blood-soaked bodies of his kinsmen in the banqueting hall. Pontus would pay for this night's iniquity.

'Not far now!' he cried as the moon broke clear of the clouds and cast a pale light over the countryside.

Indeed, he could recognize the shoulder of a hill and knew that the Galatian encampment lay just beyond it.

Aphrodite was a horse's length ahead of him.

He saw her suddenly stiffen in the saddle. Then without a sound she slithered off and fell to the road. It was only then that he realized he had heard the tell-tale swish of an arrow speeding through the air just before she fell.

He heard a voice cry out in the night air.

'We're being attacked! Sound the alarm!'

Deiotaros reined in his horse, causing it to rear back on its hind legs. The action saved his life as two more arrows sped by him in quick succession.

In that moment he was aware that the cry had been made in his own language.

'Stop! Fools! Do you not know me? Deiotaros of the Tolistoboii! Stop shooting, I say!'

There was a moment of stunned silence.

Then a voice cried.

'I know his voice. It *is* Deiotaros. Quickly, bring a torch.'

Suddenly, from the hillside a couple of burning brand torches were ignited and shadows came racing down from the darkness. He could hear the clink of metal on metal, of sword and shield.

Deiotaros swung from his mount as a breathless young man came up, followed by several armed warriors.

'Deiotaros! You have escaped!'

By the light of the burning torch, Deiotaros recognized Brogitarios, a petty chieftain of the Trocmi.

'And you, also, have escaped,' he replied dourly. Then he added: 'But your arrows have hit the girl.'

Deiotaros turned towards Aphrodite's fallen form. He knelt down, calling for a torch to be brought nearer.

It needed no expert examination to see that Aphrodite was now beyond any human aid. The arrow had pierced through her heart.

Deiotaros gazed up with a look of anguish.

'She helped me to escape after the slaughter.'

Brogitarios bit his lip. His face was anguished.

'It was my arrow that brought her down. I thought we were under attack from the soldiers of Mithridates. The gods have played a foul trick on us this night.'

Deiotaros stood up, even now aware of the dangers that could threaten any minute that they delayed in that place.

'How did you get away?'

Brogitarios, one of the younger chiefs of the Trocmi, was scarcely seventeen. His voice was unsteady as he replied.

'I was in the feasting hall, the wine was circulating a little too freely. I went outside to urinate and, as the fates would have it, it was at that moment that the warriors of Pontus offered sacrilege by attacking us. I grabbed a sword and was just about to return to the hall when I beheld the carnage. I saw the slaughter of the chieftains and I knew it was no use throwing my life away for I was the only one armed against so many. Even so, I was hard pressed by the two assassins sent to kill me. I fought them off, ran for my horse. I managed to get away . . . I was the only one that did so from that accursed place! But now here you are. You must command us, Deiotaros. We must get back to Galatia and rouse the tribes before the army of Pontus strikes at us.'

'That we will!' affirmed Deiotaros. 'Are the men ready?'

'We were about to ride when we heard the sound of your horses.' Brogitarios hesitated and glanced down at the body of the girl, curiously. The heavy cloak and veil had been torn aside in Aphrodite's fall. 'She does not look like a Hellene. Who was she?'

'I only know the name that she was given as slave.'

'Her death lies heavily on me,' muttered Brogitarios. 'I had a sister once. Her name was Berlewen. She was captured by a Hellenic raiding party and taken away as a slave. She was not much more than ten years old at the time. She must have died in captivity. This girl is of the age that Berlewen would have been had she lived. This night I swear vengeance for all Galatian blood shed by Pontus, for Berlewen's death and the death of this unknown girl. Maybe her soul will carry my oath to my sister in the Otherworld?'

Deiotaros regarded the body of the girl with sadness.

'We will not leave her. She wanted so badly to return to her own people by the sacred River Halys.'

'Then she was of my tribe, the Trocmi?' Brogitarios asked.

'I believe so. She spoke of the Halys.'

'Then as surviving chieftain of the Trocmi, I swear we shall take her body back to our fortress at Ancyra.'

Deiotaros laid an approving hand on Brogitarios' shoulder.

'Indeed; let her cairn be built at Ancyra and let our future generations pay tribute to her there. Her cairn will be the symbol for our people to rally in freedom against Pontus. *And we shall be free*. I, Deiotaros, swear it on the soul of this brave Galatian girl!'

He turned and swung up on his horse, waiting while they gathered the body of the girl, and placed it across the horse she had been riding.

There was a hint of dawn in the eastern sky as Deiotaros paused on the hill crest and looked back across the plains towards the city of Mithridates. For a moment he thought of Metis. For a while he had truly thought love had blossomed there. But no love could exist with one who could so grossly betray honour and human decency.

He gazed up at the pale dawn sky and saw the bright light of the morning star, the star the Galatians called Berlewen. Then he found himself thinking of the girl Aphrodite. He was not sure why he had connected her with thoughts of the morning star. Then he realized that Aphrodite was the Hellenic goddess of love. It was the name sometimes given to the morning star, the star the Romans called Venus. Deiotaros frowned slightly. Berlewen? Someone had mentioned that name recently but he was too confused and tired to recall who and when. Ah! He wished he had known the girl's real name. Whatever her name was, Aphrodite had been a Galatian. Now she was a Galatian heroine; simple, honourable and unselfish.

Her cairn – the cairn of 'the morning star' – would be raised at Ancyra and would become the symbol of a free people for as long as Galatia existed.

THE PREPARATION

Naomi Mitchison

Deiotaros, the hero of the last story, remained an ally of Rome but sided with Pompey against Julius Caesar. He was captured by Caesar's troops and brought to trial, but was successfully defended by Cicero and restored to his kingdom of Galatia. By this time Julius Caesar was all powerful in Rome, and his conquest of Gaul confirmed his position. From Gaul, Caesar looked toward the rich and fertile lowlands of Britain, his next point of conquest.

In the following story, Naomi Mitchison (b. 1897), one of Britain's grandes dames of historical fiction, considers the years just before Caesar's invasion of Britain, during the conquest of Gaul. The extract comes from her first novel, The Conquered *(1923), and the events are set in the year 57* BC.

Titus Veturius Barrus had grown up very much under his grandfather's influence; he was taught to disapprove of scent and pretty clothes and Greek singers and frivolous poetry. And at nineteen he did not quite realize that one political party has very seldom any more principles than another.

He had been educated chiefly at home, under approved tutors, though once he went to Greece and loved it and would have liked to stay longer, but his grandfather sent for him back, fearing the enervating effect of Greek society. He was shy and had very few friends of his own age; they found him a little dull, a little too full of the early Roman virtues. So instead of amusing himself with women and politics among his contemporaries, he stayed at home and read a good deal; his grandfather did not altogether like Aristotle and the Neo-Pythagoreans, but if he didn't read Greek, what was he to read? Ennius was rather impossible; Catullus was equally impossible – in other ways. Of course there was always Varro on agriculture; but Varro was quite often at the house himself; he disapproved of the way Caius Barrus ran his estate.

But by this time Titus Barrus was beginning to be bored. And the more he found out that his grandfather was not, after all, the most perfect type of civilization, the more his grandfather delighted in him and gave him everything he asked for. The old man had visions of his grandson reforming society, reviving the citizen spirit, putting back the aristocracy into its right place, restoring order and stability, the good old days. . . . But Titus wanted to go soldiering, just as his father had done; and he wanted to go somewhere where there was a real war; and he had been very much excited by the campaigns against the Helvetii and the Germans; and, in fact, he wanted to go to Gaul. Which was all very distressing, because the proconsul Julius Caesar was the most terrible radical, the worst enemy the state had ever had – worse than his Uncle Marius even! But Titus meant to go; he was a very persistent young man, and go he finally did. It was to be hoped that his admirable upbringing would counteract the evil influences he was sure to meet with in Gaul.

In early April, when all the vines were budding, Titus Barrus rode north through Italy; he wore his new armour a little self-consciously and his military knowledge was only theoretical. But he had the best horse money could buy, and an old servant went with him. At night he stayed with friends of his grandfather's in country houses among flowering orchards; there was more than one pretty daughter who would have taken a kiss in a corner from him, but he never looked her way.

He found Gaul vastly interesting; he wanted to stop everywhere, see everything, observe the customs of the country, collect the very charming native enamel work, and learn Gallic. But the Belgians were arming in the North; he had to hurry. He arrived at Vesontio, reported, and was told to keep out of the way till some one had time to show him what to do. For the first few weeks, of course, he was a thorough nuisance, though not so much so as some of the young officers, as he was modest, attentive and sensible, had a good memory, and was very keen on becoming efficient.

He learnt something about quickness in their hurried march north, that ended on the bank of the Axona; and he learnt much – admiringly – about Caesar, when he saw him receive and welcome the envoys from the friendly Remi. He knew enough to carry messages at the battle of the bridge-head, and was very glad to have something to do. He had never seen a dead body near by, only at the safe and unreal distance of the theatre, and that not often. Once he had ridden at a gallop through a little wood and a gap in a turf wall, straight into a knot of Belgians. He drew his sword and slashed at them as he plunged through, and found it afterwards dripping with a new red. His servant congratulated him on it afterwards; he was one of Caesar's officers and had killed an enemy of the Republic! If he had killed him: which was unlikely.

After that battle, which broke up the power of the Belgic League, he wrote a long letter to his grandfather; it took nearly a month to get South. Caius Barrus, forgetting to be calm, tore it open with shaking hands, and read it through, murmuring the words over to himself. The boy was finding himself then! He would be like his father – how well the old man remembered *his* first letter! He took it out of the cedar-wood box and looked at them together; the writing was much the same, they used the same phrases. Twenty years ago – no, it was more: how short it seemed . . . he thought of his wife reading over that first letter with him, the mother's tears and laughter and pride: so it should be. But she was dead long ago; and his pretty daughter-in-law had died too, when Titus was a baby. . . . He turned back to the letter to read it more attentively.

Titus was well; he had been to the doctor with a cut leg, but it was nothing (he'ld be sure to say that, even if it was bad). He thought he was beginning to be some use (of course!). His horse was splendid. The barbarians were brave but easily discouraged: they would not hold out much longer; he was learning their language but found it difficult. He liked most of his fellow officers and thought they liked him; there was a Tribune called Quintus Velanius (now who could he be? It seemed a respectable name: he must find out), they had shared a tent for two or three nights and had made friends; Quintus had read Thucydides and they had discussed history together.

The next sheet. He was very favourably impressed with his superior officers. He had heard so much against the proconsul before he went out, but it was entirely his doing that the battle was won, still more that it was followed up afterwards – the most important thing of all. Quintus Velanius believed in him too. He wished his grandfather would tell people in Rome that he had been misjudged – after all, politics were not everything, and Caesar had reorganized the army, Caesar had seen to the engineers, Caesar was so wonderful with the barbarians, Caesar this and Caesar that!

Caius Barrus frowned: what had come over the boy? At this rate he would be a radical before he came home! He sat down and wrote

to his grandson, thanking him for his news, telling him about their
friends, the state of the crops, the latest intelligence from the East,
then going on about Cicero's return from exile, at last, only to find
his house in Rome burnt, his country villas plundered – such was
the respect paid nowadays to true patriotism! He ended up with
a few scandals about that profiteer Crassus, a few remarks about
Caesar's morals, and an assurance that now the democrats would
soon be out of power and right would triumph in the end.

Titus Barrus got the letter just before the battle with the Nervii,
so nearly lost, but so completely won! – and all through Caesar. He
was growing experienced by now: thus rapidly did the proconsul's
young men learn. And after all that slaughter, so wide a clemency:
the survivors allowed to keep all their lands and villages, and given
protection, now they were helpless, against their neighbours! Then,
after that, came the siege of the city of the Atuatuci; the town had
capitulated on the usual terms, but nearly half the arms had been
kept back; in the night the garrison rushed on the Romans, thinking
to take them unawares, but were surrounded and cut to pieces. As
a punishment, the whole of the townspeople, some fifty thousand,
they heard, were sold as slaves: a severe sentence, thought Titus,
but well justified against treachery. After that the rest of the Belgian
tribes gave in altogether, surrendering on almost any terms, and the
campaign was over for the year.

Titus read his grandfather's letter over again; it seemed almost
incredible that people should think and speak so of Julius Caesar!
He took it over in the evening to his new friend, Quintus Velanius;
he found him in his tent, a tall, open-faced young man with a brown
skin, freckled across the nose. He read the letter and threw it back
to Titus with a laugh: 'You don't suppose they understand about
him in Rome? My dear man, they don't begin to! They give him
a thanksgiving when he's beaten two nations in four months, and
then forget all about him! We know, of course, and any one else who
has anything to do with him; but the Alps take a deal of crossing.
Even your grandfather's bound to find out about Caesar some day,
though. Only, don't let him change you in the meantime.'

'Oh, it'll take more than a letter to do that! But I'm glad Cicero's
back in Rome.'

'Caesar'll be glad too. Good men get together. Titus, I'm
going to get leave to go to one of the warm springs in the
South if things are quiet this Autumn. Those Germans got
me a bad arm last year; every one says these springs are the
best thing for stiffness. If you can get off too, will you come
with me?'

'I'd like nothing better. They're in the Arvernian country, aren't they?'

'Yes: up in the hills. All very friendly, I believe. You'ld be able to pick up plenty of your old pots and pans there!'

'Well, it seems to me to be good art – for barbarians.'

He wrote back to his grandfather that he was glad about Cicero's return, and they had just won the most splendid victory over the Belgians; also that he was going to visit some of the towns in southern Gaul that Autumn. And he sent him a Belgian slave, but the man fell sick and died on the journey, and that was so much money wasted: not that prisoners were at all expensive just then, but still it was a pity.

In Autumn, after Caesar's rather casual annexation of Gaul, the two young officers set out with their servants and horses; everywhere the country people stared at them – they were just beginning to realize the Romans as a fact in their lives. The corn was all in stooks in the Arvernian fields, and the fruit was mostly gathered, as they rode up along that very fertile valley which runs north and south through the hills. The warm springs were high up among the pines, with big, straggling villages all round them, continually filling and refilling with sick people. The Romans installed themselves in a long, low house of pine logs with a thatched roof and good stables, that lay in a sunny hollow of the woods, a little south of the springs. Quintus Velanius consulted the local doctor and made offerings at the local shrines, which were many. He was prescribed for with much ceremony: baths, waters to drink, exercise, massage by a very pretty little slave with soft, strong hands and two long plaits that were always dropping over her face and tickling the patient's arm. Titus began by taking the waters too, but found them much too nasty and so had baths instead, went for long rides in the country, and made friends with various Gauls. He was learning Gallic fairly quickly, and, better still, he was never shy of talking a foreign language, even if he only knew a few words; he was much more awake since leaving his grandfather. Besides, the Gallic nobles could generally speak some Latin or Greek, and even read it.

Autumn was always the best time of year at these springs; the small wars were mostly over, and so was the busiest season of the harvest; but it was still warm enough to lie out in the sun under the pines or sit on the stone steps by the springs, talking to one's friends and throwing little pine cones at the slave-girls who came to dip out the water. Titus was sitting there one afternoon, looking out over the hazy valley, and observing, out of the tail of his eye, two young Arvernian nobles who were standing on the steps a little to his right;

he thought he saw the beginnings of a promising quarrel. Neither of them was much older than himself and they were a good-looking pair. One stood on the top of the steps, his hands on his hips, in coat and breeches of tartan, with heavy golden tassels on the plaid; his thick hair was held in place by a circle of leather, which dangled on to his forehead, and over his ears bright squares of Haeduan enamel, dark blue and brilliant red. The other looked up at him, frowning; he wore a different tartan with more yellow in it, and on a chain round his neck swung a silver cock with crest and eyes of garnet. They both had swords and daggers and seemed as if they might use them.

Titus tried to make out what they were saying and caught scraps of it; they seemed to have been having a boasting-match – a very Gallic thing to do! – and now they were both talking at once about their own possessions, their own places, Curdun, Gergovia. The Roman looked round at that, thinking that the man from Gergovia must be the young chief Vercingetorix, lover of civilization, encourager of trade and the Greek artists – he wore a finely-cut Grecian emerald on his right hand – one of the Gauls whom Caesar had charmed to be his friend. He heard him say, 'And I've a black colt, Coré, that I'll back against anything of yours!' The other answered scornfully, 'You and your colts! Haven't you a better test than that? Or are you afraid?' Both had their hands on their swords now, and Titus was frankly staring at them; there was a clear space, level both ways, at the top of the steps; they went up, and the drawn steel flashed in the sun. 'To the death, Ardorix?' said Vercingetorix, softly, and 'Yours!' the chief of Curdun threw back at him.

They moved about, light-footed, sword in the right hand, dagger in the left, each trying to get the sun into the other's eyes. Titus watched from the steps: this was more exciting than the arena! But he didn't want to be drawn into it himself. Then suddenly everything happened with a rush: the fighters closed, with the whickering clash of steel on steel; a girl with a baby in her arms ran screaming past him up the steps, straight at the fight, right on to the swords! Titus leapt the top steps after her, trying to stop her being killed; he found himself in the thick of it, stammering Gallic at the top of his voice, a man's wrist in one hand, the other dripping blood from a cut palm. Every one was shouting, plunging about – barbarians! Two other men were separating the fighters; and then the girl collapsed heavily on to Titus' shoulder. There was a deal of blood everywhere; it was dripping steadily from his hand, which he clenched to stop the flow; the girl? She was unhurt; but as she undid the plaid there was wail on wail from the child, its face all crumpled up with pain, its hands

clutching at air. The mother sank to her knees, tearing at the brooch
to get her dress open; the baby fastened on to her breast with a sob,
and sucked hard for a minute before it started screaming again; its
soft little arm was cut from elbow to shoulder.

They had it bandaged up in a minute; quite wonderfully soon
it quieted down and was sucking happily but for a little sobbing
moan from time to time, as the girl rocked herself to and fro with
it. But if Ardorix was angry before, he was raging now. 'My son,'
he cried, 'my son – you've hurt him! You coward, you shall pay
for this!' and then, furiously, to the man who held him back, 'Let
be, Caltane! Where's my sword? I'll have his heart out!'

Caltane, his cousin, kicked the sword further away and held
on to him still: 'Why were you fighting? Who was here? What
happened?'

And Vercingetorix, panting, said, 'I never meant this – on my
honour I never meant it! How could I know there was a child?'

'My son – my baby son – he may die of it! That on you!'

'I'll give you any satisfaction you ask.'

Caltane and the other man cried out at this, 'That's fair, that's
honest dealing! Ardorix, listen to what he says – put a fine
on him!'

The baby was nearly asleep, the sudden, heavy sleep of exhaustion;
his mother's hair fell over him, she was crying like a child herself.
Ardorix knelt beside her, stroking the back of her neck: 'What fine,
Guemoné?'

She whispered back, passionately, 'Nothing – kill him!'

But the moment was passed; he turned to the others, a little
doubtful: 'Caltane —? Molhir —?'

But they shook their heads: 'No, no, a fine! Name it, we'll see
he gives it!'

Vercingetorix picked up his sword and laid it down at Guemoné's
small feet: 'Let the child take this when he's grown; he'll be proud
to have it then – my sword.'

Ardorix got to his feet slowly, surprised: 'You give your
sword?'

'A sword for a right arm. And here —' He pulled off the rings
from his right hand, the emerald among them.

'A good fine,' said Caltane; but Guemoné glowered, with a white,
tear-streaked face: 'My eldest son can be wounded then, if his father
is paid for it!'

Ardorix looked uncertainly from one to the other; all at once
Molhir said, 'Make the Roman judge! He was here before
any of us.'

They all turned to Titus, and Guemoné saw his cut hand. 'Oh,'
she cried, 'you're hurt too – trying to help! Yes, I'll take your word
over this.'

Titus did not in the least want to be judge, but he felt as if this
was perhaps the best chance he would ever have of impressing the
Gauls with Roman justice and dignity. He asked them to come with
him to his house, hoping that they might all have calmed down by
then. They agreed; Guemoné got up from the ground very carefully
so as not to wake the baby; Molhir and Caltane picked up the sword
and the rings.

At the house, wine was offered, Quintus Velanius sent for the
doctor to see the baby, and the two Romans listened to the whole
story. It was obviously not in their interest to make enemies on either
side; they compromised, with many words and much soothing down
of the angry barbarians. In the end Guemoné was the only one who
was not satisfied, and they gave her a pot of ointment for the child,
which had come all the way from Egypt, and seemed to pacify her
a little. Titus watched her sideways; she was a pretty girl – oh, very
pretty! – hardly full grown as yet, fifteen years old perhaps, not
more; her hair was curled in a yellow fleece across her back and over
her temples; her blue, resentful eyes matched the blue stones of her
necklace; how creamy-white her breast had been as she suckled the
child! He liked these blonde, firm-limbed Gallic women: something
to bite on. . . . The doctor came and pronounced favourably on
the baby, but he began to fret again, and Guemoné rose to go.
The chief from Curdun and the chief from Gergovia were quite
friendly as they went out, and the Roman officers congratulated
one another on a good day's work; this was the way to make their
rule welcome in the new province; this was how Caesar would have
wished them to be.

Vercingetorix went back to Gergovia the next week. The others
stayed on rather longer; Ardorix used to go about a great deal with
his cousin Caltane, but yet they were not too good friends. The
baby got well, but his right arm was never so strong as his left,
and the red scar was always there to keep his mother angry every
time she saw it.

Molhir of the Carnutes was going to be a Druid; he was learning
the ritual and the hymns, all their unguessable and complicated
secrets; but it would be months yet before he could make his first
sacrifice. In the meantime he travelled and observed and made
friends; it was all part of his preparation to learn what men were
like. He liked these Arvernians less than he liked the Celts of the
north, the Veneti, Meromic and his sister for instance. And he liked

the Romans, as a whole, even less; he felt them a menace to druidism, these straightforward, deliberate people; they were hard to frighten, hard to influence; they would think nothing of laying axes to the sacred groves if they had the will to do it.

The Romans went back, too, at the end of Autumn; Quintus Velanius was actually rather better, and thought himself even more so. Publius Crassus, the Legate under whose command they were, had quartered his legions among the friendly people in northern Gaul. Titus was beginning to be quite happy; he liked the camp life, the long lines of huts with fires in front of them, the sound of marching feet, the trumpet calls on winter evenings. And he liked dealing with the Gauls, getting in food, buying horses, settling disputes between them and the soldiers. He only wished he could do something about his servant; this old freedman of his grandfather's had the greatest objection to anything out of the way, particularly the Gallic stuffs and ornaments which Titus wanted to have decorating his hut; and he somehow made it difficult for Titus to ask a guest to come in. Particularly a she-guest. Perhaps it was only that he reminded that young man of his grandfather; but he was certainly trying.

Corn was beginning to run short and could not be had locally; there was the same trouble at some of the other winter-quarters. So a few of the officers were sent off to requisition it from the further tribes. Quintus Velanius and Titus Barrus rode out of the camp together, with a small following of soldiers, army accountants and slaves; they headed north-west, bound for the barley-growing cantons of Aremorica. It was the depth of winter, and the paths were sometimes hard to find, but they could always get guides from one village to the next. Titus watched his friend at work in a couple of places: it seemed easy; the landowners, chiefs and magistrates, with whom they had to deal, were on the whole willing to sell the corn at a reasonable price. He went on by himself, half afraid of the responsibility, half delighted to have it; he used to ride alone in front of his men, watching the seagulls wheeling above the frozen fields, and feeling intensely proud of being a Roman and one of Caesar's officers.

He went from town to town of the Veneti, bargaining, drawing up contracts, hiring horses to send the corn back on; he always tried to be as friendly as possible with the Gauls, modelling himself on his great commander, and very soon he could speak Gallic well enough never to need an interpreter. But, as he went up among the Veneti, further and further from his base, he began to notice that they were getting less friendly. He would perhaps get his corn, but the country people would throw stones at him; one or two of his men got killed in quarrels with the natives, and it seemed impossible to find out who had done it or get justice from the local chief. He began to be uneasy and thought he would turn back at once; he had nearly the full tale of corn.

He was in a small town near the coast, waiting to put through the last of his negotiations; the chief had made some delays, but finally the corn had appeared and was duly being weighed and checked by the accountants in the market-place. Titus had left them to it and was walking up and down the main street, which was unusually full of Gauls; his own men were just a handful, standing together beside the corn-sacks or leading the horses about to keep them warm. It was a chill, bright day; the ruts all along the street were frozen into hard edges with thick ice on the pools between; every now and then Titus slipped and cursed his nailed boots. On each side there was a long row of mud and wattle huts, with thatch hanging in deep eaves over the doors; in front of one there would be salted fish for sale, cheese or cloth in front of another.

The street sloped up, round a dozen sharp corners, towards the chief's house at the end, a big, scrambling place with a tower at each side, all round it sheds, hay-stacks, barns and stables, and finally a five-foot turf wall, wide enough to walk along, and a ditch that was frozen over except in one place where the ice had been broken for cattle to drink. Titus heard a horseman coming up behind; the hoofs rang on the hard ground as he trotted past and on to the castle; Titus thought he must be a messenger from the chief's over-lord, Kormiac the Wolf, partly because of the way every one stared after him, partly because of the wolf's head in black on the pennon at the end of his lance. The news might be anything, of course, but still Titus felt a little uneasy and turned to go back.

A glance at the castle showed him a score of armed horsemen riding down; he began to hurry along the slippery street. A couple of men came out of one of the huts with some story of pack ponies to sell, and, when he told them he didn't want any, caught him by the sleeve to keep him. He shook them off and went on down the street; an old woman came up to him and stopped him, saying that one of his soldiers had broken into her house and ill-treated her and her daughter – what compensation would he give her? He bade her come along with him and show him which man it was; she hobbled beside him, talking all the time. For a moment he kept pace with her, then broke away again, bidding her follow. Then it was more people with things to sell, crowding all round him, getting in his way, shouting so that he couldn't hear if there were horses coming up behind him or not! He told them to come after him to the market-place, where he would settle with them all; they were still thick in front of him and he drew his sword, nervously, to clear a passage. He felt like running but tried not to show it, and only walked as fast as he could. Suddenly he slipped again and fell on his back, hitting his head on the edge of the rut. His sword flew out of his hand, he rolled over in a desperate clutch at it, but the whole town was on top of him! He fought them furiously, biting and kicking, and was nearly up once, but they knocked all the breath out of him and kept him down; he was gagged before he could shout twice, and elbows and wrists were tied behind him. The horsemen from the castle were all round him, with the chief himself at their head, who hoisted him up in front of his saddle, with a great shout of laughter and 'Come along, baby!'

Titus Barrus blushed from ear to ear: he had fallen into the trap so easily! What would Quintus Velanius say? What would his Legate think? – and Caesar – and his grandfather! His helmet had fallen off, and some one reached over and put it on to him back-side-foremost: the abominable Gallic sense of humour! He was an ambassador too, or as good, come on an errand of peace; it was contrary to all right – even the barbarians must know it! What did they mean to do with him? The final humiliation was when his nose started bleeding: after that he felt as if nothing else they could do to him would matter.

They came to the market-place; first of all the chief, with Titus very conspicuously a prisoner, and then the horsemen with a great mob of townspeople, all more or less armed, behind them. The accountants and slaves almost all dropped the corn-sacks and weights and money-bags, and fell on their knees, holding out their hands for mercy; the half-dozen soldiers ran together and faced the Gauls, with drawn swords and a very Roman firmness. The chief undid the piece of stuff from over Titus' mouth, saying, 'Speak to them. We don't want bloodshed.'

Titus looked round: he hadn't the least chance of being rescued. 'What terms do you give them?' he asked.

'Their lives, and they'll not be badly treated.'

'Very well.' So he shouted to his men to surrender, as they were far outnumbered. They threw down their swords, and the Gauls took them and the others off to the castle, not always even troubling to tie their hands.

Titus said nothing at first; he was trying to hear what the Gauls were saying to one another, and also wondering what exactly he ought to do; it wasn't a situation he had ever considered. The Gauls were too irritatingly pleased with themselves; the chief wagged his great red beard and told his men how Kormiac would praise them all. One of them rode up with a sack of corn across his horse's back behind, a bag of gold in front; he shouted, 'I've been marketing with the Romans!' They all laughed and the chief poked Titus in the ribs. At the castle gate they dismounted and marched him up between them to the hall, where all the women had collected; he heard the story of his capture repeated with comic additions, and the young maids crowded round to stare at him and stick bits of hay into his hair. He was then put into chains, which were heavy but not so painful as the ropes, and, besides, left him enough liberty to move his arms and walk.

The chief sat down in a great carved chair, close to the fire, and started drinking at once. Titus was brought up to him and began, with his heart rather in his throat, by blaming his captor for using violence on one who should have been safe by all the laws of nations, and then asked why he had done it. The chief pointed a large hairy forefinger at him and said, 'If you Romans think we don't know all about you, you're wrong. Who wants to go to Britain and take all our trade away? You! Who thinks we're going to lie down under it? You! Who's going to get a surprise? You!' and he very cheerfully offered Titus a drink. It was no good trying to get information out of him; he was obviously acting under orders. But he treated Titus and his men very well; it would have been a different matter if they'd been taken prisoner during a war, but just now the Gauls were in a good temper.

Later in the evening a man ran breathlessly up the hall, and threw himself in front of the chief with a message which set all the drinkers shouting and clashing their swords. Quintus Velanius had been taken, and news was coming in from the Aremorican chiefs in all the cantons that the rest of the Roman officers who had been sent to buy corn were safely prisoners. Titus was almost glad; if he had been an idiot, at least it was in good company. But what was it all about? Suddenly he remembered that Crassus had hostages from all these tribes; so presumably the intention was that they should be exchanged for the hostages. Not that a Roman General would ever let himself be dictated to like that by barbarians! But in the meantime he could eat and drink with these Gauls. Their clothes were rougher – more skins and less woven stuff; their houses were much more primitive; he felt he had lost touch with even that half civilization there always was among the Arvernians and Haeduans he had been seeing lately.

A week later another of the messengers came, this time for him to be taken off to the over-lord, Kormiac; he had to leave his men

behind, and went off himself on a pony between armed guards.
They rode out from the town on to a wind-swept moor where they
seemed to be guided by the rare trees they passed from time to time.
The snow was not very deep, though sometimes it had drifted into
hollows where the ponies stumbled; once three of them fell and he
was thrown off and got rather uncomfortably tangled in his chains.
They stayed the night in a bothy where the shepherd's wife fed them
on rye-bread and strips of dried meat. Towards the afternoon of
the next day they came to their journey's end; a thaw had set in,
with slanting rain, and all the burns in heavy spate and dangerous
to cross; soon they and the ponies were mud from head to foot and
soaking wet. Titus heard the sea roaring in front of him and caught
a glimpse of it, grey and forbidding under the rain, as they came up
on to the cliffs.

The house stood rather by itself, without the usual surrounding
village, but there were any amount of out-buildings on each side;
it was built of wood with great blocks of granite as a foundation,
round three sides of a courtyard where the maids splashed across
with their skirts up to their knees; the walls were all lime-washed
and the doors outlined in red, but it didn't look cheerful in this
weather. Inside it was rather dark; most of the windows had been
shuttered against the wet, and the fires only lighted the two ends of
the hall. He and his guard went up to the further one, and waited,
dripping on to the floor and warming their chilled hands. At the
other side of the fire several women were standing round a loom,
where already the upper third of the stuff was woven; two of them
were altering the weights that held down the warp threads; another
held the shuttle and directed them. Further from the fire a slave girl
with matted hair stood spinning wool, the distaff under her left arm;
her twisting spindle rose and fell quickly and regularly; the creamy
wool shone in the firelight. The three at the loom looked round it
at the prisoner – tall, kindly girls, one fair head and two brown.
They had long skirts with embroidered hems, short-sleeved bodices
of fine wool, and leather brogues; bracelets were bronze and coral;
their hair was loose. The fair one had gold ear-rings, each with a
coral bead, and swung on a leathern thong, a pendant of bronze;
she looked up and smiled at Titus as she and her women went back
to their work.

They had been waiting about half an hour, and were beginning
to get warm, though not yet dry, when a big, loose-limbed boy ran
in, shaking the rain out of his hair; he was younger than Titus, but
taller already. The fair girl called to him and he came over, glancing
at guards and prisoner, then pulled off his clinging wet shirt and

trousers and threw them down in front of the fire. He kept on his shoes and a great golden necklace, all finely wrought with twists and spirals, and roundels of scarlet enamel. 'Father's coming back,' he said, 'but the bay mare's slipped her shoulder; the road's all mud outside.'

'Oh,' said the girl, 'he won't like that!'

'He doesn't. So you'd better keep out of the way, Fiommar.' And he went off himself.

A few minutes later there was a great stir; the women looked at one another questioningly, and Titus turned to see his real captor, Kormiac the Wolf, who came in with great strides, a huge man; the scabbard of his sword clattered against the door jamb, his plaid swung behind him. The guards brought Titus forward, a hand on each shoulder; he felt rather small. Kormiac stuck his chin out frowning at him: 'So this is the man, is it? Take him off at once and see he's chained fast. Why in God's name couldn't you have done it already?' The man stammered apologies; Kormiac turned his back, with 'Don't talk. Get on with it.'

But suddenly the girl spoke: 'Father, you're surely not going to send him down to the prison like this! It's not dry, and he's wet: he'll die of cold!'

'What's that to you? Do you suppose our hostages have any better quarters? You wouldn't talk like that if I'd had to send Meromic!'

But Fiommar went up to her father, put her arm round his neck and looked up at him with calm eyes: 'Now, father, don't be hasty! You must let him get dry. He hasn't even had anything to eat.'

At this Kormiac swung off to 'What were you doing not to feed him, then?'

'I was waiting for you to come home; now we can have supper.'

She called to the slave girl, who dropped her distaff and ran out, and then set herself to soothing her father down, so that by the time the food was on the table he was almost in a good temper. And she sent for dry clothes for Titus, who was shivering with the beginnings of a chill, and watched him change, much to his embarrassment.

They ate together, but Kormiac was still moody, and Titus was much too frightened of him to do any talking himself. Meromic came back rather late, but he didn't talk either, except in undertones to the man next him; and he went out early with a muttered excuse about riveting a shield-grip. Fiommar tried to keep the old Wolf on to pleasant subjects, but after a whole jar of mead to himself, he remembered the mare with a start and a curse, and bade them take the Roman down, and chain him to a staple.

So they marched him off, one man ahead with a flare to light them down stone steps and along passages that dripped water on their heads. The place where they chained him was a sort of cave hollowed in the rock, sloping up from the main tunnel; there was a barred opening four feet up, on the level of the ground outside, and gusts of rain blew in through it. The mud floor was streaming with cold trickles, and the bundle of straw they brought with them was soon sopped. For five days Titus Barrus lay there wretchedly in the grip of his chill; Fiommar or one of her maids came down from time to time with food and curious medicines, but he was too ill to take much notice. He woke up on the morning of the sixth day, feeling much better; the early sun shone in brightly from outside, and he stood in front of the grating, trying to get as much of it as he could. Suddenly he heard a great baying of hounds out of sight, and in a moment they were pelting past, just at the other side, great long-legged deer-hounds, black and grey, with collars of bronze on their stretched necks! And all at once there was Meromic running in the middle of them, leaping high in the sunlight, crying loud and ringingly to the pack, his feet no heavier than theirs. Not more than time to see him, and he was gone. The prisoner shook angrily at the bars, envying that barbarian boy out there, so free and alive and careless; then he turned away, catching himself up sharply: he was a Roman officer and a patrician, and – oh, this prison couldn't last for ever!

And indeed they came the same day and brought him up; Kormiac was in a good temper again and a different man: genial, kindly, slapping the young Roman on the back, laughing monstrously at his own jokes, calling Fiommar away from her work to sing to them; he seemed only surprised that Titus did not always respond! Meromic came in from his hunting at dusk, the blood of some slain beast on his arms.

'Did you go far?' asked his father.

'We killed on the beach over by the Black Rocks; Louaven was there too.'

'Ah. We must take our guest out hunting with us some day.'

The boy looked at Titus with a broad grin; Fiommar giggled softly: father was so unaccountable! Titus himself thought he ought to say something; he went over and fingered Meromic's short spear: 'What were you after – deer?'

'Yes; but we've got wild cats in the woods to the east and boar as well; I like boar hunting.'

'And wolves?'

'Oh, no!' – the boy looked horrified. 'It would be geas for me to kill a wolf!'

'Geas —?'

'Well: not right. I couldn't – except in self-defence. I suppose you didn't know, but I'm a wolf myself – we all are; so it would be killing one's brother; the thing one mustn't do. Father's really the Wolf, you see, the head wolf; but I'm the next after him. And I think the other wolves – the wild ones – understand, because they don't come and take our sheep like they do further along.'

Titus was surprised, but he had got used to odd things among the barbarians.

After all, he never did go hunting with them, because very soon afterwards he was sent away again, this time to a strong town on the coast, where he found Quintus Velanius, who had had much the same experience. Crassus, of course, could not hold converse with an armed enemy nor exchange the hostages; his officers had to shift for themselves. Titus and Quintus both managed to escape in late winter, after heavy bribing of their guards and a boatman; a few more bribes, and they were back with the army. As soon as Caesar's orders came, they were both sent off, first to start the building of ships of war, then to raise oarsmen from the Province. They were very cautious this time, and took really adequate forces with them; but nothing happened. The fleet was assembled gradually, the legions were prepared and waiting for the word: a fine vengeance brewing against the Veneti!

THE MOUNTAIN WOLVES

John Maddox Roberts

The following story also takes place at the time of Caesar's conquest of Gaul. It is the opening sequence of a much longer work in progress to be called Wolves and Eagles *which traces the life of the hero all through the Roman world during the campaigns of Julius Caesar.*

John Maddox Roberts (b. 1947) is as well known in the world of fantasy fiction (he has written several new Conan novels based on the character created by Robert E. Howard) as in Roman fiction, where he has written eight novels featuring his Roman detective Decius Metellus, starting with SPQR *(1990).*

Great Odysseus, whom the Romans call Ulixes, spent twenty years in war and wandering before he returned to his home. I have surpassed him, for I spent twenty-three years treading, riding and sailing the lands and waters of the world. I encountered no cyclopes and I entirely missed the land of the lotos-eaters, but I saw sights as marvelous as he did, and encountered women as terrifying as Calypso and as fearsome as Circe.

But I get ahead of myself. If I am to be my own Homer, I must start at the beginning.

I was born near the city of Gades, beyond the Pillars of Herakles. Gades is a very ancient town, once the westernmost colony of the Phoenicians, those fearless mariners who yearly sent their vessels beyond the known boundaries of the world. It was founded more than a thousand years ago and was for centuries the world's great market for tin and amber. Later the Carthaginians, a people who had raised another Phoenician colony to the dignity of empire, took Gades for their own. Then the Romans, who seize everything that lies before them, captured Gades in the second of their savage wars with Carthage.

The people there are of many bloods, both native and foreign. The Punic strain predominates in the city and the nearer countryside; dark of hair and eye, with skin olive-tinged, their speech full of guttural sounds and abrupt stops. In the hills of the interior live the wild, untamed tribes who speak a tongue related to that of Gaul. They are darker than the Gauls, but paler than the descendants of the Phoenicians and Carthaginians. Their language contains many pleasing, liquid sounds; a language for boasting and tale-telling and making love.

Here and there are to be found the very ancient folk who peopled Iberia even before the Phoenicians arrived. They are a small people, hard-faced, keeping to themselves in their villages, separated from their neighbors by a speech so incomprehensible that only one born of their race can hope to understand more than a few words.

And always, as in every city touched by the sea, there are Greeks. The Greeks of Gades were always merchants, teachers and priests, for the Greeks export their gods as other people export their local wines. Like coffers of ivory and alabaster the temples of the Olympian deities dotted the coastal plane of southern Hispania, and I was raised in one of them.

My name is Glaucus. It is a nickname I was given in childhood because of my gray-green eyes, and I never knew any other until, many years later, I discovered the secret of my real name. My foster parents were an aged priest of Apollo named Dolon and his wife, Myrrhine.

The temple was no larger than a big farm house, but its proportions were so exquisite that it shamed the city's garish temple of Mars, built a hundred years before by the Romans. Its slender columns with their Ionic capitals were fluted like the graceful pleats in the gown of a goddess. Its pediment bore a sculptured scene of the bright god quelling the battle between the rude Lapiths and the drunken centaurs.

'Regard this, child,' Dolon said to me, when I was old enough for minimal understanding. 'The god with outflung arm stills the raging of the rustics and the violence of the savage man-beasts. What does this mean to you?'

I considered it. I was perhaps seven or eight years old at the time. The god stood in the center, upright where the others were contorted, nude as they were but clothed in divinity. His head was

held high, magisterial, his right arm stretched forth on a line straight
from the shoulder, level as his terrible gaze. His form was human
but he had the unapproachability of perfect beauty.

'The god doesn't like it that they are fighting and hurting each
other,' I said. 'People shouldn't act that way in the presence
of a god.'

'You speak with the understanding of a child. You know
the story?'

'The Lapiths invited the centaurs to a great wedding. The centaurs
got drunk and there was a brawl. And then . . . I think Apollo came
down and made them stop.'

Dolon smiled and settled himself more comfortable, on the
stone bench beneath the stately cypress, one of a pair flanking
the granite-paved walk leading to the temple.

'No, Glaucus. In the tale, Theseus of Athens and his friend,
Prince Perithoos of the Lapiths, wrought a great slaughter among
the centaurs. It is a violent and rather vulgar story, typical of the
earliest legends.'

'Then why is Apollo there?' I asked, pointing up at the triangular
pediment.

'Glaucus, these stories are myths. Do you know what a myth is?'
He smiled still, but it was a serious smile, adding to the dignity of
his kindly, white-bearded face.

I thought about that for a while. I knew the word, and I had
thought it to mean the tales of heroes and gods from ancient times.
but upon reflection I realized that it must have another meaning.

'No,' I admitted.

'Excellent,' Dolon said, approvingly. 'It is good that you stop and
think before you answer. Fools think they know everything and their
words spring from their mouths without thought or reflection. And,
in a way, that is what this beautiful scene signifies.'

I did not understand what this meant, so I said nothing.
Unknowingly, I was displaying yet more precocious wisdom. In
my unsettled life since that time, I have often saved myself from
disaster by keeping my mouth shut when confronted by my own
ignorance.

'Myths,' Dolon explained, 'are things that never happened, but
are always true.' He sat with his hands folded atop his walking
stick, and now he used the stick to point at the sculptured
group. 'See how upright and masterful the god stands! His
is the power of pure thought. The god's power resides in his
mind. The Lapiths and the centaurs are creatures of unbridled emotion and brute strength. Their legs and their bodies

are contorted in their fury, their mindless desire to rend and kill.

'What a contrast is Apollo! His legs hold him erect, his body is vertical, in the noble pose of the orator. Nothing of him moves save the head and the arm. This is the mastery of the upper plane, for the head creates and expresses thought, and the arm and hand carry out the dictates of the will. This is the plane of the divine, which is the plane of the most perfectly human. The belly and loins are the realm of the animal. They must be severely controlled.'

The part about the belly I understood. I had a few years yet to be concerned about the other part.

'And is that a myth?' I asked.

'A myth is a way of explaining things,' Dolon said. 'Philosophers try to come at the truth by worrying endlessly at questions with the tool of pure reason. Myth is a way to make manifest the truths of the cosmos in the form of tales or images. Men of intelligence do not truly believe that the gods seduce mortal women or each other's wives or take a personal hand in the wars of mortal men. The demigod Herakles, whom you have learned to call Hercules, did not slaughter his wife and child, nor did he lie with the fifty daughters of King Thespius in a single night. If in truth, he existed at all.'

I found this not only confusing but alarming. 'You mean there never was a Hercules?' Hercules was one of my favorites.

'That does not mean he is not real.' With a thin finger he tapped his brow, just below the shining dome that once had been graced with hair. 'He lives here. And here,' he tapped his heart. 'Herakles is a creation of necessity. He is courage, strength and warlike ferocity harnessed to thought and purpose. He slays the monsters of nightmare, making the world a fit place for civilized men. He is a protector of those who would build and conduct their lives in peace. But he is half a god, and that is a frightening thing, so men give him human appetites and human frailties.'

'But what about Apollo?' I asked. 'And the Lapiths and centaurs? Did it really happen?'

'It is always happening,' Dolon said. 'Apollo is mind and reason triumphing over brute nature. He tames the senseless turmoil of nature and makes possible civilization, culture and all that is good and seemly in life. This is the virtue and genius of Attica. The Lapiths are uncultivated men of Thessaly and the centaurs are a part of the retinue of Dionysus, the lord of barbarous Thrace. Dionysus is a great and terrible god. Do not confuse him, as the Romans have, with their drunken Bacchus. Dionysus is the embodiment of riotous, mindless nature and he and his followers must ever be quelled if we are not to be drawn back from the light, into the dark morass of the earth cults.'

I cannot say that I truly understood this, although I remembered his words, and Dolon knew better than to try to teach me too deeply at so early an age. There were to be many more such lessons, and most of them I was to absorb into myself. I grew to revere the splendid culture of Greece, especially that of Athens, which created art of a beauty that was more than human, and whose philosophies freed men from the shackles of ignorance and superstition, giving them the power to think like gods.

But in another way he was unsuccessful, for I never lost my fascination with the mystery cults, those dark, hidden coils of power that promise knowledge deeper than thought, where worship, fear, bloodshed and ecstasy are one. Throughout my life I have sought out those sects of terror and enlightenment. Both the bright sky of Apollo and the dark underworld of Dionysus have brought me to an understanding of myself and my fellow men and women, we creatures who like the centaurs are half-god and half-animal, and who must dwell neither in the sky nor underground, but upon the surface of the earth, yearning for the one and fearing the other.

These deep matters did not press greatly upon me in those early years. I was far more concerned with the fascinating business of life, which meant climbing trees and raiding the neighbors' orchards and evading my teachers. The temple was the center of a small complex which included the house and household of Dolon, the stables, storehouses and a fine garden and vineyard. There were about twenty inhabitants, slave and free. As children will, I saw myself as the center of all this. It was a countryside of small farms and a few large plantations and horse-breeding establishments. The city was about four miles away, an hour's easy walk on the straight, beautifully kept Roman road.

One of my earliest memories was the day the Roman came. Our temple served mainly the Greek population of the district. We rarely saw the Roman overlords. I must have been about five years old. I was sitting on the edge of the steps of the temple, watching the smoke of the morning sacrifice rise from the altar. The sound of hoofbeats drew my attention down the double row of poplars to the road that connected Gades with Carthago Nova. I blinked and shouted for Dolon to come quickly.

I thought that this must be a visitor from Olympus, so brightly did he gleam. As he drew nearer I saw that the rider was clad in a cuirass of bronze burnished to a dazzling luster. On his head was a helmet covered in silver and gold and resplendent with scarlet feathers. The latest series of Hispanic wars had been over for three years, but Roman officials were still under military discipline, as I learned later.

'Stay where you are, boy,' Dolon said as he came from within the temple and descended the steps. The godlike Roman dismounted with a swirl of his blue cloak and Dolon greeted him. The two spoke together for a while but I was too far away to understand them. Something distracted me then – I think it was an especially fascinating caterpillar that crawled along the step by my thigh. Then something blocked the sunlight and I looked up to see the Roman towering over me.

'So you are Glaucus, eh?' I understood him because I had been learning Latin right along with Greek. He placed his hands under my arms and raised me high, studying me as if I was up for purchase. His helmet was off by this time, and I saw that he had short, sandy hair and a face made up of hard planes and angles. It was a forbidding face, of a type I was to discover to be typically Roman.

'You are well named,' he said, and he smiled, making him seem less frightening. 'I can see you have straight limbs, and Dolon tells me you learn well. Tell me, boy, which would you rather be? A Greek or a Roman?'

I looked at aged, bald-headed Dolon with his white beard and his walking stick. Then I looked at this gleaming demigod who held me aloft in his strong hands. 'A Roman!'

He threw back his head and laughed. I was to know that Roman laugh well in later years. If a human voice can come close to the sound of a sword clashing against armor, it is in the Roman laugh. I would have cried then, but he set me on my feet and reached into a pouch that hung from the scarlet sash that wrapped his cuirass. His hand came out with a packet wrapped in fine white cloth.

'For you, boy.'

I took it eagerly and unwrapped the cloth. It was full of sweets; honeyed figs and seed cakes rolled in crushed almonds, just the sort of thing my nurse, Gorgo, never allowed me.

'What do you say, child?' Dolon prodded.

'Thank you, sir!' Then I began stuffing them into my mouth. The Roman ruffled my hair and the two men walked away into the temple, leaving me with my prize. I went about my childish business, which included seeing how many new chicks had hatched that morning. From the chicken yard I saw Dolon and the Roman walking through a nearby field. The Roman stopped and drew a fold of his cloak over his head and stooped to look at something. Then he straightened and the two men walked on.

The Roman left perhaps an hour later. I watched him go from my perch in a favorite plane tree. For a long time I thought of the Romans as looking like him: splendid, lordly men like the bronze-girt heroes of Homer. When I finally saw legionaries, I was disappointed, for they were for the most part short men with hard, peasant faces, all of them wearing dingy iron and faded woolen tunics. Only the officers wore the resplendent bronze breastplates embossed with the muscles of an athlete and covered with griffons or gorgons or eagles worked in silver. I was also to learn that appearance had little to do with efficiency.

Myrrhine was younger than her husband, a grave, gracious lady who conducted the affairs of the temple household with quiet efficiency. I thought for a time that she was my mother, but when I was old enough to understand, she told me that I was a foundling. She had come upon me crying in the bushes after the armies had passed through the countryside in the recent wars. The roads had been full of refugees in those days; people fleeing from some sacked town or devastated countryside hoping to find a place of safety.

'You lay in the arms of a dead woman who must have been your mother, Glaucus,' she told me as I sat upon her knee. 'Her body was still warm, so recently had she died. She was a beautiful woman, and we knew that she must have been of good family, for her hands were smooth and her skin was unblemished by the sun. Her clothes were of fine quality. Your own wrappings were of the finest cloth and you wore amulets of gold.'

She stroked my cheek and smiled to soften her words. 'So you see, Glaucus, you must not call me Mother. That would show disrespect for your true parents, and that is a thing hateful to the gods. Your mother's ashes are buried behind the olive orchard, and when you are old enough you will have to go there and perform the proper rites for the repose of her shade.'

This saddened me, and my simple world became more complicated than I had thought.

'Then who is my father?' I asked.

She looked out the window. 'He may have been a soldier. Perhaps he was one of the senators who supported Sertorius in the great rebellion. Many high-born men were killed in the years following that war. You have no idea how terrible the last twenty years or more have been. Only for the last three have we had anything like true peace. So you see, Glaucus,' she spoke with utmost seriousness, the afternoon sun striking silver glints from her dark hair, 'you must never speak of these things to other people. Your family may have been one of the ones proscribed. Victors seldom forgive.'

Not long after this I went behind the olive grove and Myrrhine showed me my mother's grave marker. It was one of perhaps thirty, all of them severely plain in the Greek fashion. Carved upon it in Greek letters was a single name, Glaukia, the Greek feminine form of my own.

'If she was dead, how did you know her name?' I asked.

'She had eyes like yours. It seemed fitting.'

I asked her about the other graves. 'Some are people who lived and worked here at the temple. These three . . . ' she showed me three small markers side by side, '. . . were our own children.' The names on the small stones were Ariston, Callias and Phryne. 'Our two sons, and our daughter. None of them lived to be as old as you. Childhood fevers are terrible. They rob us of all our hopes.' She smiled down at me. 'But the gods brought you to comfort us in our old age.'

It seemed to me only fitting that the gods should show a special generosity to their priest and his wife. 'And the others?' I asked.

'Most of them were people who died nearby with no kin or friends to claim them, like your mother. One must always show respect for the dead. Never leave them unburied, without rites. Their shades can never know rest and they will stay on earth to torment the living.'

As she said these words I looked around at the nearby fields, at the temple and, just beyond the last olive tree at the corner of the orchard, I saw the chicken yard. I realized that this was where I had seen Dolon and the Roman strolling that day. What had the two of them been doing visiting a grave yard? I remembered the Roman's curious gesture and I was about to ask Myrrhine what it meant when I stopped myself. Something told me that this was a subject I should not broach, so I held my tongue. I thought about it often in later years, when I went out at the proper times to put wine and meal and oil upon my mother's grave.

As I grew, tutors arrived to give me lessons in a number of subjects. Dolon himself taught me the culture and lore of Greece and I grew up speaking that language. Others taught me Latin along with the oratorical skills the Romans consider so necessary. I learned music, poetry and the rites required by the gods. I also learned to ride, and my joy in this accomplishment surpassed all others. It was the education of a gentleman: an odd thing since I was a boy without parents, but it did not seem odd at the time.

My nurse was a Spartan. That harsh state had not been of political or military importance for nearly four hundred years, but Spartan nurses were still esteemed above all others. This is because they never spoil children, a virtue unappreciated by me at the time. She was attentive enough, I suppose, but any serious misbehavior was sufficient reason for a thrashing. She did not concern herself with my progress in my lessons, but she was alert for lapses in manners and disrespect toward my elders.

As Gorgo never tired of telling me, the Spartans have a festival at which, before the altar of Athene, boys are flogged into insensibility and frequently die of the treatment. Her whippings were not quite that severe, but the priests of Athene have stronger arms. One advantage of having such a nurse is that if later in life you are taken prisoner and made a slave, the whips of the overseers are nothing you have not experienced before.

At the time I took her sternness to be simple cruelty, but that was not so. Unlike so many mothers and nurses she did not try to quell my high spirits. For women who must toil all their lives managing a house and many children, the misbehavior of one is an intolerable distraction. Gorgo had no task save to raise me, and she could be surprisingly patient. She was not a slave but a freeborn woman, widowed young and not inclined to remarry. Sparta is one of the few places in the world where a woman without a man is not helpless and without hope, for the demand for Spartan nurses is always high and such women demand and receive good compensation.

But they cannot invest their hearts. The iron Spartan discipline would not allow her to show more than the most perfunctory affection and I thought her to be without feelings for me. Later I would come to realize that her life would have been one of endless sorrow if she had allowed herself to become closely attached to her employers' children, for she had only a few years with each before moving on to the next family.

Truthfully, she allowed me to get away with a great many things that most mothers would have punished, such as raiding the neighbors' fruit. This was a fine old Spartan tradition of which she approved, although if the neighbors complained she whipped me for being caught. But she reserved her utmost severity for disrespect. She drew a fine line between minor impudence and outright insolence, and the latter she punished. The Spartans prized above all a modest, respectful demeanor before one's elders and social superiors, and she would countenance no breach of manners.

Aside from frequent savage thrashings, though, it was a near idyllic upbringing for a boy. The moment I got away from my lessons, I was outdoors. From the time I was about nine years old, my steps took me swiftly to the stables. Iberia is a land of horses. Within a few miles of our temple there were studs that bred horses for riding, horses for war and horses for pulling chariots in the races. Our stable had stalls for four horses. They were of a local breed, sleek little blacks and bays, and all of them were gentle mares or geldings.

The stableman was a slave named Virro. He was a hill tribesman whose people had chosen the wrong side in the Sertorian rebellion of a few years before. Virro was not his real name, which was barbarous and difficult for Greeks and Romans to pronounce, so his captors had given him a shortened form they could live with. He would never tell me his true name, for he believed that it would give his masters further power over him. He regarded his slave name as something of a trick he had pulled on them.

Virro understood horses in a way that no man can understand other human beings. A part of him lived within their equine minds. He knew their feelings from the sound of their breathing and he detected their ailments long before any overt signs became evident. He rode them bareback with no more than a nose halter, controlling their movements with subtle pressures of knee and shifting body weight. He disliked bits and considered spurs an abomination. But more than anything else he controlled them with his mind and his constant, wordless communication. He strove to teach me to ride the same way.

'Nothing should come between a man and his horse,' he used to say. 'Even a loincloth is too much.' He wore none beneath his tunic.

He considered this skin-to-skin contact to be of paramount importance in understanding and communicating with one's mount. 'A saddle is a Roman thing,' he said. 'Romans are always masters, never friends. A saddle is like an overseer for them. It stands between them and their slaves and helps them to control. Romans do not bother to understand, they just demand obedience.'

He always spoke to me in the Gallic tongue of the Iberian hill people. He never had more than rudimentary Latin and Greek. Some of the other slaves spoke it as well, and I grew up with it as my third language. The hills were not far away, and once I asked Virro why he never tried to run away.

'My tribe is no more,' he said. 'I would just be made a slave by another tribe and they would treat me far worse than the priest. If I must be a slave, this is a good place and Dolon is a good master. I am not starved or beaten, and I have horses to work with. It could be much worse.' He ran his fingers through his short crop of thick, black hair. 'When I was taken prisoner they cut my hair. They slashed off my warrior plaits and took away my weapons. I can run away, but I will never be a free warrior again. It is better to be a comfortable slave than a wretched fugitive.'

Wisdom comes in many forms and from many sources. There were times when Virro's simple words sustained me better than all the volumes of Aristotle.

When I was about thirteen a number of things changed. I am vague about my age because I never knew exactly when I was born. The Romans make the date of birth an important occasion, because they have strict age qualifications for holding their various offices. Few other peoples bother with this observance and I assumed that we were among those who did not.

There are more ways to mark the passing of years than by the calendar, though. During all my previous years I had grown only in height. But then many other changes took place. My shoulders began to broaden, so that my arms no longer hung straight at my sides but inches away from them. My thin arms and legs filled out with muscle and my voice no longer piped. The most fundamental change altered not only my appearance, but my entire outlook, and gave me some unfamiliar preoccupations.

For some time I had noticed new sensations, especially when riding bareback. Warm, thrilling tingles radiated up from between my legs. At first, I thought they were coming from the horse. One day while making water I noticed that something else had changed. Previously, I had needed only my thumb and forefinger to direct my stream. Now I required almost my whole hand. My pea-sized, all but unnoticeable testicles, which had hugged my body in their tiny bubble of skin, were now like two olives and hung down in a very discernible sac. Two or three thin hairs curled at the base of my penis, which soon began to display a will of its own. It began to stand up and demand attention.

One day, only two or three months later, I was in my tiny room, my tunic off, examining this new prodigy. It rose like one of the temple columns, veined like marble porphyry, its base hidden in a now dense and luxuriant nest of fleece. I pulled it this way and that, seeking to relieve its strange, almost painful tension. I felt I was well on the way to accomplishing something when Gorgo came in, and I learned at once that terror drove the spirit from my independent member.

For a few seconds her stony Spartan face betrayed nothing, then she said: 'Get dressed and come with me.'

Relief flooded over me. She always made me take my clothes off for a beating. I followed her from the house and past the temple, to a field nearby where Dolon and Myrrhine were overseeing the planting of a new garden. On its border stood a herm; a crude statue without arms or legs, just a pillar supporting the torso and head of a satyr-like man whose penis jutted up just as mine so recently had. I had seen this statue and many others like it all my life, but it had never occurred to me to wonder at this phenomenon. I resolved to ask about it.

Dolon and Myrrhine looked up at our approach. 'What is it?' he asked.

Gorgo pushed me forward. 'It is time for the palaestra.' Then she turned around and walked away. I never saw her again.

Freed from my nurse's tyranny, I began to train for manhood. The local Greek community maintained a modest palaestra about two miles from the temple. A middle-aged slave named Kriton was assigned to be my pedagogue but his task was to supervise me and keep me out of trouble. He had no power to punish.

The first day, Dolon took me personally to enroll me in the palaestra. It was a beautiful morning, and with Kriton walking behind us, carrying a satchel with vials of oil, scraper and towels, we walked along the smooth paving of the Roman road. The smell of fresh-turned earth made the air rich and men were out pruning the fruit trees.

'You have been schooled in manners and in the accomplishments of the mind,' Dolon told me. 'But that is not enough. A gentleman must cultivate the body as well. Now you are of an age to take up physical pursuits hallowed by long tradition. You will practice running, the javelin, the discus and other exercises. You will learn wrestling, but on no account are you to box. It was once a gentlemanly accomplishment, but it has become degraded by professional athletes. Of the sports of the palaestra the noblest is running, but you are not to neglect the others.'

The palaestra was a long, low building next to a small river. We passed through its entrance and I discovered that it was no more than an enclosure surrounding a broad, rectangular exercise yard in which perhaps a hundred men and boys ran and leapt and wrestled. They were all naked except for a few older instructors who wore wraps and carried long canes which they used as pointers and employed to separate wrestlers who grew ardent in their combat.

Dolon sighed. 'Enjoy your youthful years in the palaestra,' he said. 'They will be the happiest of your life.' A graying man came to us and Dolon introduced him. 'This is Perdiccas. He is master here. He will assign you to your peer group. You are to obey him in all things.'

The two men talked for a while and I studied my new surroundings. I now saw that not everyone was involved in strenuous athletics.

In one corner an extraordinarily handsome young man was playing a lyre before an audience of rapt admirers. In fact, there seemed to be quite a few men who just watched the others.

'I will leave you here now,' Dolon said. 'Remember, your Latin composition lesson will be this afternoon as usual. Only your mornings are different now.'

He left and I followed Perdiccas. I gave my tunic to Kriton and he went to take his place on a bench along one wall, where twenty or thirty other pedagogues whiled away the hours while their well-born charges sweated and rolled in the dust. I was led to an area where boys my age and a little older were put through their paces by trainers. The boys studied me and I was distinctly uncomfortable. I had been raised as if I were an only son. There had been no slave children near my own age. I was unused to being a part of a group.

'This is Glaucus, the foster son of the priest Dolon. He is to be your group mate.' With that perfunctory introduction, Perdiccas walked away.

'We were about to begin our morning run,' a trainer said. He was a man of about thirty, splendidly built, his hair just beginning to thin and show gray threads. 'Can you run?'

'Of course I can run, sir,' I said, amazed that he should ask. It seemed to me that I had done little except run and ride, attend lessons and sleep. I never walked save indoors.

He smiled, showing white teeth in a bronze face. 'Good. You will need to know how.' A boy came up with a double flute, which he bound around his head by its tapes. 'Keep with the others,' the man told me, 'and run in time with the flute.'

The flute player began a shrill, repetitive series of up-and-down notes and the trainer trotted toward the entrance with the boys behind him. I fell in with them, expecting the steady trot to open into a real run. Outside, we took a path parallel to the Roman road. Still we maintained that steady trot. The dirt was coarse beneath my bare feet so I stepped over onto the smooth stone of the road.

'Don't run on the pavement!' the trainer shouted. His ears must have detected the different sound my feet made against the stone. 'You'll destroy your ankles and knees before you are old enough to bear arms.' I fell back amid laughter, my face flaming.

We passed the first milestone, still jogging along to the rising and falling notes of the flute, the trainer's steadily clapping hands. They called this running? I was tempted to dash out ahead of them all and show them what running really was, but I had been schooled in obedience and so I held the pace.

After the third milestone I began to breathe hard and to sweat.

By the fourth I was puffing and my stomach churned. My side felt as if someone had thrust a lance through it. Nobody else seemed to be so distressed. My legs became wobbly as my chest burned and spots swam into my vision. Still we trotted along at that maddeningly slow pace. It didn't seem so slow any more. I began to fall back. The others jeered at me as they passed me. I didn't care. I began to cough.

Abruptly, I was on all fours. My stomach was heaving, my eyes streaming, and strings of mucus dripped from my lips to the dusty ground. A great whiteness blossomed before me and then I was full length on the ground, retching and gasping at the same time. Then for a while all was blackness.

When I came back to myself I had enough strength to crawl to a nearby milestone and sit with my back against it. So this was the first day of what were to be the happiest years of my life? The palaestra must have changed since the days of Dolon's youth. I wiped the tears from my eyes and studied the milestone. They were planted along every Roman road, one every thousand paces. Each one gave the number of miles to the nearest cities, plus the distance to the Golden Milestone in the Forum Romanum, the center of the world.

A short while later the boys came back. They laughed and hooted and pointed at me. I wanted to die. The trainer stepped out and came to where I half-lay against the stone, my chest not yet working steadily. He squatted by me and his skin shone with oil and sweat, but he breathed easily.

'You see why I asked you if you knew how to run?'

I nodded.

'You thought you could run, but you have always run as boys do, heedlessly and at top speed. That is only good for the dash. Here you must learn to run as a man runs, with steady pace and controlled breathing. You can run all day this way, and when the time comes you will be able to do it in armor, with a shield on your arm. Come, can you stand?'

My limbs were like boiled dough, but I did not want to admit it. He took my arm and pulled me to my feet. For a few seconds I swayed dizzily, then my vision cleared and I was able to take a few wobbly steps. Soon I was walking beside him.

'The palaestra is a place where you test your limits,' he told me. 'Here you seek *arete*, personal excellence. It is also where you learn to deal with your peers. All the boys of your group are free born. Some are aristocrats and will think themselves better than you, but all are equal. You may have to prove it to them.'

I nodded. I was beginning to feel a little better. 'I will,' I said.

'Good. My name is Myron. I am trainer to the juniors.' He put an arm across my shoulders and with the other hand he gestured easily as he spoke. 'It will be hard at first, very hard. But if a man is to be master of himself he must first master his own body. I will help you all I can, but I cannot show favoritism. In the palaestra you are just one of the boys, and you will have to work your own way to excellence. Do you understand this?'

'Yes.'

'If you train your body well from early youth, treat it well but sternly, it will serve you excellently all your life, until age finally takes you.'

'Like a horse,' I said.

'Exactly. If you exercise a horse every day, and train it well, it becomes a creature of your will and serves you at need. Leave it in a stall and feed it grain, and not only does it become worthless but it will die young.'

We returned to the palaestra as the morning was ending. Myron took us to the little river and we plunged in, washing away the morning's accumulation of sweat, oil and dust while we were given a brief swimming lesson. As a beginner, I was merely taught how not to sink beneath the water. It looked frightening at first, but I was determined not to disgrace myself again before these who were to be my peers. To my surprise, I found the water to be immensely enjoyable.

While we sat on rocks drying ourselves I watched the other boys. Most of them seemed to defer to one slightly bigger than the rest, a dark-haired boy with a sullen mouth. Now he came up to me with a half-dozen other boys close behind him. He stood a pace or two in front of me and looked me up and down.

'You don't look like a Greek,' he told me. 'You look like some sort of bastard Gaul. Who are your parents?'

He had touched upon several sore spots at once, as he was perfectly aware. Besides my strangely colored eyes I was paler than most of the Greeks and Iberians who dwelled nearby. My hair was a sandy color between brown and blond. My squarish face was neither the small-chinned Greek triangle nor the long oval of the Iberian. I had no idea who my parents were. I knew vaguely that orphans were held in low esteem, and I believed that I was an orphan.

'I am the son of Dolon the priest and Myrrhine,' I said, stung.

'Foster son,' he corrected. 'You're probably Dolon's whelp by some slave girl.'

Of course I attacked him. I had been taught to defer to my elders. Nobody had said anything about my peers. I went in with arms flailing, my legs still unsteady from the morning run. The boy sidestepped easily and the next thing I knew I was on the ground, with a great numbness in the side of my face and a ringing in my ears. I tried to get up but I fell back, blood streaming from my nose and mouth. The boy's friends were laughing but he winced, shaking his hand as if he had burned it. This, I understood, was the boxing I was not supposed to learn. Somebody helped me to get up.

'You've just met Photius,' said my helper. 'He has made himself a sort of leader. Don't worry, everybody gets the same welcome.'

I looked at him. He seemed to be my age, with a snubbed nose and hair that bore a reddish tinge. 'Leader?' I said. 'Myron told me all are equal.'

'And he told you you would have to prove it, didn't he?' He grinned, displaying a gap between his front teeth. 'I'm Idas. I went through the same thing on my first day here. Just remember never to back down from him. Pretty soon a newer boy will come along to distract him.'

I dressed and returned home. No one remarked upon my appearance, then or later. Even at the best of times the sports of the palaestra could be rough, and at least they never damaged your clothes.

In time I came to enjoy the palaestra, and to glory in the growing power of my body, and my mastery of it. Myron taught me a useful trick, and one time when Photius took a swing at me I ducked my head so that instead of hitting my face he struck the thick bone of my crown, breaking three knuckles and rendering his hand useless for two months. Soon, he lost interest in me.

A short time after this the household went into Gades to attend a festival in honor of the city's 'deliverance' from the Carthaginians a century and a half before. There were sacrifices at all the major temples and chariot races and theatrical performances and all the usual holiday activities. I wanted to go immediately to the races, but Dolon made me first sit through a performance of *The Libation Bearers* in the town's fine theater.

Iberia is famous for its dancers, and Gades produced the most famous troupes in Iberia. These performers were in demand all over the world, and there were a dozen or more such troupes displaying their art upon platforms all over the city. I watched spellbound as they performed stories out of legend in a combination of rhythmic pantomime and gymnastics that strained the very limits of the human body, all of this to the music of flute, lyre and drums, tiny cymbals and clicking wooden instruments. They did not wear masks, but performed with their faces as much as with their bodies, conveying the minutest gradations of feeling with exquisite subtleties of expression which they nonetheless managed to convey clearly even to spectators some distance away.

Watching one such troupe, I lost all interest in chariot races. They were all women, performing before the altar of Aphrodite. They wore diaphanous gowns slit from hem to hip on both sides, girded with golden belts and spangled all over with silver moon-crescents, sacred to the goddess. Their motions were relatively decorous, but were nonetheless infused with a wanton sensuality that held me rapt.

There were ten women in the group, ranging in age from two who were no more than ten years old to a stunningly accomplished woman in her middle thirties. I forgot all of them, though, when one girl came from the rear line and before the others danced the story of Aphrodite and Adonis. Since this was originally a Phoenician tale (the Phoenicians called Aphrodite, Astarte), it was a great favorite in Gades. But I was not thinking of that at the time. I had no thought for anything but the dancing girl.

She was about my own age, with skin the color and purity of honey just pressed from the comb. Her eyes, artfully enlarged with kohl, were as black as the glossy hair that fell in rippling waves to her waist. Her face had the solemn beauty that is at its height when it is in perfect repose. Beneath the inwardly turned gravity of her face, her body and limbs moved with a freedom that was the absence of weight, making the motions of courting swallows seem gross and clumsy by comparison. She was like a creature made of air.

Tiny bells ringed her ankles and her feet seemed not to touch the platform as she mimed the famous myth, from the meeting of the goddess and the beautiful young hunter, through their passionate affair, to her unspeakable heartbreak and mourning over his ravaged corpse. So powerfully evocative were her stylized movements that I could almost see the god-youth in her embrace in their moments of transport and lying dead in her arms as her tears fell upon him. Many in the crowd, at the climax of her dance, wept openly in sympathy with her grief.

She broke the spell when she looked up from the body of her perished lover, straight into my eyes. Later I blushed to think what she must have seen before her: the veriest bumpkin of an awkward boy staring at her with his mouth open.

There was a tugging at my shoulder. I tore my eyes away from her for a moment. 'What?'

'Come along,' Idas said. 'We're going to miss the races.' He frowned in puzzlement as he caught my moonstruck expression, then he looked up on the platform and displayed his gap-toothed grin. 'So that's what's taken your mind off the races!'

'Who is she, Idas? Do you know her name?'

'The spectacular one? That's Yeroshabel, the leader of the troupe. They're called the troupe of Eshmun, because they're from the temple of Eshmun quarter.'

'No, the young one who danced the part of Aphrodite.'

'I can find out,' he said. 'But you'll have to lend me a sestertius to bet at the circus.'

I had the coin out and pressed into his palm before the last word was out of his mouth.

And so we went to the races. I have no memory of who won or lost, nor even if there were any spectacular crashes. The next day, Idas took me aside at the palaestra.

'She's Yeroshabel's youngest daughter,' he said. 'Her name is Asabel.'

'Asabel,' I breathed. It was a name that was to haunt me for the rest of my life.

Asabel. Asabel. The name sang in my ears. I repeated it endlessly, giving it the rolling meter of Homeric verse. I went about in a permanent daze, unable to banish that face and that name from my mind – not that I wanted to. Needless to say, I acted the part of the lovesick swain and became an odious burden to everyone around me. I seized every opportunity to travel into the city to see the Eshmun troupe perform. Asabel was always there, along with her sisters, her mother and the other members of the troupe, but I did not see them, only Asabel.

In the fashion of the time I sent her gifts: tame birds, bangles, wretched verses of my own composition in praise of her beauty and perfection. She sent them all back. This I attributed to her superior taste and high standards. I was pampered and indulged, as befitted a young gentleman, but I could afford no gifts truly worthy of Asabel. I longed to give her fine jewelry and horses and vineyards. Perhaps then she would notice me.

I was so besotted with Asabel that I took no notice of events in the greater world around me. I would have done well to have paid more attention. Across the mountains, in Gaul, the Romans were reducing that land to submission with unprecedented butchery. Gallic slaves began to appear in the markets in great numbers and dirt cheap. This was a boon to the plantation owners and anyone else whose enterprises called for much hand labor. The mines prospered mightily.

But with the Romans so occupied with their long warfare in Gaul, the local mountain tribes became bolder, raiding into the lowlands for loot and just for the sport of it. Scarcely a month went by that we did not receive word of a plantation devastated, a village sacked and all its women and children carried off into slavery. The governors of the Iberian provinces petitioned the Senate for reinforcements to chastise the fractious tribesmen, but were told that eight full legions were already engaged in Gaul, and two more were being raised for that war. Rome had no soldiers to spare. On the contrary, the Roman commanders in Gaul wanted yet more Iberian horsemen to help them chase the Gallic rebels and their German allies.

I paid little heed to these distant rumblings. My world had narrowed to the distance between myself and my beloved. Even now I marvel at the thoroughness with which first love reduces a young man's brain to the semblance of barley porridge.

Thus I pursued a long summer of yearning and frustration. In the palaestra we switched to the shield-race, Pyrrhic dance and some rudimentary formation drill with shields and spears, in case we should be called up for the defense of the district. We marched and wheeled and faced about, lowered our spears and advanced. As military drill it had been obsolete for more than two centuries, but was still used to instil a sense of order and discipline in utterly untrained levies. As one of the youngest, I was in the rear rank but I would have found even this exciting had I not been so preoccupied.

I sought any excuse to get close to Asabel, even to pressing Dolon, urging that he engage the Eshmun troupe to perform at the temple.

'No ceremony in the worship of Apollo calls for an all-female dance troupe,' he said firmly. 'These are more characteristic of the cults of the Earth divinities. I am sure these ladies are fully engaged throughout the year at the temples of Demeter and Dionysus and Aphrodite, not to mention those of the various Oriental gods.'

Myrrhine took me aside and put it more succinctly. 'Glaucus, you are plainly infatuated with one of those dancers. Are you aware that dancing girls, whatever their skills and accomplishments, are regarded as little better than prostitutes?'

'No, I didn't know,' I admitted, having even less knowledge of prostitutes than of dancers.

'It is unbefitting a young man of your station in life to associate with such people. You may admire their art, even –' she reddened slightly, '– even hire their services, but you must not become involved with them.'

That brought up another point. 'Just what *is* my station in life?'
'You are a noble youth of priestly family, and you are not to
forget it. Association with a woman of low character would bring
disgrace upon us all.'

She might as well have been addressing the marble statue of Apollo
that stood in the temple. My mind had descended, as Dolon might
have put it, from the upper plane, the plane of the divine. I was in
the grip of more basic, earthly forces.

In the late summer of that year my palaestra class held a sympo-
sium. These parties were traditional and each class held at least one
each year. Every member was expected to make a contribution to
cover food, wine and entertainment. The older men's associations
might hire singers to declaim the verses of Homer or Pindar, or
some old philosopher to lecture upon points of abstruse lore.

No such tedious gravity was expected of the younger men. By
long tradition, we were permitted considerable license in our choice
of entertainment, and we took full advantage of our privilege. My
joy was unbounded when I learned that the troupe of Eshmun had
been engaged for the evening. Immediately, I was jealous as well:
Other men would be looking upon *my* Asabel. (Obviously, I was not
precisely sane. The nature of this mental disorder is much debated
but it is greatly celebrated in legend, verse and drama. Often it is
deemed to be a malicious prank of the gods and its victims usually
come to a bad end. A similar infatuation resulted in the destruction
of Troy.)

That evening, I was accompanied by Kriton. My pedagogue
carried my contribution to the night's festivities: a jar of good
native wine, a sack of honeyed figs, seed-cakes and oil. I also
carried a few silver denarii to pay my share of the hire of the
dancers and musicians.

By the time we arrived at the palaestra the exercise yard was
deserted, the last of the patrons having long since departed for
home. Others were just arriving and we repaired to the dining hall
where rush lights and oil lamps were being lighted as the light faded
from the sky. We gave our contributions to the slaves to prepare and
arranged ourselves on the couches that ran around the periphery of
the hall. As one of the youngest I took a place almost at the end on
one line of couches, near the entrance. I was so taut with anticipation
that I would not have traded my lowly place for the editor's box at
the circus.

It was a sultry evening. The smell of flowers was heavy in the air
and insects still buzzed lazily among the blossoms. A cool breeze
began to relieve the heat of the day. Our slaves took our sandals

and we slipped our chitons from our shoulders and left them draped loosely about our waists with the vain nonchalance of body-proud young men.

The older boys drew lots for the title of master of ceremonies. To my relief, Photius did not draw the winning lot. Had he won, he would have been in a position to propose games for the evening's entertainment, games sure to be degrading to his favorite victims, me among them. Instead, Ariston won. He was a generous, well-favored youth who excelled at singing and playing the lyre, the son of a man who owned vast vineyards nearby. Photius was disappointed and his face showed it.

I shared a couch with Idas and another boy whose name I no longer remember. The serving girls draped ivy wreaths around our necks to forestall drunkenness and set upon our heads chaplets of acorn-studded oak leaves intertwined with wild roses. Thus adorned we felt powerfully sophisticated, in the immemorial fashion of boys playing at being men.

The slaves brought in the first course, which I barely tasted. Nor did I pay much attention to the subsequent courses, even though they included lamb cooked with mint and parsley, a rare treat after the austere table of Dolon, who considered an occasional fish to be a luxurious indulgence. My customary diet consisted of porridge, bread, cheese and fruit. With dinner we drank wine heavily watered. When the platters were cleared away Ariston exercised his authority as master of the mixing bowl and decreed that the wine be mixed with only two parts of water, an inordinate strength for so young a group. Dolon would have been shocked.

'I wish we did this more often,' Idas said, idly caressing the shoulder of the other boy who shared our couch. Here and there other couples showed similar affection, but this was not general. As ephebes, we were more often objects of the passions of older men than initiators of it.

'We could not afford many such evenings,' I said, but I understood his enthusiasm. This was my initiation into masculine society, far more so than joining the palaestra, with its rigid hierarchies of age and status. Here I was among my peers, even if some of them thought they were my betters.

Musicians came in and played upon flute and lyre while we conversed among ourselves of the inconsequential things important only to the very young. My mouth tingled with the resin-tinged savor of the wine and the fumes mounted swiftly to my head. Either the wreaths were not performing their task or I was unaccustomed to the drink, probably the latter. The room took on an otherworldly glow and the faces of my companions, flushed with wine and merriment, had the aspect of masks, all their features exaggerated into a mockery of human visage. Their voices were too loud, their words scarcely intelligible.

Then the music changed. The classic, traditional flute and lyre were joined by the rhythmic percussive instruments native to Iberia; the tiny cymbals worn on the fingers, the resounding sticks of hard wood, the little wooden clappers that set up a daemonic clatter, stirring to the blood. The youths on the couches fell silent with expectation and now the instruments were supplemented by clapping of the dancers as they entered the hall, the smack of flesh on flesh adding a subtly sensuous counterpoint to the mechanical noise of wood and metal.

For long minutes I forgot to breathe as the women whirled around the room, their movements as fluid as water. Some wore veils, some wore wreaths of ivy draped around neck and waist, none wore very much. Their bodies and limbs glistened with oil in which rose petals had steeped, and as their exertions warmed them the scent of roses suffused the still air of evening and brought yet another sense into play.

They were not dancing any particular story. This was an exhibition of the dancer's art, a display of virtuosity that was a sacred hymn to Terpsichore, in which voice and words were replaced by movements so difficult yet so graceful that it seemed impossible that mere human bodies could be pushed to such an extreme.

All of the dancers were exquisite, but my eyes were only for Asabel. She was the youngest of the troupe, for the girls not yet nubile did not perform at these private parties. Once in a while my vision would darken, reminding me to inhale again. Besides bells at wrist and ankle, she wore tiny golden shells upon her nipples and from a thin golden chain circling her narrow waist depended a brief apron of pearls. These were for adornment, not modesty. Iberian dancing girls have no more qualms about nudity than do Greek men.

Their first dances were whirling, swift and athletic. Soon the musky scent of female sweat mixed headily with the rose-scented oil and droplets flew from their flailing limbs, spattering us like warm rain. A drop struck my lower lip and I licked it off, relishing the salty tang, hoping that it came from Asabel.

The lovely Yeroshabel, wearing only a spiral of ivy twining her body from knee to shoulder, leapt to the center of the hall and raised her arms as if in adoration of the sun. A wiry girl perhaps a year or two older than Asabel sprang to Yeroshabel's shoulders, then placed her hands upon the older woman's upturned palms and unwound into a handstand. We applauded the feat, but more was to come.

For a moment the slender, gleaming body was as straight as an arrow, then her back began to arch while the other dancers clapped rhythmically. Her spine assumed the curve of a drawn bow, a sight almost painful to behold. For the moment, I actually ceased to watch Asabel. I fancied that I could hear the cracking of bones as the young woman's back bent nearly into a full circle. Her smiling face was perfectly vertical as her small, taut buttocks came to rest atop her head and her calves lowered until she crossed her feet beneath her chin.

We roared with approval, clapping and slapping the tables. There was something wildly, perversely exciting about the unnatural contortion. The sight of a woman's intimate parts in such deranged juxtaposition suggested heady possibilities to one who had never even experienced the more prosaic acts of union between man and woman.

After this the dancers ceased their frantic whirling. The insistent pounding of the instruments slowed to a languorous throb as elemental as a beating heart. The movements of the dancers became a slow, boneless writhing. Some, with arms held out from their sides, rolled their hips forward, back, to each side, each movement flowing into the next so perfectly that the eye could not follow nor the mind anticipate. Others stood perfectly still, feet apart and unmoving, like shining, painted statues except for their bellies, which rolled and writhed as if they were animals somehow separate from the women in whose bodies they were set.

Asabel was one of the latter, and by chance or intent her final steps had left her standing three feet in front of me when this bewitching stage of the dance began. She stood in perfect stillness, her arms at her sides, turned slightly so that her palms faced forward as if making an offering of herself, her head slightly back, her eyes half shut. Only her pale belly moved in time to the music, at first undulating in a continuous roll from bottom to top, like a wave on the ocean. Then the whole broad muscle that stretches from pubis to breastbone fluttered like a curtain in a breeze. Then she repeated the wavelike undulation, this time from side to side.

Finally she did something I would not have thought possible. From the base of her belly a roll of muscle ascended the left side, crossed over to the right just beneath her breasts and descended back to the base of her pelvis to reascend on the left. It looked like a small animal running around an oval track beneath a sheet. It was a dazzling display of muscular control and at that moment my draped chiton concealed an erection as shameless as a herm's. I suspect that I was not alone in this state.

Abruptly, the music changed tempo again and the women spun into a final, frenzied few minutes of dance that had them holding hands, weaving like an animated ribbon beneath each other's arms and legs until, at the last second, they all stood in a circle back to back, still holding hands with their arms raised high, resembling some exotic, many-petalled flower. Then they simultaneously bowed deeply as the music came to a rattling halt.

Amid wild applause and whooping, the women filed from the hall, walking as primly as a line of respectable Roman matrons processing to the temple of Juno for one of the more staid ceremonies.

Conversation began to resume, but fitfully. All were trying to act as if this were a familiar experience, but I noticed that many of us were breathing as if we had just run the shield race. I snatched at my wine cup and drained it, trying to will my all too visible excitement to subside so that I might go outside and speak with Asabel before she left.

In most parts of the world dancing girls are hired for the evening and, after performing, are made available to the guests. But this is not true of the very accomplished and expensive troupes of Gades. If there were those in our district who could afford to demand more intimate entertainment from a troupe like Yeroshabel's, we were certainly not among them.

As soon as I could rise from my couch without embarrassment I did so, and I was not alone. Several of us had experienced a sudden urge to take the air out in the exercise yard. There we found the dancers behaving just like athletes after a major effort. Most were walking up and down the yard, cooling off and stretching over-exerted muscles to forestall cramping. Yeroshabel strolled about with one hand pressed against her lower back, which seemed to pain her. Her other arm was around the shoulders of a magnificent young woman who resembled her so closely that I judged her to be one of the troupe leader's elder daughters. The wiry little contortionist stood balanced on one foot, the other extended straight above her head while she smiled and conversed with Ariston and another youth just as if she were clothed and standing like a normal human being.

Then I saw Asabel. She leaned against a pillar, fanning herself with a fan of woven palm shaped like an acanthus leaf. One foot was on the ground, the other propped against the pillar behind her, the thigh and knee extended outward in a sculpturesque pose of relaxation after strenuous effort. I walked over to her, glad that the moonlight would not reveal the flaming color of my face. Her eyes were heavy-lidded but they registered my presence when I halted in front of her.

'I – I am Glaucus, son of Dolon the priest,' I said.

'At last we meet,' she said, noncommittally. This close, I could see that she streamed with sweat and the moisture from her body darkened the ground beneath her, as if she had created a miniature rain storm.

'I understand why you've rejected my gifts,' I said.

She smiled faintly. 'Do you?'

'Yes. I know that you must have other suitors, wealthier and better born than I, men able to afford gifts worthy of your beauty. I want you to know that I understand.'

Now she smiled fully. To my amazement she stretched out her hand and cupped my cheek. 'Glaucus, you are a handsome boy, and at another time I might be more receptive, but what would be the point? In three days I will be gone from here.'

My heart dropped. 'Gone? What do you mean?'

She sighed. 'In three days we sail for Sicily, to dance in the festivals. Then we go to Crete, to Cyprus, to Eleusis to dance in the Mysteries, to the great Dionysia in Athens – Glaucus, we may not be back for two or three years. By then you'll have a beard and probably a wife and you'll have forgotten me.'

'Never!' I protested. 'Well, the beard probably, but I will not marry. I'll wait for you.'

Now she laughed, but without malice. 'You flatter me. I confess I do not have a great many suitors, certainly not from priestly families.'

'But, you can't go!' I protested inanely, as if she had some sort of choice. It didn't occur to me that I was not a particularly compelling reason for her to stay. A philosopher once told me that each of us is the center of his own cosmos. It takes time to learn that other people fail to share our conviction of centrality. Some never learn.

'I am a dancer, Glaucus. This will be my first great tour with the Troupe of Eshmun. We will be seen by the most important people in the world. Consuls and senators and kings and tyrants attend the Mysteries. The king of Cyprus is brother to Ptolemy of Egypt and if we please him we may dance before the court of Alexandria!'

Even in my youthful egoism I knew I had little to offer by comparison with such personages. I was in despair. 'But I must see you again!'

She took pity upon my distress. 'Do you know the shrine of Artemis?'

'I've been there,' I assured her. 'It's just outside the Cartago Nova gate, in a grove of laurel.'

'If you really want to see me again before I leave, be there tomorrow night just after moonrise. I can bribe the guard to let me out through the postern. It won't be forever, but it will be an hour or two, anyway.' She smiled and touched my face again.

'I'll be there!' I all but barked.

'Don't leave me languishing in the grove,' she warned. 'I won't forgive you for that.'

'Never! I'll be there if it costs . . .'

'Girls!' Yeroshabel called. 'Get dressed, we are going back to the city.' The women went to a bench where their robes were neatly folded and donned them.

Asabel pushed away from her pillar and kissed me lightly on the cheek. 'Tomorrow night,' she said. 'Be there.' She walked past me, still sweating profusely. So smitten was I that I thought she even perspired beautifully.

When I returned to the hall the party was in full roar, with a contest going to see who could hurl the lees of his wine the farthest and still strike a tilted kylix. Most could not have hit the floor. Two boys had stripped and were wrestling clumsily amid much laughter. These manly amusements had very little appeal for me at that moment. I gathered up my belongings, shook Kriton awake and returned home.

The next day my tutor sought to teach me something or other, but I have no memory whatever of the subject. All I could think of was Asabel and the night to come. I am sure that Dolon and Myrrhine were mystified by my manner, but I do not remember what they said to me. In the years since I have regretted that that day was so thoroughly blotted from my memory.

After dinner I lay upon my bed and tried to will the sun to dip below the horizon. Never had twilight lingered so long. But in time the buzzing of the bees ceased and the chirping of crickets began and I rose, put on my tunic and stole from my room.

At the stable Virro was still awake. He rose blinking from his bed of straw. 'What is it?'

'Bring Sparrow,' I ordered.

'You are going riding after sunset?' Then he chuckled. 'A woman, eh? Well, ride the back way, around the orchard. If Dolon hears you riding out he'll want my hide for it.'

'Don't worry,' I said, fidgeting impatiently while he bridled the little mare. It irked me that he found me so transparent, but then, for what other reason would I be going out so late?

Mounted, I rode from the temple estate and onto the road to Gades. My exhilaration mounted with each mile, my whole body tingling, the warm, muscular touch of Sparrow against my lower parts a portent of things to come. I had to restrain myself from urging her to a gallop. I did not want to arrive smelling like horse sweat.

Less than an hour brought me within sight of the city walls. Like most cities, outside the walls of Gades lay an expanse of cemeteries and the precincts of small temples and shrines. The shrine of Artemis was one such. It was a place where ceremonies to the goddess were held at intervals, but since it was not a temple it had no permanent staff. The shrine was in the form of a small, circular edifice with slender Ionic columns and a conical roof. As I approached it I could just make out the bronze image of the goddess within. She was depicted nude, armed with her bow and accompanied by her hunting dogs. Despite her virgin aspect, Artemis is a goddess of fertility and her shrines are much frequented by lovers and newlyweds.

I dismounted and held Sparrow's reins, waiting anxiously. My eyes swept the grounds, straining to see Asabel's approach. I glimpsed shadowy forms moving among the laurel, and I knew that I was not alone on my mission. From one direction came gentle laughter. From another I heard a sudden, almost violent outburst of gasping and moaning, accompanied by rhythmic slappings of flesh on flesh. My excitement grew yet more intense.

Then I saw a slender, incredibly graceful figure coming silently toward me, swathed in a close-fitting cloak and veil. I knew it was Asabel. My heart pounded in my throat as she stopped before me.

'You are easy to find,' she said. 'Not many come here on horseback.'

'I didn't want to waste any time,' I said, my voice trembling.

She took my hand. 'Come. There is a place a little way from here where you can tether your horse and we can be alone.' We walked close by the wide-spreading laurel whence came the vigorous sounds. As we passed there came a high, birdlike cry and a deep groan, then just a heavy panting, as of two runners who have collapsed after a long, hard race.

Asabel squeezed my hand. 'Another victory for the principle of life over the underworld. Demeter triumphs over Hades.' Then she added, sadly: 'But Hades always wins in the end.' I did not know what to say to this, so I said nothing. Beneath the bright half-moon the air was charged with the principle of which she spoke. There are certain magical places like this, where generations of lovers have dedicated their passion to a deity or spirit, and where it lingers in the atmosphere and in the earth of that place.

We came to a wall of laurel that appeared impenetrable, but Asabel stepped unerringly between two of the fragrant bushes and there was a path so narrow that the bristling leaves brushed Sparrow's flanks. Then we were in a tiny clearing and the moon shone on a little stream down its center. To one side was a poplar sapling, and to this I tied Sparrow's bridle.

Asabel was standing by the water, which flowed in perfect silence along its level bed of sand. She turned at my approach and lowered her veil. The moon struck silver sparks from her night-black hair. I took her in my arms and our lips came together. Hers parted beneath mine and our tongues touched, sending a shock through my body like the vibration of a plucked lyre string. I ground her against me, my control shredding, and she felt my urgent prodding against her lower belly.

She pulled her face back and pushed me away. 'Glaucus! Control yourself!' She was breathing a little heavily. 'There is no call for urgency. Before we go further, I want you to promise me something.'

'Anything!' I gasped. At that moment, I meant it.

'I am a dancer and I have many full seasons ahead of me. A woman cannot dance if she is carrying a child. Do you understand that?'

'Yes,' I said weakly, wondering if this meant I was doomed to disappointment.

'Good. You must let me be the guide. That way, this will be a joyous night for both of us and there will be no consequences to fear. Leave me in control and all will be well. Otherwise, I will leave instantly.'

'I agree!' I said desperately.

'Then come to me again,' she breathed, 'and don't try to treat me like a horse to be broken.'

This time we drifted together like two leaves caught in the same eddy and our touch was gentle, exploring each other like travelers discovering a strange land. Her lips were like moist feathers, touching my face all over. I smelled the headiness of her perfume as I combed her long hair with my fingers, touched the tip of my tongue to the complex shell of her ear, felt the serried knobs of her spine.

Asabel's hands slid within the short, wide sleeves of my tunic and caressed my arms and shoulders, then her palms touched my chest and her thumbs flicked over the tiny nipples that until that instant I did not know were sensitive. My breath shuddered and my hands slid down her back until they cupped her small, hard buttocks. I drew her closer to me and she came willingly. More than willingly.

She took her hands from within my tunic and touched the clasps at her shoulders. Her gown slithered down and lay in a pale puddle at her feet. I had seen her wearing almost nothing when dancing. But she was not dancing now, and her arousal rendered her far more than merely naked. It was in her breath and the trembling of her hands and the sharp, intoxicating scent that rose from the folds and creases of her flesh to mingle with the musk of her perfume.

Our touching became more intimate as she stripped off my tunic and we sank down to lie upon our clothes and our recumbent position allowed easier access to one another's bodies. I marveled at the texture of her inner thighs, so unbelievably soft in contrast to the steely muscles that lay beneath the white sheath. Her fingertips defined the outline of my erection, slipped beneath to cup my testicles, which had drawn up tight against the jointure of my thighs and had developed a deep, sweet ache. I sucked her nipples into my mouth, relishing their hardness.

Asabel moaned, made little sounds that were not quite speech as my fingers probed between her legs and found heat and dampness. She wriggled her way beneath me and I found myself atop her, supporting much of my weight on spread hands while she guided me within her. The sensation was overwhelming, so unexpected that I immediately lost control and went into a paralytic spasm. She had been expecting it, for her hands moved quickly between us. One finger pressed hard, almost painfully, against a spot just behind my scrotum as the frantic pulsing began in my groin. Her other hand withdrew me and held me fast against her belly as the finger released its pressure. I gasped in relief and wonder as I erupted a silvery geyser across the whiteness of her flesh.

I began to collapse upon her but a hand pushed me back a little and she chuckled; a low, sensuous sound from deep within her throat. Slowly, carefully, she squeezed the last drops from me and then guided me back once more to her magical grotto.

'Now,' she sighed in my ear, 'more slowly this time.' And her legs came up to encircle my waist as I reentered her.

Hours later I awoke and looked up at the hard brilliance of the stars. How long had I been sleeping? It could not have been long, for Asabel and I had coupled joyously for hours with the appetite and stamina of youth. She knew refinements of which I could not have dreamed and each time I thought I was utterly drained she would bring me back to full, robust activity. Finally, we had collapsed into a panting heap and slept.

As I sat up, the taste of her still upon my tongue, I felt the secretions

of her body on every part of me, smelled her scent mingled with mine.
I possessed a sense of fulfillment such as few men experience in a
lifetime. Asabel was no longer beside me but her gown was. I looked
for her and my eyes tracked the sounds coming from the little stream.
The moon had set but the stars provided enough light to see that she
was sitting in the water, and the splashing was caused by her hands
doing female things between her legs.

She saw me and smiled, the white of her teeth outshining the stars.
'Just in case,' she said. 'I don't think you could have quickened me,
but it pays to be sure. My mother says that it takes very little to
make a baby, despite what men think.'

It disturbed me to hear her speak so clinically, and to realize that
I was not her first lover. Still, I knew that, considering their calling,
Yeroshabel would have been a fool not to have given her daughters
the most thorough education in these matters.

I got up and walked to the little stream. I hated to wash the traces
of Asabel from my body but I knew that in the heat of day they would
lose their allure. I stood before her, then sat in the stream so that the
soles of our feet touched, like two children bathing in the same tub.
The coolness of the water raised goosebumps on my flesh. I cupped
it in my hands and raised it to cascade from my shoulders over my
chest and back.

'Are you pleased with our night together?' Asabel asked with a
lazy smile. Her lips were over-full, her face slightly puffy, her eyes
heavy-lidded. At that moment she looked far older than her years
and incomparably worldly.

'More than I can say.' Unbelievably, I felt myself begin to stir and
harden yet again. Sitting there with the water lapping about her hips,
her face that of an Eastern fertility goddess, only the soles of her feet
touching mine, she seemed the very embodiment of carnality.

'I am glad, because it will have to last you a long time.' Apparently
satisfied that none of my seed lay within her, she stood and the water
ran down her thighs and the subtle curves of her calves. I rose and
took her in my arms.

'But surely this is not the last time,' I protested, knowing
that it was.

She looked down and clapped her hands together. 'Oh, no! Not
again! I must get home, Glaucus, I . . .' She looked up past my
shoulder and the playful look left her face. 'Is it dawn already?
Surely not.'

I turned to see the red glow in the east. 'We must be in for a storm,'
I said hesitantly. 'But . . . that can't be. It's too early.' There was
something unnatural about the glow. Then I saw another, smaller

redness to the northeast. That was when the great alarm gong over the city gate began to bang and reverberate, again and again. In moments, gongs were sounding all over the city. Asabel's eyes went wide with terror.

'The hillmen!' she cried. 'They are raiding the countryside!' She rushed from the stream and ran to her clothes. Even in my confusion and growing terror, I found the sight of her twinkling buttocks enchanting. All too soon, her body was covered. I joined her and resumed my own garments.

'We have to get into the city before the raiders cut us off,' she said.

'But the alarm has sounded,' I pointed out. 'The gates are being barred right now.'

'The gatekeeper will let people in through the postern until the raiders are within sight,' she insisted. 'You must come with me. You'll be safe inside the city.'

'No, I have to go get my parents. There are horses there. We can ride back here before daylight.'

'Don't be a fool,' she said. 'Dawn can't be more than an hour away. Your temple is probably already burning!' Her terror was too great to be gentle in saying it.

'I have to go to them,' I said.

'Then don't detain me. Come on.' I untethered Sparrow and she took my hand once more and led the way out of the little copse. The other lovers must already have left, for we were alone in the grove of the shrine. We ran down the paved lane lined with cedars that connected the shrine with the road. I held Sparrow a little off the pavement so that his hoofs would not ring loudly on the stone. We came to the edge of the grove and looked around, holding our breath.

Fires burned in the distance, most of them mere glows but some of them near enough to discern individual flames. I thought I saw a few mounted figures silhouetted against the fires, but I could not be sure. The frantic alarm gongs of the city drowned out all other noise.

'They don't seem to be close to the city,' Asabel said, perhaps too hopefully. 'Are you sure you will not come with me?'

'I cannot,' I said.

'Then farewell, Glaucus.' Quickly she kissed me, then she was a swirl of robes running toward the nearest city gate. In seconds the blackness swallowed her.

With a trembling in my bowels and a tight constriction in my throat, I led Sparrow out onto the road. Without Asabel to show off for I did not feel brave and noble. I felt that I had made a foolish decision. I grasped Sparrow's mane, kicked high and pulled myself over her back, wincing slightly, for my nether regions were somewhat sore. Mounted, I was torn, frantic with worry for Asabel's safety, equally fevered with concern for my home.

At the end of my moments of futile worry I knew that I could do nothing to get Asabel within the city more swiftly or surely than she could contrive for herself, so I kicked Sparrow into a gallop, headed for the little temple of Apollo.

In the gloom I could see little, but the sounds of chaos were everywhere. I heard screams, the crackling of fires as I passed blazing farmsteads and villas, the terrified bleatings and lowings and neighings of alarmed livestock. There was no clash of arms, for the raiders were meeting little armed resistance, perhaps none at all.

It occurred to me that I was making a target of myself by keeping to the road, but it was the quickest way and in any case the raiders did not seem to be bothering with the road, busying themselves instead with pickings to be had in the inhabited countryside. I wondered at the time why there was so much burning. It seemed to me that surely they must be destroying a great deal of valuable plunder.

The sky was gray when at last I came in view of the temple. My heart sank. The temple stood in pristine whiteness but all around it was swirling black smoke. I urged my tired mare to even greater speed, unheedful that with the end of night I was growing more visible by the minute. As I rode down the lane between the poplars the red upper rim of the sun broke over the eastern horizon and flooded the courtyard with light, revealing all that I most dreaded to see.

The fired had burned down to embers, and heavy smoke blew across the enclosure with the vagrant breezes, but there was never enough smoke to hide the bodies that littered the ground. Numb with horror, I identified them, one by one. All were people I had known my whole life. Most were slaves of the household, but not all.

Dolon lay by the altar that stood before the steps of the temple, as if he had been trying to save the sacred precincts from profanation. A great wound stained the front of his robe, made by a sword or spear. At the time I knew too little of wounds to tell the manner of their infliction. Myrrhine was in their bedroom. Dolon must have told her to stay there when he went out to investigate the commotion. One side of her head was partially crushed, struck by a heavy club.

I have difficulty remembering the next few hours. I did a great deal of dragging, trying to get all the bodies out to the burial ground. It was a hopeless task, for it never occurred to me to use Sparrow to drag them with a rope. I did note that all the dead, like

Dolon and Myrrhine, were elderly. Those young enough to work had been taken away.

I tried to remember the rites for the dead. There was also the cremation to consider. Unlike barbarians who bury corpses we burned our dead on a funeral pyre. I wondered where I could find so much wood. Could there be enough unburnt timbers among the household buildings? Probably not. And the nearest woods were too far. I knew of no dead trees in the orchard. I seated myself on a grave marker, my body quivering with exhaustion and shock, to ponder the problem. I was still sitting there when the raiders returned.

I first noticed them when I saw a line of horses' hoofs a few feet in front of me. Idly, not greatly interested, I looked up to see who they were. There were nine or ten of them, most clean shaven, wearing a variety of armors and bronze helmets. All were heavily armed and most bore the serpentine slashing sword called a *falcata*. Some wore the long plaits hanging from their temples that proclaimed they were warriors. They were men of several tribes and one or two did not look Iberian at all.

'Come with us, pretty boy,' said a man who spoke Latin with a Celtic accent. He wore a fine breastplate embossed with a wolf's mask and a helmet with a high, oval crest. He seemed to be their leader.

'You don't understand,' I said. 'I have to bury my parents. And these others. Their shades will not know rest if they aren't buried.'

'Leave them,' the man said. 'The scavengers will come down from the hills and eat them. This will release their spirits and they will ascend to the sky as birds.' He did not snarl as one would expect of such a savage. He spoke rather gently. He turned to one of the others. 'Take the horse. It's a fine one.' The other went to the tree where I had tethered Sparrow.

'You can't do that,' I said, inanely.

'Yes we can,' said the bandit. 'You are our slave now.'

He said this with great simplicity and finality. Another man dismounted and drew my hands behind me where he bound my wrists with a heavy thong. I did not resist. I was unarmed and unutterably tired. Even so I was amazed that the thing could be accomplished so easily. I had always known that some people were free and some slave. It had not occurred to me that the transition from one state to the other could be so swift and unceremonious.

A halter was tied around my neck and its other end made fast to a saddle. As I scurried off behind the horse I turned and took a last look at the bodies of my parents. Perhaps the bandit was right.

EMPTY

Perhaps the ceremonies were unimportant. I hoped so. But I made a vow to myself that I would return and raise their grave stele and sacrifice for their repose.

At least, I thought, the last night of my freedom had been the most pleasant of my life. Thus began the first day of my servitude. It was also to be the first day of a quest that would consume twenty-three years and take me beyond the farthest reaches of the world we know.

THE RISE OF AUGUSTUS

Allan Massie

It was Gaius Octavius who was the first Roman Emperor, not Julius
Caesar as some believe. He was the son of Julius Caesar's niece, Atia,
and Caesar named him his heir in his will. Between the time of
Caesar's death in 44 BC and 27 BC, when he was granted the titles
Augustus (by which name he is better known) and Imperator, as
both Head of State and Commander of the Roman Army, Octavian
continued to consolidate his position.

In his book Augustus (1989), Allan Massie (b. 1938) successfully
recreates the life of the first Emperor and the world that he established. Augustus may have been able to build upon the successes
of Julius Caesar, but that should take nothing away from his own
skill and power. He created an Empire that survived him by over
four hundred years, and a title that, along with its later incarnation
as the Holy Roman Emperor, lasted for eighteen hundred years.

I am afraid my father's account of his Gallic Wars is among
the dullest books ever written. I remember, Gaius, how your
tutor once expressed indignation when you complained of its
tedium. But you were quite right though it seemed to me then
inexpedient to admit as much, and I only suggested to your
tutor that he make due allowance for the ardour of youth.
One reason why it is unsatisfactory is Caesar's pompous tone,
and this owes much to his unfortunate decision to write of
himself in the third person: 'Caesar did this, Caesar did that,
Caesar acted to save the situation . . .'; it grows more wearisome

and seems even more self-admiring than the perpetual 'I' of autobiographers.

Then that much-praised first sentence: 'All Gaul is divided into three parts', has really only the single virtue of lucidity. It is far from accurate, for the divisions of Gaul are more numerous and much deeper than he suggests.

In fact the book is fundamentally untruthful. Not surprising; it was written for an immediate political purpose – when did a manifesto ever speak the truth? The Triumvirate formed by Caesar, Pompey and Crassus had broken up. Caesar's enemies in Rome were baying for his blood and demanding his recall. He appealed to public opinion with this vainglorious account of his Gallic conquests: he would show them what he had done for Rome. It worked. Even the dullness of which you complained was deliberate; many had thought Caesar flashy; now they should be soothed by the impressive sobriety of his prose.

So, my dear Gaius, and Lucius, too (for I cannot imagine your tender imagination responded to Caesar's prose, though you would be too mild and mannerly to complain), your early criticism was justified. 'On the spot', as you would say yourself. It has always seemed to me an example of how not to write your memoirs. There is no personal voice. What you hear is an actor. Of course it's also true that Julius Caesar was always acting: the real Caesar, if he existed by the time I knew him, was buried deep beneath layers of artifice. Still, most of the parts he chose to play were livelier and wittier than the role he wrote for himself in his 'Gallic War'.

All the same, now that I bring myself to write this account of my own life, for you – for your instruction and, I hope, pleasure – I confess that the pompous tone is hard to avoid. Autobiography sets out to recapture experience, but the business of writing it requires the author to abstract himself from the self that lived these experiences, and to construct a figure that can hardly fail to be, as it were, theatrical. To put it another way: the self you write is never quite the self that lived. (I hope you don't find that concept too difficult. It's a modern idea of course which you certainly won't find in the authors you have studied and I am only too sadly aware of the inadequacy of my attempts at philosophical exposition.) I was anyway struck with this when I wrote a first sketch of my life about twenty years ago when I was stuck in a small town in the Pyrenees recovering from an illness. I found it heavy going, I assure you. It began, if I recall, with a genealogical chapter. Everyone is interested in his ancestry of course, but I could not bring mine to life. It was profoundly unsatisfactory.

So, engaging on this book for you, my boys, I propose to imitate

Homer or follow his advice at least. He recommends you start in the middle of action.

Therefore: here we are: Greece, late March, blustery and cold, snow on the mountains, in my nineteenth year.

As we lay in the rest-room after our baths Maecenas ran his hand over my thigh.

'You see, my dear, I was quite right. Red-hot walnut shells are absolutely it. You have such pretty legs, ducky, it's a shame to spoil them with fuzz.'

And then, with his hand still stroking me just above the knee, and Agrippa snorting something about bloody effeminate dirt from the next couch – then – it is a scene I hold clear as a vase-painting – the curtain was thrown aside, and a slave burst in, with no ceremony at all.

'Which of you is Gaius Octavius Thurinus?' he cried.

'This one is,' Maecenas said, not moving his hand. But I sat up, shaking him off. When slaves forget their manners, all the more reason to behave decently. The man thrust a letter into my outstretched hand, and disappeared without waiting for a reward. (I know why he did that; he was aware he was the bearer of bad news – slaves always know what their missives contain, I suppose they check with the secretaries and it is passed down the line – but in this case of course he could hardly have failed to know what the whole world would ring of – and he had all the Greek superstitious fear of the fate that waits the bringer of evil tidings.)

I turned it over. 'It's from my mother,' I said.

'Oh God,' Maecenas said, 'mothers.'

'That's no way to talk,' Agrippa said.

'Well, who's little Miss Good Citizen now?'

Their bickering is memory's sour accompaniment to the solo of my mother's letter. It was short enough for something that shook the world:

> *My son, your uncle Julius was this day murdered in the Senate House by his enemies. I write that bluntly because there is no way to prepare such news. And I say merely 'his enemies' because all here is uncertainty. No one knows what may happen, whether this is the beginning of new wars or not. Therefore, my child, be careful. Nevertheless the time has come when you must play the man, decide and act, for no one knows or can tell what things may now come forth.*

I let the letter drop. (One of the others picked it up and what they read silenced them.) I let my fingers play over my smooth legs and bare chin, and wondered if I was going to cry. I have always cried easily, but I had no tears for Julius either then or later.

Very soon there was a clamour without. We dressed hurriedly in some apprehension. One does in such circumstances. No one likes to be caught naked when there is danger of sword-play. My mind was full of all that I had heard and read of the proscriptions in the struggle between Sulla and Marius; how Julius himself had nearly lost his life then, for, said Sulla, 'in that young man there are many Mariuses.' I could not be certain that the slave who had brought the message was not the precursor of those who had constituted themselves my enemies as well as Julius's. I was his next-of-kin; it would make sense to dispose of me. I was indeed prudent to have such fears, for my death would have been an act of prudence on their part.

They should have killed me. I wonder when they realized that themselves. It is known that they regretted not putting Antony to death at the same time as my uncle. Cassius, wise man, wished to do so. The ostentatiously virtuous Marcus Brutus over-ruled him. The truth is, there was never so thoughtless a conspiracy. They imagined, these self-styled Liberators, these besotted idealists, these disgruntled fools, that if they killed Julius, the Republic would resume its old stability of its own accord. They were futile men, without foresight.

That night in Illyria Agrippa organized a guard for me, alert to our peril. I had gone out before the crowd and stilled their tumult. To express grief for Julius, I tore my clothes (Maecenas having first thoughtfully run a knife along the seam). I begged the crowd, whose grief I knew to be as great as mine – they liked that assurance – to go home and leave me to mourn. To my surprise it worked. They were a poor lot and even more confused than I was myself.

'Well,' I said to Maecenas when we were alone.

He stopped plucking his eyebrows, a task he would normally have left to a slave.

'Well,' I said, 'I am head of the family. Julius had no other heir. I am almost his adopted son.'

'You are only eighteen,' he said. 'There are other leaders of the Popular Party. Mark Antony and his brother Lucius.'

'They may have killed Antony too,' I said. 'Why shouldn't they? It's five days since Julius was murdered. Anything could have happened. My mother tells me to act the man. But how?'

'We must go to Italy,' he said. 'You are in no more danger there than here. And whatever you do, nobody will believe you plan to do nothing. So you might as well act with decision. The Gods,' his tongue flickered on his lips, 'have thrown the dice for you. You must pick them up, and roll again. Tell Agrippa to see to a ship, employ his vast administrative talent. As for me, well, Nikos tells me he has a new consignment from Asia. He has promised me a Phrygian boy with a bottom like a peach. It would be a shame not to pluck it before we sail. Nothing, my dear, is sadder than the remembrance of lost fucks.'

You will wonder, I am sure, why I tolerated Maecenas; he is hardly the type you would find around me now, is he? Of course I have grown staid and respectable with years, but even then your natural father Agrippa could not understand it. He often rebuked me for this friendship and inveighed against Maecenas, of whom he was intensely jealous, and whom he would call 'a pansy whoremaster'. You will wonder too why I record the light nonsense of Maecenas' lascivious conversation, that quip about my legs for instance. To tell the truth, I am surprised to find myself doing so. I can only say that nothing brings back those last moments of boyish irresponsibility so keenly to me as the echo in my memory of that affected drawl.

And to answer the first question: no one in my life ever gave me more consistently good advice.

Agrippa couldn't stand that knowledge either.

Certainly not my mother's husband Philippus.

We had arrived in Brindisi in an April dawn. The sun was just touching the mountains of Basilicata. Even this early though, the port was in a ferment. It swarmed with disbanded or disorganized legionaries – we were told that a ship bringing back some of the last remnants of Pompey's men had docked the day before, and the streets round the fishmarket were thronged with these veterans who had no idea what to do with themselves. Ours seemed an unpropitious arrival.

Then, so quickly does news get about, a century of legionaries in good marching order wheeled round the corner of the harbour offices, the crowd falling back. Their centurion halted them on the quayside, as if they constituted a guard of honour; or possibly, as I remarked to Maecenas, a prisoner's escort.

The centurion boarded the ship, followed by a couple of his men. He called out in a loud voice:

'I have information that Gaius Octavius Thurinus is on board.'

I saw the captain of the vessel hesitate. I drew back the cloak with which I was covering my face, and stepped forward.

'I am he.'

The centurion saluted with a great flourish.

'Publius Clodius Maco, centurion of the fifth cohort of the twelfth legion, served in Gaul, fought at Pharsalus and Munda, wounded and decorated in the latter battle, at your service, sir. I have brought my century as your escort, sir.'

I advanced towards him.

'Welcome, friend. I am happy to see you.' Then I raised my voice so that I could be heard by the troops drawn up on the quay. 'You are all Caesar's soldiers and colleagues. I am Caesar's adopted son. You wish to avenge your general, I seek to avenge my father. You offer me your protection on the road to Rome. I offer you my name and my father's name as a talisman, and I grant you my protection in all you do. Caesar living brought us first together. Caesar's blood, shed in most foul murder, has united us to death or victory . . .'

They gave a great cheer, without breaking ranks, a good sign. The two soldiers who had boarded the ship behind Maco hoisted me to their shoulders and bore me to the quay. I bade them set me down, and, taking a risk, announced that I would inspect the guard, my first command. It was a risk worth taking. If they had shrunk from that assertion of my authority, they would have been useless for my purpose. But they didn't. They drew themselves up, set their shoulders back. I was relieved and impressed. They were serious men, and their leather was polished, their brass and weapons shining. Maco was a good centurion to have seen to it that his men were in such fine condition in a world that was crumbling into uncertainty.

'Where now?' asked Agrippa.

'To the magistrates,' I said. 'It is important that they realize why we are here.'

'What's all this about being Caesar's adopted son?' – Agrippa was full of naïve questions when we were young – 'First I've heard of it.'

'It must be in the will. If I'm not that, we're sunk.'

'My dear boy, nobody admires your spirit more than I do.' My stepfather leant back in his arbour overlooking the Campagna and toyed with a mug of his own yellow wine; the fingers of his left hand played little drumming tunes on his swollen paunch; the mug almost vanished in the fat of his face. 'Nobody, not even your dear mother, who dotes on you and who has been in tears, floods,

I assure you, since it happened. But, dear boy, consider the facts. Look at yourself. You're scarcely more than a child. I don't want to be rude, but there simply are times when a chap must tell the truth. How old are you? Sixteen?'

'Eighteen,' I said.

'Well, eighteen, eighteen, and you want to set yourself up against chaps like Gaius Cassius. To say nothing of Mark Antony. Oh I know he's meant to be a Caesarean, but Caesar's dead, my dear. And I know you think I'm an old fogey, but still even you must admit that old fogeys have seen a thing or two. And I know Antony, know him well. He has beardless boys for breakfast. And, take my word for it, what Antony is now is an Antonian, nothing less . . . no,' he sighed deeply before resuming his wearying unwearied flow of counsel, 'take the money old Jules left you. Take that like a shot naturally, but waive the political inheritance. Just say you're too young and inexperienced. Let them look elsewhere. They'll be relieved as like as not. I don't expect either Cassius or Antony really wants to cut your throat.'

'There's that danger,' I said, 'I'm not too inexperienced to recognize that. There was a cohort sent south to arrest me, you know. I turned them round and they're on my side now, but it shows . . .'

'Only,' he sighed, 'because you will insist on drawing attention to yourself. Once announce that all you want is a quiet life, and no one will trouble you. Chaps don't come trying to clap irons on me, you know . . . Besides, you must admit, the whole Julian connection is fortuitous. A bit thin, what? I mean, if your mother's father hadn't married his sister Julia, what would you be? Nothing. Nothing significant. Decent folk of course, but small town worthies. That's all. Your own dad was the first of your family to enter the Senate, you know, and only because of the connection. What do you think all the really top families make of that? You know they sneer at Cicero as a parvenu, and he's a man of genius. You're only a boy, and your grandfather was a moneylender.'

'Let's say banker.' I kept a smile in my voice. 'Do you think my banking blood should be potent enough to persuade me to take the money and do nothing else? Do you think anyone would believe I was satisfied with that? What do you think my own soldiers would say?'

'Your own soldiers?' He sighed and poured himself wine. 'It's a fantasy, child, a boy's game, but it will end in blood, your blood, I fear. Well, your mother can't say I didn't try to dissuade you.'

*   *   *

It is hard to make you, my beloved boys, who have been brought
up in peace and order, understand the mood of a crumbling state,
of an incipient revolution. If I talk of fear and uncertainty, what
can these be but words to you children of sunshine? In the same
way, you know me as a man on the verge of old age; you can hardly
remember your natural father Agrippa. You, Gaius, were only eight
when he died; you, my dear Lucius, an infant of five. I myself could
never imagine Julius young, and yet I saw him in dangerous action.
And you have been brought up in the Republic which I restored;
how can you imagine a world that was falling apart, where no man
knew his friend?

I trusted Agrippa and Maecenas of course. Apart from affection,
they had nowhere else to go. But I trusted no other man above the
rank of centurion, and not always them either. Even Maco said to
me, 'You know, sir, my brother's with Antony. I could get him to
let us know the feeling in his camp . . .' I assented of course, but
how could I be sure of the honesty of any answer? And it wasn't
really true either that Agrippa and Maecenas were bound to me;
traitors are always welcome, for a time at least. Yet I had to act as
if their affection, of which I was sure, could continue to determine
their interest; which was more doubtful.

There were at least five parties or factions in the State, including
my own.

Antony had inherited part of Caesar's following. He was consul
which assured him direct command of at least five legions, and,
even more important, gave him legitimate authority.

The chief of the self-styled Liberators, Marcus Brutus and Gaius
Cassius, still posing as true friends of the Republic, had withdrawn
in panic from the city which had vociferously rejected their gift of
blood. Though they had only been assigned in the previous elections
the unimportant provinces of Crete and Cyrene respectively, within
a few weeks it was known that Brutus had gone to Macedonia,
Cassius to Syria, where they were raising rebellious armies in the
name of Liberty and Republican virtue.

Lurking in Sicily was Sextus Pompey, unworthy son of an
over-rated father. Pompey the Great had cleared the sea of pirates;
Sextus was little better than a pirate himself. Yet he had attracted
to him the most irreconcilable remnants of the old Optimate party,
those who, unlike the Liberators, had never made their peace with
Caesar.

In Rome itself you could find the constitutionalists; their chief was
Cicero. He was at least a voice, a marvellous and fecund organ.

And then, myself. I had got the nucleus of an army. It burned to revenge Caesar, and would continue to burn as long as I could pay it.

'Money,' Maecenas said, 'money is how it is done.'

Agrippa snorted, but I knew Maecenas was right. To this extent anyway; without money it couldn't be done.

Mark Antony had grown. That was the first surprise. I have since seen other men contract in office, as if the possession of authority revealed their deficiencies to them. His manner too had changed. He had treated me before like a younger brother. I had disliked his assumption of intimacy; he had had a habit of putting his arm round my shoulders and hugging me towards him which I found particularly offensive. Now he lay back on a couch, with two greyhounds resting beside him, and, having dismissed the slaves, looked me straight in the face.

'You're making trouble,' he said. He spoke as if I was a defaulter, and didn't ask me to sit down. Nevertheless I took the other couch. (Perhaps he regretted not having had it removed.) In the silence the babble of the morning forum rose up to us.

'I grant you,' he said – and I felt I had won the first round by compelling him to make the running in the conversation – 'that you have secured the south. I even grant it was well done. But the stories you permit to be circulated can only serve our enemies.'

'Our enemies?'

'Yes,' he said. 'I want those soldiers you have. How many is it? A legion? Half a legion? You realize of course that as consul I have the right to command them, and that you as a private citizen are acting illegally. You have no official position, and at your age you can't have one. You can't command an army anyway, you've no experience, and I need the troops. Decimus Brutus is loose in Cisalpine Gaul, the other buggers are raising armies the other side of the Adriatic. I need those troops.'

'And what will you offer me?' I asked.

'A place on my staff. A consulship years before you're qualified. Safety. After all, boy, if I fail, you're done for.'

He may even have been frank. Certainly, for Antony was the sort of optimist who believes that the expression of a desire is miraculously translated into its achievement, he seemed to think that my silence betokened consent. At any rate, he now called on a slave to bring us wine, drank off a cup himself, and began to give me a survey of the strategical situation; Julius had once told me not to underestimate Antony: for all his flamboyance he was a good staff officer, with a grasp of detail you don't often find in drunkards.

'There's another thing,' I said. 'My inheritance. Caesar's will . . .'

He closed up, walked over to the window; and I knew at that moment I would have to fight him to be anything. Antony was a chronic debtor. Having a treasure like Caesar's at his disposal was a new and exhilarating experience. Even if he had not needed the money, which Caesar had left me, to pay his troops and buy popularity, he couldn't have brought himself to relinquish something so novel and delightful.

'You are right,' I said to Maecenas that evening. 'Money is how it's going to be done. I'll have to pay my soldiers from my own resources. See what you can do about it. And meanwhile make me an appointment to see Balbus. He financed my father; let him finance me too.'

Agrippa said: 'I don't know that you were wise to turn down his offer. After all we're all Caesareans. We've got common enemies. We can sort things out between us when we've dealt with them. And Antony is consul. He has got a right to command.'

I said: 'You don't understand. There are no Caesareans. It's a meaningless term since the Ides of March.'

I couldn't blame Agrippa. He wasn't alone in his failure to understand. Yet in that general failure, in the confused incomprehension of how things actually were, lay the strength of my position; it was that which gave me freedom to manoeuvre. I despatched Agrippa into Campania to raise more troops – he had a genius for recruiting, and I knew they would come in an orderly fashion. Meanwhile, I had Maecenas, with all the considerable ostentation of which he was capable, pay Caesar's legacies from my own fortune and credit (people laugh at a banking background, but it's invaluable when you have to raise money in a hurry). And I resolved to woo Cicero.

Cicero is at most a name to you, my sons, because I have never permitted you to study his writings. You may, in the course of this narrative, come to understand why. Yet, if you are to make sense of my account of the next few months, I must tell you something about this man of the greatest genius – for another time and another city.

Marcus Tullius Cicero was the cleverest man I have ever known; yet I outwitted him at every turn. He was born in the municipality of Aroinum in the year 106 BC, so that he was by now an old man. The events of this terrible year show however that, if he was failing, it was in judgement, not energy of mind or body. I had sympathy and respect for Cicero, even affection. We were both after all from the same sort of background, and he too had risen by his own genius. He was consul in 63, the year that saw the conspiracy of Catiline, which he suppressed with vigour and, it must be said, a fine disregard for the legality he spent the rest of his life claiming to uphold. For this exploit he was granted the title 'Father of his Country', which, as you know, the Conscript Fathers have thought fit to bestow on me also. Yet he never learned the lesson of his own consulship: that power makes its own rules. Nobody was more aware than Cicero of the decrepitude of the Republic, nobody analysed it more acutely. He saw that the extraordinary commands entrusted to the Republic's generals enabled them to create armies loyal to themselves but not to the Republic; yet he never saw how this had come about. His proposed cure was preposterous: he believed that if all the 'good men' would come together and co-operate, they could restore the old virtues of the Republic as in the day of Scipio – if not that stout old peasant Cincinnatus. He did not see that the structure itself was rotten. Yet he had proved it in his own life: to combat Caesar he had been forced to propose that Pompey receive one of those extraordinary commands that were destroying what Cicero loved; crazy.

I envied him his love for the idea of the Republic; he was infatuated with virtue. (But, my sons, you know the root of that verb 'to infatuate', don't you? You realize I have chosen it with the utmost precision to describe its effect on this man of genius.) He had beautiful manners too. Having discussed the matter with Maecenas, I went to visit Cicero taking with me humble and homely presents – a pot of honey from the Alban hills, a caciocavallo cheese, the first (very early, for it was a marvellous benign spring) wood strawberries from Nemi. He received me with a dignity that did honour to us both.

He began by speaking of Caesar. 'You must not think I did not respect him,' he said, 'even love him. Who could fail to admire his abilities? What a power of reasoning, what a memory, what lucidity, what literary skill, what accuracy, profundity of thought and energy! His conquest of Gaul! Even though, as you will understand, I cannot think of it in its consequences as other than disastrous for the Republic, nevertheless, what an achievement! His genius was great, well-nigh unparalleled of its type; yet, my boy, and I say this with tears in my eyes, consider the consequence of his illustrious career: he brought this free city, which we both love – do we not? – to a habit of slavery. That is why I opposed him. That is why I welcomed his death. It is painful for me to say this; it is painful for you to hear it. Yet I must be honest if we are to work together, as I hope we may.'

'It is my hope too, sir,' I said.

'These gifts you have brought me, so aptly and significantly chosen, they give me assurance that that hope may not be vain. There is measure and restraint in your choice; a just severity of judgement.'

I said: 'They are nothing. I merely hoped they might be pleasing to the Father of our Country, who saved Rome from the mad wolf Catiline.'

His manner, which had been public, ornate, rhetorical and insincere, changed.

'Ah,' he said, 'you know about that. I can never believe they teach any history now. My own sons and my nephew would have known nothing if I had not instructed them myself. And indeed you see truly what Catiline was . . . But what else is Antony?'

I was amazed at his audacity, for I had been accustomed to hear men mock his timidity. I had not known before how some men become bolder as their future shortens.

'Do you know what Rome is?' he said. 'Ah, how could you, child? But come.'

He took me by the sleeve and led me over to where we could look down on the city. The sky was of the most intense blue; the temples on the Capitol glittered. Below the hill rose the hum of the city, a constant movement, a coming and going, a jostling animation; law courts were babbling, baths teeming, libraries attended, cook-shops and taverns sizzling. We withdrew into the cool of the atrium.

'It is a city of free men,' Cicero said, 'with liberty of discussion and debate, where none legally wears arms or armour; a city of noble equals; and that mad dog, whom I shall not dignify with Catiline's name of wolf, that drunken pirate, threatens to stop our mouths with the swords of his legionaries.'

'I have legions too, sir.'

The first smile lit up his face; he chuckled.

'Of course you have, dear boy. That's why you are here, child. The question is, what will you do with them?'

'My legions are at the service of the Republic,' I said.

He let a long silence of sceptical memories fill the air.

'But,' I continued, 'what are the intentions of the Republic towards me?'

'I am not sure,' he said, 'that just at the moment the Republic can be said to have any intentions. It is as bereft of will as it is of legions. That, dear boy, is the crux of the matter.'

*   *   *

When Antony promised me safety if I delivered my legions to him, there was mockery in his voice. There was an even harsher note: contempt. He believed I would indeed be ready to buy safety. 'You, boy,' he would say, 'with your banker's blood, who owe everything to a name . . .' Such an assumption on his part hardly caused me to respect his intelligence: did he truly fail to realize that I too had let the dice fly high when I chose to accept Julius' legacy and acknowledged Maco's salute at Brindisi?

Cicero praised me in the Senate. His words would have overwhelmed me if my vanity had approached his own. Agrippa was hugely impressed. He repeated over and over again that we had really arrived: 'I don't see that they can now deny you legitimate authority. Not after such advocacy.' Maecenas I saw smirking. 'You don't agree, do you?' I said. 'Oh,' he said, 'who am I to speak? Remember I am not a true Roman. I don't understand your Senates and Assemblies. My ancestors were Kings in Etruria. So it is hard for me to estimate the effect of oratory on a body like the Senate. But we have a saying in my family: beware the man who speaks well of you. Besides, haven't you heard the story that's going about? Someone said to Cicero, "Why on earth do you praise that young man?" The old boy looked over his shoulder to see who might overhear, and replied, "The young man must be praised." "Must be?" asks his chum. "Must be," says Cicero, "he must be praised, decorated and . . . disposed of . . ." What we mustn't forget, my dears, is that Cicero was cheating serpents before our daddies were weaned.' I looked at Maecenas. 'We must never let Cicero suspect that we guess what he has in mind. He is our dearest friend and essential ally.'

It was a spring of the utmost delicacy. The wild weather of the March of Julius' murder was scattered by a sun that promised more than we could find time to enjoy. I had got myself an army, but hesitated whether to use it or disband it for the moment. Antony returned to Rome about 20 May, bringing with him a bodyguard of thugs ready to control any vote in the popular assembly. With money that was rightfully mine he bought the alliance of Cicero's son-in-law Dolabella. At the beginning of June he staged a plebiscite to prolong his own provincial command for three years.

We met again in a house that had once belonged to Pompey; whether he or Antony was responsible for its vulgarity, I could not tell. But I had time enough to study it, for Antony had the insolence to keep me waiting. No doubt he thought to disturb me.

When he at last granted me an interview his insolence continued. He again absolutely refused to disgorge Julius' money.

I accepted his insolence in silence. Do not, my children, ever underestimate the value of silence. It disconcerts bluster and distorts judgement.

When I left his presence I let it be known that I would pay all Julius' legacies; 'If it costs me my last penny,' I asserted. I wrote to my friends in the legions in Macedonia complaining that Antony was refusing to avenge Caesar.

This was not strictly true, for by midsummer Antony was actually besieging Decimus Brutus in Mutina. This disturbed Agrippa. 'It seems to me wrong that we're not working with Antony,' he kept saying. 'I tell you our centurions don't understand what you're up to. They don't like it. They joined us to avenge Caesar and here you are fucking about with the Senate and that old woman Cicero.'

'Run away and practise your sword-play, ducky,' Maecenas said. 'We do have heads on our shoulders. We're not just blundering about.'

'Well,' Agrippa glowered at me, 'that's what it fucking well looks like. If you've got a plan, perhaps you'd be kind enough to tell me what it is?'

I thought about that.

'There you go again,' he said. 'You just sit there like a little owl, and let him make fun of me. You don't tell me anything, but it's me as has to go out and find you soldiers, and then try to keep 'em happy. But they're not happy, they're bleeding not. So what's your flaming plan?'

'I don't have one,' I said, 'not the sort of plan you could write down.'

And this was true. I have talked to you about this, Gaius and Lucius, but I have never put it in writing for you. The value of planning diminishes in accordance with the complexity of the state of affairs. Believe me: this is true. It may seem paradoxical. You may think that the more complicated a situation is, the more necessary a plan to deal with it. I shall grant you the theory. But practice is different. No plan can be equal to the complexities and casualties of political life. Hence, adherence to a plan deprives you of the flexibility which you need if you are to ride the course of events; for a moment's reflection should enable you to see that it is impossible (even with the help of the wisest soothsayers and mathematicians) to predict what will happen; and it is folly to pretend that you can control the actions of other men with any certainty. Therefore a plan is only suitable for the simple operations of life; you can plan a journey to your country house, but you cannot plan a battle or a political campaign in any detail. You must have a goal, my sons, but to achieve it, nothing is more important than that you retain fluidity of thought. Improvisation is the secret of success in politics, for most political action is in fact and of necessity reaction.

So I said now to Agrippa, 'I have no plan but I have purposes. I intend to avenge Caesar and to restore the Republic. And first I intend to safeguard our position. All my manoeuvring is directed towards these aims. You ask about Antony? You call for a reunion of the Caesareans. Well, so do I. But does Antony? As far as he is concerned, Caesar is dead and Antony is his successor. He must be persuaded that it is not so, and that he, Antony, is less than half our party.'

Meanwhile, as Maecenas was quick to tell me, Antony was doing all he could to destroy my reputation. He spread many rumours about me. I shall set them down, because I am not ashamed to have been slandered.

He let it be known that I had played the role of catamite to Caesar to encourage him to adopt me. He added that, subsequently, I had submitted to the lusts of Aulus Hirtius, Procurator of Spain, in return for 3000 gold pieces: 'The boy lends out his body at interest,' he said, 'it's his banker's blood, no doubt.' He accused me of effeminacy and sent agents among my troops to ask why they let themselves be commanded by a boy-whore.

The accusations were false of course; it was ridiculous to suppose that Caesar would so reward a boy who behaved in such a disgusting way. As for Aulus Hirtius, he was so repulsive that one of his slave-boys hanged himself rather than endure his embraces. (The boy was a Gaul too, and everyone knows that Gallic boys think it no shame to sleep with mature men; the Druid religion encourages youths to prostitute themselves to the priests, and Gallic warriors are accustomed to choose the boys who look after their war-horses for their good looks.) Besides, it was absurd to suppose that 3000 gold pieces would attract a young man of my fortune.

Curiously these allegations did me no harm with the troops. They didn't believe them. Even if they had, Antony should have known that soldiers take pleasure in the vices of their commanders. Caesar's legionaries had delighted in the story of their general's seduction by King Nicomedes. They had even sung a dirty song about it, which I shall not repeat to you.

Agrippa of course was furious. He told me I was bound to have such stories made up about me as long as I associated with a pansy like Maecenas. He said that even if my men chose not to believe them, the senators whose support I was seeking would hardly like it to be thought that they were associating with a tart.

'Don't be so silly,' I said, 'there's nothing to worry about. Everyone knows Antony is a liar.'

All the same I was displeased myself, though my displeasure was mixed with the satisfaction that the circulation of such absurd and malicious rumours showed that Antony was taking my rivalry seriously. Nevertheless, I thought it as well to do what I could to disprove the lies. I stopped shaving my legs for one thing, and grew a beard too; and I took care to let pretty slave-girls be seen round my quarters. Maecenas introduced me to one Toranius, a dealer who was able to supply me with the most delectable fruits of the market.

I tell you these things, my sons, not for any pleasure I feel in the memory – to speak the truth I look back on them with a mixture of amusement and distaste – but for two reasons: first, that you may learn from my own lips what manner of man I have been, and so be able to discount the malicious and disreputable rumours with which I am sure you will be fed; and, second, because you may learn in this way how much prudence, self-control and decision are necessary to manipulate public opinion. I was careful to arrange that Maco should see a Circassian girl slip shiftless from my tent as he awaited an interview. I knew he would go back and say, 'He's a right boy, our general, you should have seen the bit of fluff he had last night . . .'

Antony was fighting only for himself; but I had a vision of Rome. No one knows how ideas are formed, what influences operate on the mind, to what extent a man creates a world-view for himself. These are deep matters which I have discussed with philosophers, and, as the poet says, 'evermore came out, by that same door wherein I went'; and with Virgil, who was something more profound than a philosopher, a true poet. Here let me say a word on the subject of poets. Most of them are no more than versifiers. Any gentleman should of course be able to turn a verse; you, Lucius, have written elegiacs that please me. Beyond that, when it becomes a profession, there is too often something despicable in the craft. It encourages conceit and extravagant behaviour, monkey-tricks. True poetry has a moral value, most verse none; some is frankly immoral. Occasionally however you find a poet who offers more even than that. He is a man possessed of insight, a man through whom the Gods have chosen to speak. (By the way, I am glad that I have never heard you mock the Gods; only those with no rudder, men who trust complacently to their own natural buoyancy, do that. I fear the man who does not fear the Gods, for he lacks proportion.) I am fortunate to have known one such poet, Virgil. The spirit of Rome inhabited him; he saw what was hidden from other men. There is no man I have more deeply revered. I am sometimes tempted to believe that the core of my political thought derives from Virgil. And yet this is false. I was moving in that direction before I ever talked with him. Is it possible that ideas can exist, as it were, in the air?

Caesar was naturally an inspiration. Yet, speaking under my breath to you, my sons, let me confess I never cared for Julius. There was something meretricious in him, something rotten. He revealed the full decadence of the Republic; when he led his legions across the Rubicon in that winter dawn, it was as if he tore a veil away from a shrine and discovered to all that the God had abandoned it. He was a great general; his conquest of Gaul and defeat of Pompey were imperishable feats. But what did he do then? He was tempted by monarchy – I have it on good authority that when Antony three times presented him with a kingly crown on the occasion of the Feast of the Lupercal, both Caesar and Antony expected that the crowd would hail him as king, and thus allow him to accept the crown. Inept politicians! Not to have arranged that the wind would blow that way! There was a vanity to him; he wore the high red boots of the old kings of Alba Longa; can you imagine me behaving so absurdly? But there was room for such vanity – it filled a vacancy at the heart of his imagination. Having achieved supreme power, he did not see that he was only at the beginning of his labours.

I often talked of Julius with Cicero that long summer ago. When he sensed – oh he had the sharp intuition of the great cross-examiner he was – that I too had my doubts about my father, Cicero let slip the cloak of discretion which he always wore as if it chafed him. He ran his hand through his grey hair, leaned forward and thrust his scraggy neck towards me:

'The truth is,' he said, 'he was an adventurer, a gambler. He had no purpose beyond the immediate. He had no sense of history, no sense of the relationship that must exist between the past, the present and the future. He had never analysed the causes of his own elevation because he believed it had been achieved by fortune and his own merit; his genius in short. Such nonsense!'

'Do you think,' I said – I made a habit of seeking Cicero's opinion even when I had no need of it – 'do you think that there was any deep purpose behind his admission of Gauls to the Senate?'

Cicero flushed: 'There was certainly a purpose, but it was simply

ALLAN MASSIE

to insult the senators by making us associate with barbarians. Can you imagine anything more contemptuous?'

'No, sir,' I said, shaking my head and keeping my face straight, 'but tell me how in your view, garnered from your life's distinguished harvest, the Free State can be restored.'

Cicero sighed: 'I had almost come to believe it impossible. Perhaps, my dear boy, you have been sent by the gods to make it possible. What is needed is resolution, and the agreement of all good men throughout society to work together, and obey the laws. There is no fault in our laws. The fault, Octavius, lies in our own natures. Let me give you two examples. Have you ever heard of Verres?'

'Who, thanks to your sublime oratory, has not heard of Verres?'

'Well, yes, my prosecution made some stir in its time. I am glad it is still read. You remember what I said? Let me at any rate refresh your memory. I dislike quoting myself, but I know no other way to make my present point . . .'

And he did; it lasted half an hour (all from memory of course) and he was (as I guessed) hardly half-way through when he was suddenly taken by old man's weakness and had to leave me to empty his bladder. I shan't weary you with his speech: suffice to say that Verres was a dishonest and extortionate Governor of Sicily, whom Cicero had very properly prosecuted (nowadays of course a modern Verres would not be able to commit even a quarter of the offences of the original, and we have more efficient ways of dealing with such malpractice than by public trial).

I had thought the interruption might spare me the rest of the speech. Not a bit of it; he was in full flow before he was properly back in the room, doubtless lest I should change the subject.

Eventually he paused a moment. 'My peroration,' he said, 'has been called sublime.' And he gave it to me elaborate and fortissimo. (I would never advise anyone to copy his magniloquent and excessively mannered style of oratory. It was, I suppose, superb or sublime, if you like; but prolix and too carefully prepared to convince. All right in its time I daresay, but terribly dated and disgustingly florid in my view. However, I applauded as was only polite.)

Then he said: 'Now look on the other side. I myself have been a Governor too. In Cilicia, a province lamentably looted by my predecessors. I refused to follow their example. No expense was imposed on the wretched provincials during my government, and when I say no expense, I do not speak hyperbolically. I mean, none, not a farthing. Imagine that. I refused to billet my troops on them. I made the soldiers sleep under canvas. I refused all bribes. My dear boy, the natives regarded my conduct with speechless admiration and astonishment. I tell you it was all I could do to prevent them from erecting temples in my honour. Innumerable babies were named Marcus, I could hardly object to that. When I took slaves in my campaigns I deposited in the Treasury the 12 million sesterces I received for their sale. That's how to govern; that's the way it should be done. Not like Verres, not like Marcus Brutus.' He broke off to giggle. 'Do you know, dear boy, what interest he charged the wretched Cypriots under his care? No? You won't believe it. Forty-eight per cent. That's right, it's true. Forty-eight per cent. Imagine. But, dear boy, you see what I mean? There is nothing wrong with the Republic that a change of heart and a return to the stern morality of our ancestors will not put right. Meanwhile though, we have this wild beast Antony to account for. The stories he has spread about you! It's shameful. An old man like myself can stand slander; it must always hurt the young.'

Such optimism, such naïvety, in one who had seen so much!

ONE OF
CLEOPATRA'S NIGHTS

Théophile Gautier

There were several queens of Egypt called Cleopatra, but only one is remembered today and that is Cleopatra VII, who ruled (nominally with her brothers and later her son), from 51 BC, when she was eighteen, until her death in 30 BC. Her association first with Julius Caesar, and more especially with Mark Antony, threatened the very fabric of the Roman world, and it was the war between Antony and Octavian (later Augustus) that subsequently established the Roman empire. One cannot help but wonder what direction the Roman world would have taken had Cleopatra not existed.

Théophile Gautier (1811–1872) was a French poet and one of the leading exponents of the Romantic movement. He wrote a number of historical novellas, including Le roi Candaules (1844), based on the story of Gyges reprinted earlier in this anthology. He wrote his own interpretation of the Cleopatra story in Une nuit de Cléopâtre (1838).

I

A magnificently gilded and painted cangia was descending the Nile as rapidly as fifty long flat oars, which seemed to crawl over the furrowed water like the legs of a gigantic scarabæus, could impel it.

This cangia was narrow, long, elevated at both ends in the form of a new moon, elegantly proportioned, and admirably built for speed. The figure of a ram's head surmounted by a golden globe, armed the point of the prow, showing that the vessel belonged to some personage of royal blood.

In the center of the vessel arose a flat-roofed cabin – a sort of *naos*, or tent of honor, colored and gilded, ornamented with palm-leaf moldings, and lighted by four little square windows.

Two chambers, both decorated with hieroglyphic paintings, occupied the horns of the crescent. One of them, the larger, had a second story of lesser height built upon it – like the *châteaux gaillards* of those fantastic galleys of the sixteenth century, drawn by Della-Bella; the other and smaller chamber, which also served as a pilot-house, was surmounted with a triangular pediment.

In lieu of a rudder, two immense oars, adusted upon stakes decorated with strips of paint, which served in place of our modern rowlocks – extended into the water in rear of the vessel like the webbed feet of a swan; heads crowned with *pshents* and bearing the allegorical horn upon their chins, were sculptured upon the handles of these huge oars, which were manoeuvred by the pilot as he stood upon the deck of the cabin above.

He was a swarthy man, tawny as new bronze, with bluish surface gleams playing over his dark skin, long oblique eyes, hair deeply black and all plaited into little cords, full lips, high cheekbones, ears standing out from the skull – the Egyptian type in all its purity. A narrow strip of cotton about his loins, together with five or six strings of glass beads, and a few amulets, comprised his whole costume.

He appeared to be the only one on board the cangia, for the rowers bending over their oars, and concealed from view by the gunwales, made their presence known only through the symmetrical movements of the oars themselves, which spread open alternately on either side of the vessel, like the ribs of a fan, and fell regularly back into the water after a short pause.

Not a breath of air was stirring; and the great triangular sail of the cangia, tied up and bound to the lowered mast with a silken cord, testified that all hope of the wind rising had been abandoned.

The noonday sun shot his arrows perpendicularly from above, the ashen-hued slime of the river banks reflected the fiery glow, a raw light, glaring and blinding in its intensity, poured down in torrents of flame; the azure of the sky whitened in the heat as a metal whitens in the furnace; an ardent and lurid fog smoked in the horizon. Not a cloud appeared in the sky – a sky mournful and changeless as Eternity.

The water of the Nile, sluggish and wan, seemed to slumber in its course, and slowly extend itself in sheets of molten tin. No breath of air wrinkled its surface, or bowed down upon their stalks the cups of the lotus-flowers, as rigidly motionless as though sculptured; at long intervals the leap of a bechir or fabaka expanding its belly, scarcely caused a silvery gleam upon the current; and the oars of the cangia seemed with difficulty to tear their way through the fuliginous film of that curdled water. The banks were desolate, a solemn and mighty sadness weighed upon this land, which was never aught else than a vast tomb, and in which the living appeared to be solely occupied in the work of burying the dead. It was an arid sadness, dry as pumice stone, without melancholy, without reverie, without one pearly grey cloud to follow toward the horizon, one secret spring wherein to lave one's dusty feet; the sadness of a sphinx weary of eternally gazing upon the desert, and unable to detach herself from the granite socle upon which she has sharpened her claws for twenty centuries.

So profound was the silence that it seemed as though the world had become dumb, or that the air had lost all power of conveying sound. The only noises which could be heard at intervals were the whisperings and stifled 'chuckling' of the crocodiles, which enfeebled by the heat, were wallowing among the bullrushes by the river banks; or the sound made by some ibis, which – tired of standing with one leg doubled up against its stomach, and its head sunk between its shoulders – suddenly abandoned its motionless attitude, and brusquely whipping the blue air with its white wings, flew off to perch upon an obelisk or a palm-tree.

The cangia flew like an arrow over the smooth river-water, leaving behind it a silvery wake which soon disappeared, and only a few foam-bubbles rising to break at the surface of the stream bore testimony to the passage of the vessel, then already out of sight.

The ochre-hued or salmon-colored banks unrolled themselves rapidly like scrolls of papyrus between the double azure of water and sky – so similar in tint that the slender tongue of earth which separated them seemed like a causeway stretching over an immense lake, and that it would have been difficult to determine whether the Nile reflected the sky, or whether the sky reflected the Nile.

The scene continually changed: at one moment were visible gigantic propylæa, whose sloping walls, painted with large panels of fantastic figures, were mirrored in the river; pylons with broad-bulging capitals; stairways guarded by huge crouching sphinxes, wearing caps with lappets of many folds, and crossing their paws of black basalt below their sharply projecting breasts; palaces, immeasurably vast, projecting against the horizon the severe horizontal lines of their entablatures, where the emblematic globe unfolded its mysterious wings like an eagle's vast-extending pinions; temples with enormous columns thick as towers, on which were limned processions of hieroglyphic figures against a background of brilliant white; all the monstrosities of that Titanic architecture. Again the eye beheld only landscapes of desolate aridity – hills formed of stony fragments from excavations and building works – crumbs of that gigantic debauch of granite which lasted for more than thirty centuries; mountains exfoliated by heat, and mangled and striped with black lines which seemed like the cauterizations of a conflagration; hillocks humped and deformed, squatting like the criocephalus of the tombs, and projectng the outlines of their misshapen attitude against the sky-line; expanses of greenish clay, reddle, flour-white tufa, and from time to time some steep cliff of dry rose-colored granite, where yawned the black mouths of the stone quarries.

This aridity was wholly unrelieved; no oasis of foliage refreshed the eye; green seemed to be a color unknown to that nature; only some meagre palm-tree, like a vegetable crab, appeared from time to time in the horizon – or a thorny fig-tree brandished its tempered leaves like sword blades of bronze – or a carthamus-plant, which had found a little moisture to live upon in the shadow of some fragment of a broken column, relieved the general uniformity with a speck of crimson.

After this rapid glance at the aspect of the landscape, let us return to the cangia with its fifty rowers, and without announcing ourselves enter boldly into the *naos* of honor.

The interior was painted white with green arabesques, bands of vermillion, and gilt flowers fantastically shaped; an exceedingly fine rush matting covered the floor; at the further end stood a little bed, supported upon griffin's feet – having a back resembling that of a modern lounge or sofa, a stool with four steps to enable one to climb into bed, and (rather an odd luxury according to our ideas of comfort!), a sort of hemicycle of cedar wood, supported upon a single leg, and designed to fit the nape of the neck so as to support the head of the person reclining.

Upon this strange pillow reposed a most charming head – one look of which once caused the loss of half-a-world – an adorable, a divine head; the head of the most perfect woman that ever lived – the most womanly and most queenly of all women; an admirable type of beauty which the imagination of poets could never invest with any new grace, and which dreamers will find forever in the depths of their dreams: it is not necessary to name Cleopatra.

Beside her stood her favorite slave Charmion, waving a large fan
of ibis feathers; and a young girl was moistening with scented water
the little reed blinds attached to the windows of the *naos*, so that
the air might only enter impregnated with fresh odors.

Near the bed of repose, in a striped vase of alabaster with a slender
neck and a peculiarly elegant, tapering shape – vaguely recalling the
form of a heron – was placed a bouquet of lotus-flowers, some of
a celestial blue, others of a tender rose-color, like the finger-tips of
Isis, the great goddess.

Either from caprice or policy, Cleopatra did not wear the Greek
dress that day: she had just attended a panegyris, and was returning
to her summer palace still clad in the Egyptian costume she had
worn at the festival.

Perhaps our fair readers will feel curious to know how Queen
Cleopatra was attired on her return from the Mammisi of Hermonthis
whereat were worshipped the holy triad of the god Mandou, the
goddess Ritho, and their son, Harphra: luckily we are able to satisfy
them in this regard.

For headdress, Queen Cleopatra wore a kind of very light helmet
of beaten gold, fashioned in the form of the body and wings of the
sacred partridge: the wings, opening downward like fans, covered
the temples, and extending below almost to the neck, left exposed
on either side through a small aperture, an ear rosier and more
delicately curled than the shell whence arose that Venus whom
the Egyptians named Athor – the tail of the bird occupied that
place where our women wear their chignons: its body covered with
imbricated feathers, and painted in variegated enamel, concealed the
upper part of the of the head; and its neck, gracefully curving forward
over the forehead of the wearer, formed together with its little head a
kind of horn-shaped ornament, all sparkling with precious stones – a
symbolic crest designed like a tower, completed this odd but elegant
headdress. Hair dark as a starless night flowed from beneath this
helmet, and streamed in long tresses over the fair shoulders whereof
the commencement only, alas! was left exposed by a collarette or
gorget adorned with many rows of serpentine stones, azodrachs,
and chrysoberyls; a linen robe diagonally cut – a mist of material,
of woven air, *ventus textilis* as Petronius says – undulated in vapory
whiteness about a lovely body, whose outlines it scarcely shaded with
the softest shading. This robe had half-sleeves, tight at the shoulder,
but widening toward the elbows like our *manches-à-sabot*, and
permitting a glimpse of an adorable arm and a perfect hand; the arm
being clasped by six golden bracelets, and the hand adorned with a
ring representing the sacred scarabæus. A girdle whose knotted ends

hung down in front, confined this free-floating tunic at the waist; a short cloak adorned with fringing completed the costume; and if a few barbarous words will not frighten Parisian ears, we might add that the robe was called *schenti* and the short cloak *calisiris*.

Finally we may observe that Queen Cleopatra wore very thin light sandals, turned up at the toes, and fastened over the instep, like the *souliers-à-la-poulaine* of the mediæval *châtelaines*.

But Queen Cleopatra did not wear that air of satisfaction which becomes a woman conscious of being perfectly beautiful and perfectly well dressed: she tossed and turned in her little bed; and her rather sudden movements momentarily disarranged the folds of her gauzy *canopeum* which Charmion has often rearranged with inexhaustible patience, and without ceasing to wave her fan.

'This room is stifling,' said Cleopatra – 'even if Pthah the God of Fire established his forges in here, he could not make it hotter: the air is like the breath of a furnace!' And she moistened her lips with the tip of her little tongue, and stretched out her hand like a feverish patient seeking an absent cup.

Charmion, ever attentive, at once clapped her hands; a black slave clothed in a short tunic hanging in folds like an Albanian petticoat, and a panther-skin thrown over his shoulders, entered with the suddenness of an apparition; with his left hand balancing a tray laden with cups and slices of water-melon, and carrying in his right a long vase with a spout like a modern teapot.

The slave filled one of these cups – pouring the liquor into it from a considerable height with marvelous dexterity – and placed it before the queen. Cleopatra merely touched the beverage with her lips, laid the cup down beside her, and turning upon Charmion her beautiful liquid black eyes lustrous with living light, exclaimed, 'O Charmion, I am weary unto death!'

II

Charmion at once anticipating a confidence, assumed a look of pained sympathy, and drew nearer to her mistress.

'I am horribly weary!' continued Cleopatra, letting her arms fall like one utterly discouraged – 'this Egypt crushes, annihilates me; this sky with its implacable azure is sadder than the deep night of Erebus – never a cloud! never a shadow, and always that red sanguine sun which glares down upon you like the eye of a Cyclops. Ah, Charmion, I would give a pearl for one drop of rain! From the inflamed pupil of that sky of bronze no tear has ever yet fallen upon the desolation of this land; it is only a vast covering for a tomb – the dome of a necropolis – a sky dead and dried up like the mummies it hangs over; it weighs upon my shoulders like an over-heavy mantle; it constrains and terrifies me; it seems to me that I could not stand up erect without striking my forehead against it. And moreover, this land is truly an awful land – all things in it are gloomy, enigmatic, incomprehensible! Imagination has produced in it only monstrous chimeræ and monuments immeasurable; this architecture and this art fill me with fear; those colossi, whose stone-entangled limbs compel them to remain eternally sitting with their hands upon their knees, weary me with their stupid immobility – they trouble my eyes and my horizon. When indeed shall the giant come who is to take them by the hand and relieve them from their long watch of twenty centuries? For even granite itself must grow weary at last! Of what master, then, do they await the coming, to leave their mountain-seats and rise in token of respect? Of what invisible flock are those huge sphinxes the guardians, crouching like dogs on the watch, that they never close their eye-lids and forever extend their claws in readiness to seize? Why are their stony eyes so obstinately fixed upon eternity and infinity? What weird secret do their firmly locked lips retain within their breasts? On the right hand, on the left, whithersoever one turns only frightful monsters are visible – dogs with the heads of men; men with the heads of dogs; chimæras begotten of hideous couplings in the shadowy depths of the labyrinths; figures of Anubis, Typhon, Osiris; partridges with great yellow eyes that seem to pierce through you with their inquisitorial gaze, and see beyond and behind you things which one dare not speak of – a family of animals and horrible gods with scaly wings, hooked beaks, trenchant claws – ever ready to seize and devour you should you venture to cross the threshold of the temple, or lift a corner of the veil.

'Upon the walls, upon the columns; on the ceilings, on the floors; upon palaces and temples; in the long passages and the deepest pits of the necropoli – even within the bowels of the earth where light never comes, and where the flames of the torches die for want of air; for ever and everywhere are sculptured and painted interminable hieroglyphics, telling in language unintelligible of things which are no longer known, which belong, doubtless, to the vanished creations of the past – prodigious buried works wherein a whole nation was sacrificed to write the epitaph of one king! Mystery and granite! – this is Egypt; truly a fair land for a young woman, and a young queen!

'Menacing and funereal symbols alone meet the eye – the emblems of the *pedum*, the *tau*, allegorical globes, coiling serpents, and the scales in which souls are weighed – the Unknown, death, nothingness! In the place of any vegetation only *stelae* limned with weird characters; instead of avenues of trees avenues of granite obelisks; in lieu of soil vast pavements of granite for which whole mountains could each furnish but one slab; in place of a sky ceilings of granite – eternity made palpable – a bitter and everlasting sarcasm upon the frailty and brevity of life! – stairways built only for the limbs of Titans, which the human foot cannot ascend save by the aid of ladders; columns that a hundred arms cannot encircle; labyrinths in which one might travel for years without discovering the termination! – the vertigo of enormity – the drunkenness of the gigantic – the reckless efforts of that pride which would at any cost engrave its name deeply upon the face of the world!

'And, moreover, Charmion, I tell you a thought haunts me which terrifies me – in other lands of the earth, corpses are burned, and their ashes soon mingle with the soil. Here, it is said that the living have no other occupation than that of preserving the dead; potent balms save them from destruction; the remains endure after the soul has evaporated – beneath this people lie twenty peoples – each stands upon twenty layers of necropoli – each generation which passes away leaves a population of mummies to a shadowy city; beneath the father you find the grandfather and the great-grandfather in their gilded and painted boxes, even as they were during life; and should you dig down forever, forever you would still find the underlying dead.

'When I think upon those bandage-swathed myriads – those multitudes of parched specters who fill the sepulchral pits and who have been there for two thousand years, face to face in their own silence which nothing ever breaks, not even the noise which the grave-worms make in crawling, and who will be found intact after yet another two thousand years with their crocodiles, their cats, their ibises, and all things that lived in their lifetime – then terrors seize me, and I feel my flesh creep! What do they mutter to each other? – for they still have lips; and every ghost would find its body in the same state as when it quitted it, if they should all take the fancy to return!

'Ah, truly is Egypt a sinister kingdom, and little suited to me, the laughter-loving and merry one! – everything in it encloses a mummy: that is the heart and the kernel of all things. After a thousand turns you must always end there – the pyramids themselves hide sarcophagi. What nothingness and madness is this! Disembowel the sky with gigantic triangles of stone – you cannot hereby lengthen your corpse an inch. How can one rejoice and live in a land like this, where the only perfume you can respire is the acrid odor of the naphtha and bitumen which boil in the cauldrons of the embalmers, where the very flooring of your chamber sounds hollow because the corridors of the hypogea and the mortuary extend even under your alcove? To be the queen of mummies – to have none to converse with but statues in constrained and rigid attitudes – this is in truth a cheerful lot! Again, if I only had some heartfelt passion to relieve this melancholy – some interest in life; if I could but love somebody or something – if I were even loved! but I am not!

'This is why I am weary, Charmion: with love this grim and arid Egypt would seem to me fairer than even Greece with her ivory gods, her temples of snowy marble, her groves of laurel and fountains of living water. There I should never dream of the weird face of Anubis, and the ghastly terrors of the cities under ground.'

Charmion smiled incredulously. 'That might not, surely, to be a source of much grief to you, O queen; for every glance of your eyes transpierces hearts, like the golden arrows of Eros himself.'

'Can a queen,' answered Cleopatra, 'even know whether it is her face or her diadem that is loved? The rays of her starry crown dazzle the eyes and the heart – were I to descend from the height of my throne, would I even have the celebrity or the popularity of Bacchis or Archianassa? – of the first courtesan from Athens or Miletus? A queen is something so far removed from men – so elevated, so widely separated from them – so impossible for them to reach! What presumption dare flatter itself in such an enterprise? It is not simply a woman: it is an august and sacred being that has no sex, and that is worshipped kneeling without being loved. Who was ever really enamoured of Hera, the snowy-armed, or Pallas of the sea-green eyes? – who ever sought to kiss the silver feet of Thetis or the rosy fingers of Aurora? – what lover of the divine beauties ever took unto himself wings that he might soar to the golden palaces of heaven? Respect and fear chill hearts in our presence; and in order to obtain the love of our equals, one must descend into those necropoli of which I have just been speaking!'

Although she offered no further objection to the arguments of her mistress, a vague smile which played about the lips of the handsome Greek slave, showed that she had little faith in the inviolability of the royal person.

'Ah,' continued Cleopatra, 'I wish that something would happen to me – some strange unexpected adventure! The songs of the poets, the dances of the Syrian slaves, the banquets, rose garlanded, and prolonged into the dawn, the nocturnal races, the Laconian dogs, the tame lions, the humpbacked dwarfs, the brotherhood of the

Inimitables, the combats of the arena, the new dresses, the byssus robes, the clusters of pearls, the perfumes from Asia, the most exquisite of luxuries, the wildest of splendors – nothing any longer gives me pleasure; everything has become indifferent to me – everything is unsupportable to me!'

'It is easily to be seen,' muttered Charmion to herself, 'that the queen has not had a lover, nor had anyone killed for a whole month.'

Fatigued with so lengthy a tirade, Cleopatra once more took the cup placed beside her, moistened her lips with it, and putting her head beneath her arm, like a dove putting its head under its wing, composed herself for slumber as best she could. Charmion unfastened her sandals, and commenced to gently tickle the soles of her feet with a peacock's feather; and Sleep soon sprinkled his golden dust upon the beautiful eyes of Ptolemy's sister.

While Cleopatra sleeps, let us ascend upon deck and enjoy the glorious sunset view. A broad band of violet color, warmed deeply with ruddy tints toward the west, occupies all the lower portion of the sky; encountering the zone of azure above, the violet shade melts into a clear lilac, and fades off through half-rosy tints, into the blue beyond: afar, where the sun, red as a buckler fallen from the furnace of Vulcan casts his burning reflection, the deeper shades turn to pale citron hues, and glow with turquoise tints. The water rippling under an oblique beam of light, shines with the dull gleam of the quicksilvered side of a mirror, or like a damascened blade: the sinuosities of the bank, the reeds, and all objects along the shores are brought out in sharp black relief against the bright glow. By the aid of this crepuscular light you may perceive afar off, like a grain of dust floating upon quicksilver, a little brown speck trembling in the network of luminous ripples. Is it a teal diving? – a tortoise lazily drifting with the current? – a crocodile raising the tip of his scaly snout above the water to breathe the cooler air of evening? – the belly of a hippopotamus gleaming amid-stream; or, perhaps a rock left bare by the falling of the river: for the ancient Opi-Mou, Father of Waters, sadly needs to replenish his dry urn from the solstitial rains of the Mountains of the Moon.

It is none of these. By the atoms of Osiris so deftly resewn together! it is a man, who seems to walk, to skate upon the water! Now the frail bark which sustains him becomes visible – a very nutshell of a boat – a hollow fish! – three strips of bark fitted together (one for the bottom and two for the sides), and strongly fastened at either end by cord well smeared with bitumen. The man stands erect with one foot on either side of this fragile vessel, which he impels with a single oar that also serves the purpose of a rudder; – and although the royal cangia moves rapidly under the efforts of the fifty rowers, the little black bark visibly gains upon it.

Cleopatra desired some strange adventure, something wholly unexpected; this little bark which moves so mysteriously seems to us to be conveying an adventure, or at least an adventurer. Perhaps it contains the hero of our story – the thing is not impossible.

At any rate he was a handsome youth of twenty, with hair so black that it seemed to own a tinge of blue, a skin blond as gold, and a form so perfectly proportioned that he might have been taken for a bronze statue by Lysippus – although he had been rowing for a very long time he betrayed no sign of fatigue, and not a single drop of sweat bedewed his forehead.

The sun half sank below the horizon; and against his broken disk figured the dark silhouette of a far distant city, which the eye could not have distinguished but for this accidental effect of light; his radiance soon faded altogether away; and the stars – fair nightflowers of heaven – opened their chalices of gold in the azure of the firmament. The royal cangia closely followed by the little bark, stopped before a huge marble stairway, whereof each step supported one of those sphinxes that Cleopatra so much detested. This was the landing place of the summer palace.

Cleopatra, leaning upon Charmion, passed swiftly like a gleaming vision between a double line of lantern-bearing slaves.

The youth took from the bottom of his little boat a great lion-skin, threw it across his shoulders, drew the tiny shell upon the beach, and wended his way toward the palace.

III

Who is this young man, balancing himself upon a fragment of bark, who dares to follow the royal cangia and is able to contend in a race of speed against fifty strong rowers from the land of Kush, all naked to the waist, and anointed with palm-oil? What secret motive urges him to this swift pursuit? That, indeed, is one of the many things we are obliged to know in our character of the intuition-gifted poet, for whose benefit all men, and even all women (a much more difficult matter), must have in their breasts that little window which Momus of old demanded.

It is not a very easy thing to find out precisely what a young man from the land of Kemi – who followed the barge of Cleopatra, queen and goddess Evergetes, on her return from the Mammisi of

Hermonthis two thousand years ago – was then thinking of. But we shall make the effort notwithstanding.

Meïamoun, son of Mandouschopsch, was a youth of strange character; nothing by which ordinary minds are affected made any impression upon him. He seemed to belong to some loftier race, and might well have been regarded as the offspring of some divine adultery. His glance had the steady brilliancy of a falcon's gaze, and a serene majesty sat on his brow as upon a pedestal of marble; a noble pride curled his upper lip, and expanded his nostrils like those of a fiery horse – although owning a grace of form almost maidenly in its delicacy, and though the bosom of the fair and effeminate god Dionysos was not more softly rounded or smoother than his, yet beneath this soft exterior were hidden sinews of steel, and the strength of Hercules – a strange privilege of certain antique natures to unite in themselves the beauty of woman with the strength of man!

As for his complexion, we must acknowledge that it was of a tawny orange color – a hue little in accordance with our white-and-rose ideas of beauty, but which did not prevent him from being a very charming young man, much sought after by all kinds of women – yellow, red, copper-colored, sooty-black, or golden skinned; and even by one fair white Greek.

Do not suppose from this that Meïamoun's lot was altogether enviable – the ashes of aged Priam, the very snows of Hippolytus, were not more insensible or more frigid – the young white-robed neophyte preparing for the initiation into the mysteries of Isis led no chaster life – the young maiden benumbed by the icy shadow of her mother was not more shyly pure.

Nevertheless, for so coy a youth, the pleasures of Meïamoun were certainly of a singular nature – he would go forth quietly some morning with his little buckler of hippopotamus hide, his *harpe* or curved sword, a triangular bow and a snakeskin quiver, filled with barbed arrows; then he would ride at a gallop far into the desert upon his slender-limbed, small-headed, wild-maned mare until he could find some lion-tracks – he especially delighted in taking the little lion-cubs from underneath the belly of their mother. In all things he loved the perilous or the unachievable; he preferred to walk where it seemed impossible for any human being to obtain a foothold, or to swim in a raging torrent; and he had accordingly chosen the neighborhood of the cataracts for his bathing place in the Nile: the Abyss called him!

Such was Meïamoun, son of Mandouschopsh.

For some time his humors had been growing more savage than

ever: during whole months he buried himself in the Ocean of Sands, returning only at long intervals. Vainly would his uneasy mother lean from her terrace, and gaze anxiously down the long road with tireless eyes. At last after weary waiting, a little whirling cloud of dust would become visible in the horizon; and finally the cloud would open to allow a full view of Meïamoun, all covered with dust, riding upon a mare gaunt as a wolf with red and blood-shot eyes, nostrils trembling, and huge scars along her flanks – scars which certainly were not made by spurs!

After having hung up in his room some hyena or lion skin, he would start off again.

And yet no one might have been happier than Meïamoun: he was beloved by Nephthe, daughter of the priest Afomouthis, and the loveliest woman of the Nome Arsinoïtes. Only such a being as Meïamoun could have failed to see that Nephthe had the most charmingly oblique and indescribably voluptuous eyes, a mouth sweetly illuminated by her ruddy smile; little teeth of wondrous whiteness and transparency: arms exquisitely round, and feet more perfect than the jasper feet of the statue of Isis – assuredly, there was not a smaller hand nor longer hair than hers in all Egypt. The charms of Nephthe could have been eclipsed only by those of Cleopatra. But who could dare to dream of loving Cleopatra? Ixion, enamoured of Juno, strained only a cloud to his bosom, and must forever roll the wheel of his punishment in hell.

It was Cleopatra whom Meïamoun loved.

He had at first striven to tame this wild passion; he had wrestled fiercely with it, but love cannot be strangled even as a lion is strangled, and the strong skill of the mightiest athlete avails nothing in such a contest. The arrow had remained in the wound, and he carried it with him everywhere – the radiant and splendid image of Cleopatra with her golden-pointed diadem and her imperial purple, standing above a nation on their knees, illumined his nightly dreams and his waking thoughts like some imprudent man who has dared to look at the sun and forever thereafter beholds an impalpable blot floating before his eyes – so Meïamoun ever beheld Cleopatra. Eagles may gaze undazzled at the sun, but what diamond eye can with impunity fix itself upon a beautiful woman – a beautiful queen?

He commenced at last to spend his life in wandering about the neighborhood of the royal dwelling, that he might at least breathe the same air as Cleopatra – that he might sometimes kiss the almost imperceptible print of her foot upon the sand (a happiness, alas! rare indeed): he attended the sacred festivals and *panegyris* striving to obtain one beaming glance of her eyes – to catch in passing one stealthy glimpse of her love-lines in some of its thousand varied aspects. At other moments filled with sudden shame of this mad life, he gave himself up to the chase with redoubled ardor, and sought by fatigue to tame the ardor of his blood and the impetuosity of his desires.

He had gone to the panegyris of Hermonthis, and in the vague hope of beholding the queen again for an instant as she disembarked at the summer palace, had followed her cangia in his boat – little heeding the sharp stings of the sun – through a heat intense enough to make the panting sphinxes melt in lava-sweat upon their reddened pedestals.

And then he felt that the supreme moment was nigh – that the decisive instant of his life was at hand, and that he could not die with his secret in his breast.

It is a strange situation, truly, to find one's self enamored of a queen; it is as though one loved a star – yet she, the star, comes forth nightly to sparkle in her place in heaven. It is a kind of mysterious rendezvous – you may find her again, you may see her, she is not offended at your gaze! O, misery! to be poor, unknown, obscure, seated at the very foot of the ladder – and to feel one's heart breaking with love for something glittering, solemn, and magnificent – for a woman whose meanest female attendant would scorn you! – to gaze fixedly and fatefully upon one who never sees you, who never will see you – one to whom you are no more than a ripple on the sea of humanity, in nowise differing from the other ripples, and who might a hundred times encounter you without once recognizing you! – to have no reason to offer, should an opportunity for addressing her present itself, in excuse for such mad audacity, neither poetical talent, nor great genius nor any superhuman qualifications – nothing but love, and to be able to offer in exchange for beauty, nobility, power, and all imaginable splendor, only one's passion and one's youth – rare offerings, forsooth!

Such were the thoughts which overwhelmed Meïamoun. Lying upon the sand, supporting his chin on his palms, he permitted himself to be lifted and borne away by the inexhaustible current of reverie – he sketched out a thousand projects, each madder than the last. He felt convinced that he was seeking after the unattainable, but he lacked the courage to frankly renounce his undertaking; and a perfidious hope came to whisper some lying promises in his ear.

'Athor, mighty goddess,' he murmured in a deep voice – 'what evil have I done against thee that I should be made thus miserable?

– art thou avenging thyself for my disdain of Nephthe, daughter of the priest Afomouthis? – hast thou afflicted me thus for having rejected the love of Lamia, the Athenian hetaira, or of Flora, the Roman courtesan? Is it my fault that my heart should be sensible only to the matchless beauty of thy rival, Cleopatra? Why hast thou wounded my soul with the envenomed arrow of unattainable love? What sacrifice, what offerings dost thou desire? Must I erect to thee a chapel of the rosy marble of Syene with columns crowned by gilded capitals, a ceiling all of one block, and hieroglyphics deeply sculptured by the best workmen of Memphis and of Thebes? Answer me!'

Like all gods or goddesses thus invoked, Athor answered not a word, and Meïamoun resolved upon a desperate expedient.

Cleopatra, on her part, likewise invoked the goddess Athor. She prayed for a new pleasure, for some fresh sensation; as she languidly reclined upon her couch, she thought to herself that the number of the senses was sadly limited, that the most exquisite refinements of delight soon yielded to satiety and that it was really no small task for a queen to find means of occupying her time. To test new poisons upon slaves, to make men fight with tigers, or gladiators with each other, to drink pearls dissolved, to swallow the wealth of a whole province – all these things had become commonplace and insipid!

Charmion was fairly at her wit's end and knew not what to do for her mistress.

Suddenly, a whistling sound was heard, and an arrow buried itself, quivering, in the cedar wainscoting of the wall.

Cleopatra well-nigh fainted with terror. Charmion ran to the window, leaned out, and beheld only a flake of foam on the surface of the river. A scroll of papyrus encircled the wood of the arrow; it bore only these words written in Phœnician characters, 'I love you!'

IV

'I love you,' repeated Cleopatra, making the serpent-coiling strip of papyrus writhe between her delicate white fingers; 'those are the words I longed for; what intelligent spirit, what invisible genius has thus so fully comprehended my desire?'

And thoroughly aroused from her languid torpor, she sprang out of bed with the agility of a cat which has scented a mouse, placed her little ivory feet in her embroidered *tatbebs*, threw a byssus tunic over her shoulders, and ran to the window from which Charmion was still gazing.

The night was clear and calm; the risen moon outlined with huge angles of light and shadow the architectural masses of the palace, which stood out in strong relief against a background of bluish transparency; and the waters of the river wherein her reflection lengthened into a shining column, was frosted with silvery ripples: a gentle breeze, such as might have been mistaken for the respiration of the slumbering sphinxes, quivered among the reeds and shook the azure bells of the lotus flowers; the cables of the vessels moored to the Nile's banks groaned feebly; and the rippling tide moaned upon the shore like a dove lamenting for its mate. A vague perfume of vegetation, sweeter than that of the aromatics burned in the *anschir* of the priests of Anubis, floated into the chamber. It was one of those enchanted nights of the Orient, which are more splendid than our fairest days; for our sun can ill compare with that Oriental moon.

'Do you not see far over there, almost in the middle of the river, the head of a man, swimming? See! he crosses that track of light, and passes into the shadow beyond! – he is already out of sight!' And supporting herself upon Charmion's shoulder she leaned out, with half of her fair body beyond the sill of the window, in the effort to catch another glimpse of the mysterious swimmer. But a grove of Nile acacias, dhoum-palms, and sayals flung its deep shadow upon the river in that direction, and protected the flight of the daring fugitive. If Meïamoun had but had the courtesy to look back, he might have beheld Cleopatra, the sidereal queen, eagerly seeking him through the night gloom – he, the poor obscure Egyptian! the miserable lion-hunter!

'Charmion! Charmion! send hither Phrehipephbour, the chief of the rowers; and have two boats dispatched in pursuit of that man!' – cried Cleopatra, whose curiosity was excited to the highest pitch.

Phrehipephbour appeared – a man of the race of Nahasi, with large hands and muscular arms, wearing a red cap not unlike a Phrygian helmet in form, and clad only in a pair of narrow drawers diagonally striped with white and blue. His huge torso, entirely nude, black and polished like a globe of jet, shone under the lamplight. He received the commands of the queen and instantly retired to execute them.

Two long narrow boats so light that the least inattention to equilibrium would capsize them, were soon cleaving the waters of the Nile with hissing rapidity under the efforts of the twenty vigorous rowers; but the pursuit was all in vain. After searching the river banks in every direction, and carefully exploring every patch of reeds, Phrehipephbour returned to the palace; having only succeeded in putting to flight some solitary heron which had been sleeping on one leg, or in troubling the digestion of some terrified crocodile.

So intense was the vexation of Cleopatra at being thus foiled, that she felt a strong inclination to condemn Phrehipephbour either to the wild beasts, or to the hardest labor at the grindstone. Happily Charmion interceded for the trembling unfortunate who turned pale with fear despite his black skin. It was the first time in Cleopatra's life that one of her desires had not been gratified as soon as expressed; and she experienced in consequence a kind of uneasy surprise – a first doubt, as it were, of her own omnipotence.

She, Cleopatra, wife and sister of Ptolemy – she who had been proclaimed goddess Evergetes, living queen of the regions Above and Below, Eye of Light, Chosen of the Sun (as may still be read within the cartouches sculptured on the walls of the temples) – she to find an obstacle in her path! to have wished aught that failed of accomplishment! to have spoken and not been obeyed! As well be the wife of some wretched Paraschistes – some corpse-cutter – and melt natron in a cauldron! It was monstrous, preposterous! – and none but the most gentle and clement of queens could have refrained from crucifying that miserable Phrehipephbour!

You wished for some adventure, something strange and unexpected: your wish has been gratified. You find that your kingdom is not so dead as you deemed it. It was not the stony arm of a statue which shot that arrow – it was not from a mummy's heart that came those three words which have moved even you – you who smilingly watched your poisoned slaves dashing their heads and beating their feet upon your beautiful mosaic and porphyry pavements, in the convulsions of death-agony! – you who even applauded the tiger which boldly buried its muzzle in the flank of some vanquished gladiator!

You could obtain all else you might wish for: chariots of silver starred with emeralds; griffin-quadrigeræ; tunics of purple thrice-dyed; mirrors of molten steel, so clear that you might find the charms of your loveliness faithfully copied in them; robes from the land of Serica so fine and subtly light that they could be drawn through the ring worn upon your little finger; orient pearls of wondrous color; cups wrought by Myron or Lysippus; Indian paroquets that speak like poets – all things else you could obtain, even should you ask for the Cestus of Venus or the *pshent* of Isis; but most certainly you cannot this night capture the man who shot the arrow which still quivers in the cedar wood of your couch.

The task of the slaves who must dress you tomorrow will not be a grateful one; they will hardly escape with blows: the bosom of the unskillful waitingmaid will be apt to prove a cushion for the golden pins of the toilette; and the poor hairdresser will run great risk of being suspended by her feet from the ceiling.

'Who could have had the audacity to send me this avowal upon the shaft of an arrow? Could it have been the Nomarch Amoun-Ra who fancies himself handsomer than the Apollo of the Greeks? – what think you, Charmion? – or perhaps Cheâpsiro, commander of Hermothybia, who is so boastful of his conquests in the land of Kush? Or is it not more likely to have been young Sextus, that Roman debauchee who paints his face, lisps in speaking, and wears sleeves in the fashion of the Persians?'

'Queen, it was none of those: though you are indeed the fairest of women, those men only flatter you; they do not love you. The Nomarch Amoun-Ra has chosen himself an idol to which he will be forever faithful; and that is his own person: the warrior Cheâpsiro thinks of nothing save the pleasure of recounting his victories – as for Sextus, he is so seriously occupied with the preparation of a new cosmetic that he cannot dream of anything else. Besides he had just purchased some Laconian dresses, a number of yellow tunics embroidered with gold, and some Asiatic children which absorb all his time. Not one of those fine lords would risk his head in so daring and dangerous an undertaking – they do not love you well enough for that.

'Yesterday in your cangia, you said that men dared not fix their dazzled eyes upon you; that they knew only how to turn pale in your presence – to fall at your feet and supplicate your mercy; and that your sole remaining resource would be to awake some ancient, bitumen-perfumed Pharaoh from his gilded coffin. Now here is an ardent and youthful heart that loves you: what will you do with it?'

Cleopatra that night sought slumber in vain; she tossed feverishly upon her couch, and long and vainly invoked Morpheus the brother of Death – she incessantly repeated that she was the most unhappy of queens – that everyone sought to persecute her – and that her life had become insupportable: woeful lamentations which had little effect upon Charmion, although she pretended to sympathize with them.

Let us for awhile leave Cleopatra to seek fugitive sleep, and direct her suspicions successively upon each noble of the court – let us return to Meïamoun – and as we are much more sagacious than Phrehipephbour, chief of the rowers, we shall have no difficulty in finding him.

Terrified at his own hardihood, Meïamoun had thrown himself into the Nile, and had succeeded in swimming the current and gaining the little grove of dhoum-palms, before Phrehipephbour had even launched the two boats in pursuit of him.

When he had recovered breath, and brushed back his long black locks, all damp with river foam, behind his ears, he began to feel more at ease – more inwardly calm. Cleopatra possessed something which had come from him; some sort of communication was now established between them: Cleopatra was thinking of him – Meïamoun! Perhaps that thought might be one of wrath; but then he had at least been able to awake some feeling within her – whether of fear, anger, or pity: he had forced her to the consciousness of his existence. It was true that he had forgotten to inscribe his name upon the papyrus scroll; but what more could the queen have learned from the inscription – *Meïamoun, Son of Mandouschopsh*? In her eyes the slave or the monarch were equal. A goddess, in choosing a peasant for her lover, stoops no lower than in choosing a patrician or a king: the Immortals from a height so lofty can behold only love in the man of their choice.

The thought which had weighed upon his breast like the knee of a colossus of brass, had at last departed: it had traversed the air; it had even reached the queen herself – the apex of the triangle – the inaccessible summit! It had aroused curiosity in that impassive heart – a prodigious advance, truly, toward success!

Meïamoun indeed never suspected that he had so thoroughly succeeded in this wise; but he felt more tranquil – for he had sworn unto himself by that mystic Bari who guides the souls of the dead to Amenthi, by the sacred birds Bermou and Ghenghen, by Typhon and by Osiris and by all things awful in Egyptian mythology, that he should be the accepted lover of Cleopatra though it were but for a single night – though for only a single hour – though it should cost him his life, and even his very soul.

If we must explain how he had fallen so deeply in love with a woman whom he had beheld only from afar off, and to whom he had hardly dared to raise his eyes – even he who was wont to gaze fearlessly into the yellow eyes of the lion – or how the tiny seed of love, chance-fallen upon his heart, had grown there so rapidly and extended its roots so deeply, we can answer only that it is a mystery which we are unable to explain – we have already said of Meïamoun – The Abyss called him.

Once assured that Phrehipephbour had returned with his rowers, he again threw himself into the current and once more swam toward the palace of Cleopatra, whose lamp still shone through the window curtains like a painted star. Never did Leander swim with more courage and vigor toward the tower of Sestos; yet for Meïamoun no Hero was waiting, ready to pour vials of perfume upon his head to dissipate the briny odors of the sea, and banish the sharp kisses of the storm.

A strong blow from some keen lance or *harpe* was certainly the worst he had to fear; and in truth he had but little fear of such things.

He swam close under the walls of the palace which bathed its marble feet in the river's depths, and paused an instant before a submerged archway into which the water rushed downward in eddying whirls. Twice, thrice, he plunged into the vortex unsuccessfully; – at last, with better luck, he found the opening and disappeared.

This archway was the opening to a vaulted canal, which conducted the waters of the Nile into the baths of Cleopatra.

V

Cleopatra found no rest until morning, at the hour when wandering dreams re-enter the Ivory Gate. Amidst the illusions of sleep she beheld all kinds of lovers swimming rivers and scaling walls in order to come to her; and, through the vague souvenirs of the night before, her dreams appeared fairly riddled with arrows bearing declarations of love. Starting nervously from time to time in her troubled slumbers, she struck her little feet unconsciously against the bosom of Charmion, who lay across the foot of the bed to serve her as a cushion.

When she awoke, a merry sunbeam was playing through the window curtain, whose woof it penetrated with a thousand tiny points of light, and thence came familiarly to the bed; flitting like a golden butterfly over her lovely shoulders, which it lightly touched in passing by with a luminous kiss. Happy sunbeam, which the Gods might well have envied!

In a faint voice, like that of a sick child, Cleopatra asked to be lifted out of bed; two of her women raised her in their arms and gently laid her on a tiger skin stretched upon the floor, of which the eyes were formed of carbuncles and the claws of gold. Charmion wrapped her in a *calasiris* of linen whiter than milk; confined her hair in a net of woven silver threads; tied to her little feet cork *tatbebs* upon the soles of which were painted in token of contempt two grotesque figures representing two men of the races of Nahasi and Nahmou, bound hand and foot: – so that Cleopatra literally deserved the epithet, 'Conculcatrix of Nations' which the royal cartouche-inscriptions bestow upon her.

It was the hour for the bath; Cleopatra went to bathe accompanied by her women.

The baths of Cleopatra were built in the midst of immense gardens filled with mimosas, aloes, carob-trees, citron-trees, and Persian apple-trees, whose luxuriant freshness afforded a delicious contrast to the arid appearance of the neighboring vegetation: there, too, vast terraces uplifted masses of verdant foliage and enabled flowers to climb almost to the very sky upon gigantic stairways of rose-colored granite – vases of Pentelic marble bloomed at the end of each step like huge lily-flowers; and the plants they contained seemed only their pistils – chimeras caressed into form by the chisels of the most skillful Greek sculptors, and less stern of aspect than the Egyptian sphinxes, with their grim mien and moody attitudes, softly extended their limbs upon the flower-strewn turf, like shapely white leverettes upon a drawing-room carpet. These were charming feminine figures – with finely chiseled nostrils, smooth brows, small mouths, delicately dimpled arms, breasts fair-rounded and daintly formed; wearing earrings, necklaces, and all the trinkets suggested by adorable caprice – whose bodies terminated in bifurcated fishes' tails, like the women described by Horace, or extended into birds' wings, or rounded into lions' haunches, or blended into volutes of foliage according to the fancies of the artist or in conformity to the architectural position chosen. A double row of these delightful monsters lined the alley which led from the palace to the bathing halls.

At the end of this alley was a huge fountain-basin, approached by four porphyry stairways; through the transparent depths of the diamond-clear water the steps could be seen descending to the bottom of the basin, which was strewn with gold-dust in lieu of sand – here figures of women terminating in pedestals like Caryatides spirited from their breasts slender jets of perfumed water, which fell into the basin in silvery dew, pitting the clear watery mirror with wrinkle-creating drops. In addition to this task these Caryatides had likewise that of supporting upon their heads an entablature decorated with Nereids and Tritons in bas-relief, and furnished with rings of bronze to which the silken cords of a velarium might be attached. From the portico was visible an extending expanse of freshly humid, bluish-green verdure and cool shade – a fragment of the Vale of Tempe transported to Egypt. The famous gardens of Semiramis would not have borne comparison with these.

We will not pause to describe the seven or eight other halls of various temperature, with their hot and cold vapors, perfume boxes, cosmetics, oils, pumice stone, gloves of woven horse-hair, and all the refinements of the antique balneatory art brought to the highest pitch of voluptuous perfection.

Hither came Cleopatra, leaning with one hand upon the shoulder of Charmion; she had taken at least thirty steps all by herself - mighty effort! – enormous fatigue! A tender tint of rose commenced to suffuse the transparent skin of her cheeks, refreshing their passionate pallor – a blue network of veins relieved the amber blondness of her temples; her marble forehead – low like the antique foreheads, but full and perfect in form – united by one faultless line with a straight nose finely chiseled as a cameo, with rosy nostrils which the least emotion made palpitate like the nostrils of an amorous tigress; the lips of her small, rounded mouth, slightly separated from the nose, wore a disdainful curve; but an unbridled voluptuousness – an indescribable vital warmth – glowed in the brilliant crimson and humid luster of the under lip. Her eyes were shaded by level eyelids and eyebrows slightly arched and delicately outlined. We cannot attempt by description to convey an idea of their brilliancy; it was a fire, a languor, a sparkling limpidity which might have made even the dog-headed Anubis giddy; every glance of her eyes was in itself a poem richer than aught of Homer or Mimnermus. An imperial chin, replete with force and power to command, worthily completed this charming profile.

She stood erect upon the upper step of the basin, in an attitude full of proud grace; her figure slightly thrown back, and one foot in suspense, like a goddess about to leave her pedestal, whose eyes still linger on heaven: her robe fell in two superb folds from the peaks of her bosom to her feet, in unbroken lines. Had Cleomenes been her contemporary and enjoyed the happiness of beholding her thus, he would have broken his Venus in despair.

Before entering the water, she bade Charmion, for a new caprice, to change her silver hair-net – she preferred to be crowned with reeds and lotus-flowers, like a water divinity. Charmion obeyed; and her liberated hair fell in black cascades over her shoulders, and shadowed her beautiful cheeks in rich bunches like ripening grapes.

Then the linen tunic, which had been confined only by one golden clasp, glided down over her marble body, and fell in a white cloud at her feet, like the swan at the feet of Leda . . . .

And Meïamoun, where was he?

O cruel lot, that so many insensible objects should enjoy the favors

which would ravish a lover with delight! The wind which toys with a
wealth of perfumed hair, or kisses beautiful lips with kisses which it is
unable to appreciate; the water which envelops an adorably beautiful
body in one universal kiss, and is yet notwithstanding indifferent to
that exquisite pleasure; the mirror which reflects so many charming
images; the buskin or *tatbeb* which clasps a divine little foot – oh,
what happiness lost!

Cleopatra dipped her pink heel in the water and descended a few
steps: the quivering flood made a silver belt about her waist, and
silver bracelets about her arms, and rolled in pearls like a broken
necklace over her bosom and shoulders; her wealth of hair, lifted
by the water, extended behind her like a royal mantle – even in the
bath she was a queen. She swam to and fro, dived and brought up
handfuls of gold dust with which she laughingly pelted some of her
women – again, she clung suspended to the balustrade of the basin,
concealing or exposing her treasures of loveliness – now permitting
only her lustrous and polished back to be seen – now showing her
whole figure, like Venus Anadyomene, and incessantly varying the
aspects of her beauty.

Suddenly she uttered a cry as shrill as that of Diana surprised by
Actæon: she had seen gleaming through the neighbouring foliage
a burning eye, yellow and phosphoric as the eye of a crocodile
or lion.

It was Meïamoun who, crouching behind a tuft of leaves, and
trembling like a fawn in a field of wheat, was intoxicating himself
with the dangerous pleasure of beholding the queen in her bath.
Though brave even to temerity, the cry of Cleopatra passed through
his heart, coldly piercing as the blade of a sword: a death-like sweat
covered his whole body; his arteries hissed through his temples with
a sharp sound – the iron hand of anxious fear had seized him by
the throat, and was strangling him.

The eunuchs rushed forward lance in hand: Cleopatra pointed out
to them the group of trees, where they found Meïamoun crouching in
concealment. Defence was out of the question: he attempted none,
and suffered himself to be captured. They prepared to kill him
with that cruel and stupid impassibility characteristic of eunuchs;
but Cleopatra, who in the interim had covered herself with her
calasiris, made no signs to them to stop and bring the prisoner
before her.

Meïamoun could only fall upon his knees and stretch forth
suppliant hands to her, as to the altars of the gods.

'Are you some assassin bribed by Rome? – or for what purpose
have you entered these sacred precincts from which all men are

excluded?' – demanded Cleopatra with an imperious gesture of interrogation.

'May my soul be found light in the balance of Amenti, and may Tmeï, daughter of the Sun and goddess of Truth, punish me if I have ever entertained a thought of evil against you, O queen!' answered Meïamoun, still upon his knees.

Sincerity and loyalty were written upon his countenance in characters so transparent, that Cleopatra immediately banished her suspicions, and looked upon the young Egyptian with a look less stern and wrathful – she saw that he was beautiful.

'Then what motive could have prompted you to enter a place where you could only expect to meet death?'

'I love you!' murmured Meïamoun in a low but distinct voice; for his courage had returned, as in every desperate situation when the odds against him could be no worse.

'Ah!' cried Cleopatra, bending toward him, and seizing his arm with a sudden brusque movement – 'so then it was you who shot that arrow with the papyrus scroll! – by Omns, the Dog of Hell, you are a very foolhardy wretch! . . . I now recognize you: I long observed you wandering like a complaining Shade about the places where I dwell . . . You were at the Procession of Isis – at the Panegyris of Hermounthis: you followed the royal cangia. Ah! – you must have a queen? . . . You have no mean ambitions; you expect without doubt to be well paid in return! . . . Assuredly I am going to love you! . . . Why not?'

'Queen,' returned Meïamoun with a look of deep melancholy, 'do not rail! I am mad, it is true; I have deserved death – that is also true: be humane; – bid them kill me!'

'No: I have taken the whim to be clement to-day: I will give you your life.'

'What would you that I should do with life? – I love you!'

'Well, then, you shall be satisfied; – you shall die,' answered Cleopatra: 'you have indulged yourself in wild and extravagant dreams; in fancy your desires have crossed an impassable threshold: – you imagined yourself to be Cæsar or Mark Antony – you loved the queen! In some moment of delirium you have been able to believe that – under some condition of things which takes place but once in a thousand years – Cleopatra might some day love you. Well, what you thought impossible is actually about to happen: – I will transform your dream into a reality – it pleases me, for once, to secure the accomplishment of a mad hope. I am willing to inundate you with glories and splendors and lightnings: I intend that your good fortune shall be dazzling in its brilliancy. You were at the bottom of the ladder – I am about to lift you to the summit, abruptly, suddenly, without a transition. I take you out of nothingness; I make you the equal of a god; and I plunge you back again into nothingness: that is all – but do not presume to call me cruel or to invoke my pity – do not weaken when the hour comes. I am good to you: I lend myself to your folly – I have the right to order you to be killed at once; but since you tell me that you love me I will have you killed to-morrow instead: your life belongs to me for one night. I am generous: I will buy it from you – I could take it from you. But what are you doing on your knees at my feet! Rise; and give me your arm, that we may return to the palace.'

VI

Our world of today is puny indeed beside the antique world: our banquets are mean, niggardly, compared with the appalling sumptuousness of the Roman patricians and the princes of ancient Asia – their ordinary repasts would in these days be regarded as frenzied orgies; and a whole modern city could subsist for eight days upon the leavings of one supper given by Lucullus to a few intimate friends. With our miserable habits, we find it difficult to conceive of those enormous existences, realizing everything vast, strange, and most monstrously impossible that imagination could devise. Our palaces are mere stables in which Caligula would set quarter his horse – the retinue of our wealthiest constitutional king is as nothing compared with that of a petty satrap, or a Roman proconsul. The radiant suns which once shone upon the earth are forever extinguished in the nothingness of uniformity; above the dark swarm of men no longer tower those Titanic colossi, who bestrode the world in three paces, like the steeds of Homer – no more towers of Lylacq; no giant Babel scaling the sky with its infinity of spirals; no temples immeasurable; builded with the fragments of quarried mountains; no kingly terraces for which successive ages and generations could each erect but one step and from whence some dreamfully-reclining prince might gaze on the face of the world as upon a map unfolded; more of those extravagantly vast cities of cyclopean edifices, inextricably piled upon one another – with their mighty circumvallations – their circuses roaring night and day – their reservoirs filled with ocean-brine and peopled with whales and leviathans – their colossal stairways – their super-imposition of terraces – their tower-summits bathed in clouds – their giant palaces, – their aqueducts – their multitude-vomiting gates – their shadowy necropoli. Alas! henceforth only plaster hives upon chessboard pavements!

One marvels that men did not revolt against such confiscation of all riches and all living forces for the benefit of a few privileged ones; and that such exorbitant fantasies should not have encountered any opposition on their bloody way. It was because those prodigious lives were the realizations by day of the dreams which haunted each man by night – the personifications of the common ideal which the nations beheld living symbolized under one of those meteoric names that flame inextinguishably through the night of ages. To-day, deprived of such dazzling spectacles of omnipotent will – of the lofty contemplation of some human mind, whose least wish makes itself visible in actions unparalleled – in enormities of granite and brass – the world becomes irredeemably and hopelessly dull: man is no longer represented in the realization of his imperial fancy.

The story which we are writing, and the great name of Cleopatra which appears in it, have prompted us to these reflections – so ill-sounding, doubtless to modern ears. But the spectacle of the antique world is something so crushingly discouraging, even to those imaginations which deem themselves exhaustless, and those minds which fancy themselves to have conceived the utmost limits of fairy magnificence, that we cannot here forbear recording our regret and lamentation that we were not contemporaries of Sardanapalus – of Teglathphalazar – of Cleopatra, queen of Egypt – or even of Elagabalus, emperor of Rome and priest of the Sun.

It is our task to describe a supreme orgie – a banquet compared with which the splendors of Belshazzar's feast must pale – one of Cleopatra's nights! How can we picture forth in this French tongue, so chaste, so icily prudish that unbounded transport of passions – that huge and mighty debauch which feared not to mingle the double purple of wine and blood – those furious outbursts of insatiate pleasure, madly leaping toward the Impossible with all the wild ardor of senses as yet untamed by the long fast of Christianity?

The promised night should well have been a splendid one; for all the joys and pleasures possible in a human lifetime were to be concentrated into the space of a few hours – it was necessary that the life of Meïamoun should be converted into a powerful elixir, which he could imbibe at a single draught. Cleopatra desired to dazzle her voluntary victim, and plunge him into a whirlpool of dizzy pleasures – to intoxicate and madden him with the wine of orgie; so that death, though freely accepted, might come invisibly and unawares.

Let us transport our readers to the banquet-hall!

Our existing architecture offers few points for comparison with those vast edifices whose very ruins resemble the crumblings of mountains rather than the remains of buildings. It needed all the exaggeration of the antique life to animate and fill those prodigious palaces, whose halls were too lofty and vast to allow of any ceiling save the sky itself – a magnificent ceiling, and well worthy of such mighty architecture!

The banquet-hall was of enormous and Babylonian dimensions; the eye could not penetrate its immeasurable depth: monstrous columns – short, thick and solid enough to sustain the pole itself – heavily expanded their broad-swelling shafts upon socles variegated with hieroglyphics, and sustained upon their bulging capitals gigantic arcades of granite rising by successive tiers, like vast stairways reversed. Between each two pillars a colossal sphinx of basalt, crowned with the *pshcent*, bent foward her oblique-eyed face and horned chin, and gazed into the hall with a fixed and mysterious look. The columns of the second tier, receding from the first, were more elegantly formed, and crowned in lieu of capitals with four female heads addorsed, wearing caps of many folds and all the intricacies of the Egyptian headdress: instead of sphinxes bull-headed idols – impassive spectators of nocturnal frenzy and the furies of orgie – were seated upon thrones of stone, like patient hosts awaiting the opening of the banquet.

A third story constructed in a yet different style of architecture – with elephants of bronze spouting perfume from their trunks – crowned the edifice: above the sky yawned like a blue gulf; and the curious stars leaned over the frieze.

Prodigious stairways of porphyry, so highly polished that they reflected the human body like a mirror, ascended and descended on every hand, and bound together these huge masses of architecture.

We can only make a very rapid sketch here, in order to convey some idea of this awful structure, proportioned out of all human measurements. It would require the pencil of Martin – the great painter of enormities passed away; and we can present only a weak pen-picture in lieu of the Apocalyptic depth of his gloomy style: but imagination may supply our deficiencies – less fortunate than the painter and the musician, we can only present objects and ideas separately in slow succession. We have as yet spoken of the banquet-hall only, without referring to the guests; and yet we have but barely indicated its character. Cleopatra and Meïamoun are waiting for us: we see them drawing near . . . .

Meïamoun was clad in a linen tunic constellated with stars, and a purple mantle, and wore a fillet about his locks, like an Oriental king. Cleopatra was appareled in a robe of pale green, open at either side, and clasped with golden bees: two bracelets of immense pearls gleamed around her naked arms; upon her head glimmered the golden-pointed diadem. Despite the smile on her lips, a slight cloud of preoccupation shadowed her fair forehead; and from time to time her brows became knitted in a feverish manner. What thoughts could trouble the great queen? As for Meïamoun, his face wore the ardent and luminous look of one in ecstasy or vision – light beamed and radiated from his brow and temples, surrounding his head with a golden nimbus like one of the twelve great gods of Olympus.

A deep, heartfelt joy illuminated his every feature: he had embraced his restless-winged chimera; and it had not flown from him – he had reached the goal of his life. Though he were to live to the age of Nestor or Priam – though he should behold his veined temples hoary with locks whiter than those of the high priest of Ammon, he could never know another new experience – never feel another new pleasure. His maddest hopes had been so much more than realized that there was nothing in the world left for him to desire.

Cleopatra seated him beside her upon a throne with golden griffins on either side, and clapped her little hands together. Instantly lines of fire, bands of sparkling light, outlined all the projections of the architecture: the eyes of the sphinxes flamed with phosphoric lightnings – the bull-headed idols breathed flame – the elephants, in lieu of perfumed water, spouted aloft bright columns of crimson fire – arms of bronze, each bearing a torch, started from the walls; and blazing aigrettes bloomed in the sculptured hearts of the lotus-flowers.

Huge blue flames palpitated in tripods of brass; giant candelabras shook their disheveled light in the midst of ardent vapors: everything sparkled, glittered, beamed. Prismatic irises crossed and shattered each other in the air: the facets of the cups, the angles of the marbles and jaspers, the chiseling of the vases – all caught a sparkle, a gleam, or a flash as of lightning. Radiance streamed in torrents, and leaped from step to step like a cascade over the porphyry stairways; it seemed the reflection of a conflagration on some broad river – had the Queen of Sheba ascended thither she would have caught up the folds of her robe, and believed herself walking in water, as when she stepped upon the crystal pavements of Solomon. Viewed throughout that burning haze, the monstrous figures of the colossi, the animals, the hieroglyphics, seemed to become animated and to live with a factitious life; the black marble rams bleated ironically, and clashed their gilded horns; the idols breathed harshly through their panting nostrils.

The orgie was at its height: the dishes of phenicopters' tongues, and the livers of scarus fish; the eels fattened upon human flesh, and cooked in brine; the dishes of peacock's brains; the boars stuffed with living birds – and all the marvels of the antique banquets were heaped upon the three table-surfaces of the gigantic triclinium. The wines of Crete, of Massicus, and of Falernus foamed up in cratera wreathed with roses, and filled by Asiatic pages whose beautiful flowing hair served the guests to wipe their hands upon. Musicians playing upon the sistrum, the tympanum, the sambuke, and the harp with one-and-twenty strings, filled all the upper galleries, and mingled their harmonies with the tempest of sound that hovered over the feast: even the deep-voiced thunder could not have made itself heard there.

Meïamoun, whose head was lying on Cleopatra's shoulder, felt as though his reason were leaving him: the banquet-hall whirled around him like a vast architectural nightmare – through the dizzy glare he beheld perspectives and colonnades without end – new zones of porticos seemed to uprear themselves upon the real fabric and bury their summits in heights of sky to which Babel never rose. Had he not felt within his hand the soft, cool hand of Cleopatra, he would have believed himself transported into an enchanted world by some witch of Thessaly or Magian of Persia.

Toward the close of the repast, hump-backed dwarfs and mummers engaged in grotesque dances and combats: then young Egyptian and Greek maidens representing the black and white Hours danced with inimitable grace a voluptuous dance after the Ionian manner.

Cleopatra herself arose from her throne, threw aside her royal mantle, replaced her starry diadem with a garland of flowers, attached golden *crotali* to her alabaster hands, and began to dance before Meïamoun, who was ravished with delight. Her beautiful arms, rounded like the handles of an alabaster vase, shook out bunches of sparkling notes; and her *crotali* prattled with ever-increasing volubility. Poised on the pink tips of her little feet, she approached swiftly to grace the forehead of Meïamoun with a kiss – then she recommenced her wondrous art, and flitted around him; now backward-leaning with head reversed, eyes half closed, arms lifelessly relaxed, locks uncurled and loose-hanging like a Bacchante of Mount Mænalus; now again, active, animated, laughing, fluttering – more tireless and capricious in her movements than the pilfering bee. Heart-consuming love – sensual pleasure –

burning passion – youth inexhaustible and ever-fresh – the promise
of bliss to come: she expressed all! . . .

The modest stars had ceased to contemplate the scene: their
golden eyes could not endure such a spectacle; the heaven itself
was blotted out; and a dome of flaming vapor covered the hall.

Cleopatra seated herself once more by Meïamoun. Night advanced:
the last of the black Hours was about to take flight – a faint blue
glow entered with bewildered aspect into the tumult of ruddy light
as moonbeam falls into a furnace – the upper arcades became
suffused with pale azure tints: day was breaking.

Meïamoun took the horn vase which an Ethiopian slave of sinister
countenance presented to him, and which contained a poison so
violent that it would have caused any other vase to burst asunder.
Flinging his whole life to his mistress in one last look, he lifted to
his lips that fatal cup in which the envenomed liquor boiled up,
hissing.

Cleopatra turned pale, and laid her hand on Meïamoun's arm to
stay the act. His courage touched her – she was about to say – 'Live
to love me yet: I desire it! . . .' when the sound of a clarion was
heard. Four heralds-at-arms entered the banquet-hall on horseback;
they were officers of Mark Antony, and rode but a short distance
in advance of their master. Cleopatra silently loosened the arm
of Meïamoun. A long ray of sunlight suddenly played upon her
forehead, as though trying to replace her absent diadem.

'You see the moment has come: it is daybreak; it is the hour
when happy dreams take flight,' said Meïamoun. Then he emptied
the fatal vessel at a draught; and fell as though struck by lightning.
Cleopatra bent her head; and one burning tear – the only one she
had ever shed – fell into her cup to mingle with the molten pearl.

'By Hercules, my fair queen! I made all speed in vain – I see I have
come too late,' cried Mark Antony, entering the banquet-hall – 'the
supper is over. But what signifies this corpse upon the pavement?'

'Oh, nothing!' returned Cleopatra with a smile – 'only a poison
I was testing with the idea of using it upon myself should Augustus
take me prisoner – My dear lord, will you not please take a seat
beside me, and watch those Greek buffoons dance?'

THE CHARIOT RACE

Lew Wallace

Part of the fascination with the early decades of the Roman Empire is its clash with the growth of Christianity, a thread that unravels in a number of the following stories. One of the most popular of all books set at the time of Christ was Ben-Hur, or the Days of the Messiah *(1880) by the American general and statesman Lew Wallace (1827–1905). Wallace set out to write a story about the Three Wise Men and ended up producing a blockbuster that was to sell over three million copies in the United States alone. Its events run alongside the life of Christ and follow the adventures of Judah Ben-Hur in Palestine and Rome. Both the epic film adaptations in 1926 and 1959 were famous for the staging of the chariot race, but as the book is little read these days few will remember the original account, which is reprinted here.*

I

The Circus at Antioch stood on the south bank of the river, nearly opposite the island, differing in no respect from the plan of such buildings in general.

In the purest sense, the games were a gift to the public; consequently, everybody was free to attend; and, vast as the holding capacity of the structure was, so fearful were the people, on this occasion, lest there should not be room for them, that, early the day before the opening of the exhibition, they took up all the vacant spaces in the vicinity, where their temporary shelter suggested an army in waiting.

At midnight the entrances were thrown wide, and the rabble, surging in, occupied the quarters assigned to them, from which nothing less than an earthquake or an army with spears could have dislodged them. They dozed the night away on the benches, and breakfasted there; and there the close of the exercises found them, patient and sight-hungry as in the beginning.

The better people, their seats secured, began moving towards the Circus about the first hour of the morning, the noble and very rich among them distinguished by litters and retinues of liveried servants.

By the second hour, the efflux from the city was a stream unbroken and innumerable.

Exactly as the gnomon of the official dial up in the citadel pointed the second hour half gone, the legion, in full panoply, and with all its standards on exhibit, descended from Mount Sulpius; and when the rear of the last cohort disappeared in the bridge, Antioch was literally abandoned – not that the Circus could hold the multitude, but that the multitude was gone out to it, nevertheless.

A great concourse on the river shore witnessed the consul come over from the island in a barge of state. As the great man landed, and was received by the legion, the martial show for one brief moment transcended the attraction of the Circus.

At the third hour, the audience, if such it may be termed, was assembled; at last, a flourish of trumpets called for silence, and instantly the gaze of over a hundred thousand persons was directed towards a pile forming the eastern section of the building.

There was a basement first, broken in the middle by a broad arched passage, called the Porta Pompae, over which, on an elevated tribunal magnificently decorated with insignia and legionary standards, the consul sat in the place of honour. On both sides of the passage the basement was divided into stalls termed *carceres*, each protected in front by massive gates swung to statuesque pilasters. Over the stalls next was a cornice crowned by a low balustrade; back of which the seats arose in theatre arrangement, all occupied by a throng of dignitaries superbly attired. The pile extended the width of the Circus, and was flanked on both sides by towers which, besides helping the architects give grace to their work, served the *velaria*, or purple awnings, stretched between them so as to throw the whole quarter in a shade that became exceedingly grateful as the day advanced.

This structure, it is now thought, can be made useful in helping the reader to a sufficient understanding of the arrangement of the rest of the interior of the Circus. He has only to fancy himself seated on the tribunal with the consul, facing to the west, where everything is under his eye.

On the right and left, if he will look, he will see the main entrances, very ample, and guarded by gates hinged to the towers.

Directly below him is the arena – a level plane of considerable extent, covered with fine white sand. There all the trials will take place except the running.

Looking across this sanded arena westwardly still, there is a pedestal of marble supporting three low conical pillars of grey stone, much carven. Many an eye will hunt for those pillars before the day is done, for they are the first goal, and mark the beginning and end of the race-course. Behind the pedestal, leaving a passage-way and space for an altar, commences a wall ten or twelve feet in breadth and five or six in height, extending thence exactly two hundred yards, or one Olympic stadium. At the further, or westward, extremity of the wall there is another pedestal, surmounted with pillars which mark the second goal.

The racers will enter the course on the right of the first goal, and keep the wall all the time to their left. The beginning and ending points of the contest lie, consequently, directly in front of the consul across the arena; and for that reason his seat was admittedly the most desirable in the Circus.

Now if the reader, who is still supposed to be seated on the consular tribunal over the Porta Pompae, will look up from the ground arrangement of the interior, the first point to attract his notice will be the marking of the outer boundary-line of the course – that is, a plain-faced, solid wall, fifteen or twenty feet in height, with a balustrade on its cope, like that over the *carceres*, or stalls, in the east. This balcony, if followed round the course, will be found broken in three places to allow passages of exit and entrance, two in the north and one in the west; the latter very ornate, and called the Gate of Triumph, because, when all is over, the victors will pass out that way, crowned, and with triumphal escort and ceremonies.

At the west end the balcony encloses the course in the form of a half-circle, and is made to uphold two great galleries.

Directly behind the balustrade on the coping of the balcony is the first seat, from which ascend the succeeding benches, each higher than the one in front of it; giving to view a spectacle of surpassing interest – the spectacle of a vast space ruddy and glistening with human faces, and rich with vari-coloured costumes.

The commonalty occupy quarters over in the west, beginning at the point of termination of an awning, stretched, it would seem, for the accommodation of the better classes exclusively.

Having thus the whole interior of the Circus under view at the moment of the sounding of the trumpets, let the reader next imagine the multitude seated and sunk to sudden silence, and motionless in its intensity of interest.

Out of the Porta Pompae over in the east rises a sound mixed of voices and instruments harmonized. Presently, forth issues the chorus of the procession with which the celebration begins; the editor and civic authorities of the city, givers of the games, follow in robes and garlands; then the gods, some on platforms borne by men, others in great four-wheel carriages gorgeously decorated; next them, again, the contestants of the day, each in costume exactly as he will run, wrestle, leap, box, or drive.

Slowly crossing the arena, the procession proceeds to make circuit of the course. The display is beautiful and imposing. Approval runs before it in a shout, as the water rises and swells in front of a boat in motion. If the dumb, figured gods make no sign of appreciation of the welcome, the editor and his associates are not so backward.

The reception of the athletes is even more demonstrative, for there is not a man in the assemblage who has not something in wager upon them, though but a mite or farthing. And it is noticeable, as the classes move by, that the favourites among them are speedily singled out: either their names are loudest in the uproar, or they are more profusely showered with wreaths and garlands tossed to them from the balcony.

If there is a question as to the popularity with the public of the several games, it is now put to rest. To the splendour of the chariots and the superexcellent beauty of the horses, the charioteers add the personality necessary to perfect the charm of their display. Their tunics, short, sleeveless, and of the finest woollen texture, are of the assigned colours. A horseman accompanies each one of them except Ben-Hur, who, for some reason – possibly distrust – has chosen to go alone; so, too, they are all helmeted but him. As they approach, the spectators stand upon the benches, and there is a sensible deepening of the clamour, in which a sharp listener may detect the shrill piping of women and children; at the same time, the things roseate flying from the balcony thicken into a storm, and, striking the men, drop into the chariot-beds, which are threatened with filling to the tops. Even the horses have a share in the ovation; nor may it be said they are less conscious than their masters of the honours they receive.

Very soon, as with the other contestants, it is made apparent

that some of the drivers are more in favour than others; and then
the discovery follows that nearly every individual on the benches,
women and children as well as men, wears a colour, most frequently
a ribbon upon the breast or in the hair: now it is green, now yellow,
now blue; but, searching the great body carefully, it is manifest that
there is a preponderance of white, and scarlet and gold.

In a modern assemblage called together as this one is, particularly
where there are sums at hazard upon the race, a preference would be
decided by the qualities or performance of the horses; here, however,
nationality was the rule. If the Byzantine and Sidonian found small
support, it was because their cities were scarcely represented on the
benches. On their side, the Greeks, though very numerous, were
divided between the Corinthian and the Athenian, leaving but a
scant showing of green and yellow. Messala's scarlet and gold
would have been but little better had not the citizens of Antioch,
proverbially a race of courtiers, joined the Romans by adopting the
colour of their favourite. There were left then the country people,
or Syrians, the Jews, and the Arabs; and they, from faith in the
blood of the sheik's four, blent largely with hate of the Romans,
whom they desired, above all things, to see beaten and humbled,
mounted the white, making the most noisy, and probably the most
numerous, faction of all.

As the charioteers move on in the circuit, the excitement increases;
at the second goal, where, especially in the galleries, the white is the
ruling colour, the people exhaust their flowers and rive the air with
screams.

'Messala! Messala!'

'Ben-Hur! Ben-Hur!'

Such are the cries.

Upon the passage of the procession, the factionists take their seats
and resume conversation.

'Ah, by Bacchus! was he not handsome?' exclaims a woman,
whose Romanism is betrayed by the colours flying in her hair.

'And how splendid his chariot!' replies a neighbour, of the same
proclivities. 'It is all ivory and gold. Jupiter grant he wins!'

The notes on the bench behind them were entirely different.

'A hundred shekels on the Jew!'

The voice is high and shrill.

'Nay, be thou not rash,' whispers a moderating friend to the
speaker. 'The children of Jacob are not much given to Gentile
sports, which are too often accursed in the sight of the Lord.'

'True, but saw you ever one more cool and assured? And what
an arm he has!'

'And what horses!' says a third.

'And for that,' a fourth one adds, 'they say he has all the tricks of the Romans.'

A woman completes the eulogium.

'Yes, and he is even handsomer than the Roman.'

Thus encouraged, the enthusiast shrieks again, 'A hundred shekels on the Jew!'

'Thou fool!' answers an Antiochian, from a bench well forward on the balcony. 'Knowest thou not there are fifty talents laid against him, six to one, on Messala? Put up thy shekels, lest Abraham rise and smite thee.'

'Ha, ha! thou ass of Antioch! Cease thy bray. Knowest thou not it was Messala betting on himself?'

Such the reply.

And so ran the controversy, not always good-natured.

When at length the march was ended, and the Porta Pompae received back the procession, Ben-Hur knew he had his prayer.

The eyes of the East were upon his contest with Messala.

II

About three o'clock, speaking in modern style, the programme was concluded except the chariot-race. The editor, wisely considerate of the comfort of the people, chose that time for a recess. At once the *vomitoria* were thrown open, and all who could hastened to the portico outside where the restaurateurs had their quarters. Those who remained yawned, talked, gossiped, consulted their tablets, and, all distinctions else forgotten, merged into but two classes – the winners, who were happy, and the losers, who were grum and captious.

Now, however, a third class of spectators, composed of citizens who desired only to witness the chariot-race, availed themselves of the recess to come in and take their reserved seats; by so doing they thought to attract the least attention and give the least offence. Among these were Simonides and his party, whose places were in the vicinity of the main entrance on the north side, opposite the consul.

As the four stout servants carried the merchant in his chair up the aisle, curiosity was much excited. Presently some one called his name. Those about caught it and passed it on along the benches to the west; and there was hurried climbing on seats to get sight of the

man about whom common report had coined and put in circulation
a romance so mixed of good fortune and bad that the like had never
been known or heard of before.

Ilderim was also recognized and warmly greeted; but nobody knew
Balthasar or the two women who followed him closely veiled.

The people made way for the party respectfully, and the ushers
seated them in easy speaking distance of each other down by the
balustrade overlooking the arena. In providence of comfort, they
sat upon cushions and had stools for footrests.

The woman were Iras and Esther.

Upon being seated, the latter cast a frightened look over the Circus,
and drew the veil closer about her face; while the Egyptian, letting
her veil fall upon her shoulders, gave herself to view, and gazed
at the scene with the seeming unconsciousness of being stared at,
which, in a woman, is usually the result of long social habitude.

The new-comers generally were yet making their first examination
of the great spectacle, beginning with the consul and his attendants,
when some workmen ran in and commenced to stretch a chalked
rope across the arena from balcony to balcony in front of the pillars
of the first goal.

About the same time, also, six men came in through the Porta
Pompae and took post, one in front of each occupied stall; whereat
there was a prolonged hum of voices in every quarter.

'See, see! The green goes to number four on the right; the Athenian
is there.'

'And Messala – yes, he is in number two.'

'The Corinthian –'

'Watch the white! See, he crosses over, he stops; number one it
is – number one on the left.'

'No, the black stops there, and the white at number two.'

'So it is.'

These gatekeepers, it should be understood, were dressed in tunics
coloured like those of the competing charioteers; so, when they
took their stations, everybody knew the particular stall in which
his favourite was that moment waiting.

'Did you ever see Messala?' the Egyptian asked Esther.

The Jewess shuddered as she answered no. If not her father's
enemy, the Roman was Ben-Hur's.

'He is beautiful as Apollo.'

As Iras spoke, her large eyes brightened and she shook her jewelled
fan. Esther looked at her with the thought, 'Is he, then, so much
handsomer than Ben-Hur?' Next moment she heard Ilderim say to
her father, 'Yes, his stall is number two on the left of the Porta

Pompae;' and, thinking it was of Ben-Hur he spoke, her eyes turned that way. Taking but the briefest glance at the wattled face of the gate, she drew the veil close and muttered a little prayer.

Presently Sanballat came to the party.

'I am just from the stalls, O sheik,' he said, bowing gravely to Ilderim, who began combing his beard, while his eyes glittered with eager inquiry. 'The horses are in perfect condition.'

Ilderim replied simply, 'If they are beaten, I pray it be by some other than Messala.'

Turning then to Simonides, Sanballat drew out a tablet, saying, 'I bring you also something of interest. I reported, you will remember, the wager concluded with Messala last night, and stated that I left another which, if taken, was to be delivered to me in writing to-day before the race began. Here it is.'

Simonides took the tablet and read the memorandum carefully.

'Yes,' he said, 'their emissary came to ask me if you had so much money with me. Keep the tablet close. If you lose, you know where to come; if you win' – his face knit hard – 'if you win – ah, friend, see to it! See the signers escape not; hold them to the last shekel. That is what they would with us.'

'Trust me,' replied the purveyor.

'Will you not sit with us?' asked Simonides.

'You are very good,' the other returned; 'but if I leave the consul, young Rome yonder will boil over. Peace to you; peace to all.'

At length the recess came to an end.

The trumpeters blew a call at which the absentees rushed back to their places. At the same time, some attendants appeared in the arena, and, climbing upon the division wall, went to an entablature near the second goal at the west end, and placed upon it seven wooden balls; then returning to the first goal, upon an entablature there they set up seven other pieces of wood hewn to represent dolphins.

'What shall they do with the balls and fishes, O sheik?' asked Balthasar.

'Hast thou never attended a race?'

'Never before; and hardly know I why I am here.'

'Well, they are to keep the count. At the end of each round run thou shalt see one ball and one fish taken down.'

The preparations were now complete, and presently a trumpeter in gaudy uniform arose by the editor, ready to blow the signal of commencement promptly at his order. Straightway the stir of the people and the hum of their conversation died away. Every face near-by, and every face in the lessening perspective, turned to the

east, as all eyes settled upon the gates of the six stalls which shut
in the competitors.

The unusual flush upon his face gave proof that even Simonides
had caught the universal excitement. Ilderim pulled his beard fast
and furious.

'Look now for the Roman,' said the fair Egyptian to Esther, who
did not hear her, for, with close-drawn veil and beating heart, she
sat watching for Ben-Hur.

The structure containing the stalls, it should be observed, was
in form of the segment of a circle, retired on the right so that its
central point was projected forward, and midway the course, on the
starting side of the first goal. Every stall, consequently, was equally
distant from the starting-line or chalked rope above mentioned.

The trumpet sounded short and sharp; whereupon the starters,
one for each chariot, leaped down from behind the pillars of the goal,
ready to give assistance if any of the fours proved unmanageable.

Again the trumpet blew, and simultaneously the gatekeepers threw
the stalls open.

First appeared the mounted attendants of the charioteers, five
in all, Ben-Hur having rejected the service. The chalked line was
lowered to let them pass, then raised again. They were beautifully
mounted, yet scarcely observed as they rode forward; for all the time
the trampling of eager horses, and the voices of drivers scarcely less
eager, were heard behind in the stalls, so that one might not look
away an instant from the gaping doors.

The chalked line up again, the gate-keepers called their men,
instantly the ushers on the balcony waved their hands, and shouted
with all their strength, 'Down! down!'

As well have whistled to stay a storm.

Forth from each stall, like missiles in a volley from so many
great guns, rushed the six fours; and up the vast assemblage arose,
electrified and irrepressible, and, leaping upon the benches, filled the
Circus and the air above it with yells and screams. This was the time
for which they had so patiently waited! – this the moment of supreme
interest treasured up in talk and dreams since the proclamation of
the games!

'He is come – there – look!' cried Iras, pointing to Messala.

'I see him,' answered Esther, looking at Ben-Hur.

The veil was withdrawn. For an instant the little Jewess was brave.
An idea of the joy there is in doing an heroic deed under the eyes
of a multitude came to her, and she understood ever after how, at
such times, the souls of men, in the frenzy of performance, laugh
at death or forget it utterly.

The competitors were now under view from nearly every part of the Circus, yet the race was not begun; they had first to make the chalked line successfully.

The line was stretched for the purpose of equalizing the start. If it were dashed upon, discomfiture of man and horses might be apprehended; on the other hand, to approach it timidly was to incur the hazard of being thrown behind in the beginning of the race; and that was certain forfeit of the great advantage always striven for – the position next the division wall on the inner line of the course.

This trial, its perils and consequences, the spectators knew thoroughly; and if the opinion of old Nestor, uttered what time he handed the reins to his son, were true–

> 'It is not strength, but art, obtained the prize,
> And to be swift is less than to be wise'–

all on the benches might well look for warning of the winner to be now given, justifying the interest with which they breathlessly watched for the result.

The arena swam in a dazzle of light; yet each driver looked first thing for the rope, then for the coveted inner line. So, all six aiming at the same point and speeding furiously, a collision seemed inevitable; nor that merely. What if the editor, at the last moment, dissatisfied with the start, should withhold the signal to drop the rope? Or if he should not give it in time!

The crossing was about two hundred and fifty feet in width. Quick the eye, steady the hand, unerring the judgement required. If now one look away! or his mind wander! or a rein slip! And what attraction in the *ensemble* of the thousands over the spreading balcony! Calculating upon the natural impulse to give one glance – just one – in sooth of curiosity or vanity, malice might be there with an artifice; while friendship and love, did they serve the same result, might be as deadly as malice.

The divine last touch in perfecting the beautiful is animation. Can we accept the saying, then these latter days, so tame in pastime and dull in sports, have scarcely anything to compare to the spectacle offered by the six contestants. Let the reader try to fancy it; let him first look down upon the arena, and see it glistening in its frame of dull-grey granite walls; let him then, in this perfect field, see the chariots, light of wheel, very graceful, and ornate as paint and burnishing can make them – Messala's rich with ivory and gold; let him see the drivers, erect and statuesque, undisturbed by the motion of the cars, their limbs naked, and fresh and ruddy with the healthful polish of the baths – in their right hands goads, suggestive of torture dreadful to the thought – in their left hands, held in careful separation, and high, that they may not interfere with view of the steeds, the reins passing taut from the fore ends of the carriage poles; let him see the fours, chosen for beauty as well as speed; let him see them in magnificent action, their masters not more conscious of the situation, and all that is asked and hoped from them – their heads tossing, nostrils in play, now distended, now contracted – limbs too dainty for the sand which they touch but to spurn – limbs slender, yet with impact crushing as hammers – every muscle of the rounded bodies instinct with glorious life, swelling, diminishing, justifying the world in taking from them its ultimate measure of force; finally, along with chariots, drivers, horses, let the reader see the accompanying shadows fly; and, with such distinctness as the picture comes, he may share the satisfaction and deeper pleasure of those to whom it was a thrilling fact, not a feeble fancy. Every age has its plenty of sorrows; heaven help where there are no pleasures!

The competitors having started, each on the shortest line for the position next the wall, yielding would be like giving up the race; and who dared yield? It is not in common nature to change a purpose in mid-career; and the cries of encouragement from the balcony were indistinguishable and indescribable; a roar which had the same effect upon all the drivers.

The fours neared the rope together. Then the trumpeter by the editor's side blew a signal vigorously. Twenty feet away it was not heard. Seeing the action, however, the judges dropped the rope, and not an instant too soon, for the hoof of one of Messala's horses struck it as it fell. Nothing daunted, the Roman shook out his long lash, loosed the reins, leaned forward, and, with a triumphant shout, took the wall.

'Jove with us! Jove with us!' yelled all the Roman faction, in a frenzy of delight.

As Messala turned in, the bronze lion's head at the end of his axle caught the fore-leg of the Athenian's right-hand trace-mate, flinging the brute over against its yoke-fellow. Both staggered, struggled, and lost their headway. The ushers had their will at least in part. The thousands held their breath with horror; only up where the consul sat was there shouting.

'Jove with us!' screamed Drusus frantically.

'He wins! Jove with us!' answered his associates, seeing Messala speed on.

Tablet in hand, Sanballat turned to them; a crash from the course below stopped his speech, and he could not but look that way.

Messala having passed, the Corinthian was the only contestant on the Athenian's right, and to that side the latter tried to turn his broken four; and then, as ill-fortune would have it, the wheel of the Byzantine, who was next on the left, struck the tail-piece of his chariot, knocking his feet from under him. There was a crash, a scream of rage and fear, and the unfortunate Cleanthes fell under the hoofs of his own steeds; a terrible sight, against which Esther covered her eyes.

On swept the Corinthian, on the Byzantine, on the Sidonian.

Sanballat looked for Ben-Hur, and turned again to Drusus and his coterie.

'A hundred sestertii on the Jew!' he cried.

'Taken!' answered Drusus.

'Another hundred on the Jew!' shouted Sanballat.

Nobody appeared to hear him. He called again; the situation below was too absorbing, and they were too busy shouting, 'Messala! Messala! Jove with us!'

When the Jewess ventured to look again, a party of workmen were removing the horses and broken car; another party were taking off the man himself; and every bench upon which there was a Greek was vocal with execrations and prayers for vengeance. Suddenly she dropped her hands; Ben-Hur, unhurt, was to the front, coursing freely forward along with the Roman! Behind, them, in a group, followed the Sidonian, the Corinthian, and the Byzantine.

The race was on; the souls of the racers were in it; over them bent the myriads.

III

When the dash for position began, Ben-Hur, as we have seen, was on the extreme left of the six. For a moment, like the others, he was half blinded by the light in the arena; yet he managed to catch sight of his antagonists and divine their purpose. At Messala, who was more than an antagonist to him, he gave one searching look. The air of passionless hauteur characteristic of the fine patrician face was there as of old, and so was the Italian beauty, which the helmet rather increased; but more – it may have been a jealous fancy, or the effect of the brassy shadow in which the features were at the moment cast, still the Israelite thought he saw the soul of the man as through a

glass, darkly: cruel, cunning, desperate; not so excited as determined
– a soul in a tension of watchfulness and fierce resolve.

In a time not longer than was required to turn to his four again,
Ben-Hur felt his own resolution harden to a like temper. At whatever
cost, at all hazards, he would humble this enemy! Prize, friends,
wagers, honour – everything that can be thought of as a possible
interest in the race was lost in the one deliberate purpose. Regard
for life even should not hold him back. Yet there was no passion on
his part; no blinding rush of heated blood from heart to brain, and
back again; no impulse to fling himself upon Fortune – he did not
believe in Fortune; far otherwise. He had his plan, and, confiding
in himself, he settled to the task never more observant, never more
capable. The air about him seemed aglow with a renewed and perfect
transparency.

When not half-way across the arena, he saw that Messala's rush
would, if there was no collision, and the rope fell, give him the wall;
that the rope would fall, he ceased as soon to doubt; and, further,
it came to him, a sudden flash-like insight, that Messala knew it
was to be let drop at the last moment (prearrangement with the
editor could safely reach that point in the contest); and it suggested,
what more Roman-like than for the official to lend himself to a
countryman who, besides being so popular, had also so much at
stake? There could be no other accounting for the confidence with
which Messala pushed his four forward the instant his competitors
were prudentially checking their fours in front of the obstruction –
no other except madness.

It is one thing to see a necessity and another to act upon it.
Ben-Hur yielded the wall for the time.

The rope fell, and all the four but his sprang into the course under
urgency of voice and lash. He drew head to the right, and, with all
the speed of his Arabs, darted across the trails of his opponents,
the angle of movement being such as to lose the least time and
gain the greatest possible advance. So, while the spectators were
shivering at the Athenian's mishap, and the Sidonian, Byzantine,
and Corinthian were striving, with such skill as they possessed,
to avoid involvement in the ruin, Ben-Hur swept around and took
the course neck and neck with Messala, though on the outside. The
marvellous skill shown in making the change thus from the extreme
left across to the right without appreciable loss did not fail the sharp
eyes upon the benches; the Circus seemed to rock and rock again with
prolonged applause. Then Esther clasped her hands in glad surprise;
then Sanballat, smiling, offered his hundred sestertii a second time
without a taker; and then the Romans began to doubt, thinking

Messala might have found an equal, if not a master, and that in an Israelite!

And now, racing together side by side, a narrow interval between them, the two neared the second goal.

The pedestal of the three pillars there, viewed from the west, was a stone wall in the form of a half-circle, around which the course and opposite balcony were bent in exact parallelism. Making this turn was considered in all respects the most telling test of a charioteeer; it was, in fact, the very feat in which Orestes failed. As an involuntary admission of interest on the part of the spectators, a hush fell over all the Circus, so that for the first time in the race the rattle and clang of the cars plunging after the tugging steeds were distinctly heard. Then, it would seem, Messala observed Ben-Hur, and recognised him; and at once the audacity of the man flamed out in an astonishing manner.

'Down Eros, up Mars!' he shouted, whirling his lash with practised hand – 'Down Eros, up Mars!' he repeated, and caught the well-doing Arabs of Ben-Hur a cut the like of which they had never known.

The blow was seen in every quarter, and the amazement was universal. The silence deepened; up on the benches behind the consul the boldest held his breath, waiting for the outcome. Only a moment thus: then, involuntarily, down from the balcony, as thunder falls, burst the indignant cry of the people.

The four sprang forward affrighted. No hand had ever been laid upon them except in love; they had been nurtured ever so tenderly; and as they grew, their confidence in man became a lesson to men beautiful to see. What should such dainty natures do under such indignity but leap as from death?

Forward they sprang as with one impulse, and forward leaped the car. Past question, every experience is serviceable to us. Where got Ben-Hur the large hand and mighty grip which helped him now so well? Where but from the oar with which so long he fought the sea? And what was this spring of the floor under his feet to the dizzy eccentric lurch with which in the old time the trembling ship yielded to the beat of staggering billows, drunk with their power? So he kept his place, and gave the four free rein, and called to them in soothing voice, trying merely to guide them round the dangerous turn; and before the fever of the people began to abate, he had back the mastery. Nor that only; on approaching the first goal, he was again side by side with Messala, bearing with him the sympathy and admiration of every one not a Roman. So clearly was the feeling shown, so vigorous its manifestation, that Messala, with all his boldness, felt it unsafe to trifle further.

As the cars whirled round the goal, Esther caught sight of Ben-Hur's face – a little pale, a little higher raised, otherwise calm, even placid.

Immediately a man climbed on the entablature at the west end of the division wall, and took down one of the conical wooden balls. A dolphin on the east entablature was taken down at the same time.

In like manner, the second ball and second dolphin disappeared.

And then the third ball and third dolphin.

Three rounds concluded: still Messala held the inside position; still Ben-Hur moved with him side by side; still the other competitors followed as before. The contest began to have the appearance of one of the double races which became so popular in Rome during the later Caesarean period – Messala and Ben-Hur in the first, the Corinthian, Sidonian, and Byzantine in the second. Meantime the ushers succeeded in returning the multitude to their seats, though the clamour continued to run the rounds, keeping, as it were, even pace with the rivals in the course below.

In the fifth round the Sidonian succeeded in getting a place outside Ben-Hur, but lost it directly.

The sixth round was entered upon without change of relative position.

Gradually the speed had been quickened – gradually the blood of the competitors warmed with the work. Men and beasts seemed to know alike that the final crisis was near, bringing the time for the winner to assert himself.

The interest which from the beginning had centred chiefly in the struggle between the Roman and the Jew, with an intense and general sympathy for the latter, was fast changing to anxiety on his account. On all the benches the spectators bent forward motionless, except as their faces turned following the contestants. Ilderim quitted combing his beard, and Esther forgot her fears.

'A hundred sestertii on the Jew!' cried Sanballat to the Romans under the consul's awning.

There was no reply.

'A talent – or five talents, or ten; choose ye!'

He shook his tablets at them defiantly.

'I will take thy sestertii,' answered a Roman youth, preparing to write.

'Do not so,' interposed a friend.

'Why?'

'Messala hath reached his utmost speed. See him lean over his chariot-rim, the reins loose as flying ribbons. Look then at the Jew.'

The first one looked.

'By Hercules!' he replied, his countenance falling. 'The dog throws all his weight on the bits. I see, I see! If the gods help not our friend, he will be run away with by the Israelite. No, not yet. Look! Jove with us, Jove with us!'

The cry, swelled by every Latin tongue, shook the *velaria* over the consul's head.

If it were true that Messala had attained his utmost speed, the effort was with effect; slowly but certainly he was beginning to forge ahead. His horses were running with their heads low down; from the balcony their bodies appeared actually to skim the earth; their nostrils showed blood-red in expansion; their eyes seemed straining in their sockets. Certainly the good steads were doing their best! How long could they keep the pace? It was but the commencement of the sixth round. On they dashed. As they neared the second goal, Ben-Hur turned in behind the Roman's car.

The joy of the Messala faction reached its bound: they screamed and howled, and tossed their colours; and Sanballat filled his tablets with wagers of their tendering.

Malluch, in the lower gallery over the Gate of Triumph, found it hard to keep his cheer. He had cherished the vague hint dropped to him by Ben-Hur of something to happen in the turning of the western pillars. It was the fifth round, yet the something had not come; and he had said to himself, the sixth will bring it; but, lo! Ben-Hur was hardly holding a place at the tail of his enemy's car.

Over in the east end, Simonides' party held their peace. The merchant's head was bent low. Ilderim tugged at his beard, and dropped his brows till there was nothing of his eyes but an occasional sparkle of light. Esther scarcely breathed. Iras alone appeared glad.

Along the home-stretch – sixth round – Messala leading, next him Ben-Hur, and so close it was the old story:

> 'First flew Eumelus on Pheretian steeds;
> With those of Tros bold Diomed succeeds;
> Close on Eumelus' back they puff the wind,
> And seem just mounting on his car behind;
> Full on his neck he feels the sultry breeze,
> And, hovering o'er, their stretching shadow sees.'

Thus to the first goal, and round it. Messala, fearful of losing his place, hugged the stony wall with perilous clasp; a foot to the left, and he had been dashed to pieces; yet, when the turn was finished, no man, looking at the wheel-tracks of the two cars, could have said, here went Messala, there the Jew. They left but one trace behind them.

As they whirled by, Esther saw Ben-Hur's face again, and it was whiter than before.

Simonides, shrewder than Esther, said to Ilderim, the moment the rivals turned into the course, 'I am no judge, good sheik, if Ben-Hur be not about to execute some design. His face hath that look.'

To which Ilderim answered, 'Saw you how clean they were and fresh? By the splendour of God, friend, they have not been running! But now watch!'

One ball and one dolphin remained on the entablatures; and all the people drew a long breath, for the beginning of the end was at hand.

First, the Sidonian gave the scourge to his four, and, smarting with fear and pain, they dashed desperately forward, promising for a brief time to go to the front. The effort ended in promise. Next, the Byzantine and Corinthian each made the trial with like result, after which they were practically out of the race. Thereupon, with a readiness perfectly explicable, all the factions except the Romans joined hope in Ben-Hur, and openly indulged their feeling.

'Ben-Hur! Ben-Hur!' they shouted, and the blent voices of the many rolled overwhelmingly against the consular stand.

From the benches above him as he passed, the favour descended in fierce injunctions.

'Speed thee, Jew!'

'Take the wall now!'

'On! loose the Arabs! Give them rein and scourge!'

'Let him not have the turn on thee again. Now or never!'

Over the balustrade they stooped low, stretching their hands imploringly to him.

Either he did not hear, or could not do better, for half-way round the course, and he was still following; at the second goal even still no change!

And now, to make the turn, Messala began to draw in his left-hand steeds, an act which necessarily slackened their speed. His spirit was high; more than one altar was richer of his vows; the Roman genius was still president. On the three pillars only six hundred feet away were fame, increase of fortune, promotions, and a triumph ineffably sweetened by hate, all in store for him! That moment Malluch, in the gallery, saw Ben-Hur lean forward over his Arabs, and give them the reins. Out flew the many-folded lash in his hand; over the backs of the startled steeds it writhed and hissed, and hissed and writhed again and again; and though it fell not, there were both sting and menace in its quick report; and as the man passed thus from quiet to resistless action, his face suffused, his eyes gleaming, along the reins he seemed to flash his will; and instantly not one, but the four as one, answered with a leap that landed them alongside the Roman's car. Messala, on the perilous edge of the goal, heard, but dared not look to see what the awakening portended. From the people he received no sign. Above the noises of the race there was but one voice, and that was Ben-Hur's. In the old Aramaic, as the sheik himself, he called to the Arabs,–

'On, Atair! On, Rigel! What, Antares! dost thou linger now? Good horse – oho, Aldebaran! I hear them singing in the tents. I hear the children singing and the women – singing of the stars, of Atair, Antares, Rigel, Aldebaran, victory! – and the song will never end. Well done! Home to-morrow, under the black tent – home! On, Antares! The tribe is waiting for us, and the master is waiting! 'Tis done! 'tis done! Ha, ha! We have overthrown the proud. The hand that smote us is in the dust. Ours the glory! Ha, ha! – steady! The work is done – soho! Rest!'

There had never been anything of the kind more simple; seldom anything so instantaneous.

At the moment chosen for the dash, Messala was moving in a circle round the goal. To pass him, Ben-Hur had to cross the track, and good strategy required the movement to be in a forward direction; that is, on a like circle limited to the least possible increase. The thousands on the benches understood it all: they saw the signal given – the magnificent response; the four close outside Messala's outer wheel; Ben-Hur's inner wheel behind the other's car – all this they saw. Then they heard a crash loud enough to send a thrill through the Circus, and, quicker than thought, out over the course a spray of shining white and yellow flinders flew. Down on its right side toppled the bed of the Roman's chariot. There was a rebound as of the axle hitting the hard earth; another and another; then the car went to pieces; and Messala, entangled in the reins, pitched forward headlong.

To increase the horror of the sight by making death certain, the Sidonian, who had the wall next behind, could not stop or turn out. Into the wreck full speed he drove; then over the Roman, and into the latter's four, all mad with fear. Presently, out of the turmoil, the fighting of horses, the resound of blows, the murky cloud of dust and sand, he crawled, in time to see the Corinthian and Byzantine go on down the course after Ben-Hur, who had not been an instant delayed.

The people arose, and leaped upon the benches, and shouted and screamed. Those who looked that way caught glimpses of Messala, now under the trampling of the fours, now under the abandoned cars. He was still; they thought him dead; but far the greater number followed Ben-Hur in his career. They had not seen the cunning touch of the reins by which, turning a little to the left, he caught Messala's wheel with the iron-shod point of his axle, and crushed it; but they had seen the transformation of the man, and themselves felt the heat and glow of his spirit, the heroic resolution, the maddening energy of action with which, by look, word, and gesture, he so suddenly inspired his Arabs. And such running! It was rather the long leaping of lions in harness; but for the lumbering chariot, it seemed the four were flying. When the Byzantine and Corinthian were half-way down the course, Ben-Hur turned the first goal.

And the race was WON!

The consul arose; the people shouted themselves hoarse; the editor came down from his seat, and crowned the victors.

The fortunate man among the boxers was a low-browed, yellow-haired Saxon, of such brutalized face as to attract a second look from Ben-Hur, who recognized a teacher with whom he himself had been a favourite at Rome. From him the young Jew looked up and beheld Simonides and his party on the balcony. They waved their hands to him. Esther kept her seat; but Iras arose, and gave him a smile and a wave of her fan – favours not the less intoxicating to him because we know, O reader, they would have fallen to Messala had he been the victor.

The procession was then formed, and, midst the shouting of the multitude which had had its will, passed out of the Gate of Triumph.

And the day was over.

CALIGULA THE GOD

Robert Graves

Although it was unfortunate for Rome that so many of the early emperors were either weak or mad, it also adds to the fascination with the period. The two most notorious were Caligula and Nero. Caligula became emperor in AD 37. His name was a nickname meaning little boots, arising, apparently, from an incident when he was only two when soldiers dressed him up in miniature army gear. His real name was Gaius Germanicus, named after his father, a hero in the eyes of the Romans and the nephew of Tiberius. At the start of his reign Caligula undertook some very popular measures and many worshipped him. However, it was not long before some malady began to affect him. In the following extract from I, Claudius (1934), in which Claudius is the narrator, Robert Graves (1895–1985) explores Caligula's growing madness. It begins on Caligula's attempt to conquer Britain.

Caligula swore that he was about to fight a war against the Germans that would only end in their total extermination. He would piously complete the task begun by his grandfather and father. He sent a couple of regiments over the river to locate the nearest enemy. About 1,000 prisoners were brought back. Caligula reviewed them and after picking out 300 fine young men for his bodyguard he lined up the remainder against a cliff. A bald-headed man was at either end of the line. Caligula gave Cassius the order: 'Kill them, from bald head to bald head, in vengeance for the death of Varus.' The news of this massacre reached the Germans and they withdrew into

their thickest forests. Caligula then crossed the river with his entire
army and found the entire countryside deserted. The first day of his
march, just to make things more exciting, he ordered some of his
German bodyguard into a neighbouring wood, and then had news
brought to him at supper that the enemy was at hand. At the head
of his 'Scouts' and a troop of Guards Cavalry he then dashed out
to the attack. He brought back the men as prisoners, loaded with
chains, and announced a crushing victory against overwhelming
odds. He rewarded his comrades-in-arms with a new sort of military
decoration called 'The Scouts' Crown', a golden coronet decorated
with the Sun, Moon, and stars in precious stones.

On the third day the road lay through a narrow pass. The army
had to move in column instead of in skirmishing order. Cassius said
to Caligula, 'It was in a place rather like this, Caesar, that Varus
got ambushed. I shall never forget that day so long as I live. I was
marching at the head of my company and had just reached a bend
in the road, as it might be this one we are coming to, when suddenly
there was a tremendous war-cry, as it might be from that clump of
firs yonder, and three or four hundred assegais came whizzing down
on us . . .'

'Quick, my mare!' called Caligula in a panic. 'Clear the road.'
He sprang from his sedan, mounted Penelope (Incitatus was at
Rome, winning races) and galloped back down the column. In
four hours' time he was at the bridge again, but found it so
choked with baggage-wagons and was in such a hurry to cross
that he dismounted and made soldiers hand him in a chair from
wagon to wagon until he was safely on the other side. He recalled
his arms at once, announcing that the enemy were too cowardly to
meet him in battle, and that he would therefore seek new conquests
elsewhere. When the whole force had reassembled at Cologne he
marched down the Rhine and then across to Boulogne, the nearest
port to Britain. It so happened that the heir of Cymbeline, the King
of Britain, had quarrelled with his father and, hearing of Caligula's
approach, he fled across the Channel with a few followers and
put himself under Roman protection. Caligula, who had already
informed the Senate of his total subjugation of Germany, now wrote
to say that King Cymbeline had sent his son to acknowledge Roman
suzerainty over the entire British archipelago from the Scilly Islands
to the Orkneys.

I was with Caligula throughout this expedition and had a very
difficult time trying to humour him. He complained of sleeplessness
and said that his enemy Neptune was plaguing him all the time with
sea-noises in his ears, and used to come by night and threaten him

with a trident. I said: 'Neptune? I wouldn't allow myself to be browbeaten by that saucy fellow if I were you. Why don't you punish him as you punished the Germans? You threatened him once before, I remember, and if he continues to flout you, it would be wrong to stretch your clemency any further.'

He looked at me, uncomfortably, through narrowed eyelids. 'Do you think I'm mad?' he asked, after a time.

I laughed nervously. '*Mad*, Caesar? You ask whether I think you *mad*? Why, you set the standard of sanity for the whole habitable world.'

'It's a very difficult thing, you know, Claudius,' he said confidentially, 'to be a God in human disguise. I've often thought I was going mad. They say that the hellebore cure at Anticyra is very good. What do you think of it?'

I said: 'One of the greatest Greek philosophers, but I can't remember now which of them it was, took the hellebore cure just to make his clear brain still clearer. But if you are asking me to advise you, I should say, "Don't take it! Your brain is as clear as a pool of rock-water."'

'Yes,' he said, 'but I wish I could get more than three hours' sleep at night.'

'Those three hours are because of your mortal disguise,' I said. 'Undisguised Gods never sleep at all.'

So he was comforted and the next day drew up his army in order of battle on the sea-front: archers and slingers in front, then the auxiliary Germans armed with assegais, then the main Roman forces, with the French in the rear. The cavalry were on the wings and the siege-engines, mangonels, and catapults planted on sand-dunes. Nobody knew what on earth was going to happen. He rode forward into the sea as far as Penelope's knees and cried: 'Neptune, old enemy, defend yourself. I challenge you to mortal fight. You treacherously wrecked my father's fleet, did you? Try your might on me, if you dare.' Then he quoted from Ajax's wrestling match with Ulysses, in Homer:

> Or let me lift thee, Chief, or lift thou me.
> Prove we our force . . .

A little wave came rolling past. He cut at it with his sword and laughed contemptuously. Then he coolly retired and ordered the 'general engagement' to be sounded. The archers shot, the slingers slung, the javelin-men threw their javelins; the regular infantry waded into the waters as far as their arm-pits and hacked at the little waves, the cavalry charged on either flank and swam out some way, slashing with their sabres, the mangonels hurled rocks, and the catapults huge javelins and iron-tipped beams. Caligula then put to sea in a war-vessel and anchored just out of range of the missiles, uttering absurd challenges to Neptune and spitting far out over the vessel's side. Neptune made no attempt to defend himself or to reply, except that one man was nipped by a lobster, and another stung by a jelly-fish.

Caligula finally had the rally blown and told his men to wipe the blood off their swords and gather the spoil. The spoil was the sea-shells on the beach. Each man was expected to collect a helmet-full, which was added to a general heap. The shells were then sorted and packed in boxes to be sent to Rome in proof of this unheard-of victory. The troops thought it great fun, and when he rewarded them with four gold pieces a man cheered him tremendously. As a trophy of victory he built a very high lighthouse, on the model of the famous one at Alexandria, which has since proved a great blessing to sailors in those dangerous waters.

He then marched us up the Rhine again. When we reached Bonn Caligula took me aside and whispered darkly: 'The regiments have never been punished for the insult they once paid me by mutinying against my father, during my absence from this Camp. You remember, I had to come back and restore order for him.'

'I remember perfectly,' I said. 'But that's rather long ago, isn't it? After twenty-six years there can't be many men still serving in the ranks who were then there. You and Cassius Chaerea are probably the only two veteran survivors of that dreadful day.'

'Perhaps I shall only decimate them, then,' he said.

The men of the First and Twentieth Regiments were ordered to attend a special assembly and told that they might leave their arms behind, because of the hot weather. The Guards cavalry were also ordered to attend but instructed to bring their lances as well as their sabres. I found a sergeant who looked as though he might have fought at Philippi, he was so old and scarred. I said, 'Sergeant, do you know who I am?'

'No, sir. Can't say that I do, sir. You seem to be an ex-Consul, sir.'

'I am the brother of Germanicus.'

'Indeed, sir. Never knew that there was such a person, sir.'

'No, I'm not a soldier or anyone important. But I've got an important message for you fellows. *Don't leave your swords too far away when you go to this afternoon's assembly!*'

'Why, sir, if I may ask?'

'Because you may need them. Perhaps there will be an attack by the Germans. Perhaps by someone else.'

He stared hard at me and then saw that I really meant it.

'Much obliged to you, sir; I'll pass the word around,' he answered.

The infantry were massed in front of the tribunal platform and Caligula spoke to them with an angry, scowling face, stamping his feet and sawing with his hands. He began reminding them of a certain night in early autumn, many years before, when under a starless and bewitched sky ... Here some of the men began sneaking away through a gap between two troops of cavalry. They were going to fetch their swords. Others boldly pulled theirs out from under their military cloaks where they had been hiding them. Caligula must have noticed what was happening, for he suddenly changed his tone, in the middle of a sentence. He began drawing a happy contrast between those bad days, happily forgotten, and the present reign of glory, wealth, and victory. 'Your little playfellow grew to manhood,' he said, 'and became the mightiest Emperor this world has ever known. No foeman, however fierce, dares challenge his unconquerable arms.'

My old sergeant rushed forward. 'All is lost, Caesar,' he shouted. 'The enemy has crossed the river at Cologne – three hundred thousand strong. They're out to sack Lyons – then they'll cross the Alps, and sack Rome!'

Nobody believed this nonsensical story but Caligula. He turned yellow with fear, dived from the platform, grabbed hold of a horse, tumbled into the saddle, and was out of the camp like a flash. A groom galloped after him and Caligula called back to him, 'Thank God I still hold Egypt. I'll be safe there at least. The Germans aren't sailors.'

How everyone laughed! But a colonel went after him on a good horse and caught him before very long. He assured Caligula that the news was exaggerated. Only a small force, he said, had crossed the river and had been beaten back: the Roman bank was now quite clear of the enemy. Caligula stopped at the next town and wrote a dispatch to the Senate, informing them that all his wars were now successfully over and that he was coming back at once with his laurel-garlanded troops. He blamed those cowardly stay-at-homes most severely for having, from all accounts, lived life in the City just as usual – theatres, baths, supper-parties – while he had been undergoing the severest hardships of campaign. He had eaten, drunk, and slept no better than a private soldier.

The Senate was puzzled how to pacify him, being under strict orders from him to vote him no honours on their own initiative. They sent him an embassy, however, congratulating him on his magnificent victories and begging him to hasten back to Rome where his presence was so sadly missed. He was dreadfully angry that no triumph had been decreed him even in spite of his orders, and that he was not referred to as Jove in the message but merely as the Emperor Gaius Caesar. He rapped his hand on his sword-pommel and shouted: 'Hasten back? Indeed I will, and with this in my hand.'

He had made preparations for a triple triumph: over Germany, over Britain, and over Neptune. For British captives he had Cymbeline's son and his followers, to which were added the crews of some British trading vessels whom he had detained at Boulogne. For German captives he had 300 real ones and all the tallest men he could find in France, wearing yellow wigs and German clothes and talking together in a jargon supposed to be German. But, as I say, the Senate had been afraid to vote him a formal triumph, so he had to be content with an informal one. He rode into the City in the same style as he had ridden across the bridge at Baiae, and it was only on the intercession of Caesonia, who was a sensible woman, that he refrained from putting the entire Senate to the sword. He rewarded the people for their alms-giving generosity to him in the past by showering gold and silver from the Palace roof. But he mixed red-hot discs of iron with this largesse, to remind them that he had not yet forgiven them for their behaviour in the amphitheatre. His soldiers were told that they could make as much disturbance as they pleased and get as drunk as they liked at the public expense. They took full advantage of this licence, sacking whole streets of shops and burning down the prostitutes' quarter. Order was not restored for ten days.

This was in September. While he was away the workmen had been busy on the new temple on the Palatine Hill at the other side of the Temple of Castor and Pollux from the New Palace. An extension had been made as far as the Market Place. Caligula now turned the Temple of Castor and Pollux into a vestibule for the new temple, cutting a passage between the statues of the Gods. 'The Heavenly Twins are my doorkeepers,' he boasted. Then he sent a message to the Governor of Greece to see that all the most famous statues of Gods were removed from the temples there and sent to him at Rome. He proposed to take off their heads and substitute his own. The statue he most coveted was the colossal one of Olympian Jove. He had a special ship built for its conveyance to Rome. But the ship was struck by lightning just before it was launched. Or this, at least, was the report – I believe, really, that the superstitious crew burned it on purpose. However, Capitoline Jove then repented of his quarrel with Caligula (or so Caligula told us) and begged him to return and live next to him again. Caligula replied that he had now practically completed a new temple; but since Capitoline Jove had apologized so humbly he would make a compromise – he would build a bridge over the valley and join the two hills. He did this: the bridge passed over the roof of the Temple of Augustus.

Caligula was now publicly Jove. He was not only Latin Jove but Olympian Jove, and not only that but all the other Gods and Goddesses, too, whom he had decapitated and re-headed. Sometimes he was Apollo and sometimes Mercury and sometimes Pluto, in each case wearing the appropriate dress and demanding the appropriate sacrifices. I have seen him go about as Venus in a long gauzy silk robe with face painted, a red wig, padded bosom, and high-heeled slippers. He was present as the Good Goddess at her December festival: *that* was a scandal. Mars was a favourite character with him, too. But most of the time he was Jove: he wore an olive-wreath, a beard of fine gold wires, and a bright blue silk cloak, and carried a jagged piece of electrum in his hand to represent lightning. One day he was on the Oration Platform in the Market Place dressed as Jove and making a speech. 'I intend shortly,' he said, 'to build a city for my occupation on the top of the Alps. We Gods prefer mountain-tops to unhealthy river-valleys. From the Alps I shall have a wide view of my Empire – France, Italy, Switzerland, the Tyrol, and Germany. If I see any treason hatching anywhere below me, I shall give a warning growl of thunder so! [He growled in his throat.] If the warning is disregarded I shall blast the traitor with this lightning of mine, so!' [He hurled his piece of lightning at the crowd. It hit a statue and bounced off harmlessly.] A stranger in the crowd, a shoemaker from Marseilles on a sight-seeing visit to Rome, burst out laughing. Caligula had the fellow arrested and brought nearer to the platform, then bending down he asked, frowning: 'Who do I seem to you to be?' 'A big humbug,' said the shoemaker. Caligula was puzzled. 'Humbug?' he repeated. '*I* a humbug!' 'Yes,' said the Frenchman. 'I'm only a poor French shoemaker and this is my first visit to Rome. And I don't know any better. If anyone at home did what you're doing he'd be a big humbug.'

Caligula began to laugh too. 'You poor half-wit,' he said. 'Of course he would be. That's just the difference.'

The whole crowd laughed like mad, but whether at Caligula or at the shoemaker was not clear. Soon after this he had a thunder-and-lightning machine made. He lit a fuse and it made

a roar and a flash and catapulted stones in whatever direction he
wanted. But I have it on good authority that whenever there was a
real thunderstorm at night he used to creep under the bed. There is a
good story about that. One day a storm burst when he was parading
about dressed as Venus. He began to cry: 'Father, Father, spare your
pretty daughter!'

The money he had won in France was soon spent and he invented
new ways of increasing the revenue. His favourite one now was to
examine judicially the wills of men who had just died and had left
him no money: he would then give evidence of the benefits that
the testators had received from him and declare that they had been
either ungrateful or of unsound mind at the time of drawing their
wills and that he preferred to think that they had been of unsound
mind. He cancelled the wills and appointed himself principal heir.
He used to come into Court in the early morning and write up
on a blackboard the sum of money that he intended to win that
day, usually 200,000 gold pieces. When he had won it, he closed
the Court. He made a new edict one morning about the hours of
business permitted in various sorts of shops. He had it written in
very small letters on a tiny placard posted high on a pillar in the
Market Place where nobody troubled to read it, not realizing its
importance. That afternoon his officers took the names of several
hundred tradesmen who had unwittingly infringed the edict. When
they were brought to trial he allowed any of them who could do so
to plead in mitigation of sentence that they had named him as co-heir
with their children. Few of them could. It now became customary for
men with money to notify the Imperial Treasurer that Caligula was
named in their wills as the principal heir. But in several cases this
proved unwise. For Caligula made use of the medicine chest that he
had inherited from my grandmother Livia. One day he sent round
presents of honied fruits to some recent testators. They all died
at once. He also summoned my cousin, the King of Morocco, to
Rome and put him to death, saying simply: 'I need your fortune,
Ptolemy.'

During his absence in France there had been comparatively few
convictions at Rome and the prisons were nearly empty: this meant
a shortage of victims for throwing to the wild beasts. He made the
shortage up by using members of the audience, first cutting out their
tongues so that they could not call out to their friends for rescue.
He was becoming more and more capricious. One day a priest was
about to sacrifice a young bull to him in his aspect of Apollo. The
usual sacrificial procedure was for a deacon to stun the bull with a
stone axe, and for the priest then to cut its throat. Caligula came in

dressed as a deacon and asked the usual question: 'Shall I?' When
the priest answered 'Do so,' he brought the axe down smash on the
priest's head.

I was still living in poverty with Briseis and Calpurnia, for though
I had no debts, neither had I any money except what little income
came to me from the farm. I was careful to let Caligula know how
poor I was and he graciously permitted me to remain in the Senatorial
Order though I no longer had the necessary financial qualifications.
But I felt my position daily more insecure. One midnight early in
October I was awakened by loud knocking at the front door. I put
my head out of the window. 'Who's there?' I asked.

'You're wanted at the Palace immediately.'

I said: 'Is that you, Cassius Chaerea? Am I going to be killed, do
you know?'

'My orders are to fetch you to him immediately.'

Calpurnia cried and Briseis cried and both kissed me good-bye
very tenderly. As they helped me to dress I hurriedly told them
how to dispose of my few remaining possessions, and what to do
with little Antonia, and about my funeral, and so on. It was a most
affecting scene for all of us, but I did not dare prolong it. Soon I
was hopping along at Cassius's side to the Palace. He said gruffly,
'Two more ex-Consuls have been summoned to appear with you.'
He told me their names and I was still more alarmed. They were rich
men, just the sort whom Caligula would accuse of a plot against him.
But why me? I was the first to arrive. The two others came rushing
in almost immediately after, breathless with haste and fear. We were
taken into the Hall of Justice and made to sit on chairs on a sort of
scaffold looking down on the tribunal platform. A guard of German
soldiers stood behind us, muttering together in their own language.
The room was in complete darkness but for two tiny oil lamps on
the tribunal. The windows behind were draped, we noticed, with
black hangings embroidered with silver stars. My companions and
I silently clasped hands in farewell. They were men from whom I
had had many insults at one time or another, but in the shadow of
death such trifles are forgotten. We sat there waiting for something
to happen until just before daybreak.

Suddenly we heard a clash of cymbals and the gay music of
oboes and fiddles. Slaves filed in from a door at the side
of the tribunal, each carrying two lamps, which they put on
tables at the side; and then the powerful voice of a eunuch
began singing the well-known song *When the long watches of
the night*. The slaves retired. A shuffling sound was heard and
presently in danced a tall ungainly figure in a woman's pink

silk gown with a crown of imitation roses on its head. It was
Caligula.

> *The rosy-fingered Goddess then*
> *Will roll away the night of stars . . .*

Here he drew away the draperies from the window and disclosed
the first streaks of dawn, and then, when the eunuch reached the
part about the rosy-fingered Goddess, blowing out the lamps one
by one, brought this incident into the dance too. Puff. Puff. Puff.

> *And where clandestine lovers lie*
> *Entangled in sweet passion's toils . . .*

From a bed which we had not noticed, because it was in an alcove,
the Goddess Dawn then pulled out a girl and a man, neither of them
with any clothes on, and in dumb show indicated that it was the
time for them to part. The girl was very beautiful. The man was
the eunuch who was singing. They parted in opposite directions as
if profoundly distressed. When the last verse came:

> *O Dawn, of Goddesses most fair,*
> *Who with thy slow and lovely tread*
> *Dost give relief to every care . . .*

I had the sense to prostrate myself on the ground. My companions
were not slow in following my example. Caligula capered off the
stage and soon afterwards we were summoned to breakfast with
him. I said, 'O God of Gods, I have never in my life witnessed any
dance that gave me such profound spiritual joy as the one I have
just witnessed. I have no words for its loveliness.'

My companions agreed with me and said that it was a million
pities that so matchless a performance had been given to so tiny
an audience. He said, complacently, that it was only a rehearsal.
He would give it one night soon in the amphitheatre to the whole
City. I didn't see how he would manage the curtain-drawing effect
in an open-air amphitheatre hundreds of yards long, but I said
nothing about that. We had a very tasty breakfast, the senior
ex-Consul sitting on the floor alternately eating thrush-pie and
kissing Caligula's foot. I was just thinking how pleased Calpurnia
and Briseis would be to see me back when Caligula, who was in
a very pleasant humour, suddenly said: 'Pretty girl, wasn't she,
Claudius, you old lecher?'

'Very pretty indeed, God.'

'And still a virgin, so far as I know. Would you like to marry her? You can if you like. I took a fancy to her for a moment, but it's a funny thing, I don't really like immature women any more . . . Or any mature woman, for that matter, except Caesonia. Did you recognize the girl?'

'No, Lord, I was only watching you, to tell the truth.'

'She's your cousin Messalina, Barbatus' daughter. The old pander didn't utter a word of protest when I asked for her to be sent along to me. What cowards they are, after all, Claudius!'

'Yes, Lord God.'

'All right, then, I'll marry you two to-morrow. I'm going to bed now, I think.'

'A thousand thanks and homages, Lord.'

He gave me his other foot to kiss. Next day he kept his promise and married us. He accepted a tenth of Messalina's dowry as a fee but otherwise behaved courteously enough. Calpurnia had been delighted to see me alive again and had pretended not to mind about my marriage. She said in a businesslike way: 'Very well, my dear, I'll go back to the farm and look after things for you there again. You won't miss me, with that pretty wife of yours. And now you have money you'll have to live at the Palace again.'

I told her that the marriage was forced on me and that I would miss her very much indeed. But she pooh-poohed that: Messalina had twice her looks, three times her brains, and birth and money into the bargain. I was in love with her already, Calpurnia said.

I felt uncomfortable. Calpurnia had been my only true friend in all those four years of misery. What had she not done for me? And yet she was right: I *was* in love with Messalina, and Messalina was to be my wife now. There would be no place for Calpurnia with Messalina about.

She was in tears as she went away. So was I. I was not in love with her, but she was my truest friend and I knew that if ever I needed her she would be there to help me. I need not say that when I received the dowry money I did not forget her.

Messalina was an extremely beautiful girl, slim and quick moving, with eyes as black as jet and masses of curly black hair. She hardly spoke a word and had a mysterious smile which drove me nearly crazy with love for her. She was so glad to have escaped from Caligula and so quick to realize the advantages that marriage with me gave her, that she behaved in a way which made me quite sure that she loved me as much as I loved her. This was practically the

first time I had been in love with anyone since my boyhood; and
when a not very clever, not very attractive man of fifty falls in love
with a very attractive and very clever girl of fifteen it is usually a
poor look-out for him. We were married in October. By December
she was pregnant by me. She appeared very fond of my little Antonia,
who was aged about ten, and it was a relief to me that the child now
had someone whom she could call mother, someone who was near
enough to her in age to be a friend and could explain the ways
of society to her and take her about, as Calpurnia had not been
able to do.

Messalina and I were invited to live at the Palace again. We arrived
at an unfortunate time. A merchant called Bassus had been asking
questions of a captain of the Palace Guards about Caligula's daily
habits – was it true that he walked about the cloisters at night
because he could not sleep? At what time did he do this? Which
cloisters did he usually choose? What Guard did he have with him?
The captain reported the incident to Cassius and Cassius reported
it to Caligula. Bassus was arrested and cross-examined. He was
forced to admit that he had intended to kill Caligula but denied
even under torture that he had any associates. Caligula then sent
a message to Bassus' old father, ordering him to attend his son's
execution. The old man, who had no notion that Bassus had been
planning to assassinate Caligula or even that he had been arrested,
was greatly shocked to find his son groaning on the Palace floor,
his body broken by torture. But he controlled himself and thanked
Caligula for his graciousness in summoning him to close his son's
eyes. Caligula laughed. 'Close his eyes indeed! He's going to have no
eyes to close, the assassin! I'm going to poke them out in a moment.
And yours too.'

Bassus's father said: 'Spare our lives. We are only tools in the
hands of powerful men. I'll give you all the names.'

This impressed Caligula, and when the old man mentioned the
Guards' Commander, the Commander of the Germans, Callistus
the Treasurer, Caesonia, Mnester, and three or four others, he
grew pale with alarm. 'And whom would they make Emperor in
my place?' he asked.

'Your uncle Claudius.'

'Is he in the plot too?'

'No, they were merely going to use him as a figure-head.'

Caligula hurried away and summoned the Guards' Commander,
the Commander of the Germans, the Treasurer, and myself to a
private room. He asked the others, pointing to me: 'Is that creature
fit to be Emperor?'

They answered in surprised tones, 'Not unless you say so, Jove.'

Then he gave them a pathetic smile and exclaimed, 'I am one and you are three. Two of you are armed and I am defenceless. If you hate me and want to kill me, do so at once and put that poor idiot into my place as Emperor.'

We all fell on our faces and the two soldiers handed him their swords from the floor, saying, 'We are innocent of any such treacherous thought, Lord. If you disbelieve us, kill us!'

Do you know, he was actually about to kill us! But while he hesitated I said: 'Almighty God, the colonel who summoned me here told me of the charge brought against these loyal men by Bassus' father. Its falsity is evident. If Bassus had really been employed by them, would it have been necessary for him to question the captain about your movements? Would he not have been able to get all the necessary information from these generals themselves? No, Bassus' father has tried to save his own life and Bassus' by a clumsy lie.'

Caligula appeared to be convinced by my argument. He gave me his hand to kiss, made us all rise, and handed the swords back. Bassus and his father were thereupon hewn to pieces by the Germans. But Caligula could not rid his mind of the dread of assassination, which was presently increased by a number of unlucky omens. First the porter's lodge at the Palace was struck by lightning. Then Incitatus, when he was brought in to dinner one evening, reared up and cast a shoe which broke an alabaster cup that had belonged to Julius Caesar, spilling the wine on the floor. The worst omen of all was what happened at Olympus, when, in accordance with Caligula's orders, the temple workmen began to take the statue of Jove to pieces for conveyance to Rome. The head was to come off first, to be used as a measure for the new head of Caligula that would be substituted when the statue was reassembled. They had got the pulley fixed to the temple roof and a rope knotted around the neck and were just about to haul, when suddenly a thunderous peal of laughter roared out through the whole building. The workmen rushed away in panic. Nobody could be found bold enough to take their places.

Caesonia now advised him, since by his immovable rigour he had made everyone tremble at the very sound of his name, to rule mildly and earn the people's love instead of their fear. For Caesonia realized how dangerously he was placed and that if anything happened to him she would certainly lose her life too, unless she was known to have done her best to dissuade him from his cruelties. He was behaving in a most imprudent way now. He went in turn to the Guards' Commander, the Treasurer, and the Commander of the

Germans and pretended to take each of them into his confidence, saying, 'I trust *you*, but the others are plotting against me and I want you to regard them as my deadliest enemies.' They compared notes; and that is why when a real plot was formed they shut their eyes to it. Caligula said that he approved Caesonia's advice and thanked her for it; he would certainly follow it when he had made his peace with his enemies. He called the Senate together and addressed us in this strain: 'Soon I shall grant you all an amnesty, my enemies, and reign with love and peace a thousand years. That is the prophecy. But before that golden time comes heads must roll along the floor of this House and blood spurt up to the beams. A wild five minutes that will be.' If the 1,000 years of peace had come first, and then the wild five minutes, we should have preferred it.

BETRAYED

Juliet Dymoke

The Romans finally conquered the southern part of Britain in AD *43, under Claudius. Until then, it was easy to imagine that the ancient Britons were a primitive and uncivilized race. They were quite the opposite in fact. Britain was a highly prosperous island, trading throughout Europe, and this had led to a wealthy aristocracy amongst the leading tribes. Two of the biggest tribes, between them quite capable of defeating the Romans, were the Catuvellauni, who occupied most of the East Midlands and what is now East Anglia, and whose king was Caractacus, and the Brigantes, who occupied most of what is now Yorkshire and Northumbria, and who were ruled by Queen Cartimandua. If Caractacus and Cartimandua had been allies, the history of the world might have been so very different. Instead the following story, set in the year* AD *15, reveals what did happen.*

Juliet Dymoke (b. 1919) is the author of over thirty historical novels, mostly with a Napoleonic or Georgian setting, but she began her writing career with a Roman novel, Sons of the Tribune *(1956). The following story is adapted from her other Roman novel,* Prisoner of Rome *(1975).*

It was dark in the forest, the first rays of the sun barely penetrating the deep gloom. The men lay where they had sprawled in the sleep of exhaustion, exactly where they had fallen last night; those who had bearskin cloaks huddled under them, for the autumn night had been cold.

When Cefn awoke all was quiet. On opening his eyes, there was a
young deer, seeing no danger in these still creatures, sniffing among
the rough undergrowth. Cefn sat up and the animal fled down the
rough track worn by the feet of many hunters and woodmen. He
was sorry he had no weapon but the knife stuck in his belt, for the
deer might have provided food for a few days. His stomach was so
empty it seemed clamped against his back. Looking round he saw
that a little way off their Chief was also awake and sitting with his
back against a tree, he too so still he had not disturbed the deer,
his eyes staring broodingly into the gloom of the forest.

Cefn got up and went over to him. This morning he felt older
than his sixteen years. Tentatively he asked, 'Did you not sleep
last night?'

'I slept,' the older man answered, 'until an hour or so ago. Is
there anything left to eat?'

'I'll look,' Cefn said, but found only an apple from the few picked
yesterday. Others were waking now, brushing fallen leaves from
their tunics, swinging their skins over their shoulders. They were
nearly all seasoned fighting men, short but very strong, with legs
like oak trees, broad shoulders, brawny arms.

The King stood up. He was the tallest there, of powerful build,
gold bracelets on his sunburned arms, a gold amulet on a chain about
his neck. His hair, long and fair, was kept back from his forehead by
a golden band, and he had a thick drooping moustache though only
a fair stubble on his chin which in general he kept shaved. A man
of towering personality, a leader of men, and despite, or perhaps
because of his expertise in battle, he took pride in his appearance,
never forgetting his royal birth. To Cefn he was near enough a god,
everything Cefn wished to be when he was older. His own father
having been killed in the fighting against the Romans some seven
years ago, his mother long dead, Cefn had lived in the King's care
and the King's lady had been a mother to him, the daughter of the
house a sister.

Caractacus himself was the eldest son of Cunobelinus, King of the
Catuvellauni tribe on the eastern side of the country. The capital,
Camulodunum, had been, Cefn thought, a large and very fine camp
with what seemed a palace for the king, but at last the Romans had
taken that too, sacked it and killed Cunobelinus. Caractacus and his
brothers had fled west with the remains of their men, his wife and
daughter left behind, undergoing who knew what horrors, though
Caractacus had said through tight lips that as they had fallen into the
hands of Marcus Ostorius Scapula, son of the Governor of Britain,
they should be safe enough. Marcus was renowned for his fighting

skills, but he was also known for fair dealing and it was likely he would honour such prisoners.

Caractacus seemed to trust Marcus Ostorius, Cefn thought, though he was not sure why. The Romans were their enemies, invading their country long before Cefn was born, taking their lands, their gold, their weapons, their women, and he had been part of the fighting force resisting them since he was twelve. But things had gone against them. Pushed back into the west, the King, in three years of sporadic fighting, had joined with the Silures tribe to harry the Romans where and whenever they could. But always they were pushed back, and a few days ago, having turned north to link up with another tribe, the Ordovices, had found themselves confronting a large army of the enemy.

As always with an eye to a good position Caractacus had chosen his ground carefully, posting his men on a steep hill, fortifying it as well as he could, filling the approaches with piles of large boulders, strengthening the natural outcrop of rocks. But it hadn't stopped the Romans, nor had the shower of missiles and darts hurled down on them. The Romans simply closed ranks, locked their long shields above their heads, and made an impenetrable roof to protect themselves. Nothing, it seemed, could stop them. Tearing down the stone ramparts they came on, and a fierce battle ensued. Amid the noise, the clash of arms, the yelling of the tribesmen, the screams of the wounded, Cefn conducted himself, he hoped, as a man should. He had driven his spear into one enemy, finding a gap between helmet and neck, saw the blood spurt, the soldier fall with a croaking sound, and leapt over his body at another. He was struck on the leg, but in his frenzy barely noticed it; his spear broke and, wrenching his sword from his belt, he lunged at another soldier. But the tide of red-clad fighting men was turning them back. Stumbling over some stones, a blow on the head sent him reeling into oblivion.

When he came to himself it was to find he was being carried like a sack over the shoulder of Rudin, a great burly fellow and one of Caractacus' most devoted followers. Rudin's head was bleeding but he did not seem to notice it, and when Cefn spoke and said he would walk, Rudin told him gruffly to bide where he was. It was a headlong flight and when Cefn was at last set down, he realized he was still dizzy and could not have kept the pace; the blood from his head was dry on his face.

They had nothing to eat, but that evening came upon a group of huts occupied by a few small men, some women and children, covered with little more than rags – still they shared what they had with the fleeing warriors. It was little enough, but the King thanked them as if it had been a feast and promised them a reward when he could send it.

Now as his men woke, stood stretching and yawning, Cefn asked where they were going.

'To the Brigantes,' Caractacus spoke through grim lips. 'To Queen Cartimandua.'

They had been joined by two other men, only slightly older than Cefn: Beric, who had been his friend from boyhood, and Jorst, who had come to Camulodunum with his family from over the seas. No one had any idea what had happened to his parents in the sack of the city, and Jorst had made Caractacus his master. These three had, somewhat to the King's amusement, constituted themselves his bodyguard. 'Aren't they a warlike tribe?' Jorst asked now. 'As for their Queen I've heard she is ferocious toward an enemy and not much better to her friends.'

They had been joined by the rest of the men, crowding round to know what they should do next and an argument broke out as to the wisdom of going to the Brigantes.

Caractacus held up his hand and such was his authority that an instant silence fell. 'There is nowhere else to go unless we cross the sea,' he pointed out,' but this is our land and I won't give it up. We're only a small remnant, we need food, arms, men, and we must trust to Queen Cartimandua to help us.'

'Well, I wouldn't trust a Brigantian as far as I could see him,' a grey-haired man muttered. 'I remember in my father's day –'

'Your father's day is over,' Caractacus broke in sharply. 'Do you forget my wife and daughter were taken, and my brother Cunobel? I cannot cross the sea while they are in Roman hands.'

Not given to venturing an opinion among his elders nevertheless Cefn muttered to Beric 'But won't the Governor treat them well? He just said –'

'There's no such thing as an honest Roman,' Beric answered, crushingly. 'We have to rescue them and if Queen Cartimandua will aid us maybe we can.'

'That is my thought,' Caractacus picked up their talk. 'Cefn, does your head hurt?' He had a long cut on his own cheek though now dry and healing.

'It aches,' Cefn answered, 'but it's nothing.' The wound on his leg hurt more, but he was not going to admit it.

'We can't be far from the Brigantian camp now.' The King looked round his small band. 'A day's march maybe.'

They moved off, twenty or so hungry, wounded and dispirited

men, yet, Cefn thought, as long as their Chief led them they wouldn't
lose heart. He walked awkwardly but at least he was alive and on
his own two feet.

By late afternoon as the sun went down a mist crept over the
land, and as they came out into an open stretch they saw a river,
moving sluggishly, and a ford. Crossing it with the water only up
to their knees, Cefn found it stinging to his wound for it was very
cold. On the far side was a grassy slope, a wooded hill and beyond
that rolling moors.

'We must be almost there,' Caractacus said – then held up his hand,
either his acute hearing or an unerring instinct warning him to stop.
Out of the wood plunged a band of some thirty men, wild-looking
and brandishing spears, long hair flying as they shouted menacingly
at the small company of fugitives. Cefn and Jorst, who still had
knives stuck in their belts, drew them, prepared if need be to make
a stand.

'Hold,' the King said loudly. 'Those are Brigantians.' He went
forward without hesitation, a proud figure despite his torn and
bloodied tunic, and the men came to a halt staring. It seemed that
one at least guessed who he was for he stepped forward to ask if
he was the Chief of the Catuvellauni.

'I am,' Caractacus answered. 'I seek shelter with Queen
Cartimandua.'

The man nodded. 'Aye, we heard a rumour of another triumph
for the Romans. You couldn't stop them, eh?'

Cefn could sense the Chief's anger, but with admirable calm
Caractacus merely answered, 'We were outnumbered. Now I wish
to be taken to the Queen.'

'She is expecting you.'

'How can that be?'

The Brigantian gave a superior snort. 'Oh, she has men keeping
watch for her in a great many places.'

It seemed to Cefn an odd thing to say. A tribe was a tribe and
stayed within its own confines, or used to until the Romans came.
He hated them for taking what was not theirs; they killed and
conquered, had slain his own father, and it seemed to him that
only Caractacus was able to stand up to them, only he could
lead the combined tribes. Individually they could do nothing.
But they had not gone so far north before and he knew nothing
of the Brigantes, nor what they might or might not do in this
situation.

The man who had spoken to Caractacus motioned to him to come
forward with the air at least of conducting a guest and the rest of the

Brigantes surrounded the little group, indicating that they should follow.

'I suppose this is what the Chief wants,' Cefn murmured to his friends. 'But I don't like it. I wouldn't trust any of them.'

'We shall soon see the Queen and then we shall know,' Beric answered.

'Well, I can't bear that the Chief should go begging to Cartimandua. If she is in the least like men say –'

'You talk too much,' Beric told him. 'He won't beg from anyone.'

Jorst pointed, 'Look!'

Ahead of them lay a very large encampment, the largest any of them had seen, a great many huts within a wooden pallisade, smoke rising from fires where women were preparing the evening meal. Wild-eyed children scampered everywhere, not a few of them with red hair, and they paused to stare at the newcomers, jabbering away as they passed through the camp. Men and women gathered round, and as always it was the King who drew all eyes to himself.

'We may be fugitives,' Cefn said stoutly, 'but he will never look anything but a king.'

In the centre was a big wooden building, the roof thatched, a door at one end open wide. Caractacus was ushered in and Cefn, Beric and Jorst followed ahead of the rest, considering it their duty to attend him and pushing two curious Brigantes out of the way in the process. But inside they came to a sudden halt. Cefn, remembering the the King's house at Camulodunum, saw that this too was a palace, for he could hardly call it less. The walls were hung with shields and spears, with gold chains and strips of brightly coloured cloth; on the long table in the centre were shining silver jugs filled with ale, bowls ready for the meat that was being roasted, the smell of it tantalizing to hungry men. In the hall, awaiting their supper, were the tribe's noblemen, dressed in colourful tunics with flowing moustaches and beards while below them were the lesser men, noisy and shaggy, talking and arguing, and hunting dogs running freely, pushed and kicked out of the way by all and sundry. The children were mostly dressed in skins stitched into rough tunics and several were engaged in playing with wooden skittles, but they stopped to stare at these strangers, one child gazing, finger in mouth, at the leader. Marched the length of the hall Cefn saw there, on a wooden platform raised above the earth floor, a curious stone chair and sitting on it a startling woman. She had red hair streaming loose below the binding of a gold fillet and when she rose she was seen to be tall and generously built. Her gown was crimson trimmed with gold thread, her arms encased in gold bracelets, a white bearskin cloak hanging from her shoulders. Brilliant and very hard blue eyes swept over the refugees before coming to rest on Caractacus.

'You are the Chief of the Catuvellauni?'

'I am,' Caractacus answered proudly, 'and King since the death of my father at Roman hands. You are Queen Cartimandua?'

But it was not really a question, Cefn thought. How could she be otherwise?

'You are still in arms?'

'I am,' the King repeated the brief phrase.

'But,' her gaze swept round again, 'with few followers.'

'I have been accustomed to lead a great host,' he answered proudly, 'With my own tribe and the Silures in Wales, the Ordovices further north, I have harassed the Romans often enough, but this time they sent a large army. We were overcome a few days ago. However, I will raise another army and am come for your help, most gracious Queen.'

For a moment they measured each other. Sustaining a long gaze she took in the magnificent stature of her visitor, the strong sunburned arms flecked with golden hairs and clasped by bracelets, the lean face, the firm mouth. There was a gleam of appreciation as at last she said, 'I will need to know more before I send my Brigantes into battle against the Romans. They have not yet come as far north as this.'

'They will,' was Caractacus' terse comment. 'What the Roman sees he covets.'

'Perhaps.' Her eyes narrowed. 'You are welcome, King of the Catuvellauni. We will eat together.'

There was a sudden bustle in the hall, as serving men and women hurried about with great platters of meat, pitchers of mead and ale, slabs of flat bread. A great cauldron of potage was set in the middle of the long table where men were now pushing for places, the more important at the top. There were some squabbles, one importunate fellow pushed off his bench to tumble on the floor among the snapping dogs, everyone seizing what he wanted. Only at the high table was there some deference paid to the Queen.

Cefn was uncertain what to do. Usually he, with Beric, attended Caractacus, standing behind him and serving his needs, only eating their supper when he dismissed them, but perhaps here the Queen would order her own attendants to serve the guest. However, Caractacus, sensing the uncertainty, beckoned the two young men to their usual places, Cefn seizing a pitcher of wine from a reluctant servant as he went. Beric brought bread for their master and a faint smile lifted the Queen's lips.

The talk, most of which Cefn understood though the Queen spoke with a strange accent, was naturally of the Romans and what to do about them. 'They must be driven out,' Caractacus maintained. 'All of us must band together. They shall never take our land from us.'

One of the highborn men, his ringed fingers twisted around a mug of mead, spoke mockingly. 'You have had a taste of their methods, King Caractacus. Their army is well trained, well armed – what do we have?'

'Our spears, our swords, our courage,' a fierce young man put in. 'And our war chariots. Have you seen them, Chief?'

'I have,' was the King's brief reply and Cefn thought of the great vehicles he had seen in the courtyard with their huge, shiningly evil spikes sticking sideways out from the wheels to slice a man's leg off. A terrifying weapon, was Cefn's reaction and he hoped he would never confront one in battle.

An older man said, 'I was in the south when Caesar came and we couldn't stop him. Only our weather drove him away.'

'All he came for was to be given some of our pearls, our silver and our gold. By the gods, he has surely enough!' another warrior exclaimed. 'But the Romans are greedy, may they be cursed for ever. They take and take.'

'But they trade,' a white-haired man joined in the talk. 'They need our tin, our precious metals and our corn and they pay for those. What do you think, King Caractacus? Would we not be wise to make peace and trade with them?'

Caractacus paused, looking down at the remains of the duck he had dismembered. Deliberately tearing a piece of bread he mopped up the herb-flavoured juice in his bowl before he answered. 'You mistake the matter. Trade must be from a position of strength, not as a conquered people. If we are beaten, they will take what they want anyway. If we stand up to them they will barter with us.'

'And you, King Caractacus, have driven them off more than once,' one of the noblemen put in with a courteous gesture towards the guest.

'And will do so again. But I need men, weapons, chariots. Shall I find them here?'

A dozen voices answered, 'Aye, Aye,' while others shook their heads. The white-haired man spoke up, saying, 'I have lived my life fighting for us Celts. I've lost three sons, and two grandsons to Roman swords. No more, I say, no more!'

'The fight has gone out of our old men,' a belligerent fellow jeered. 'What do you say, most noble Queen, will you give your young men leave to join the King, with yourself at our head in your chariot?'

She had been listening intently to all this talk, her penetrating eyes moving from one to the other. 'It is a matter than must be debated,' she agreed smoothly. 'We will speak of it tomorrow.'

He was not sure why, but Cefn detected a menace in her voice and felt uneasy. When she rose he stood back respectfully, watching as the men at the high table dispersed. Bearskins were laid out on the floor for sleeping and down the hall the trestle table was dismantled and put against the wall so that men, women, and children, could settle themselves for sleep. Two of the older serving men stayed by the fire to take it in turns to keep it alight during the night. Except for one or two of Caractacus' senior men, the rest were taken out to be housed in huts around the courtyard. Only the Queen and Caractacus remained together by the table. 'We have much to talk of,' she said in a low voice, 'and I am glad you have become known to me, Chief of the Catuvellauni. We are well matched, I think.' She was looking directly at him, letting her gaze sweep over his strong body, herself only a few inches shorter and an equally impressive figure. Then she added, 'You may lie with me on my couch tonight.'

Cefn, who with Beric was still waiting in the shadows for any request from their chief, caught his breath at these astonishing words. They seemed more an order than a request, and casting a surreptitious glance at the King he wondered how he would answer.

As always Caractacus measured his words. Then in a low voice for her ear only he said carefully, 'You are gracious, noble lady. I esteem you mightily as a great leader of your people, but while my wife is a captive in Roman hands I have made a vow not to pleasure myself elsewhere. Her rescue is my sole desire.'

Terrified, yet at the same time proud of his Chief, Cefn wished himself at the other end of the hall, not daring to look at the Queen. But to his astonishment she shrugged and turned away. Yet he thought her answer ominous.

'You are a man of high notions, my friend, but I am a woman and a Queen, who does not grant favours lightly. Sleep where you will.' She threw these words over her shoulder and crossing to a recess hidden by hangings, went in to her own bed, two young women hurrying after her.

Caractacus stood where he was for a moment and then became aware of his paralysed henchmen. 'Find a place to sleep,' he said curtly and making his way to a corner where skins and covers were laid out threw himself down and prepared for sleep.

'We had better stay close,' Beric said. 'I don't trust her.'

'Nor do I,' Cefn answered, and they slept against the wall below the platform, as near as they dared. Jorst joined them and hearing what had happened, his response was a snort.

'Ye gods, I'd not like to lie with that woman. More likely you'd get a knife in your back if she'd a mind to it.'

Three very tense days followed. Caractacus went hunting with several noblemen, Cefn, Beric and Jorst attending him. He cocked an eyebrow at his youngsters as he gathered up spear and knife.

'Are you watching my back?' he asked, in some amusement.

'Yes,' Jorst said stolidly, and Cefn added: 'Wherever you go we'll guard you.'

Caractacus laughed outright. 'Oh, I am well served with three younglings to take on my enemies!'

'Do you think the Brigantes are our enemies?' Beric put the question hesitantly. Like Cefn, to serve Caractacus was all he cared for.

'Who knows?' the King answered, weighing the spear in his hand only to reject it and pick up another from the pile in the courtyard. 'But we need them. In the mean time we hunt a four-footed foe.'

'I wish we'd not come here,' Jorst muttered. 'We'd have done better to stay in the west with the tribes there, or what's left of them.'

'What do you know?' Cefn turned on him. 'More than the Chief?'

A Brigantian youth came up to them. He had red hair and a belligerent look. Choosing a large spear he glanced at Cefn and said, 'Too heavy for you, eh? You don't look as if you could throw it.'

'I may not be very big,' Cefn retorted, 'but I fought in a battle a week ago. Have you done that? I'll wager you haven't. You're all talk.'

The youth threw down the spear and launched himself at Cefn. There was a few minutes of satisfying scrapping, for small though he was Cefn was strong and rightly judged the Brigantian. He had him on the ground when a hand seized him by the back of his tunic and dragged him off, while an older Brigantian hauled his assailant away.

'Enough,' Caractacus said sharply. 'What use are you to me if you brawl like dogs over a bone?'

Cefn went scarlet and followed in silence as his master strode off.

'You are a donkey,' Beric told him. 'Fight such stupid fellows if you must but not almost under the feet of the Chief.'

They returned with two deer slung from poles, as well as a wild boar and two smaller pigs. 'Good food for a few days,' a Brigantian told the Queen and she ordered a feast for the following evening. But there had been no further discussion as to what should be done, Caractacus' request smoothly put aside. There seemed to Cefn to be an atmosphere in the hall as they assembled for the feast, as if they were being watched. And he noticed that the rest of the King's men were being assembled to eat their meal outside by one of the fires. Something was going on, he was sure of it. Had the Queen taken mortal offence at his King's refusal to lie with her? Why had she made the offer?

During the meal Cefn stood as usual beind his King, ready to serve him, and thankful that the talk at the high table was on safer lines, old wars, of trading, of building more houses and roads. A little lulled by this, when he was no longer needed he prepared to enjoy the feast. The slain animals had been roasted, there was wine and mead and ale in plenty, freshly baked bread, roasted apples smothered in honey, all of it appetizing, and after a while Queen Cartimandua said amiably, 'Go down to the board, young men, and eat your fill. My own will serve your master.'

There was no mistaking her tone, however friendly. One did not, it seemed, argue with the Queen. Caractacus gave them an imperceptible nod and they went down into the body of the hall, where the food was piled high. Sitting together they stuffed themselves hungrily, and drank deep. The ale was strong and Cefn always seemed to have a full cup, various hands refilling it from the big pitchers. The feast grew riotous, there was singing and laughter, talk and shouts, arguments, friendly and otherwise. The firelight flickered and across the hall Cefn saw a girl. She too had red hair and he wondered if she was one of the Queen's children that they had heard about, though Cartimandua had no husband.

The girl's yellow robe fell from the neck over large breasts and Cefn had a sudden desire to fondle them, to lay his head there. She was looking towards him, a lazy provoking smile on her full mouth. He turned to see if she was directing it at anyone else, but it seemed not. He hesitated for barely a moment. Amid the wildness of the feast, in the hot light of the fire, he saw Beric fondling another girl, while Jorst had been drawn away to play at dice with several others. He wouldn't do well, Cefn thought, he looked too drunk.

Almost stumbling over a lurcher chewing his discarded bone of pork, and aware that he too was more than half drunk, he made his way over to the red-haired girl. For a moment they stood looking at each other. He put out a hand and touched her, and then with barely a pause she put her mouth to his in a manner that sent his blood racing.

'Come,' she said with a tempting smile, and took his hand to lead him outside. It was a clear night, the harvest moon low and bright. The cold air cleared his head a little but only briefly. In a shelter leaning against the wall of the hall was a place for animals in bad weather. None was there tonight and she led Cefn inside where it was dark and hidden. There, sinking back against the straw she pulled him down beside her, putting her arms round him as he bent to caress those large warm breasts, to lay his head on them. In turn she moved her hands about his head, sending fire into him until there was no sense left in him. He had never felt quite like this, previous fumblings paling into insignificance.

Astride her now, almost crowing with delight in his manhood, he took her triumphantly, lost himself in her until he collapsed into a sleep of inebriated bliss.

When he woke, hours later, it was to a sudden and inexplicable sense of danger. He was alone. Below his head he felt the vibration of many marching feet, a sound he instantly recognized and springing up he ran out. The open space was filled with men gesticulating, shouting, as a long line of Roman soldiers marched across it and into the hall, some with diagonal spears holding back the tribesmen, though these seem to have been told to make no trouble.

Catapulted from the pleasure of the night into fear, Cefn pelted across the courtyard, pushing his way through the curious crowd of Brigantes, dodging the Romans streaming into the hall. One struck him aside but he was on his feet and making for the platform. Ye gods, what were they doing here? Coming in without hindrance? Terror and fear for his Chief shook him.

At a glance he saw that none of his fellow tribesmen were in the hall, presumably they were herded outside, but Beric and Jorst were scrambling up, shaking off the fumes of last night's carousal, only to find themselves seized, Roman spears at their throats. On the raised part of the hall a dozen men had surrounded Caractacus where, roused from sleep, he stood with his back against the wall. The Queen stood aloof, watching the capture of her guest with an oddly satisfied look.

Cefn flung himself foward, shrieking, 'Don't! Don't! Oh, stop!' Hurling himself at the nearest Roman he too was seized and thrown aside like a tiresome child. Once again he fell heavily and was pushed beside Jorst and Beric, two Romans standing menacingly over them. Beric was nursing a cracked skull.

'Oh what have we done?' Cefn cried out. 'How could we let him be taken?'

'Don't you see?' Jorst shook him. 'That fiendish woman. She set her people on to separate us last night with women and drink. It was all planned to keep us from the King.'

'Why, why? Not surely because he refused to bed with her?'

Beric looked at him severely. 'That was only part of it. She wants to deal with the Romans, not fight them. You've only to look round this place to see her greed for gold. I wonder what her reward will be?'

They had not long to wait to find out. The Romans were bringing their royal captive down into the body of the hall now, amid the jeers and yells of the Brigantes, where he stood proud and dignified to face them all. And Cefn, looking at him, wished he had died before letting this happen. 'We failed you,' he cried out. 'We weren't there when you needed us.'

'Lad,' the King gave him a brief warm look. 'Do you think I'd have wanted you slain? This was base treachery. Look!'

At the far end of the hall half a dozen Romans were entering carrying two great iron clad chests. These they set down and opened. Inside one lay gold and silver coins, in the other gleaming jewels, bracelets and pendants, fillets fit for a Queen's adornment.

'She sold him,' Cefn could hardly bring out the words. 'How could she be so – so –' he could think of nothing bad enough to say of her, tears of anger and fury running down his face

Queen Cartimandua came down into the centre of the hall and bending dipped her hand into one chest, letting the coins run through her fingers, into the other to pick out a large pearl set as a brooch, letting it sparkle in the freshly kindled firelight. 'A Queen's bargain,' she said and looked across at the man she had betrayed. 'You are a fool, Caractacus, not to have known where your good lies.'

Her double meaning sent an angry flush to his cheeks. 'Not with you, lady.' He threw the words at her. 'I am glad I did not ally myself, in any way, with a scheming fickle whore.'

Her breath hissed. 'Take him out, take him away. Do what you like with him – hang him if you wish.'

The Roman commander, listening to this exchange, put an end to it, by stepping forward to say 'I am Tribune Marcus Ostorius Scapula, son to the Governor of Britain. He sent me in order to see our bargain sealed, but I do not know what will be done with the prisoners. My father has sent to the Emperor in Rome to know his pleasure.'

'Let him be put in the circus there,' she commanded, having

learned enough of the Roman language to deal with them. 'Let your gladiators make an end of him.'

Marcus Ostorius was a giant of a man, dark-haired, with firm features, the oak-leaf wreath that he wore as a fibula to fasten his scarlet cloak the highest award that could be won for bravery. Having summed up the situation, for his own preference he would have preferred to ally himself with the famously brave King of the Catuvellauni. What might they not have achieved together in this country of mists and dark forests and untold riches? Instead he had to deal with this perfidious woman. Coldly, he said, 'His fate is in the hands of the Emperor. You have your part of the bargain.'

She dipped her hand again into the box of gleaming precious stones and picked out a another large pearl, though not set in anything. 'Take this to the Emperor,' she said loudly, 'a token of a Queen's good will.'

Marcus took it, his face betraying an expression of disgust, but he merely said, 'It shall be handed to him,' and then turning his back he nodded to the centurion to march the captives marched away down the hall.

On the way Cefn, prodded by a spear, saw the girl who had lured him out last night. He understood it now and shouted at her. 'Bitch! Treacherous whore! I wish I could kill you.'

She laughed jeeringly at him and that laughter seemed to pass through him, stiffen him. His life might end in the courtyard, or wherever he was taken but if he survived, by all the weird gods of the woods, he swore to himself that he would come back and avenge this terrible morning's work. But for the moment he and the others were tied, roped together, to march out between lines of Romans, behind their betrayed leader.

It was some months later that the British prisoners arrived in Rome. For Cefn and his companions the voyage was a new experience and he would have enjoyed it enormously if it had not been for the circumstances. But at least at the Roman fort of Londinium, on the bank of a great river, the King and his wife and daughter were reunited. She was a quiet determined lady, matching her husband in dignity, and at this reunion when she had thought never to see him again she stood proudly beside him, ready to share his fate. The only lighter moment was when his little daughter, thrown up on his shoulder laughed and cried aloud in delight, unencumbered by thoughts of the future. Caractacus' brother, Cunobel, shared the reunion and later sought all the details of what had happened from Cefn and the others.

Marcus Ostorius was a courteous captor. He treated Caractacus with respect, invited him to his table and saw him housed in a cabin next to his own. Cefn sensed he did not want to see his prisoner thrown to the wild animals in the Roman circus. The rest of the prisoners were kept on deck but reasonably fed. Cefn was glad he was not one of the slaves handling the massive oars, their legs in chains, and the horrid thought struck him that possibly he and Beric and Jorst might be sent to serve on the galleys.

Disembarking at Ostia they were marched through a pleasant countryside of farms and villas, dark-leaved trees and vineyards. So far Marcus had refused to shackle his noble prisoner, but now at the outskirts of the city, with obvious reluctance, he had the chains set on him, while Marcus himself mounted a magnificent war chariot to lead the procession. His men tramped behind, the Catuvellauni in their midst, while they bore banners, the great SPQR standard, others with golden snakes twisted around poles, still others blowing trumpets to announce their coming. In front of them girls scattered flower petals under the hooves of the white chargers that pulled the chariot. All the panoply of a Roman Triumph was here, the people lining the streets to cheer them forward. And there were wonderful streets here, fine buildings, libraries, law courts, meeting places of all sorts. The Catuvellauni gazed in amazement.

'I never dreamed . . .' Cefn began and for the life of him could say no more, only stare, as the gleaming sand-coloured stone houses and the shops took his breath away. He had never seen wine and fruit, eggs and cheese and vegetables laid out for sale, counters inside some shops for silk and cloth of all kinds, the men and women lining the way well dressed, some in white togas, the women in charming gowns, with hair well dressed and curling about their foreheads. It was a world none of the prisoners had ever envisaged. They were .narched towards some steep steps that led to a pillared platform, part of the royal palace and open to the sunny Italian skies. There was a throne set here and on it, in a white toga, sat the Emperor Claudius. If he had not been Emperor, Cefn might have thought little of him, as an unimpressive, rather ugly little man, but he saw only the power and the pomp of Rome.

Marcus Ostorius dismounted and himself led the captive king up the long flight of steps to come to a halt at the top. There he presented his captive, without excessive triumph and in a courteous manner, for during the long journey the two men had grown to respect each other.

Predictably it was Caractacus who spoke first as he faced the Emperor of all the known world, and to the astonishment of the assembled courtiers who had looked to see a wild barbarian captive, it seemed that this King of a remote and beaten tribe was as proud and dignified as the man he faced. In a loud voice, he said, 'Had my lineage and rank been accompanied by only moderate success I should have come here as friend rather than prisoner. As it is, humiliation is my lot, glory yours. You want to rule all men, Emperor of Rome, but why should I and my people become slaves? We have done you no harm.' Claudius looked at him intently for a moment before answering, 'You are a King, Caractacus of the Catuvellauni. You have defended your own and you speak nobly.'

'Yet you want my death?'

Again Claudius paused, clearly impressed by the man facing him, shackled though he was. He beckoned Marcus to his side and they spoke quietly together. Then Claudius said, 'I think not. I cannot return you to your country where you would no doubt continue to wage war on my soldiers, but you do not deserve death. You and your wife and family shall be lodged on an estate nearby with servants for your needs. I believe you and I will have some pleasant converse togther.'

Caractacus had stepped back involuntarily, clearly staggered by this, though he was acute enough to see that he would still be a virtual prisoner,. His followers were scarcely less amazed. Marcus, however, was smiling broadly. Recovering himself, Caractacus said, 'You are generous, Emperor of the Romans. If I may have my three young attendants here –?'

Claudius nodded. 'I see no objection to that, if they will live by our laws.'

The King glanced at the three, a few steps below, waiting with his family, and at a look from him they bowed in agreement. That his Chief should think of him and Beric and Jorst at such a moment nearly unmanned Cefn, but he held back the threatening tears.

So they were not to die, nor was his beloved Chief to be made a spectacle! How he wished he could fling this unexpected end to their journey into Cartimandua's face, taunt the girl who had seduced him – but for the present, who knew what life in this amazing city might hold for him and the others?

It seemed Caractacus' thoughts were on the same lines. He looked all round at the brilliant scene, the buildings such as he had never seen before, the splendid Imperial Guard dressed in black and gold and encircling the platform, the courtiers and their ladies all in finest silks, a great crowd below gazing upwards. Then a slow smile creased his face.

'I wonder, most noble Emperor, that you who have all this, should covet our poor huts!'

CAPTAIN LEOPARD

L. Sprague de Camp

We now return to the growing impact of Christianity upon Rome.
In the following story, which is more of a reflection upon events,
L. Sprague de Camp questions the very origins of Christianity based
on the teachings of the philosopher Celsus who lived around AD
180. This is an original story, specially written for this anthology.
L. Sprague de Camp (b. 1907) has long been a noted authority
on the ancient world. Not only has he written five novels set in
Greece and Rome, starting with An Elephant for Aristotle (1958)
and including The Bronze God of Rhodes (1960) and The Arrows
of Hercules (1965), but he also produced several scholarly books
on the technology of the ancients, including The Ancient Engineers
(1963) and Great Cities of the Ancient World (1972).

This tale is based upon a lost work by the second-century Platonic
philosopher Kelsos or Celsus, who wrote a treatise called A True
Word, attacking Christianity and presenting the story of Panthera
and Miriam. We know most of the content of Celsus' work because
the Church father Origenes wrote a verbose attack on it, Against
Celsus, which survives.

Herondas waved me to the new table and chairs in his vinarium,
behind the counter. 'After all,' he said, 'you talked me into installing
them. Whether they are worth the extra rent I have to pay for the
space remains to be seen. Space in Damascus is hellishly costly.'
  I had scarcely sat down when this burly, gray-haired centurion

in full Roman legionary accouterments appeared. I knew he was a centurion by the transverse crest on his helmet.

Herondas instantly became the cringing courtier: 'Oh, Captain! I have just the place for you!' He waved to the other chair at my little table. 'I have some delicious Falernian . . .'

When the centurion made for the vacant chair, I rose, expecting him to want the table to himself. But he carefully laid his helmet on the table and said:

'No, no, sit down, my good man! There's no sense in having one of those fine chairs go to waste.' Then to Herondas: 'A *sextarius* of that Falernian, please.'

The accent of his Latin said 'Greek Alexandria!' as plainly as if it had been painted on his forehead. Since his manners were better than one expects of an officer in an army of occupation, I said:

'*Milete Hellēniká?*'

'Oh, good! You speak Greek,' he replied in that tongue. 'So there are at least two civilized men in Damascus. I am Gaius Julius Panthera, *Posterior hostatus* of the third cohort of the Sixth Legion Ferrata. In the original Greek it was *Pardalis*, meaning that big spotted cat they fetch from Africa for shows in the arena. But the Romans translated it when I enlisted. And you, my good sir?'

'Nobody; just Claudius Dion, factor for Maesius the importer. In Latin they bobtail my name to Dio. Pleased to meet you, Captain Leopard.'

By now the centurion had drunk a large goblet of Herondas' Falernian, enough to affect one's balance. But the centurion, being an old soldier, showed no effects. He signaled for a second, indicating one for me as well. While waiting, he said:

'Friend Dion, you may be just the man I am looking for. You see, my twenty years are up in a few days, so I am looking for a safe place to invest my *peculium*.' He meant his discharge bonus.

'You are not staying on, then?'

The centurion tossed back his head. '*Ouchi!* There's a rumor that the Ironclad Sixth is to be shifted back to Judaea, and I saw all I wanted of that country when we were posted there thirty years ago . . .'

For a while we talked of Maesius' business, with its far-flung import accounts and its profits and losses. Somehow Panthera's service in Judaea came up again. He said:

'Besides, going back there might subject me to certain – ah – domestic embarrassments.'

'Indeed?'

'Yes, sir! You see, I formed an attachment there to a Jewish girl.

L. SPRAGUE DE CAMP

She'd be an aging woman now, of course, but my present mate is looking forward to a proper wedding as soon as I'm paid off. She would take umbrage if my long-ago light-o'-love came back into our lives. My mate of many years is a fiery Galatian Celt. Are you married, Dion?'

'Yes. Three children, plus one that died of a sickness.'

'Then you know what I mean.'

'Sure. Who was this onetime light-o'-love?'

'Just a pretty little Jewish girl named Miriam, the betrothed of a carpenter named Joseph. During our love affair, she became pregnant. When her state became obvious, the carpenter dumped her. The Jews have an official procedure for breaking a betrothal, like a divorce, and the carpenter took advantage of it.'

'What happened then?'

'She took her infant, our baby son, to Egypt looking for work. This child she named Yeshua, a good Jewish name, which becomes *Jesous* in Greek and *Jesus* in Latin, since those languages have no *sh* sound.

'Anyway, I understand, this kid grew up in Egypt. Miriam managed to get him an education of sorts on her slim housekeeper's pay, at one of the temples, where they worship gods with the heads of lions, hippopotami, and other beasties. The priests who tutored the lad, finding him a promising youth, taught him some of the tricks they use to beguile their worshipers into thinking they can do real magic and miracles.

'In time, Miriam and Yeshua came back to Judaea. To make a living, Yeshua showed off some of his Egyptian tricks and soon had a following who would swear he could work genuine miracles.

'So, they reasoned, he must be some sort of demigod, with a divine father. Since his followers were mostly Jews, they got the idea that this divine parent must be Yahveh, the bad-tempered, bloodthirsty Judaean chief god. I've heard that, when they asked Yeshua about it, he gave evasive answers.

'Eventually all this talk of a half-divine son of Yahveh came to the ears of the Sanhedrin, a council of Jewish priests who had jurisdiction in some criminal and civil cases. Since a main tenet of Judaism is that Yahveh is the one and only real god in existence, you can see why they would not put up with this demigod fable.

'Of course, in the Mediterranean world we are used to demigods. Asklepios, the founder of medicine, they say was the child of Apollo and the mortal maid Koronis – unless this Koronis got herself pregnant the same way my Miriam did and then blamed it on the first god who came to mind. After all, if your daughter tells you she lost her virginity to a god, you don't dare punish her severely. She just might be telling the truth, in which case the god in question might resent your chastisement of one of his light loves.

'But the Jews are funny that way. Nowadays most educated people know that men make gods in their own image. As Xenophanes said, if horses had gods, those gods would have manes and hooves. So we civilized folk don't take theological disputes seriously.

'But things are different in this part of the world. Many Jews take their theology very seriously indeed, especially those who call themselves Pharisees. I wish we had more of them in the Sixth. They are fierce fighters and, I think, more trustworthy than the general run of folk. If you give one an order, in plain, definite language, he'll carry it out or die trying.

'But the Jews have persuaded the Emperors to excuse them from military duty. The reason they give is that they would have to swear Roman oaths, which they consider against their religion.'

'What became of Yeshua?'

'*Lipon* ... It's a sad story. The Sanhedrin persuaded the Procurator, Pontius Pilatus, to arrest him so they could try him for heresy. This is a serious matter to the Jews, and one convicted thereof is deemed worthy of death.

'Pilatus was a strict disciplinarian who went by the letter of the law, and a strong believer in doing things the old Roman way. He had caused disturbances before – something about bringing army standards, with their little statues on poles, into Jerusalem. Some Jews thought that an outrage, violating their ancient prohibition of works of art. When there were riots, with people sworded to death, Rome sent Pilatus a warning to be more careful of these people's religious sensitivities.

'So his soldiers rounded up young Yeshua, who had been promoting some kind of reformed Judaism, with doctrines of extreme altruism. If someone assaulted you to rob you, he preached, you shouldn't resist but let him have his way. To any manly Greek – or Roman, either – that would seem crazy advice; but that's what they say he said.

'After a hearing, Pilatus said he did not think Yeshua had committed any offense grave enough to merit punishment. But the Sanhedrin made a fuss about the heretic's violation of their sacred creed. So Pilatus, rather than risk another riot, gave in and let the fellow be crucified.'

'What became of that Procurator?'

Panthera shrugged. 'He was recalled to Rome when some people complained about him to the Emperor. You know how things are.

Under the Empire, anyone who gets into a position of authority at once becomes the object of plots, conspiracies, and complaints, whether he has done anything wrong or not.

'Anyway, Pilatus survived until Emperor Tiberius died and Gaius, the crazy one, succeeded him. During that character's reign, Pilatus killed himself – though whether the mad Emperor ordered him to do so, or whether he simply got tired of life in imperial Rome, where everybody's hand is out for a bribe, I know not.'

'What became of this Miriam?'

Panthera shrugged again. 'No contact for many years. Twenty-odd years ago, I was quite besotted with her. I said I'd support her as my concubine until my hitch ended, and then I would legally marry her.

'You know, I suppose, that the divine Augustus ordained that soldiers may not marry during active service. The reasons they give for the law, such as the fact that soldiers can be ordered anywhere in the Empire, you probably know. But for individuals it can become damned inconvenient. One can for a small bribe, however, usually find a centurion willing to let the soldier and his woman go through some little local barbarian rite of marriage.

'I had just been promoted to *optio*, but even the extra pay didn't convince Miriam. No, the real objection was that I was of the *goyim*, the non-Jewish nations. A proper Jew looks down upon all such people much as we Greeks look down upon all non-Greeks as barbarians. Living in sin with a real Jew would have been bad enough; but with a "gentile" it was out of the question.

'I even looked into the possibility of becoming a Jew myself. But I should have had to spend endless hours studying their hairsplitting laws under one of their teachers, follow their complicated dietary rules, and undergo that disgusting mutilation of my personal parts that they insist on. Besides, since I couldn't prove direct descent from Abraham, it would have made me only a second-class Jew and would have interfered with my military duties. So my centurion would never have allowed it.

'So there we were. When we parted finally, she said she really loved me, too; but the obstacles were imposed by their irascible god, Yahveh, and there was nothing to be done about it. She was going to Egypt, taking our little son with her, for she had heard that well-born Egyptian women don't go in for swarms of slaves the way Romans do. They will hire people like her, poor free women, as housekeepers, to sweep and clean and make the beds and mind the children and wash the dishes. Besides, the city she was going to had a substantial Jewish settlement, with a temple and all. So that was that.'

The centurion gave me a funny little crooked smile. 'I sometimes wonder what would have happened if Miriam had remained in Judaea. I should have been – I suppose you might say – the stepfather of a demigod. It would be interesting to find out, but of course it's too late for that.

'I wonder, too, what would have happened if the Sixth had still been stationed in Judaea when young Yeshua and his mother came back from Egypt. I might have come to know the lad, and perhaps I could have steered him away from some of his impractical notions.

'Then again, perhaps not. You know how young men are, sure they know everything and that nothing a man of the older generation has to say could have anything to do with the real world of their own time.

'It might not have been so impossible if he had had a real, civilized education. But his upbringing had been narrowly Jewish. I'd wager he thought the world was flat and that he had never even heard of people like Aristotle and Demokritos, who investigated the world to find out how it actually worked.'

'What of that carpenter Miriam was betrothed to before she took up with you?'

'I daresay he's long dead. He was a widower, old enough to be Miriam's father, with a houseful of children by his first wife. Needless to say, they would not have been friendly to me, or to young Yeshua either – though I believe that, after Yeshua's execution, one of that family, a certain Yakov, was converted to Yeshua's following and became a leader of the Jerusalem faction of the sect.

'This was not only after Yeshua's death, but also after that Jew from Tarsus, who Romanized his name to Paulus, went around preaching a complicated new theology to support the Yeshuites, or as they are now called, Christians, meaning followers of the Anointed One.

'This Paulus voyaged all over the Inner Sea, they say, carrying his message and starting up little groups of Christians in the cities he visited. He must have been a man of extraordinary energy and magnetic personality, though I confess the logic of his complex theology escapes me. But then, it seems likely that it would also escape anyone brought up on Aristotle, as I was. So I am sure these Christians will prove just one more little sect, which will soon fade away and be forgotten.

'Now tell me more about Maesius' business. I really should not talk so much about my personal affairs. The barbarians say that the Greek national vice is not sodomy but garrulity.'

'But about Maesius' business: you understand, of course, that I would not sign any hard-and-fast agreement on the basis of a conversation in a wine bar. I shall want to look around for other possibilities first.'

Panthera was evidently a cautious fellow, which made him a likely partner for Maesius. The importer was getting old and did not have a son to break in to the business. After another hour, with the help of Herondas' wine, we had pretty much roughed out an agreement, provided that I could sell the idea to Maesius. He would of course want to meet Panthera himself before committing himself to anything.

And that, essentially, is how I came to be the factor for the partnership of Maesius and Panthera. When Maesius dies, Panthera has promised me his place. When the centurion became a full partner, he asked me not to discuss the tale of him and Miriam, on the ground that it would be bad for business.

'I've dealt with religious enthusiasts,' he told me. 'One thing I do know is that it does no good whatever to argue with them, no matter what evidence you adduce. They will brush it aside and sometimes go for you with a dagger, to punish you for casting slights on their sacred beliefs. If they kill you, Christians are sure the world is about to end any day now – certainly before Roman law could bring you to book. So what have they to lose?

'Can you imagine what it would do to the trade, with a squad of pious Jews screaming "Heretics!" at a squad of Christians, who scream back: "Unbelievers! Atheists!" Then someone starts picking up our merchandise and throwing it . . .'

SWORD OF FREEDOM

E. C. Tubb

Gladiatorial combat is one of the most lasting images of ancient Rome. It is perhaps difficult to imagine how the Romans, who seemed so civilized and pleasure-seeking on the one hand, could be so brutal and savage on the other. The Emperor Claudius, one of the better emperors of the first century, took immense delight in studying the expressions of the victims in the arena as they died. In the following story, E. C. Tubb (b. 1919) gets inside the mind of a gladiator who has become the champion of Nero. The story has been extracted and revised from Tubb's novel Atilus the Gladiator *(1975).*

I was in the exercise yard of the Ludus Magnus when Agonestes brought the news. Before me stood a post as thick as a man's body, the timber wrapped with straw which flew in chaff beneath the impact of the gladius I swung against it. Victory in the arena and the adulation which came with it had made me soft. There had been too many parties, too much wine, good food, lack of exercise. That time was over and I needed to regain my former condition if I hoped to survive. The Great School held the equipment for me to do it. The equipment and the grim reminder of what would happen to those who grew careless or forgot their status as slaves: the whipping block, the stocks, the cross on which rebels were crucified. Something I had witnessed and could never forget and straw flew thicker as anger rose within me. If only the post was Rome itself. If only I could kill it with a single blow.

Dreams – Rome was eternal.

'Atilus!' The Greek was excited as he came to stand at my side. 'You've heard that Claudius is dead?'

'Yes.'

Sweat covered my body and ran into my eyes, blurring my vision. The post became a man, balding, weak-legged, grotesque in his regalia. Claudius, who had invaded Britain, whose soldiers had conquered my people, raped and killed my mother, who had sold me into slavery to become a gladiator. A man regarded as little more than a beast. One destined to fight or die for the amusement of the mob.

Mushrooms had killed him, so the rumours had said. A dish of them, one larger and more tempting than the rest. Agrippina had eaten from the same dish leaving the best for the Emperor. After eating he had fallen into convulsions and died despite the ministrations of his physicians.

'But have you heard the rest?' Agonestes stepped closer. 'The Praetorian guard have proclaimed Nero the new Emperor. The Senate has bowed to their demands and accepted him. It was done by bribery, of course, a fortune was shared between the officers and men and more has been promised.'

The sword froze in my hand. 'Are you certain of that?'

'I had it from Paccius.' His patron would know the truth. Hesitating he added, 'You were close to Nero, weren't you? His servant, wasn't it? His companion?'

He was being kind. I had attracted Nero's attention and had been used to entertain at his parties and to protect his person when wandering the city at night. I had even saved his life. In return he had sworn to grant me my freedom. A theatrical gesture performed before the lares and having little substance for, as an Imperial slave, my freedom was not his to grant. Nor was my presence longer required. Shortly afterwards I had abruptly been returned to the school.

Agonestes told me more. Agrippina had been cunning. Not only had she won the support of the Praetorian guard, she had also arranged for Nero to marry Octavia, the daughter of Claudius, and so enhance her son's position. The marriage-promise had won over reluctant Senators. Britannicus, the son of Claudius, had been pushed aside and my recent charge was now the ruler of Rome.

'Atilus!' Agonestes caught my arm. 'Are you well?'

'Yes.'

'Your face! You looked as if you'd just seen a vision.' His eyes were concerned as he examined me. 'The sun,' he decided.

'You've been overdoing the exercises. Let me get you into the shade.'

'I'm all right.'

'Well, you should know.' His hand touched my arm. 'Take care of yourself, my friend. Soon you could be back in favour.'

'I want only my freedom.'

'May it come soon.'

Smiling I returned the grip of his hand. Agonestes meant well and he couldn't know that I was as good as free. Soon now, surely, Nero would remember his oath.

My hope faded as the days passed. Great things were happening in Rome, but they washed over the school without leaving a trace. Men previously banished were returning to the city. Families which had been in disgrace now basked in favour. Crimes against the state were forgiven to those close to the new ruler. A holiday atmosphere pervaded the streets and valleys of Rome.

Grimly I concentrated on the exercises, rebuilding muscle and stamina, working until the heavy practice sword felt like a wand, the shield a scrap of parchment, the helmet a cap of wool. One road to freedom had seemingly closed, but another still lay open. To fight and win and win again until I gained the coveted rudis. The wooden sword which would give me all I craved to own.

One night Callus Caecina came to visit me in my room. The lanista was old enough to be my father and wise in the ways of the arena. He was wearing a dark cloak, a hood shielding his face, and was alone.

'I've news, Atilus.'

'Word from the Emperor?'

'In a way.' He sat on the edge of the bed, making no comment on my expectation of a personal message. 'I've been instructed to put you into the arena. A big munera has been arranged to celebrate the Emperor's marriage to Octavia. There'll be no trainers, whips or hot irons. The best of gladiators have been obtained and a point was made that you should be matched against a certain opponent. The chances –' He broke off then said, abruptly, 'I like you, Atilus, and I think you've earned better than what you're getting. I'll do my best, but the rest is up to you. Do you understand?'

He was trying to tell me something, but I couldn't guess what. A warning? But what need was there of that? I would fight and win and the rest would follow.

I drew in my breath as I realized what could be intended. Nero, dominated by his mother, would be advised not to free a gladiator, without apparent justification, especially one who had been his

personal guard. There would be gossip and those who suspected
Claudius had been poisoned would be alert for any suspicious acts.
Caution would account for the delay in keeping his promise. It was
essential for him to be discreet, but no one would think it odd that
a gladiator should be given the rudis.

And Nero would have kept his word.

Just prior to the munera it became obvious that things, for me,
were not normal. I was not permitted to join the others at the
customary feast held before the start of the games. I ate alone and
was kept in isolation. When I was due to fight, I was hurried to the
arena in a closed sedan.

It was the old amphitheatre built by Titus Statilius Taurus. The
preparation rooms were small and cramped, overcrowded now with
throngs of gladiators, trainers, attendants, officials and slaves. Under
the direction of Gallus Caecina I was hastily prepared. The helmet
with its masking lattice was the first item of equipment to be fitted
on me; normally it would have been the last. Flavus, the slave who
usually attended me, was nowhere to be seen.

I was alone, unrecognized, unknown.

As we moved towards the row of gods for me to make the
customary offering, Caecina who accompanied me, said, quietly,
'A man is a fool to neglect the gods. A bigger fool to forget the past.
Remember what you did the last time you fought. Ready now?'

A hint? If so its meaning eluded me. Everything had been
abnormal, the preparation, the obvious intention to keep me from
sight, all made no sense. If they had wanted to kill me then why
not poison my food or use a dagger in the night?

But why should anyone want me dead?

As we reached the opening of the Gate of Life the trumpets
sounded, clear notes echoing to the sky. The podium was thick with
dignitaries: ambassadors, prefects, magistrates, the Vestal Virgins,
the Emperor himself. Nero wore purple, his red hair curled and
oiled, touches of rouge brightening his cheeks. Rings weighed his
fingers and a naked boy crouched at his feet holding a lyre. Octavia,
his wife, sat at his right, a slip of a girl looking little more than a
child. On his left Agrippina dominated the scene.

On the sand, waiting, stood my opponent.

A retiarius as I was a secutor. Tall, a Nubian, long-limbed, eyes
like smoked amber, net and trident snug in his hands, his left shoulder
armoured, the apron of fine leather, the broad belt bright with silver
ornaments in the shape of a fish. A dagger rested in its sheath.

Selim – a man I had fought before.

No one shouted as I walked towards him and turned to lift

my sword in salute to the Emperor and his party. That added to the strangeness. Always before, since I had shown my worth, my amatores in the stands would yell their encouragement. Every proven gladiator had their followers, and I was no raw beginner, but a tried and tested fighter. The only explanation for the silence was that the assembled crowd didn't know who I was.

Now I realized why things had been handled as they had. I was an inconvenience, a nuisance, someone better out of the way. Nero? His mother? I looked to where she sat, remembering the task she had given me before I had been returned to the school. To buy a phial of something from a noted witch. Had it held poison? Had she used it against her husband? Reason enough to want me dead and where safer than in the arena?

And Selim would do the killing.

He was the perfect choice; I had beaten him once and he had been lucky to escape with his life. A thing he would never forget. He had been bested, humiliated, shamed before the crowd. His pride and reputation had been hurt and I had been the cause.

He sneered as he uttered the traditional chant.

'I do not hunt you. I seek a fish. Why do you swim away – Atilus?'

The name was spoken in a whisper, but loud enough to let me know that he knew who I was. To tell me, also, that I could expect no mercy. He would down me and kill me regardless of the verdict of Nero or the crowd.

The lash of his net was like the barb of his tongue, but I dodged it easily, standing poised on the balls of my feet, moving as the net fell to catch the thrust of the trident on my sword. Preliminary touches as we circled each other. Selim stood well clear. This time he wouldn't underestimate me and fall victim to his own conceit.

I edged close, cut, withdrew, feeling the sting of weights on my naked back. The trident darted at my eyes, but I wasted no effort in beating it aside. The lattice I wore protected them.

The protection which helped to even the odds between a retiarius and a secutor. The lash of a weight in an eye and the combat would be as good as over. The barbs of the trident thrusting at a naked face would engage the full attention of an opponent and make him vulnerable to the cast of the net. The weight of the shield would slow him down. The gladius with its straight blade was designed to thrust and chop, not to slash. The careful balancing of armour and weapons which made our combat an almost-even dance of death.

Almost – Selim still held the advantage.

He moved like oil, gracefully, his body gleaming in the sun. I

caught the flash from his armour, the lift of his left shoulder. I
saw the gleam of barbs and swung my sword as they came lancing
up to thrust at my neck. The edge slammed against the shaft and I
weaved, the thrown net hitting my shield, the trident stabbing again
at my exposed side.

Net and trident working in harmony, opposed by shield and
sword and rapid movement.

'Selim! Selim! Selim!'

The crowd yelled as he cast his net, the mesh opening, falling,
jerked to one side by the thong attached to his wrist. It touched my
helmet and settled over my shield, tightening as he pulled.

I turned to my right, the sword sweeping up and over, the edge
drawn back as it met the strands. A sica would have cut through
it; the gladius did little more than fray the mesh, lifting it up and
throwing it to one side.

The trident came at me, the barbs aimed for my thigh, clashing
as they hit my upraised greave.

A move which left him open, but standing on one foot I could
get little power into the blow without losing my balance. Even so
it would have cut his arm to the bone had he not lunged forward
to take it on the armour protecting his shoulder.

I spun as he passed me to run clear, to stand, panting, as he
faced me.

'You are fast, Atilus,' he said. 'Faster than you were, but still
not good enough to beat me. Yield now and I promise you a quick
ending.'

Talk to gain time, to distract my attention as he readied his net.

'Just then you almost fell. Luck alone saved you. How long can
it last? It is only a matter of time before you bite the sand.'

An experienced fighter talking from conviction. Down, I would
add another silver ornament to his belt.

Another life to Rome.

Then, as had happened before, it came.

There is a state of mind essential to anyone who fights in the
arena. A concentration, a dedication, a determination to win, to
kill. Anger and hate could help bring that about, but rage had to
be controlled, channeled, mastered and used as a tool.

The roar of the crowd dimmed, the faces, the straining bodies,
all vanished from my sight. Now there was nothing but Selim, a
man like a beast determined to kill me. Who would kill me unless
I killed him first.

Training would have given him certain reflexes, actions taken
without the need of conscious thought. A trait which had proved

its worth in previous bouts. He would rely on them, use them –
how could I turn them against him?

How to get in close so the sword could reach out and meet
living flesh?

I moved, noted his reaction, backed to advance again and repeat
the same move. The trident lifted to block the sword as my shield
rose to block the net. I exaggerated the movement, lifting the shield
higher each time, tilting it up and away from my body to expose
the naked flesh beneath.

Three times, five times – on the seventh he lunged.

I was ready. As the barbs stabbed at my torso I swayed to my right,
felt the shock and burn of metal and then I was moving forward, my
blade glittering as it flashed in the sun, the edge falling towards his
head, his face. A blow aimed to slash flesh and splinter bone. He
threw himself backward; the point slicing through his cheek and
opening his chest in a long, shallow gash.

'Habet!' The crowd yelled their appreciation of the wound as he
backed, sand pluming beneath his bare feet. The roar changed as I
followed, becoming wild, savage, and ugly. 'Verbera! Verbera!'

Strike! Strike! Smash the sword on living flesh and bone. Bury
the edge, the point, let blood flow like a fountain.

Kill! Kill!

The demand of Rome – the law of the arena.

Selim turned, taking a slash across the back as he raced over
the sand. A burst of energy which carried him beyond my reach
and gave him time to regain his stance. Then, like a whirlwind,
he attacked.

I felt the jar as the barbs hit my lowered helmet, the upper rim of
my shield. Powerful thrusts that would rip through the lattice given
time. All I could do was to divert the blows, knock aside the trident,
and lunge forward within its reach.

Twice I tried – the third time he trapped my blade.

As the sword slipped between the tines he twisted the shaft,
catching the weapon and tearing it from my hand to send it
spinning high in the air, to fall well to one side, hilt uppermost,
the point buried in the sand.

'Now, Atilus,' he gloated. 'You die!'

He spoke with certainty; arrogance made him slow to claim his
victory.

I feigned an attempt to run to the sword and he moved to stand
in front of it. That gave me time to rip the shield from my arm and
to send it, spinning, edge on towards his face. As he ducked I ran
forward, grabbed the end of the net, and pulled.

Trapped by the thong around his wrist, he staggered after me as I ran over the sand. I gave him no chance to use the trident. Once the net was taut I halted, swung the mesh in a circle and pulled him after it as if he was a weight attached to the end of a line. Intent on staying on his feet he threw aside the trident, snatched at his dagger, to slash free the thong.

Too late.

He was moving too fast and we were too near the surrounding wall of the arena. With an effort which took all the power of back and shoulders I swung him, released the net, sent him to crash headlong against the wall.

The crowd shrieked their delight as he fell, head and face a pulped mess, brains and blood showing grey and red on his skin and the sand.

A sight which triggered memory and, suddenly, I recognized Caecina's hint for what it was. Quickly I tore the helmet from my head the lattice from my face. Turning to where Nero sat I raised my arm in salute.

'Atilus!' The crowd had recognized me. Their shouts were like thunder. 'Atilus! Atilus!'

I saw Nero's eyes, his sudden start of recognition. He hadn't known. Now that he did I would surely be given my promised freedom. Then a warning yell rose from the crowd.

'Atilus! Behind you!'

A pair of Thracians were running towards me, armed with the curved sica, carrying their small, round shields both intent on my death. Agrippina's plan to eliminate me should I win the bout?

Anger burst in me like a flame. Selim was down, but his net was intact and his dagger lay close by. I snatched it up, freed the net, spun it as the Thracians drew near. It wasn't attached to my wrist and travelled further than they had expected, but one of them dodged to one side as it settled over the helmet and blade of his companion. As he paused, calculating his next move, I ran forward, stooped, snatched up a handful of sand, and threw it into his face.

Blinded he staggered back, trying to clear his eyes. Before he could succeed I was on him, my left hand gripping his right wrist, trapping his sword as I drove the dagger past his shield and into his stomach.

As he fell I ran to the trident lying on the sand.

The other man cut himself free as I reached it. He glanced once at his companion, then advanced, blade and shield at the ready, handling them both with trained skill. I responded with fury. My discarded helmet lay to one side. I turned the man so that his back was towards it, then forced him to retreat with vicious thrusts of the barbs. He met my attacks with calm efficiency, using shield and sica as a defence as he waited for the moment when I must weaken and give him his chance. One which never came. His foot hit the helmet and, as he toppled, I drove the trident into his eyes, the tines grating on bone as they passed through the sockets to penetrate the brain.

Tearing it free I raised the blood-smeared weapon and ran towards the podium where Nero sat.

'Your oath!' I yelled. 'Nero, remember your oath!'

He didn't hear me. He couldn't. From all sides came a sound unique to Rome; a screaming roar vented by hysterical men and women gripped in the frenzy born of the spectacle of blood and pain.

Then officials came to stand before the podium blocking those who sat in it from the threat of the trident. One negated as Gallus Caecina took it from my hand. He clapped me on the shoulder, his face wreathed in smiles.

'You've done it, Atilus! He's giving you your freedom. You've won the rudis!'

Nero held up the wooden sword, smiling as he rose to his feet, lifting one hand for silence. His voice was loud and clear as he made the presentation, but I didn't hear a word. I saw nothing but the wooden sword he held, uplifted, before throwing it at me to catch.

The rudis!

My freedom!

Around me rose the sound again, the cheers, yells, shouts and cries. The noise of the people. The voice of Rome.

THE LAST LETTER

Derek Wilson

The spread of Christianity throughout the Roman Empire was the work of the apostles, and none is more famous than Paul, originally Saul of Tarsus. At one time he was a persecutor of Christians, but on the way to Damascus had a vision of Christ that revealed that he was the man to take the Word to the Gentiles. Paul travelled throughout the Mediterranean world and is believed to have ended up in Rome, but just what did become of him has never been satisfactorily resolved. In the following story, Derek Wilson, a historian and author of the Tim Lacy art-world mysteries, sets another of the apostles on the trail of Paul.

Dear Theophilus,

Five years have passed since I attempted, at your request, to provide an orderly account of the spread of the message about the Kingdom of God from its beginnings in Jerusalem to its open proclamation in the capital of the Empire. I was an eye witness of many of the events I recorded then and, for the rest, I had information directly from those possessing first-hand knowledge. Nothing was hearsay; nothing gossip. My concern, as with my earlier report on the life and teaching of Jesus, was to present you with a true and trustworthy narrative.

I have not been impervious to your entreaties that I should continue the chronicle as far as our own troubled times, and, particularly, that I should record accurately what befell Paul after the lifting of his detention in Rome. Family business in Philippi and my own indifferent health prevented me for some time from complying with your request. It was only fifteen months ago that I realized that I must delay no longer. After the great fire in Rome, responsibility for which was unjustly fastened on the Christians, the vilest calumnies were spread from the centre to the very rims of the Empire. In the chaos of denunciations and persecutions many believers fled, carrying with them confused and confusing stories about Paul, Peter, Apollos and others. Thus it became imperative for me once more to set out upon my travels in search of the truth.

Even when I had ascertained all that I could I hesitated to write to you. The posts are frequently tampered with and my letter might have attracted to you the unwelcome attentions of over-zealous officials. Now that the arch-enemy of the Christians is dead by his own hand* and discredited it is safe to convey to you those facts which I have been able to gather. My own involvement in the work of God through his servants has always been insignificant but on this occasion I shall have to place myself at the centre of the action so that you will understand the remarkable happenings as I was able to unravel them.

I set out with extreme anxiety about Paul. Apart from one brief letter passed on to me by the church elders at Philippi, my only sources of information were rumours. Some claimed that he had died in Rome on Nero's orders; others that he was still in distant Spain; and I frequently came across reports that he had been seen in various locations – Ephesus, Crete (where he supposedly was being hidden by Titus, the leader of the churches on the island) and even – most unlikely of all considering his reputation there – Corinth. On one occasion when I visited Thessalonica, the elders there showed me with great pride a letter that one of their number had recently brought back from Asia. It was a copy of a message addressed to Timothy, whom you met as a young man when we stayed in your house all those years ago, and it purported to be from Paul. I scanned it eagerly for clues about our friend's health and whereabouts. Alas, it was a disappointment. I, who have taken down many letters at Paul's dictation, could recognize little of his style, and you may imagine my surprise when I read that I was among the writer's present companions. Parts of this missive may, indeed, have come from Paul or his immediate circle but they had certainly been mixed up with passages from other hands. In these times of discord, when few of the Lord's first followers remain to provide guidance, there are leaders who resort to all manner of stratagems

---

* Nero committed suicide in June 68.

to bolster their own authority. As you assuredly know, some have even claimed that Peter and others went from Jerusalem to Rome to organize the church there. I concluded that, rather than follow up any of these dubious leads, I should start my investigations in the place where I had last seen my dear friend.

I remembered very clearly the comfortable little house on the Caelian Hill with its garden running right up to the city wall. Here, for two years, Paul had held court in a manner scarcely less busy than that of the emperor. Day after day, Roman Christians, visitors from all over the world and even men and women from Caesar's own household visited us to receive instruction, convey gifts and messages and to pray with the prisoner. We waited for his accusers to come from Jerusalem with their false accusations of sedition but they never appeared. It was one thing to stir up mobs in Judaea and exert political pressure on weak procurators. It was quite another to confront a Roman citizen with cogent evidence before the judgement seat of Caesar himself. During the two years of Paul's incarceration I presented several petitions to the office of the Praetorian Prefect Burrus requesting that Paul's case be heard without further delay. However, it was only when the Prefect of the City and an official of the Praetorian guard made representations that the lawyers took action. The military and police chiefs complained about the waste of resources involved in keeping prisoners like Paul under house arrest.

By then Gaius Ofonius Tigellinus, the emperor's friend and no one else's, had taken over from Burrus. He heard the case personally in the justice hall of the Palatine palace. We could expect little from a man who had already begun a purge of Caesar's suspected enemies. Paul had prepared a detailed defence but instead had to listen to a long harangue from the Prefect. When the charge had been read Tigellinus called for the evidence to be presented. There was silence. The hall was packed, mostly with Paul's friends, but not a single person beneath the wide, star-decorated dome spoke up.

Tigellinus banged with his staff on the marble floor. 'I see this is another of these disputes between rival Jewish factions. You people seem to think you can waste the court's time with impunity. You have your own laws and legal processes. Use them! You, prisoner, stand forth!'

Paul stood before the Prefect, manacled to a centurion.

'All this is your doing. When this case was presented in Judaea you claimed the privileges of a Roman citizen. For some unaccountable reason the Procurator, the late Porcius Festus, supported your appeal to Rome. Why were you not content to stand trial in your own country?'

Paul spoke up in that high-pitched, cracked voice of his which held so many audiences spellbound. 'Your Excellency, I appealed to the impartial justice of Rome from the bias and violence of the Jewish Sanhedrin. They hate the followers of Jesus the Christ. Only recently news has come from Jerusalem of the murder of the leader of the Christian church there.'*

'You see, it is as I thought,' Tigellinus shouted. 'Petty disputes among pestilential, uncouth subjects. If I had been the Procurator of Judaea I'd have had the lot of you flogged and sent about your business.'

'It is not permissible to flog Roman citizens who stand condemned of no crime, your Excellency.'

Paul's boldness in thus addressing the chief justice shocked the entire court into silence. We all looked to see how Tigellinus would react.

For several seconds he stared, wide-eyed at the prisoner, his colour rising, his free hand tightly gripping the braided edge of his toga. 'You insolent little Jew! You dare to lecture me on the law? I'll tell you about Roman citizenship: it is squandered on vermin like you! There are far too many members of subject races granted precious privileges. People like you should be kept firmly in your place, alongside slaves and barbarians.'

I saw the familiar smile on Paul's face that meant only one thing, that he saw an opportunity to speak boldly about the Lord Jesus. 'You are right, most wise Tigellinus,' he began. 'It is proper that all men should know their place. Jew and Roman, citizen and slave, civilized and barbarian – we must all stand in the judgement hall of God. And he has appointed an advocate for us – Jesus Christ. He alone can plead our cause. He alone . . .'

'Silence!' Tigellinus was not to be lulled by that voice that had persuaded many to faith. 'There'll be no preaching of foreign blasphemies in my court room. Hold your tongue and listen to the sentence pronounced in *my* judgement hall. Paul, you have twenty-four hours to leave Rome. You are never to return – on pain of death. Guard, take him away!'

The rest of that day was a time of mingled joy and sorrow. A crowd of Paul's friends led him to the house of old Urbanus. They celebrated his release but grieved that he was to leave them.

* The Apostle James, the brother of the Lord, was stoned to death by a mob incited by the Sanhedrin.

Paul himself was jubilant. 'You see, brothers, how God answers our prayers. For months I have asked to be allowed to travel to the very edge of the world, to Spain, with the Gospel. Now, God not only releases me from bondage, but he pushes me forth on my journey without another day's delay.'

I was unable to share his enthusiasm. Paul was a man already past his sixtieth year. His physical strength was remarkable for a man of his age but his body bore the scars of many beatings and mishaps. The enforced rest of his imprisonment had brought the four humours back into balance, so that, in most respects, he was healthier than he had been when he came to Rome. But he was almost blind. I had couched the cataracts in both his eyes in the early days of his captivity but this had provided only a temporary respite. What he laughingly referred to as his 'thorn in the flesh' had not proved a serious disability as long as he was under house arrest. Even when he was not chained to a guard he could feel his way around his familiar confines. If, now, he was to set out on his travels again he would be totally dependent on his companions and he would be without the advice of his physician. I had ignored several urgent entreaties from Macedonia but I could not indefinitely set aside my family responsibilities and certainly I could not journey farther westwards. Paul understood my situation. Indeed, he urged me, on more than one occasion to return home. Yet, I still felt that I was deserting him.

The following day was the saddest of my life. Several of us brought Paul, riding in a cart, down to the port of Ostia, where he found passage on a ship carrying grain to Corsica. It was the only west-bound vessel leaving on the next tide. Paul would have preferred a more substantial ship, rigged and provisioned for a longer journey but since we were accompanied by a troop of the Praetorian Guard intent on seeing him clearly underway from Latium he had no choice. He had selected as his travelling companion Eubulus, a young Roman Christian who had been converted through Paul's preaching. I knew him to be an educated but robust fellow well able to withstand the rigours of the journey as well as the abuse and hardship that Paul's fearless preaching frequently attracted. More importantly I judged that he would cope with our friend's frequent changes of mood. Paul was a visionary leader, an inspiring teacher and a bold proclaimer of the Gospel but he was certainly not the easiest of men to live with.

An hour before the ship was due to sail Paul gathered us all on the quayside. He warned that persecutions would grow worse – and exhorted us to stand firm until the coming of the Lord Jesus. Then he prayed and bade us all farewell. Many wept, knowing that they would see him no more. Such were my memories as, five years later, I began my journey back to Rome.

I took ship to Cenchriae on the Isthmus of Corinth, planning, like most travellers, to cross to the port of Lechaion on the opposite shore. Unlike Paul, I was never a good sailor. Impatient voyager that he was, he habitually chose the quickest route to his desired destination careless of the consequences. He sometimes boasted about having been in four shipwrecks – or, rather, he boasted of the God who had preserved him in these calamities. I am of less value to the Almighty and prefer not to put him to the test. My dreams are still haunted by the terrifying, tempest-tossed days and nights we spent being driven across the central Mediterranean from Crete, before being cast up on the island of Malta. So you will understand, Theophilus, why I had no stomach for braving the stormy southern tip of the Peloponnesos.

My cautious itinerary involved a stay of several days in what our ancient poets aptly call 'wealth-corrupted Corinth'. It is not a city that I like. It seems to attract the worst elements of every one of the cosmopolitan communities drawn there by its agricultural and commercial affluences. There are temples to every conceivable deity, both Greek and foreign. Jewish shops with their overpriced goods dominate the agora. Bath houses and their attendant vices are everywhere and, to pander to the depraved tastes of Roman settlers, they have recently built an amphitheatre for gladiatorial fights and contests between wild animals.

It was not easy to seek out fellow Christians. Those that I knew or to whom I had introductions had either fled in the recent troubles or were cautious of any stranger who came asking questions about their meeting places or customs. It was in Corinth that I first learned of the revolt in Judaea. On my second day in the city I made my way to the synagogue, meaning to institute cautious enquiries about followers of the true Messiah. I found the small building boarded up and a notice nailed to it forbidding the assembly of Jewish people for any purpose. It was in a tavern out on the Lechaion road that I fell in with a group of centurions who reported the dismal events in Rome's least favourite and least successful province. They explained that a decree had been issued restricting the activities of Jewish communities to prevent them sending financial aid to the rebels. They were on their way from Italy to Syria with reinforcements for Gallus, the legate, and they told of troops being hastily conveyed from Parthia (with whom peace had recently been concluded), the eastern border, Spain and other parts of the empire to the latest trouble spot.

'We'll crush them this time, for sure,' one of them, a bulky Illyrian, insisted.

His colleague, a red-haired giant from one of the Gallic tribes, agreed. 'I did a tour there a dozen years back – my worst posting ever. Show me a Jew and I'll show you a crafty, stubborn fanatic. Have you ever been to Palestine, friend?'

I told him, cautiously, that I had visited the land.

'Then you'll know what a barren, dusty country it is. No city or town worthy of the name. The earth is so poor that it can't support its own people. That's why you find them all over the empire. They worship a primitive god who obviously hasn't done much for them. Yet they refuse the benefits of civilization and actually claim to be a chosen, favoured race, destined to rule the world. I don't know why we've put up with them so long.'

'Well, they're for it, now. The emperor has sent Titus Flavius Vespasian to suppress this revolt. He's a soldier's soldier. I served under him in Britain. He won't stand any nonsense. Mark my words, within ten years there'll be no Jewish land or people.'

As we talked I noticed that one of the centurions said little. Prompted by the Holy Spirit I surreptitiously made the sign of the fish in a puddle of spilled wine. Our eyes met briefly before I brushed the liquid from the table with the back of my hand.

He stayed behind when his companions left and we embraced eagerly. He was a young man, recently promoted, from the colony of Arles in Narbonese Gaul. I was excited to learn of his origins in the western empire and asked if he had heard anything of Paul. Yes, he said, fellow believers from his home town had written to him about eighteen months before to say that the great apostle had passed through Arles and preached in the agora. My new friend, whose name was Licinius Rufus, knew nothing of Paul's movements after that. It mattered not. The important fact was that I had a place to start looking, a place where Paul had been seen, alive and well, as recently as eighteen months ago. Licinius gave me the name of a contact in Arles who would be able to tell me more. The soldier, for his part, was eager to learn from me all that I could tell him about Jesus and, unlike his colleagues, was delighted to be going to the land where the Lord had taught, healed, suffered, died and risen to new life. I soon discovered that the young man had received little tuition since his baptism. We talked long into the night. I told him how Jesus, over thirty years ago, had prophesied those very evils which were now befalling his people; how he had spoken of false messiahs who would only lead their followers to destruction; how he had forewarned that Jerusalem would be surrounded by armies and overrun; how the great temple would be invaded by heathen soldiers and then totally destroyed. These, along with the persecution of Christians throughout the empire, were signs of the end of all things and the return of Jesus in the clouds. When would this happen, Licinius urged me to say, but I could only pass on to him the Lord's own instructions, 'Watch and pray for you do not know when the time will come.'

It was Licinius who provided my contact with Corinthian Christians. Before leaving Rome he had been given the address of a meeting place. It was in the cellar of a merchant's house near the newly built courtyard of Apollo, a place for public gatherings. On the last day of the week Licinius and I went to locate it, so that we would be in good time for worship the following day. As we watched we observed several people, singly or in pairs, enter the shop and make their way through to the premises at the rear. Eventually we presented ourselves at the door. We were greeted civilly if warily by the Jewish tradesman and his wife who introduced themselves as Herodion and Rachel. They indicated the rows of copper and bronze vessels on shelves within but regretted that, this being their holy day, they could not serve us. We revealed ourselves as Christians but this brought forth no warm welcome.

'You are Gentiles,' the swarthy Herodion observed. 'Have you, then, been circumcised into the faith?'

'We have been baptized,' I told him. 'That is all the Lord requires.'

'The Lord requires what is written in his holy law. What you speak sounds like the heresy of Paul, that Gentiles and Jews are equally acceptable to God. We want none of that nonsense here. We will be obliged if you will leave us.'

We left the shop and began to walk disconsolately along the street. After a few paces Rachel hurried after us. 'Bibulus, the potter,' she announced breathlessly. 'His house is alongside the east wall.' Then she retreated to her own home.

The following day, Sunday, we presented ourselves at the place the woman had mentioned and were joyfully received by Bibulus and over fifty believers who had gathered for the breaking of bread. It soon became clear what had happened in Corinth. The Christian community, always prone to factions and divisions, had recently been swamped by exiles from Palestine. Such Judaizers had always been Paul's most tenacious enemies, confronting him in public, working behind his back to subvert his teaching. Now they had taken over in Corinth, forcing out those who refused their 'purer', law-based religion.

We spent several happy hours in fellowship with those of the true faith. There was no one there who could give me any reliable information about Paul but I did meet a man who shared my concern for him. Manaus was an Asian Jew from the province of Lycia-Pamphylia. Like Paul he had studied in the university at Tarsus. Like me he was a doctor. I found him a charming and cultured companion with whom I had much in common. He was on his way to Rome to talk with the remarkable army surgeon, Dioscorides, and had stopped in Argolis to visit the famous Asclepieion at Epidaurus. What did I think, as a Greek and a Christian, about this ancient centre of healing associated with the pagan hero-god Asclepios, he asked.

It was a subject I had often considered and often discussed with Paul. My own studies, long before my conversion, had, of course been based on the philosopher-physicians such as Hippocrates, Aristotle and Theophrastus as well as the cult practices associated with the god of healing. My interest in Jesus had been first aroused by the stories believers told about the cures he achieved of several bodily and spiritual disorders. They certainly resembled the miracles claimed by those who prayed and made offerings at the temples of Asclepios and especially at the great sanctuary at Epidaurus. Manaus and I obviously had much to discuss. I suggested that he accompany me as far as Rome and he accepted.

My new companion was sympathetic to my feelings about the sea and readily agreed on the short Adriatic crossing to Brindisi rather than the long voyage around Italy to the port of Ostia on the far coast. Our journey from there along the Appian Way was, inevitably, hindered by the demands of patients. A physician cannot appear in a town or village without the maimed, the sick and those who fancy themselves sick requiring (sometimes *demanding*) attention. And here were we, *two* doctors, travelling together. News of our approach went ahead of us and it became the settled pattern that where we had resolved to spend a single night we ended up passing two or three days, setting broken bones, issuing drugs, blood-letting, prescribing diets and even performing minor operations such as tonsillectomy and treatment of goitre. Frequently our time was wasted by customers who, dissatisfied with the diagnosis one of us had given, paid a second fee to be examined by the other. Romans may sneer about medicine being a calling only fit for slaves and foreigners but they are eager enough for our services when their own health is impaired.

Long discussion on medical theory and observation of each other's working practices made plain fundamental professional differences between Manaus and myself. He was a Dogmatist, one who, having learned the principles enunciated by Hippocrates and certain Jewish masters, believed in their universal application. Disease, he asserted, was physiological and, since all bodies were, medically speaking, identical, so treatment could not vary from patient to patient. When I asked how he explained the connection Jesus made between disease and sin, he insisted that the Lord had been misunderstood on the subject. Jesus, he insisted, being a man of God had an intuitive understanding of all human disorders and on this rested the healing successes which some regarded as miraculous. This was a view I had encountered among several non-Christian Jews who were happy to recognize Jesus as holy man and prophet but not Messiah. It was not surprising that Manaus should be affected by this scepticism.

I have observed in the Christian churches which have grown up in all parts of the world how believers interpret the facts about Jesus in terms of their own cultures and habits of rational thought. This is as true of me as any others. As a Greek, I tend to look for those points of convergence between the teachings of the ancients and those of the Lord Jesus. The priests of Asclepios long ago recognized that physical disfunction is not simply a bodily failing but a matter of psychic disharmony.

> Pure must he be who enters the fragrant temple;
> Purity means to think nothing but holy thoughts.

So runs the inscription over the magnificent entrance to the sanctuary at Epidaurus. It was an insight Paul readily recognized. 'Whatever 's pure, what is holy and of good report – set your mind on these things', he often taught; and in his letters he was always exhorting believers to find wholeness through being 'spiritually minded' and letting the Holy Spirit direct their thoughts. His own remarkable mind was able to embrace every new proposition presented to it. Yet, at the same time, he could with needle-sharp accuracy transfix the error in an argument or locate its essential truth.

But where was he now? In a world that was falling apart and hastening to its end was he safe? Every fresh demand upon my time increased my impatience to reach Rome where, I felt sure, someone would have reliable news of his whereabouts.

When we finally reached the city after more than a month on the road I was shocked by the changes that had taken place since I had left it five years before. The centre as I had known it was quite vanished. Where streets of houses and shops, ancient temples and public buildings had once stood there were now piles of blackened rubble or large areas cleared and swarming with hundreds of slaves, like so many ants. The house where Paul had been held was no more. The whole area from the Caelian Hill to the Palatine had been razed in order to create space for Nero's new palace. The Golden House was already complete and gangs of slaves were laying out over two-hundred acres of gardens, lakes, pavilions, colonnades and fountains for the emperor's exclusive pleasure. People told me about – but I deliberately did not go to see – the immense gilded statue of himself that Nero had set up to overlook the forum.

Yet it was not so much the material changes to Rome that impressed most visitors. There was, everywhere, an air of gloom, anger and fear. Thousands of citizens had had their property confiscated to make way for the imperial vulgarities. Businesses had disappeared, leaving their owners destitute. Hundreds of people had perished in the fire. Though no one dared say so openly because of the secret police, the general opinion was that the emperor was responsible for the conflagration. I heard men who despised 'Christian atheists' express sympathy for those who had been made scapegoats and punished for the blaze. But it was not religious minorities and mere slaves who suffered. The emperor's agents were assiduous in seeking out all who appeared to constitute a threat to the First Citizen. Tigellinus, now Nero's closest confidant, had revised the treason laws and used them to put to death several nobles.

Wherever I went I could feel oppressive evil and decay. There could be no doubt that all this was the work of Satan. Just as diseases of the body had their origin in spiritual conflict, so in the state crimes and outrages committed by men were the outward manifestations of warfare in the heavens between the divine cohorts and what Paul called 'the rulers of the present world darkness'.

After a couple of days in the city I located old Persis, a dear friend and leader of the church, until partial paralysis confined him to his villa at Trastevere, across the river. I introduced Manaus to him and we sat in his lemon grove, drinking honeyed Falernum from his vineyards in the Campagna and talking over old times. Persis sat in his chair in the shade, a battered straw hat tied with string on top of his thick, white hair to stop it blowing off in the breeze. He provided a sad catalogue of men and women who had died on the emperor's orders or fled.

'We expected the Lord's return long since,' he said. 'When his people were slaughtered so cruelly and the numbers sleeping in the Lord grew we said to ourselves, "Surely he can delay no longer." I certainly did not expect to taste death before his coming, but now,' he gestured with his good arm, 'it seems I must rest in the catacombs with so many of my friends.'

'The catacombs?'

'When the persecution became really severe we had an enormous burial problem – scores, hundreds of interments to make. We received permission to extend the chambers alongside the Appian Way. Now there are several long tunnels – or so they tell me; I cannot get there to see for myself. Even in this, the Lord blessed us: these underground chambers make good meeting places. When it became too dangerous to gather inside the city some of the brothers took to meeting in the catacombs. They said they were carrying out funerary rites. The authorities were too superstitious to interfere with them.'

'Do they still meet there?' I asked.

'Some, yes. But there are several secret places for worship. There have to be. Despite the emperor's attempts to destroy us – or perhaps because of this – our numbers grow.'

'Is there any news of Paul?' Manaus asked the question which I had been leading up to.

The old man stared at us. 'You haven't heard? I felt sure that you, of all people . . .'

'I have heard many things but none that I could prove true.'

Persis shook his head sadly. 'Our dear Paul was executed just over two years ago.'

'Two years ago? Persis, are you sure about that?'

'Yes. He was somewhere in Gaul, I believe, when he heard about the terrible things happening here. He decided to return to strengthen the church in the capital. Of course, he took no thought for his own safety; you know what he was like. Our friends did their best to keep him hidden but he insisted on visiting the bereaved and gathering groups together for teaching. He was arrested after he had been here about two weeks.'

'How was he? His eyes – was there any sight left?'

'Oh, I didn't see him.'

'What? You mean Paul came to Rome and didn't visit one of his oldest friends?'

'I'm sure he intended to but there were other more urgent matters . . .'

Although Persis brushed the matter aside it was obvious that he was saddened and surprised that Paul had not called upon him. To me it was incomprehensible.

The old man quickly concluded his story. There was not much more to tell. Refusing to skulk in back streets and catacombs, Paul had been soon arrested. By returning to Rome he had broken the law and there could be only one penalty. On a fine spring dawn a troop of soldiers had marched him out through the Ostian Gate and as far as the third milestone on the harbour road. There, in a small grove a few paces from the highway, he was bound to a slab of stone which was chest high to a kneeling man. Paul began to sing a hymn. I could imagine that unmusical, powerful voice penetrating the morning air. He was, Persis reported, singing up to the moment the sword struck.

I asked what had happened to the body. Had it been taken to the catacombs?

'The guards were under orders not to release it,' Persis said. 'They didn't want Paul's remains to be buried where they could become a focus of pilgrimage. Tigellinus was furious that the little Christian preacher had disobeyed him and he had no intention of turning Paul into a martyr. The body was disposed of secretly.'

My old friend was tired and obviously distressed at recalling these events. Manaus and I left shortly afterwards. Before departing I asked Persis about the Sunday worship and whether we should present ourselves at the catacombs. We could do so, he said, and he would give us a letter of introduction in case no one recognized me. Alternatively, we were welcome to return to the villa. A small group gathered there every week and, so far, had not attracted the attention of the authorities.

As we made our way back with sad, slow steps towards the Sublicio Bridge, Manaus said, 'It seems that your quest is at an end.'

'It seems so.'

However, I was not wholly convinced. If what Persis said was true, then Licinius' information was inaccurate. Of course, the centurion had only passed on hearsay. But, then, I reasoned, so had Persis. Neither had direct proof of Paul's whereabouts.

'You still think there's any doubt?' Manaus asked.

'I suppose I'm trying to persuade myself – clinging to a hope that isn't really a hope.'

As I met other members of the brotherhood I asked them what they knew of Paul. All, without exception, told the same story. On Sunday Manaus and I made our way to Trastevere at daybreak for the customary celebration of the Lord's rising. Persis had said that there would only be a small gathering. In fact, over a hundred men and women crowded into the paved atrium of the villa. Many of them had come to meet me, knowing of my connection with Paul. I was asked to speak and, although I am no orator, I tried to share with these brave disciples some of my memories of Paul and of others who had actually seen and spoken with the Lord. My audience had many eager questions with which they plied me all through the fellowship meal which followed our worship. Although several slaves left to return to their duties, the sun was high overhead before the gathering finally dispersed.

The man who presided over the meeting was called Linus. He was unknown to me but his authority seemed to be accepted without question and he appeared to be both forceful and clear-headed. He walked back with Manaus and me to the city centre. He told us that he came from southern Italy, had been a Christian for about ten years and had been the leader of the church in his home town. Shortly before Paul's death, he said, the apostle had entrusted the Roman church into his hands. The man had obvious leadership qualities, yet, for a reason I could not identify, I did not feel at ease with him.

I asked Linus if he could tell me any more about Paul's last days. He could not.

'What happened to Eubulus?' I enquired.

'Eubulus?'

'Paul's companion. I assume he returned with Paul?'

'Oh, yes, of course.' Linus was obviously uncomfortable. 'He managed to escape.'

He was not inclined to elaborate and I did not press him. Manaus and I returned to our lodging and I spent several hours in prayer and thought trying to decide what to do next.

That evening, shortly before nightfall, our host came to the room to say that someone was outside asking for me. I donned my sandals, collected my staff and went down with him. When Manaus tried to come as well the lodging-house keeper said that the caller was insistent that Dr Luke should go alone. Outside, I discovered Linus. With very few words he led the way to a poor quarter of the city where mean houses backed onto the river. We entered one and ascended to an upper room. In answer to Linus' knock it was opened – by Eubulus.

I was shocked as much by the young man's appearance as by his being there at all. He was thin and hollow-cheeked. His eyes lacked lustre and his skin was pale. We embraced and I could feel the lack of strength in his arms.

When we were all seated on the room's sparse furniture it was Linus who began the explanation. 'I'm sorry we tried to deceive even you but I'm sure you'll understand that it was necessary. When the trouble broke out here three years ago you can guess who was behind it.'

'The Jews?'

'As ever. Things were coming to a head in Judaea. Tigellinus was about to organize a purge in the city. The synagogue leaders responded by stirring up a riot and denouncing the Christians as responsible. This suited the emperor's purpose ideally. He needed someone to blame for the fire and . . . well, the rest you know. Over the following months the Jews were feverishly active, spying on us, laying information against us – anything to deflect attention from themselves.

'The church was decimated and demoralized. Most of our elders had been sacrificed in the circus and the arena. Those who were left spent much time in prayer and the Holy Spirit appointed me to take over the leadership. Slowly things quietened down but we were not safe and we still aren't. There was one man above all others that our enemies wanted to lay their hands on.'

'Paul?'

'Of course. He was the Jews' arch-enemy. As for Tigellinus he bore a personal grudge and regretted having let Paul get away. Our greatest comfort during the worst days was knowing that our beloved Paul was miles away and beyond the clutches of his foes in Rome. Imagine then how appalled we were when, suddenly, Eubulus arrived to tell us that Paul was on his way back to the city.'

The young man took up the story. 'We had a wonderful time in Tarraconensis [the province of North and Central Spain] particularly in the coastal towns. The people were anxious to hear the Gospel and we stayed a year baptizing and instructing and appointing elders. Then Paul felt the Holy Spirit calling us to the nearby province of Narbonensian Gaul. We made our way over the mountains. It was terrible. The weather turned bad and Paul grew weak. I had to carry him on the steeper sections. Then I fell ill with a fever. I don't remember clearly how we survived. All I do recall is Paul's amazing strength of spirit. Not once did he despair. Always he was thinking of the next town where he could preach the Gospel. But he was exhausted and when we reached a place called Toulouse he had to rest completely. After a couple of months we were on the road again. In the proconsular capital of Narbonne Paul's challenge to the priests at the temple of the divine emperor resulted in a beating, a night in the jail and an armed escort out of town. It was when we reached the port of Marseilles that we heard of the troubles in Rome. Paul was broken-hearted at the stories the fugitives were bringing and he was also concerned that the church in the capital should be strong. He was convinced that Rome would in future be the centre for Christian mission rather than Jerusalem. We must return immediately, he said, and I could not dissuade him.' He looked at me appealingly. 'You know how useless it was to argue with him. Fortunately, he was too weak to make the sea voyage and he knew it. He insisted that I go on ahead and tell the brothers in Rome that he was on his way. I didn't want to leave him, truly I didn't, but he told me it was the Lord's will, so having engaged a local family to look after him I came here by the fastest ship in the harbour.'

'Of course, we were horrified,' Linus explained. 'For Paul to enter the city was certain death. We sent Eubulus back straight away and two of our people went with him with instructions to prevent Paul from reaching Rome. They would have used force if necessary.'

Linus paused and exchanged doleful glances with Eubulus. I sensed they were coming to the unhappy climax of their story.

'We couldn't find him,' Eubulus muttered. 'We reached Marseilles to discover that Paul had left over a week previously. He had simply settled up with his hosts and gone, without saying where he was going.'

'Did he have no one with him?' I asked.

'As far as we could discover, no. We looked feverishly in all the neighbouring towns and villages. We tried the harbours, large and small. It seemed most likely that he was already headed for Rome. But no one had seen him, or, if they had, they had not noticed him. Who would pay any attention to an old, near-sightless man stumbling through the streets with the aid of a stick? He would have been dismissed as just another beggar.'

Linus added, 'Naturally, we kept a careful watch for him here. Some of the brothers work on the docks at Ostia and would have reported if Paul had arrived. But he didn't.'

'Then, why this elaborate story of him being arrested and beheaded?' I asked.

'For his own safety. His enemies were everywhere. Still they arrive from time to time, looking for him. We deliberately spread the story of Paul's death and, because so many Christians were killed and others disappeared and there was general confusion, it was believed. Wherever Paul is now he should be safe from Satan's hounds.'

'Did you seek him in Arles?' I asked Eubulus.

'Arles? No, that is many miles from Marseilles, much of it over marshy, inhospitable country. Why would Paul want to go there?'

'It's an important administrative centre and there is already a church there. I have a reliable report that Paul was there a few months ago. We must start a new search in Arles.'

Suddenly Linus put a finger to his lips. He hurried across to the door, threw it open and looked out. He came back, shaking his head.

'I thought I heard a creak on the stair. There are spies everywhere. We have to be so careful.'

We made our plans swiftly and put them into execution the next day. Eubulus and I went to Ostia and obtained passage three days later on a coastal trader calling at Marseilles. From there we journeyed by road to Arles. It took several days of cautious enquiry to locate the small Christian community but when we did we had immediate success. Paul had, indeed, visited the city, had preached in the streets and the market place and had made an immediate impact, particularly among some of the military families. Thanks to influential friends and converts he had been protected from those who wanted to commend themselves to the authorities in Rome by deliberately seeking out exponents of the new religion.

Of course, the question we wanted an answer to was 'Where is Paul now?' The answer was Nimes, some twenty miles away. He had, some four months earlier, become very weak, having narrowly survived a bout of fever. At the same time, orders had arrived from Rome, that all preachers of unauthorised cults were to be arrested and, if found guilty, executed. As soon as Paul was well enough to be moved, his friends had taken him to Nimes. The city, established by Augustus as a veteran college, enjoyed several privileges, including independence from the proconsul at Narbonne and exemption from some of the more tiresome imperial government directives. There, Paul would be safe.

We thanked our informant, a veteran of the Tenth Legion, and asked for letters of introduction so that we might be reunited with our old friend and I could tend his sick body.

The reply was a shock. 'There's no need. His personal physician is with him. He arrived two days ago and went straight on to Nimes.'

'Who was this physician?' I asked.

The old man struggled to remember. 'He was a Jew, like Paul; a very pleasant, courteous man; rather dark complexion. What was his name? Ah, yes; Manaus, that was it.'

I turned to Eubulus. 'We must go, now! We have to stop Manaus.'

He looked puzzled. 'But I thought . . .'

'That he was one of us? Yes, so did I. He fooled me thoroughly – not just once; every day for months.'

As we hurried along the dusty road I asked myself over and again how I could have been so easily duped. I now saw Manaus for what he was – an agent sent from Jerusalem to be revenged on Paul and, through Paul, on Jesus. He had feigned membership of the church in order to find information and attached himself to me knowing that I of all people would discover the truth. I had no doubt what he would do if he found Paul. There would be no reliance on Roman justice this time.

We reached Nimes as darkness was falling. The guards at the Augustus Gate refused to let us in. We argued for over half an hour. It was no use. We were obliged to lodge at a tavern outside the walls and spend a sleepless night waiting, probably within a few hundred paces of our friend yet unable to warn him of his danger.

In the morning as soon as the gate was opened we went straight to the house close by the temple of Diana to which we had been directed. The door was opened by a slave girl who was plainly terrified at being confronted at such an hour by two strangers demanding to see her master. I could not understand her anxiety until I recalled that the day was a Sunday. All the family would be attending secret worship and she was under strict orders to tell no one of their whereabouts.

Did she, I asked, know anything about a man called Manaus? She nodded, obviously relieved at being asked a question she could answer. 'He was staying here, Sir, but he left about half an hour ago. I heard him say he would be going out by the South Gate.'

Leaving Eubulus to locate the church meeting, I hastened through the quiet streets and squares and out through the gateway overlooking a wide plain. There was, as yet, little traffic passing in and out of the town and travellers could be seen some way ahead along the road.

I found Manaus, at last, about a mile from Nimes, sitting on a rock. It was as though he was waiting for me.

'Good morning,' he said as I approached. 'I'm glad to be able to see you again before my return to Judaea. I have enjoyed our companionship enormously and I was genuinely sorry to have to deceive you.'

'Where is Paul? What have you done with him?' I demanded.

'He is where he can do no more harm with his blasphemous teaching.'

'You have killed him?'

Manaus shook his head. 'I would like to be able to claim that privilege. Perhaps I will when I report to the Sanhedrin. But because of our long weeks of friendship you deserve the truth.' He stood up and walked a few paces from the highway, beckoning me to follow.

He pointed down at a rectangle of newly turned earth. 'He died five days ago – very peacefully, they tell me. His friends actually boasted of how, at the end he quoted one of my people's prophets–

> "Death where is your sting;
> death where is your victory?"

It is a pity he did not die in pain, fully aware of his failure. But, really, it matters little. All that does matter is that the world has heard the last of Paul of Tarsus.'

I know not how long I stayed at the spot, vision blurred with grief, memories cascading through my mind.

Even now, more than a year later, the letters grow indistinct as I write them and tears splash onto the page. Manaus was right: the world will soon forget Paul but for those of us who knew him he will always have a place in our hearts.

Farewell,
Luke

THE LAST DAY OF POMPEII

Edward Bulwer-Lytton

The eruption of Vesuvius on 24 August AD 79, which resulted in the destruction of Pompeii and Herculaneum, must be the best known volcanic event in history.

Edward Bulwer (1803–1873), who became Lord Lytton in 1866, was one of the most popular writers of the early Victorian age. His work ushered in an age of sensational literature. He shocked the establishment by writing two books – Paul Clifford (1830) and Eugene Aram (1832) – which idealized the villain. With this reputation, his books sold in vast quantities and he produced a number of historical novels, including The Last Days of Pompeii (1834), from which the following extract is taken.

The main hero of the story is the Greek Glaucus, who is in love with Ione, but who falls foul of the magician, Arbaces and is accused of murder. As a result, Glaucus is arrested and forced to fight in the arena on the very day Vesuvius is about to erupt.

I

Glaucus and Olinthus had been placed together in that gloomy and narrow cell in which the criminals of the arena awaited their last fearful struggle. Their eyes, of late accustomed to the darkness, scanned the faces of each other in this awful hour: and by that dim light, the paleness, which chased away the natural hues from either cheek, assumed a yet more ashen and ghastly whiteness. Yet their brows were erect and dauntless; their limbs did not tremble;

their lips were compressed and rigid. The religion of the one, the pride of the other, the conscious innocence of both, and, it may be, the support derived from their mutual companionship, elevated the victim into a hero!

'Hark! hearest thou that shout? They are growling over their human blood,' said Olinthus.

'I hear; my heart grows sick; but the gods support me.'

'The gods! Oh, rash young man! in this hour recognize the One God. Have I not taught thee in the dungeon, wept for thee, prayed for thee? In my zeal and in my agony, have I not thought more of thy salvation than my own?'

'Brave friend!' answered Glaucus, solemnly, 'I have listened to thee with awe, with wonder, and with a secret tendency towards conviction. Had our lives been spared, I might gradually have weaned myself from the tenets of my own faith, and inclined to thine; but, in this last hour, it were a craven thing, and a base, to yield to hasty terror what should only be the result of lengthened meditation. Were I to embrace thy creed, and cast down my father's gods, should I not be bribed by thy promise of heaven, or awed by thy threats of hell? Olinthus, no! Think we of each other with equal charity; I honouring thy sincerity, thou pitying my blindness or my obdurate courage. As have been my deeds, such will be my reward, and the Power of Powers above will not judge harshly of human error, when it is linked with honesty of purpose and truth of heart. Speak we no more of this. Hush! Dost thou hear them drag yon heavy body through the passage? Such as that clay will ours be soon.'

'O Heaven! O Christ! already I behold ye!' cried the fervent Olinthus, lifting up his hands. 'I tremble not; I rejoice that the prison-house shall be soon broken.'

Glaucus bowed his head in silence. He felt the distinction between his fortitude and that of his fellow-sufferer. The heathen did not tremble; but the Christian exulted. The door swung gratingly back; the gleam of spears shot along the walls.

'Glaucus the Athenian, thy time has come,' said a loud and clear voice, 'the lion awaits thee.'

'I am ready,' said the Athenian. 'Brother and co-mate, one last embrace! Bless me; and – farewell!'

The Christian opened his arms; he clasped the young heathen to his breast; he kissed his forehead and cheek; he sobbed aloud; his tears flowed fast and hot over the features of his friend.

'Oh, could I have converted thee, I had not wept. Oh, that I might say to thee, "We two shall sup this night in Paradise!" '

'It may be so yet,' answered the Greek, with a tremulous voice.

'They whom death parted not may meet yet beyond the grave. On the earth – on the beautiful, the beloved earth – farewell for ever! Worthy officer, I am ready.'

Glaucus tore himself away; and when he came forth into the air, its breath, which, though sunless, was hot and arid, smote witheringly upon him. His frame, not yet restored from the effects of the deadly draught, shrank and trembled. The officers supported him.

'Courage!' said one, 'thou art young, active, well-knit. They give thee a weapon! despair not, and thou mayst yet conquer!'

Glaucus did not reply; but ashamed of his infirmity, he made a desperate and convulsive effort, and regained the firmness of his nerves. They anointed his body, completely naked, save by a cincture round the loins, placed the stilus – vain weapon! – in his hand, and led him into the arena.

And now, when the Greek saw the eyes of thousands and tens of thousands upon him, he no longer felt that he was mortal. All evidence of fear – all fear itself – was gone. A red and haughty flush spread over the paleness of his features – he towered aloft to the full of his glorious stature. In the elastic beauty of his limbs and form; in his intent but unfrowning brow; in the high disdain, and in the indomitable soul, which breathed visibly – which spake audibly – from his attitude, his lips, his eye; he seemed the very incarnation, vivid and corporeal, of the valour of his land – of the divinity of its worship – at once a hero and a god.

The murmur of hatred and horror at his crime, which had greeted his entrance, died into the silence of involuntary admiration and half-compassionate respect; and, with a quick and convulsive sigh, that seemed to move the whole mass of life as if it were one body, the gaze of the spectators turned from the Athenian to a dark uncouth object in the centre of the arena. It was the grated den of a lion!

'By Venus, how warm it is!' said Fulvia, 'yet there is no sun. Would those stupid sailors* could have fastened up that gap in the awning.'

'Oh! it is warm, indeed. I turn sick – I faint!' said the wife of Pansa: even her experienced stoicism giving way at the struggle about to take place.

The lion had been kept without food for twenty-four hours, and the animal had, during the whole morning, testified a singular and restless uneasiness, which the keeper had attributed to the pangs of hunger. Yet its bearings seemed rather that of fear than of rage; its roar was painful and distressed; it hung its head – snuffed the air

---

* Sailors were generally employed in fastening the *velaria* of the amphitheatre.

through the bars, then lay down, started again – and again uttered its wild and far-resounding cries. And now, in its den, it lay utterly dumb and mute, with distending nostrils forced hard against the grating, and disturbing, with a heaving breath, the sand below on the arena.

The editor's lip quivered, and his cheek grew pale; he looked anxiously around – hesitated, delayed; the crowd became impatient. Slowly he gave the sign; the keeper, who was behind the den, cautiously removed the grating, and the lion leaped forth with a mighty and glad roar of release. The keeper hastily retreated through the grated passage leading from the arena, and left the lord of the forest – and his prey.

Glaucus had bent his limbs so as to give himself the firmest posture at the expected rush of the lion, with his small and shining weapon raised on high, in the faint hope that *one* well-directed thrust – for he knew that he should have time but for *one* – might penetrate through the eye to the brain of his grim foe.

But, to the unutterable astonishment of all, the beast seemed not even aware of the presence of the criminal. At the first moment of its release it halted abruptly in the arena, raised itself half on end, snuffing the upward air with impatient sighs; then suddenly it sprang forward, but not on the Athenian. At half-speed it circled round and round the space, turning its vast head from side to side with an anxious and perturbed gaze, as if seeking only some avenue of escape; once or twice it endeavoured to leap up the parapet that divided it from the audience, and on failing, uttered rather a baffled howl than its deep-toned and kingly roar. It evinced no sign either of wrath or hunger; its tail drooped along the sand instead of lashing its gaunt sides; and its eye, though it wandered at times to Glaucus, rolled again listlessly from him. At length, as if tired of attempting to escape, it crept with a moan into its cage, and once more laid itself down to rest.

The first surprise of the assembly at the apathy of the lion soon grew converted into resentment at its cowardice, and the populace already merged their pity for the fate of Glaucus into angry compassion for their own disappointment. The editor called to the keeper –

'How is this? Take the goad, prick him forth, and then close the door of the den.'

As the keeper, with some fear but more astonishment, was preparing to obey, a loud cry was heard at one of the entrances of the arena; there was a confusion, a bustle – voices of remonstrance suddenly breaking forth, and suddenly silenced at the reply. All eyes turned, in wonder at the interruption, towards the quarter of the disturbance; the crowd gave way, and suddenly Sallust appeared on the senatorial benches – his hair dishevelled, breathless, heated, half exhausted. He cast his eyes hastily round the ring. 'Remove the Athenian!' he cried, 'haste – he is innocent! Arrest Arbaces, the Egyptian – HE is the murderer of Apæcides!'

'Art thou mad, O Sallust?' said the prætor, rising from his seat. 'What means this raving?'

'Remove the Athenian! Quick! or his blood be on your head. Prætor, delay, and you answer with your own life to the emperor! I bring with me the eye-witness to the death of the priest Apæcides. Room there! stand back! give way! People of Pompeii, fix every eye upon Arbaces – there he sits! Room there – for the priest Calenus!'

Pale, haggard, fresh from the jaws of famine and of death – his face fallen, his eyes dull as a vulture's, his broad frame gaunt as a skeleton – Calenus was supported into the very row in which Arbaces sat. His releasers had given him sparingly of food; but the chief sustenance that nerved his feeble limbs was revenge!

'The priest Calenus! – Calenus!' cried the mob. '*Is* it he? No – it is a dead man!'

'It *is* the priest Calenus,' said the prætor, gravely. 'What hast thou to say?'

'Arbaces of Egypt is the murderer of Apæcides, the priest of Isis; these eyes saw him deal the blow. It is from the dungeon in which he plunged me – it is from the darkness and horror of a death by famine – that the gods have raised me to proclaim his crime! 'Release the Athenian – *he is* innocent!'

'It is for this, then, that the lion spared him. A miracle! a miracle!' cried Pansa.

'A miracle! a miracle!' shouted the people. 'Remove the Athenian – *Arbaces to the lion!*'

And that shout echoed from hill to vale – from coast to sea – '*Arbaces to the lion!*'

'Officers, remove the accused Glaucus – remove, but guard him yet,' said the prætor. 'The gods lavish their wonders upon this day.'

As the prætor gave the word to release, there was a cry of joy – a female voice – a child's voice – and it was of joy! It rang through the heart of the assembly with electric force – it was touching – it was holy – that child's voice! And the populace echoed it back with a sympathizing gratulation!'

'Silence!' said the grave prætor – 'who is there?'

'The blind girl – Nydia,' answered Sallust, 'it is her hand that has raised Calenus from the grave, and delivered Glaucus from the lion.'

'Of this hereafter,' said the prætor. 'Calenus, priest of Isis, thou accusest Arbaces of the murder of Apæcides?'

'I do!'

'Thou didst behold the deed?'

'Prætor – with these eyes –'

'Enough at present – the details must be reserved for more suiting time and place. Arbaces of Egypt, thou hearest the charge against thee – thou hast not yet spoken – what hast thou to say?'

The gaze of the crowd had been long riveted on Arbaces, but not until the confusion which he had betrayed at the first charge of Sallust and the entrance of Calenus had subsided. At the shout, 'Arbaces to the lion!' he had indeed trembled, and the dark bronze of his cheek had taken a paler hue. But he had soon recovered his haughtiness and self-control. Proudly, he returned the angry glare of the countless eyes around him; and replying now to the question of the prætor, he said in that accent, so peculiarly tranquil and commanding, which characterized his tones –

'Prætor, this charge is so mad that it scarcely deserves reply. My first accuser is the noble Sallust – the most intimate friend of Glaucus! my second is a priest; I revere his garb and calling – but, people of Pompeii! ye know somewhat of the character of Calenus – he is griping and gold-thirsty to a proverb; the witness of such men is to be bought. Prætor, I am innocent!'

'Sallust,' said the magistrate, 'where found you Calenus?'

'In the dungeon of Arbaces.'

'Egyptian,' said the prætor, frowning, 'thou didst, then, dare to imprison a priest of the gods – and wherefore?'

'Hear me,' answered Arbaces, rising calmly, but with agitation visible in his face, 'This man came to threaten that he would make against me the charge he has now made, unless I would purchase his silence with half my fortune: I remonstrated – in vain. Peace, there – let not the priest interrupt me! Noble prætor – and ye, O people! – I was a stranger in the land – I knew myself innocent of crime! but the witness of a priest against me might yet destroy me. In my perplexity I decoyed him to the cell whence he has been released, on pretence that it was the coffer-house of my gold. I resolved to detain him there until the fate of the true criminal was sealed, and his threats could avail no longer; but I meant no worse. I may have erred – but who amongst ye will not acknowledge the equity of self-preservation? Were I guilty, why was the witness of this priest silent at the trial? – *then* I had not detained nor concealed him. Why did he not proclaim my guilt when I proclaimed that of Glaucus? Prætor, this needs an answer. For the rest, I throw myself on your laws. I demand their protection. Remove hence the accused and the accuser. I will willingly meet, and cheerfully abide by, the decision of the legitimate tribunal. This is no place for further parley.'

'He says right,' said the prætor. 'Ho! guards – remove Arbaces – guard Calenus! Sallust, we hold you responsible for your accusation. Let the sports be resumed.'

'What!' cried Calenus, turning round to the people, 'shall Isis be thus contemned? Shall the blood of Apæcides yet cry for vengeance? Shall justice be delayed now, that it may be frustrated hereafter? Shall the lion be cheated of his lawful prey? A god – a god – I feel the god rush to my lips! *To the lion – to the lion with Arbaces!*'

His exhausted frame could support no longer the ferocious malice of the priest; he sank on the ground in strong convulsions – the foam gathered to his mouth – he was as a man, indeed, whom a supernatural power had entered! The people saw and shuddered.

'It is a god that inspires the holy man! *To the lion with the Egyptian!*'

With that cry up sprang – on moved – thousands upon thousands! They rushed from the heights – they poured down in the direction of the Egyptian. In vain did the ædile command – in vain did the prætor lift his voice and proclaim the law. The people had been already rendered savage by the exhibition of blood – they thirsted for more – their superstition was aided by their ferocity. Aroused – inflamed by the spectacle of their victims, they forget the authority of their rulers. It was one of those dread popular convulsions common to crowds wholly ignorant, half free and half servile; and which the peculiar constitution of the Roman provinces so frequently exhibited. The power of the prætor was as a reed beneath the whirlwind; still, at his word, the guards had drawn themselves along the lower benches, on which the upper classes sat separate from the vulgar. They made but a feeble barrier – the waves of the human sea halted for a moment, to enable Arbaces to count the exact moment of his doom! In despair, and in a terror which beat down even pride, he glanced his eyes over the rolling and rushing crowd – when, right above them, through the wide chasm which had been left in the velaria, he beheld a strange and awful apparition – he beheld – and his craft restored his courage! He stretched his hand on high; over his lofty brow and royal features there came an expression of unutterable solemnity and command.

'Behold!' he shouted with a voice of thunder, which stifled the roar of the crowd, 'behold how the gods protect the guiltless! The fires of the avenging Orcus burst forth against the false witness of my accusers!'

The eyes of the crowd followed the gesture of the Egyptian, and beheld a vast vapour shooting from the summit of Vesuvius, in the form of a gigantic pine-tree; the trunk, blackness – the branches, fire; a fire that shifted and wavered in its hues with every moment, now fiercely luminous, now of a dull and dying red, that again blazed terrifically forth with intolerable glare!

There was a dead, heart-sunken silence, through which there suddenly broke the roar of the lion, which, from within the building, was echoed back by the sharper and fiercer yells of its fellow-beast. Dread seers were they of the Burden of the Atmosphere, and wild prophets of the wrath to come!

Then there rose on high the universal shrieks of women; the men stared at each other, but were dumb. At that moment they felt the earth shake beneath their feet; the walls of the theatre trembled; and beyond, in the distance, they heard the crash of falling roofs; an instant more, and the mountain-cloud seemed to roll towards them, dark and rapid, like a torrent: at the same time, it cast forth from its bosom a shower of ashes mixed with vast fragments of burning stone! Over the crushing vines – over the desolate streets – over the amphitheatre itself – far and wide, with many a mighty splash in the agitated sea, fell that awful shower!

No longer thought the crowd of justice or of Arbaces; safety for themselves was their sole thought. Trampling recklessly over the fallen, amidst groans, and oaths, and prayers, and sudden shrieks, the enormous crowd vomited itself forth through the numerous passages. Whither should they fly? Some, anticipating a second earthquake, hastened to their homes to load themselves with their more costly goods, and escape while it was yet time! Others, dreading the showers of ashes that now fell fast, torrent upon torrent, over the streets, rushed under the roofs of the nearest houses, or temples, or sheds – shelter of any kind – for protection from the terrors of the open air. But darker, and larger, and mightier, spread the cloud above them. It was a sudden and more ghastly Night rushing upon the realm of Noon!

II

Stunned by his reprieve, doubting that he was awake, Glaucus had been led by the officers of the arena into a small cell within the walls of the theatre. They threw a loose robe over his form, and crowded round in congratulation and wonder. There was an impatient and fretful cry without the cell; the throng gave way, and the blind girl, led by some gentler hand, flung herself at the feet of Glaucus.

'It was *I* who have saved thee,' she sobbed, 'now let me die!'

'Nydia, my child! – my preserver!'

'Oh, let me feel thy touch – thy breath! Yes, yes, thou livest! We are not too late! that dread door; methought it would never yield! And Calenus – oh! his voice was as the dying wind among tombs; we had to wait – gods! it seemed hours, ere food and wine restored to him something of strength; but thou livest! – thou livest yet! And I – *I* have saved thee!'

This affecting scene was soon interrupted by the event just described.

'The mountain! the earthquake!' resounded from side to side. The officers fled with the rest; they left Glaucus and Nydia to save themselves as they might.

As the sense of the dangers around them flashed on the Athenian, his generous heart recurred to Olinthus. He, too, was reprieved from the tiger by the hands of the gods; should he be left to a no less fatal death in the neighbouring cell? Taking Nydia by the hand, Glaucus hurried across the passages; he gained the den of the Christian. He found Olinthus kneeling, and in prayer.

'Arise! arise! my friend,' he cried. 'Save thyself, and fly! See! Nature is thy dread deliverer!' He led forth the bewildered Christian, and pointed to the cloud which advanced darker and darker, disgorging forth showers of ashes and pumice stones; and bade him hearken to the cries and trampling rush of the scattered crowd.

'This is the hand of God – God be praised!' said Olinthus, devoutly.

'Fly! seek thy brethren! Concert with them thy escape. Farewell!'

Olinthus did not answer, neither did he mark the retreating form of his friend. High thoughts and solemn absorbed his soul; and in the enthusiasm of his kindling heart, he exulted in the mercy of God rather than trembled at the evidence of His power. At length he roused himself, and hurried on, he scarce knew whither.

The open doors of a dark desolate cell suddenly appeared on his path; through the gloom within there flared and flickered a single lamp; and by its light he saw three grim and naked forms stretched on the earth in death. His feet were suddenly arrested; for amidst the terrors of that drear recess – the spoliarium of the arena – he heard a low voice calling on the name of Christ!

He could not resist lingering at that appeal; he entered the den, and his feet were dabbled in the slow streams of blood that gushed from the corpses over the sand.

'Who,' said the Nazarene, 'calls upon the Son of God?'

No answer came forth; and, turning round, Olinthus beheld, by the light of the lamp, an old grey-headed man sitting on the floor, and supporting in his lap the head of one of the dead. The features of the dead man were firmly and rigidly locked in the last sleep, but over the lip there played a fierce smile – not the Christian's smile of hope – but the dark sneer of hatred and defiance. Yet on the face still lingered the beautiful roundness of early youth. The hair curled thick and glossy over the unwrinkled brow; and the down of manhood but slightly shaded the marble of the hueless yet iron cheek. And over this face bent one of such unutterable sadness – of such yearning tenderness – of such fond and such deep despair. The tears of the old man fell fast and hot, but he did not feel them; and when his lips moved, and he mechanically uttered the prayer of his benign and hopeful faith, neither his heart nor his sense responded to the words: it was but the involuntary emotion that broke from the lethargy of his mind. His boy was dead, and had died for him! And the old man's heart was broken!

'Medon!' said Olinthus, pityingly, 'arise, and fly! God is forth upon the wings of the elements! the new Gomorrah is doomed! Fly, ere the fires consume thee!'

'He was ever so full of life! he *cannot* be dead! Come hither! place your hand on his heart! – sure it beats yet!'

'Brother, the soul has fled! we will remember it in our prayers! Thou canst not reanimate the dumb clay! Come, come! Hark! while I speak, yon crashing walls! hark! yon agonizing cries! Not a moment is to be lost! – Come!'

'I hear nothing!' said Medon, shaking his grey hair. 'The poor boy, his love murdered him!'

'Come, come! forgive this friendly force.'

'What! Who would sever the father from the son?' and Medon clasped the body tightly in his embrace, and covered it with passionate kisses. 'Go!' said he, lifting up his face for one moment. 'Go! we must be alone!'

'Alas!' said the compassionate Nazarene, 'death hath severed ye already!'

The old man smiled very calmly. 'No, no, no!' he muttered, his voice growing lower with each word, 'death has been more kind!'

With that his head dropped on his son's breast – his arms relaxed their grasp. Olinthus caught him by the hand – the pulse had ceased to beat! The last words of the father were the words of truth – *Death had been more kind!*

Meanwhile Glaucus and Nydia were pacing swiftly up the perilous and fearful streets. The Athenian had learnt from his preserver that Ione was yet in the house of Arbaces. Thither he fled, to release – to save her! The few slaves that the Egyptian had left at his mansion when he had repaired in long procession to the amphitheatre, had been able to offer no resistence to the armed band of Sallust; and when afterwards the volcano broke forth, they had huddled together, stunned and frightened, in the inmost recesses of the house. Even the tall Ethiopian had forsaken his post at the door; and Glaucus (who left Nydia without – the poor Nydia, jealous once more, even in such an hour) passed on through the vast hall, without meeting one from whom to learn the chamber of Ione. Even as he passed, however, the darkness that covered the heavens increased so rapidly that it was with difficulty he could guide his steps. The flower-wreathed columns seemed to reel and tremble; and with every instant he heard the ashes fall cranchingly into the roofless peristyle. He ascended to the upper rooms, breathless he paced along, shouting out aloud the name of Ione; and at length he heard at the end of a gallery, a voice – *her* voice, in wondering reply! To rush forward – to shatter the door – to seize Ione in his arms – to hurry from the mansion – seemed to him the work of an instant! Scarce had he gained the spot where Nydia was, than he heard steps advancing towards the house, and recognized the voice of Arbaces, who had returned to seek his wealth and Ione, ere he fled from the doomed Pompeii. But so dense was already the reeking atmosphere, that the foes saw not each other, though so near – save that, dimly in the gloom, Glaucus caught the moving outline of the snowy robes of the Egyptian.

They hastened onward – those three! Alas! whither? They now saw not a step before them; they were encompassed with doubt and horror; and the death he had escaped seemed to Glaucus only to have changed its form and augmented its victims.

III

The sudden catastrophe which had, as it were, riven the very bonds of society, and left prisoner and gaoler alike free, had soon rid Calenus of the guards to whose care the prætor had consigned him. And when the darkness and the crowd separated the priest from his attendants, he hastened, with tembling steps, towards the temple of his goddess. As he crept along, and ere the darkness was complete, he felt himself suddenly caught by the robe, and a voice muttered in his ear –

'Hist! Calenus! an awful hour!'

'Ay! by my father's head! Who art thou? thy face is dim, and thy voice is strange!'

'Not know thy Burbo? – fie!'

'Gods! how the darkness gathers! Ho, ho! – by yon terrific mountain, what sudden blazes of lightning! How they dart and quiver! Hades is loosed on earth!'

'Tush! thou believest not these things, Calenus! Now is the time to make our fortune!'

'Ha!'

'Listen! Thy temple is full of gold and precious mummeries! – let us load ourselves with them, and then hasten to the sea and embark! None will ever ask an account of the doings of this day.'

'Burbo, thou art right! Hush! and follow me into the temple. Who cares now – who sees now – whether thou art priest or not? Follow – and we will share!'

In the precincts of the temple were many priests gathered around the altars, praying, weeping, grovelling in the dust. Imposters in safety, they were not the less superstitious in danger! Calenus passed them, and entered the chamber yet to be seen in the south side of the court. Burbo followed him – the priest struck a light. Wine and viands strewed the table, the remains of a sacrificial feast.

'A man who has hungered forty-eight hours,' muttered Calenus, 'has an appetite even in such a time.' He seized on the food, and devoured it greedily. Nothing could, perhaps, be more unnaturally horrid than the selfish baseness of these villains; for there is nothing more loathsome than the valour of avarice! Plunder and sacrilege, while the pillars of the world tottered to and fro! What an increase to the terrors of nature can be made by the vices of man!

'Wilt thou never have done?' said Burbo, impatiently; 'thy face purples, and thine eyes start already.'

'It is not every day one has such a right to be hungry. O Jupiter! what sound is that? the hissing of fiery water! What! does the cloud give rain as well as flame! Ha! – what! shrieks? And, Burbo, how silent all is now! Look forth!'

Amidst the other horrors, the mighty mountain now cast up columns of boiling water. Blent and kneaded with the half-burning ashes, the streams fell like seething mud over the streets in frequent intervals. And full – where the priests of Isis had now cowered around the altars, on which they had vainly sought to kindle fires and pour incense, one of the fiercest of those deadly torrents, mingled with immense fragments of scoria, had poured its rage – over the bended forms of the priests it dashed: that cry had been of death – that silence had been of eternity! The ashes – the pitchy stream – sprinkled the altars, covered the pavement, and half concealed the quivering corpses of the priests!

'They are dead,' said Burbo, terrified for the first time, and hurried back into the cell, 'I thought not the danger was so near and fatal.'

The two wretches stood staring at each other; you might have heard their hearts beat! Calenus, the less bold by nature, but the more griping, recovered first.

'We must to our task and away!' he said, in a low whisper, frightened at his own voice. He stepped to the threshold, paused, crossed over the heated floor and his dead brethren to the sacred chapel, and called to Burbo to follow. But the gladiator quaked and drew back.

'So much the better,' thought Calenus, 'the more will be *my* booty.' Hastily he loaded himself with the more portable treasures of the temple; and thinking no more of his comrade, hurried from the sacred place. A sudden flash of lighning from the mountain showed to Burbo, who stood motionless at the threshold, the flying and laden form of the priest. He took heart; he stepped forth to join him, when a tremendous shower of ashes fell right before his feet. The gladiator shrank back once more. Darkness closed him in. But the shower continued fast – fast; its heaps rose high and suffocating – deathly vapours steamed from them. The wretch gasped for breath; he sought in despair again to fly; the ashes had blocked up the threshold; he shrieked as his feet shrank from the boiling fluid. How could he escape? He could not climb to the open space – nay, were he able, he could not brave its horrors. It were best to remain in the cell, protected, at least, from the fatal air. He sat down and clenched his teeth. By degrees, the atmosphere from without – stifling and venomous – crept into the chamber. He could endure it no longer. His eyes, glaring round, rested on a sacrificial axe which some priest had left in the chamber: he seized it. With the desperate strength of his gigantic arm, he attempted to hew his way through the walls.

Meanwhile, the streets were already thinned; the crowd had hastened to disperse itself under shelter; the ashes began to fill up the lower parts of the town; but, here and there, you heard the steps of fugitives cranching them warily, or saw their pale and haggard faces by the blue glare of torches, by which they endeavoured to steer their steps. But ever and anon the boiling water, the straggling ashes, or mysterious and gusty winds rising and dying in a breath, extinguished these wandering lights, and with them the last living hope of those who bore them.

In the street that leads to the gate of Herculaneum, Clodius now bent his perplexed and doubtful way. 'If I can gain the open country,' thought he, 'doubtless there will be various vehicles beyond the gate, and Herculaneum is not far distant. Thank Mercury! I have little to lose, and that little is about me!'

'Holloa! – help there – help!' cried a querulous and frightened voice. 'I have fallen down – my torch is gone out – my slaves have deserted me. I am Diomed – the rich Diomed – ten thousand sesterces to him who helps me!'

At the same moment Clodius felt himself caught by the feet. 'Ill fortune to thee; let me go, fool!' said the gambler.

'Oh, help me up! – give me thy hand!'

'There – rise!'

'Is this Clodius? I know the voice! Whither fliest thou?'

'Towards Herculaneum.'

'Blessed be the gods! our way is the same, then, as far as the gate. Why not take refuge in my villa? Thou knowest the long range of subterranean cellars beneath the basement – that shelter, what shower can penetrate?'

'You speak well,' said Clodius, musingly, 'and by storing the cellar with food, we can remain there even some days, should these wondrous storms endure so long.'

'Oh, blessed be he who invented gates to a city!' cried Diomed. 'See! they have placed a light within yon arch; by that let us guide our steps.'

The air was now still for a few minutes; the lamp from the gate streamed out far and clear: the fugitives hurried on – they gained the gate – they passed by the Roman sentry; the lightning flashed over his livid face and polished helmet, but his stern features were composed even in their awe! He remained erect and motionless at his post. That hour itself had not animated the machine of the ruthless majesty of Rome into the reasoning and self-acting man! There he stood amidst the crashing elements: he had not received the permission to desert his station and escape!

Diomed and his companion hurried on, when suddenly a female form rushed athwart their way. It was the girl whose ominous voice had been raised so often and so gladly in anticipation of 'the merry show!'

'Oh, Diomed!' she cried, 'shelter! shelter! See' – pointing to an infant clasped to her breast – 'see this little one! – it is mine! –

the child of shame! I have never owned it till this hour! But *now* I remember I am a mother! I have plucked it from the cradle of its nurse: *she* had fled! Who could think of the babe in such an hour but she who bore it! Save it! save it!'

'Curses on thy shrill voice! Away, harlot!' muttered Clodius, between his ground teeth.

'Nay, girl,' said the more humane Diomed, 'follow if thou wilt. This way – this way – to the vaults!'

They hurried on and arrived at the house of Diomed – they laughed aloud as they crossed the threshold, for they deemed the danger over.

Diomed ordered his slaves to carry down into the subterranean gallery, before described, a profusion of food, and oil for lights; and there Julia, Clodius, the mother and her babe, the slaves, and some frightened visitors and clients of the district, sought their shelter.

IV

The cloud which had scattered so deep a murkiness over the day had now settled into a solid and impenetrable mass. It resembled less even the thickest gloom of a night in the open air than the close and blind darkness of some narrow room. But, in proportion as the blackness gathered, did the lightnings around Vesuvius increase in their vivid and scorching glare. No rainbow ever rivalled their varying and prodigal dyes. Now brightly blue as the most azure depth of a southern sky; now of a livid and snakelike green, darting restlessly to and fro as the folds of an enormous serpent; now of a lurid and intolerable crimson, gushing forth through the columns of smoke far and wide, and lighting up the whole city from arch to arch – then suddenly dying into a sickly paleness like the ghost of its own life!

In the pauses of the showers you heard the rumbling of the earth beneath, and the groaning waves of the tortured sea; or, lower still, and audible but to the watch of intensest fear, the grinding and hissing murmur of the escaping gases through the chasms of the distant mountain. Sometimes the cloud appeared to break from its solid mass, and, by the lightning, to assume quaint and vast mimicries of human or of monster shapes striding across the gloom, hurtling one upon the other, and vanishing swiftly into the turbulent abyss of shade, so that to the eyes and fancies of the affrighted wanderers the unsubstantial vapours were as the bodily forms of gigantic foes – the agents of terror and of death.

The ashes in many places were already knee-deep; and the boiling showers which came from the steaming breath of the volcano forced their way into the houses, bearing with them a strong and suffocating vapour. In some places immense fragments of rock, hurled upon the house-roofs, bore down along the streets masses of confused ruin, which yet more and more with every hour obstructed the way; and, as the day advanced, the motion of the earth was more sensibly felt; the footing seemed to slide and creep; nor could chariot or litter be kept steady, even on the most level ground.

Sometimes the huger stones, striking against each other as they fell, broke into countless fragments, emitting sparks of fire which caught whatever was combustible within their reach; and along the plains beyond the city the darkness was now terribly relieved – for several houses, and even vineyards, had been set in flames; and at various intervals the fires rose sullenly and fiercely against the solid gloom. To add to this partial relief of the darkness, the citizens had, here and there in the more public places, such as the porticoes of temples and the entrances to the forum, endeavoured to place rows of torches, but these rarely continued long; the showers and the winds extinguished them, and the sudden darkness into which their sudden birth was converted had something in it doubly terrible and doubly impressing on the impotence of human hopes – the lesson of despair.

Frequently, by the momentary light of these torches, parties of fugitives encountered each other, some hurrying towards the sea, others flying from the sea back to the land, for the ocean had retreated rapidly from the shore; an utter darkness lay over it, and upon its groaning and tossing waves the storm of cinders and rock fell without the protection which the streets and roofs afforded to the land. Wild, haggard, ghastly with supernatural fears, these groups encountered each other, but without the leisure to speak, to consult, to advise; for the showers fell now frequently, though not continously, extinguishing the lights which showed to each band the deathlike faces of the other, and hurrying all to seek refuge beneath the nearest shelter. The whole elements of civilization were broken up. Ever and anon, by the flickering lights, you saw the thief hastening by the most solemn authorities of the law, laden with, and fearfully chuckling over, the produce of his sudden gains. If in the darkness wife was separated from husband, or parent from child, vain was the hope of reunion. Each hurried blindly and confusedly on. Nothing in all the various and complicated machinery of social life was left save the primal law of self-preservation!

Through this awful scene did the Athenian wade his way,

accompanied by Ione and the blind girl. Suddenly a rush of hundreds, in their path to the sea, swept by them. Nydia was torn from the side of Glaucus, who, with Ione, was borne rapidly onward; and when the crowd (whose forms they saw not, so thick was the gloom) were gone, Nydia was still separated from their side. Glaucus shouted her name. No answer came. They retraced their steps – in vain; they could not discover her. It was evident that she had been swept along some opposite direction by the human current. Their friend, their preserver, was lost. And hitherto Nydia had been their guide. *Her blindness rendered the scene familiar to her alone.* Accustomed through a perpetual night to thread the windings of the city, she led them unerringly towards the sea-shore, by which they had resolved to hazard a escape. Now, which way could they wend? – all was rayless to them – a maze without a clue. Wearied, despondent, bewildered, they, however, passed along, the ashes falling upon their heads, the fragmentary stones dashing up in sparkles before their feet.

'Alas! alas!' murmured Ione, 'I can go no farther; my steps sink among the scorching cinders. Fly, dearest! – beloved, fly! and leave me to my fate!'

'Hush, my betrothed! my bride! Death with thee is sweeter than life without thee! Yet, whither – oh! whither can we direct ourselves through the gloom? Already it seems that we have made but a circle, and are in the very spot which we quitted an hour ago.'

'O gods! yon rock; see, it hath riven the roof before us. It is death to move through the streets!'

'Blessed lightning! See Ione – see! the portico of the Temple of Fortune. Let us creep beneath it; it will protect us from the showers.'

He caught his beloved in his arms, and with difficulty and labour gained the temple. He bore her to the remoter and more sheltered part of the portico, and leant over her, that he might shield her with his own form from the lightning and the showers! The beauty and the unselfishness of love could hallow even that dismal time.

'Who is there?' said the trembling and hollow voice of one who had preceded them in their place of refuge.

'Yet, what matters! – the crush of the ruined world forbids to us friends or foes.'

Ione turned at the sound of the voice, and with a faint shriek, cowered again beneath the arms of Glaucus; and he, looking in the direction of the voice, beheld the cause of her alarm. Through the darkness glared forth two burning eyes – the lightning flashed and lingered athwart the temple – and Glaucus, with a shudder, perceived the lion to which he had been doomed crouched beneath the pillars; – and, close beside it, unwitting of the vicinity, lay the giant form of him who had accosted them – the wounded gladiator, Niger.

That lightning had revealed to each other the form of beast and man; yet the instinct of both was quelled. Nay, the lion crept nearer and nearer to the gladiator, as for companionship; and the gladiator did not recede or tremble. The revolution of Nature had dissolved her lighter terrors and her wonted ties.

While they were thus terribly protected, a group of men and women, bearing torches, passed by the temple. They were of the congregation of the Nazarenes; and a sublime and unearthly emotion had not, indeed, quelled their awe, but it had robbed awe of fear. They had long believed, according to the error of the early Christians, that the Last Day was at hand; they imagined now that the Day had come.

'Woe! woe!' cried, in a shrill and piercing voice, the elder at their head. 'Behold! the Lord descendeth to judgment! He maketh fire come down from heaven in the sight of men! Woe! woe! ye strong and mighty! Woe to ye of the fasces and the purple! Woe to the idolator and the worshipper of the beast. Woe to ye who pour forth the blood of saints, and gloat over the death-pangs of the sons of God! Woe to the harlot of the sea! – woe! woe!'

With a loud and deep chorus, the troop chanted forth, along the wild horrors of the air – 'Woe to the harlot of the sea! – woe! woe!'

The Nazarenes paced slowly on, their torches still flickering in the storm, their voices still raised in menace and solemn warning, till, lost amid the windings in the streets, the darkness of the atmosphere and the silence of death again fell over the scene.

There was one of the frequent pauses in the showers, and Glaucus encouraged Ione once more to proceed. Just as they stood, hesitating, on the last step of the portico, an old man, with a bag in his right hand, and leaning upon a youth, tottered by. The youth bore a torch. Glaucus recognized the two as father and son – miser and prodigal.

'Father,' said the youth, 'if you cannot move more swiftly, I must leave you, or we *both* perish!'

'Fly, boy, then, and leave thy sire!'

'But I cannot fly to starve; give me thy bag of gold!' And the youth snatched at it.

'Wretch! wouldst thou rob thy father?'

'Ay! who can tell the tale at this hour? Miser, perish!'

The boy struck the old man to the ground, plucked the

bag from his relaxing hand, and fled onward with a shrill yell.

'Ye gods!' cried Glaucus, 'are ye blind, then, even in the dark? Such crimes may well confound the guiltless with the guilty in one common ruin. Ione, on! – on!'

V

Advancing, as men grope for escape in a dungeon, Ione and her lover continued their uncertain way. At the moments when the volcanic lightnings lingered over the street, they were enabled, by that awful light, to steer and guide their progress: yet, little did the view it presented to them cheer or encourage their path. In parts the surface of the earth presented a leprous and ghastly white. In other places, cinder and rock lay matted in heaps, from beneath which might be seen the half-hid limbs of some crushed and mangled fugitive. The groans of the dying were broken by wild shrieks of women's terror – now near, now distant – which, when heard in the utter darkness, were rendered doubly appalling by the crushing sense of helplessness and the uncertainty of the perils around; and clear and distant through all were the mighty and various noises from the Fatal Mountain; its rushing winds; its whirling torrents; and, from time to time, the burst and roar of some more fiery explosion. And ever as the winds swept howling along the street, they bore sharp streams of burning dust, and such sickening and poisonous vapours, as took away, for the instant, breath and consciousness, followed by a rapid revulsion of the arrested blood, and a tingling sensation of agony trembling through every nerve and fibre of the frame.

'Oh! Glaucus, my beloved– my own! take me to thy arms. One embrace – let me feel thy arms around me – and in that embrace let me die – I can no more!'

'For my sake, for my life – courage yet, sweet Ione. My life is linked with thine; and see – torches – this way! Lo! how they brave the wind! Ha! they live through the storm – doubtless, fugitives to the sea! – we will join them.'

As if to inspire the lovers, the winds and showers came to a sudden pause; the atmosphere was profoundly still; the mountain seemed at rest, gathering, perhaps, fresh fury for its next burst: the torch-bearers moved quickly on. 'We are nearing the sea,' said, in a calm voice, the person at their head. 'Liberty and wealth to each slave who survives this day! Courage! – I tell you that the gods themselves have assured me of deliverance. On!'

Redly and steadily the torches flashed full on the eyes of Glaucus and Ione, who lay trembling and exhausted on his bosom. Several slaves were bearing, by the light, panniers and coffers, heavily laden; in front of them – a drawn sword in hand – towered the lofty form of Arbaces.

'By my fathers!' cried the Egyptian, 'Fate smiles upon me even through these horrors, and amidst the dreadest aspects of woe and death, bodes me happiness and love. Away, Greek! I claim my ward, Ione!'

'Traitor and murderer!' cried Glaucus, glaring upon his foe, 'Nemesis hath guided thee to my revenge! – a just sacrifice to the shades of Hades, that now seem loosed on earth. Approach – touch but the hand of Ione, and thy weapon shall be as a reed. I will tear thee limb from limb!'

Suddenly, as he spoke, the place became lighted with an intense and lurid glow. Bright and gigantic through the darkness, which closed around it like the walls of hell, the mountain shone – a pile of fire! Its summit seemed riven in two; or, rather, above its surface there seemed to rise two monster shapes, each confronting each, as Demons contending for a World. These were of one deep blood-red hue of fire, which lighted up the whole atmosphere far and wide; but *below*, the nether part of the mountain was still dark and shrouded – save in three places, adown which flowed, serpentine and irregular, rivers of the molten lava. Darkly red through the profound gloom of their banks, they flowed slowly on, as towards the devoted city. Over the broadest there seemed to spring a cragged and stupendous arch, from which, as from the jaws of hell, gushed the sources of the sudden Phlegethon. And through the stilled air was heard the rattling of the fragments of rock, hurtling one upon another as they were borne down the fiery cataracts – darkening, for one instant, the spot where they fell, and suffused, the next, in the burnished hues of the flood along which they floated!

The slaves shrieked aloud, and, cowering, hid their faces. The Egyptian himself stood transfixed to the spot, the glow lighting up his commanding features and jewelled robes. High behind him rose a tall column that supported the bronze statue of Augustus; and the imperial image seemed changed to a shape of fire!

With his left hand circled round the form of Ione – with his right arm raised in menace, and grasping the stilus which was to have been his weapon in the arena, and which he still fortunately bore about him – with his brow knit – his lips apart – the wrath and menace of human passions arrested, as by a charm, upon his features – Glaucus confronted the Egyptian!

Muttering to himself, Arbaces turned his eyes from the mountain – they rested on the form of Glaucus! He paused: 'Why,' he muttered, 'should I hesitate? Did not the stars foretell the only crisis of peril to which I was subjected? – Is not that peril past?'

'The soul,' cried he aloud 'can brave the wreck of worlds and the wrath of imaginary gods! By that soul will I conquer to the last! Advance, slaves! – Athenian, resist me, and thy blood be on thine own head! Thus, then, I regain Ione!'

He advanced one step – it was his last on earth! The ground shook beneath him with a convulsion that cast all around upon its surface. A simultaneous crash resounded through the city, as down toppled roof and pillar! – the lightning, as if caught by the metal, lingered an instant on the Imperial Statue – then shivered bronze and column! Down fell the ruin, echoing along the street, and riving the solid pavement where it crashed! The prophecy of the stars was fulfilled!

The sound – the shock, stunned the Athenian for several moments. When he recovered, the light still illumined the scene; the earth still slid and trembled beneath! Ione lay senseless on the ground; but he saw her not yet – his eyes were fixed upon a ghastly face that seemed to emerge, without limbs or trunk, from the huge fragments of the shattered column – a face of unutterable pain, agony, and despair! The eyes shut and opened rapidly, as if sense were not yet fled; the lips quivered and grinned – then sudden stillness and darkness fell over the features, yet retaining that aspect of horror never to be forgotten!

So perished the wise Magian – the great Arbaces – the Hermes of the Burning Belt – the last of the royalty of Egypt!

VI

Glaucus turned in gratitude but in awe, caught Ione once more in his arms, and fled along the street, that was yet intensely luminous. But suddenly a duller shade fell over the air. Instinctively he turned to the mountain, and behold one of the two gigantic crests, into which the summit had been divided, rocked and wavered to and fro; and then, with a sound the mightiness of which no language can describe, it fell from its burning base, and rushed, an avalanche of fire, down the side of the mountain! At the same instant gushed forth a volume of blackest smoke – rolling on, over air, sea, and earth.

Another – and another – and another shower of ashes, far more profuse than before, scattered fresh desolation along the streets.

Darkness once more wrapt them as a veil; and Glaucus, his bold heart at last quelled, sank beneath the cover of an arch, and, clasping Ione to his heart – a bride on that couch of ruin – resigned himself to die!

Meanwhile Nydia, when separated by the throng from Glaucus and Ione, had in vain endeavoured to regain them. In vain she raised that plaintive cry so peculiar to the blind; it was lost amidst a thousand shrieks of more selfish terror. Again and again she returned to the spot where they had been divided – to find her companions gone, to seize every fugitive – to inquire of Glaucus – to be dashed aside in the impatience of distraction. Who in that hour spared one thought to his neighbour? Perhaps, in scenes of universal horror, nothing is *more* horrid than the unnatural selfishness they engender! At length it occurred to Nydia that, as it had been resolved to seek the seashore for escape, her most probable chance of rejoining her companions would be to persevere in that direction. Guiding her steps, then, by the staff which she always carried, she continued, with incredible dexterity to avoid the masses of ruin that encumbered the path – to thread the street – and unerringly (so blessed now was that accustomed darkness so afflicting in ordinary life!) to take the nearest direction to the sea-side.

Poor girl! her courage was beautiful to behold! – and fate seemed to favour one so helpless! The boiling torrents touched her not, save by the general rain which accompanied them; the huge fragments of scoria shivered the pavement before and beside her, but spared that frail form; and when the lesser ashes fell over her, she shook them away with a slight tremor, and dauntlessly resumed her course.

Weak, exposed, yet fearless – supported but by one wish, she was a very emblem of Psyche in her wanderings – of Hope, walking through the Valley of the Shadow – of the Soul itself, lone but undaunted, amidst the dangers and the snares of life!

Her path was, however, constantly impeded by the crowds that now groped amidst the gloom, now fled in the temporary glare of the lightnings across the scene; and, at length, a group of torch-bearers rushing full against her, she was thrown down with some violence.

'What!' said the voice of one of the party, 'is this the brave blind girl? By Bacchus, she must not be left here to die? Up, my Thessalian! So – so. Are you hurt? That's well! Come on with us! we are for the shore!'

'O Sallust! it is thy voice! The gods be thanked! Glaucus! Glaucus! have ye seen him?'

'Not I! He is doubtless out of the city by this time. The gods who saved him from the lion will save him from the burning mountain.'

As the kindly epicure thus encouraged Nydia, he drew her along with him towards the sea, heeding not her passionate entreaties that he would linger yet awhile to search for Glaucus; and still, in the accent of despair, she continued to shriek aloud that beloved name, which, amidst all the roar of the convulsed elements, kept alive a music at her heart.

The sudden illumination, the burst of the floods of lava, and the earthquake, which we have already described, chanced when Sallust and his party had just gained the direct path leading from the city to the port; and here they were arrested by an immense crowd, more than half the population of the city. They spread along the field without the walls, thousand upon thousands, uncertain whither to fly. The sea had retired far from the shore; and they who had fled to it had been so terrified by the agitation and preternatural shrinking of the element, the gasping forms of the uncouth sea things which the waves had left upon the sand, and by the sound of the huge stones cast from the mountain into the deep, that they had returned again to the land, as presenting the less frightful aspect of the two. Thus the two streams of human beings, the one seaward, the other *from* the sea, had met together, feeling a sad comfort in numbers – arrested in despair and doubt.

'The world is to be destroyed by fire,' said an old man, in long loose robes, a philosopher of the Stoic school: 'Stoic and Epicurean wisdom have alike agreed in this prediction; and the hour is come!'

'Yea; the hour is come!' cried a loud voice, solemn but not fearful.

Those around turned in dismay. The voice came from above them. It was the voice of Olinthus, who, surrounded by his Christian friends, stood upon an abrupt eminence on which the old Greek colonists had raised a temple to Apollo, now time-worn and half in ruin.

As he spoke, there came that sudden illumination which heralded the death of Arbaces, and glowing over that mighty multitude, awed, crouching, breathless – never on earth had the faces of men seemed so haggard! – never had meeting of mortal beings been so stamped with the horror and sublimity of dread! – never, till the last trumpet sounds, shall such meeting be seen again! And above rose the form of Olinthus, with outstretched arm and prophet brow, girt with the living fires. And the crowd knew the face of him they had doomed to the fangs of the beast – *then* their victim, *now* their warner; and through the stillness again came his ominous voice – 'The hour is come!' The Christians repeated the cry. It was caught up – it was echoed from side to side – woman and man, childhood and old age, repeated, not aloud, but in a smothered and dreary murmur – 'THE HOUR IS COME!'

At that moment, a wild yell burst through the air – and, thinking only of escape, whither it knew not, the terrible tiger of the desert leaped amongst the throng, and hurried through its parted streams. And so came the earthquake – and so darkness once more fell over the earth!

And now new fugitives arrived. Grasping the treasures no longer destined for their lord, the slaves of Arbaces joined the throng. One only of their torches yet flickered on. It was borne by Sosia; and its light falling on the face of Nydia, he recognized the Thessalian.

'What avails thy liberty now, blind girl?' said the slave.

'Who art thou? Canst thou tell me of Glaucus?'

'Ay, I saw him but a few minutes since.'

'Blessed by thy head! where?'

'Crouched beneath the arch of the Forum – dead, or dying! – gone to rejoin Arbaces, who is no more!'

Nydia uttered not a word; she slid from the side of Sallust; silently she glided through those behind her, and retraced her steps to the city. She gained the Forum – the arch; she stooped down – she fell around – she called on the name of Glaucus.

A weak voice answered – 'Who calls on me? Is it the voice of the Shades? Lo! I am prepared!'

'Arise! follow me! take my hand! Glaucus, thou shalt be saved!'

In sudden hope, Glaucus arose – 'Nydia still! Ah; thou, then, art safe!' The tender joy of his voice pierced the heart of the Thessalian, and she blessed him for his thought of her.

Half leading, half carrying Ione, Glaucus followed his guide. With admirable discretion, she avoided the path which led to the crowd she had just quitted, and, by another route, sought the shore.

After many pauses and incredible perseverance, they gained the sea, and joined a group who, bolder than the rest, resolved to hazard any peril rather than continue in such a scene. In darkness they put forth to the sea; but, as they cleared the land and caught new aspects of the mountain, its channels of molten fire threw a partial redness over the waves.

Utterly exhausted and worn out, Ione slept on the breast of Glaucus, and Nydia lay at his feet. Meanwhile the showers of dust and ashes, still borne aloft, fell into the wave, and scattered their snows over the deck. Far and wide, borne by the winds, those showers descended upon the remotest climes, startling even the swarthy African; and whirled along the antique soil of Syria and of Egypt!

VII

And meekly, softly, beautifully, dawned at last the light over the trembling deep! – the winds were sinking into rest – the foam died from the glowing azure of that delicious sea. Around the east, thin mists caught gradually the rosy hues that heralded the morning; light was about to resume her reign. Yet still, dark and massive in the distance, lay the broken fragments of the destroying cloud, from which red streaks, burning dimlier and more dim, betrayed the yet rolling fires of the mountain of the 'Scorched Fields.' The white walls and gleaming columns that had adorned the lovely coast were no more. Sullen and dull were the shores so lately crested by the cities of Herculaneum and Pompeii. The darlings of the deep were snatched from her embrace! Century after century shall the mighty mother stretch forth her azure arms, and know them not – moaning round the the sepulchres of the Lost!

There was no *shout* from the mariners at the dawning light – it had come too gradually, and they were too wearied for such sudden bursts of joy – but there was a low, deep *murmur* of thankfulness amidst those watchers of the long night. They looked at each other and smiled; they took heart; they felt once more that there was a world around, and a God above them! And in the feeling that the worst was past, the over-wearied ones turned round, and fell placidly to sleep. In the growing light of the skies there came the silence which night had wanted; and the barque drifted calmly onward to its port. A few other vessels, bearing similar fugitives, might be seen in the expanse, apparently motionless, yet gliding also on. There was a sense of security, of companionship, and of hope, in the sight of their slender masts and white sails. What beloved friends, lost and missed in the gloom, might they not bear to safety and to shelter!

In the silence of the general sleep, Nydia rose gently. She bent over the face of Glaucus – she inhaled the deep breath of his heavy slumber – timidly and sadly she kissed his brow – his lips; she felt for his hand – it was locked in that of Ione; she sighed deeply, and her face darkened. Again she kissed his brow, and with her hair wiped from it the damps of night. 'May the gods bless you, Athenian!' she murmured, 'may you be happy with your beloved one! – may you sometimes remember Nydia! Alas! she is of no further use on earth!'

With these words she turned away. Slowly she crept along by the *fori*, or platforms, to the farther side of the vessel, and pausing bent low over the deep; the cool spray dashed upward on her feverish brow. 'It is the kiss of death,' she said, 'it is welcome.' The balmy air played through her waving tresses – she put them from her face, and raised those eyes – so tender, though so lightless – to the sky, whose soft face she had never seen!

'No, no!' she said, half aloud, and in a musing and thoughtful tone, 'I cannot endure it; this jealous, exacting love – it shatters my whole soul in madness! I might harm him again – wretch that I was! I have saved him – twice saved him – happy, happy thought – why not *die* happy? – It is the last glad thought I can ever know. Oh! sacred Sea! I hear thy voice invitingly – it hath a freshening and joyous call. They say that in thy embrace is dishonour; that thy victims cross not the fatal Styx; be it so! – I would not meet him in the Shades, for I should meet him still with *her*! Rest – rest – rest! there is no other Elysium for a heart like mine!'

A sailor, half dozing on the deck, heard a slight splash on the waters. Drowsily he looked up, and behind, he fancied he saw something white above the waves; but it vanished in an instant. He turned round again, and dreamed of his home and children.

When the lovers awoke, their first thought was of each other – their next of Nydia! She was not to be found – none had seen her since the night. Every crevice of the vessel was searched – there was no trace of her. Mysterious from first to last, the blind Thessalian had vanished for ever from the living world! They guessed her fate in silence; and Glaucus and Ione, while they drew nearer to each other (feeling each other the world itself), forgot their deliverance, and wept as for a departed sister.

MARCELLUS TAKES THE BISCUIT

Leopold Spero

The following story takes us away from major events in Roman history to the everyday life of the Roman senator and his family.

Leo Spero wrote a short series about Marcellus for Chambers's Journal *in the late 1940s. He considered what must have been a formidable problem at the time – the influx of the savage British into the Roman world.*

This story is set during the reign of the Emperor Trajan, about AD *100.*

Marcus Naso, that eminent Roman legislator, had been in Rome for a fortnight on Senatorial affairs. His wife Julia, welcoming him on the steps of their pleasant country villa in the Alban Hills, was all agog for the latest news from the capital. But as she kissed him, with the tenderness of twenty-seven years' unclouded devotion, she had a sense of deep unease. Something was wrong. Marcus was never a man of lively manner, though he would have deeply resented any implication that he was ever glum or dull. She did not expect to see him beaming or humming the latest popular song, for that was not his way. But this was not his customary gravity. Senator Marcus Naso was worried.

Julia took his arm. 'The journey has tired you, *dilectissime*, eh? Rome takes too much of my dear husband. Why must you attend so many meetings of the Senate, Marcus?'

Marcus sighed. 'Because I am a Senator.'

'But, darling, they surely don't need you as badly as all that? What you need, *meum cor*,' said Julia firmly, 'is a glass of Falernian.' She clapped her hands, and the immense head-butler, black as night and of incredible majesty, appeared from nowhere in particular, and took his mistress's order with head reverentially bowed and palms outstretched.

'We'll have it in the *aula*,' she said. 'Bring a dish of the Neapolitan *buccellata* as well.'

'*Imperasti, praestantissima!*'

Julia put her hand to her mouth, suppressing her giggles with difficulty until the ebony giant was out of hearing. Then she exploded.

'Julia!'

'I – I can't help it, Marcus. His *accent*! And those long words he uses! How he loves them!'

'He holds our noble Roman speech in honour,' said Marcus, sitting down as though he had lumbago.

'Husband, dearest! Why so severe?'

Marcus took her hand and squeezed it. 'I didn't mean to be severe. Not with my own beloved wife.'

'And I didn't mean to be flippant . . . but I do love a good laugh. Maconis wouldn't mind my laughing at him. These Numidians are so good-humoured – just like nice children. Of course, a head-butler has to be dignified. But it's only on the surface. I won't laugh at him when he comes back, Marcus.'

'With the *buccellata*?'

'And the new Falernian.'

'You mean the old Falernian, I hope?'

'Of course I do. The first bottle this year.'

'Then why take Army biscuit with it?'

This time Julia burst out laughing without restraint. 'Army biscuit, beloved?'

'That's what you ordered, isn't it?'

'Oh, dear!' Julia sat back and wiped her eyes helplessly. 'Did you think I meant real *buccellata*, my love? These are something unique, from that new Syrian bakery in Neapolis – the most exquisite, delicate little cakes you ever tasted. Iasonides has a peculiar sense of humour, however.'

'Iasonides? I thought you said he was a Syrian?'

'He is, darling. But you can't do business in Neapolis with a Syrian name, can you?'

'How should I know? I'm no merchant.'

'Well . . . you can't. I mean – the Greeks are *smart*.'

'I've met smart Syrians.'

'But that's not what I mean. The Syrian has the brains, I'll grant
. . . but not the *style*, darling. Greece *invented* style.'

The butler, preceded by a slave with a tray, an unusual Etruscan
piece of great though over-elaborated beauty, interrupted the argument. The Falernian held lovely winking fires enclosed in its cool
depths. Beside it reposed half a dozen crisp brown confections, thinly
ribbed, oblong, squares, diamonds, and circles. Marcus conveyed
one to his lips, and waved to Maconis to set the tray on the little
table beside him.

'Mmmm!'

'Nice, darling?'

The Senator licked his lips. 'Not exactly Army biscuit. I've never
tasted anything quite like these.'

'I'm sure you haven't. What of the wine, *o mi vir*?'

'Give me a chance, *dilecta*.' Marcus poured out a careful glass,
held it up to the afternoon light, and winked back at it as he took
his first critical sip. 'Ah-h-h!' A long-drawn-out sigh of unalloyed
pleasure escaped from the aristocratic thin lips. No matter what
troubles and disturbances threatened the mind, one could still reach
out to divine Falernian comfort through the palate.

Marcus laid down his *calix* on the splendid little agate table. He
nibbled at another of the biscuits. 'They really are – how would
Maconis phrase it? – *praestantissima*. But what a name to give
them, dearest wife! Why not call them by some name worthy of
the fine art of the *pistor*? For, Apollo bear me witness, I've tasted
no more delicate confection in all my days?'

'I'm so glad, *carissime*. Give me one. *Gratias tibi, marite*. But
don't you see, it's so *clever*.'

'What's so clever?'

She held the little oblong flake at arm's length. 'Calling these
delightful cakes by a name like *buccellatum*.'

'What's clever about it, *Julia pulcerrima*?'

'I'm surprised at you, dear husband! A man of your intelligence
must surely appreciate the subtlety of giving the name of a coarse
and tasteless soldier's ration to an exquisite creation worthy of some
Olympian banquet. Do you suppose Licinius Lucullus himself ever
served such biscuits at his table, even though he did live in Neapolis?
Doesn't it add to your enjoyment, my own sweetheart, to be told
you're going to get *buccellata* . . . and to get *these*?'

Marcus shrugged his shoulders. 'It looks to me like a typical Syrian trick. Besides, we Romans shouldn't encourage these confounded foreigners to lead us into ways of luxury. But there' – he squeezed her hand – 'what a way to talk to a wife like mine! And me enjoying every last crumb! Still . . .' he stuffed another biscuit into his mouth '. . . you remember the verses of Quintus Horatius Flaccus?' The Senator sat back and declaimed to the landscape of purple and gold which stretched in rolling delight before his eyes. ' "*Persicos odi, puer apparatus* . . ." How right he was, Julia! What an instinct that man had for the perfect phrase!'

Julia frowned. 'Horatius Flaccus? You mean that *common* little man my grandfather used to speak about? Why, his father was no more than a *praeco* – a low auctioneer. Born a slave, what's more. How can you quote the sentiments of such a person?'

'Because he was a great poet, my darling. Never mind what his father may or may not have been. Quintus Horatius was and is one of the abiding glories of eternal Rome. Well might he say of himself' – Marcus puffed out his chest once more in the pride of renewed quotation – ' "*Exegi monumentum aere perennius.*" Yes, in truth – more lasting than bronze. Not bronze . . . gold, my dearest wife. Golden verses. Golden songs of the blessed countryside, where true happiness resides within simple walls with such meagre fare as a man of simple tastes may look for.'

Julia chuckled. 'Don't tell Maconis that, darling. He won't appreciate your quotations. Besides, Quintus Horatius was just a common fat little man. My grandfather said so, and *he* knew *all* the *best* people He wasn't so simple, either, any more than you are. He was a perfect glutton, which my Marcus is not – except perhaps for Neapolitan biscuits. And his table manners! My dear! There was one time, at dinner with that extraordinarily nice man who was so good to him . . . tut-tut! the name escapes me, though I've heard the venerable Sempronius speak it again and again when I was a child – he lived on the Esquiline – a most marvellous home, quite unique in those days so they say – surely you can think who he was, Marcus?'

'Not Cilnius Maecenas?'

'Of course! Maecenas. That's it. Well, he took him up, as you know, and made an immense fuss of him all his life. But what I say is, you can't make a silk purse out of a sow's ear. And one day at dinner, in front of all Rome, so to speak – '

Marcus laughed indulgently. 'Don't speak so, dear wife. Let it go at that. As for the silk purse . . .' He paused and frowned.

Julia glanced at him. His face was clouded, and he had pushed his goblet of Falernian aside. She was alarmed, not by his words, but by his looks. She strove to keep her composure, for she was a Roman matron of the Patrician Order, and granddaughter of Titus Sempronius Piso, Old Pea-Face of Misenum, who was himself also of the *gens Calpurnia*, and thus a connection by marriage of Gaius Julius, first and greatest of the Caesars. All this confused but unquestionably authentic farrago of genealogy ran through her brain as she made her wild guesses about what was in her husband's mind. She could hardly have made a less fortunate preparation for what he did have to tell her.

'Engaged?' whispered Julia. 'Actually *engaged*?'

Marcus sighed. 'Not the slightest doubt of it. I never knew the boy more determined about anything. And opposition from either of us – at this stage, at any rate – would only make things worse. I'm quite sure of that.'

'So am I.' There were tears in Julia's eyes, but her voice was firm. 'Has he told anyone else?'

'I don't think so. It isn't a thing one can talk about. And where would it take him, if he did?'

'*She's* been blabbing, I expect,' suggested Julia viciously.

'I don't think so. They're a secretive people, you know.'

'The British? Secretive?'

Marcus bit his thumb. 'Their religion makes them so. Or maybe it's the eternal fog they live in. They're proud, too. They keep themselves to themselves. They've got a certain . . . er . . . *dignity*: almost like Romans.'

'Marcus!' Julia's voice was well-nigh sharp.

'Yes, my dear?'

'Is our son as good a talker as all that?'

'I – I don't know what you mean.'

'Oh yes, you do. Marcellus has talked you into something. What is it?'

'He hasn't talked me into anything.'

'But you say he proposes to marry this creature?'

'I wouldn't call her a creature, *dilectissima*.'

'A blue-painted slave-girl . . . a noble wife indeed for Marcellus, son of Marcus Naso!'

Marcus sighed. 'She's not a slave, my dear.'

'Indeed? What is she then? A free-born Roman? They're cheap enough nowadays, goodness knows! And growing cheaper every day, from what I can see.'

He sighed again. 'Legally, I suppose Guenifra *is* a slave.'

'Guenifra? What sort of a name is that? How d'you pronounce it?'

'You said it very nicely, *Julia mea*.'

Julia's fine eyes filled with tears. 'I never thought my husband could vex me so.'

Hastily, full of repentance, he sought to soothe her, caressing her hand, wiping the tears away with his kerchief. 'Don't cry, *deliciae meae*. I can't bear to see you in tears. But I could cry myself, almost. *Per Iovem immortalem*, but our son has indeed delivered us into trouble.'

'It's not his fault at all!' cried Julia. 'We alone are to be blamed, you and I: his parents, who should have found a suitable wife for the boy long since. And now . . . oh, what shall we do?'

'We can't do much, my love. I've reasoned with him, but he's very obstinate . . . and very much in love.'

'Even so,' sobbed Julia, 'he needn't *marry* her. He *can't* marry her. It would be a public scandal. Our laws would not allow it. You are a Senator, Marcus. you should know that. If he won't obey you, then at least he'd have to obey the Emperor. Can't you see His Majesty about it?'

'Too late, my dearest. Marcus has seen *Her* Majesty, and the girl is to have her freedom. It looks as though we've got a British daughter-in-law on our hands. One day we'll have . . . British grand – '

Julia put her hands. '*Don't!* I can't *bear* it!'

The Senator gazed at his wife with the helpless affection of a dog watching its owner in distress beyond aid. He loved her very dearly, and she relied on him completely. Well, a wife should rely on a husband; a Roman wife above all. But it wasn't always so, not in these degenerate days. Yes, they were degenerate. Not so bad as they had been, of course. The divine Trajan had pulled Rome out of the worst morasses into which his predecessors had led her. But even he had been unable to restore the grand old days before Rome knew any Emperor, the dry and rigid morale of the Republic. Rome was not a world capital then; but she was something better – a world example. There were Catos in those days. Now, there was only Empire, with all its pomp and glitter, its vast and ever-increasing treasure, its endless variety of luxuries and epicurean indulgences, its imports of so much the old Rome never knew, and if it had known, would have scorned – particularly the human importations who were made Roman citizens before a true Roman could call upon his household gods to ask the reason why.

A British daughter-in-law. Grandchildren whose blood-stream of

Naso and Calpurnia would mingle with wild tribesmen's thick and muddy descent. And yet . . . the girl was a beauty, no doubt of that. Divinely tall, and most divinely fair, as one might have said had one been a poet. Great dignity, a fine reserve . . . and, of course, all the pride in the world.

'D'you mind, my love, if I take another glass of wine?'

Julia looked at him apprehensively. 'You *will* tell me all, husband? You won't hide anything?'

'Have I not told you enough?' Marcus filled the *calix* with affectionate care, and held it up against the afternoon sunlight so that its ruby sparkle might prolong the pleasures of anticipation. He turned to see Julia wringing her hands, silent but all the more piteous.

There *is* something else,' she said. 'I know there is, I *know* it. He's married her, Marcus. Hasn't he – *hasn't* he?'

Marcus gave a short laugh. 'Nonsense, my dearest wife. Those fears at least are groundless.'

'But how do you know?'

'Because he promised me. He took oath before our family gods that he would take no further step without advising me first . . . and you. She agreed.'

'*She* agreed? Was *she* present?'

'But of course. After all, the discussion concerned her too.'

'No wonder you took another cup of wine,' sobbed Julia. 'You needed it, to tell me *that*. No, go away! Leave me alone!' She tried to fend off her husband's comforting arm.

'But . . . Julia! Listen, *carissima*.'

'Listen to what? To how my husband, Marcus Naso, Senator of Imperial Rome, took counsel and instruction in his family affairs from a Trinobantian slave-wench?'

'She's not a Trinobant at all,' corrected Marcus. 'She's of the Iceni.'

'Wh-what's the difference?'

'A great deal, as you'll admit when you see her.'

'*See* her!' Julia sprang to her feet. Drawn up to full height, indignation seeming to add inches to her always-impressive stature, she flamed like an offended goddess.

Marcus felt the warmth of the wine mellowing the blood in his veins. This also was a beautiful woman, and an angry one. The whole world seemed to be full of beautiful women being angry with Marcus Naso; blonde yesterday, brunette to-day. It was the wrong kind of life for his station and dignity . . . but it was exciting . . . and it was not entirely *unpleasant*.

* * *

'Come and sit by me, *o bellissima, amantissima, felicissima mulierum omnium*! Let us take counsel together in this trouble. For this is a truly beautiful young person whom our son has found for himself. And if her status is that of a slave by our law, be sure she does not recognize it. She has been brought up from birth in a noble house, and if she was not born in Rome, that was . . . just bad luck. Had Junius Brutus Galea not been on service in Londinium at the time, Guenifra's parents might have come to Rome with him, and their daughter might have been born in Rome . . . a free woman. She regards herself as a free woman, as it is.'

'They've spoiled her. She should be whipped.'

The Senator started. 'What did you say, *cara mea*?'

'You heard,' said Julia. 'Whipped.'

'Yes, I heard. But if you meet her – *when* you meet her, Julia – '

'I refuse to meet her, Marcus. I thought I'd made that plain.'

'Very well. When, despite your refusal, and no doubt most undutifully, our son brings his affianced British bride to see his parents, which he is fully determined to do, don't mention the subject of whipping, my beloved I'm not *asking* you now, you see. With all affection, but as a Roman husband and father exacting his prerogative of obedience, I'm just *telling* you, dearest wife. *Absit omen* – we've troubles enough to go on with – but whipping must not be mentioned, even in the course of casual domestic news.'

Julia stared at him. 'Are you in your right senses, Marcus? What has happened to you? Why are you talking like this? You're not ill, are you?'

'I'm not very well, *cor meum*,' replied the Senator. 'I think I'll go and lie down. Dinner at the third hour, please.'

'Against the day when our future daughter-in-law comes to dine with us for the first – and last – time,' said Julia, 'I think you had better see about another hostess.'

But Guenifra never came to dinner at the villa. Instead, four days after his mother's ultimatum, Marcellus arrived, dusty and travel-stained, roaring for wine and food even as he embraced his parents. When these came, he ate and drank greedily, and would not speak until he was sated. Then he wiped his mouth in a rough fashion which Julia felt with horror must be German manners, not yet forgotten in Court attendance, stood up and stretched his powerful limbs, glared at the quiet and unworried afternoon, shook himself like a dog after a bath, and sank back into his seat.

Julia watched him with keen anxiety. She knew he had picked up bad manners in the German forests, but this boorishness was too much. She felt she could scream as he sat and glared, ever more gloomily, still silent, at the rich lands which he would one day inherit, and to which he proposed to bring his lovely savage from beyond Gaul. Marcus, more sensitive to the situation, pursed his lips and waited with greater patience than his wife.

'Well,' said Marcellus, at length. 'It's all over. No doubt you'll be relieved, pleased perhaps. But don't show it too plainly, and don't take too much notice of a son who hasn't the manners to be gracious to the best parents a man ever had. I know I'm behaving like a Teuton pig, but I'm . . .' He paused, and suddenly buried his head in his hands.

'What's the matter, my dearest son?' Julia was at his side, stroking the strong young head, bending down with caresses, murmuring comfort.

'She won't have me.' Marcellus looked up, and there was grievous hurt in his eyes. 'Guenifra is not to be my wife, after all. You've seen her, father, and you know what I've lost. Mother doesn't. I dare say, o *dilectissima mater mea*, you imagined, from what you'd heard, that I intended bringing a crude young barbarian creature into your home.'

'I imagined nothing of the kind!' cried Julia indignantly. 'From all your father told me, I gathered that she was a lovely, talented, dignified, high-spirited young woman, just the kind of wife you *would* choose, *fili mi*.'

Marcus bit his thin lips, but made no comment.

'I"m done with women,' declared Marcellus. His voice sounded miserable. 'I know of just one woman who's worth a second thought, and that's my own darling mother.' He got up, walked a couple of paces up and down, then resumed his seat. 'No, I mustn't be unjust to Guenifra. She had her reasons for what she's done. She told me what they were, with her usual honesty. Why, oh why did I have to include Claudius Varro amongst my ancestors? Tell, me, that, o *mi pater*.'

'It wasn't my fault,' Marcus retorted. 'But Claudius Varro was a highly eminent person, a good soldier, a public man of distinction. And anyway, what has that to do with whatever trouble has occurred between you and the lady from Britain?'

'You may well ask,' said Marcellus. 'Why she took it upon herself to look into my family history is a puzzle to me — well, maybe she was within her just rights, even so. With a lineage like hers, Guenifra would naturally wish to examine the descent

of the man she was going to marry. You know what her descent
is, I suppose?'

Marcus shrugged his shoulders. 'How should I?'

'But didn't I tell you? Guenifra is the great-granddaughter of the
noble Boudicca. D'you hear that, mother?'

'I hear it, son, but it conveys nothing to me. Who was
Boudicca?'

'Father will tell you,' said Marcellus.

Julia turned to her husband with a look of enquiry.

The Senator sighed. 'I'm not well up in Imperial history,' he
explained, 'but I take it that our son is referring to an extremely
troublesome local chieftainess in the east of the main British
island – '

'She was a queen,' snapped Marcellus. 'Queen of the Iceni, an
admirable and highly civilized people. Guenifra told me all about
them. The greatest queen they ever had, greater than Britain has
ever seen before or since.'

'She was a nuisance,' Marcus snapped back, just as shortly as his
son. 'That would have been bad enough. She was a rebel, which
was worse. But by far the worst of all, she was a successful rebel.
She defeated the legions of Rome in battle.'

'I remember now,' said Julia. 'Didn't she recapture Londinium,
and some other British towns we'd settled, and massacre a whole
lot of our colonists? An awful massacre, they say . . . thousands
and thousands.'

'Never mind the massacre,' exclaimed Marcus. 'Civilians have to
take that risk when they settle in foreign and savage parts. But the
point was, this woman defeated the armies of Rome . . . and that
was unforgivable.'

'Unforgivable!' Marcellus was on his feet now. 'It was glorious.
It was immortal.'

'Marcellus!' The Senator was appalled. 'Does my son speak
reason?'

'Your son,' answered Marcellus, 'pays tribute to a noble creature,
who had been shamefully used, for no better reason than that she
loved her country.'

'What!' cried the Senator, in a rare fury. 'You would make a
heroine out of a savage like that?'

Marcellus faced his father with an anger equal to his, but colder,
more level, more bitter. 'The savage, as you call her, had been
scourged by our officers, whipped like a dog. And why? Because,
when she no longer had a husband to defend her, we Romans,
civilized Romans, stole her country from her and enslaved her

people. She was their queen, father, and she behaved like a queen. She was a mother ... Do you know what happened to her daughters? Guenifra would tell you. I've lived among these primitive people, father, *You* haven't. They may have their faults, but they can teach us something about family devotion. I've lived in Rome for the past eight months without learning more than enough about our so-called civilization. Morals? There's not a tribe beyond the Alps that can't teach us what morality means. The gods know I'm no ascetic. But Rome to-day ... ugh!'

Calmer now, Marcus found himself quite stirred by the young man's spirited sermon. But it would never do to let him know as much. 'You've met my friend Cornelius Tacitus, have you not, my son? The historian?'

Marcellus' eyes lighted up. 'The man who wrote that wonderful *De Germania*? The only book I've ever read, pretty well. Is he a friend of yours? Could I meet him, father? Oh, but you *must* let me meet him. There are one or two points on tribal custom around the Confluentes that he – well, he's not exactly *wrong*, you see, but he's *missed* things. I could – I could *tell* him.'

'You *shall* meet him, my son. And you shall correct his ethnography, if you wish.'

'Not *correct*, father,' said Marcellus, in horrified tones. 'Correct the author of *De Germania*! A fine fool I should look doing that!'

'Not at all, Marcellus. My friend Publius Cornelius is not too proud to accept technical advice from the man who knows, the man on the spot. But before you talk about the tribes of Rhenus, ask him how many Romans were slaughtered by this marshland queen of yours in Britain. Publius Cornelius has put the total at seventy thousand. Think that over, my son. Seventy thousand Romans.'

Marcellus looked at his father in anger again. 'There were eighty thousand of the Iceni killed in battle afterwards, when Suetonius Paulus brought his army up against them. Think that over, my father. Eighty thousand Britons.'

'If you were not my only beloved son,' snapped Marcus, 'and had you not always been so dutiful, I would have thought that last remark of yours impertinent.'

'What *is* all this mathematics?' asked Julia. She slipped an arm through the arm of husband and son with equal affection. 'And what has it to do with this nice barbarian girl we were going to have in the family?'

'She's no barbarian, mother,' said Marcellus sulkily.

'Well, darling' – she chuckled, and squeezed his hand – 'this beautiful British denizen, eh? What's she got to do with the story, which I confess begins to bore me?'

'Only this, mother' – Marcellus still looked hurt – 'that she's found out that Claudius Varro was my great-uncle, and he was the young centurion who gave the order – the *actual* order – for Queen Boudicca to be scourged. After that, well, I ask you!' Much as she loved me, how could any girl of spirit bring herself to marry me?'

Julia sighed, happily. 'How, indeed? Why, Marcellus, I expect she thought it was in the blood. You might be wanting to whip *her* before you'd been married a month.'

His mouth opened. He stared. 'Say that again.'

She laughed. 'Don't take it too seriously, darling. All I meant was that your Guenifra might have thought she'd made a mistake, and let herself in for the kind of husband she wasn't expecting. Only a joke, of course. But – girls are funny about these little things – and you're no simple addition sum, my pet.'

'Mother,' begged Marcellus, 'tell me something frankly, will you?'

'I'm always frank, love. Ask your father if I'm not.'

'Well, then – why did Guenifra refuse to marry me? Was it because she was afraid of me?'

Julia hesitated. 'Not exactly.'

'Come, mother,' Marcellus pleaded, in a disappointed tone. 'You promised frankness.'

'Very well, my son. Your Guenifra was not afraid of you . . . she was afraid of Rome.'

'Of Rome? But what bearing has that on our marriage?'

'A great deal – especially with your ancestry, and hers. Oh, I know that you find our great city degenerate, and lacking in the stark virtues which you say are so typical of the tribes along the Germanic rivers, in the meadows of the Belgae, or in your horrifying Britain with its mists and swamps and trackless jungle. Yes, and it's easy to admire what you call freedom, but I call wild and irresponsible social aimlessness, especially when you know better, and can come away to something better whenever you please. I'm no politician, *Marcelle mi*, but Rome stands for Law and Order and you, my dear, not merely because you're a Roman soldier, but because you are yourself, son of Marcus the Senator, with the blood of Sempronius Piso and of Claudius Varro in your veins, also stand for Law and Order. In the world of to-day, Rome takes you in, or shuts you out. There's no half-and-half about it. Whatever you are, Dacian,

Greek, Syrian or Jew, Scythian or Numidian, Egyptian or – yes, even Briton, you're one of two things: for Rome, or against Rome. All sensible people, even among the barbarians themselves, realize this. Guenifra, finding you so good a listener, and so intelligent on tribal custom and religion, doubtless mistook you at first for something you were not. Is that not possible, my son?'

Marcellus screwed up his face, an endearing habit which made his mother want to hug him. After all, what was he still but her puzzled small boy, puzzled and hurt? 'I don't understand you, *mater mea*.'

'Well, Marcellus . . . Rome is full of cranks, people with queer, unorthodox ideas, social, religious, political. Good cranks and bad cranks, by which I mean the sincere ones, who are the more dangerous, and the common-minded ones, who are just contemptible. For example, I call these awful young women who think it clever to dress up in armour and make a show of themselves in the sports arenas nothing but vulgar cranks – yet they belong to our leading families, worse luck. And those shameful old women who run after young men when they should be offering sacrifices in the temples for the boon of a serene and dignified twilight; they're vulgar cranks too. But they're not dangerous, like those fanatical religious agitators – Christians, they call themselves: I don't expect you've met any yet, though some quite nice people have taken their ideas up.'

'But – but I don't have anything to do with any such people, mother.'

'No, my dear. But with all your interest in these Germans of yours, and now with the Britons, it did seem as though you'd absorbed some of the new-fangled ideas about the rights of barbarians, and so forth.'

'But haven't barbarians any rights?'

'Of course not: except to place themselves under the tutelage of Rome, and be glad of the chance.'

'Then do we have to ill-treat them?'

'Not at all. Merely keep them in their place. – Isn't that so, Marcus?'

'Of course it is,' agreed the Senator. 'Guenifra's young, and as your mother has said, she's been more than a little spoiled. No Roman girl, I imagine, could have had a nicer upbringing, or a better education. And mind you, I don't say she's not turned out well, in a way – quite a credit to the kind family who have befriended her.'

'She must have been,' said Julia, 'to secure so favourable an opinion in the eyes of Her Imperial Majesty. But to think she can

change Eternal Rome, and make a softy out of a Roman officer –
well, all the barbarian beauty and intelligence in Britain wouldn't
justify that. She tried to use you, dear boy, and you've been lucky
not to fall into the trap.'

'I can't bear to think of the trouble she might have made for
us all,' said Marcus. 'She'd have been trying to Briticize the whole
family before long. No, it wouldn't have done.'

'And she saw she'd never have succeeded,' Julia concluded, 'so
she took the best way out.'

'The only *dignified* way,' added the Senator.

'I – I suppose you're right,' Marcellus admitted, with a still
troubled look. He took up a cake from the table beside him.
'What are these, mother? I say, they're jolly good. Not like the
Army biscuit we got in Germany.'

'No, darling,' said Julia. 'And they don't teach that kind of cookery
in Britain either. All the same, don't spoil your dinner, my love.'

FORTUNATUS

R. H. Stewart

We remember Hadrian because of Hadrian's Wall, that magnificent piece of Roman engineering which stretches from coast to coast and effectively established the border between the Roman Empire in Britain and the wild untameable world of the Picts beyond. Even if we don't particularly think about Hadrian himself, his name holds a certain fascination. In fact although he was able to strengthen the Roman Empire during his reign, from AD 117–38 and undertook a marvellous programme of rebuilding works, most Romans distrusted him, and he ended his reign in ignominy. Although R. H. Stewart (b. 1938) was born in Surrey, she grew up in County Durham, and later moved to Cumbria where she and her husband ran a farm just north of the Roman wall.

You've come a good way to find me, young man, that I'll say.

Want to know about me, do you? Fortunatus the famous charioteer. Huh. What's it to be then – this book of yours? Oh, 'Annals' – I beg your pardon. Yes, we agreed: I'll give you an outline. Anything for an easy life!

You carry the wine; I'll bring the cups. We'll go outside under the pergola, where there's shade but the heat can get at my arthritis. I'll stretch out on the daybed. You wouldn't believe the pain in my back and shoulders – right down the arms into my hands. Then the palms split. See? Easy as wink. Open your hand incautiously and away she goes again. Comes of all the gripping and sawing of the reins.

That's better. Help yourself.

You have the table, d'you see – spread out your tablets and
papers and you can make notes. I want a flat fee, mind – but
you can negotiate that with my son-in-law before you leave. Ah
... well ... there's no such thing as a free lunch, is there? And you
don't fob me off with some titchy royalty on volumes sold: how in
Hades do I know what sort of interest your stuff'll command?

How the air shimmers here, when you look out across the land.
Hispania. Baetica. The Ulpians' own Province, you might say. I
love gazing at it: buildings, paddocks, the wide herd grazings full
of shifting horses. It's a handsome spread. One of the finest of all
the Imperial stud farms. And myself titular master of the lot – under
the Emperor, of course. My son-in-law, mind you, who helps me, is
one of the shrewdest judges of bloodstock, bar none.

They are clever girls – both my daughters. Take after their mother.
The other one married a career soldier. I call him the Hairy Bear!
(Full beard and all that.) But he has prospects they tell me: might
well make Legate.

Their mother ... now there was a woman! A mind as bright
and clear as rock crystal – and looks to match. She was the love
of my life, Aurelia, and I do not hide it. I miss her appallingly –
each sunset ... every dawn. But I'll catch up with her eventually,
on the other side of Styx. I'm sure of that. Yes – quite correct – she
was distantly related to the Imperial family. You would say that did
me no harm. Of course not. But I was a Chieftain's son born, and
always ambitious. I grafted; I didn't fling my prize monies away like
autumn leaves as so many of them do. I invested and prospered on
my own account. And Hadrian favoured me. Equestrian ring, see?
Narrow stripe. Hadrian himself conferred the status. The Divine
Hadrian: I find it hard to remember that he is dead too, now.

Fortuna favours the brave, they say. 'Fortunatus' was the name
Aurelia gave me at the beginning of my driving career. When she
was about thirteen, I think.

I am, as you so politely pointed out at luncheon, something of
what the Greeks would term a phenomenon: a true one-off. I see
no reason not to be quite proud of that. Shall we start?

I was British born. Which is a novelty in itself, because to the
very best of my knowledge I was, and remain, the only one of my
kind ever to race-drive in Rome. Mostly they are Greek, or Hispanic
with a sprinkling of North Africans thrown in.

Not only am I British by origin, but I was born outwith the Empire,
since in the time of the Divine Trajan its northern limit had yet to be
defined. Where we dwelt, it was all debatable territory. As I said:
I was a Chieftain's son and I was born two years after Trajan

assumed the Purple – 'with the century', as those nutty Christians put it, meaning one hundred years on from their strange Jewish god. They named me Morgan, then.

We were Brigantian by tribe, but because my father would not sign accommodations with Rome he was sequestered of much good land to the south and east of what is now the Imperial boundary. They forced him north – taking his warriors and dependents – right up into the last extremity of our tribal country, where it abuts that of the Selgovae to the west and the Votadini to the east. They squeezed us tight into a round bulge with much alien tribal pressure at our backs and Rome ranged firmly in front of us across the whole neck of Britain from sea to sea. We lived proud – but we lived constrained and deprived of much former wealth.

I blamed my sister for our capture and slavery. Yes, I blamed Deirdre. But I don't know . . . you can't go on like that for ever. She paid for it, poor soul, and without it none of the rest would have happened.

She was sixteen: I was ten. Father had given me a pony of my own to celebrate my birthday. I took the pony's reins from Father and he batted me affectionately on the shoulder – then I sprang on board, to try her out. Deirdre was riding with me 'to keep an eye on me', as we cantered high-spiritedly away into the wind and sunshine – and neither of us returned home.

She was supposed to be marrying some long thin drink of water from Selgovia – only his mean relatives kept haggling over six extra mangy head of cattle on the bride-price.

Dee was always bonny and full of wild courage – like Pa himself, really. What none of us knew until she trailed me with her to meet him that day, was that she was already carrying on with a Roman officer. Pa would have killed her for it – literally – with his bare hands.

I spotted this chap up ahead, waiting, on a tall horse – all crimson and brass-inlay. No slouch, for sure. I was aghast. All Dee would admit to was part of his name: Marcus Lepidus Something – but she couldn't remember the 'Something'. I ask you!

I got ferociously sworn to silence and made to hold the ponies. They disappeared behind the bushes. I left the ponies to graze, sat down on sun-warmed rock and must have dozed off. The next thing I knew, I was meshed up in a big net and being wound steadily in like a trapped salmon. Dee was already shackled and dejected – her gown torn and with bruises growing on her face and body. Her fancy man, Marcus, was riding round us with a big sneer, telling two highly muscular slave dealer's ferrets exactly what they could do with us. When I protested, I got a boot in my belly. They clamped us into collars and leg-irons linked by running chain and took us away in a mule wagon, which was otherwise loaded with cut brushwood that they could hide us under. They weren't meant to be trading like this within thirty miles. It had to be a set-up.

The irony was, we passed within a spit of our Father's garth – but these fellows knew the tricks and they went cautiously, detouring herds widely. No one saw us.

We were camped two nights. They went through Selgovan country – right into Novantia – westwards. I saw the boundary cairns. No vestige of Roman law was operative there.

On a grey beach somewhere far out along our great estuary, but on its northern shore, they robbed us of all we had down to the remnants of our underwear – and filed us aboard a big slaver, custom-built. Dee and me, and several hundred others: children, the lot of us.

Have I ever been back? Yes. Once. While on tour with the Divine Hadrian. He sometimes took me abroad with him – trusted me as a skilled personal driver in foreign parts. Well, you never know, do you? Then, also, we would take chariots and racing teams with us in order to give exhibition matches. I've often wondered if they'd take to racing in Britain.

I asked permission, and while Hadrian was planning his frontier, I went visiting my family. It was a great mistake. You find yourself dismayed, you know, at the stranger you have become. Ma was long dead – naturally. Pa, whom I'd remembered only in his vigour as a Prince, was a blind, querulous antique bypassed in a corner. My sisters-in-law fingered me with curiosity as though I were some outlandish kind of pudding, while my brothers – none of whom cared to recall much about me – scowled and spat suspicion into the hearth flames. I gave them money – awkwardly – on the excuse of needing a breeding pair of brindled wolfhounds – and left them to it.

Besides, I found the sheer dirt turning my stomach.

I cannot tell you how I survived the voyage. Anger, perhaps. I said the ship was custom-built, which meant we were chained down in rows to benches and long wooden ledges, cramming the hold. There was this little chap, a Novantian called Cei next to me – couldn't have been more than six or seven. He either grizzled or sucked his thumb the whole time. Nearly drove me daft! I talked, or played silly mind games with him in the end, just to stop the girning and slurping. After which he looked up to me, as a 'big 'un'.

Deirdre was racked up tight almost opposite to me across the hull. When we hit this terrible great storm and began heaving and wallowing, she started bleeding and miscarried. Which explained a lot. M. Lepidus had certainly had his fun. She knew she dared not turn to Pa. Lover-boy wasn't minded to have his military career shadowed by official reprimand – Dee was a Chieftain's daughter, after all, and the territorial situation delicate – nor did he wish to be dunned by the natives for maintenance.

I had to watch her die; through shock, I suppose, and the battering, and the unstaunched loss of blood, and I could do nothing.

She hung lifeless two days in her fetters before they unlatched her and dragged her up on deck to chuck overboard. Perhaps it was as well, even so. You can guess what she'd have been sold into, in Rome.

We must have been a sight when they landed us at Ostia: filthy, infested and covered in sores and bruises. Thin, besides, from rubbish food and seasickness.

They put us in quarantine for a bit, in an old army training base: shaved our heads and ran us through the bathhouse like a regular stampede of little wild cattle. Then the students from the medical schools arrived to slap stinging green ointment on us. We got kitted out with scratchy, short grey tunics. But at least they fed us: decent bread, cheese, and a meat stew every evening. They had to, to get a return. Trajan's campaigns were glutting the market and they'd have made no prices at all for bags of bones too weak to function. Children are a niche with steady turnaround, of course: they either break down or grow up.

Once we recovered we were sorted into batches and sent upstream on Tiber barges, to be landed at dawn on the Emporium quays. Then they trotted us in chained lines through the empty early morning streets to the auctioneers' stances.

Before going on to the sale platforms, auction house assistants chalked your tunic with a name, working alphabetically: Arrius, Burrus, Cnaeus, Decimus, Ennius and so on. I got Gaius. It could have been worse – the boy before me was 'Fuscus', and Cei, behind me, who had wet himself and was thumbsucking worse than ever, was marked, sardonically, 'Hero'.

Welcome to Rome.

Though I knew nothing about her at the time, Fortuna, the Good Goddess, intervened there and then. Or someone up there did.

I was sold into the hands of an elderly Greek-born steward called Philostratos and became the property of the noble senator T. Aurelius Ulpius Marcianus. Heard of him? No, you are too young, I daresay.

He was quite famous in his time: a dutiful, exemplary, rather solitary man. He was a distinguished judge – a noted tryer of difficult or sensitive cases, an austere sniffer-out of corruption.

He had big estates out here in Baetica; above all, as the patronymic denotes, he was a cousin of the Emperor Trajan.

When in Rome, Marcianus lived elegantly on the Pincian Hill amid extensive gardens and pleasances where he cultivated magnificent roses. He was unusually devoted to the memory of his late wife, who had died quite young. She herself had been related, and close to, Trajan's Empress Plotina.

Physically, Marcianus rather resembled his Imperial cousin: tall, lean, clean-shaven – a full head of well-cut hair which, they said, had turned white early in the Ulpian manner. He was thin-featured with high cheekbones, and that archetypal beaky 'Roman' nose.

They tried me out as houseboy for a year but my cleaning and polishing never quite met Philo's exacting standards, and I sometimes dropped dishes at meals. Worse: I had discovered horses at the end of Marcianus' parks, and persistently bunked off to watch them being exercised. Someone was always having to haul me back and beat me for unwarranted absence.

Something Had To Be Done, you might say. Scrubbed, dried, combed and into my best tunic (the one with silver-lace edging), Philo took me for interview with the man himself.

I stood facing the Senator's huge study table, scuffling my toes inside my sandals and wondering what would happen. Up till then, he had hardly appeared to notice me. He brooded at me a long time in silence, then cleared his throat.

'We keep having occasional trouble, don't we, boy?'

'Yes, Dominus. I am sorry, Dominus.'

'It's not as though you are stupid: you keep yourself clean and tidy and you've picked up Latin well. But just not prepared to buckle down enough to the more boring jobs – eh?'

'I'll try better, Dominus.'

'No, you won't! Although Philo has persuaded me not to send you back for resale, you may be thankful to hear. I had considered transferring you to some client or acquaintance with a smaller, less demanding house – but then I could not think of one who might relish having pheasant seethed in hot, spiced sauce cascaded all across his lap!'

'I took punishment for that mistake, Dominus.'

'So I should hope.'

His mouth twitched. It did cross my mind that perhaps he was trying not to smile.

'Which leaves me two more options. One was to pass you on to my sister's son, whom I have adopted to be my heir – but at present he is on foreign posting with the army and won't be back here for at least two years.'

My stomach lurched. Possibly I flinched. Marcianus was watching me shrewdly.

'I know of your story of capture,' he stated kindly. 'My nephew's name – until he takes up mine – is Lucius Annius and he serves in a place called Syria.'

'Yes, Dominus.'

'Do not carry inward scars for life, boy. Nor imagine that all Roman officers are devious and unscrupulous. Well . . . I shan't lecture.'

'Thank you, Dominus.'

'Which brings me to my solution: since it seems you are attracted to our Blue Faction racing stables, like metal filings to what the Greeks term electrified iron – horses you shall have. Your household duties are ended, thus saving me from permanent damage at dinner! Gather your belongings and prepare to move,' he handed me a little round ivory plaque with writing on and a hole through it, 'Here is your pass in and out from stables. It will go on your neck-chain next to your nameplate – Philo will see to it. You remain my property, but I have required Heracles, the Master of Horse, to set you on as stable boy. Try not to think of it as demotion.'

Demotion! It promised bliss to me! I had never seen such animals as they had over there.

'Yes, Dominus. No, Dominus. Thank you, Dominus!'

My excitement caused him dry amusement.

'I perceive you consider this a sideways move! So be it. I daresay I shall see you on occasion, when I make inspection. I administer all Blue racing, you see, on behalf of the State – which is to say, my Imperial cousin.'

Belongings. I had none, bar an old abandoned comb on which a porter had roughly scored GAIUS for me, and the clay money pig which had been my year's end Saturnalia gift from the Dominus. This now contained two battered copper bits that I had picked out of street gutters while on purchasing errands with Philo.

He opened and closed a link in my chain to add my pass disk.

They fed me in the kitchens – imminent departure causing Cooky (who was always emotional) to at last forgive me the pheasant.

Philo took me across the park. At the last moment he thrust into my hand a small statuette of Fortuna.

'Here. Take her. That she may protect you. She has been good to

me, one time and another. Look after yourself, Gaius. I do believe
we'll miss you!'

The stables were a self-contained two-storey block built in a square,
enclosing a spacious courtyard and an unsabotageable water supply.
There was one large, guarded entrance through solid double doors
and an archway. Security was maximum. Despite Philo's presence
they looked me up and down three times, read my nameplate and
scrutinized the pass, sent in the written order from Marcianus and
called someone who called someone else, who brought Heracles in
person.

'Oh. Righ'. Gaius, is it? In, then. Thanks, Philo. Demetriu'? Here
a mo. Show this one where to go an' aw abou' it, eh?'

Noisy open dormitories; prickly straw pallets on loosely strawed
timber flooring – we were above the stalls and boxes and harness
rooms, along with the hay and bedding and feedstuffs.

They roused you out at dawn and worked you non-stop until
noon stand-easy, a meal and two hours rest; then it was evening
stables all over again until supper.

For three months I did nothing else at all but pick up, sweep and
cart away muck.

But the horses! Ye gods: the fine-legged, fleet-footed, dark-eyed,
soft-muzzled, quivering, dancing beauties! Demi-gods, in themselves
– surely.

Fortuna had noticed me. I was in my element.

It was an enclosed life. We lived behind those stout walls, heavy
roofs and big timber doors much as if it had been a small fortress.
Heracles ruled: severely but fairly. There was no thieving or bullying
to speak of. If he caught you out in something underhand, you might
get one chance but never two: after that you were on your way back
to the City auction houses, usually, it was said, with an unpleasant
recommendation as to future employment.

Just like a fort, we had bakers and cooks and a bathhouse
arrangement. There were farriers and harness makers and a Greek
doctor with an Egyptian sidekick, whose skills were split equally
between equine and human patients. In a crunch, the horses came
first. And there was a chariot workshop.

Wine was permitted in moderation, but no women. Drivers and
senior grooms got regular time off to go into the City, but we younger
fry had to stay put, short of exceptional reason, or a wander in
Marcianus' parkland at stand-easy. But Heracles never let anyone
stagnate. Every six months, he reviewed the whole establishment

– switching jobs; weeding out the unsatisfactory; moving people up, down or sideways. All except principal drivers. It kept you on your toes.

Heracles himself you had to have seen to have believed! He was once a brilliant driver – absolutely the best, apart from his great friend and rival, Teres. But he'd had this dreadful smash-up which put paid to his career, and which he barely survived. He was lumps and bumps and scar tissue from head to foot, and had this way of herpling about in sudden rushes on cranky, bent-out legs! Also, his face was misshapen and he had these gold-covered false teeth on wires which meant he couldn't talk properly. When he got livid – which was often – he used to drag the teeth from his mouth, throw them down and jump on them, before bellowing even more loudly, but even less coherently! Yeah – but he knew horses down to an inch – and loved 'em. Which was why Trajan had personally footed the bills to have him patched up and convalesced, then slotted him into the Blue Faction training job.

Do you know about racing organization? Not a lot. Well – we shan't bore your potential readership out of their skulls. On the other hand, there might be a few persons in far-flung places who would be mildly interested.

Briefly then: racing in Rome is a state industry – right? – out of which the Treasury is always happy to extract the relevant taxes and betting levies. Contrary to cynical received opinion, racing is actually run efficiently and mostly honestly. That surprises people, but to do it well benefits the Treasury far more than corruption would. Also – psychologically – it is an entertainment in which people really love to feel that their little flutter is a genuine risk, and not one big fix. You know how they are in Rome; if the populus decided one day that the whole thing was a huge scam, there'd be riots into eternity! So it falls to upright old bods like T. A. U. Marcianus to run the show and they do a decent job, and blood on the streets is thereby minimized.

Now then: customarily racing has always been carried out by four 'Colours' – Red, White, Blue and Green – except that in the past because of some economies and much security, Blue subsumed Red, and Green subsumed White. But: simply to race Blue against Green all the time leads to monotony, and people like the tradition of cheering on Red and White as well – so these colours are used, and aspiring drivers and riders often emerge for Blue through Red and for Green through White.

Blue stables held a big complement: full chariot teams for both Blue and Red, plus spares, plus a number for ridden races, plus a

few horses just beginning to race – say sixty or thereabouts. They
were changed regularly from the big stud farms and breaking schools
like this one. Green/White were set up just the same. Does that give
a picture?

After three months of mucking out I did a stint in the tack rooms,
cleaning leather. I found myself surrounded by horses to look at but
had not yet been allowed to touch one. I used to console myself by
creeping off in the rest hours, nicking titbits, and going down the
stalls making equine friends. Heracles caught me at it of course.

'Won'ered why me carro' bins kep' goin' down! Gaius Rufus.'

He was sitting quietly on a bran tub waiting for me to manifest.
He called me Rufus on account of what was then my dark red
hair – and to distinguish me from five other Gaiuses on the
strength.

But he'd been watching me cajole a little North African filly,
not long arrived. She had the prettiest head and by all accounts a
fabulous turn of speed, but she was picky and nervous, and trying
to get gear on her resulted in squeals and kicks and bargings, and
all manner of nervous frenzy.

'Name of Zephyr,' said Heracles laconically, ''N you go' 'er
gentled where no one else's manage'. Wew done. How long you
been on tack?'

'Near three months, Master.'

'Junio' groom, then. Wi' Demetriu'. He'll show you.'

'Yes, Master!'

Marcianus made regular, thorough inspections – usually alone – but
occasionally in company with his most illustrious relatives – if they
were in Rome. Trajan inspected Green as well, of course – he was
supposed to be impartial.

I got used to turning out in line, in a brand new tunic, right
arm and fist thumped across my chest in salute and head bowed,
while the Imperial party drifted by on a wave of perfume and light
conversation. Sometimes I even got to lead out a horse they might
particularly want to see.

Trajan and his Empress had no children of their own. Yes,
thank you, I remember what the smart joke used to be: they never
managed it because he persistently forgot to turn her the right way
round first.

But there was always a clutch of youths and girls – related in one
degree or another – whom they had in wardship, to be polished for
glittering careers, or marital alliances.

Once, when I was about fourteen, the Senator came with Empress Plotina and two girls.

The Augusta was a most striking lady: tall and slender with elaborately piled-up black hair. She favoured dressing in white and silver. She really was something to look at – though you weren't supposed to stare. These girls were the latest family acquisitions from Spain or Gaul, cousins to each other, as well as her: the ladies Marcia and Aurelia. Marcia was twelve, I think; Aurelia about eight or nine. They never liked each other much. Aurelia hopped and skipped a lot and toted a model horse and chariot, with a driver-figure pegged into it.

Heracles was for demonstrating a new light cart he'd had made, and which he thought Marcianus might use about the park, or on the exercise tracks. The Empress was interested. I came to know later that she could, and did, drive herself very competently – single or a pair.

I led out one of the pair to be harnessed, and once everything was satisfactorily yoked and buckled, we all trooped out through the archway for Marcianus to give the outfit a whirl.

I can hear the Augusta now, as she commented coolly: 'It's rather smart, Titus! Do you think I might try it too?'

The girls weren't best pleased at being told to keep well out of the way. They had some ineffectual waiting woman with them.

I gazed up the road back toward the house, and there were bright splodges of red which were Praetorian Guardsmen stationed every few yards along it.

Aurelia asked: 'Oh, Aunt Augusta, can't we go in it?' On being refused, she hopped about some more and trundled her toy along the ground on a string. Marcia, who was bored and petulant, picked a squabble.

There were reasons for the Senator's superb rosebeds and arbours and one of them stood not far from us: item, one monumental clamp of well-matured horse muck which we continually added to at one end, while the gardeners quarried away at the other. Like everything else there, it was done and undone with method and forethought.

The equipage was going happily away from us at the trot. The next thing I knew was a sharp cry of fury and anguish from the Lady Aurelia because the Lady Marcia had pinched her plaything and hurled it with devastating accuracy right on top of the dunghill. Before anyone could open their mouths, let alone stop her, the Lady Aurelia went pell-mell after it. She clawed her way upward using the steps and shelves that the gardeners had cut in the 'old' end.

She slipped and slithered, but picked herself up and clambered relentlessly on.

The maid had hysterics. Heracles swore and dispatched my fellow groom along the road after the disappearing chariot. And I knew, I just knew, precisely what was going to happen. The toy was visible – perched toward the stable end where all the stuff was new and steaming and crumbly. I went after Aurelia.

By the time I came rapidly up over the dry end, she was well along the top, bent on retrieving her valuable.

'Got it!' she shrieked, 'Yah Boo! Mingy Marcia!' She did a wardance, broke the crust and sank: 'Yah – ooh, errgh!'

I flattened myself and belly-crawled after her.

I was a stranger to her; and I suppose also she was instinctively aware of a need to restore some manner of dignity. We surveyed each other close-to. She was trying not to be scared. She had fairish hair, and wide grey-blue eyes.

'I'm so sorry,' she said, 'But I do seem to have gone rather far in.'

I stuffed her precious model inside the top of my tunic and took hold of her.

'Don't try to struggle – you'll only sink worse.'

I got her in a sort of rescue lift under the arms so that she could hang down over one shoulder and wormscrewed her out. Everything shifted and settled. We inched backwards. She'd lost a shoe. I plunged in an arm above the elbow, scrabbled, found it, emptied it out and restored it to her.

'Thank you so much. And your name is . . .?' she enquired with imperious politeness.

'Gaius, lady.'

'Oh yes? I'm Aurelia. How do you do?'

I couldn't exactly bow, so we clasped arms, formally.

'I am most grateful. Truly. 'Cos it's awfully stinky here, don't you find? And then, you know, I might have sunk into oblivion!'

By the time I had got her safely down, the Empress and Marcianus were back. Order and good sense prevailed. A bath was decided upon – at 'Uncle Titus' house'.

Aurelia sang my praise.

'This is Gaius, Aunt Augusta, and he is most tremendously brave for rescuing me. So please, please, don't be cross with anyone but me – although really, you know, it was Marcia's fault at the beginning . . .'

I handed over the toy.

Her small, plastered, straw-stuck figure went walking up the

road beside the Empress, still talking: 'Gaius's eyes are *green*, Aunt
Augusta, isn't that unusual? And don't you think his dark red hair
is beautiful? I do.'

The Augusta looked back at me, murmuring to her.

Marcianus cleared his throat: 'Makes a change from pheasant,'
he remarked pleasantly, stepping up once more into his chariot and
urging away his horses.

Heracles said: 'Phaw! Wha' a niff! You. Clean up. Now. Unner
the pump. You jammy li'ul beggar!'

I favoured my mother's side in colouring. It's all faded now.

Is that the flagon finished? Amazing. They don't make these things as
deep as they used to, I swear it! The boy can fetch us out another.

I had thought I could ride at home. Heracles disabused me of that.
He bullied us into straight backs and sitting deep with a grip of the
thighs like glue, instead of what he called, 'shooglin' abou' like ne's
o' cabbages.'

Once you had achieved the basics and could be entrusted with
exercising pairs – riding one and leading the other – he set about
teaching racing posture and tactics. You ride crouched forward in
the arena, remember, with your knees higher and bent. The turns
are all left-handed – there's only one way round Circus Maximus.
You have to keep the horse on the proper leg and subtly shift your
balance, so that it can't run out or very wide.

'YOU'RE AWFU'!' he'd roar after us. 'WHA' ARE YOU? SOME DAF'
OL' BIDDY'S PE' MONKEYS – OR WHA'?'

One way and another, his teeth took a terrible pounding. But
it all paid off, the day you got to clatter proudly down the Via
Flaminia, wearing your Colour and Phrygian-style cap, to show
you were truly a part of Roman racing. You can't make traffic
jams – we always had to turn off and work our way across to the
Circus by skirting the city and threading through back lanes. These
little kids would come out to shout and wave and rush along trying
to keep up.

Trajan had not long spent a mint on enlarging and doing the
Circus all out in stone. Well, it was safety really – the old timber
stands with shops and lock-ups underneath were gutted by a fire.

And riding or driving, there is nothing – nothing in the entire
world – quite like when they sound the trumpets and you make
that very first emergence from the under-cover horse lines into the
grand procession that starts a festival.

Some lads begin race riding at thirteen – I was a year older. It depends how your physique develops really. Practice gallops are one thing; being bumped, bored, lashed, or having your knees crunched, is quite another. It was a year before I won anything significant. Ridden races are pipe-openers and fillers, of course: they keep bums on seats between the big chariot matches. But that autumn, celebrating the end of a long campaigning season, Trajan personally sponsored a week's festival of races and entertainments. There was a jockey's championship with substantial prize money.

Heracles told me I could ride Blue – fourth jockey – which left me well down the betting. But he gave me Zephyr. Zephyr was still a dubious quantity. She could blister her way round gallops, but in harness she was trouble, and picky about her neighbours. Yet, she was a compact creature, naturally neat on the turn, and she would sometimes do more for me than anyone else. If I could get her balanced; keep her legs right; set her flying – I had a chance. I camped out in her box the night before, and sweet-talked her for hours.

On the opening days my sections of the heats went by with never a soul noticing. But I was placed often enough to be listed for a quarter-final, and that we won.

'Wew done,' said Heracles tersely.

By the fifth day I was the only Blue entered for the second semi-final. The field was smaller because by then the quasi amateurs – senatorial younger sons, business syndicate freelancers and military couriers on furlough – had been weeded down.

Zephyr churned and fretted at the start, but the moment the rope dropped she sprang away in front. I tucked her in close to the spina, so she could nip round the ends with never an inch wasted. We won – still from in front – by two good lengths. I couldn't believe it: when I pulled her up, we were being cheered – personally!

'You' up in the beh'ing now aw righ', Rufe,' said Heracles. 'Don' leh me down.'

The other remaining Blue into the final – on the afternoon of the last day – was riding No. 1 for us. Plainly, if it came to tactics, he expected me to give way to him. I kept my mouth shut and let him think it. Beyond telling us briefly to do our best, Heracles didn't give any instructions.

It was a much tougher race. Zephyr kept getting barged during the middle laps. On the other hand this made her squeal, and eventually she bored her way through a narrow gap that a larger, less coordinated animal might have baulked at. I sat tight and crooned at her until her ears flicked – then she poured out the speed like cream. At the last half-lap turn some character from White tried putting her off with his whiplash. I hit back, fled past, and beat our No. 1 by half a length with my reins dropped on Zephyr's lathered neck.

I had the crowd on its feet, the palm, and five hundred sesterces in good, round silver.

When the mounted stewards escorted me up in front of the Imperial seating, one small person was leaping up and down in huge delight, crying out: 'Gaius! Gaius Rufus! It's *me* . . . remember?'

The Emperor passed out the bag of cash. Augusta Plotina, smiling and congratulating me, was supposed to hand me the palm.

'You have a fervent admirer, Gaius Rufus, as you see,' and she allowed the lady Aurelia to assist in giving it to me.

'Gaius Rufus – Victor – many congratulations,' piped Aurelia with awesome formality and a heavy frown, then she grinned widely and added: 'Oh you're absolutely splendid! Please can you go on being my friend?'

Marcia scowled behind her head.

I bent my head and said: 'The Domina Aurelia does me great honour. Thank you,' and having saluted her gallantly went away on my lap of applause.

There was the usual monumental party to celebrate. Thinking myself all sorts of a dog, I drank rather a lot and discovered just how friendly some young ladies might be. When I came to, next morning, it was to find my fellow Victors had put me down for every last piece of my winnings with the tradesmen, to help subsidise the bean-feast.

'Oh yes . . . that's the custom,' they choroused, standing there with their hands out and their faces barely straight, 'Rookie Victors always pay the most.' The caterers, the wine merchants' men, the agent in charge of 'flute girls'. I'd even got stuck with the bill for some useless article's fancy prancing horse carved out of ice – which had melted everywhere. I thought: 'Never again!'

Zephyr and I won several matches and it seemed we might settle into a dominant partnership – but Fortuna had other ideas.

When I was sixteen, Ulpius Marcianus died.

The household was put into hired mourning. The heir, Lucius Annius, who was a staff officer to Hadrian Caesar, was given compassionate leave to see to the funeral and execute the Will. I had permission to attend, along with Philo and a whole crowd of servants.

We had an appropriately bleak day with a swirling wind, and rain, and I felt bereft somehow.

The Augusta – elegant as always in full black with a small blaze of diamonds – read out a superb eulogy on behalf of the Emperor, who was out in Antioch. Though she never lost her poise, she was pale and hollow-eyed with grief, and I thought she seemed strained. She looked at me once with a sort of musing expression – then her eyes filled with tears, so she turned sharply away. I was surprised at how much that affected me.

Lucius Annius – who was now also Aurelius Ulpius Marcianus – sent for me to go up to the house. To this day, I tend to be faintly allergic to the military, but this one, in his early thirties, was brisk and forthright.

The upshot was: the old chap had left a codicil specifically naming me among the slaves to be manumitted at his death. I was free.

'Sign here,' instructed the lawyer. 'Erm . . . well . . . put your mark.'

I crabbed out GAIUS. I've always been awkward with a pen – though I had myself taught to read and number fluently as soon as I could afford to.

They explained in words of one syllable that I had remained Marcianus' property when he 'sent me down the road', whereas most of the slaves in stables were Imperial. Had I been aware of that? Right.

'And – um – twenty in silver, Gaius. For you. This may seem odd – tiny in relation to your winnings – but at the time it was intended to stake you: clothes, food, somewhere to lay the head. No longer 'all found' – what? Well done. All the best.'

I asked if I might adopt the name Aurelianus, in compliment to my late benefactor. It seemed only fair to offer his Shade something in return – besides, it reminded me of someone. Annius seemed offhandedly pleased. The notary went scribble, scribble on his document and tetchily set things out afresh.

They took off my neck-chain and I only just remembered in time to reclaim the ivory pass.

Gaius Aurelianus Rufus: freedman. It sounded all right.

Heracles went distinctly glum.

He had just begun trying me in a learner's wicker cart with a single horse. I'd had two lessons. I could, with luck, manage a wide, simple turn at the trot.

'What's wrong?' I demanded.

Everything, seemingly. Slaves 'lived in'; slaves got the tuition; amateurs might ride, but – with rare exceptions – slaves drove racing chariots. That at least was how you came into the game, even if you grew rich and astute enough to buy yourself free later on, and not many did. There were Regulations.

'Jupiter! What am I to do? I don't know anything else. I don't *want* anything else! Help me, Heracles.'

'Don' russ me, don' russ me! *I* wan' you, Rufe – you go' deffnut ponenshul.'

He took private pupils. There was always some sprog Praetorian having lessons so he could show off to his society girlfriends, or some nutter determined to set world speed records down twenty-five measured miles of the Via Appia. I would pay. What with? Winnings. What winnings? He couldn't race me any more. He couldn't really employ me in stables any more: the arrangement with Marcianus was over. And there were Regulations.

'You nee' Imperiaw backin'. We takin' this to the top.'

'How? Who?'

'Augusta.'

'I can't ask *her*!'

'Why no'? Very lovely lady. You don' – I wiw. Awrigh'?'

She was coming on inspection, he assured me, before going out to join the Emperor – no one else to do it at the moment.

'By the way,' he added cannily, 'if you' stoppin' I wan' ten in silver on accoun'.'

'On account of what?'

'Boar' an' lodgin', sunshine.'

Empress Pompeia Plotina arrived looking composed in pale grey and white, with pearls threaded through her hair. There was no small girl at her side. Instead, she was accompanied by a brand new Captain of the Guard, blindingly burnished as to armour. He had cold eyes, ostrich plumes which filled the front of his helmet crestbox like a thunder cloud and when he closed his mouth, it set like a rat-trap. Something about him made all my neck hairs lift.

'Don' you dare disappear, awrigh'?'

I lingered nervously in out-of-the-way places until sent for to Heracles' own rooms.

'I have explain',' Heracles hissed at me as he lurched discreetly away.

The officer was also dismissed out of doors.

The Augusta told me crisply that she understood my predicament and that since Marcianus had been in cousinship, she felt, in a sense, responsible. For the time being, she would undertake the expenses of my keep and tuition, since Heracles seemed convinced that I might do well in the arena.

I bowed. I boiled over with relief and thanks, which she brushed aside.

'Learn,' she said. 'I look forward to results.'

I asked if she might wish me to repay her out of prize money in the future, but she flicked me an amused glance and tweaked her stola straight and said: 'Oh, I daresay you will, you know . . . one way or another. Gaius Aurelianus Rufus.'

She inclined her head, and I followed her out into the courtyard. If there were nuances, I did not understand them.

Heracles came herpling back. She offered him her hand and he stooped awkwardly to kiss it.

'Blue seems in excellent order,' I listened to her say, 'and I shall be happy to inform the Emperor accordingly. Now: where is my Tribune?'

Unbelievably, he was beside the central water basin, ruffling through the curly hair of a youngster newly joined. The boy was chewing.

The Augusta frowned.

'I wish he wouldn't do that,' she complained to Heracles. 'He collects them – carries sweetmeats with him in a bag, like dog biscuit. I find it disconcertingly at odds with all the rest of him.' She raised her voice to retrieve the officer's attention: 'Tribune,' she announced, 'Marcus Lepidus Gratianus . . .'

And instantly I knew why it was that I detested him.

Heracles worked my backside off. But I got the full treatment: a cubby hole to live in all to myself; the best food; baths and massage; physical exercise for strengthening; even occasional leave to go into the City. And daily he taught me, until I could take the practice tracks flat out and spin carts on a coin. Single horses, then pairs. I learned to work with all the spare of the reins wrapped snugly round my waist; to lean my weight into turns; to keep animals balanced and running in harmony. He tried me out with a triga – which is difficult: the yoked pair have a tracer, Etruscan-style – a third horse running in front on the near side. He didn't reckon me strong enough yet for a quadriga, but he let me borrow reserve fours now and again after meetings, and with an established Blue driver in beside me, we'd have practice sessions in the eerily empty arena. I was appearing quite regularly using singles carts or pairs in novice events, by the time the Imperial party came home from bashing the Parthians, with the imminent onset of winter.

*   *   *

There was talk in the City that the Parthians obstinately refused to stay bashed – that the Emperor's health had suffered – that he increasingly took refuge in wine. Hadrian Caesar was never far from him.

'Your lady-friend's here,' said Demetrius, 'Heracles' office.'

'Who? Haven't got one! Only Lucilla at parties . . .'

'No? I reckon you've got two, actually – not counting Lucilla, who's everyone's at parties. Go on – you're wanted!'

The Augusta was seated in Heracles' high-backed basket chair, scrutinizing accounts. Behind her, the lady Aurelia, twelve and shooting up, gave me a beam and a thumbs-up. The Praetorian this time was a hawk-like centurion. There was a muffled-up waiting woman who sneezed.

'Good . . .' said the Empress abstractedly, and emerged from columns of figures, 'Gaius Aurelianus, you appear to be doing rather well. I find that pleasing.'

She had had them yoke up a pair to the late Marcianus' light cart. She cloaked herself, saying: 'Come. Shall we try what you can do?'

There was some anxious footwork behind her.

'Augusta? With permission . . . and the young lady, also?'

'Would there be room? Oh, I suppose – at a pinch! Very well, child.'

We went for a spin in the park and I found myself rigorously assessed. The inevitable soldiers were dotted here and there. I wondered where Lepidus was.

We finished on the practice tracks, where I went round the 'arena oval' for them at a cracking pace.

'Most invigorating,' the Empress commented. 'And I hear you have had novice wins. Master Heracles is right: you could be good, given time.'

She had not touched me once – rarely looked at me – yet something – a spark, an unstated current – had come into being. And the lady Aurelia, her eyes all eloquence between us, was for once unaccountably subdued.

I received Trajan's permission to appear next season in full matches, at the Master of Horse's discretion.

'You jammy beggar!' they all said.

Spring is the busiest time in professional racing: the best weather and with loads of official and semi-official games and festivals crowding the calendar.

One of our Blue quadriga drivers took a smash, and died. I was in funds at the time, so I managed to negotiate the take-over of his rented rooms at the Circus. For those who will never see it, the stands are built up on massive arch supports, right? Underneath there are honeycombs of partitioned-off premises all for lease. Anything from eating stalls and cheap boutiques, through to drivers' 'sets' and the long rows of cubicles that the girls and fellows work from. Lucilla was in those. Freelance, because she had her head screwed on.

I was in the horselines cautiously feeling for possible heat in a fetlock one day when this spindly, shambling creature clad in haphazard filthy rags arrived with a skip and a muck fork. The only remotely clean bit on his whole person was his heavily calloused right thumb.

'Oi! You! 'Ero!' shouted an angry voice from farther up. 'You've missed some!'

He went dully away and came dully back, head down. 'Cei?' I asked, 'Where've you been?'

It took him a long painful while to sort me out. 'Aw . . .' he said at last. 'Red hair . . . that boat, eh? Morgan – is it? You done well then – lookin' at you.'

'What happened to you?'

'Don't ask! Grew too big, anyway. They dumped me here. Poo-shifter. Just about my dab.'

He had to be coming fourteen. He was certainly one of life's losers. But he was a Brit. Though it lowered my silver level drastically once again, I dug out the overseer, slid him a backhander, and bought Cei over, cheap.

I had his hair de-matted and took him for the full treatment in the Baths and we kitted him out in some decent second-hand gear that Lucilla found. 'Ah . . . the pore soul!' she exclaimed, gazing at him in dismay, and promptly took him to her heaving bosom. She heaved it rather well, actually. There was a distinct improvement. He danced shy attendance on Lucilla if she came for supper on one of her rare evenings off.

He wouldn't talk about himself. Apart from sucking his thumb, he had behaviour problems at night, and I had to be firm about him sleeping alone. Luckily my 'set' was two small rooms. I made allowances because in the bathhouses I had seen the marks all over him. Fed and cheered up, he did whatever I asked of him unquestioningly, and guarded my little space against all comers. Because he didn't steal, I passed on the clay money pig and gave him bits of pocket money once a month.

Two months on, he was standing with his arms full of harness for me, while I was bridling a horse when he made a curious, scared whimper, dropped the stuff – to my annoyance – and

scarpered at top speed. I looked about. There were the usual
grooms and drivers at work. But at the far end of the lines, a
thick-set hard-faced individual was approaching carrying a big
wine flagon, and drinking as he walked. He wore civilian clothes.
He trailed a small, depressed-looking child tied to his tunic belt by
a length of thin rope. The child was chewing. I slid behind my horses
and watched him pass. Marcus Lepidus Gratianus – 'out of uniform
and out of hours' – as the army says.

I called a groom to stand by and legged it home. Cei was in a
corner huddled beneath his blanket, shaking.

'I know that man!'

'So do I,' I said feelingly.

'You won't let him get me, will you?'

'He's gone. No. I promise. What in all Hades did he do
to you?'

'Nothin'. But I seen what he can do!'

'Where were you these seven years?'

'Don't ask – please!' said Cei – and was sick.

Two bodies turned up, flung among the junk in some midden outside
the City. Children. Manacled, it was said, and grotesquely done
to death. But nobody missed them. It might have been a summer
season wonder, but after a bit there was a third. And then a fourth.
Awkwardly, the dump overseer, distressed at such grim little relics,
swore black-was-white that it happened each time after dust-carts
brought rubbish down from the Palatine. The magistrates decided
on inquiry.

All the world remembers Trajan died that August. Way out
in Mesopotamia somewhere. Empress Plotina came sadly home
alone.

It was said that she had survived some politically delicate moments
in the East, getting Hadrian hailed and accepted as Emperor. Though
he was the groomed and obvious successor, Trajan had never quite
got round to finally confirming him as heir. Plotina smoothed his
transition, then discreetly left. All the old gossip came up about
Hadrian having been her lover in his youth. Perhaps. He certainly
held her in high regard – but who couldn't?

At home she sent for me and asked if, when I wasn't racing, I might
take her out for drives, to help recuperate. She had her own vehicle
and horses. We covered miles – day after day – through parkland
or out in the country. Goodness knows what her staff thought: there
was only me with her. When I commented on this, she answered,

surprised: 'But I trust you, Gaius. Besides, I'm a private citizen really. There is a new Empress now.'

There was: Vibia Sabina was a quarrelsome shrew. Hadrian's *modus vivendi* was to meet her as infrequently as possible, and to turn to other company.

'Gaius,' she had said – as to an established friend. I began listening to nuances.

She seemed depleted. But gradually she started talking of Trajan and her memories of him. She never spoke without affection and honour – so there had been much between them. Which knocked *that* gossip firmly on the head.

'You're a very calming person – do you know that?' she told me, 'I come out all fretted and in no time, I am at peace. No wonder horses respond to you so!'

She took the reins from me and chirruped the animals into a controlled canter.

'Domina Augusta,' I teased, 'You are a great fraud!'

'How so?'

'You do that as well as I can. You don't need me here at all!'

'But I like you here . . . Gaius.'

She slowed them down.

'Where are you living now? They tell me you have left Blue stables.'

I explained about the rooms in Circus Maximus. She thought about it.

'I could do better for you than that,' she said, and handed me back the horses.

I said I owed her much already and she answered sharply that she wasn't in the business of collecting debts.

'It is a matter of what you might want,' she added obliquely.

I was silent, not knowing how to go on.

'Is there someone?' she wanted to know. 'I would not be so selfish as to wish to intervene.'

I said no. As sure as eggs, Lucilla wasn't going to miss me. 'Perhaps you think of me as being old,' she said, diffidently.

Trajan was sixty-something when he died, and although she was very considerably younger that still made her well into her forties. I am neither blind nor stupid, and I was at the time standing close up to her. But she had kept herself superbly, and I knew what could be done about hair colour. Lucilla changed hers radically every other week.

'Lady,' I answered, 'often I dream about you, at nights.'

'Do you? But perhaps you might do more than merely dream. Gaius?'

I found reason to drive on with her sheltered inside the crook of my arm and gently she leaned her body up against mine. When I ventured to kiss the angle of her neck and shoulder – which was soft and fragrant – she said: 'You see? I knew I could trust you, all along.'

You can stop that smirk: thank you! I loved and honoured that lady. Still do. Every year without fail I make an offering for her Shade, on her birthday. And she taught me much about her philosophy of the inextinguishable soul. She was a marvellous, intelligent, essentially beautiful person.

I collected a second ivory pass, made myself known to Augusta Plotina's Chamberlain and was allotted a coldly magnificent room adjoining her suite of apartments. I kept the 'set' because it was paid up, and the toe-hold was convenient on racing days. Anyway – not even the three-headed dog of Hell could persuade Cei to come with me.

'Have you come to live?' Aurelia demanded. 'Oh, scrumptious! We're all down here, look,' and dragged me away by the hand to go and see. She played complicated, self-invented games using the black and white tiles of the immense corridor floors as boards, and people for counters. The penalties often included having to stand on one leg. Wobblers were 'out'. Laughter usually persuaded the Augusta to join in.

Once when I returned from a successful match in a privately sponsored race card, she surveyed the bag of loot and asked: 'What will you do with that?'

It wasn't easy – trying to keep money by me; trying not to have it pinched; just plain keeping it. The Augusta furnished me there and then with an introduction to her bankers – and, believe me, going to them was the wisest single move I ever made!

I asked Aurelia one day: 'Where's that Tribune gone? Marcus Lepidus?' He hadn't been about.

'Oh, him! Aunt Augusta doesn't like him. He gives *me* goose pimples! Um ... he's busy with an inquiry of some kind. I think ...'

When we were alone, the Augusta confirmed it: 'Yes. He's leading the inquiry into those child murders. Hideous business! From our end. Assisting the civil magistrates. Why?'

'*He* is leading the inquiry? Marcus Lepidus Gratianus is?'

'So I believe.'

I told her what I had witnessed – and Cei's reaction. She frowned.

'You would swear to this in law?'

'Yes, Lady.'

'Not a suitable person. I shall look into it; take the matter to the Emperor.'

Palaces have a million ears. We had precipitated something.

When I returned from racing the following afternoon, the apartments were humming with people searching everywhere, and the Augusta stricken. The ladies Marcia and Aurelia had gone missing – not seen since midday. She herself had been out visiting friends. No one had thought to look until she returned.

'Domina – where is the Tribune Lepidus?'

'No idea! The wretched man . . . we can't find him, either!' Her hand flew up and we stared at each other sharing a terrible thought.

'Who can you trust in your Guard?'

'Me, Domina Augusta,' said the hawklike centurion, saluting, 'I have men assembled. We'll take Rome apart, if needs be.'

Lepidus was long gone from his duty quarters, which were neat and empty. No clues. Think. Think. He had to have true concealment – perhaps a place where extraneous noise might obliterate sound? We went down to the Circus and swept through it like a wind. Nothing. The dump overseer had sworn the bodies materialized out of rubbish brought down from the Palatine.

Cei knew the man. Cei wouldn't go to the Palatine. I picked up a cringing Cei. All the way back to the Palace, I kept getting mind pictures of Aurelia in deep distress.

I dumped Cei at the Augusta's feet, saying angrily: 'He knows something. I'd swear he knows where. Tell us! Just tell us, you daft loon!'

But he cried and sicked up and went silly.

She knelt down and wiped his face.

'Do you know who I am, boy?' she asked gently. He snivelled yes – he'd seen her once, outside.

'Then will you help us? Two young lives depend upon it.' He kept protesting that 'the man would get him' but she promised him the safety of her own presence, as well as that of the soldiers – if he would only show us.

He hiccupped and nodded, and she swept him with us. He had mentioned having heard horses. We began at the Imperial stables. Cei cast round like a thin hound. We trailed through yards, abandoned kitchens, shrines, out-offices, rubbish collection points. He picked up familiarity: 'Here. This way, look . . . along here . . . down. Down there and down them steps. Aw . . .' he shivered and clung to the Augusta.

A private building in a short, private street. Nondescript. It might have been a temple conversion job. Secure and tightly shuttered. We had come round in a curve. When a horse whinnied in its stall, we all heard it.

'It's a club,' Cei explained. 'When they brung us up from where we lived, they always said it was Club Night.'

Praetorians swung a heavy baulk of timber from out of a nearby builder's yard and burst the metal-shod door. Inside . . . was like a walk into the caverns of Hell.

'Lady, this is no place for you,' I said hastily.

'Never mind,' she set her mouth. 'We must find the girls. Centurion: proceed!'

Lepidus had them to himself.

Marcia was wandering about free – falling drunk and giggling. Aurelia was hung in shackles and he was trying drunkenly to feed her something, interspersed with slops of wine. She glistened with bruises, but she was still resisting, twisting from him and spitting out.

The centurion swore disgustedly. Empress Plotina commanded implacably: 'Arrest this man!', and removing her stola, wrapped it gently round Aurelia's straining body. An optio swiped Lepidus' keys and unlocked her, talking soothingly. She came down stiffly into my arms and I carried her carefully away.

Perhaps it had begun as some half crazy notion of hostage holding, because of whatever his informant had whispered. But with Lepidus, having them there to himself was temptation – and his viciousness overcame him.

When I went out to race the next day, Heracles said we had a case of cracked ribs in Blue, leaving a quadriga empty.

'Now's your chance, Rufe.'

I was running No. 3. I drew 7 by lot for the carceres. The handlers backed me steadily in, soothed the horses until the last minutes and slid off, closing the doors. I heard the bolt scrape home. All the line settled. My horses trampled and mouthed, froth flying. The warning trumpet went, up on the roof. I suppose the starter dropped his white cloth; the mechanism lad banged down the lever, springing the bolts – and the doors flew apart. I shouted: 'Fortuna and Aurelia! Go, boys, go,' at the team, cracked my whip and we surged out into daylight. Seven and a half laps: the full distance. I drove with such a concentration of controlled fury that we led from start to finish. 'Awesome!' said the clerk, writing down results.

When it was over, and I'd bathed and looked respectable, I presented myself to the Augusta.

'How is she?' I asked.

'Better. Come and see. She asks for you. The doctors seem satisfied and she has rested well.'

Aurelia bounced up in bed.

'Ow!' she said, and, 'Did you win?'

'Yes, Domina – specially for you!'

'I knew you'd come, Gaius Rufus – I knew you'd come! When it got bad, I prayed to the Good Lady and I remembered what you'd told me about horses understanding things in pictures – so I sent you pictures into your mind. Did you see them?'

'I saw them. Urgently.'

'There you are, then! If you are going to be rich and famous, you should have a racing name – like they do.'

'Then you shall name me. I will drive under your designation.'

'Oh lovely!' She thought for a bit and decided, 'If you follow Fortuna what better than Fortunatus? Do you think?'

I bowed my head and she reached out her arms and hugged me tight.

'Thank you so much,' she said – and wouldn't be undone. She said: 'I don't want any secrets – not between us three. I know you love Aunt Augusta now – and that's all right because she is a lovely person, and I'm not grown up. But after that, Gaius – when I *am* grown up – and when you are really rich and famous – might you marry me?'

I kissed her hair – a child still at thirteen – yet roughly dragged to the very threshold of adulthood. I looked at the Empress who smiled a little and shrugged helplessly.

'Yes, I shall,' I said – knowing I meant it, 'I promise you.'

But that was ten years off.

I shan't go reeling off all the details of what I won and where. Go and look at the monument to my horses that I set up along the hill, yonder. It's all listed. Anything else – ask my secretary.

Lepidus? Court-martialled. They broke him from the Guard with ignominy. Hadrian made his estates forfeit. Then they sent him to Trajan's interrogation centre – Castra Peregrina – where they boiled some names out of him. Then they pitched him off to the metal mines somewhere, in slavery. So there is some justice.

The Emperor spent the winter cleaning out a right little Senatorial nest of vipers – and it didn't help that one or two of them turned out to be implicated in a plot against him. Hadrian got in first, fast and hard – so I don't think the Senate ever really quite forgave him.

Cei? He survived. I had him with me for years. He's buried here. He worshipped the ground Aurelia trod.

How did I come to marry her? Ah . . . that's another story. Money, if you like – what else? Look here! Caius Apuleius Diocles whose driving coincided with mine, all bar about four years, won thirty-five million, eight hundred thousand sesterces. That is a world record. I didn't do quite so well, because I kept being sidetracked by Imperial persons wanting transport – but I didn't do badly. And I had the advantage of Empress Plotina's bankers.

When Aurelia came of age, Hadrian had her married to this well-born sprig. We'd expected that. He was an amiable ninny, really. She made rings round him.

I went travelling with Hadrian. He had these strange theories about government: that the Empire should be less of an Empire and more a collection of like-minded nations in a commonwealth. I'm not going into politics. All I shall tell you is, he landed himself in a real pickle one time, and needed a lot of money, very fast, to extricate himself diplomatically. I supplied it. He was very blunt and upfront, was Hadrian.

'I can't pay you back. Not without waves in the Senate.'

'Don't,' I told him. 'That's all right. It's a gift.'

He brooded for a bit.

'What does make it square?' he wanted to know.

'Your cousin Aurelia.'

'That means divorce for her – and Equestrian for you, plus a new job.'

'Right,' I said, 'there's enough gold in my coffers for me to qualify – and then some.'

So he did it.

What was that old chestnut from Socrates that the Empress taught me once – in between peeling grapes? 'Three masters – Time, Pain and the Royalty in the Blood have taught me: Patience.'

Think about it.

THE WALKING
WALLS OF ROME

Keith Taylor

The following story is also set during the reign of the Emperor Hadrian and explores the conflicts leading up to the building of the wall. Keith Taylor (b. 1946) is an Australian writer with a keen interest in Britain's early history. He has written a series of books, starting with Bard (1981), *which explore Britain and Ireland in the years after the fall of the Roman Empire.*

I

May: Sixth Year of Hadrian's Reign

'The Emperor!' The round eyes in Constance's heart-shaped face grew rounder yet. 'The divine Hadrian coming to Britain! Tarmundus, we must spend the summer in the city . . . we may have a chance to pay our respects . . . and Caius Faninus will present us if an opportunity comes, won't you, tribune?'

'If an opportunity comes, lady, yes.' That committed him to nothing. 'I'd be pleased to. But probably it will not come. Granted, I may see the Emperor when he inspects the frontier, but that will not be a social occasion, and I daresay you won't be present. The procurator could be of more help than I.'

Constance bit her lip, stricken. Coiffured like a praetor's wife, she wore a stola that gave her goosebumps despite the heating system under the floor. (They had fired it. Nights were cold even in the season that passed for spring among the inhabitants of this damned, damp isle.) Her daughter had more sense. Besides being warmer, the native long-sleeved gown and belted woollen over-tunic suited her far better.

Irnic, Constance's brother-in-law, grinned in blatant derision. 'It's very true, sister. The tribune is not the man to get you introductions to the mighty. Not since his precious Ninth Legion broke and ran in the heather. This same divine Hadrian cashiered it.'

'Irnic, that's enough.' Tarmundus spoke loudly. 'The Ninth may have been all but destroyed –'

'All but destroyed for the third time in Britain.' Irnic bit into an apple, crunchingly. Seeds flew and a bit of skin stuck in his sweeping moustache. Neatly, fastidiously, he removed it. 'Boudicca mauled it the first time. The second it was caught by surprise in a night attack on a fool's expedition north. Never lucky, the Ninth Hispana.'

'– but our guest was one of those who kept the remnants in order and brought back the standard safe. He was hurt nearly to death and the scars are all in the front. And by Arthur himself, there's more to boast of in his legion's performance than there is in your manners tonight.' A big, slope-shouldered man with a horselike face, he turned to look at Caius. 'Tribune, I regret my brother's insult.'

Caius shrugged. 'Nothing.'

'What the Emperor needs to subdue the Painted People for all time is a legion of British men.' Irnic warmed to the subject. 'He probably knows it, too. They were British legions he led to conquer Dacia. I'll bet this gold ring on my arm that he raises a new one when he arrives, and turns Caer Lluel* into a legionary fortress.'

'I should take you,' Caius said crisply. 'A poor tribune can always use gold, and the lesson might improve your mind.'

'You think your Emperor won't?'

'I know my Emperor won't. Legions are not that lightly raised, and in any case he is bringing the Sixth Victrix with him, to serve in Britain.'

'And replace the Ninth.'

'And replace the Ninth.' Caius smiled coldly. Compact and swarthy, shaved smooth, his barbered black hair pressed close to his head by the frequent and prolonged pressure of his helmet, he made a sharp contrast to the shaggy barbarians around him. 'By Jupiter's thunder! You will speak of that legion less often if you're wise. Which of course you're not. Remember, little man, it was unrest and stirrings of revolt in your own tribe that brought the

* Carlisle

Painted People in as allies, and made it needful for us to march
north against them.'

'Our clan was not among those that caused it,' Tarmundus
said grimly. 'We've had a feud with that whole faction since my
grandfather's time.'

'I know it. The Governor is not so sure. Nor do I think, despite his
being my uncle, that he'd give weight to my judgement in the matter.'
Caius spoke harshly, trying to embody in his single presence all that
was most chilling of Rome's authority. 'I perceive,' he said to Irnic,
'which side had *your* support. Conceal it better. It's nothing to me
what disaster you bring on yourself, but I assume you wish your
kinsmen well.'

Irnic's eyes flashed blue fire. The lines of tattooing on his bare
arms moved as his muscles hardened. 'Some would say that called
for the sword.'

Caius looked at him with contempt. 'I'll not play your game –
here. However, if it pleases you, we might go hunting one day,
north of Luguvalium; Caer Lluel, if you prefer. And take our swords
with us.'

Someone laughed loudly. It was Calgaich, the warrior who had
been a gladiator in the east. Tarmundus' right-hand man was
smiling, too. An old soldier, he had served under Trajan until
his discharge and return home. Tarmundus liked having men
like that around him, who could give him a picture of the
broader world.

Irnic began to rise. His face indicated trouble. A hothead never
enjoys being called a hothead. Caius was prepared to give him all
the trouble he wanted; just not here and now, where it would ruin
Constance's dinner party. That had been one remark too many
about the Ninth Legion.

Before Irnic could explode, a woman's face appeared by his
shoulder and a long white hand rested on his arm. The other
topped his drinking cup with wine. Caius received an impression
of height, red hair, and bright blue eyes very like Irnic's own. Their
expression was scornful.

'He isn't worth it, uncle. Let him live. He could not even give
you a good fight.'

'Radona!' Constance was furious. 'You talk like a child and a
fool! You insult Rome in the person of the tribune!'

'Yes,' Tarmundus growled. 'Irnic, you swaggering cock, this is
your work. Bad manners are as catching as sneezes. Both of you,
ask pardon of Caius Faninus, or leave the hall and don't show your
faces again while he's here.'

Calgaich, the ex-gladiator, said softly, 'If you want to argue about that, Irnic, you can step outside and argue with *me*.'

Irnic sneered, unmoved. Looking at Caius, he increased the sneer. 'Tribune, forgive me for hurting your feelings.'

It was so childish that Caius was suddenly tempted to laugh. He repressed the urge. 'You exaggerate your own powers. They are not so easily hurt.'

The girl walked forward. Caius saw her clearly now. She was tall, strong and supple, as tall as he to within a quarter-inch. Her figure made a man begin thinking at once how rewarding it would be to undress her. Her hair wasn't coppery, or chestnut, or any other poetic description of Celtic locks, but simply red as brickdust. She had the freckles that usually went with it. Caius didn't care for freckles, and there were traces of her father's equine looks in her long nose and jaw, too, but those bright blue eyes were striking. Her figure looked better every second. There was a pride and grace to her carriage that would have been hard to ignore anywhere . . .

Caius caught himself. It wouldn't do for Radona's kinsmen to notice him ogling her like some girl on the streets of a garrison town. Neither, he found, did he want to confirm the opinion the girl herself no doubt had of Romans.

'Tribune Faninus,' she said, 'I ask your pardon for my bad manners.' Then, recklessly, she added, 'But you are lucky the quarrel did not go forward, for you do not know my uncle.'

'No,' Caius agreed. Pride impelled him to add dryly, 'Though you may be a little in error concerning my own qualities as a fighter.'

Radona bowed and returned to her place near her uncle. Caius wondered if she made a point of refusing to recline on a couch at the low central table because it was Roman in style. A pity if she inclined to the ideals and sympathies of Irnic's group.

'Noble tribune,' Constance gushed, 'forgive my daughter; I fear that, like Irnic, she will never be civilized.'

Caius was inclined to agree. Constance came from the south, of course, the country of the Atrebates. She must miss it. These dark Pennine hills with their dark dales, dark mists, dark caves and dark, bloody past, encouraged dark thoughts and dark deeds.

Later, as Vanddar the bard sang a song about some ancient king of Britain called Bran the Blessed, the girl listened with shining eyes. Caius considered the story ridiculous, filled with crass impossibilities, although if a man could stop his ears to the words, there was pleasure to be derived from Vanddar's harping. He had skill.

'I was a spark in fire,
I was wood in a bonfire;
I am not one who does not sing;
I have sung since I was small!
I sang in the army of the trees' branches
Before the ruler of Britain.'

Caius saw everything in the smoky hall clearly as the harp-music
surged and the old phrases rang. Tarmundus' low slate-topped table,
surrounded by couches in the Roman manner, was of course there
to please Constance, like the hypocaust beneath the tiled floor. But
spears and long British swords hung on the walls. Caius suspected
that head-hunting trophies had been removed before he came, in
discreet good manners. Yes, Constance was right. Her daughter
and brother-in-law would never be civilized. Her husband, maybe.
But Caius doubted even that, in spite of his liking for Tarmundus.
Dark mists, dark past, dark deeds. In this place the old ways were
a force that might not be ignored except at one's own risk.

II

May: Sixth Year of Hadrian's Reign

Mist clung to the high ground, undaunted by the weak sunlight.
Ponies stamped in the stable yard. Irnic moved sluggishly, wine still
clogging his head, his gaudy checked trousers and ornamented belt
making him conspicuous. Caius saw that he wore a long, gold-hilted
sword slung across his back.

He carried his own blade in the same fashion. Tarmundus
had advised it. There were blood feuds seventy years old in
these dales.

He hadn't known Radona would be present, and he blinked in
astonishment as he noticed her. The woman was dressed for the hunt!
Or undressed, more like. Her pale doeskin tunic stopped a hand's
breadth short of her knees. Under it she wore a green wool kirtle,
and there were gartered wrappings around her calves. Two huge
bounding dogs reared up to place their front paws on her shoulders.
Radona wrestled back and forth with them, laughing, until they slob-
bered her face too wetly. Then she thrust them away and grabbed a
spear she had left leaning against the wattle-and-daub stable wall.

'Tribune!' she greeted him. 'Why the blank face? Did you not
know I was coming? I like a wolf hunt, and this pair has been killing

our sheep for a year. They raided folds in the winter with their whole pack! Not again, for we know the place of their lair now. They hid it cunningly, those two. The bitch must have chosen it.'

Caius lifted a black eyebrow. 'I take it you believe her mate would not have the wit.'

'He might. But there is always more at stake for a woman in choosing the place of her home, isn't there?' When Caius failed to respond, she frowned. 'I feel a chill now that's not from the early hour! Oh. My words last night?'

'I wasn't,' Caius said dryly, 'so deeply hurt that I should still be brooding upon them now. But I did receive the impression that Tarmundus' daughter is a brat with no manners.'

She reddened until her freckles all but vanished. It made the bright blue eyes conspicuous.

'I had to say something to placate my uncle.' She glanced quickly in Irnic's direction. He was paying little attention to anything but his spears – and, it was likely, his throbbing head. Still, Radona lowered her voice. 'He wanted to fight you.'

'Yes. The prospect terrified me.'

'I said you did not know him! You don't. Listen to me, tribune; two years ago, he went across Micklefell to visit a man who seduced his cousin. Now the man was no pup. A noted warrior. Irnic challenged him in his master's hall and brought back his dripping head. I have not heard that anybody stood in his way as he left.' She studied Caius's face with a direct, savage, unabashed flax-flower gaze. 'But taking your head would be a different matter. The price of it would be higher than we could pay. I didn't speak to insult you. I spoke to avoid that.'

After a moment she added. 'Uncle Irnic's fond of me. He let himself be mollified when he thought I despised you. Father's ordering him about just put his back up higher. If no harm was to be done, he had to feel someone was on his side.'

'He apparently did.'

Caius was not impressed by the story. No doubt Irnic had coloured it. He still considered the man a barbaric dandy who talked a fierce battle.

'He hates Rome as wolves hate those dogs of mine,' she said, low, 'and he has to fight. Do not let him provoke you.'

'And what's your feeling, Radona?' Caius asked sardonically. 'Do you love Rome?'

'I wish none of you had ever come to this island,' she said frankly. 'But you did come, and you are not going to go away, and nothing will be the same again. We have to make the best of it.'

They left Tarmundus' hall and village as the sun rose higher
through the mists. Grey cloud covered most of the sky, as usual,
but at least it was not raining. The river ran clear. Leaves rustled
everywhere in the wooded valley, and a herd of swine moved out
of their way, grunting, deeper into the trees.

Beyond the falls and to the north lay open heath. Tarmundus
pointed to a distant low hill, one side of it steep and rocky, almost
a cliff. 'That's where our wolves lair,' he said. 'Their pack killed
one of my shepherds when he was out looking for lost sheep in the
snow. They dug the sheep out of their snowdrift, too, and left but
the red bones.'

'They won't do that again, if the place of their lair has been
marked aright,' Caius answered. 'Not after today.'

'Tach! They're cunning as shape-shifters, but we'll have them in
the end, and the rest of their pack, tribune. They have lived at our
cost too long.'

A cutting wind began to blow across the heath from the north,
tearing the low clouds to rags. Strips of pale blue sky showed
through. The hunting party's cloaks pressed against their chests
and fluttered out behind them. It stung Caius' face and made his
dark eyes water, but he didn't mind.

Good, he thought. *The quarry will never scent us coming. They
will not even hear us. Not if they're at home.*

The Britons moved up the hill at a half-run, converging from all
sides. They poked into gorse and ling with spears, in case the wolves
had another way out of their lair. Caius found himself beside Pendor,
the former legionary who had served on the Danube. Radona rushed
ahead of them both, and Caius was well content to let her take the
lead, just for the sight of her long springy legs thrusting against the
heath. Just the backs of her knees and fleeting glimpses of smoothly
muscled thigh were more attractive than the entire persons of most
women . . .

Think about wolves, he told himself. *Besides being a chief's
daughter, she doesn't care for Romans. And she's well liked.*

Someone called out, 'Lord, they are not here!'

'Not here?' Pendor repeated. He turned to Caius with disappointment in his face. 'Hades, noble tribune! If the fools who spied out
the lair let the wolves know they had been discovered, they won't
come back. They would take the warning and find a new home
sharp. This is a clever pair.'

Radona spun about. Her brickdust hair blew in the wild wind.
'Old armyboots, I was one of those fools! We were careful. I'll take
oath the wolves did not spy us.'

Calgaich heard the exchange. 'So? It's a sign, lady, and not to my liking! I feel as I used to feel when I stepped out on the sand.'

'Are you sure, Calgaich?' Radona's voice was sober with respect. She took the rascal's premonition seriously, Caius realized. Britons!

'Sure,' Calgaich repeated. He spat into the heather and wiped palms on his breeches. 'The only wolves we will see this day have two legs.'

His words summoned the event.

Armed men rose out of the heather where they had lain. They charged up the hill, shouting the war-cry of their clan. Others, more distant, came riding hard on shaggy ponies to join the ambush. Caius made a soldier's quick estimate of their numbers. Twenty.

Twenty or so against a dozen.

'Otter Sept men!' Tarmundus shouted. 'Blood enemies, tribune! Keep together, all of you, and get out of this before the trap closes!'

'Run from them?' Irnic barked laughter. He drew his long sword hissing from the sheath. 'Brother, we have you and I, we have Calgaich, we have Pendor ... even the tribune may be useful! Why run?'

'And how do you know these are all?' Caius snapped. 'Or that others are not burning your home at this moment? Retreat as the chieftain says, you supreme fool.'

Clutching her spear, Radona muttered, '*They* scared the wolves off! Scouting the hill and setting their trap – for us – they frightened them away.'

Women, Caius thought. *We're all threatened with death and she's trying to show it was not her fault the quarry escaped! Well, we are the quarry now.*

He cantered at Tarmundus' left side. Radona was on her father's right, Irnic a little behind them. The hunters who went afoot kept up with the ponies at a light-footed run. They were used to covering rough ground quickly.

Fifteen wild shapes bounded up from the heather, directly in their path, naked except for trousers or kilts. Their weapons were barbed spears, round bullhide shields and hand-axes. They were painted blue. They shrieked like ghosts.

Picts.

Javelins flew. Knowing the Pict, Caius dropped down his pony's flank, casting an arm around its neck. Something hissed through the air where his throat had recently been. Tarmundus' pony crashed down, screaming, a spear in its chest. Tarmundus rolled clear, shoulder-long hair spreading out around his bald crown.

Radona was there, yelling. She rammed her spear at an eager Pict who rushed to split her father's skull. It went in between his ribs. Planting her feet, she twisted the spear.

Caius finished him with a backhand slash, then turned on another Pict who was hamstringing a pony with deft cuts of his hand-axe. He opened the painted belly. Howling, the man dropped in the ling, but he threw his arms around Caius' knees and clung tenaciously, heedless of the fact that he was dying. When two other men rushed upon the tribune, it looked bad for him until Irnic, roaring, killed his own adversary and whirled around, striking down both warriors from behind, his great sword whirling left and right, leaving a trail of red drops on the air.

Radona had not erred, after all. Caius had underestimated her uncle as a fighter; but he still saw no reason to revise his opinion of the man's brains.

After that, and for an endless time, Caius simply relived the retreat of the Ninth's remnants, on a smaller scale. Mile by dreadful mile they battled across the fell. Sometimes their enemies hung back, sometimes they attacked in fury. The folk of Tarmundus' Ram Sept stayed tenaciously together, exchanged blows, took wounds and gave them, killed when they could – and one by one left their dead on the heath.

First to fall was a mere boy. Next was a huntsman whose name Caius did not know, and after him, a long, grim time later, Pendor who had served in the legions. Tarmundus blew his horn for help again and again, until he had no breath to spare from fighting.

Once, the tightly-knit group was broken apart and the ambush party swarmed over them, avid to finish the slaughter. Caius used all his powers to bring the band back together while any of them survived. Both Radona's mighty wolfhounds died, but before they were killed, they did their share of killing. Four more men also fell.

By then, five times wounded, Caius knew nothing but confused, fleeting images. He remembered Irnic with a barbed spear in his thigh, and the Pict who held it twisting like man trying to land a fish, until Caius swung his sword and almost severed the savage's head. He remembered Radona, holding her uncle up while he lurched and hopped along; the leader of the attackers calling for the death of the Roman above all; Calgaich beside him, using every lethal trick of combat he had learned on the bloody sand; Radona with her spear, standing firm beside the men, a long gash on her hip; and at last, at long last, a score of men from Tarmundus' hall racing to their rescue, afoot and in chariots.

Caius, his senses reeling, subsided into the back of a chariot unsure whether or not he was bleeding to death. He saw the cloudy British sky, felt drops of rain, and a long time later he looked with fogged comprehension at a raftered ceiling. The Britons' care for him was well-intentioned, but he always thought he did well to survive until his cohort surgeon reached him.

III

July: Sixth Year of Hadrian's Reign

A month later he was watching his centurions put the garrison of Vindolanda through a long, demanding drill parade. Standards had slackened in his absence, but on the whole nothing was wrong with the fort that couldn't be quickly put right. Caius had felt bitter, originally, at being given the command of a cohort of barbarian auxiliaries (Germans in the main, with some Gauls and Scythians) seeing it as a setback to his career. But now he was proud of them. He had led them for three years. He was prepared to match them, not only for fighting spirit, toughness and faith, but also for turnout and drill, with any cohort (except the First) of a regular legion.

The parade ended. Caius ate in his quarters, while planning duty rosters and patrols for the next month. He flexed and turned his left foot as he worked; a slash in his calf muscles on the day of the wolf hunt had left them stiff, but they had healed well, and he was determined to banish all trace of a limp from that leg.

A knock at his door interrupted him. It was one of the centurions, a man named Valitharius, his German name having taken Latin form early in his service.

'Yes, centurion?'

'A party of Britons at the south gate, sir. They ask for refuge. The leader has his wife and daughter with him. He says his name is Tarmundus, that he's a noble, and known to the commander.'

'*Tarmundus*? A big, strong-looking man, bald at the crown, with a face somewhat like a horse's? His wife is small for a British woman, and the daughter tall.'

'Yes, sir. They are the ones.'

'I know them. Asking for refuge?' Caius wanted to know a great deal more about this. 'What sort of general look do they have about them?'

'Worn and stained, sir. They have come a long way in a hurry, and the smell of smoke clings to them. Their attendants, too – about twenty armed warriors, a hard lot, and they have seen recent fighting. They appear angry.'

'Let them in, give them food. Don't disarm them. Twenty British warriors won't make trouble with a cohort, unless they are insane, but put them by the parade ground. Have the century that made the poorest showing this morning turned out for extra drill, sword, shield and pilum. Make sure the gate and wall sentries are especially alert. Bring the chieftain and his family to me at once.'

'Sir.'

Valitharius had described their condition accurately. They had fought hard, travelled hard and slept little; their eyes were red, their mouths grim. Caius found his gaze leaping to Radona's face the second she entered between her tall brothers. With conscious effort, he looked back at Tarmundus.

'Jupiter's thunder, man! What happened?'

'They burned our home!' raged the younger son. 'Cattle driven off – our people killed!'

'We barely escaped!'

A trifle strenuous, life among the Brigantes. Caius said crisply, 'Chieftain?'

'It's so.'

'Who did these things?' He raised a hand. 'Let one speak at a time.'

'Otter Sept warriors, and others,' Tarmundus answered. 'Some were at feud with us, some not. All belonged to the faction that hates Rome.'

'Drem was there, tribune,' Radona interjected. 'He was in the forefront, laughing.'

'Drem,' Caius repeated. 'He led those who ambushed us the day of the wolf hunt.'

'The same, tribune,' Tarmundus endorsed. 'All gods curse him! I saw. I have witnesses with me who saw.'

'A useful identification. I made a report of the wolf hunt that mentions his name. He's on record as an enemy of Rome.' *Even though the governor, my esteemed uncle, did nothing.* 'He burned your home?'

'Down to the foundations.'

Constance ground her teeth, all the gushing imitation Roman matron vanished from her bearing. Caius liked to think of himself as unsentimental, but he thought of the vulgar warmth of that raftered hall where he had been a guest – despite Irnic's insults –

and felt a pang of regret. Irnic was dead, anyhow, and he had saved Caius' hide before dying. There was no question that he owed this family a debt of honour. Yes, but what a time for them to appear at his gate claiming it, with the Emperor in Britain and on his way north – at Eboracum, in fact, according to the last reliable word Caius had received.

'I am sorry. Were Picts with him?'

'Not this time.'

'A pity. That would make it a matter of keeping the frontier secure, but if I have my way, this robber Drem will feel the hand of Rome for his crimes.'

Cattle-raiding and burning a man's home in the course of a feud hardly ranked as crimes in the eyes of wild Britons. Tarmundus had done the same things, more than once, no doubt, and would be as sorry as Drem to give them up when law became firmly established in the north, but that was by the way.

After free use of the bath-house and changes of clothing for the chieftain's family, they came to dinner with Caius and his officers. Although rough – the women's had come from a nearby farm-house – the garments were adequate. Caius and his centurions wore plain tunics as a courtesy.

'It was a night attack,' Tarmundus grunted. 'Men from the Lune, Nidd and Ure, as well as Drem's parts. We saw their faces clearly by the light of our own burning roof! Although we'd have known them all by moonlight alone. They have been feud enemies of ours since Cartimandua's day. You know I am a grandson of hers?' Caius did. 'Aye, well. When she handed over Caractacus to Rome, and had to fight two wars with her husband as a result, there were feuds and factions established that we are still dealing with.'

'Politics,' Caius remarked. 'It's as much of the present as the past. Drem has a claim to be king of the Brigantes, and so do your sons, chieftain. They cannot be preferred to him if their throats are cut. I'd rather see them rule, but there is nothing in that to warrant the intervention of Rome. It's a tribal matter.'

'Would-be kings like Drem often go beyond their tribe for help, tribune,' Valitharius offered. He understood barbarian politics well. His father had counselled a king. 'He has connections among the Picts. He brought Picts across the frontier to help kill his enemies. Isn't that Rome's concern?'

'Drem knowingly tried to murder you, noble tribune,' Constance said indignantly. 'Surely that makes him Rome's concern! He ought to be a long time dying if you catch him.'

Caius nearly smiled. Drem's crime was that he had threatened

Constance's family and burned her house. The kind, fussy hostess trying so hard to be a Roman matron was not now in evidence.

'True,' he owned. 'Since I escaped to tell the tale he's an outlaw; if I take him I can execute him without going higher. Still he has brothers, sons and nephews, all as eligible for kingship as he, if they can gain support – two of those sons married to Pictish princesses.'

'Wipe them all out, then,' Tarmundus said harshly. 'None of that breed will ever do the peace of Rome good.'

'Probably not. I shouldn't greatly object to wiping them out,' Caius said, his dark face saturnine in the lamp-light. 'There are new scars on my body that itch when I think of them. But the weighty consideration is not Drem and his kindred, or you, chieftain, or me; not to Rome. Wipe them out, and in ten years or thirty the situation would recur with a new gang. It's too easy for tribes, and factions within tribes, to join hands across the frontier. After all, the frontier is nothing more than a road with some forts beside it. It's not a wall. The garrisons are the walls, walking walls, and they cannot be everywhere. If it were not so easy –' He shrugged. 'Again, that's a matter too high for me to decide. But I believe my standing is enough to have your wrongs redressed.'

It wasn't, he thought – at any rate not with his illustrious uncle by marriage, Quintus Falco, Governor of Britain – but Falco would not be governor till the world ended. And that was as well. It occurred to him that in the swaggering Irnic, Radona had not possessed a bad uncle, after all. He'd felt such affection for her that she could wrap him around her finger even when he was eager to quarrel. This was a good deal more than Caius could say.

IV

July: Sixth Year of Hadrian's Reign

After dinner, Caius took Radona and her younger brother to the ramparts with him, by the north gate of Vindolanda, beside the catapults. He had more than enough to concern him, with the Emperor coming to inspect the frontier, and he wondered a little why he was doing it; but their parents had both drunk too much wine and the elder brother was moody. Anyhow, the cool night air was pleasant.

They looked towards the great starlit slopes of the heather lands. The road below ran east and west through the gap. A pale ribbon under the stars, it seemed to Caius like a line between the created world and chaos. He considered for a moment how it might seem to the Britons. Radona had told him frankly that she would rather the legions, the procurators and governors were anywhere but here. He wondered if she still felt that way now that her home was rain-soaked cinders – the doing of other Britons, not of Rome's soldiers.

'It's a narrow line,' young Clydno said at last, 'and only the strength of the legions makes it mean anything. In the dales we call them Rome's walking walls.'

'It's a phrase I like. Sometimes I use it. I have marched this country from sea to sea, more than once, and it seems to me that here would be a good place to build long walls, stone walls that do not walk, so that the frontier would be hard to cross unless Rome permitted it.'

'Hard,' Radona said with a touch of defiance. 'Never impossible.'

'Never impossible,' Caius agreed. 'Still, even a great Pictish host that swarmed across could then be contained, forced back and trapped against the stone wall by those other walls, the walking walls you spoke of. The frontier would be more secure, and your father's enemies cut off from their painted allies. It would be better for all of us except Drem.'

'Could it truly be done?' Clydno sounded eager. Radona was silent.

'It's done all the time. Hadrian ordered the entire frontier organized anew in Germany, and the legions did it. When a hill stands in your way, you tear down the hill. When a marsh lies across your path, you drain or fill the marsh. It would be a simpler matter here, I think – and if it is, our Emperor will see it. But it is foolish to pretend to speak for emperors.'

'Father could become King of the Brigantes, then, and reign secure,' Clydno said thoughtfully.

'By permission of Rome.'

'Rome permits kings within her borders, Radona,' Caius told her, 'so long as they own the Emperor's sovereignty and godhead. It doesn't permit such acts as the burning of your home. You had to come to a Roman fort to be safe. You could not be safe in your own dales.'

'No. That's true, we could not.' Fury seethed in her words. 'Our own neighbours would not take us in. Drem struts and thinks he rules the dales! All fear him.'

'My cohort does not.'

'Ha! I'll own I wished you were there with your cohort, the night they came! You'd have enjoyed settling with him for his murder attempt on you! And I should have liked seeing it. Irnic would have been avenged.'

Savage, Caius thought, amused – and a feeling stirred in him that was not amusement.

'He may be yet,' he answered, 'but whether or not Drem is ever taken, he will not be King of the Brigantes now. Your father would make a good one.'

Radona leaned on the rampart and sighed, a melancholy sound in the dark. 'It was Irnic who had a passion to be king.'

'Irnic made a better warrior-hero,' Caius said. 'It's in my mind that he died as he would wish to die.' He hesitated, not sure of what to say next or how to say it. Radona had loved her uncle. Rather lamely, he finished, 'He saved my skin. He did much to save all our skins.'

'You tried to save his,' Clydno recalled. 'You are a good man of your hands, tribune.'

Caius shrugged.

'We caught the wolves,' Radona said. 'Remember? The ones we missed that day?'

'Yes, I remember. The crafty pack leader and his mate.'

'They had cubs. We killed all but one. I nearly killed him, too, but then I thought how the first kings of Rome were fostered by a she-wolf. He's a fine cub. Would the tribune Caius Faninus like to have him?'

There was a basket by Radona's feet. She reached into it, to haul out a squirming bundle of fur that snapped at her with sharp milk teeth. There was a triangle of whitish fur on the grey chest, and another patch, like a skullcap, between the pricked ears. They glimmered in the starlight.

'By Mars, what a little warrior!' Caius felt absurdly touched. Briefly, he wondered what his cohort of barbarian hard-cases would think of such a pet, given by a British girl. Well, discipline would not suffer as a result – he'd see to that – and he wasn't going to reject a gift that seemed meant as some sort of peace offering. *Not from the daughter of a potential tribal king*, he told himself a bit cynically.

'Tribune, can we stay here if the Emperor is likely to travel the length of the frontier?'

Boy's question, boy's awe. Caius tried to remember if he had ever been that young. Not since well before the Ninth was destroyed in the heather, surely.

'He's sure to do so, and I wish you to stay. If the Emperor should ask about your presence, I believe I can satisfy him.'

Radona asked shrewdly. 'What about the Governor?'

'His Excellency the Governor is my father's sister's husband.'

The flat tone was meant to close the subject, and rather to Caius' astonishment, it did. Radona might know something, but candid and tactless as she was, even she chose not to blurt out: *He has treated you as a disgrace to the family and pretended you are not alive, ever since you came back with the remnant of the Ninth.*

Caius fondled the squirming cub with its frosty patches. What in the name of Mars was he going to do with a pet wolf? No matter. It provided him with a welcome change of subject.

'Thank you for my gift,' he said. 'You brought him all this way with death behind you? Then I shall have to treasure him.' *One cannot make a pet of a wolf. I shall have to kill him or turn him loose before he's half grown.* 'Have you named him?'

Radona said shyly, as though she expected him to think it foolish, 'I call him Silver Hat, but there may be one you like better.'

'No. Silver Hat is a good enough name. Probably this entire cohort will take him to their hearts as a mascot.'

'Tribune Faninus, listen!' The words tumbled out of Radona. 'I'm glad you will take him! Since I saw him I knew he was yours. Now that you have accepted him, he will bring you luck, and your plans and wishes for the future will succeed. I'm not foresighted, but I *knew.*'

'Then I'll take triply good care of him.'

Caius returned the cub to his basket, knowing that despite his private thoughts, those sensible and realistic private thoughts, he was going to do what he had said and . . . treasure the animal.

V

September: Sixth Year of Hadrian's Reign

It had been some time since Caius had taken such unalloyed pleasure in a day. Riding upstream, the way they had gone on the fearful day that Irnic died, he thought how much had changed for the better since then – and very likely for no greater reason than that an emperor had enjoyed his breakfast. Hadrian had spoken to Tarmundus with benign interest, and commended Caius for taking him in, and personally despatched three centuries under Valitharius to punish Drem. Nor was that all he had done. His actions and commands before he left had exceeded Caius' highest hopes. Smiling, he turned to Tarmundus, who rode almost knee to knee with him. His much-indulged daughter was on the chieftain's other side.

'A season since, we'd have been wary of riding that wooded valley without a strong force, Tarmundus.'

'Agreed. A man could ride alone, now! Your cohort routed out Drem in short time!'

'Come, do not flatter us,' Caius said, grinning. 'I have lived here for some time. Drem may have vanished for the present, and taken the worst of his followers with him, but he will be back from wherever he's skulking.'

'I hope so,' Tarmundus answered. His lip lifted from his teeth, giving him the look of a stallion ready to fight. 'I've sworn to have his head, and the heads of ten of his henchmen, as the price for Irnic's.'

'My best wishes,' Caius said lightly, 'but if I meet him first, I shall claim him first.' He looked across at Radona. 'I think you are foresighted, lady. With your wolf cub came the best luck I have known in years. I'm to have a part in building this great new wall and its forts. New auxiliary cohorts are to be raised in the island and set to the task; there could not be a better one for hammering them into shape. It will train them as masons, engineers, a dozen trades, and there will be fighting, too, before all is done. By the end, I may receive a legionary posting again, if I do well.'

'It's in my mind that you will,' Radona said. She lifted her red head. 'Just do not suppose that the feuds and the raiding will stop because the frontier is fortified from end to end, tribune! You won't see an end to that. Neither will your children.'

Caius looked up at the cloudy sky, his cloak blowing in the raw wind. 'My children,' he said with determination, 'if I have any, will be born in a warmer land.'

'Guard your back well while you build your wall.' Tarmundus advised, 'else you may not live to have children. There are many proud tribesmen north and south of the frontier who will be angry that Rome means to curb their movements.'

'Oh, I know about their anger. They have written some of their protests on my hide. In the end they will have to endure it.'

Radona laughed aloud. Caius enjoyed the sound. 'I shouldn't complain, tribune. Not now. You proved yourself our friend when you took us in, but this is no time for looking grim! You say it yourself, you have great work ahead of you that you were longing to do, and hopes of a legionary posting! At least this new governor, the Emperor's friend, what's his name –'

'Nepos. Aulus Platorius Nepos.'

'Yes. At least he doesn't have personal reasons to be against the idea of advancing you!'

'True. My beloved uncle Quintus is as happy to be out of Britain as I was to see him leave, and prospects are a good deal more hopeful because of it. But that's by the way. Tarmundus, I should like to visit you more often, in friendship, in the future –'

'We'd all like that, tribune.'

'Caius. I have been making free with your name for some time.'

Radona said with far too innocent and candid a look, 'My mother would like it most of all, perhaps.'

Recent events, and the way he bore himself during them, had started Caius thinking that he was Achilles' own equal for valour. The picture of Constance with a match-making gleam in her eye revealed to him that he wasn't as courageous as he believed. He was tempted to run then and there – and from Radona's chortle she was aware of it.

'Your mother,' Tarmundus told her, 'didn't birch you often enough when you were little.'

They came to the slope above the river where Tarmundus' hall stood. Its stone foundations and cellar had survived the burning, though the floor of Constance's prized atrium had needed new tiles. Everything else had been rebuilt quickly enough, and the fresh thatch shone like gold in the daylight.

'Your man Valitharius brought back our beasts, too,' Tarmundus said. 'All of them, and enough more to constitute a fair honour-price, not to mention the sheep and swine he drove up to the frontier to fee your soldiers . . . which I say was no more than reasonable and fair, so don't punish him.'

'I never mentioned it. It has often seemed to me since I achieved rank that a fair part of command wisdom lies in knowing when to look the other way.'

Constance, still settling into her rebuilt home, was full of endless questions on how to furnish it in the height of Roman fashion. Whenever she was not quizzing Caius on that subject, it seemed, she was speculating about the possibilities of becoming Queen of the Brigantes or trying to throw Caius and Radona together. He felt rather glad, by the time his visit ended, that it hadn't been longer.

'Mother mine, have you no pride?' Radona demanded, once Caius was out of earshot. 'I believed the next thing you would do was fall on your knees and beg him to marry me!'

'He's handsome and brave and he seems to like you.'

'You must be the only one, apart from his mother, to have ever called him handsome!' Radona thought the rest over. 'He's courageous, yes, and a man of his hands; Uncle Irnic might have got along with him better, if he'd lived. But like me? He thinks I'm one notch more civilized than a Pict.'

'You've given him reason,' Tarmundus pointed out.

'I don't want to marry him, and he wants a posting to a regular legion – and he's hoping for one in Spain, where his father came from. So that ends it.'

Oddly enough, Caius enjoyed a somewhat similar, though more impersonal, exchange with the new Governor of Britain at their next meeting. Aulus Platorius did not say much on the subject. A tough-minded, demanding little man with sharp cheekbones and a lined forehead, he was far more concerned with the great project of the wall, and the engineering abilities of the men who would be working on it. But he spared a few moments to discuss Tarmundus and his kin.

'Even with the frontier under closer control, it will be a couple of generations yet before the north is tamed – if it happens then. However, a friendly king of the Brigantes would do something to keep the pot from boiling over. What is your opinion of this man Tarmundus, tribune?'

'He's worthy, sir. Good-natured, more concerned for his children and kindred than the kingship, which I suspect in his heart he regards as more nuisance than it's worth. But he'd take it if he could get it, rather than let his blood enemies have it. He would trouble neither you nor his tribe needlessly, which I'd be prepared to say of few others.'

'If Rome backs him, he can certainly get it. It's evident that his wife and daughter think well of you.'

'Sir? His wife Constance thinks well of anything Roman. As for the daughter – I gave them refuge and she brought me a wolf cub for a present.' He added. 'She is not delighted by all things Roman.'

The governor shrugged. 'A man who intended to settle in Britain could do worse than consider her. She's at least partly civilized and her father may become a king.' He studied Caius's face for a moment. 'I can see that the notion of contracting dropsy appeals to you more, so let us talk of more important things.'

Caius willingly did so.

EPILOGUE

June: Tenth Year of Hadrian's Reign

Silver Hat had become a fully grown dog-wolf of independent mind. He lay in his favourite position on Vindolanda's ramparts by the north gate, in the shade of a catapult. He was the least of all that had changed.

'When was it that you really decided you wanted me for a wife?' Radona asked.

Caius remembered well. 'After I left building the wall to take command of the governor's personal cohort. I discovered that the Roman ladies in London were more polished than you, more urbane than you, in some cases more beautiful than you – and that they all bored me to Tartarus. Oh, it delighted them to go to the games, turn down their dainty thumbs and watch some beaten mirmillo daggered, but it came to my mind, more and more, how little use they would be in a running fight against odds. None of them would ever give a man a wolf cub as a peace offering, either. So when Nepos' time as governor ended, I asked him to assign me to my auxiliaries again.'

'You were lucky to find me unmarried still. I had more than one suitor.'

'Lucky, yes. Why were you?'

'I thought you'd come back,' Radona said calmly. 'Not even a Roman could be that stupid. Mind you, Caius Feninus, I shouldn't have waited till the sun died.'

Caius cocked an eyebrow. 'Shredding her bed-covers, sobbing in fits, hurling furniture and fighting with anything that looked her way. Unmoved else. I am quoting your brothers. Both of them. For their safety's sake, let me assure you they only spoke these colourful phrases in their cups, and after we had been married.'

'They will be laid out for burial when I see them next! So, that was all?'

'Not quite all. It occurred to me that I had better ask for you while there was still doubt that Tarmundus would become king. Otherwise, you might have believed that I took you only to form a useful connection.'

'I'm not that unsure of my worth.'

'I know that now. Your modest and timid manner misled me in the beginning.'

Radona glanced swiftly around to be sure no legionaries were watching. Then she fisted Caius in the ribs. He coughed. Silver Hat lifted his head, glanced their way, and resumed dozing. Had he seen his mistress strike any other man, even lightly, he would have been a picture of raised hackles and snarling menace in an instant. When Caius had first returned from London, there had been no exception made even for him, but the wolf accepted him now.

'It's bad for discipline,' Caius said, 'for the commander to correct his wife's lapses in public. My quarters are private. I suggest we go there.'

He looked into bright blue eyes and had difficulty breathing. Even after two years. Radona's throat moved slowly.

'I shall go,' she murmured. 'After all, a great-grand-daughter of Cartimandua is not afraid of anything a Roman might do.'

ÆOLF THE MARTYR

A. W. Marchmont

Christian persecution in Rome reached its peak during the reign of the Emperor Diocletian. In AD 303 he issued an edict ordering the destruction of all churches throughout the Empire, and followed this with an edict that commanded all Christians to sacrifice to the old Roman gods (whose worship Diocletian had reinstated) on pain of death. The following poignant piece is about the fate of one young man who died for a faith he never followed.

Arthur Marchmont (1852–1923) was a journalist, newspaper editor and lawyer before he turned to writing as a career.

Æolf a Christian: all Rome smiled at the idea and the smile deepened into raucous laughter when it was said that he was to die for the faith.

Not that the man feared death. He had faced it, smiling, a hundred times in the arena, from the moment when the gaping crowd had thronged the Appian Way to mark the triumph of Aucanius Mistor, and had greeted with loud-tongued admiration the captive Briton's towering form as he strode along behind the victorious general's car, his mighty limbs wearing, like so many tinkling baubles, the heavy fetters that clanked on his bulging arms and decked his massive legs.

Who could not recall a score of wondrous tales of his strength which no man could withstand, no wild dissipation sap, and no mad riotous excess diminish?

But a Christian – and to be thrown to the beasts!

Yet it was true as truth or love; and, indeed, because of both.
For it was the work of the Christian witch, Dorcas.

He was not to die for lack of the chance of being allowed to live,
however.

Even on the very eve of the day he was to die, every temptation
that a cunning Prefect's subtlety could devise had been tried for his
weakening.

He was alone in his dungeon loaded with chains, when soldiers
came and struck them off, leading him to a room where all was
light, brilliance, and luxury, and his old companions revelled and
feasted. Brave comrades thronged around him, pressing him to give
up his mad craze and join again in the glorious life ever open to the
strong men of Rome.

Of all he was as heedless as of the dead. To love or sneer, caress
or jibe, wrath, or entreaty, he held the same attitude of unshakable
indifference.

Once only was he moved. They brought in Dorcas, and Vulpia
(the most beautiful, the most vicious and the most jealous of all
the women present) sneered blasphemously at them both.

Then Æolf saw Dorcas shrink and cower as if struck.

He leapt to his feet, and the flowers were scattered and trodden
by the girls who fled, laughing but frightened, from the blaze of
rage in his face. All but Vulpia, who stood sneering and insolent,
as she glanced from one to the other.

He seized her by the arm, gripping it in his anger till the delicate
bones were like to crack beneath the pressure.

'Peace, girl,' he said, between his teeth, 'a pinch of my finger on
your throat will stop your tongue for ever.'

She screamed with pain and baffled wrath, for she had loved
him in her way.

'Coward,' she cried; then to the men around she called, 'Is every
one of you cowed by a woman-beater?'

Two of the brawniest came running forward at the cry.

'Hands off, Æolf,' cried one.

The Briton's eyes flashed fire, and, rejoicing to have something
on which to vent his rage, he turned on them and smote one with
clenched fist with all his force. The man went down and lay senseless
as a log. The scent of fight roused the animal in Æolf and he turned
to the second.

'Æolf!' a thin white hand was laid on his quivering arm, and the
Christian girl's eyes sought his face.

At the touch and the look he changed, and stood like a
stricken child.

But the sight of this influence maddened Vulpia, and, going swiftly to Dorcas, she struck the girl twice in the face.

'Bah, thou Christian cat! That makest a coward thy burly lover!'

Æolf, mad at the sight of the blow, made as if to thrust or even throw the angry woman aside.

'It is but till tomorrow, Æolf,' said the girl, in her sweet, clear, cool voice. 'There is no pain in this now that I know thou art steadfast.'

'Steadfast!' began Vulpia again, with a loud mocking laugh; but the others closed round her then, and for their old comrade's sake forced her to be silent; and the two were left apart together and the revels were hushed, until Æolf and Dorcas had been taken back to their dungeons.

They did not meet again till the next day, when the victims for the day's carnival of slaughter were huddled together awaiting the signal for the butchery in the arena to begin.

By then, a painful change had been wrought in Dorcas. Fear of the wild beasts had broken her. Their staring eyeballs, gaping blood-flecked jaws, and cruel, gleaming fangs grinned at her from every corner of her cell. She seemed even to feel their hot breath as they crouched in readiness for their spring. Memory brought back the horrors she had been forced to witness when others of the faith had died; and out of the awful blackness came echoes of the gasps and screams of pain and terror which the moment of attack had wrung from even the staunchest.

All through the hanging hours of the terrible vigil her senses were harrowed by these terrors till the nerves, overtaxed, gave way.

Her fear was not of death, but of the manner of compassing it; and as she had Æolf knelt apart from the others in the ante-chamber of slaughter, she faltered out this confession to him.

Just as she finished the recital the noise of the raging beasts was borne in upon their ears, and the girl shrank and shuddered as she clung to her companion to stay her from falling to the ground, and her face was grey and seamed with lines of terror, while the sweat stood in cold beads on her forehead.

'Pray for me, Æolf; pray for me; pray for me to have strength,' she cried, through her chattering teeth, as she clutched him, and moved her livid lips in swift, soundless prayer.

'Death is but a puny thing, Dorcas, after all,' he said.

'It is not death I fear, but the dying, Æolf. The beasts, the beasts,' she answered, and cowered close to him, as the roar of the brutes

came again. 'God, help me to be strong. Christ, help me. Pray for
me, Æolf. Pray for me.'

'Not death, but the dying,' repeated the man to himself, under
his breath, and slowly, for the words had started a thought.

Then he set to praying as though fervently; but to save her by
human means from the torture she dreaded was more in his thoughts
than the idea of any help from Heaven.

Vulpia's scorching scorn had, indeed, gone near the truth.

He was to die for the faith, indeed; but his own faith was shallow
enough. His God was the shivering, timorous, beautiful girl by his
side; and his faith, the love he bore her. It had pleased her to make
him a Christian; and Christian he would be to the death, since to
turn back would but grieve her.

That such a fragile thing as the girl at his side should have such
horror of the beasts was natural enough; but he would have thought
better of the God she worshipped so fervently if He had given her
an end more suited to the dainty slightness of her strength. Save
her life, he could not. No power in Rome could do that, save the
Emperor, and the Emperor was stone. But he had a plan.

'I can save you from the beasts, Dorcas,' he said.

'You!' and her face shone for a moment with the light of
wistful hope.

'I cannot save you from death, dear.'

'It is not death I fear, but the beasts.'

'I can save you from them.'

'By what means?'

'I cannot say,' he returned, but then, seeing the light of her eyes
fade, he thought a moment and – lied.

'I won the right to save one victim each year, when I overthrew
the big Greek, Clytos, in the games a year ago.'

It did not occur to her to doubt the truth of this, and he rose
and crossed to one of the guards, who had been a close comrade,
and spoke earnestly. When he returned, his manner showed no
hesitancy.

'It is well, Dorcas,' he said simply. 'You must go with the rest
into the arena, but then all will be well.'

Under the assurance the girl grew calm, and soon could rise and
move about among the rest, exhorting them, comforting them, and
soothing their fears.

When the signal came that the butchery was to commence, he
drew her to his side.

'We two are to go last,' he said.

As they passed between the lines of soldiers along the dim corridor,

at the end of which, through the narrow gate, she could see a part of
the huge sea of eager, expectant faces and hear the hisses and howls
of execration which greeted the appearance of the first victims,
she trembled for an instant and closed her eyes. But Æolf took
her hand.

'Your death will be easy, love,' he whispered; and at the assurance
she lifted her lids and smiled, and then went out.

The gate they passed through was fashioned of heavy iron bars,
and, standing next to it, and last in the line of guards, was the
soldier to whom Æolf had spoken.

As he neared the gate, Æolf lingered a pace or two, letting Dorcas
get first into the arena. Then with a swift sudden movement he sprang
upon the soldier who made only a faint resistance, wrenched the
short sword from him, and, springing through the door, closed it
with almost superhuman strength.

A cry of surprise, starting in a shout from the soldiers, spread
like a fire all round the vast concourse of people, and the shouts
deepened into a roar of wonder and expectation when it was seen
that the gladiator whom all Rome had come to see die had armed
himself and held the gate against the soldiers. Then the guards at
the other side, mistaking the signals, opened the dens and let the
beasts into the arena.

Æolf saw this, too, and left the gate.

'Come now, if you dare,' he cried to the guard with a bitter
smile.

He hurried to Dorcas, who was standing shuddering in dismay
and panic, as the beasts with snarling stealth began to close on their
victims. Every man and woman of the pent thousands had marked
his act and waited in eagerness to see what he would do.

Did he mean to fight the beasts? Were they to have a combat
between the strongest gladiator in all Rome and these ravening
brutes, already crouching to sate their starvation-spurred hunger
on the beggarly Christians? Or had he turned craven when it came
to the death?

He was not long in showing what he meant. His one thought
was for Dorcas.

'You are not to look at the beasts, Dorcas. I am to guard you
from them; but your hour has come, child, though how you die
you will not see. It will be a painless death. Quick, kiss me once.'

She put up her face, and for an instant his towering head bent
over her from behind and his lips rested on hers, while all the
world and all eternity were alike for that instant and in that only
kiss, forgotten.

'Now, turn your face to the Emperor and pray your last prayer. It must be short. Quick. I am between you and the beasts, love.'

She turned her head to the Emperor's seat, sank on her knees, and, closing her eyes, lifted her hands in prayer. Æolf glanced round uneasily and saw the beasts were close upon them.

Then he turned again to her and, the next instant, with a swift dexterous stab drove the sword right through her heart with so true an aim that she rolled forward without even a moan, dead.

At the sight of this a terrific shout went up from the multitude, while the scent of the blood drove the beasts to a frenzy.

He had saved the girl from them in his own barbarian fashion.

Then, that not a man should call him craven, he tossed the soldier's sword far from him and stood firm with folded arms till, with a loud roar, a huge lion sprang upon him, giving the signal for the general carnage, and pulled him down.

So died Æolf, the martyr, for the faith that was never in him.

THE TEMPLE OF DEATH

A. C. Benson

*This story and the next look at the growth of Christianity in
the Roman world and the inevitable tension between the newly
authorized Christians and the remaining pagans.*

*A. C. Benson (1862–1925), eldest brother of the better-known
E. F. Benson, and perhaps best known as the author of the words*
Land of Hope and Glory *to Elgar's* Pomp and Circumstance *music,
considers the life and perils of one such missionary in the early days
of Christendom.*

It was late in the afternoon of a dark and rainy day when Paullinus left
the little village where he had found shelter for the night. The village
lay in a great forest country in the heart of Gaul. The scattered folk
that inhabited it were mostly heathens, and very strange and secret
rites were still celebrated in lonely sanctuaries. Christian teachers, of
whom Paullinus was one, travelled alone or in little companies along
the great high roads, turning aside to visit the woodland hamlets, and
labouring patiently to make the good news of the Word known.

They were mostly unmolested, for they travelled under the
powerful name of Romans, and in many places they were kindly
received. Paullinus had been for months slowly faring from village
to village, without any fixed plan of journeying, but asking his way
from place to place, as the Spirit led him. He was a young man,
a very faithful Christian, and with a love of adventure and travel
which stood him in good stead. He carried a little money, but he
had seldom need to use it, for the people were simple and hospitable;

he did not try to hold assemblies, for he believed that the Gospel must spread like leaven from quiet heart to quiet heart. Indeed he did not purpose to proclaim the Word, but rather to prepare the way for those that should come after. He was of a strong habit, spare and upright; when he was alone he walked swiftly, looking very eagerly about him. He loved the aspect of the earth, the green branching trees, the wild creatures of the woodland, the voices of birds and the sound of streams. And he had too a great and simple love for his own kind, and though he had little eloquence he had a plentiful command of friendly and shrewd talk, and even better than he loved to speak he loved to listen. He had a sweet and open smile, that drew the hearts of all whom he met to him, especially of the children. And he loved his wandering life in the free air, without the daily cares of settled habit.

He had spent the night with an old and calm man, who had been a warrior in his youth, but who could now do little but attend to his farm. Paullinus had spoken to him of the love of the Father and the tender care that Jesus had to His brothers on earth; the old man had listened courteously, and had said that it sounded fair enough, but that he was too old to change, and must stand in the ancient ways. Paullinus did not press him; his custom was never to do that. In the morning he had gone to and fro in the village, and it was late before he thought of setting out; the old man had pressed him to stay another night, but something in Paullinus' heart had told him that he must not wait, for it seemed to him that there was work to be done. The old man came with him to the edge of the forest, and gave him very particular directions to the village he was bound for, which lay in the heart of the wood. 'Of one thing I must advise you,' he said. 'There is, in the wood, some way off the track, a place to which I would not have you go – it is a temple of one of our gods, a dark place. Be certain, dear sir, to pass it by. No one would go there willingly, save that we are sometimes compelled.' He broke off suddenly here and looked about him fearfully; then he went on in a low voice: 'It is called the Temple of the Grey Death, and there are rites done there of which I may not speak. I would it were otherwise, but the gods are strong – and the priest is a hard and evil man, who won his office in a terrible way, and shall lose it no less terribly. Oh, go not there, dear stranger!' and he laid his hand upon his arm.

'Dear brother,' said Paullinus, 'I have no mind to go there – but your words seem to have a dark meaning behind them. What are these rites of which you speak?' But the old man shook his head. 'I may not speak of them,' he said, 'it is better to be silent.'

Then they took a kind leave of each other, and Paullinus said that he would pass again that way to see his friend, 'for we are friends, I know.' And so he went into the wood. It was a wood of very ancient trees, and the dark leaves roofed over the grassy track making a tunnel. The heavens too grew dark above, and Paullinus heard the drops patter upon the leaves. Generally he loved well enough to walk in the woodways, but here it seemed different. He would have liked a companion. Something sinister and terrible seemed to him to hide within those gloomy avenues, and the feeling grew stronger every moment. But he said to himself some of the simple hymns with which he often cheered his way, and felt again that he was in the hands of God.

Presently he passed a little forest pool that was one of the marks of his way. Upon the further bank he was surprised to see a man sitting, with a rod or spear in his hand, looking upon the water. He was glad to see another man in this solitude, and hailed him cheerfully, asking if he was in the right way. The man looked up at the sound. Paullinus saw that he was of middle age, very strong and muscular – but undoubtedly he had an evil face. He scowled, as though he were vexed to be interrupted, and with an odd and angry gesture of the hand he stepped quickly within the wood and disappeared. Paullinus felt in his mind that the man wished him evil, and went on his way somewhat heavily. And now the sun began to go down and it was darker than ever in the forest; Paullinus came to a place where the road forked, and thinking over his note of the way, struck off to the left, but as he did so he felt a certain misgiving which he could not explain. He now began to hurry, for the light failed every moment, and the colour was soon gone out of the grass beneath his feet, leaving all a dark and indistinguishable brown. Soon the path forked again, and then came a road striking across the one that he had pursued of which he did not think he had been told. He went straight forward, but it was now grown so dark that he could no longer see his way, and stumbled very sadly along the wet path, feeling with his hand for the trees. He thought that he must by this time have gone much further than the distance between the villages, and it was clear to him that he had somehow missed the road.

He at last determined that he would try to return, and went slowly back the way that he had come, till at last the night came down upon him. Then Paullinus was struck with a great fear. There were wolves in those forests he knew, though they lived in the unvisited depths of the wood and came not near the habitations of men unless they were fierce with famine. But he had heard several times a strange snarling cry some way off in the wood, and once or twice he had thought he was being softly followed. So he determined to go no further, but to climb up into a tree, if he could find one, and there to spend an uneasy night.

He felt about for some time, but could discover nothing but small saplings, when he suddenly saw through the trees a light shine, and it came across him that he had stumbled as it were by accident upon the village. So he went forward slowly towards the light – there was no track here – often catching his feet among brambles and low plants, till the gloom lifted somewhat and he felt a freer air, and saw that he was in a clearing in the wood. Then he discerned, in front of him, a space of deeper darkness against the sky, what he thought to be the outline of the roofs of buildings; then the light shone out of a window near the ground; but presently he came to a stop, for he saw the light flash and gleam in the ripples of a water that lay in his path and blocked his way.

Then he called aloud once or twice; something seemed to stir in the house, and presently the light in the window was obscured by the head and shoulders of a man, who pressed to the opening; but there was no answer. Then Paullinus spoke very clearly, and said that he was a Roman, a traveller who had lost his way. Then a harsh voice told him to walk round the water to the left and wait awhile; which Paullinus did.

Soon he heard steps come out of the house and come to the water's edge. Then he heard sounds as though someone were walking on a hollow board – then with a word of warning there fell the end of a plank near him on the bank, and he was bidden to come across. He did so, though the bridge was narrow and he was half afraid of falling; but in a moment he was at the other side, a dark figure beside him. He was bidden to wait again, and the figure went out over the water and seemed to pull in the plank that had served as a bridge; and then the man returned and bade him to come forward. Paullinus followed the figure, and in a moment he could see the dark eaves of a long, low house before him, very rudely but strongly built; then a door was opened showing a lighted room within, and he was bidden to step forward and enter.

He found himself in a large, bare chamber, the walls and ceiling of a dark wood. A pine torch flared and dripped in a socket. There were one or two rough seats and a table spread with a meal. At the end of the room there were some bricks piled for a fireplace with charred ashes and a smouldering log among them, for though it was still summer the nights began to be brisk. On the walls hung some implements; a spade and a hoe, a spear, a sword, some knives and javelins. He that inhabited it seemed to be part a tiller of the soil and part a huntsman; but there were other things of which Paullinus could not guess the use – hooks and pronged forks. There were skins of beasts on the floor, and on the ceiling hung bundles of herbs and dried meats. The air was pungent with pine-smoke. He recognized the man at once as the same that he had seen beside the pool; and he looked to Paullinus even stranger and more dangerous than he had seemed before. He seemed too to be on his guard against some terror, and held in his hand a club, as though he were ready to use it.

Presently he said a few words in a harsh voice: 'You are a Roman,' he asked, 'how may I know it?' 'I do not know,' said Paullinus, trying to smile, 'unless you will believe my word.' 'What is your business here?' said the man, 'are you a merchant?' 'No,' said Paullinus, 'I have no business, I travel, and I talk with those I meet – perhaps I am a teacher – a Christian teacher.' At this the man's sternness seemed a little to relax. 'Oh, the new faith?' he said, rather contemptuously, 'well, I have heard of it – and it will never spread; but I am curious to know what it really is, and you shall tell me of it.' But suddenly his angry terrors came upon him again, and he said, with a frown, 'But where were you bound, and whence come you?'

Paullinus, with such calmness as he could muster, for he felt himself to be in some danger, he scarcely knew what, mentioned the names of the villages. 'Well, you have missed your way,' said the man. 'Why did you come here to the Temple of Death?' Paullinus had a sudden access of dread at the words. 'Is this the Temple?' he said, 'it is the place I was bidden to avoid.' At this the man gave a fearful kind of smile, like a flash of lightning out of a sombre cloud, and he said, with a certain dark pride, 'Ay, there are few that come willingly; but now you must abide with me tonight – unless,' he added, with a savage look, 'you have a mind to be eaten by wolves.' 'I will certainly stay,' said Paullinus, 'I am not afraid – I serve a very mighty God myself, who guards his servants if they guard themselves.' 'Ay, does He?' said the man, with a flash of anger, 'then He must needs be strong; – but I wish you no evil,' he added in a moment. 'I think you are a brave man, perhaps a good one – I fear you not.' 'There is no need for you to fear me,' said Paullinus, 'my God is a God of peace and love – and indeed,' he added with a smile, looking at the man's great frame, 'I should have thought there was little need for you to fear any one.' This last word seemed to dissolve the man's evil mood all at once, for he put away the club he held, in a corner of the room, and bade Paullinus eat and drink, which he did gladly. The meat was a strongly flavoured kind of venison, and

there was a rough bread, and a drink that seemed both sweet and
strong, and had the taste of summer flowers. He praised the food,
and the man said to him, 'Ay, I have learnt to suit it to my taste.
I live here in much loneliness, and there is none to help me.'

After the meal the man asked him to tell him something of the
new faith, and Paullinus very willingly told him as simply as he
could of the Way of Christ.

The man listened with a sort of gloomy attention. 'So it is this,'
he said at last, 'which is taking hold of the world! well, it is pretty
enough – a good faith for such as live in ease and security, for women
and children in fair houses; but it suits not with these forests. The god
who made these great lonely woods, and who dwells in them, is very
different,' – he rose and made a strange obeisance as he talked. 'He
loves death and darkness, and the cries of strong and furious beasts.
There is little peace here, for all that the woods are still – and as for
love, it is of a brutish sort. Nay, stranger, the gods of these lands
are very different; and they demand very different sacrifices. They
delight in sharp woes and agonies, in grinding pains, in dripping
blood and death-sweats and cries of despair. If these woods were
all cut down, and the land ploughed up, and peaceful folk lived here
in quiet fields and farms, then perhaps your simple, easy-going God
might come and dwell with them – but now, if he came, he would
flee in terror.'

'Nay,' said Paullinus, but somewhat sadly, for the man's words
seemed to have a fearful truth about them, 'the Father waits long
and is kind; the victory of love is slow, but it is sure.'

'It is slow enough,' said the man; 'these forests have grown here
beyond the memory of man, and they will stand long after you and
I have been turned to a handful of dust – and so I will serve my
gods while I live. But you are weary,' he added, 'and may sleep;
fear not any hurt from me; and as for the way you speak of, well,
I will say that I should be content if it had the victory. I am sick
at heart of the hard rule of these gods – but I fear them, and will
serve them faithfully till I die.'

And then he brought some skins of beasts and heaped them in a
corner of the room for Paullinus, who lay down gladly, and from
mere weariness fell asleep. But the priest sat long before the fire
in thought; and twice he went to the door and looked out, as if
he were waiting for some tidings.

Once the opening of the door aroused Paullinus; and he saw the
dark figure of the priest stand in the doorway, and over his head
and shoulders a dark still night, pierced with golden stars; and once
again, when he opened the door a second time, the pure gush of

air into the close room woke Paullinus from a deep sleep; again he saw the priest stand silent in the door, with his hands clasped behind him; and through the door Paullinus could see the dim ring of dewy woods, that seemed to sleep in quiet dreams; and over the woods a great pale light of dawn that was coming slowly up out of the east.

But Paullinus fell back into sleep again from utter weariness, as a man might dive into a pool. And when at last he opened his eyes he saw that day was come with an infinite sweetness and freshness; the birds called faintly in the thickets; and the priest was going slowly about his daily task, preparing food; and Paullinus, from where he lay, smiled at him, and the priest smiled back, as though half ashamed, and presently said, 'You have slept deeply, sir; and to sleep as you have done shows that a man is brave and innocent.'

Then Paullinus rose, and would have helped him, but the man said, 'Nay, you are my guest; and besides, I do things in a certain order, as all do who live alone, and I would not have anyone to meddle with me.' He spoke gruffly, but there was a certain courtesy in his manner.

Presently the priest asked him to come and eat, and they sat together eating in a friendly way. The priest was silent, but Paullinus talked of many things – and at last the priest said, 'I thought I loved my loneliness, but it seems that I am pleased to have a companion. I believe,' he added, 'that I would be content if you would dwell with me.' And Paullinus smiled in answer, and said, 'Ay, it is not good to live alone.'

A little while after Paullinus said that he must set out on his way, and that he was very grateful for so gentle a welcome; but the priest said, 'Nay, but you must see the sights of my house and of the temple. Few folk have seen it, and never a foreign man. It is not a merry place,' he added, 'but it will do to make a traveller's tale.'

So he led him to the door, and they went out. Paullinus saw that the house where he had spent the night stood on a little square island, with a deep moat all round it, filled with water; the island was all overgrown with bushes and tall plants, except that in one place there were some pens where sheep and goats were kept; and a path led down to the landing-place where he had crossed it the night before. But what at once seized and held the eyes and mind of Paullinus was the temple. He thought he had never seen so grim a place; it rose above the bushes and above the houses. It was of very rough stone, all blank of windows, with a roof of stone; the blocks were very large, and Paullinus wondered how they had been brought there. In front there was a low door, and over it a hideous carving, that seemed to Paullinus to be the work of devils. Apart from the temple, rising among the bushes, stood a rough sculptured figure, with a leering evil face, very roughly but vigorously cut, with an arm raised as though beckoning people to the temple. This figure, of a kind of reddish stone, seemed horrible beyond words to Paullinus. It seemed to him like a servant of Satan, if not Satan himself, frozen into stone.

The priest looked at Paullinus, who could not help showing his horror, with a kind of pride. Then he said, 'Will you go further? Will you enter the temple with me, and see what is therein? Perhaps you will after all bow your head to the gods of the forest.' And Paullinus said, 'Yes, I will go,' and he said a silent prayer to the Lord Christ that He would guard him well. Another path paved with stone led from the landing-place to the temple, along which they went slowly; the priest leading. Arrived at the door, the priest made another strange obeisance, lifting his hands slowly above his head and closing his eyes; then he opened the door into the temple itself. There came out a foul and heavy smell that shuddered in the nostrils of Paullinus and left him gasping somewhat for breath. The priest looked at him with a sort of curious wonder, which made Paullinus determine to go further.

The temple itself was large and dark, a sickly light only filtering in through a hole in the roof. The floor was paved, and the roof was supported by great wooden columns, the trunks of large forest trees. The greater part of the building was shut off by a large wooden screen, about the height of a man, close to them, so that they stood in a kind of vestibule. The whole of the building, walls, roof, and floor, had been painted at some time or other a black colour, which was now faded and looked a dark slaty grey. Over the screen in the centre was seen the head of what seemed an image, very great and horrible. The light, which came from an opening immediately above the image, showed a horned and bearded head, misshapen and grotesque. Possibly at another time and place Paullinus might have smiled at the ugly thing; but here, peering at them over the screen, in the fetid gloom, it froze the blood in his veins.

And now behind the screen were strange sounds as well, a kind of heavy breathing or snorting, and what seemed the scratching of some beast. The priest went up to the screen and opened a sort of panel in it; this was followed by a hoarse and hideous outcry within, half of fear and half of rage. The priest took from an angle of the wall a long pole shod with iron, and leaned within the opening, saying in a stern tone some words that Paullinus did not understand. Presently the noises ceased, and the priest, using a great effort, seemed to pull or push at something with the pole, and there was the sound as of a great gate turning on its hinges. Then he drew his head and arms out, and said to Paullinus, 'We may enter.' He then threw a door open in the middle of the screen and went in. Paullinus followed.

In front of them stood a great statue on a pedestal; the figure of a thing, half-man half-goat, crouched as though to spring. The smell was still more horrible within, and it became clear to Paullinus that he was in the lair of some ravenous and filthy beast. There lay a mess of bones underneath the statue. To the left, in the wall, there was a strong oaken door, made like a portcullis, which seemed to close the entrance of a den; something seemed to move and stir in the blackness, and Paullinus heard the sound of heavy breathing within. The priest, still holding the pole in his hand, led the way round to the back of the statue. Here, set into the wall, were a number of stone slabs, with what seemed to be a name upon each, rudely carved.

The priest pointed to these and said, 'Those are the names of the priests of this shrine. And now,' he went on, 'I will tell you a thing which is in my mind – I know not why I should wish to say it – but it seems to me that I have a great desire to tell you all and keep nothing back; and I tell you this, though you may turn from me with shame and horror. We have a law that if a man be condemned to death for a certain crime – if he have slain one of his kin – he is bound to a tree in the forest to be devoured piecemeal by the wolves. But if there seem to be cause or excuse for the deed that he has done, then he is allowed to purchase his life on one condition – he may come to this place and slay the priest who serves here, if he can, or himself be slain. And if he slay him he reigns in his stead until he himself be slain. And the rites of this place are these: all of this tribe who may be guilty of the slaying of a man by secret or open violence without due cause are offered here a sacrifice to the god – and that is the task that I have done and must do till I am myself slain. And here in a den dwells a savage beast – I know not its name and its age is very great – that slays and devours the guilty. What wonder if a man's heart grows dark and cruel here; I can only look into my own heart, black as it is, and wonder that it is not blacker. But the gods are good to me, and have not cursed me utterly.

'And now I will tell you that when I saw you by the pool, and when you called to me in the night, I thought that perchance you had come to slay me – and then I saw that you were alone, and not guarded as a prisoner would be; but even then my heart was dark, because the god has had no sacrifice for many a month, and seems to call upon me for a victim – so I had it in my heart to slay you here. And now,' he said, 'I have opened the door of my heart, and you have seen all that is to be seen.'

And then he looked upon Paullinus as if to know his judgment; and Paullinus, turning to the priest, and seeing that in his heart he desired what was better, and abode not willingly in the ways of death, said, 'Brother, with all my heart I am sorry for you – and I would have you turn your heart away from these dark and evil gods – who are indeed, I think, the very spirits of hell – and turn to the Father of mercy of whom I spoke, with whom there is forgiveness and love for all His sons, when once they turn to Him and ask His help.'

The priest looked very gently at Paullinus as he spoke; but there came a horrible roaring out of the den, and the beast flung himself against the bars as if in rage.

Then the priest said, 'For twenty years I have heard no speech like this; for twenty years I have lived with death and done wickedness, and all men turn from me with fear and loathing, and speak not any word to me: I have never looked in a kindly human eye, nor felt the hand of a friend within my own. Judge between me and my sin. I had a brother, an evil man, who made it his pleasure to trouble me. I was stronger than he, and he feared me. I loved a maiden of our tribe, and she loved me; and when my brother knew it he went about to do her a hurt, that it might grieve me. One day she went through the forest alone, and never returned, and I, in madness ranging the wood to find her, found the mangled bones of her body. I knew it by the poor torn hair – she had been devoured by wolves – but burying the bones I saw that the feet were tied together with a cord, and then I knew that someone had bound her by violence and left her to be devoured.

'Then as I returned from burying her, I came upon my brother in a glade of the wood, and he looked upon me with an evil smile, and said, 'Hast thou found her?' And I knew in my heart what he had done, and I slew him where he stood – and then I returned and said what I had done. Then they imprisoned me – for my brother was older than myself, and my enemies said that I had done it to win his inheritance – and at last, after long consulting, they gave me the choice to be devoured of wolves or to become the priest of Death. I chose the latter, because I was mad and hated all mankind. I came to this place at sundown, and my guards left me. I swam the ditch, and knocked at the priest's door; he was an old man and piteous, who abhorred his trade – and there I seized him and slew him with my hands – he was weak and made no resistance – and I flung his

body to the beast and carved his name. That is my bitter story –
and since then I have lived, accursed and dreaded. These gods are
hard taskmasters.' He made a wild gesture of the hand and turned
his bright eyes upon Paullinus, who stood aghast.

'The tale is told,' said the priest. 'I who have kept silence all these
years have babbled my story to a stranger. Why did I tell you? I
thought that with all your talk of mercy and forgiveness you might
have a message for my bitter and tired heart – but you shrink from
me, and are silent.'

'Nay,' said Paullinus, 'shrink from you! – not so – nay, I cling to
you more than ever; come and claim your part in the forgiveness
that waits for all – you have suffered, you have repented – and the
God whom I serve has comfort and peace for you and for all; His
love is wide and deep – claim your share in it.' And he took the
priest's hand in both of his own.

There was a horrible roaring behind them as they stood: the
great beast behind them struck at the bars, but the priest took
no heed.

'If I could,' he said, with his eyes fixed on Paullinus' face.

'Nay then,' said Paullinus, 'if you would it is done already, for
He reads the very secrets of the heart.'

There broke out a loud fierce crashing sound behind them; the
great oaken gate heaved and splintered, and a monstrous beast
as huge as a horse appeared at the mouth of the den; his small
head was laid back on his hairy shoulders, his little eyes gleamed
wickedly, and his red mouth opened snarling fiercely. The priest
turned, and met the rush of the beast full. In a moment he was
flung to the ground with a dreadful rending sound. 'Save yourself!'
he cried. The huge brute glared, with his foot upon the fallen form,
and seemed to hesitate whether to attack his second foe. Paullinus,
hardly knowing what he did, seized the great iron-pointed pole,
and with a firmness of strength which he had not known himself
to possess drove it full into the monster's great throat as it opened
its mouth towards him. It made a wild and sickening cry; it raised
one foot as though to strike, then it beat the air and struck once at
the head of the prostrate form; then, with a gurgling sound, spitting
out a flood of hot blood, it collapsed, rolled slowly on one side.
Paullinus, watching it intently and still holding the pole, thrust it
further in with all his might. It quivered all over, and in a moment
lay still. Paullinus made haste to drag the priest out from beneath –
but he saw that all was over; the last blow of the beast had battered
in the skull – and besides that the body was horribly mangled and
crushed. The limbs of the priest were heavy and relaxed; his hands

were folded together as though in prayer, and he drew one or two little fluttering breaths, but never opened his eyes.

Paullinus was like one in a dream at this sudden horror; but he kept his senses; once or twice the great beast moved, and drummed on the pavement with a horny paw. So Paullinus drew the prostrate body of the priest outside the screen and closed the door. Then he went with swift steps out of the temple and to the water's edge; he drew up a little water in his hand, looking into the dark and cool moat. Then he came back with a purpose in his mind. He sprinkled the water on the poor mangled brow; and then, choosing the name of the Apostle whom Jesus most loved, he said, 'John, I baptize thee, *in nomine*, &c.' It was like a prisoner's release; the straining hands relaxed, and with a sigh the new-made Christian presently died. 'I doubt I have done right,' said Paullinus to himself. 'He was coming to the Saviour very swiftly, and I think was at His feet; and if he was not in heart a Christian, the Lord will know when he meets Him in the heavenly places.'

When Paullinus went back to the hut he found a rough mattock. First he dug a great hole; the earth was black and soft, and water oozed soon into the depths; then with much painful labour he dragged the great beast thither, and covered him in from the eye of day; and then he toiled to dig a grave for the priest – once he stopped to eat a little food, but he worked with unusual ease and lightness. But the night came down on the forest as he finished the grave – for he did not wish that the priest should lie within the dreadful temple.

Then he went back, very weary but not sad; his terrors and distresses had drawn slowly off from his mind, as he worked in the still afternoon, under the clear sky, all surrounded by woods; the earth seemed like one who had come from a bath, washed through and through by the drench of wholesome rains, and the smell of the woods was sharp and sweet.

Paullinus slept quietly that night, feeling very close to God; but in the morning, when the dawn was coming up, he was awakened by a shouting outside. His sleep had been so deep and still that he hardly knew at first where he was, but it all came swiftly back to him; and then the shouting was repeated. Paullinus rose to his feet and went slowly out.

On the edge of the water, where the causeway crossed it, he saw two men standing, that from their dress seemed to be great chiefs. Behind them, with his hands bound, and attached by a rope held in the hand of one of the chiefs, was a young man of a wild and fierce aspect, in the dress of a serf, a rough tunic and leggings. His

head was bare, and he looked around him in dismay, like a beast
in a trap. Behind, at the edge of the clearing, stood four soldiers
silent, with bows strung and arrows fitted to the string. Over the
whole group there seemed to be the shadow of a stern purpose. At
the appearance of Paullinus, the two chiefs hurriedly bent together
in talk, and looked at him with astonishment. Paullinus came down
to the water's edge, when one of the chiefs said, 'We have come for
the priest; where is he? For he must do his office upon this man,
who hath slain one of his kin by stealth.'

'It is too late,' said Paullinus; 'he is dead, and waits for burial.'

Then the chiefs seemed again to confer together, and one of them,
with a strange reverence, said, 'Then you are the new priest of the
temple? And yet it seems strange, for you are not of our nation.'

'Nay,' said Paullinus, 'I am a wanderer, a Roman. It was not I
who slew him – it was the great beast who lived in the den yonder;
and the beast have I slain – but come over and let me tell you all
the tale.'

So he made haste to put out the bridge, and the two chiefs came
over in silence, leaving the prisoner in the hands of the guards who
surrounded him. Paullinus led them to the temple, which he could
hardly prevail upon them to enter, and showed them the dead body,
which was a fearful sight enough; then he showed them the broken
gate and the empty den, and then he led them to the mound where
the beast lay buried, and offered if they would to uncover the body.
'Nay, we would not see him,' said the elder chief in a low voice; 'it
is enough.'

Paullinus then led them to the hut and told them the story from
beginning to end. The chiefs looked at him with surprise when he
told them of the beast's death, and one of them said, 'I doubt, sir,
you slew him by Roman magic – for he was exceedingly strong, and
you look not much of a warrior.' 'Nay,' said Paullinus, smiling, 'I
doubt he was his own death, as is often the end of evil – he leapt
upon the pole: I did but hold it, and the Lord made my hand
strong.'

When he had done the story the chiefs spoke together a little in
a low tone. Then one of them said, 'This is a strange tale, sir. And
it seems to us that you must be a man whom the gods love, for you
stayed here a night with the priest – who was a fierce man and no
friend of strangers – and received no hurt. And then you have slain
the Hound of Death, unarmed. But we will ask you to go with us,
for we cannot decide so grave a matter until we have taken counsel
with our tribe. Be assured that you shall be used courteously.'

'I will go very willingly,' said Paullinus. 'My God did indeed send me hither to do a work which He had prepared for me to do, and I would serve His will in all things.'

So they first buried the body of the priest in his grave, and then they went together to the village, and messages were sent to the chiefs of the tribe, who came in haste, ten great warriors; and they sat and debated long in low voices. And Paullinus sat without wondering that he could feel so calm, for he knew that he was in jeopardy.

So when they had talked a long while they called Paullinus into the council, and the oldest chief, an ancient warrior with silver hair, much bowed with age, told him that they saw that he was a man favoured of God. 'I hide it not from you,' he said, 'that some of my brethren here would have it that death should be your portion, because you have meddled with sacred and secret things. But I think that it is clear that you have done no wrong, or otherwise you would have been slain; you spoke but now of the God you serve, and we would hear of Him; for now that the priest is dead and the beast dead, we say with reverence that a cloud is lifted from us, and that we have served dark gods too long.'

So Paullinus spoke of the Father's love and the coming of the Saviour on to the earth; and when he had finished the chiefs thanked him very courteously, and then they asked him to abide with them and speak again of the matter. So Paullinus abode there and made many friends, as his manner was.

Then came a day when the chiefs again held council, and they told Paullinus that if he would, he should be the priest of the temple and teach what he would there, and that the temple should be cleansed; and they said that they would not ask him to be the slayer of such as had killed a man, for that, they said, seems to belong rather to a warrior than a priest.

So Paullinus said that he would abide with them, but that he must first go and be made a priest after his own order; and he departed, but soon returned, and the Temple of Death was made a Church of Christians.

Paullinus is an old man now; you may see him walk at evening beside the water, under the shadow of the church. The images have been broken and defaced; but Paullinus often stops beside a mound, and thinks of the bones of the great beast that lie whitening below – and then he stands beside a grave which bears the name of John, and knows that his brother, that did evil in the days of his ignorance, but that suffered sore, will be the first to meet him in the heavenly country, with the light of God about him; 'and perhaps,' says Paullinus to himself, 'he will bear a palm in his hand.'

THE GREAT WORLD AND THE SMALL

Darrell Schweitzer

The fourth century saw Rome coming increasingly under the threat of the Germanic and other tribes that were sweeping across Europe. In AD 330, the Emperor Constantine re-established his capital at Byzantium, which he renamed Constantinople, and the power and protection of the imperial guard and the army drained from Rome. Although Constantine restored Christianity and made it the religion of Rome, there were many supporters of the old religion, and when Rome wasn't under attack from outside its borders, it was under threat from different factions within. The following story looks at one such power struggle between followers of the old religion and the new and its effect on two brothers.

Darrell Schweitzer (b. 1952) is best known for his fantasy stories and novels, especially The Mask of the Sorcerer (1995). The stories in We Are all Legends (1981) follow the fated travels of a medieval knight, and conjure up a doomed and decaying image of the Middle Ages, an image that is equally appropriate for this story.

I did not kill my brother. In time, I hope we'll be able to joke about it, and say that for all fratricide is the most venerable of Roman traditions aside from, possibly, rape, I couldn't bring myself to emulate Romulus. My Remus survives yet. I never carried off any Sabine women either.

I remember telling him stories, more than anything else. That was how our childhood passed. Each summer the family would flee the heat of the City and seek refuge with grandfather, Serenus Falco, who had an estate in the north of Italy, in the foothills of the Julian Alps. Every night, all summer, Flavius and I slept in a broad, low room up under the tiled eaves. It was a spooky place, filled with ghosts, I was certain, but I was not afraid of them, and it was *there* that I could lie in the darkness listening to the wind among the mountain peaks, or to the secret conversations of the owls in nearby trees.

There I could well imagine that the world had never changed because everybody decided to worship a dead Jew, that the mysteries were still alive, that the gods still gazed down on us from Olympus, that the ancient heroes dwelt among the gods and looked down on us also, to inspire us to imitate mighty deeds.

There.

'It's time for a story,' I would say, and sometimes my brother, when he was very young, would whimper, or when he was older protest, 'No, that's wicked,' or when he was older still, dismiss it as 'pagan rubbish'.

But he always listened, silently, more fascinated than he dared to admit to himself, even when the telling turned to monsters and restless shades of the wronged dead, and the terrible Strix beyond imagining, I was *certain* that the gods actually spoke to me then. They called out to me in the night. I heard their voices distinctly, but I could not make out their words. It was a kind of miracle, I decided. I wondered if Flavius could hear them too. Once, in the morning, I actually asked him, and he thought I was telling him another silly story.

But when I return to those nights again and again, in my memory, as if I were reading once more from an old and beloved book, I know why, for all he should have become my enemy, I could not kill my brother.

He was my audience.

He should have been my enemy. Though he was but five years my junior, my brother was the product of another time, another world. I was our father's son, he our mother's. I think that in the early years of their marriage, our parents called a truce in their constant bickerings long enough to divide up the spoils. Mother got Flavius, raising him a Christian, naming him, as is increasingly fashionable, after the sainted emperor Flavius Constantinus, whom the Christians call the Great.

But Father taught me to revere the old gods and the old ways.

When my brother and I were boys, we fought like boys, made up, played, fought again, and the difference did not seem so great, but later, it became a chasm. We were torn apart even as the world is torn apart.

But first, we grew up. I put on the toga of manhood and tried to make a career as Father had, as our ancestors had all the way back to the days of the Republic: pleading cases, managing our estates, hunting, riding, hearing the complaints of tenants. I read old books and wrote poetry in the approved manner, which literary men said recalled the ancient masters. Soon I was to marry a girl of a lineage fully as venerable as my own. Father had arranged it.

Meanwhile, in the world beyond our immediate lives, Abrogastes, Master of Troops in the West, slew Valentinian Augustus and set up one Eugenius in his place. This Eugenius was the first emperor since Julian to worship the gods of Rome. He restored the altar of Victory in the Senate.

But he was also a usurper and the puppet of a murderer. His methods were those of his kind. He and his master swore they would turn the churches on the Vatican Hill into stables. Given time, they would have started heaving Christians to what few starving lions the circuses still possessed.

Yet Father went to serve the new regime. I remember how it was when the word reached our house.

Mother shrieked and wept. Flavius tried to comfort her. I had just come in from the law courts, and stood as still as one of the numberless commemorative statues in the Forum, trying to look dignified in my toga.

Father dragged me into the library, shut the door, checked to make sure no one was listening, then said to me, 'It is time to join the great world, my son. It is the end of being small.'

'But –'

'Despite everything, it is Rome's last chance. I am certain of that. Truly the last.'

I was to act as if nothing had happened, and to deny all knowledge of his actions and preserve the family wealth if fate went against us. He made me swear a solemn oath to obey him. I protested that this was unnecessary. But his look was hard and fierce, as if he were animated by the spirit of some ancient hero. I tried to believe he was. I swore.

Then he gave me certain, other instructions. And so, in the summer of my eighteenth year, while the most Christian Theodosius Augustus marched from the East to do battle with Eugenius and the world awaited the outcome, I made my last trip to Grandfather

Falco's. I rode on horseback, trailed by servants and a dozen pack mules laden with books and accounts and gifts. Behind them, Flavius lolled in a cart, prostrate with the heat.

When we got to Aquilea, the great city was filled with soldiers and with refugees from the coming battle. Smoke rose from sacrificial altars. Christian churches were closed. Flavius said the gods were devils and the stench of burning animals made him sick.

Ostensibly we were going to set our grandfather's affairs in order, since he was very old now, and his mind clouded. I tried to pretend it was nothing more than that. At night, I even told Flavius a few stories, for all he was in no mood to listen.

I hoped he would never find out that I bore letters for partisans of Eugenius. It was all we could do not to quarrel, since we'd both lived our lives weary of our parents quarrelling. But he was old enough to have his own ideas, and for me not to trust him.

Somewhere north of Aquilea, the thing happened.
We had been on the road most of the day, hours beyond the last inn or posting station, when suddenly the woods around us exploded with screaming men waving swords and spears. One grabbed my horse's bridle. I kicked him in the face and sent him tumbling. Flavius awoke with a shout, then started striking bravely on every side with a rake that happened to be in the cart with him. Once I saw him turn and stumble, and for a horrible second I thought he was transfixed with an arrow.

All was confusion, shouting. A servant screamed, his head cloven with an axe. The cart-horse reared up and the cart tipped over. Flavius went flying. Someone was on the horse behind me, but I shoved him off with a vicious jab of my elbow. A burly man in military armor went for my bridle again. I swerved away from him. He cursed in what sounded like German, drew his sword, slashed, missed.

I saw my brother struggling with three men who were trying to hold him down. One, my horse trampled. The other two rolled to either side. Flavius reached up with his hand. I caught him, hauled him up in front of me, and sped off.

I glanced back once to see the servants standing helplessly about while the robbers tore through the luggage, hurling papers into the air.

We galloped along a narrow path, up a rugged hillside, trailing dust. All the while Flavius was draped over the saddle like a blanket, his head one way, his feet the other. He struggled to sit up. I helped him. My hand brushed the arrow in his tunic.

'Are you hurt?'

He pulled the arrow out. It was merely through a fold in the tunic, not through him. 'I don't think so.'

'Jupiter be praised.'

He didn't even upbraid my paganism then. We rode for a while longer, along a ridge line, looking down over the vast countryside, the city of Aquilea below, and beyond it, the Adriatic. The world looked quiet, empty of armies and robbers.

The horse slowed to a walk. 'Who were they?' Flavius asked.

I shrugged. 'Soldiers. Allies, deserters, brigands. It's hard to tell.'

'But whose?' He meant, of course, Christians or pagans, men of Theodosius or of Eugenius, friends or foes.

Toward evening, we looked down on Grandfather Falco's villa and farm, which seemed undisturbed, but was surrounded by hundreds of campfires.

'We can't go there,' I said.

'They might be friends –'

'*Whose* friends?'

He saw the problem at once. For his age, I think he saw a great deal. But he didn't know what to say, and only managed a feeble, 'I don't know.'

'Besides, it wouldn't make any difference if they thought we had any money,' I said.

So we turned away, walking down, Flavius leading the horse. There was nothing to do but find a secluded spot and camp for the night. In time we came to a little hollow, where water trickled among some boulders.

But we did not dare make a fire. Instead, we sat still beneath the trees, listening to the wind, gazing up at the darkening sky.

'Titus, what is going to happen to us?' my brother asked, and for a minute he sounded like a frightened child. It seemed as if the years were as nothing, and we were in the loft again, and it was time for a story.

But Flavius interrupted. 'We should be enemies,' he said.

I stared at him, startled. 'Why?'

'Because we're on different sides. Of everything. You know perfectly well.'

Unconsciously, I fingered the letters, which I wore in a sealed packet around my neck.

'What do I know perfectly well?'

He was staring at me. As inconspicuously as I could, I withdrew my hand. But he lunged at me suddenly, and the two of us wrestled like small boys, rolling over the ground, startling our horse, while he shouted, 'Give it, you bastard!' I dug my hand into his face and shoved him away with a mighty heave, but he had hold of the letters. The string broke. He tumbled backward, clutching his prize, then stood up, tore the packet open, and tried to read.

I tackled him. We rolled again. I got the letters back as he wriggled, tried to kick me in the face, and broke free.

We sat in the dust, panting, our clothing in ruins, glaring at one another. I'd scraped my knee painfully. But I held the letters. He had produced a dagger from somewhere.

'Now what are you going to do?' I said. 'Kill me?'

'Or you me?'

'It would make a certain amount of sense.'

'You're a traitor, Titus. You and Father both.'

'Shut up. You don't know what you're talking about.'

But he did. 'Those men. They weren't robbers. They were looking for –' He pointed to the letters.

'Yes, they were. But they let us get away. Not very competent, were they?'

'They let *you* get away –'

'Do you think they would have treated you any differently?'

'It wasn't my fault –' There was nothing to argue about. I felt a sinking, helpless feeling. I cursed Father for meddling in the affairs of the great world. I was losing my brother. Now it was all coming out, like a long-festering poison.

'Consider,' I said after a while. 'We are both Romans, and the soldiers on both sides are virtually all barbarians. Not one in a hundred speaks decent Latin.'

'So?'

'That must count for something. Family must count for a lot more. Our lands, our ancestors, everything. So let us not be enemies, all right?' I held out my hand.

He clutched the dagger and drew back. 'You're trying to trick me!'

I should have killed him right then and there. Logic dictated it.

A long, difficult silence followed. The sky became fully dark, moonless, filled with stars. Around us, the owls began to speak. Flavius sat very still, his face an inscrutable mask.

After a very long time he asked, in the tone of a child again, 'What are we going to do?'

'I don't know. What do you think?'

'I think I should pray for you.'

'That's a start.'

But he did not. He sat still, listening to the sounds of the night.

'Do you hear them?' I said.

'What?'

'The voices of the gods. I heard them many times on nights like this. Sometimes when I went downstairs to piss, I'd look out a window, and see the gods up in the sky, huge as clouds, standing far away, with the stars like jewels in their cloaks.'

'You were dreaming.'

'No.'

'It was clouds then.'

'No. They spoke to me quite clearly, and said that because I still believed, I could call on them when I needed them the most, and they would answer –'

'What a crock of –'

'It wasn't the wind,' I said. 'I heard them.'

Again silence settled between us, and I listened for the voices of the gods in the night. Surely on this night, I told myself, surely now as the world hung in the balance, they would speak.

I was the one who began to pray, '*Mother Hecate, mistress of night, goddess of graves –*'

'Stop that!' Flavius hissed. 'It's devilish!' He made the old sign to ward off evil, not the Christian one.

'I think it is time for a story,' I said. 'Will you listen?'

He said nothing at all, so I began my story, telling of two brothers who were lost in the woods, and how the spirits of the old gods gathered around them to hear one of them tell a story.

'I think I *know* this story,' my brother said with heavy irony.

'No you don't. Let it continue.' All around us, the owls cried out.

In the story the brothers rose from where they sat and ran through the night, hand in hand, because one of them heard a voice calling out to him clearly, while the other, the younger, did not. The elder dragged the younger along, and the boy fought with him, and was afraid, but had lost his dagger somewhere.

In the story, he said I was bewitched, that the devil had me.

I did not kill him. I came to a cliff's edge and could have easily hurled him off.

Here a tree, there a stone. Again, the bending path. I knew the signs like something long remembered, like an old story, and the voices of the owls led me on, and shadows among the trees: a face like a man, a form not at all human.

In the story, in the story as I told it, the two of us crawled on all fours up steep hillsides, beneath thickets of thorns, until we came to a strange country where the very earth seemed transformed into crumbly ash, and the sky was black but there were no stars, and all the noises of the night were gone but for the voices of the thousand owls, which flew above us, invisible.

A single, black bird fluttered before my face; not an owl, and I saw its own face clearly: a woman's, with streaming black hair and snow-pale skin, eyes black and blind like a basalt statue.

It shrieked at me. Flavius cried out, stumbled. I caught hold of his wrist, yanked, dragged him on.

To this day I do not know if what followed was some kind of dream or an actuality, or if the distinction means anything.

Think of it as a vision. We came to a ruined temple in a valley between two hills, beneath a starless sky that was utterly dark. The owls had deserted us, and we approached the fallen columns and roofless enclosure in absolute silence.

Flames burned noiselessly in a great, bronze bowl set on a tripod. In the firelight, amid flickering shadows, I saw shrivelled corpses in heaps, and scattered bones, and great ravens rooting through the debris like robbers. My brother and I waded among them, but were not molested as they tore at the bones through fragments of fine garments, scattering jewels, scepters, diadems. Somewhere, Flavius babbled words in a whispering delirium.

At least one corpse had an animal's head, a dog, I think.

Then bones and tatters rose up before me, assembling themselves into the shape of a woman with wild black hair, her face streaked with blood, her eyes black as a statue and blind.

She groped for Flavius and caught him, quick as a striking serpent, hurling him to the ground, kneeling astride him, holding his arms down with her clawed hands. She rocked her head from side to side and hissed.

I saw that her teeth were like needles. Strix. Devourer of children. Desperate, famished, mad.

My brother's eyes met mine. 'Help me,' he said. I think he wanted to say more, but couldn't find the words. I think he wanted to say that I had brought him here deliberately, to kill him.

But I turned suddenly, looking about for a weapon. I found a staff of some sort, picked it up, struck at the monster, then stumbled with the unspent force of the blow as the staff went right through the creature as if it were made of smoke.

Flavius let out a little cry. I called on the gods then. I named them, great Jupiter, Apollo, Mercury, as many as I could think of.

Because in one of my stories there was a boy who spoke with the gods, and to whom the gods spoke. They promised to come if he called.

The temple filled with wind. Dust rose. The feasting ravens flapped their wings irritably.

In the far darkness, in the back of the temple, there was a light, like a candle before the face of a huge, seated statue. But the face turned toward me and opened its terrible eyes, and said, 'She would have your brother's life. It will do her no good. We are all dying anyway.'

'Stop her!' Even then the black hag seemed to kiss Flavius on the side of the neck.

'Stop her!'

'I have no power left to stop her. Speak to her, Titus Serenus. Remind her who she once is.'

'But – but – is she not the Strix?'

'No Not always.'

I thought I understood then, in my amazement, and if I can ever be called brave, if I ever can claim to have performed a heroic deed, it was this: I took the crone by the hand. She looked up at me, blood streaming over her chin. I spoke to her gently, my voice trembling, but I did not lose my words.

'Dread Mother of Darkness, I am honored to greet you at last.'

She rose. I crouched down and helped Flavius to his feet. He leaned on my shoulder.

Together, he and I approached the seated one, and I saw a diademed figure clad in military garb like an emperor, larger than a man, mighty of limb, but the face was filled with pain and weariness. A spear had pierced the right side. Blood pooled before the throne.

I knelt and gathered the blood into my hands and poured it out again, as an offering to Death.

'Do you not know me?' The voice was like muted thunder.

'Yes, Lord, I do.'

Flavius also knelt and dipped his fingers into the blood.

And all around us, the shadows shifted, and figures stepped out from behind the broken pillars. I saw them all, in their tattered clothing and tarnished crowns, in all their aspects and personas, those who were human in form and those who were not – the great ones, more perfect in shape than any mortal, and another, whose head was that of a startled bird, and another, green and clad in leaves – all of them feeble with age and neglect, truly, as their king had said, dying.

I cried out then, and fell prostrate, for I could no longer doubt that I was in the presence of the very gods who had made Rome a colossus, who granted immortality to heroes or smote them. The true gods, revealed to me, who was no one in particular, who was merely fond of telling stories in the dark.

I wept. The seated one leaned down and touched me on the shoulder. His touch burned, but very slightly.

'Get up,' he said. 'We are all waiting for you.'

They were my audience. The ruined temple rustled with the wind of their voices. Dust stirred, rose, settled, rose again. I could not make out any words. At times they seemed to be laughing, at times weeping. At times it was like the soft chatter of pigeons under the eaves at Grandfather Falco's.

Then they all fell silent, and I was commanded to begin. I sat where I was, in the middle of the floor, and spoke haltingly, urged on whenever I could no longer find the words; all the while amazed that anyone would want to listen to a stuttering schoolboy who had forgotten his lessons and could only mangle Hesiod and Homer and Vergil. I felt like a boy again, like I was ten years old and had slipped down from the loft to relieve myself and looked out the window and saw, or imagined I saw, the gods in the night sky.

But it didn't seem to matter. After a while I came to understand that my listeners did not care at all about the quality of my delivery. They merely wanted to be reminded of old events. I think they merely wanted to hear the names.

Much to my surprise, my brother's voice joined my own. He crouched beside me, his face drawn, his expression bewildered, but he spoke gently, and together we told of Proserpine and of the passion of Demeter, of Orpheus and his descent into the nether world; only we left the ending off that particular story and made it seem as if the poet had found his beloved among the shades and been content to remain with her.

The lady who had been the Strix and before that a goddess sank down into sleep, into the darkness, bones rattling as they scattered across the floor.

'*That was well done, for both of you.*'

I looked up.

'Come closer. I cannot rise.' And the dying god pulled the spear out of his side with a grunt, and his blood splashed over me, burning. It poured into my cupped hands, and for an instant it seemed I held a magic glass of some kind. Through it I gazed down as if from a great height on two armies in desperate combat. The place was the gorge where the river Frigidus cuts through the mountains above Aquilea.

I saw a black-bearded, red-faced man riding furiously through a forest, up a steep hillside. His horse stumbled, broke a leg, threw him; but he continued on with three or four followers, all on foot, all of them at the absolute limit of endurance.

I knew this to be the murder-soiled traitor Abrogastes, who had promised to restore the old gods. Trapped at last in a cave, he clasped his friends to him one by one, then released them, muttered something, and fell on his sword.

The man who stood beside him, who steadied him as he fell, was my father.

I let the pooled blood drip out between my fingers. The image was gone.

'Why have you shown me this?' I said at last.

'I cannot tell. There must be a reason. I do not know it any more.'

When the god spoke no more, I knew he was dead. Even as I watched, the divine flesh sublimated away, rising like golden smoke. Bones poured out of the throne in a heap. Faint lightning flickered once or twice, and then there was absolute darkness in which Flavius groped his way to me and held me tight, his face against my chest.

He said something very strange: 'What have I become?'

'You haven't changed at all. You're still my brother.' I think I had fathomed the final mystery then. I was to be a witness to the end of the great world. Only the small remained. We were to go on with our lives.

Flavius shook me awake that morning. We were still in the hollow, among mossy boulders. The horse grazed nearby.

'You've burned your hands,' he said.

I looked at them dumbly. 'They must have fallen into the fire.'

'But we didn't make a fire.' He turned his head to one side, wincing with pain. 'Ow. I think a scorpion stung me.'

'Do you know what happened, Flavius?'

'I had some kind of . . . dream. It was horrible at first. But in the end I was no longer afraid, and I dreamed of the angels.'

'Really?'

He glared at me, but his fury faded into a kind of disoriented exhaustion. I didn't try to argue. I let him lead me to a stream. The cool water felt good on my hands.

I did not kill my brother. It wouldn't have mattered if I had. Not in the end.

In the end, the soldiers of Abrogastes went over to Theodosius and the Christians won the battle. Father vanished on the field or nearby. His body was never found.

But our family was spared, perhaps because as soon as Flavius and I reached Grandfather Falco's house I went straight to the kitchen and burned the letters in the oven.

My brother is not my enemy. That is all the consolation I have. If we had fought, if one of us had killed the other over the affairs of the great world, what difference would it have made, to Abrogastes and Eugenius, to Theodosius, or to the gods?

Father once told me that we are like barnacles on the hull of a ship, and the ship is the great world of Caesars and empires and gods. We live in our own small world where what matters is more a matter of the hailstorm that flattened the crops and whether or not your belly is full. The events of the great world are as remote as the thoughts of the ship's captain to the barnacles.

'But what if the ship is wrecked?' I asked.

'Then we cling to some fragment large enough that we won't notice the difference.'

'Do you believe we can?'

'No,' he said.

The ship was wrecked a few years later. Those same Goths who fought for Theodosius at Aquilea turned on the empire. On their way to Rome they ransacked Grandfather Falco's estate. He met them at the door, sword in hand, on his head the old helmet he hadn't worn in fifty years. A Goth laughed and ran him through with a spear.

The barbarians left the Queen of Cities a hollow shell. Now, though the Roman corpse may still be seated on the throne of the world, it is truly dead, its heart torn out, its limbs rotting in the sun.

I think of the old Stoic epitaph: *I did not exist. I existed. I do not exist. I care not.* So it is with all things, even the world, even the gods.

So it is in the great world, and in the small.

THE CROWN OF THE GOLDEN CHAIN

Max Pemberton

On 4 September AD 476, the Emperor Romulus Augustulus resigned
his imperial office and retired to his villa in Naples. Although the
senate sent word to Zeno, the emperor in the East, that he was
now Emperor of the whole united Empire, Zeno was too weak a
ruler to pursue the offer. Instead Odoacer, leader of the German
mercenaries, set himself up as king of Rome, and remained so until
he was defeated by Theodoric, king of the Ostrogoths in AD 493.
Zeno had supported Theodoric, but was never able to regain the
empire for himself, indeed he died before Odoacer. Zeno's successors
continued to rule from Constantinople which now became the base
of the Byzantine Empire. At the outset they ruled under the same laws
as the Romans, and it was to all intents a continuation of the Roman
Empire. Roman law, culture and language continued for another
generation or two, but by the reign of the Emperor Justinian, who
ruled from AD 527 to 565, the times they were a-changing. It was
during Justinian's reign that Latin ceased to be the official language,
and it was at this time that the real Roman Empire came to an end and
the Byzantine one began. The following story is set in the early days
of Justinian's reign. It is one of a series of stories that Max Pemberton
(1863–1950) wrote about the escapades of the Lady Zoë.

The reign of the Emperor Justinian, and his wife, Theodora, in
the city of Constantine, was characterized in the main by much

wholesome progress, and by no little advance in science and morals. But while it was, as all the world knows, an epoch of new laws and the codification of laws, it is yet remarkable for a story of riot and disorder surpassing in ferocity any which the more turbulent times can show.

Born in the Circus, always a centre of intrigue and faction, the record of this popular rising is, for the most part, the old story of the rival parties, the 'blues' and the 'greens,' who so long rent Constantinople with their brawls. Upon this occasion, however, the hand of 'blue' was not uplifted against 'green;' but banding together, the former rivals made common cause against the palace, and in a few hours had not only burned half the city to the ground, but had crowned a new Emperor in that very Augustaeum which erstwhile was the arena of their encounters.

Of the means by which Constantinople was delivered from this mob, of the events which saved Justinian's crown, the older books tell us little; but the lately-discovered manuscripts concerning the secret history of Theodora and her husband make the matter plain, and we owe it to their discovery that this account is possible.

Now, the trouble began in the Circus with an onslaught of 'blue' upon 'green,' and after that a charge of the mailed horsemen through the Hippodrome, and many prisoners carried to the secret dungeons of the Imperial Palace. Lacking discretion, a partisan of neither faction, the Emperor ruled that 'blue' and 'green' should hang side by side before the Monastery of St Conan; and that thus justice should be done. Such an edict stirred the city to the last point of indignation and dismay.

It is true that 'blue' cared nothing if 'green' were hanged; and 'green' would not have given an obole to have saved 'blue' from the halter; but that both 'blue' and 'green' should hang from the same gibbet surpassed the fables in wonder. Quickly, unmistakably, determinedly the clamour spread. There were a thousand 'blues' and 'greens' before the monastery door when the fateful morning came. Even the mailed horsemen could not keep the people back; no sword uplifted, no threat of guards could silence that ominous cry: 'Down with them! Down with them!'

It was a misty morning of January; heavy rain had fallen during the night; day dawned through lingering vapours steaming up from the cloud-robed seas. An old chronicler has said that it were as though the elements themselves mourned that hour of death and retribution. Whatever were men's sympathies, the bravest among them shuddered as victim after victim emerged from the cloister cells, and stood, a monk on either hand, beneath the terrible gibbet. Some cowering when They had raised their eyes to Heaven for the last time, some boldly appealing to their fellows to avenge them, the rioters died one by one for the folly of the Circus and the madness which folly had provoked. At last but three remained for the clumsy hand of the unwilling executioner. It was a supreme moment when the anger of the people passed control, and even the mailed horsemen were no longer to be feared.

Now, it has been recorded of the executioner that he was the unwilling servant of Emperor in this matter. Whatever may be truth of that story, the growing anger of the mob, the curses it showered both upon John of Cappadocia and the Prefect Eudemius, its open defiance of the guard, its contempt of the Emperor's authority, unnerved him so greatly, that when there were but three of the condemned yet to be hanged, his courage ebbed away and he could no longer perform his task.

Harassed by the people, and not a little afraid of them, he so bungled his work that the first of the three criminals, having struggled for a moment in the noose which choked him, slipped from it at last, and fell with a thud upon the wet grass at his feet. Upon which, as the account goes the mob raised angry shouts, crying that the man had suffered and that there was an end of it.

'Would ye hang him for the second time? Shall our friends suffer so? What say ye, comrades, will ye be silent under this?'

To whom others responded:

'Let Eudemius come and we will tie such a knot as the Emperor himself may not undo! Shame! Shame! Will ye bear it, friends? Have ye no arms that these things must be?'

The answer to the cry was a very forest of spears and scimitars raised high above the people's heads as silver wands upon which the rain-drops glistened.

'We'll not suffer it – let the man go free! Have ye not hanged him as the Emperor willed?'

And from others –

'The time is ripe; press on, comrades, press on!'

It was a contagious mood, and those about the monastery door did little to appease it. In spite of lowered brows and scowling faces and blades uplifted and angry cries, they bade the executioner tie up the man for the second time, and for the second time the noose slipped, and the victim fell heavily. From which moment the day was lost to Justinian and his servants. At one impulse, with one purpose, caring nothing for life, counting death but a light hazard, the mob broke the ring of mailed horsemen, and closed in upon the

gibbet. So quick was it, so sure, that even those snatched thus from
the threshold of death scarce knew that ropes were no longer about
their necks ere they found themselves borne shoulder-high above
that shrieking throng.

But the rioters themselves rushed onward to the Hippodrome;
and as one man five thousand cried:

'Nika! Victory!'

The news of the outbreak spread quickly; the clamour of it was
heard in the harbour; the story of it re-told in many a house and
many an alley to summon recruits for the cause, to swell the volume
of the cries. Rapidly as the tidings of it went, nevertheless they were
carried first to the palace of the Lady Zoë, and were there recounted
to trembling courtiers and frightened guards and all the sentinels.

'The factions are out, five thousand march to the palace; they
cry for a new king – they have overthrown the Guard, and
none withstand them. Save yourselves, friends, while there is yet
time —'

The Lady Zoë heard the uproar and quitted her apartments that
she might know the reason of it. At any other time, those she
questioned would have feared to speak so boldly before her; but
now, with a mob sweeping onward to the palace gates, there was
no time for equivocation or delay. Many, indeed, spoke together in a
wailing cry of warning and dismay when they confessed the truth.

'Save yourself, lady, we beseech you! The factions are out – they
are killing and plundering in the city. They name a new Emperor.
Save yourself while there is yet time –'

The Lady Zoë, wearing only a long white robe with a chain of
gold about her neck, and a circle of diamonds in her coal-black
hair, listened for a moment to the thundrous echoes of that human
avalanche before she answered her servants with that scorn they
feared so greatly.

'A new Emperor! Shall we cast off the purple, then, because my
servants are craven? O, devoted friends, I see truly that your first
thought is for me, that I may lead you safely out of the city to a place
of safety. Babes that ye are, shall not a woman defend you?'

And then with a new thought of prudence, she cried:

'Let Hypatius come! Must I have women for my Guard? Let
Hypatius come, and the gates be closed. Will ye open because every
slave is knocking? Shame on you that have known my service –
shame!'

Her courage, always looked for, stirred them to action and to
hope. Those who erstwhile had been dumb with fear, now began

to bustle about the palace, closing the great gates and chiding the sentinels. Others called for Hypatius; and when they had found him, they thrust the young captain forward to the great hall of audience, and so brought him to their mistress that he might answer.

Now Hypatius, the Captain of the Gate in the Imperial Palace, was nephew to Anastasius, the dead Emperor, and there were many in the city who, from time to time, when Justinian's caprice offended them, named the young soldier as his successor to the purple. Hypatius, it may be, heard them with affected displeasure, for he was craven at heart and little daring; and while he nursed secretly an ultimate hope of the supreme power, nevertheless he confessed that hope to none, and posed always as the loyal servant of the reigning dynasty.

Few, perhaps, at the Court knew the man truly; but the Lady Zoë was an exception, and no phase of that unattractive character was hidden from her. For this reason, we cannot doubt, she sent for Hypatius at the first news of the uprising; and casting the glove to him, she challenged him for the truth.

'They say that the city is up, and that five thousand march to the palace gates. Where, then, is Hypatius at such an hour?'

Now, the young soldier came wearing his helmet of brass and his brazen shield and buckler; but having no word ready for that swift event, he stood confused and hesitating, and was unable to answer as he would have wished. Zoë, meanwhile, was determined that he should speak.

'Let the truth be told,' she cried again. 'What means this cry, of what victory do they speak, Hypatius?'

The soldier stood guiltily before her; his eyes were cast down to the marble pavement at her feet. He feared her glance, had always feared it.

'It means, lady,' he said, 'that this is the last day of your cousin Justinian's reign.'

The Lady Zoë clapped her hands; the room rang with her merry laughter.

'And this from the Keeper of the Palace Gate! Oh, worthy Hypatius! Shall I not tell them of your courage?'

Indifferent to her mockery, Hypatius continued:

'Two hundred of the Guard are dead at St Conan's Gate. Terbell, the executioner, hangs at his own gibbet. There is not a boat in the harbour which can find a crew, for all have business at the Palace. "Blue" and "green" are to be seen upon one banner, Lady. There are no troops in the city, for Belisarius lingers yet at Prusa. Are not the people wise, then, to speak of victory? Should I be less than your friend if I said "save yourself from the people"?'

She could not hide her impatience.

'From the people – nay, if I am to be saved, it must be from my friends! And you first. Hypatius – shall I not save myself from you?'

He raised his eyes and looked at her with a meaning she could not mistake.

'Many months have passed since I asked favour of you,' he said slowly. 'This day may give me what the past has denied.'

And then, growing more bold, he went on:

'The people are at the gates; Belisarius is in Asia; the Guard is overthrown, the people rule. Listen to their cries; they proclaim a new Emperor. Am I not fortunate thus to win the people's favour?'

He raised his hand as though the advancing hosts would answer for him, and those in the room, listening with him, heard presently a great shout, a long resounding cry, 'Hypatius, Hypatius!' whose meaning they could not mistake. As the victory of winds, that watch-word swelled upon the breeze, it floated as an echo of great sounds over the placid seas; it was carried to the palace gates to awe those who waited and trembled there. Even the Lady Zoë was silent when she heard the voices.

'A new Emperor, a new city, such is the people's will, Zoë. Account me no prophet when I say that this day shall give me what the past has denied. Is it not life that I offer you – the half of my kingdom?'

He spoke in a low fawning voice, the words of one who avowed his purpose but was not yet unashamed of it. Craven still, he would have measured her resource by his own. Passion egging him on, he said that to-night he would hold her in his arms. What mattered it that she laughed so scornfully, or was at no pains to disguise her contempt for him? Such was the old Zoë, he said; a few hours would work miracles.

How little he knew of the brave heart contending against him, of a woman's woeful fear cloaked by that girlish laughter which feigned contempt.

'I come to you at sunset for my answer,' he went on passionately, when he found her silent: 'remember, Zoë, for you and those dear to you, there is safety in my house. But do not look for any help from others. I shall be Emperor to-morrow, and it will be mine to command. The people will it. I cannot oppose the people's will —'

Her ironical laughter put an end to his unctuous platitudes.

'O, let me crown thee, Caesar,' she cried rising suddenly, and taking the golden chain from her neck; 'behold here is the first of the fetters which thy kingdom forges for thee. Art thou not a saviour of women? – wear, then, a woman's guerdon!'

As one jesting she held the golden chain and put it about the soldier's neck. He knew not how to read her merriment; nor would he linger here at such at time.

'To-night,' he answered, 'to-night I shall return to thee.'

But to her Guards the Lady Zoë said:

'Lead out to the people the King they would crown!'

Hypatius left the Palace to go to those who proclaimed him Emperor; and the gates being shut, the Imperial household waited for the end. There was not one among them who doubted what the last terrible scene would be, or who had not already told himself that Justinian's day was done. The absence of the only military genius of the Empire, Belisarius, who lingered yet in Asia, the reckless determination of the rioters, the supineness, the divided counsels, the palsy of fear which had come upon the Palace, left the ultimate issue beyond question.

Sooner or later, at nightfall or at dawn, the gates would be burst open, the men put to the sword, the women carried to the houses of the victors.

Nothing less than a miracle could turn that supreme assault or hold that house against an enraged people. There was but one man among the Emperor's servants whose capacity for command, whose courage, whose resource might save Justinian's house. And that man was at Prusa, loitering on his homeward journey. Little wonder that every prayer which terror wrung from the gathered courtiers sent up a cry to Heaven that Belisarius might come. For Belisarius was the last hope. He alone could save them.

'He may come even yet, friends. Had not our lord news of him but three days since? He lingered at Prusa but thought much of home. Let chance befriend us, and the dawn may bring his ship —'

'Too late, too late, comrade. Those who come at dawn may wish they had not come at all. Let Justinian bow to the people's will and his servants may yet be saved. Think you that any can help him when ten thousand cry a new King! Ay, surely, his star has set, and it will never rise again.'

Others said in wailing words:

'The city burns; Irene's church is in flames, they fire the Senate House and the brazen porch. Who will see to-morrow's sun – God help us, comrades, if Belisarius does not come!'

Now, all this was the talk in the guardroom and the purlieus of the palace; neither was there any braver spirit in the Emperor's apartments nor in those of his councillors. Some, indeed, were already advocating the opening of the palace gates; others demanded that an embassy should go down to the people and make terms with them. The Emperor himself, convinced from the outset of the hopelessness of resistance, spoke of surrender and the sacrifice of his own life, if need be, that his friends, and especially the women of the household, might be saved.

One voice alone was added to the supplication of the Empress Theodora that the purple might not thus lightly be cast aside, and it was the voice of the Lady Zoë. Bravely before them all, no longer the girlish mistress of jest or laughter, she pleaded for respite, for a better resolution and a more courageous hope. And she spoke also an enigma of promise.

'Give me until midnight, and if Belisarius be not come, I myself will open the gate. My lord, I beseech you, listen to a woman's word. If courage be the gift of Kings, no less is faith a woman's right. Will you betray those who have lived and died for Justinian's name? Better to perish here when men shall say "an Emperor has fallen" than to die as a malefactor in the city you have loved. Nay, go not out, my lord, because the people cry "surrender," for to-morrow they will raise a new cry, and your name may still be heard.'

They heard her with approbation, many adding their voices and saying: 'Go not out, my lord.' The Empress herself, mounting the throne, declared that she would die in that place before any snatched the purple from her. Even the Guards, shamed to courage by a woman's word, spoke no more of surrender, but only of defiance.

'The Lady Zoë has commanded it,' they said; 'we will hold the Palace until her will be known.'

But others cried still:

'God send Belisarius, or no man shall see the dawn.'

The Palace gates were closed, the Guard was posted, the archers sent to the walls, such of the mailed horsemen as remained drawn up to meet the contemplated assault. In the city itself pandemonium now reigned. It was death, men said, to utter a word of prudence; death to cry mercy for Justinian; death to withstand that orgy of success and madness. Huddled in the cellars of the houses, flying hither, thither, some to the seashore, some to the gardens remote and the silent places, the partisans of the reigning house sought to escape the peril and the riot.

And fire now began to herald the night and the last delirious scene. From the high place by the lighthouse, from the hills beyond the Bosphorus, from many a watch-tower and many a roof, watchers

beheld the flame and crimson smoke floating as a lurid cloud above
the doomed city – in their terror they said it was the Judgment Day,
the second coming of the Christ. All seemed ended, all lost but that
supremacy of lust and slaughter.

'God!' they prayed, 'if Belisarius would come!'

Now, the Lady Zoë watched the holocaust from the windows
of her palace, and she who, at noon, had spoken an enigma to the
Emperor, spake another at sunset to her servants when she cried
of a sudden that they should go and seek John of the Cages and
command him to come to her. The Keeper of the Beasts had, indeed,
been passing by her window at the moment when she uttered this
request; and remembering her jest of old time with him, she now
sent for him that she might learn what passed in the Hippodrome.
He told her quietly and simply as an honest man who would not
chop allegiance for any parrot-cry.

'They crown Hypatius, lady, with a golden chain, and set him on
a throne of skins. The very gutters run with blood. There are ten
thousand in the Circus and ten thousand at the gates. The hospital
is burned and the brazen porch. Let the night send Belisarius, or
all is lost.'

She heard him musingly, but anon she asked a question:

'Is one man, then, so gifted that he alone can work a miracle?'

'I know not, lady, but they name him always, saying that when he
is come the army will be with him, and twenty thousand that have
fought the Persians. Such is their wisdom. Yet I do believe, truly,
that if they saw the silver armour this very night, though the General
should stand alone, nevertheless he would prevail with them.'

Again the Lady Zoë pondered the words:

'Hypatius of the craven heart has always feared Belisarius. The
people worship him as a god. If, then, Belisarius rode out to them
to-night, they would open to him and the Guard might pass in. Shall
all be lost because one is lacking? Are there not two shields of silver
in Constantine's city? Tell me truly, John of the Cages, shall this
night's work find you willing?'

He knew not what she asked of him; but she had no more faithful
friend in the city, and now he answered her in honesty:

'Lady, your will is my will: command me and I obey!'

The Lady Zoë turned and put her little hand upon the keeper's arm.

'Lead me, as once I led you,' she said, 'to the light.'

The rioters had determined to attack the palace when the sun had
set, and darkness would cloak the last assault. For which purpose

they gave the afternoon to rapine and slaughter; and afterwards, sacking the shops of the wine-merchants, they swarmed to the great Hippodrome there to crown Hypatius with the golden chain, and to cap the feast in drunken debauchery and the madness of excess. Commanding all at the sword's point, they drove the singing girls to the arena, the wrestlers to the death-throw, the women of Egypt to the foaming dance.

Never had such orgies been known since Constantine raised a city from the waste and his builders set a wall about it. The very temples quaked at the tumult of sounds, the very sky shone crimson as with the blood of the dying. It needed but the sack of the palace to finish a work so triumphant. And that would be at midnight, men said, for Hypatius, the Caesar of an hour, had so willed it.

Many applauded this pleasant resolution, and such as were driven out of the Hippodrome by the press of the people – for the throng there surpassed all reason – went early to the palace gates that they might be at hand when the pillage began and the women fell to the lot of the boldest among the adventurers. So it befell that a great multitude gathered about the walls at the hour of eleven; and fearing no longer a threat of the guard nor any consequences of their treachery, the rioters cried always for the gates to be opened and for Justinian to come out to them. Judge, then, of their astonishment when this request was answered, not by the bows and the javelins of the Imperial Guard but by a solitary herald, who opened the gate boldly and raising a torch cried in a loud voice:

'Make way, make way, the Lord Belisarius passes.'

Now, that had been a very common cry in Constantine's city in the days before the great General set out for the Persian wars; but men had not heard it for many a month, and there was no name written or known that could so quickly call the mob to fear or to dismay. Hardly daring to believe their ears, standing aghast in awe and wonder, the rioters at the palace gate waited dumfounded while the cry was repeated:

'Make way, make way, the Lord Belisarius passes.'

He had come then; had hastened back from Prusa! Or was it but a ruse, a stratagem, the last hope of the doomed within the palace? These questions the people scarce had time to ask when a figure at the gate gave them answer. Outstanding in the flare of torches, the silver armour flashing lights as of jewels, the black horse champing at the bit, the sword upraised, the crimson cross upon the helmet – ay, who should ask a second time if this were Belisarius or another? As the judgement of God upon a stricken city the figure of their General stood before them. The very ground seemed to open and to swallow them up.

'Belisarius!' they cried, 'spare us, lord, spare thy people!'

The General rode out, a company of the mailed horsemen upon either hand. No word would he speak to those who cast themselves on their knees before him; but going at his ease, he turned toward the Hippodrome, where sat the Emperor of an hour, a golden chain about his neck, a wine-cup in his hand. And as the soldier passed, he left panic in his path. Men staggered from the purlieus blindly, crying: 'The army is come back, the Lord Belisarius is here!'

Those who had been the boldest an hour ago now fled to the secret places of the city or sought ships in the harbour, the sanctuary of churches, and the refuge of cellars. Friends deserted friends, and began to avow themselves the servants of the returned General. Such soldiers as believed that their defections had not been too public took their arms and uttered Justinian's name as they ran swiftly toward the Circus. There were a thousand horsemen on Belisarius' heels when, still silent, a shining figure upon a black horse, he rode to the great gate of the Hippodrome, and there claimed obedience.

'In the name of our Lord Justinian, open!'

Now, it befell at that moment that the Egyptian women had finished their dance and the last of the dead wrestlers had been carried from the arena; and the wine being all drunk, and the mob ripe for new excesses, the mock Emperor Hypatius had risen from his throne of skins, and was about to give the command to sack the Imperial Palace. Pressing all together, in a drunken frenzy of madness, the rioters raised their shields and chanted incoherently their watchword, 'Nika! Victory!' Neither man nor woman should be spared, said the oath, until Hypatius, their god, was crowned, and Justinian and his children driven out with blinded eyes to the exile of the Isles.

The rioters being engaged in this savage anthem, some moments passed before those who ran in with the tidings could make themselves heard; and they had to repeat again and again, 'Belisarius is come, the army is here,' before silence was obtained or any word of wisdom could be spoken. But when, at last, the news was known, then such a wail of woe went up to Heaven as though every man there heard the sentence of his doom and knew that it was irrevocable.

'Belisarius is come, the army is here.'

It was a weird scene. Thousands of torches illumined the towering obelisks, the countless statues of the Hippodrome. Rank by rank, pressing together upon the sanded floor, crowding the benches and the galleries, showing awe-struck faces even from the highest pinnacles, soldiers and dancers, wrestlers and athletes, the women of the city, the keepers of the cages – such a concourse never, surely, heard in one place tidings so momentous.

It were as though a voice from Heaven had spoken to cast their new-born Empire down, to wash away the stains of it in a river of blood. For if Belisarius had come, who should hope for mercy, what grace might be expected from that master of war and vengeance, that pitiless soldier, that iron heart? Verily, had their triumph been short-lived. The story of it would be written to-morrow in crimson letters. The night must be a night of death.

They cried the tidings, and Hypatius, the Emperor of a day, reeled forward to answer them.

'Who names Belisarius?' he asked in drunken obstinacy. 'What child of the wine-vat speaks now to us?'

They echoed it, twenty together, with pale faces and hands that shook upon their swords.

'We have seen the crimson cross; Belisarius is at the gate, Master.'

He mocked them, striking one upon the mouth so that the blood flowed.

'Dreamer of dreams, go say to this Belisarius that I speak not with visions.'

'Lord, they open the gate to him. Even now he rides in to us.'

Hypatius stepped back to his throne, and waited with drawn sword. There, high above the serried ranks, he beheld the silver armour flashing, the coal-black horse, the banner of the mighty Belisarius. The sudden hush, falling upon the Circus as a hush of doubt and wonder, betrayed the failing hearts, the broken resolution of those about him. No man raised a hand to drive out the mailed horseman, who cut a lane through the ranks as through some vast field of human grass. Belisarius had come, indeed, Belisarius, the invincible.

Slowly, as one fearing nothing, conscious already of triumph, the General rode to the throne and confronted the usurper. He uttered no word, gave no sign to those who cast themselves pitifully upon their knees and craved mercy. Hypatius was his goal – and to Hypatius first the mandate went.

'Deliver up thy sword, that our lord, the Emperor, may be justified!'

Now, Hypatius heard the challenge, and not a little to the surprise of those about him, who had already given up everything for lost, he answered them, not by any plea for mercy, nor any self excuse; but stepping down from his throne, he caught the bridle of the General's horse and held it firmly.

'Thou art not Belisarius,' he said; and then again, 'thou art not Belisarius!'

The accusation was as a message of pardon to those in the Circus. Men, who thought they were about to hear a sentence of doom, sprang up from the ground and shouted: 'It is not Belisarius!' Women laughed hysterically; archers beat their shields in a clash of triumph; the frenzied shouts were heard as an echo of thunder, even at the palace where Justinian waited.

'Thou art not Belisarius!'

One, and one only in that vast assembly, read aright the enigma of the mask. Hypatius, who watched the silver armour as a hunter watches his quarry, who told himself from the first that another, not Belisarius, spoke, Hypatius whose passion had sent him out to the madness of the night – he, at least was not deceived. And he hastened now to declare his discovery in accents of a triumph assured.

'Thou art not Belisarius – thou art Zoë! Come down, then, that I may kiss thy lips.'

He stretched out his hand and would have dragged the figure down to him, but, at the first gesture, a trooper raised his scimitar, and the mock Emperor drew back affrighted.

'Is it peace or the sword?' he asked defiantly, for he knew that he had five thousand with him. 'Come you to seek mercy, or would you die before the hour appointed? Have done with this pretence, for surely I know that thou art the Lady Zoë and no other, and that Belisarius lingers yet in Asia —'

He turned to the people to carry them with him and to bring back their courage.

'Would you run for a woman, then? There sits the Lady Zoë – no other. Bear witness all, these eyes were not deceived —'

They answered him as their wish was, 'it is the Lady Zoë,' and pressing about the black horse they began to applaud the design and to mock the Guards.

'For thee, lady, grace; but to those others, your Guards, no mercy shall be shown.'

It was the surpassing moment of the night. Lusty for vengeance, fired by wine and excess, the throng sought already the death of the mailed horseman, the beginning of their terrible orgy. But now, the Lady Zoë, suddenly lifting the vizor of her helmet, addressed herself for the first time to the people.

'I am Zoë, as you say, and I come to save my children. Who, then, will hearken unto me?'

A long, resounding shout, a recognition of doubt made certainty, greeting this swift declaration. Won to humour by the ruse, dazzled by that winning figure of the woman, applauding the musical voice, the commanding gesture, the supple, graceful figure, the mob stood to cry again: 'Long live Zoë, long live our mistress!' But she, knowing that the minutes were all precious, appealed to them again:

'I come to save my children. Let those who would win pardon, go their way now, ere it be too late. If ye be my friends, accept of me this friendship. The Emperor speaks of clemency to those who hearken.'

They greeted her with a new shout of mockery, which the threat provoked.

'And if we go not – will our Lady drive us out? Ho, ho, comrades, shall a woman turn us? Let Hypatius answer – this is his affair.'

Ribald laughter, the din of shields clashing, a frenzy of reeling dancers and torches flaring and swords uplifted, drowned for some moments the words which Hypatius spoke. When silence came again a few there told themselves that the price of the masquerade was, for the Guards, death – for the Mistress of the Guards that which was worse than death. And she waged a good fight for her friends, they said; there was no braver heart in the Circus that night.

Hypatius answered the Lady Zoë, but he spoke not for the people as they had wished, but for himself and that which lay closest to his heart:

'Why hast thou come here if it be not to crave mercy of me? Thinkest thou that fifty horsemen shall affright five thousand? I tell thee if I do but raise my hand, these friends of thine shall as surely die as Justinian must this night – Justinian and those with him in the Palace.'

Her word was one of scorn:

'Hail to the prophet,' she said; 'hail to the King of the golden chain. Surely is Hypatius crowned with fetters this night.'

She made a signal to one who rode upon her right hand, and he, regardless of the place or the scene or the fear of death imminent, cast a rope suddenly and so deftly that a loop of it caught the mock Emperor by the arms and dragged him headlong to the floor. So quick was the act, so sure, that a silence of awe at the very daring of it fell for an instant upon all the arena. And in that instant Zoë spoke.

'Think ye, then, that I come here alone? Nay, a greater than Belisarius is my ally. Let those who would see to-morrow's sun, go ere the gates of life be shut.'

She faced them imperiously, the mistress of their doom; and they, listening for any sound of tidings from without, heard of a sudden a message which blanched their faces and sent women screaming from the Circus and brought strong men to their knees, and crushed the weak in that avalanche of flight.

'God!' they cried, 'the beasts are out, the cages are open!'

For more than an hour. Belisarius and his troops (for Belisarius himself reached the harbour at midnight), drove the frantic people headlong through the streets of Constantine's city, some to death in the sea, many to perish in the flaming buildings, thousands to fall under bloody scimitars and relentless javelins. When dawn came, none but the bravest dared to pass the gates of the Hippodrome, or to survey that last scene of carnage and of death. But those that went in, over the dead and the dying, beheld Hypatius, the Emperor, still upon his throne, bound there by the golden chain which yesterday had been his crown.

'So perish all craven hearts,' they said, 'for this man, surely, died of fear. Have ye not heard of it, comrades – John of the Cages whipped cubs in among them, and the cry was raised that the lions were out. So willed the Lady Zoë that she might give life to Justinian and quench the fires. To her, then, let the city's thanks be given.'

They turned away and went, with the priests and the soldiers, up to the palace that they might hear again that cry of yesterday.

'Nika! Victory!'

For this was Zoë's gift to them.

SOURCES AND ACKNOWLEDGEMENTS

Acknowledgements are accorded to the following for the rights to publish the stories in this anthology. Every effort has been made to trace copyright holders. The Editor would be pleased to hear from anyone if they believe there has been an inadvertent transgression of copyright.

'The Temple of Death', by A.C. Benson. Reprinted from *The Hill of Trouble* (London: Isbister, 1903). Copyright expired in 1976.

'The Thread', © 1980 by Vera Chapman. Reprinted from *The Phoenix Tree*, edited by Robert Boyer & Kenneth J. Zahorski (New York: Avon Books, 1980). Reprinted by permission of the author's agent, Laurence Pollinger Limited.

'The Gods Play for High Stakes', © 1951 by Langston Day. First published in *Magic Casements* (London: Rider, 1951). Unable to trace the author or representatives of the author's estate.

'Captain Leopard', © 1996 by L. Sprague de Camp. First printing, original to this anthology. Printed by permission of the author.

'Betrayed', © 1996 by Juliet Dymoke. First printing, original to this anthology. Printed by permission of the author.

'One of Cleopatra's Nights', by Théophile Gautier. Reprinted from *The Collected Works of Théophile Gautier* (New York: Walter J. Black, 1928).

'Caligula the God', © 1934 by Robert Graves. First published in *I, Claudius* (London: Arthur Barker, 1934). Reprinted by permission of Carcanet Press Ltd.